Tess of the D'Urbervilles

Tess of the D'Urbervilles

THOMAS HARDY

Edited with Notes by TIM DOLIN
With an Introduction by MARGARET R. HIGONNET

PENGUIN CLASSICS
an imprint of
PENGUIN BOOKS

PENGUIN CLASSICS

Published by the Penguin Group
Penguin Books Ltd, 80 Strand, London WC2R ORL, England
Penguin Group (USA) Inc., 375 Hudson Street, New York, New York 10014, USA
Penguin Group (Canada), 90 Eglinton Avenue East, Suite 700, Toronto, Ontario, Canada M4P 2Y3
(a division of Pearson Penguin Canada Inc.)
Penguin Ireland, 25 St Stephen's Green, Dublin 2, Ireland (a division of Penguin Books Ltd)
Penguin Group (Australia), 250 Camberwell Road, Camberwell,
Victoria 3124, Australia (a division of Pearson Australia Group Pty Ltd)
Penguin Books India Pvt Ltd, 11 Community Centre,
Panchsheel Park, New Delhi – 110 017, India
Penguin Group (NZ), 67 Apollo Drive, Rosedale, North Shore 0632, New Zealand
(a division of Pearson New Zealand Ltd)
Penguin Books (South Africa) (Pty) Ltd, 24 Sturdee Avenue, Rosebank, Johannesburg 2196, South Africa

Penguin Books Ltd, Registered Offices: 80 Strand, London WC2R ORL, England

www.penguin.com

First published 1891
Published in Penguin Classics 1998
Reprinted with Further Reading 2003
This edition published 2008

3

Introduction and Appendix III copyright © Margaret R. Higonnet, 1998
Notes, A History of the Text and Appendix II copyright © Tim Dolin, 1998
General Editor's Preface and Chronology copyright © Patricia Ingham, 1996
All rights reserved

The moral rights of the editors have been asserted

Cover design and illustration Coralie Bickford-Smith

Typeset by Rowland Phototypesetting Ltd, Bury St Edmunds, Suffolk
Printed in Great Britain by Clays Ltd, St Ives plc

A CIP catalogue record for this book is available from the British Library

978-0-141-04033-2

www.greenpenguin.co.uk

CONTENTS

ACKNOWLEDGEMENTS

I would like to acknowledge the assistance of scholars and specialists on the following electronic mailing lists: the 'Classics' list, co-ordinated by Linda Wright; the 'Victoria' list, co-ordinated by Patrick Leary; and the 'alt.architecture' newsgroup. Thanks also to Hugh Craig, Dianne Osland, Christopher Pollnitz and Lucy Dougan.

Tim Dolin

This edition uses, with one exception, the first edition in *volume* form of each of Hardy's novels and therefore offers something not generally available. Their dates range from 1871 to 1897. The purpose behind this choice is to present each novel as the creation of its own period and without revisions of later times, since these versions have an integrity and value of their own. The outline of textual history that follows is designed to expand on this statement.

All of Hardy's fourteen novels, except *Jude the Obscure* (1895) which first appeared as a volume in the Wessex Novels, were published individually as he wrote them (from 1871 onwards). Apart from *Desperate Remedies* (1871) and *Under the Greenwood Tree* (1872), all were published first as serials in periodicals, where they were subjected to varying degrees of editorial interference and censorship. *Desperate Remedies* and *Under the Greenwood Tree* appeared directly in volume form from Tinsley Brothers. By 1895 ten more novels had been published in volumes by six different publishers.

By 1895 Hardy was sufficiently well-established to negotiate with Osgood, McIlvaine a collected edition of all earlier novels and short story collections plus the volume edition of *Jude the Obscure*. *The Well-Beloved* (radically changed from its serialized version) was added in 1897, completing the appearance of all Hardy's novels in volume form. Significantly this collection was called the 'Wessex Novels' and contained a map of 'The Wessex of the Novels' and authorial prefaces, as well as frontispieces by Macbeth-Raeburn of a scene from the novel sketched 'on the spot'. The texts were heavily revised by Hardy, amongst other things, in relation to topography, to strengthen the 'Wessex' element so as to suggest that this half-real half-imagined location had been coherently conceived from the beginning, though of course he knew that this was not so. In practice 'Wessex' had an uncertain and ambiguous development in the earlier editions. To trace the growth of Wessex in the novels as they appeared it is necessary to read them in their original pre-1895 form. For the 1895–6 edition represents a substantial layer of reworking.

Similarly, in the last fully revised and collected edition of 1912–13, the Wessex Edition, further alterations were made to topographical detail and photographs of Dorset were included. In the more open climate of opinion then prevailing, sexual and religious references were sometimes (though not always) made bolder. In both collected editions there were also many changes of other kinds. In addition, novels and short story volumes were grouped thematically as 'Novels of Character and Environment', 'Romances and Fantasies' and 'Novels of Ingenuity' in a way suggesting a unifying master plan underlying all texts. A few revisions were made for the Mellstock Edition of 1919–20, but to only some texts.

It is various versions of the 1912–13 edition which are generally available today, incorporating these layers of alteration and shaped in part by the critical climate when the alterations were made. Therefore the present edition offers the texts as Hardy's readers first encountered them, in a form of which he in general approved, the version that his early critics reacted to. It reveals Hardy as he first dawned upon the public and shows how his writing (including the creation of Wessex) developed, partly in response to differing climates of opinion in the 1870s, 1880s and early 1890s. In keeping with these general aims, the edition will reproduce all contemporary illustrations where the originals were line drawings. In addition for all texts which were illustrated, individual volumes will provide an appendix discussing the artist and the illustrations.

The exception to the use of the first volume editions is *Far From the Madding Crowd*, for which Hardy's holograph manuscript will be used. That edition will demonstrate in detail just how the text is 'the creation of its own period': by relating the manuscript to the serial version and to the first volume edition. The heavy editorial censoring by Leslie Stephen for the serial and the subsequent revision for the volume provide an extreme example of the processes that in many cases precede and produce the first book versions. In addition, the complete serial version (1892) of *The Well-Beloved* will be printed alongside the volume edition, since it is arguably a different novel from the latter.

To complete the picture of how the texts developed later, editors trace in their Notes on the History of the Text the major changes in 1895–6 and 1912–13. They quote significant alterations in their explanatory notes and include the authorial prefaces of 1895–6 and 1912–13. They also indicate something of the pre-history of the texts in manuscripts where these are available. The editing of the short stories will be separately dealt with in the two volumes containing them.

Patricia Ingham
St Anne's College, Oxford

1840   2 June: Thomas Hardy born, Higher Bockhampton, Dorset,
       eldest child of a builder, Thomas Hardy, and Jemima Hand,
       who had been married for less than six months. Younger siblings:
       Mary, Henry, Katharine (Kate), to whom he remained close.

1848–56 Schooling in Dorset.

1856   Hardy watched the hanging of Martha Browne for the murder
       of her husband. (Thought to be remembered in the death of
       Tess Durbeyfield.)

1856–60 Articled to Dorchester architect, John Hicks; later his
       assistant.

late 1850s Important friendship with Horace Moule (eight years older,
       middle-class and well-educated), who became his intellectual
       mentor and encouraged his self-education.

1862   London architect, Arthur Blomfield, employed him as a
       draughtsman. Self-education continued.

1867   Returned to Dorset as a jobbing architect. He worked for Hicks
       on church restoration.

1868   Completed his first novel *The Poor Man and the Lady* but it was
       rejected for publication (see 1878).

1869   Worked for the architect Crickmay in Weymouth, again on
       church restoration.

1870   After many youthful infatuations thought to be referred to in
       early poems, met his first wife, Emma Lavinia Gifford, on a
       professional visit to St Juliot in north Cornwall.

1871   *Desperate Remedies* published in volume form by Tinsley Brothers.

1872   *Under the Greenwood Tree* published in volume form by Tinsley
       Brothers.

1873   *A Pair of Blue Eyes* (previously serialized in *Tinsleys' Magazine*).
       Horace Moule committed suicide.

1874   *Far from the Madding Crowd* (previously serialized in the *Cornhill*

Magazine). Hardy married Emma and set up house in London (Surbiton). They had no children, to Hardy's regret; and she never got on with his family.

1875   The Hardys returned to Dorset (Swanage).

1876   *The Hand of Ethelberta* (previously serialized in the *Cornhill Magazine*).

1878   *The Return of the Native* (previously serialized in *Belgravia*). The Hardys moved back to London (Tooting). Serialized version of part of first unpublished novel appeared in *Harper's Weekly* in New York as *An Indiscretion in the Life of an Heiress*. It was never included in his collected works.

1880   *The Trumpet-Major* (previously serialized in *Good Words*). Hardy ill for many months.

1881   *A Laodicean* (previously serialized in *Harper's New Monthly Magazine*). The Hardys returned to Dorset.

1882   *Two on a Tower* (previously serialized in the *Atlantic Monthly*).

1885   The Hardys moved for the last time to a house, Max Gate, outside Dorchester, designed by Hardy and built by his brother.

1886   *The Mayor of Casterbridge* (previously serialized in the *Graphic*).

1887   *The Woodlanders* (previously serialized in *Macmillan's Magazine*).

1888   *Wessex Tales*.

1891   *A Group of Noble Dames* (tales). *Tess of the D'Urbervilles* (previously serialized in censored form in the *Graphic*). It simultaneously enhanced his reputation as a novelist and caused a scandal because of its advanced views on sexual conduct.

1892   Hardy's father, Thomas, died. Serialized version of *The Well-Beloved*, entitled *The Pursuit of the Well-Beloved*, in the *Illustrated London News*. Growing estrangement from Emma.

1892–3   *Our Exploits at West Poley*, a long tale for boys, published in an American periodical, the *Household*.

1893   Met Florence Henniker, one of several society women with whom he had intense friendships. Collaborated with her on *The Spectre of the Real* (published 1894).

1894   *Life's Little Ironies* (tales).

1895   *Jude the Obscure*, a savage attack on marriage which worsened relations with Emma. Serialized previously in *Harper's New Monthly Magazine*. It received both eulogistic and vitriolic reviews. The latter were a factor in his ceasing to write novels.

1895–6 First Collected Edition of novels: Wessex Novels (16 volumes), published by Osgood, McIlvaine. This included the first book edition of *Jude the Obscure*.

1897 *The Well-Beloved* (rewritten) published as a book; added to the Wessex Novels as vol. XVII. From now on he published only the poetry he had been writing since the 1860s. **No more novels**.

1898 *Wessex Poems and Other Verses*. Hardy and Emma continued to live at Max Gate but were now estranged and 'kept separate'.

1901 *Poems of the Past and the Present*.

1902 Macmillan became his publishers.

1904 Part 1 of *The Dynasts* (epic-drama in verse on Napoleon). Hardy's mother, Jemima, 'the single most important influence in his life', died.

1905 Met Florence Emily Dugdale, his future second wife, then aged 26. Soon a friend and secretary.

1906 Part 2 of *The Dynasts*.

1908 Part 3 of *The Dynasts*.

1909 *Time's Laughingstocks and Other Verses*.

1910 Awarded Order of Merit, having previously refused a knighthood.

1912–13 Major collected edition of novels and verse, revised by Hardy: The Wessex Edition (24 volumes). 27 November: Emma died still estranged. This triggered the writing of Hardy's finest love-lyrics about their early time in Cornwall.

1913 *A Changed Man and Other Tales*.

1914 10 February: married Florence Dugdale (already hurt by his poetic reaction to Emma's death). *Satires of Circumstance*. *The Dynasts: Prologue and Epilogue*.

1915 Mary, Hardy's sister, died. His distant young cousin, Frank, killed at Gallipoli.

1916 *Selected Poems*.

1917 *Moments of Vision and Miscellaneous Verses*.

1919–20 Mellstock Edition of novels and verse (37 volumes).

1922 *Late Lyrics and Earlier with Many Other Verses.*

1923 *The Famous Tragedy of the Queen of Cornwall* (drama).

1924 Dramatized *Tess* performed at Dorchester. Hardy infatuated with the local woman, Gertrude Bugler, who played Tess.

1925 *Human Shows, Far Phantasies, Songs and Trifles.*

1928 Hardy died on 11 January. His heart was buried in Emma's grave at Stinsford, his ashes in Westminster Abbey. *Winter Words in Various Moods and Metres* published posthumously. Hardy's brother, Henry, died.

1928–30 Hardy's autobiography published (on his instructions) under his second wife's name.

1937 Florence Hardy (his second wife) died.

1940 Hardy's last sibling, Kate, died.

The Wessex of The Novels.

This map is from the Wessex Novels Edition, 1895–6

BIBLIOGRAPHICAL NOTE

The following abbreviations are used for texts frequently cited in this edition.

Biography	Michael Millgate, *Thomas Hardy: A Biography* (Oxford and Melbourne: Oxford University Press, 1982)
Collected Letters	Richard Little Purdy and Michael Millgate (eds.), *The Collected Letters of Thomas Hardy*, 7 vols. (Oxford: Clarendon Press, 1978–88)
Cox	R. G. Cox (ed.), *Thomas Hardy: The Critical Heritage* (London: Routledge and Kegan Paul, 1970)
Firor	Ruth A. Firor, *Folkways in Thomas Hardy* (New York: A. S. Barnes and Co., 1962)
Gatrell	Simon Gatrell, *Hardy the Creator: A Textual Biography* (Oxford: Clarendon Press, 1988)
Grindle and Gatrell	Juliet Grindle and Simon Gatrell (eds.), *Tess of the d'Urbervilles* (Oxford: Clarendon Press, 1983)
Laird	J. T. Laird, *The Shaping of 'Tess of the d'Urbervilles'* (Oxford: Clarendon Press, 1975)
Life	Thomas Hardy, *The Life and Work of Thomas Hardy*, ed. Michael Millgate (London: Macmillan, 1984)
Literary Notebooks	Lennart Björk (ed.), *The Literary Notebooks of Thomas Hardy*, 2 vols. (London: Macmillan, 1985)
Mitchell	Sally Mitchell (ed.), *Victorian Britain: An Encyclopaedia* (New York: Garland, 1988)
OED	James A. H. Murray *et al.* (eds.), *A New English*

Dictionary on Historical Principles, 10 vols. (Oxford: Oxford University Press, 1884–1928)

Personal Notebooks   Richard H. Taylor (ed.), *The Personal Notebooks of Thomas Hardy* (New York: Columbia University Press, 1979)

Personal Writings   Harold Orel (ed.), *Thomas Hardy's Personal Writings: Prefaces, Literary Opinions, Reminiscences* (New York: St Martin's Press, 1966)

Purdy   Richard Little Purdy, *Thomas Hardy: A Bibliographical Study* (Oxford: Clarendon Press, 1954)

apes her in her sleep. The narrator meditates that the
awakening at that hour had not 'the least inkling that
s in the hands of the spoiler' (XI).[11] Alec himself admits
nd offers to 'pay to the uttermost farthing' (XII). Such
language have provided the foundation for readers'
ess's purity of intention and the perception that 'the
gedy' is due to 'the tyranny of man ... and of social
[12]

ovoked and tantalized readers then and now, in part
use she seems to exceed the boundaries of the language
her. In an often-quoted comment, Hardy wrote on 29
: 'I am glad you like Tess, though I have not been able
er all that she is, or was, to me.'[13] From Tess as naïve
ect to economic blackmail by her shiftless parents and
pulous rake; to the proud, angry child-mother of a sickly
erved yet sensuous woman whose passion for a minister's
way her resolve not to marry; the abject, self-mutilating
r husband's prudish rejection; and finally the murderess
ns break through in a brief moment of fulfilment – the
of Tess's life shape a figure who seems to defy any
. Physically as well, she conjoins different 'phases' of
d with 'bouncing' womanliness. This heterogeneity was
objection raised by Ellen Moers, who in a 1960s review
complained that Tess is a patchwork of 'cultural stereo-
h goddess, modern woman, doomed bride of balladry,
ictorian daughter, unwed mother, murderess, and princess
Hardy's Tess is surely the all-purpose heroine.'[14]
lexity of Tess and of the determining event in her brief
y some of Hardy's most powerful strategies in the novel:
definition and multi-layered characterization, the high-
nterpreters as those who shape meaning, and resistance
conventions about the relationship between events and
ch of these strategies is centred on the representation of
but each also proliferates into other aspects of the novel.
er of 1890, probably when he was thinking about the
ough which his heroine passed, Hardy reflected that he

INTRODUCTION

(New readers are advised that this Introduction makes
the detail of the plot explicit.)

When *Tess of the D'Urbervilles* appeared in early December 1891, its
'scandalous notoriety' among some readers and impassioned popularity among others made Hardy financially secure and confirmed his
stature as one of the major writers of the nineteenth century.[1] The
passage of the United States Copyright Bill had guaranteed an income
from the American serialization in *Harper's Bazar* and from the subsequent book publication without risk of piracy, and Hardy's publishers
scrambled to reprint the novel. Readers, reviewers and the author
himself responded to the heroine as if she were a real person capable
of change through time. To one correspondent who wrote in her
praise, he answered: 'I am so truly glad that Tess the Woman has
won your affections. I, too, lost my heart to her as I went on with her
history.'[2] The sharply divided reactions to the book focused on the
heroine and on the claim made by Hardy's 'exasperating' (and exasper-
ated) subtitle (*A Pure Woman*), which he had added at the last minute
to proofs of the three-volume first edition. In his autobiography, Hardy
reported that the Duchess of Abercorn's dinner guests had been 'almost
fighting across her dinner-table over Tess's character'. Those who
thought the 'little harlot' deserved hanging were put in one group;
those who pitied her as a 'poor wronged innocent' sat in another,
together with the Duchess.[3]

Even before the novel was printed, the rejection of the manuscript
on moral grounds by three publishers in a row guaranteed that it
would be born into controversy. Accepted in censored form by the
Graphic, a family magazine, *Tess* was dismembered, with three key
episodes removed and published separately in two sketches (see Appendix V). These changes necessitated further bowdlerization; and in one
scene the heroine's modesty was rescued at the last minute by the
Graphic editor, who insisted that she be transported in a wheelbarrow
along a flooded lane, rather than carried in Angel's arms. Having

been forced earlier by publishers to adapt *The Woodlanders* and *A Group of Noble Dames*, and frustrated by this 'piecemeal mode of parturition', Hardy reacted by turning *Tess* into a vehicle for attack on 'the censorship of prudery'. Already in his 1890 article on 'Candour in English Fiction', he condemned popular magazines and lending libraries for excluding subjects (especially sexuality and childbirth) deemed incompatible with 'social forms and ordinances'.[4] In the serial version of *Tess*, which ran from July to December 1891, and yet more so in the subtly revised volume editions, Hardy deliberately and combatively obscured the question of Tess's purity. As can be seen in Tim Dolin's history of the text, through successive revisions Hardy complicated motives and compounded contradictions in Tess's relation to her 'cousin' Alec D'Urberville. He complained repeatedly about the mangling of the plot to satisfy 'the Young Girl' reader of the *Graphic*, which obliged him to substitute a mock marriage for 'the seduction pure & simple of the original MS'.[5] The serial version none the less described Tess not as a simple victim, but as a girl made 'pliable' by her economic dependence on Alec. The textual evidence indicates that throughout his revisions Hardy intended the tension between Alec's violation of Tess and her physical compliance to remain unresolved.[6] Hardy inserted many traces pointing to Tess's involvement: she confesses she 'ought to have seen sooner' the import of Alec's attentions; she has stayed on at his estate perhaps a month before deciding she would not become his 'creature' any longer (XII). In letters Hardy named her 'mistake' a 'fall', yet he maintained the 'paradoxical morality' that Tess was 'essentially pure – purer than many a so-called unsullied virgin'.[7]

Conservative readers were not convinced by his claim. Mowbray Morris, who had already rejected the manuscript for serial publication by *Macmillan's Magazine* as having 'rather too much succulence', returned to the attack in the *Quarterly Review*; there he mocked Tess's behaviour as implausible and immoral, compared Hardy's descriptions of Tess to 'a slave-dealer appraising his wares' (an insight that coincides with more recent accusations of voyeurism), and concluded that he had told 'a coarse and disagreeable story in a coarse and disagreeable manner'.[8] Similarly, R. H. Hutton in the *Spectator*, although he declared

Tess to be perhaps the most [...]
heroine's case weak in those n[...]
supposed to have had control: [...]
reluctance to persist in seeking [...]
to Alec's importunities and of [...]
'Though pure in instinct, she w[...]
concluded.[9] To such readers, T[...]
painted by a Methodist enthusia[...]
side: too 'hot' for comfort.

Once Hardy had reintegrate[...]
which Alec carries Tess off int[...]
sequence depicting the baptism [...]
tural implications of the debat[...]
apparent in the narrative. Parado[...]
ment and reassembly of his mar[...]
violation of a body, Hardy's 'Exp[...]
sion that the frankly sexual eleme[...]
of an atrocity, thus reinforcing th[...]
been violently assaulted. When H[...]
of things', defenders of Tess's pu[...]
chain of images to which Tess is [...]
restored scene in Chapter XI, wh[...]
the woods, while the narrator re[...]
doomed to receive' the 'coarse pa[...]
in Chapter LVIII of her sleeping [...]
the altar at Stonehenge now clearl[...]
the horse Prince pierced at night o[...]
hart first spared then killed in the [...]
and killed at harvest, the wounded [...]
the peasant girls to whom mailed [...]
wrong'.[10] The scenes selected for il[...]
of which were printed in *Harper's Ba*[...]
had included three of these mome[...]
moments of Alec's aggression, such [...]
forces a strawberry into her mouth. [...]
throat making her sputter and gasp[...]

that he then [...]
cottagers jus[...]
their sister w[...]
'I did wrong'[...]
imagery and[...]
defences of [...]
Woman's T[...]
circumstance[...]

Tess has [...]
perhaps bec[...]
that describe[...]
October 189[...]
to put on pa[...]
teenager sul[...]
by an unscr[...]
infant; the r[...]
son sweeps [...]
sufferer of h[...]
whose passi[...]
seven phase[...]
classificatio[...]
her childho[...]
precisely th[...]
misguidedly[...]
types': 'Ear[...]
prostitute, [...]
in disguise: [...]

The com[...]
life exempl[...]
ambiguous[...]
lighting of [...]
to narrativ[...]
endings. E[...]
Tess hersel[...]
In the wi[...]
'phases' th[...]

was 'more than ever convinced that persons are successively various persons, according as each special strand in their characters is brought uppermost by circumstances'.[15] No doubt Angel overvalues his own flawed vision when he harshly proclaims to Tess after her wedding-night confession why he cannot forgive her: 'You were one person; now you are another' (xxxv). Yet in a larger sense that Tess explains in her eloquent letter pleading for his return to her from Brazil, 'What was the past to me as soon as I met you? It was a dead thing altogether. I became another woman, filled full of new life from you' (xlviii). Hardy's focus on this principle of growth informs his resistance to insular categories and many of his breaks with established plot conventions.

The same drive toward ambiguity and complication visible in Hardy's treatment of Tess's violation announces itself even in minor issues of naming. From the first sentence, the narrator offers two names for Tess's birthplace – the Vale of Blakemore or Blackmoor; in the same scene, the antiquarian Parson Tringham salutes Jack Durbeyfield with an ironic second appellation, 'Sir John D'Urberville'. In turn, we learn that Alec's family has usurped the D'Urberville name and crest to displace their original name of Stoke, which might be too well remembered in association with his father's profits in a dubious trade (and which may remind us of his glowing cigar, or of the steam-driven threshing machinery that forces Tess to work ceaselessly). A forger of his mother's signature and a self-conscious performer, Alec appears unannounced in a farmhand's smock amid the burning couch-grass of the Marlott vegetable plots to work with a pitchfork next to Tess, to whom he leeringly names himself the 'old Other One'; ever generous, even toward the man who represents the 'tragic mischief' in her life, Tess replies, 'I never said you were Satan' (l).

Above all Tess herself eludes naming, though she courageously assumes her own identity, the 'poor wounded name' of the epigraph from Shakespeare. Hardy actually considered giving her his own name – in which case the novel would have been entitled 'Tess of the Hardys'. Mocking, teasing or benighted, the men in her life insistently rebaptize her with names such as 'Coz', 'my pretty' (like the names of two cows), 'Artemis' or 'maidy'. She steadily replies, 'Call me Tess.'

Having become Mrs Angel Clare in name only, and forced to rely on arduous field labour at a starve-acre farm, she sheds her husband's surname, reverting to simple 'Tess' in order to protect his reputation. In the end Angel (whom his father considers 'misnamed') finds her only after a postman hits upon the link between Durbeyfield and D'Urberville, and only after he himself has become simply 'Angel'.

This difficulty of naming has for Hardy epistemological significance. In the period when he was drafting *Tess*, Hardy read Plato's *Cratylus* and noted somewhat optimistically: 'A very good way of looking at things would be to regard everything as having an actual or false name, and an intrinsic or true name, to ascertain which all endeavour should be made ... The fact is that nearly all things are falsely, or rather inadequately, named.'[16] It is not surprising therefore that he refers to the idealist philosopher Immanuel Kant when addressing the question raised by the 'faithfully presented' on the title-page: 'We don't always remember as we should that in getting at the truth we get only at the true nature of the impression that an object, etc., produces on us, the true thing in itself being still beyond our knowledge, as Kant shows.'[17] Appearances and impressions deceive: 'Nature is an arch-dissembler ... *nothing* is as it appears.'[18]

The inadequacy of labels and the uncertainty of 'intrinsic' meaning provoke a proliferation of interpretations. If the blind Mrs D'Urberville reads with assurance the bodies of her birds to discern their names, diet and state of health, other readings are far less secure. Of the stone pillar at Cross-in-Hand, the narrator notes coolly that it marks 'the site of a miracle, or murder, or both', then twice returns to the 'differing accounts' given of its 'history and purport' (XLIV–XLV); Tess shivers with the '*petite mort*' at a shepherd's account of an execution there. Similarly, when the cock crows on Tess's wedding day straight in the face of Angel, it appears to different dairy-folk to identify him as a cuckold (though the dairyman does not say so outright), to augur the suicidal despair of the milkmaids who loved him in vain or more prosaically to indicate a change of weather. Readers may find an augury that Angel will deny Tess repeatedly, as Peter does Christ.

Equal uncertainty surrounds one of the most threatening omens to foreshadow the destiny of Hardy's heroine, the legend of the

D'Urberville coach.[19] Tess's mother Joan introduces the motif in a wishful aphorism, ' 'tis well to be kin to a coach, even if you don't ride in en' (IV). The legendary coach, in which an abduction and a murder were supposed to have taken place, parodically becomes the fashionable dog-cart in which Alec forces his kisses on Tess. A few years later, with a shiver of fear Tess seems to recognize the dilapidated conveyance in which the bridal couple go to church as an uncanny echo from her past, but Angel does not explain to her the legend, or whether seeing the coach signifies death or commission of a crime (or both). On the eve of the Durbeyfield household's removal from Marlott, Alec appears as a pale rider in a white mackintosh at the very moment when Tess 'fancied it was a carriage and horses'. Like the fourth horseman of the Apocalypse, he announces the beginning of the end for Tess. When he retells the legend finally, however, the ultimate question, who killed whom, has been lost from memory: 'in the struggle he killed her – or she killed him – I forget which' (LI). Such mocking reversibility of responsibility in a murder challenges the assumption that moral judgements can be fixed absolutely and for all time.

These open-ended readings of images and events underscore the central way that the body of Tess invites and defeats readings. Dressed by her mother to obscure her youth, Tess is misread by Alec, who also underestimates her pride and independence. Angel cons 'the characters of her face as if they had been hieroglyphics', hoping to detect that her 'no' means 'yes' (XXVIII). Her melancholy expression puzzles him, 'as one deciding on the true construction of a difficult passage', for he cannot grasp her as a being separate from himself (XXXIV). After their mutual confession Angel believes (erroneously, the narrator tells us), 'her heart was not indexed in the honest freshness of her face' (XXXV). Although Tess herself seems to read character intuitively, she attracts contradictory and deceptive readings, as Patricia Ingham has argued, not only from Angel and Alec but also from the narrator, who refutes yet reimposes 'men's language' as a measure of her identity.[20]

One of Hardy's master themes, then, is the questioning of stereotypes, classifications and conventions that dictate interpretations of human character. Several passages in the novel echo his 1883 attack on condescending social classifications in 'The Dorsetshire Labourer'. For *Tess*, Hardy borrowed the discussion of 'the supposed real but highly conventional Hodge', a condescending nickname for typical rural workfolk. The falsity of any stereotype of Hodge arises in part from the extension of educational opportunities, the transformation of working conditions by new technologies and the displacement of traditional artisans, when old forms of tenancy lapse. As conditions shift, so do identities.

'Hodge', in fact, is above all in this novel the *woman* worker, Tess, who becomes the touchstone to test schematic misreadings. Freshly arrived at the dairy, Angel must learn 'to read human nature' and to differentiate the workers at Dairyman Crick's farm from 'The conventional farm-folk of his imagination – personified by the pitiable dummy known as Hodge'. Upon closer acquaintance with the men and women at Talbothays dairy, Angel's conventional image becomes 'disintegrated into a number of varied fellow-creatures' (XVIII).[21] Angel's slow apprenticeship in discrimination starts with his attunement to a 'fluty' note in Tess's voice, when she explains how she separates her body from her thoughts as she contemplates the stars. Yet as he distinguishes her from the young women with whom she works, he projects on to the figure before him idealized types of women, such as Artemis, Demeter or the virtuous woman of King Lemuel. Thus he remains the prisoner of gender and class assumptions. Proudly, to his accusation on their wedding night that she is only 'an unapprehending peasant woman', she responds, 'I am only a peasant by position, not by nature!' (XXXV). The tragic distance between Angel and Tess, which springs from his unconscious adherence to the prejudices of his milieu, can close only when he is ready to accept her with all that she has done and been, as an individual, and that moment arrives only when she has surrendered herself to death.

For Hardy the problem of constructing a portrait, a character or a novel merges with the themes of displacement and death, for to fashion an image risks fixing the complex, mutable richness of the individual. Among the many motifs that point us toward this fear of killing into art, the effigy, as an art of the dead or absent (especially in criminal law), evokes the ambiguous status of a representation that marks

INTRODUCTION

(New readers are advised that this Introduction makes
the detail of the plot explicit.)

When *Tess of the D'Urbervilles* appeared in early December 1891, its
'scandalous notoriety' among some readers and impassioned popularity among others made Hardy financially secure and confirmed his
stature as one of the major writers of the nineteenth century.[1] The
passage of the United States Copyright Bill had guaranteed an income
from the American serialization in *Harper's Bazar* and from the subsequent book publication without risk of piracy, and Hardy's publishers
scrambled to reprint the novel. Readers, reviewers and the author
himself responded to the heroine as if she were a real person capable
of change through time. To one correspondent who wrote in her
praise, he answered: 'I am so truly glad that Tess the Woman has
won your affections. I, too, lost my heart to her as I went on with her
history.'[2] The sharply divided reactions to the book focused on the
heroine and on the claim made by Hardy's 'exasperating' (and exasper-
ated) subtitle (*A Pure Woman*), which he had added at the last minute
to proofs of the three-volume first edition. In his autobiography, Hardy
reported that the Duchess of Abercorn's dinner guests had been 'almost
fighting across her dinner-table over Tess's character'. Those who
thought the 'little harlot' deserved hanging were put in one group;
those who pitied her as a 'poor wronged innocent' sat in another,
together with the Duchess.[3]

Even before the novel was printed, the rejection of the manuscript
on moral grounds by three publishers in a row guaranteed that it
would be born into controversy. Accepted in censored form by the
Graphic, a family magazine, *Tess* was dismembered, with three key
episodes removed and published separately in two sketches (see Appendix V). These changes necessitated further bowdlerization; and in one
scene the heroine's modesty was rescued at the last minute by the
Graphic editor, who insisted that she be transported in a wheelbarrow
along a flooded lane, rather than carried in Angel's arms. Having

been forced earlier by publishers to adapt *The Woodlanders* and *A Group of Noble Dames*, and frustrated by this 'piecemeal mode of parturition', Hardy reacted by turning *Tess* into a vehicle for attack on 'the censorship of prudery'. Already in his 1890 article on 'Candour in English Fiction', he condemned popular magazines and lending libraries for excluding subjects (especially sexuality and childbirth) deemed incompatible with 'social forms and ordinances'.[4] In the serial version of *Tess*, which ran from July to December 1891, and yet more so in the subtly revised volume editions, Hardy deliberately and combatively obscured the question of Tess's purity. As can be seen in Tim Dolin's history of the text, through successive revisions Hardy complicated motives and compounded contradictions in Tess's relation to her 'cousin' Alec D'Urberville. He complained repeatedly about the mangling of the plot to satisfy 'the Young Girl' reader of the *Graphic*, which obliged him to substitute a mock marriage for 'the seduction pure & simple of the original M S '.[5] The serial version none the less described Tess not as a simple victim, but as a girl made 'pliable' by her economic dependence on Alec. The textual evidence indicates that throughout his revisions Hardy intended the tension between Alec's violation of Tess and her physical compliance to remain unresolved.[6] Hardy inserted many traces pointing to Tess's involvement: she confesses she 'ought to have seen sooner' the import of Alec's attentions; she has stayed on at his estate perhaps a month before deciding she would not become his 'creature' any longer (XII). In letters Hardy named her 'mistake' a 'fall', yet he maintained the 'paradoxical morality' that Tess was 'essentially pure – purer than many a so-called unsullied virgin'.[7]

Conservative readers were not convinced by his claim. Mowbray Morris, who had already rejected the manuscript for serial publication by *Macmillan's Magazine* as having 'rather too much succulence', returned to the attack in the *Quarterly Review*; there he mocked Tess's behaviour as implausible and immoral, compared Hardy's descriptions of Tess to 'a slave-dealer appraising his wares' (an insight that coincides with more recent accusations of voyeurism), and concluded that he had told 'a coarse and disagreeable story in a coarse and disagreeable manner'.[8] Similarly, R. H. Hutton in the *Spectator*, although he declared

Tess to be perhaps the most powerful of Hardy's novels, found the heroine's case weak in those moments of her life when she might be supposed to have had control: her failure to tell Angel of her past, her reluctance to persist in seeking aid from his parents and her surrender to Alec's importunities and offers of aid to her family at the end. 'Though pure in instinct, she was not faithful to her pure instinct', he concluded.[9] To such readers, Tess was a text like the vermilion letters painted by a Methodist enthusiast on blank walls around the countryside: too 'hot' for comfort.

Once Hardy had reintegrated into the book the censored scene in which Alec carries Tess off into the wood of The Chase and the sequence depicting the baptism and death of Tess's infant, the structural implications of the debate over Tess's purity became more apparent in the narrative. Paradoxically, by describing the dismemberment and reassembly of his manuscript in terms that suggested the violation of a body, Hardy's 'Explanatory Note' conveyed the impression that the frankly sexual elements of his novel had been the victim of an atrocity, thus reinforcing the implication that Tess herself had been violently assaulted. When Hardy had restored the 'true sequence of things', defenders of Tess's purity could experience the powerful chain of images to which Tess is linked as yet another victim. The restored scene in Chapter XI, where Tess sleeps amid the leaves of the woods, while the narrator reflects on her 'feminine tissue . . . doomed to receive' the 'coarse pattern' of Alec's lust, and the image in Chapter LVIII of her sleeping body stretched out for sacrifice on the altar at Stonehenge now clearly bracketed recognizable parallels: the horse Prince pierced at night on the road, the legend of the white hart first spared then killed in the forest, the field animals cornered and killed at harvest, the wounded pheasants left to die in a wood and the peasant girls to whom mailed knights of old 'had dealt the same wrong'.[10] The scenes selected for illustration in the serial (about half of which were printed in *Harper's Bazar* and the US edition of the novel) had included three of these moments; they had already highlighted moments of Alec's aggression, such as their first encounter, when he forces a strawberry into her mouth. The drug Alec pours down Tess's throat making her sputter and gasp in the 1891 edition also implies that he then rapes her in her sleep. The narrator meditates that the cottagers just awakening at that hour had not 'the least inkling that their sister was in the hands of the spoiler' (xi).[11] Alec himself admits 'I did wrong' and offers to 'pay to the uttermost farthing' (xii). Such imagery and language have provided the foundation for readers' defences of Tess's purity of intention and the perception that 'the Woman's Tragedy' is due to 'the tyranny of man . . . and of social circumstance'.[12]

Tess has provoked and tantalized readers then and now, in part perhaps because she seems to exceed the boundaries of the language that describes her. In an often-quoted comment, Hardy wrote on 29 October 1891: 'I am glad you like Tess, though I have not been able to put on paper all that she is, or was, to me.'[13] From Tess as naïve teenager subject to economic blackmail by her shiftless parents and by an unscrupulous rake; to the proud, angry child-mother of a sickly infant; the reserved yet sensuous woman whose passion for a minister's son sweeps away her resolve not to marry; the abject, self-mutilating sufferer of her husband's prudish rejection; and finally the murderess whose passions break through in a brief moment of fulfilment – the seven phases of Tess's life shape a figure who seems to defy any classification. Physically as well, she conjoins different 'phases' of her childhood with 'bouncing' womanliness. This heterogeneity was precisely the objection raised by Ellen Moers, who in a 1960s review misguidedly complained that Tess is a patchwork of 'cultural stereotypes': 'Earth goddess, modern woman, doomed bride of balladry, prostitute, Victorian daughter, unwed mother, murderess, and princess in disguise: Hardy's Tess is surely the all-purpose heroine.'[14]

The complexity of Tess and of the determining event in her brief life exemplify some of Hardy's most powerful strategies in the novel: ambiguous definition and multi-layered characterization, the highlighting of interpreters as those who shape meaning, and resistance to narrative conventions about the relationship between events and endings. Each of these strategies is centred on the representation of Tess herself, but each also proliferates into other aspects of the novel. In the winter of 1890, probably when he was thinking about the 'phases' through which his heroine passed, Hardy reflected that he on condescending social classifications in 'The Dorsetshire Labourer'. For *Tess*, Hardy borrowed the discussion of 'the supposed real but highly conventional Hodge', a condescending nickname for typical rural workfolk. The falsity of any stereotype of Hodge arises in part from the extension of educational opportunities, the transformation of working conditions by new technologies and the displacement of traditional artisans, when old forms of tenancy lapse. As conditions shift, so do identities.

'Hodge', in fact, is above all in this novel the *woman* worker, Tess, who becomes the touchstone to test schematic misreadings. Freshly arrived at the dairy, Angel must learn 'to read human nature' and to differentiate the workers at Dairyman Crick's farm from 'The conventional farm-folk of his imagination – personified by the pitiable dummy known as Hodge'. Upon closer acquaintance with the men and women at Talbothays dairy, Angel's conventional image becomes 'disintegrated into a number of varied fellow-creatures' (XVIII).[21] Angel's slow apprenticeship in discrimination starts with his attunement to a 'fluty' note in Tess's voice, when she explains how she separates her body from her thoughts as she contemplates the stars. Yet as he distinguishes her from the young women with whom she works, he projects on to the figure before him idealized types of women, such as Artemis, Demeter or the virtuous woman of King Lemuel. Thus he remains the prisoner of gender and class assumptions. Proudly, to his accusation on their wedding night that she is only 'an unapprehending peasant woman', she responds, 'I am only a peasant by position, not by nature!' (XXXV). The tragic distance between Angel and Tess, which springs from his unconscious adherence to the prejudices of his milieu, can close only when he is ready to accept her with all that she has done and been, as an individual, and that moment arrives only when she has surrendered herself to death.

For Hardy the problem of constructing a portrait, a character or a novel merges with the themes of displacement and death, for to fashion an image risks fixing the complex, mutable richness of the individual. Among the many motifs that point us toward this fear of killing into art, the effigy, as an art of the dead or absent (especially in criminal law), evokes the ambiguous status of a representation that marks

D'Urberville coach.[19] Tess's mother Joan introduces the motif in a wishful aphorism, ' 'tis well to be kin to a coach, even if you don't ride in en' (IV). The legendary coach, in which an abduction and a murder were supposed to have taken place, parodically becomes the fashionable dog-cart in which Alec forces his kisses on Tess. A few years later, with a shiver of fear Tess seems to recognize the dilapidated conveyance in which the bridal couple go to church as an uncanny echo from her past, but Angel does not explain to her the legend, or whether seeing the coach signifies death or commission of a crime (or both). On the eve of the Durbeyfield household's removal from Marlott, Alec appears as a pale rider in a white mackintosh at the very moment when Tess 'fancied it was a carriage and horses'. Like the fourth horseman of the Apocalypse, he announces the beginning of the end for Tess. When he retells the legend finally, however, the ultimate question, who killed whom, has been lost from memory: 'in the struggle he killed her – or she killed him – I forget which' (LI). Such mocking reversibility of responsibility in a murder challenges the assumption that moral judgements can be fixed absolutely and for all time.

These open-ended readings of images and events underscore the central way that the body of Tess invites and defeats readings. Dressed by her mother to obscure her youth, Tess is misread by Alec, who also underestimates her pride and independence. Angel cons 'the characters of her face as if they had been hieroglyphics', hoping to detect that her 'no' means 'yes' (XXVIII). Her melancholy expression puzzles him, 'as one deciding on the true construction of a difficult passage', for he cannot grasp her as a being separate from himself (XXXIV). After their mutual confession Angel believes (erroneously, the narrator tells us), 'her heart was not indexed in the honest freshness of her face' (XXXV). Although Tess herself seems to read character intuitively, she attracts contradictory and deceptive readings, as Patricia Ingham has argued, not only from Angel and Alec but also from the narrator, who refutes yet reimposes 'men's language' as a measure of her identity.[20]

One of Hardy's master themes, then, is the questioning of stereotypes, classifications and conventions that dictate interpretations of human character. Several passages in the novel echo his 1883 attack

Having become Mrs Angel Clare in name only, and forced to rely on arduous field labour at a starve-acre farm, she sheds her husband's surname, reverting to simple 'Tess' in order to protect his reputation. In the end Angel (whom his father considers 'misnamed') finds her only after a postman hits upon the link between Durbeyfield and D'Urberville, and only after he himself has become simply 'Angel'.

This difficulty of naming has for Hardy epistemological significance. In the period when he was drafting *Tess*, Hardy read Plato's *Cratylus* and noted somewhat optimistically: 'A very good way of looking at things would be to regard everything as having an actual or false name, and an intrinsic or true name, to ascertain which all endeavour should be made . . . The fact is that nearly all things are falsely, or rather inadequately, named.'[16] It is not surprising therefore that he refers to the idealist philosopher Immanuel Kant when addressing the question raised by the 'faithfully presented' on the title-page: 'We don't always remember as we should that in getting at the truth we get only at the true nature of the impression that an object, etc., produces on us, the true thing in itself being still beyond our knowledge, as Kant shows.'[17] Appearances and impressions deceive: 'Nature is an arch-dissembler . . . *nothing* is as it appears.'[18]

The inadequacy of labels and the uncertainty of 'intrinsic' meaning provoke a proliferation of interpretations. If the blind Mrs D'Urberville reads with assurance the bodies of her birds to discern their names, diet and state of health, other readings are far less secure. Of the stone pillar at Cross-in-Hand, the narrator notes coolly that it marks 'the site of a miracle, or murder, or both', then twice returns to the 'differing accounts' given of its 'history and purport' (XLIV–XLV); Tess shivers with the '*petite mort*' at a shepherd's account of an execution there. Similarly, when the cock crows on Tess's wedding day straight in the face of Angel, it appears to different dairy-folk to identify him as a cuckold (though the dairyman does not say so outright), to augur the suicidal despair of the milkmaids who loved him in vain or more prosaically to indicate a change of weather. Readers may find an augury that Angel will deny Tess repeatedly, as Peter does Christ.

Equal uncertainty surrounds one of the most threatening omens to foreshadow the destiny of Hardy's heroine, the legend of the was 'more than ever convinced that persons are successively various persons, according as each special strand in their characters is brought uppermost by circumstances'.[15] No doubt Angel overvalues his own flawed vision when he harshly proclaims to Tess after her wedding-night confession why he cannot forgive her: 'You were one person; now you are another' (xxxv). Yet in a larger sense that Tess explains in her eloquent letter pleading for his return to her from Brazil, 'What was the past to me as soon as I met you? It was a dead thing altogether. I became another woman, filled full of new life from you' (xlviii). Hardy's focus on this principle of growth informs his resistance to insular categories and many of his breaks with established plot conventions.

The same drive toward ambiguity and complication visible in Hardy's treatment of Tess's violation announces itself even in minor issues of naming. From the first sentence, the narrator offers two names for Tess's birthplace – the Vale of Blakemore or Blackmoor; in the same scene, the antiquarian Parson Tringham salutes Jack Durbeyfield with an ironic second appellation, 'Sir John D'Urberville'. In turn, we learn that Alec's family has usurped the D'Urberville name and crest to displace their original name of Stoke, which might be too well remembered in association with his father's profits in a dubious trade (and which may remind us of his glowing cigar, or of the steam-driven threshing machinery that forces Tess to work ceaselessly). A forger of his mother's signature and a self-conscious performer, Alec appears unannounced in a farmhand's smock amid the burning couch-grass of the Marlott vegetable plots to work with a pitchfork next to Tess, to whom he leeringly names himself the 'old Other One'; ever generous, even toward the man who represents the 'tragic mischief' in her life, Tess replies, 'I never said you were Satan' (l).

Above all Tess herself eludes naming, though she courageously assumes her own identity, the 'poor wounded name' of the epigraph from Shakespeare. Hardy actually considered giving her his own name – in which case the novel would have been entitled 'Tess of the Hardys'. Mocking, teasing or benighted, the men in her life insistently rebaptize her with names such as 'Coz', 'my pretty' (like the names of two cows), 'Artemis' or 'maidy'. She steadily replies, 'Call me Tess.'

identity. The effigies in the family vaults at Kingsbere-sub-Greenhill represent the legacy of D'Urberville traits, which we gradually learn include pride, exploitation of the poor and weak, and impulsive, at times criminal, violence. When Tess finally reaches the abbey church at Kingsbere, she discovers those effigies have been defaced by the action of time and civil war, just as the name has been worn away to Durbeyfield. The effigies' power to represent their originals has been mutilated; their implied reincarnation in Tess can only be partial. Dispersed throughout the phases of her life, the images of the past assume spurious, legendary, mocking forms, such as that of her 'cousin' Alec.

The complex issue of shaping Tess's identity, which the narrator needs to name yet unname, becomes paradigmatic for the creative paradox of description and characterization. To some extent, Hardy suggests, generalization is necessary to all observation: 'The art of observation . . . consists in this: the seeing of great things in little things, the whole in the part – even the infinitesimal part.'[22] From a distance, the narrator presents an anonymous yet distinctive woman binding sheaves at Marlott, who 'seduces casual attention' because she 'never courts it', before he announces: 'It is Tess Durbeyfield, otherwise D'Urberville, somewhat changed – the same, but not the same.' The theme of sameness in difference is indeed the crux of the aesthetic problem and of Tess's life. Tess has become 'a stranger and an alien here, though it was no strange land' (xiv). Workers may be subsumed into the general by their tasks, when their labour is communal rather than individualized. An 'alien observer' visiting Talbothays might recondense into a singular Hodge the dairy-folk as they stoop in a serried line to weed a field (xxii). Tellingly, women are subsumed more into the type than men are: 'A field-man is a personality afield; a field-woman is a portion of the field; she has somehow lost her own margin, imbibed the essence of her surrounding, and assimilated herself with it' (xiv).

Often these momentary narrative generalizations assume a remote angle of vision that makes Tess representative. Assuming the long view, the narrator suggests that Tess, having disguised herself by snipping her eyebrows and putting on her oldest clothing, has come to seem 'a figure which is part of the landscape; a field-woman pure and simple' (xlii). This tendency to essentialize 'feminine traits' was intensified in the first edition of the novel, which introduces phrasing such as 'feminine' curiosity or 'feminine' hope. Indeed, for some feminist critics one of the more problematic features in the narrator's voice has been its reductive impetus to define Tess as the quintessence of her sex, more 'woman' than the other milkmaids, 'a whole sex condensed into one typical form' (xx), or a 'portion of one organism called sex' (xxiii). In this 'condensation', for example, Penny Boumelha finds 'the ideological elision of woman, sex, and nature' that shapes the tragic pattern of Hardy's work. As Boumelha also observes, however, there is a heightened consciousness of such stylization of womanhood that 'throws into question the ideological bases' of the novel's polarities.[23]

As a result, the narrative tension between differentiation and generalization has provoked theoretical speculation about the significance of contradictions in the narrative voice. Early readers objected to an inconsistency of register, particularly to vocabulary such as 'photosphere' or 'vitalization' held to be inconsistent with the character of Tess, understood as a focalizer or as the consciousness circumscribing the narrative. Some recent readers have argued that this inconsistency is, as it were, consistent with a more general focus in the novel on the instability of meaning. Is there more than a single narrative voice – one deeply engaged with Tess's own perceptions, empathetic and located strategically close to her, and another more detached, more critical and pessimistic, as Simon Gatrell maintains?[24] Or is there a mosaic of voices each of which adapts to the local needs of a passage? Michael Millgate has argued that Hardy's 'method is not to blend together the disparate constituents of the fiction but to leave them – individual, identifiable – in permanent suspension'.[25]

Peter Widdowson holds that Hardy's focus on differentiation and misrepresentation 'exposes *characterization* itself as a humanist-realist mystification'.[26] Casting Hardy as a modernist, he suggests that in *Tess* Hardy deliberately juxtaposed multiple registers in cubist fashion, fracturing the plane of vision to 'defamiliarize' or estrange the plot. He points to Hardy's 1890 observation:

Art is a disproportioning – (i.e., distorting, throwing out of proportion) – of realities, to show more clearly the features that matter in those realities, which, if merely copied or reported inventorially, might possibly be observed, but would more probably be overlooked. Hence 'realism' is not Art.[27]

In this view, inconsistency can be understood as a tool of the *vraisemblable*, as a way to foreground 'the features that matter' in the representation of 'realities'.

Hardy's understanding of realism in representation is indeed remarkably modern. Responding to J. M. W. Turner's watercolours exhibited in 1889 at the Royal Academy, Hardy pondered the 'strange mixtures' of light and objects through which the artist approximated the effect of the real. 'Art', he reflected, 'is the secret of how to produce by a false thing the effect of a true.'[28] Narrative structure was to be a critical tool for achieving the desired effect. One of his letters about *Tess* explains that he had violated strict notions of unity, precisely in order to achieve an effect of realism. In response to criticism of an apparently unnecessary detail, Hardy disagreed: 'It would take too long to explain why such apparently irregular modes of narrating are often to be countenanced for reasons of *vraisemblance*. The truth is that in artistic matters, literary & other, you often best keep the rules by occasionally breaking them.'[29]

Social scripts, Hardy felt, dictated literary scripts. Weak writers of 'rigidly good family and rigidly correct education', he argued, 'mostly treat social conventions and contrivances – the artificial forms of living – as if they were cardinal facts of life.'[30] In Hardy's view, these artificial forms, which he called the 'doll' of English fiction, must be 'demolished'.[31] To do so, he turned to 'apparently irregular modes of narrating' that disrupted genre conventions with their precepts of unity of plot and uniformity of tone. Throughout his career Hardy played with the ironic splicing of literary modes, perhaps most obviously in his first published novel, *Desperate Remedies* (1871), and in his most blatantly feminist novel, *The Hand of Ethelberta* (1876).

The juxtaposition of romance and melodrama, of comedy and tragedy, creates an effect of discontinuity in form that forces us to reinterpret both character and plot, as we have imagined them in anticipation. In the Talbothays courting days of Angel and Tess, for example, Hardy immerses the couple in transformative mists that encourage their mutual idealization, then disrupts the mood suddenly when they return to the house, where Dairyman Crick is expostulating to old Deborah Fyander for not washing her hands. The sharp narrative turn dissipates the romantic tone and shatters the illusions of any London folk among the readers who might be ignorant of the 'slovenly ways' of some milkers. Similarly he follows up a passionate moment in their idyll with a plebeian chapter in which the entire work force goes out to clear a field, because in the dairy's excellent milk a 'twang' of garlic has been discovered. The twang of the real briefly interrupts the transcendent movement of romance; it offers an unheeded warning to Angel and to Tess as well. *Et in Arcadia ego* – I too am in Arcadia, says Death.

Hardy achieves a similar effect of interrogation by repeating an image of expansive joy in the very different circumstances of alcoholic release. As she crosses the threshold of the Var valley to begin work in the dairy at Talbothays, Tess's reviving hopes mingle with the sunshine in 'an ideal photosphere', preparing us for the 'luminous gloom' (xx) of affection that will temporarily envelop and protect her from the wolves of fear and shame that menace her engagement to Angel Clare (xxxi). The couple's perception of a phosphorescent gleam that illuminates them both is not so very different, it would seem, from the 'sort of halo, an occidental glow', that comes over her mother Joan Durbeyfield at the alehouse, enabling her to shut out pressing needs and to see in her defective husband an ideal lover (iii). Drink has transformed the villagers sitting there, so that 'their souls expanded beyond their skins, spreading their personalities warmly' and gilding their surroundings (iv). At the market town of Chaseborough too, after an evening of drink and dance, 'however terrestrial and lumpy' to the uninebriated eye the workfolk might be, to themselves they seemed to soar, 'themselves and surrounding nature forming an organism of which all the parts harmoniously and joyously interpenetrated each other', their shadows surrounded by a beatific halo (x).[32] Violence, however, immediately follows the scenes of drunken release. And the transfiguration of Angel and Tess by love will have its own gothic sequel in the honeymoon at Wellbridge, when Angel in his conscious hours ruthlessly rejects his wife and in his unconscious hours mourns over her enshrouded body as if she were dead.

It is no accident that this ecstatic rendition of pastoral love should be so shot through with notes of dark admonition, or that the currents of *eros* and *thanatos* should converge under an irresistible law. To John Addington Symonds Hardy wrote in 1889: 'All comedy, is tragedy, if you only look deep enough into it.'[33] Despite Tess's clinging to principle, to her vow not to marry after her violation by Alec, she is carried forward by her desire for happiness, by Angel's insistent coaxing and by the surroundings that 'impregnate' them both. She attempts to tell him her experiences, in the face of his condescension, 'loving satire', and interruptions. But she is swayed to accept the silence he presses on her by her appetite for joy, 'as the tide sways the helpless weed' (xxx). As weeks pass she delays a decision. 'In reality, she was drifting into acquiescence . . . every wave of her blood, every pulse singing in her ears, was a voice that joined with nature in revolt against her scrupulousness' (xxviii). The drive toward joy, which Freud would call the 'pleasure principle', and the desire to preserve this moment of happiness, of 'perpetual betrothal', prevent her from speaking as she yields to the tides of life.

Yet here too, in this 'flux and reflux', Hardy converts the language of ecstasy into a premonition of loss to come. The imagery of Tess's surrender turns subliminally against her happiness, threatening her with submersion as if she were Ophelia: 'Her feelings almost filled her ears like a babble of waves, and surged up to her eyes' (xxxi). As the water rises, squirts through the weirs and booms in a 'multitudinous intonation', Tess fatalistically is 'carried along . . . without the sense of a will'; 'she accordingly drifted into that passive responsiveness to all things her lover suggested' (xxxii).[34] Self-annihilation looms ahead, whether through the suppression of her most significant experience, or through an honest declaration whose price will be her happiness.

Hence the feelings that lift Tess also drown her. Her instinct for self-preservation impels her toward candour and toward self-destruction. Hardy elaborates a Keatsian duality in the courtship, in which 'the thread of her life was so distinctly twisted of two strands, positive pleasure and positive pain' (XXVIII). Tess takes refuge from Angel's entreaties in a willow thicket where she lies moaning on a bed of spear-grass, her 'palpitating misery broken by momentary shoots of joy' (XXVIII). The seesawing mixture of pleasure and pain tears her, and alienates her from those who cannot understand her dilemma. The mixture of misery and joy, dark and light, seems the inevitable extension of the uncultivated twilit garden in Chapter XIX, strangely reminiscent of Hieronymus Bosch with its dazzling but malodorous weeds, thistle-milk and slug-slime, the air filled with floating pollen, where the two are first brought together by the thin music of Angel's harp.

If the imagery of a green world that suffuses the Talbothays romance is idyllic, it is also anti-romantic. Where opposites touch they become entangled or suspended momentarily in equilibrium, but not (as Coleridge would have it) reconciled. Tess's oscillation between joy and agony draws on bitter references to romantic poetry, especially to Wordsworth and Coleridge. From the outset, Wordsworth's lyrical ballad about 'nature's holy plan' provokes a sharp rejoinder, in light of the vulnerability of the weak to the Darwinian struggle for survival. Fecundity does not guarantee the survival of the individual, as the Malthusian Tess early comes to understand in contemplating her parents' improvidence. The pathos of Tess's younger siblings – left without a father, a home, or any source of food and clothing – inspires the narrator to comment on the 'ghastly satire' in Wordsworth's lines 'Not in utter nakedness/But trailing clouds of glory do we come'. More subliminal cues refer us as well to Coleridge's 'Dejection: An Ode', whose narrative line here is turned inside out, with the imagery of 'Joy the luminous cloud' as 'A light, a glory, a fair luminous cloud/Enveloping the earth' preceding Angel's desiccating intellectual reflections on his situation in a grief that is 'void, dark and drear'. The brief moment of fulfilment that the couple enjoy, when they take refuge from the police after the murder of Alec, offers its own comment on the term 'pure' in Coleridge's line, 'Joy that ne'er was given,/Save to the pure, and in their purest hour'.

Ironic juxtapositions and sharp shifts in tone quickly catch the eye of a reader. Participating in a Shakespearean tradition that sets high romance against the farce of clowns, such ruptures become naturalized as one aspect of tragic irony. More profoundly disturbing, but less patent on the surface, are romantic plots that are dismembered, inverted and dispersed across the narrative, like the legend of the D'Urberville coach. The novel is thick with such ironic allusions to Milton, medieval romance, romantic poetry, opera, country songs and folklore.

Many details in the narrative awaken the ghostly trace of familiar fairy tales, mixing Christian with pagan, including verbal touches like the description of the twilit garden whose sticky blights 'though snow-white on the apple-tree trunks, made blood-red stains on her skin' (xix). Characteristically, however, these motifs are both rearranged and turned into grotesque inversions of conventional plots. Some echoes may not have been conscious, for instance one sinister reminder of a miller's daughter in Grimm. When Tess submits to Joan's pleas and embellishments, saying 'Do what you like with me, mother', her surrender to emotional blackmail and commodification by her feckless parents casts her in the role of this classic fairy-tale heroine, able to preserve her purity even while submitting to violence and exile. Grimm's miller, who has traded his daughter to the devil in exchange for immense wealth, asks her, 'Help me in my need.' The daughter responds, 'Do with me what you will', and the father cuts off her hands. Miraculously preserved by a guardian angel, the girl leaves home, marries a king, and bears a child whom she baptizes 'Sorrowful', a name whose universality rings out in the baptism of Tess's dying infant. Unlike the miller's daughter, whose mutilated body is ultimately restored, Tess learns that 'once lost always lost' is the rule for chastity. Scattered and reordered, these motifs fracture the conventional pattern of female suffering and redemption.

Of another embedded fairy tale, 'Sleeping Beauty', which was repeatedly rewritten by Victorian adapters such as Christina Rossetti, Dinah Mulock Craik, Anne Thackeray and Jean Ingelow,[35] Hardy was undoubtedly conscious, since he parodied its most conspicuous motifs. Having fallen asleep while driving the family cart to market, Tess is awoken not by a prince but by the death of her horse Prince, sole support of the higgler's family. One of her names in the manuscript,

Rose-Mary, may evoke the Grimms' name for Sleeping Beauty, 'Briar Rose', at the moment when she is pricked by the roses that Alec, a pseudo-aristocrat, has offered her – an ill omen that displaces the traditional prick by a needle or spindle that marks the sexual rite of passage of a fairy-tale heroine. After beginning work on the D'Urberville estate, the exhausted Tess falls asleep once again – overcome by fatigue and drugged by spirits that he pours 'unawares' down her throat (a detail in the first edition that Hardy would later omit). Sleep is followed inexorably by violence, as the sexual motifs in the tale are brought to the foreground.

The power of fairy-tale plots to shape people's dreams (and vice versa) is made patent by Joan Durbeyfield's hope that Tess would restore the family fortunes by marrying a gentleman: 'It would have been something like a story to come back with' (XII). Even had Alec offered marriage to the 'farm girl' with the manners of a 'princess', however, Tess might well have responded with a refusal rather than 'a crude snatching at social salvation'. She rejects the trite social solution to her story just as Hardy in his essay 'Candour in English Fiction' rejects the 'regulation finish' that 'they married and were happy ever after'.[36]

Her true Prince is, of course, Angel, and Tess's willingness to wait indefinitely for Angel conforms to the requirements of the fairy-tale. Just as Perrault mocks his heroine for such implausible patience, an ironic attitude echoed by a number of Victorian women writers, Alec here sinisterly assures Tess that she waits in vain, and her struggle to conform to her own ideal ultimately fails. The plot of century-long female virtue rewarded by a happy ending has disintegrated. Legends inevitably erode: 'So does Time ruthlessly destroy his own romances' (XLIX).

While Tess's tendency to fall asleep just before a catastrophe has often been noted, the transference of the sleep motif to Angel has been less fully commented on. Angel, whose unconscious submission to social convention and romantic ideals is responsible for his misreading of Tess, believes in the romance of a virginal maid whom he awakens by kissing, behind the screen of a willow thicket.[37] Symbolically, Angel wrestles against the reality principle in his sleep, pummelling his travelling trunk, as he dreams it to be a crude farmer who has commented that Tess is comely enough but not a 'maid'. Tess awakens him from this sleepwalking episode. On the second occasion, after their mutual confessions of prior sexual experience, Angel wraps Tess in her sheet, then carries her outdoors, across a narrow footbridge, to the overgrown ruin of the nearby Wellbridge Abbey-church, where he places her in the stone coffin of an abbot, kisses her, then falls into 'the deep dead slumber of exhaustion' (XXXVII). Again, Tess rouses him to protect him from the winter's chill. Angel's difficulty in distinguishing waking from sleeping corresponds to his more general difficulties of self-definition and understanding of the world.

A counterpart to women's novels such as Jane Austen's *Northanger Abbey* or George Sand's *Indiana* that mock their heroines for reading life through the lens of fiction, Hardy's novel presents Angel as prey to belief in the romantic plot. Angel's return home to Tess is guided by his narcissistic recollection of their wedding day: 'How her eyes had lingered upon him; how she had hung upon his words as if they were a god's!' (XLIX). His delusion that he is a prince charming who will awaken Tess sexually is exploded by her confession. Her 'mishap', he recognizes, should be the subject of satire, not of tragic suicide. But his awakening leaves him sleepwalking: although he is 'no longer passion's slave', he is not yet 'enfranchised' (XXXV). The plot he is caught in is not the one he thought he was writing.

The anti-romantic thrust of Hardy's narrative experimentation finds a comic representative in the story-telling voice of the farmer who runs the dairy at Talbothays. 'Dairyman Crick's stories had the peculiarity of seeming to be ended when they were not really so' (XXI). While churning on a hot summer's day, the dairyman tells the comic tale of Jack Dollop, a ''hor's-bird of a fellow' who had once worked at the farm. Like the cream, which resists turning into butter (and like Tess herself, who wishes for a 'perpetual betrothal'), Crick's tale of milker Dollop thrives on delays. Doing all the voices with great vivacity, he recounts how the wily Dollop hid in the churn from the mother of a young milkmaid he had deceived, apparently eluding her. Crick pauses for comments before then continuing with the mother, who once she discovered the hiding place angrily winched the churn. Rattled about inside, Jack finally promised to make it right, 'And so it ended that day.' Dairyman Crick hints that his ending may be merely provisional, valid perhaps for but a day, since every narrative is a fragment extracted from the continuum of life.

Hardy, we recall, rejected the 'regulation finish' of conventional plots, the '*dénouement*' which he knew to be 'indescribably unreal and meretricious, but dear to the Grundyist and subscriber'.[38] Already spun out beyond its first apparent conclusion, the tale of Jack Dollop returns to haunt Tess, for his courting adventures were not really over. Several weeks later, the dairyman reports that Jack did not marry the girl he had wronged but a rich widow instead, whose income lapsed upon her remarriage. The simple story of the reformed rake receives a twist, turned into a perpetual 'cat-and-dog' domestic conflict, once the deceiver has been deceived.

The dairyman's jocular account stands out because of its powerful impact on Tess. Listeners offer a variety of moral comments: Mrs Crick reflects that the widow 'should have told him sooner that the ghost of her first man would trouble him'; assorted milkmaids suggest (depending on their character) the widow should have told the suitor at the last minute, refused him or knocked him down with a rolling-pin. Choking, Tess perceives her own impossible choice before her. 'What was comedy to them was tragedy to her' (xxix). In this characteristic moment, Hardy turns a humorous narration inside out, making the sorrow embedded in the tale apparent. While the pregnant girl's tears elicit laughter from the listeners, Tess, reminded of her own experience of violation by a rake, steps outside, overcome by faintness and distress. In 1888, Hardy jotted in his notebook (anticipating what he wrote to Symonds): 'If you look beneath the surface of any farce you see a tragedy; and, on the contrary, if you blind yourself to the deeper issues of a tragedy you see a farce.'[39] Commonplace as the observation is, it records a vision of the world that shapes many of the leitmotifs and narrative twists of *Tess*.

Even though she is remote from the nameless widow, Tess enters painfully into her dilemma, 'this question of a woman telling her story'.[40] Angel's dismissiveness, the accident of a rug's placement and her own passion for him prevent her from telling her own history before their wedding night, but she knows full well that the ghost of the past will trouble her. Later she senses that an 'implacable past' still engirdles her, and 'Bygones would never be complete bygones till she was a bygone herself' (XLV).

The question of a woman telling her own story, then, lies at the core of Tess's own narrative. The experiences with Alec that Tess confides to her mother on her return are not recorded. Silently the narrative passes from what 'was to be' on the night in The Chase to daybreak several weeks later, when Tess is bearing not only the basket on her arm but the burden of her pregnancy. Again, when Tess writes out her story in a four-page letter to Angel, the envelope goes astray under a rug, and we do not hear the details that would explain why she was 'more sinned against than sinning'. On her wedding night, the blank page of her story marks the unforgiving gap between the phase of her courtship and the phase entitled 'The Woman Pays': 'Her narrative ended; even its re-assertions and secondary explanations were done' (XXXV).

Tess's unrecorded and unread story, like the tale told by Dairyman Crick or the tale of the white hart, repeatedly seems to be ended when it is not so. After the death and burial of the infant Sorrow, Tess sets off to try her hand at milking, and the narrator defiantly declares, 'Let the truth be told – women do as a rule live through such humiliations, and regain their spirits' (XVI). Thus begins 'Phase the Third, The Rally'. Probably what shocked readers even more in Hardy's radical recasting of narrative convention was the double violation of their expectations in the final phase, 'Fulfilment'. For there, contrary to their desires for a 'regulation finish' (readers wrote asking him to let Tess live), and after her protracted struggle to resist his lust, Tess agreed to become the 'Providence' of her little sisters and brothers by returning to Alec as his mistress. Furthermore, if the murder of Alec is a 'fulfilment' of a kind, repaying his admitted wrongs to her, Tess's return the same morning to Angel's embrace undoes the priggish image of the cuckolded husband who had rejected her. Perhaps Tess had not forgotten Angel's despair when he learned that Alec was still alive. In any case, the brief happiness she finds on her final pilgrimage from Sandbourne to Stonehenge, from tinselly modernity to a primordial past, baffled readers' belief in the outcomes permitted to a heroine who had committed a fundamentally immoral act.

The narrative silence at the major junctures in Tess's life, compounded by Angel's inability to hear her reiterated insistence on telling her 'history', indicts Victorian censorship of her experiences. The original trauma of her defloration by Alec, enveloped in the vapours of night and drug, remains unassimilable, haunting her as she haunts the Marlott woods at dusk, when 'the plight of being alive becomes attenuated to its least possible dimensions' (x111). For in such a trauma, the mental wound, unlike a physical one, has come 'too soon, too unexpectedly, to be fully known'.[41] The silence itself stubbornly bears witness to the repressed wound that cries out, whose truth buried deep in darkness, sleep and ignorance remains unavailable for mourning and drives Tess forward toward her death. Each of Angel's slighting gestures re-enacts her repression; each attempt to retell her story attempts to voice a history that is socially inaccessible. Gaps also insistently invade the space of their love-making, breaking Tess's sentences into fragments and condensing her story into a single name: 'I – I – am not a Durbeyfield, but a D'Urberville –' (xxx). These breaks, like her dry sobs, mark the violence that cannot be told but will be re-enacted through a chain of repetitions that seems overdetermined by ancestry, character and the casual workings of a rural economy in decay. The trauma repeats itself unremittingly.

In our resistance to these silences, we may find one of the secrets to Hardy's apparent ability to conjure a living heroine, even one larger than life. Tongue in cheek, Hardy acknowledged in his Preface to the Fifth Edition the contribution to the creative process made by readers' 'own imaginative intuition' (Appendix I). As we undertake our writerly task of reconstituting Tess's figure, we may return to consider her many other forms of expression: the counterpoint of her whistling to the bullfinches, her sublime recitation of the baptismal rites, her weeping empathy with the dying pheasants and her two eloquent letters to Angel. The voice of her letters, heard first as an anguished cry for help, then (in reverse order) as the awakening of Angel's consciousness, takes on life by virtue of its reception. What it tells us is not a sequence of events, but a sequence of feelings, not 'things done', but 'impulses' and 'things willed'. By her final words, Tess assumes control of events. Her execution will forestall any recriminations by Angel in the future. With the simple phrase 'I am ready', she gathers the strands of her life together.

Margaret R. Higonnet

Notes

1. *Life*, 255; *Biography*, 322–3.

2. *Collected Letters*, I, 249.

3. *Life*, 255, 258.

4. 'Candour in English Fiction', in *Personal Writings*, 129, 130.

5. *Collected Letters*, I, 246.

6. See Laird; Gatrell; and Patricia Ingham, *Thomas Hardy* (Atlantic Highlands: Humanities Press International, 1990), pp. 86–7.

7. *Collected Letters*, I, 251, 267.

8. 'Culture and Anarchy', Cox, 220–21.

9. Cox, 193.

10. The trail of blood is brilliantly traced by Tony Tanner, 'Colour and Movement in Hardy's *Tess of the d'Urbervilles*', *Critical Quarterly* 10 (Autumn 1968), 219–39.

11. The allusion to 'spoilers' (Judges 2: 14) prepares the reader for Tess's revenge on Alec, as Jael avenges her people on Sisera the spoiler (Judges 5: 24–30). Alec has already foreshadowed his own end by promising Tess: 'I'll never do it again against your will. My life upon it now!' (VIII). See 'A History of the Text' on modifications in later editions to the scene in The Chase.

12. Unsigned review, *Pall Mall Gazette*, 31 December 1891, Cox, 182.

13. *Collected Letters*, I, 245.

14. Ellen Moers, 'Tess as Cultural Stereotype', in *Twentieth Century Interpretations of 'Tess of the d'Urbervilles': A Collection of Critical Essays*, ed. Albert J. LaValley (Englewood Cliffs: Prentice-Hall, 1969), pp. 99–100.

15. *Life*, 241.

16. *Life*, 226.

17. *Life*, 261–2.

18. *Life*, 182.

19. Hardy's friend Horace Moule reported to the local antiquarian society

on the legend of the Turberville 'spectre-coach', according to which 'none can see this ghostly coach of the Turbervilles who have not Turberville blood in their veins'. Hardy inserted this tale relatively late into the manuscript (Michael Millgate, *Thomas Hardy: His Career as a Novelist* (Houndmills: Macmillan, 1994), p. 400n). Laird argues that the D'Urberville motifs in the serial versions and in the 1891 edition build up the sense of impending doom, hereditary recklessness and violence, and give Tess a romantic 'aura' (Laird, 114–16).

20. Ingham, *Thomas Hardy*, pp. 68, 72–3.

21. The novel also borrows information from 'The Dorsetshire Labourer' about women's labour for the sections about hiring practices and technological change at Flintcomb-Ash and the description of moving on Lady-Day.

22. *Life*, 262.

23. Penny Boumelha, *Thomas Hardy and Women: Sexual Ideology and Narrative Form* (Totowa, N.J.: Barnes and Noble, 1982), pp. 122–3. See also Ingham, *Thomas Hardy*, p. 73; and Mary Childers, 'Thomas Hardy, the Man Who "Liked" Women', *Criticism* 23 (1981), 219–39.

24. Gatrell, 101. Gatrell finds further contradictions within the detached narrator, when he makes ironic, non-authoritative narratorial interventions (p. 104).

25. Millgate, *Thomas Hardy: His Career as a Novelist*, p. 278.

26. Peter Widdowson, ' "Moments of Vision": Postmodernising *Tess of the d'Urbervilles*; or, *Tess of the d'Urbervilles* Faithfully Presented by Peter Widdowson', in *New Perspectives on Thomas Hardy*, ed. Charles P. C. Pettit (Houndmills: Macmillan, 1994), p. 97. See also Kathleen Blake, 'Pure Tess: Hardy on Knowing a Woman', *Studies in English Literature* 22 (1982), 689–705.

27. *Life*, 239.

28. *Life*, 226.

29. *Collected Letters*, I, 274.

30. *Life*, 222.

31. *Collected Letters*, I, 250.

32. The Chaseborough dance scene elaborately expands this experience of luminous haze, in which the elements blend and bodies meet: see Appendix V.

33. *Collected Letters*, I, 190. See *Life*, 224.

34. In the Fifth Edition of 1892, this image reappears in Chapter LV (see note 5). Hardy thus connects the different forms of her suicidal self-division.

35. See U. C. Knoepflmacher, 'Repudiating Sleeping Beauty', in *Girls, Boys, Books, Toys*, ed. Beverly Clark and Margaret Higonnet (Baltimore: Johns Hopkins University Press, 1998).

36. *Personal Writings*, 127–8.

37. Like Perrault's prince, who notices that Sleeping Beauty was dressed like his grandmother, Angel on the wedding night recognizes similarities between Tess and her granddames in the portraits built into the wall of Wellbridge Manor; it is he, however, who has created the *décolleté* effect in order to set off the jewels he gives her.

38. *Collected Letters*, I, 195; *Personal Writings*, 130.

39. *Life*, 224.

40. See Margaret R. Higonnet, 'A Woman's Story: Tess and the Problem of Voice', in *The Sense of Sex: Feminist Perspectives on Hardy*, ed. Margaret R. Higonnet (Urbana: University of Illinois Press, 1993), pp. 14–21.

41. Cathy Caruth, *Unclaimed Experience: Trauma, Narrative, and History* (Baltimore: Johns Hopkins University Press, 1996), p. 4.

Bayley, John, *An Essay on Hardy* (Cambridge: Cambridge University Press, 1973)

Bernstein, Susan David, 'Confessing and Editing: The Politics of Purity in Hardy's *Tess*', in *Virginal Sexuality and Textuality in Victorian Literature*, ed. Lloyd Davis (Albany: State University of New York Press, 1993)

Boone, Joseph A., *Tradition Counter Tradition: Love and the Form of Fiction* (Chicago: University of Chicago Press, 1987)

Boumelha, Penny, *Thomas Hardy and Women: Sexual Ideology and Narrative Form* (Totowa, N.J.: Barnes and Noble, 1982)

Bronfen, Elisabeth, *Over Her Dead Body: Death, Femininity, and the Aesthetic* (New York: Routledge, 1992)

Casagrande Peter J., *Tess of the d'Urbervilles: Unorthodox Beauty* (New York: Twayne, 1992)

Claridge, Laura, 'Tess: A Less than Pure Woman Ambivalently Presented', *Texas Studies in Literature and Language* 28 (1986), 324–38

Elbert, Monika, 'Malinowski's Reading List: Tess as Field Guide to Woman', *Colby Library Quarterly* 35.1 (1999), 49–67

Garson, Marjorie, *Hardy's Fables of Integrity: Woman, Body, Text* (Oxford: Clarendon Press; New York: Oxford University Press, 1991)

Gatrell, Simon, *Thomas Hardy and the Proper Study of Mankind* (Houndmills: Macmillan, 1993)

Goode, John, *Thomas Hardy: The Offensive Truth* (Oxford: Blackwell, 1988)

Hennelly, Mark, 'The "Original Tess": Pre-Texts, Tess, Fess, Tesserae, Carnivalesque', *Thomas Hardy Yearbook* 25 (1998), 26–68.

Higonnet, Margaret R. (ed.), *The Sense of Sex: Feminist Perspectives on Hardy* (Urbana: University of Illinois Press, 1993)

Ingham, Patricia, *Thomas Hardy* (Atlantic Highlands: Humanities Press International, 1990)

Jacobus, Mary, 'Tess: The Making of a Pure Woman', in *Tearing the*

Veil: Essays on Femininity, ed. Susan Lipshitz (London: Routledge and Kegan Paul, 1978), pp. 72–92

Kramer, Dale (ed.), *The Cambridge Companion to Thomas Hardy* (Cambridge: Cambridge University Press, 1999)

—(ed.), *Critical Essays on Thomas Hardy: The Novels* (Boston: G. K. Hall, 1990)

—, *Thomas Hardy: 'Tess of the d'Urbervilles'* (Cambridge: Cambridge University Press, 1991)

Law, Jules, ' "A Passing Corporeal Blight": Political Bodies in *Tess of the D'Urbervilles'*, *Victorian Studies* 40.2 (1997), 245–70

Miller, J. Hillis, *Fiction and Repetition: Seven English Novels* (Cambridge, Mass.: Harvard University Press, 1982)

Millgate, Michael, *Thomas Hardy: His Career as a Novelist* (1971; Houndmills: Macmillan, 1994)

Page, Norman (ed.), *Oxford Reader's Companion to Hardy* (Oxford: Oxford University Press, 2000)

Pettit, Charles P. C. (ed.), *New Perspectives on Thomas Hardy* (Houndmills: Macmillan; New York: St Martin's Press, 1994)

Poole, Adrian, 'Men's Words and Hardy's Women', *Essays in Criticism* 31 (1981), 328–45

Riquelme, John Paul (ed.), *Tess of the d'Urbervilles: Complete, Authoritative Text with Biographical and Historical Contexts, Critical History, and Essays from Five Contemporary Critical Perspectives* (Boston, Mass.: Bedford, 1998)

Springer, Marlene, *Hardy's Use of Allusion* (Lawrence: University Press of Kansas, 1983)

Tanner, Tony, 'Colour and Movement in Hardy's *Tess of the d'Urbervilles'*, *Critical Quarterly* 10 (Autumn 1968), 219–39

Widdowson, Peter, *'Tess of the d'Urbervilles'* (New York: St Martin's Press, 1993)

—(ed.), *Tess of the d'Urbervilles* (New Casebooks) (Houndmills: Macmillan; New York: St Martin's Press, 1993)

Williams, Melanie, '*Tess of the D'Urbervilles* and the Law of Provocation', in *Law and Literature*, ed. Michael Freeman and Andrew Lewis (Oxford: Oxford University Press, 1999), pp. 167–90

See also books listed in the Bibliographical Note.

In early December 1891, *Tess of the D'Urbervilles* was published in a three-volume edition of 1,000 copies by Osgood, McIlvaine and Co. Hardy had been occupied with the novel for more than four and a half years – since at least mid 1887, when he signed a contract for a serial story with Tillotson and Son, the newspaper fiction syndication bureau based in Bolton, Lancashire.[1] During that time it underwent a complex metamorphosis. The phases of *Tess*'s composition and publication can be traced through the manuscript (British Museum), the serial versions of the novel and its 'dismembered' parts, the *Life* and Hardy's correspondence. After the first edition of 1891 (used as the copy-text here) *Tess* went through further substantial changes, particularly for the one-volume edition of 1892 ('Fifth Edition'); the 1895 Osgood, McIlvaine 'Wessex Novels' edition; the 1900 Harper Paperback Edition; the 1902 Macmillan Uniform Edition; and the 1912 Macmillan Wessex Edition. The most significant textual variations both leading up to and following the publication of the first edition are discussed in broad terms in a later section ('The 1891 *Tess*') and in further detail in the explanatory notes. Readers looking for more-complete accounts of the novel's composition, publication and revision should consult Juliet Grindle and Simon Gatrell's 1983 critical edition and J. T. Laird's *The Shaping of 'Tess of the d'Urbervilles'* (see 'Bibliographical Note').

COMPOSITION AND PUBLICATION

On 16 March 1887, Tillotson's offered Hardy 1,000 guineas for a story of 'the same length as *The Woodlanders*'.[2] Hardy duly agreed, and on 29 June an agreement was signed stating that Tillotson's would purchase 'the exclusive serial right of Publication together with the right

of supply to America of Advance Sheets.' In return four instalments
were to be delivered 'on or before the Thirtieth day of June 1889; and
the remainder by weekly instalments, until completed'.[3] The route to
volume publication was not so simple.

Having settled the contract with Tillotson's Hardy turned his attention to other work: poetry; the slowly evolving *Dynasts*; and short stories,
the writing and publishing of which would parallel his novel writing
throughout the 1880s and 1890s. Notwithstanding these commitments,
Hardy had begun *Tess* by February 1889 (or so he wrote to Tillotson's),[4]
drawing upon impressions and ideas he had gathered on a visit to two
of the novel's principal scenes of action, 'The Valley of the Great Dairies'
on the river Froom and 'The Valley of the Little Dairies' in the Vale of
Blackmoor,[5] at the end of the previous September.

Hardy could not meet the 30 June deadline for the first four
instalments, and sometime after February he negotiated a later date.
By mid July he could report that the promised novel would be entitled
'The Body and Soul of Sue';[6] and by late July or early August he was
working intensively on it.[7] Only a few weeks later he had progressed
far enough to sketch out a short (and circumspect) summary of the
story and announce a new title. In a letter to James Osgood, who was
overseeing from London the American serial publication in *Harper's
Bazar* (as part of Tillotson's syndication arrangements), he wrote:

The title I have thought of is

'Too late, Beloved!'

They tell me it is a very good magazine title, if not good in itself.

I can hardly describe the story in brief. The heroine of the narrative is a
young country girl, a milkmaid, who is, however, a lineal descendant of one
of the oldest county families in the kingdom – of Norman blood and name.
But this is only by the way – her personal character & adventures being, of
course, the immediate source of such interest as the tale may have. I should
say that her position is based on fact.[8]

On 9 September 1889 Hardy despatched 'a portion of the MS' of
'Too Late Beloved' (note the change of punctuation from his working
title) – 'equal to about one-half' of the novel.[9] This was quickly set in

type and the first proofs pulled before anyone at Tillotson's actually read what Hardy had written. Not surprisingly they 'were distinctly taken aback' when they did read it (this was a firm with strong Nonconformist roots), and they immediately asked for substantial changes, suggesting 'that the story should be recast and certain scenes and incidents deleted entirely'.[10] Hardy strenuously objected to these suggestions, and Tillotson's promptly refused to publish, even at the risk of having to pay out the contracted fee. Hardy, however, was content for the contract to be cancelled, and the publishers returned the manuscript, proofs and three prepared illustrations. He and Tillotson's remained on amicable terms, moreover, with Hardy writing 'The Melancholy Hussar' for them almost immediately, and in February 1890 signing an agreement to write another serial (which became 'The Pursuit of the Well-Beloved').[11]

The reason for Hardy's decision not to accept the Tillotson changes, and the thinking behind the puzzling series of negotiations he subsequently entered into concerning the unfinished manuscript, remain open to speculation. As Juliet Grindle and Simon Gatrell point out, 'Hardy had a long record of willingness to alter his texts to suit the sensibilities of serial publishers',[12] so he must have had good reason to refuse on this occasion. It is generally agreed that only the financial success of *Tess* (still two years away) freed Hardy from dependence upon the considerable added income that serial publication usually provided. And he had resigned himself early in his career to the inevitability of bowdlerization for middle-class periodicals. If he became an expert self-bowdlerizer, this was in order to forestall the censorship of editors and ensure that he himself did not develop habits of unthinking self-censorship. As he grew older Hardy increasingly drew his readers' attention to these conditions, deliberately producing one text for serial consumption and quite another for volume publication, and openly remarking upon the enforced 'dismemberment' or 'mutilation' of his manuscripts and their subsequent 'restoration'.[13] In other words, Hardy was perfectly prepared to compromise with the serials if he felt that he could preserve some 'original' version of the text for reconstitution as the volume edition.[14] In this way, financial pragmatism was reconciled with artistic principle. Grindle and Gatrell argue that because *Tess* was unfinished when it was submitted to Tillotson's, and because Hardy was 'more closely involved as a writer with his heroine than with the central figure of any of his earlier books', he felt unwilling 'to agree to destroy his original conception for the sake of financial gain'.[15] But Tillotson's demands also put him in the position of not only having to change what he had already written but being compelled to adapt the remainder of the story to their strict requirements as he was completing it.

Just as importantly, as far as both the money and the principle were concerned, Hardy knew that he could afford to wait, finish the manuscript and proceed with the self-imposed process of bowdlerization with which he felt more comfortable. This was because in late October 1887, late February 1888 and again in February 1889, Arthur Locker of the *Graphic* had written to him requesting a serial novel. Hardy declined all of these offers, preferring to 'wait for some future opening' in this popular illustrated weekly.[16] As he told Locker in February 1888,

I find it would be impossible for me to enter into any arrangement at present, owing to my uncertainty as to the time at which I shall finish the undertakings I mentioned in my last letter. But I never forget an editor's offer, & I shall be sure to write to you as soon as I feel courage enough to commit myself anew.[17]

When Tillotson rejected *Tess*, therefore, and Hardy allowed the contract to be dissolved, Locker's repeated offers must have been in his mind: he knew that he had a certain buyer for the serial rights.

What Hardy did next may also be explained by this same desire to remain firmly in control of the novel and the process of its temporary 'dismemberment' and to justify his own role as a bowdlerizer for the middle-class family serials. Hardy wrote to Locker in October or November 1889 shrewdly offering to 'substitute a serial story for the short one' he had arranged with them – that is, 'A Group of Noble Dames' – while adding that 'as the date at which I could send in the short one suits you I will consider that as settled'.[18] Rightly confident of securing the contract, he proposed beginning the serial in January 1891, which Locker, when he responded immediately with the expected offer, pushed back to July 1891.[19] With a good portion of the work already completed, this gave Hardy more than eighteen months to finish *Tess*.

When, having secured the breathing space he needed, Hardy was finalizing terms with Locker, however, the unfinished manuscript was being read by Edward Arnold with a view to publication in the monthly *Murray's Magazine*. Hardy had written to Arnold in late September or early October 1889 (this letter has been lost), offering the story and suggesting terms. In reply, Arnold had written that both 'Mr. Murray and I are most anxious to secure your novel if possible', but that '£50 a month is more than we are in the habit of paying'. Arnold also asked to see the manuscript before deciding, and Hardy must have sent it off shortly before he wrote to Locker. On 15 November he heard back from Arnold, who regretted that the novel was 'not, in our opinion, well adapted for publication in this magazine' on the grounds of its 'frequent and detailed reference to immoral situations'.[20]

A couple of days after receiving the manuscript back from Arnold, and having secured the contract with the *Graphic*, Hardy sent it out again, this time to Mowbray Morris at *Macmillan's Magazine*, who likewise advised in a reply of 25 November that 'it would be unwise for me to publish it in my magazine'. Morris's long letter finds no 'theological offence' in *Tess*, but adds:

But there are other things which might give offence, &, as I must frankly own to think, not altogether unreasonably. Of course, you will understand that I write only of the fitness of the story for my magazine, beyond which I have neither the right nor the wish to go. My objection . . . is general rather than particular. Perhaps an instance or two may explain my meaning. It is obvious from the first page what is to be Tess's fate at Trantridge; it is apparently obvious also to the mother, who does not seem to mind, consoling herself with the somewhat cynical reflection that she may be made a lady after if not *before*. All the first part therefore is a sort of prologue to the girl's seduction which is hardly ever, & can hardly ever be out of the reader's mind. Even Angel Clare, who seems inclined to 'make an honest woman' of Tess, has not as yet got beyond a purely sensuous admiration for her person. Tess herself does not appear to have any feelings of this sort about her; but her capacity for stirring & by implication for gratifying these feelings for others is pressed rather more frequently & elaborately than strikes me as altogether convenient, at any rate for my magazine. You use the word *succulent* more than once to describe the general appearance & condition of the Frome Valley. Perhaps I might say that the general impression left on me by reading your story – so far as it has gone – is one of rather too much succulence. All this, I know, makes the story 'entirely modern' . . .

He also criticizes:

some passages in your manuscript where neither the thought nor the language is very clear to me; & words sometimes of which I am not sure that I understand the meaning. This you will doubtless say, & possibly with justice, is my stupidity. But you also sometimes use words which do not seem to me English at all. *Venust*, for example, on p. 214. The meaning is clear enough, of course; but surely the word is no English one. Surely one might as well say of a brave man that he was *fort*, or of a learned man that he was *doct*, as of a pretty woman that she was *venust* . . .

I make no doubt that your story will find many admirers, & certainly no one can deny its cleverness; but I have also no doubt that it would be unwise for me to publish it in my magazine.[21]

Morris's patronizing tone echoes comments of Leslie Stephen in the 1870s. In his commendation of the rural scenes over those of 'entirely modern bearings', Hardy must have felt, as he did earlier, that he was being sent back to Dorset to write about sheepfarming.[22]

It has been suggested by Grindle and Gatrell that Hardy, secure in the certainty of publication in the *Graphic*, knowing what Morris's response to the novel would be and guessing at Arnold's, sent the unfinished novel to them 'to build up evidence' in preparation for his contribution to the *New Review* symposium on 'Candour in English Fiction' (published January 1890). This may be persuasive but does not explain why Hardy raised the question of payments with Arnold if he had no intention of taking things further. Another explanation suggests itself. Hardy had, after all, decided on principle to turn down Tillotson's 1,000 guineas and had already decided to agree to publish the story in the *Graphic*, which would certainly demand changes along the same lines and coerce him into unconsciously accommodating the unwritten half to the *Graphic* readership. In submitting the manuscript to Arnold and Morris, therefore, Hardy was possibly only reassuring himself that the story as he conceived it would not be publishable anywhere in serial form, and that he would therefore have absolutely no choice but to bowdlerize it himself if he wanted to publish serially.

As J. T. Laird has shown, Hardy began that process almost immediately by removing two episodes, most of which material he returned to the manuscript for the volume publication.[23] These were ultimately published separately – 'The Midnight Baptism' in *The Fortnightly Review* in May 1891 and an adaptation of the Chaseborough dance and seduction scene, 'Saturday Night in Arcady', in the *National Observer* in November 1891. In the *Life* Hardy recalled with obvious pleasure how this plan of publishing the offending passages was 'unprecedented'.[24]

Between November 1889 and May 1890, however, Hardy was mostly taken up with his earlier commitment to the *Graphic*, 'A Group of Noble Dames'. Towards the end of June Locker wrote demanding changes to make the stories 'suitable for the . . . delicate imaginations of young girls'.[25] To what extent this wearing work of expurgating 'Noble Dames' influenced 'the permanent fabric'[26] of *Tess* is an important question. If Hardy entered into the agreement with Locker knowing that he would be required to bowdlerize *Tess* quite as much as Tillotson's had originally demanded, then Locker's response to 'Noble Dames' only provided further confirmation. In preparing *Tess* for the *Graphic*, therefore, it seems likely that he would have been concentrating on easing his later task of restoring the text for volume publication. What almost certainly entered the text at this stage, however, is what Grindle and Gatrell describe as 'the increased combativeness of Hardy's defence of his heroine . . . which culminated in his appending the subtitle ["A Pure Woman"] to the first edition.'[27]

Hardy sent the manuscript to the *Graphic* in two instalments in early and late October 1890, and he had received the first proofs (about one-third of the whole) by the end of December, and the remainder by 9 February 1891. Hardy spent most of March correcting and revising the proofs,[28] and the first instalment appeared on 4 July. The novel appeared simultaneously in serials in provincial England and Australia, and two weeks later in *Harper's Bazar*. This latter edition, based on the *Graphic* proof-sheets, is of special significance since Hardy revised it differently (see following section).

As he recalled in the *Life*, Hardy 'spent a good deal of time in August and the autumn correcting *Tess of the d'Urbervilles* for its volume form, which process consisted in restoring to their places the passages and chapters of the original MS. that had been omitted from the serial publication'.[29] By November the proofs had arrived, and *Tess* was published early in December. It immediately attracted mixed reviews, but also unexpectedly vigorous sales: its modest print-run of 1,000 was quickly sold out, and the novel was reprinted in its expensive three-volume form in February and March 1892.[30] The six-shilling one-volume edition, of which 5,000 copies were printed, was published at the end of September, and by the end of the year it had gone through five impressions, selling 17,000 copies. This, the so-called 'Fifth Edition', which was substantially revised by Hardy and includes a new Preface, is of considerable textual significance.

The Harper & Brothers American edition, published in late January 1892, was, as Grindle and Gatrell have shown, set from 'a variety of copy' – both the *Harper's Bazar* version and the *Graphic* revises or sheets.[31] For their second edition, issued in May 1892, the publishers incorporated the excised passages that had been returned to the English first edition, claiming, however, that it had been 'thoroughly revised by Mr. Hardy, and . . . considerably expanded, according to the latest English edition'.[32]

Hardy's next opportunity to revise the novel came in 1894, when a uniform edition of his work was proposed by Osgood, McIlvaine.[33] *Tess*, the first in the series, was published in 1895 from the plates of the one-volume edition and Hardy made many fewer changes than in 1892, although he added a new Preface. In 1900 Harper's, who had bought out Osgood, McIlvaine, issued a sixpenny paperback edition which Hardy revised. In 1902 Macmillan issued a uniform edition of the novels based on the 1895 plates but with some significant revisions (see pp. lxi–lxii below), and in 1912 Hardy revised *Tess* again for the major Macmillan 'Wessex Edition'.

THE 1891 *TESS*

The 'shaping' of *Tess of the D'Urbervilles* has been meticulously traced and analysed by Laird (who places most emphasis on the MS.) and Grindle and Gatrell (who correspondingly emphasize the printed texts). In this summary, accordingly, I shall simply provide a survey of the most significant textual variants discussed in the explanatory notes to this edition, with a view to assisting readers who are familiar with the *Tess* of later editions (those based either on 1912 or, in the case of the Grindle and Gatrell edition, based on the MS. with all of Hardy's verified alterations superimposed). I have grouped the variants here in an approximate way to identify patterns of change in key aspects of the novel: the representation of Tess and the focal events in which she features; the representation of Alec and Angel and their relationships with her; the narrator and the narrative commentary; and important changes in language and dialect. Hardy likewise alters some of the details of social life in the novel, and these are also discussed briefly.

Before considering the 1891 edition in any detail, however, it is necessary to describe the printer's manuscript and its complicated history. Embedded in the manuscript, and identified by its distinct systems of folio-numbering, are the heavily revised sheets of the novel Hardy was writing in 1889 (and which he submitted unfinished to Tillotson's, *Murray's Magazine* and *Macmillan's Magazine*). Laird's research has also revealed that, in Grindle and Gatrell's words, it is

possible to distinguish between different layers of the *89* foliation by the name given to the heroine. She appears successively as Love, Cis, Sue, Rose-Mary and Tess; the first four names are only present on leaves with the *89* foliation, and Tess appears only as a revision on these leaves – though we know from Morris's letter that the revisions had been made by the time he saw the novel.[34]

There are therefore 'five well-defined chronological layers of material',[35] making it impossible to speak simply of the 'manuscript' version of any given reading in the notes which deal with the manuscript readings and in the summary below. However, in the interest of clarity

I do not discriminate among all five layerings. Rather I broadly distinguish between the 'Ur-*Tess*' (the layerings of the 1889 foliation) and the 'MS.' (to indicate the later manuscript readings and cancellations).

The bound manuscript which Hardy presented to the British Museum in 1911 was not the fair-copy manuscript for any one printed edition. The names of the compositors in the margins are of those who set the text for the *Graphic*, but this manuscript 'was not assembled until after the serial manuscript had been returned . . . for only then was it practical for Hardy to restore to their places the forty-seven omitted leaves and a small number of leaves that had been temporarily rewritten for serial purposes'.[36] The manuscript therefore contains traces of Hardy's earliest conceptions of the novel, over which are layered his bowdlerizations for the *Graphic*; and on these changes, in their turn, Hardy superimposed his reconstruction of the text for the first volume edition. This considerably complicates any idea of the novel 'as originally written' (to use Hardy's own misleading words from his 'Explanatory Note'). Rather, the manuscript and the revisions to the printed texts reveal that *Tess*, of all Hardy's novels, calls into question any principles of authorial origination or final intentions that may govern the production of an edited text. This novel was in a more or less constant state of evolution from the late 1880s until at least 1919, and Hardy characteristically never felt that the text came up to his 'original' (that is, ideal) conception of it. Moreover, that evolution does not represent a gradual movement towards coherence and completeness, but, as I shall show, a continual complication of motives and a compounding sense of the contradictions and conflicts present. As the novel evolves, it becomes more and more deeply involved in its 'tangle of inconsistencies'.[37] This is why the complex textual history has proved so significant, especially to feminist critics, who have shown how 'the heroine is too often caught in the middle of Hardy's own evolving ideas'.[38] For this reason, the decision to use the 1891 edition here is a compelling one: it presents *Tess* in a state of overt incompleteness, evidenced by the missing Chaseborough dance sequence, at a significant moment in the history of its conception and its reading.

The most important differences between the 1891 *Tess* and later editions concern the controversial rape–seduction scene. It had been omitted altogether from the *Graphic* where it was replaced by the bogus-marriage plot, in which Alec tricks Tess into going through a form of marriage before a fake registrar. In *Harper's Bazar* (a distinct serial edition for the slightly more liberal American readership, which Hardy prepared from the *Graphic* proof-sheets), the rape–seduction is reinstated, but only as part of Tess's confession to her mother. Working from the proofs, Hardy could make only relatively modest changes for the *Bazar*, and he had to be content with this makeshift restoration. However, as a result of this restriction on the revisions, only the *Bazar* serial and the first American edition (based partly on the *Bazar*) entertain the possibility of Tess taking legal action against Alec for rape. In the *Graphic* Joan Durbeyfield responds to Tess's distressed account of the false marriage by exclaiming: 'But he can be prosecuted for this,' which Hardy left intact in the *Bazar* text, where it refers to the rape–seduction, not the marriage.

The excised chapters dealing with the incident in The Chase and Tess's baby (see Appendix V) were restored for the 1891 *Tess*, when Hardy '[pieced] the trunk and limbs of the novel together'.[39] However, in this edition the Chaseborough episode, in which Tess waits for her companions and is approached by Alec, and that in The Chase, both differ considerably from editions based on Hardy's 'final intentions'. First, the Ovidian 'Chaseborough dance' sequence, part of the Chaseborough episode as published separately in W. E. Henley's *National Observer*, was not returned to the novel until Hardy undertook the revision for the 1912 Macmillan Wessex Edition. Secondly, the rape–seduction differs markedly in 1891 from later editions. In the Ur-*Tess* Alec had rescued the heroine in his gig (perhaps referring back to the earlier sinister reverie in the Ur-*Tess* in which she had imagined his body as an extension of his gig). He has on hand a large wicker-cased household spirit-jar of his mother's, from which he forces her to drink: as in the 1891 *Tess*, she swallows instinctively to avoid the liquid spilling on her best dress. In 1891, however, Hardy substitutes a small 'druggist's bottle', which accentuates the elements of gothic melodrama in the scene, and leaves no doubt that Alec rapes Tess. The few mouthfuls of strong alcohol put an already 'inexpressibly weary' heroine to sleep in the MS., but not before she has time to despair of her vulnerability at Alec's hands; when he returns in the dark and puts his face close to her sleeping face, he detects traces of 'damp about her eyelashes' 'as if she had wept'. The drugged Tess of 1891 does not weep in Alec's absence.

The 1891 *Tess* is the only edition which contains the clear allusion to rape in 'the hands of the spoiler' (Judges). The sheets of manuscript which might have included this reference are missing: it is not known whether it appeared there. We do know that Hardy removed it from 1892 along with the druggist's bottle. In its place, he added to the dialogue of the women who discuss Tess's fate in the fields in Chapter xiv. Their conversation in 1891 turns on the remark that ' 'Twas a thousand pities that it should have happened to she, of all others.' In 1892, Hardy adds: 'A little more than persuading had to do wi' the coming o't, I reckon. There were they that heard a sobbing one night last year in The Chase; and it mid ha' gone hard wi' a certain party if folks had come along.' Hardy probably introduced this exchange to counterbalance his removal of the incriminating drug.

But it is not only the manner in which Hardy represents the rape–seduction scene which prevents readers from an unambiguous reading of the events of that night – the removal of the clumsy device of the sleeping drug obscures the incident, but Hardy also sets about complicating the relationship between Tess and Alec that leads up to and briefly follows the rape–seduction. This process occurs principally in the major revisions for the one-volume edition (the 'Fifth Edition', which I refer to as 1892). To understand these changes fully, however, we must first briefly look at the revisions leading up to 1891. Mary Jacobus has argued that Hardy's main objective in preparing the 1891 *Tess* was to demonstrate the purity referred to in his belated and combative subtitle. She believes that Tess's purity is a 'literary construct "stuck on" in retrospect . . . to meet objections the novel had encountered even before its publication in 1891'.[40] Jacobus stresses two factors in Tess's purification: the development of her 'privileged sensibility', and 'the character-assassination of Alec and Angel'. The younger, more ordinary country-girl of the Ur-*Tess* is conspicuously set apart in 1891: she is 'especially conscious of her parents' shortcomings, especially responsible, especially alert to the implications of Alec's behaviour'.[41] She is in every way the reverse of her progenitors in the Ur-*Tess* and 'Saturday Night in Arcady'. The heroine of the latter is characterized as a country-girl with the pride and self-defensiveness of Tess but whose story passes with the brutal swiftness and casual devastation of sexual assault. Big Beauty resists the 'master's' advances, is seduced or raped by him, is cowed into submissiveness and devotion by her acute economic dependency and is callously rejected by him. Her experience transforms her by destroying whatever was exceptional about her: she becomes one with dark Car and the Queen of Diamonds. This 'Tess', however, is relegated to the margins of the text: at its centre is the extraordinary heroine of the 1891 *Tess*.

If, however, the evidence of the MS.-to-1891 revisions points towards the 'making of a pure woman', the revisions after 1891 seem almost immediately to qualify or complicate Tess's purity. Why? It can be argued that Hardy responded to the reviewers' clamouring objections to the subtitle not, as might be expected, by even more vigorously defending his assertion of her blamelessness, but by further obscuring or mystifying her character. A significant example occurs in Chapter v, where in 1891 Tess wanders 'desultorily' around the grounds of The Slopes, 'eating in an abstracted half-hypnotized state whatever D'Urberville offered her'. In 1892, however, Tess is more actively engaged in what is happening to her, and she wanders around in a 'half-pleased, half-reluctant state'. When in Chapter vi Tess debates whether to take up Alec's offer of employment, she pleads (in 1891): 'But – but – I don't quite like Mr D'Urberville!' In 1892, Hardy amends this to 'But – but – I don't quite like Mr D'Uberville being there!' This removes the already qualified statement of Tess's dislike: she objects not to him but to his 'being there'.

There are further complications in 1892. When in Chapter x Alec first tries to persuade Tess to drive home from Chaseborough with him, the narrator says: 'Tess had never quite got over her original mistrust of him'. In 1892: 'Tess, though flattered, had never quite got . . .' In Chapter xii, when Alec remarks that she did not come to Trantridge for love of him, Tess replies: ' 'Tis quite true. If I had gone for love o' you, if I had ever really loved 'ee, if I loved you still, I should not so loathe and hate myself for my weakness as I do now!' In 1892, Hardy substitutes 'sincerely' for 'really' and adds: 'My eyes were dazed by you for a little, and that was all.' This change implies that Tess did 'love' Alec – insincerely – because she was 'dazed' by him: suggesting, in other words, that she was physically attracted to him against her will and better judgement. This explains better why Tess makes up her mind not to stay on longer at Trantridge than she already has: why she sees 'what I ought to have seen sooner' (XII). These alterations culminate in the account of Tess's thoughts about Alec at the end of Chapter XII: 'She had never cared for him, she did not care for him now. She had dreaded him, winced before him, succumbed to him, and that was all.' This describes fairly accurately the blackened Alec of 1891. The 1892 revisions modify this to: 'She had never wholly cared for him, she did not at all care for him now. She had dreaded him, winced before him, succumbed to a cruel advantage he took of her helplessness; then, temporarily blinded by his ardent manners, had been stirred to confused surrender awhile: had suddenly despised and disliked him, and had run away.' The 1895 revisions see Alec's advantage as 'adroit' not 'cruel'; and in 1912 Tess succumbs to 'adroit advantages', no longer implying only the rape – seduction. Tess's 'confused surrender awhile' points to her profound confusion regarding her own feelings towards Alec which Hardy accentuates in 1892, and which subtly modify 1891's defiantly pure woman. This will have crucial implications later when Angel claims that Tess's 'aims and impulses' are pre-eminent over her actions, since it seems that Hardy sets out in the 1892 revisions to obscure these 'aims and impulses' from her and from the readers.

These revisions (which complicate Tess's relationship with Alec by introducing the possibility of their mutual sexual attraction both in the early stages and later, when she returns to live with him in Sandbourne) do not compromise Tess's blamelessness. Hardy made these changes to answer criticism of his subtitle; it is this matter of 'licensed . . . meaning' that rankles him in the Preface to 1892. If the subtitle is defiant in its declaration of Tess's purity in 1891, in 1892 it represents a rejection of the idea of the 'pure' woman altogether because the phrase necessarily takes its meaning from the idea of the fallen woman. It was probably not Hardy's intention to compromise the virtue of his heroine, nor to offer, more defiantly still, even more 'inducements to his readers to refuse her the name' of 'pure woman'.[42] For Hardy the 'defiant blazon', as Margaret Oliphant described it, defies readers of the novel to define Tess. 'Let me repeat', he stresses in the 1892 Preface, 'that a novel is an impression, not an argument.'

The significant changes to Tess's relationship with Angel Clare from the MS. to the 1891 *Tess*, the 1892 revisions and later editions, also have a bearing upon this complication of Tess's character after 1891. These are most decisive in the later parts, after Tess confesses to Alec's rape–seduction and the birth of her child. The 1891 *Tess* has her assume a kind of shamed servitude towards Angel, who is himself correspondingly stiffer and more remote than we see him in later editions. But Hardy must have felt that Tess's body language gave readers the wrong signals about Angel: he is too much the moral bully. In 1891, for example, Tess consistently lowers her eyes in Angel's presence like a pattern Magdalen, and even calls him 'Mr Clare', a form more properly suited to master and servant. Hardy deletes both of these in 1892.

Hardy also makes a small but vital change to the Tess who walks to Flintcomb-Ash in fear of sexual molestation and who reluctantly makes herself over into a 'mommet of a maid' (XLII). In the 1891 *Tess*, the troublesome compliments make her feel paradoxically hopeful: 'for was it not possible that her husband might claim her even yet?' Thus, 'she was bound to take care of herself on the chance of it, and keep off lovers'. Yet in nipping her eyebrows off and tying the handkerchief around her face Tess ironically knows that in protecting herself she also risks losing what may be her last chance with her husband: her looks. The 1892 revisions accentuate Tess's loneliness and show it as in some way sexual as well as emotional. The harassing men are not 'lovers', so Hardy amends this to 'these casual lovers'. But he also alters the nature of Tess's hope, which is that 'her husband also might say these same things to her even yet'. In this way, Hardy transforms Tess's paradoxical reaction into a poignant study of her sexual longing for the absent Clare.

There are further revisions to Tess's character in the episode of her work on the threshing machine on Groby's farm (XLVII). In 1891 Tess is forced to spend the entire long day doing the back-breaking work on the vibrating platform of the machine. In 1892, Marian changes places with her for occasional half-hours.

The character of Angel Clare, too, undergoes modification in the changes in 1892, which for the most part complement the alterations between the Ur-*Tess* and 1891. Angel is less likable in the 1891 *Tess* than in any other edition: he is more priggish, and he reacts more savagely to Tess's confession. For the serials and 1891 Hardy introduced changes which rid Clare of his passionate abandon and set him on the path toward the Shelleyan 'fastidiousness' which is fixed in 1892 (XXXI). But in 1891 he does not yet have the qualities of self-criticism which temper his stringently moral character. He is the familiar man of heterodoxy here (XXV), but not yet the man of 'heterodoxy, faults, and weaknesses' of 1892. He is the infuriating 'stickler for good morals' (XXXIV), except that in 1891 he seems to exempt himself from the impurity he hates in others. In 1892, he admires spotlessness, 'even though [he] could lay no claim to it' (XXXIV). Only in 1892 does Hardy show that the turning-point in Clare's life – the remorse that 'struck into him' at the stranger's 'cursory remarks' in Brazil (XLIX) – is a moment of sudden self-knowledge. In the 1891 *Tess* Clare, recalling Izz Huett's words that Tess would lay down her life for him, realizes the extent of her love: 'How her eyes had lingered upon him; how she had hung upon his words as if they were a god's!' It is this gratifying recollection that turns Clare from a critic into an advocate of Tess. In 1892, Hardy adds several sentences that indicate Clare's acknowledgement of his own guilt: 'His own parochialism made him ashamed by its contrast. His inconsistencies rushed upon him in a flood. He had persistently elevated Hellenic Paganism at the expense of Christianity; yet in that civilization an illegal surrender was not certain disesteem. Surely then he might have regarded that abhorrence of the un-intact state, which he had inherited with the creed of mysticism, as at least open to correction when the result was due to treachery.'

These faults of Angel's in 1891 are the more striking when we look back upon the earnestness and considerateness of the younger Clare of the MS., and the physical passion of his love for Tess. Hardy may have felt that these characteristics made his rejection of Tess implausible, and by 1891, his love for Tess is 'ethereal to a fault, imaginative to impracticability' (xxxvi). To this in 1892 Hardy adds enigmatically: 'Some might risk the odd paradox that with more animalism he would have been the nobler man. We do not say it.' Many of the revisions to Angel's character in 1892 are clearly meant to endow him with a kind of nobility conspicuously absent from the 1891 *Tess*. For example, Hardy makes numbers of tiny changes to the pivotal episode in which he reacts to Tess's confession (xxxv). In 1891, Clare, shocked, recoils with a stiff and restrained formality, and his first speech reads: 'Tess, am I to believe this? From your manner I am to take it as true. You cannot be out of your mind, though you ought to be. Yet you are not. I see nothing in you to warrant such a supposition as that.' A few moments later, in response to Tess's stunned question 'But you do not forgive me?', Angel replies with unforgiving briskness: 'Forgiveness does not apply to the case. You were one person; now you are another.' The changes for 1892 introduce endearments into both of these speeches which considerably alter their tone. In the first, he exclaims, 'My wife, my Tess – nothing in you warrants . . .'; and in the second, he replies 'O Tess, forgiveness does not apply . . .' Hardy also modifies Angel's outburst to Tess from 'You are an unapprehending peasant woman' to 'You almost make me say you are an unapprehending . . .' Many more dashes and other punctuation marks are also interspersed into Clare's speech in 1892, possibly to accentuate his confusion and torment. These additions undo the hardening of Angel's character that was the result of the 1891 changes, when, for example, his demonic laugh, 'as unnatural and ghastly as a laugh in hell', was added. Readers had to wait until 1892 to have these rather damning characteristics offset by others.

In ennobling Angel's character in 1892, Hardy emphasizes his idealization of Tess. Early in their acquaintanceship, when he is looking at Tess at the Cricks' table, in 1891 Angel muses: 'What a genuine daughter of Nature that milkmaid is!' (xviii). 1892 has him observe that she is 'a fresh and virginal daughter of Nature'. In Chapter xxxii, similarly, the narrator reveals, in 1891, that he 'loved her dearly, though perhaps rather ideally than with the impassioned thoroughness of her feeling for him' (the 'impassioned thoroughness' of Clare's own character, present in the MS., was suppressed more and more). In 1892, Hardy, as he leads up to the confession scene, hints at the danger that lurks in Angel's idealization. Consequently, Angel loves her 'ideally and fancifully', suggesting the extent to which Tess is a fantasy of his own troubled inner conflict between Christian morality and the Pagan sensuousness he mythologizes in the 'natural world' of Hodge. This is most evident in a change in Chapter XXXVI, in which Angel says: 'I thought . . . I should secure rustic unsophistication as surely as I should secure pink cheeks.' In 1892, he says: 'I should secure rustic innocence as surely . . .'

In addition to these adjustments to Angel's character, Hardy by further accentuating his age introduces a certain urgency into his plans, and a fear that all his thinking and questioning has not fitted him for anything. In Chapter XVIII in the 1891 *Tess* Angel, after all his youthful rebellion, realizes that 'something had to be done' (and farming is what he decides upon); in 1892, however, something has to be done because 'he had wasted many valuable years'. When we learn later in the same chapter that his harp was bought at a sale, 1892 has Angel remark 'in a bitter humour that he might have to get his living by it in the streets some day'.

Alec's reappearance in the unlikely character of the ranting parson has troubled readers, and Hardy was again confronted with the problem that he had in the earlier chapters: how to strike and maintain the delicate balance between Alec's stagy villainy and the complexities of his relationship with Tess. Much of the burden of the latter lies with Tess's character, and the alterations Hardy makes to the earlier scenes in 1892 are mostly to her ambivalent feelings about Alec, and they inevitably reflect more favourably upon him. Hardy may therefore have felt that he needed to offset any small trace of sympathy for Alec by returning him to the diabolical villain of the piece dressed up as the convert to Christianity.

The majority of these changes were not made for another ten years, in the 1902 Macmillan Uniform Edition. The only exception to this is a consequential small amendment to the plot. In Chapter LI of the 1891 *Tess*, the Durbeyfields are evicted from their cottage and forced to pack up and move to Kingsbere because Tess has returned and is observed tending her baby's grave 'by some people of scrupulous character and great influence'. With a 'sudden rebellious sense of injustice' she scribbles the note to Angel beginning: 'O why have you treated me so monstrously'. The 1892 changes shift the circumstances for this letter to the reappearance of Alec, who incites Tess to write as a last resort by goading her that Angel will never return: 'Wait – what for? For that nice husband, no doubt. Now look here, Tess, I know what men are, and, bearing in mind the *grounds* of your separation, I am quite positive he will never make it up with you.'

1902 comprehensively demonizes Alec, transforming what is arguably his authentic religious conversion in the 1891 *Tess* – 'he was in earnest, unmistakably' (XLV) – into the 'whimsical conversion' (XLVI) of later editions. In Chapter XLV, for example, the Alec of 1902 (who attributes his conversion to remorse triggered by the sudden death of his mother) anticipates Tess's profound scepticism of these 'good new words in bad old notes' (XLV), her mistrust of his motives and her abhorrence of his cynicism. He remarks at one point: 'there is something of the ridiculous to your eyes in seeing me like this', and later inserts asides such as 'sneer if you like' and (in XLVI) 'A devil of a poor hand I shall make at the trade, no doubt.' When explaining how her unexpected appearance at the barn had unnerved him, he claims in 1891 that 'God helped me through it'; in 1902 it is his own 'will', not 'God', that helps him, 'though perhaps you think me a humbug for saying it'. The more sincere Alec of the 1891 *Tess*, who pleads, 'If you could only know, Tess, the sense of security, the certainty, you would, I am sure—', becomes the cynical Alec of 1902, who says instead: 'If you could only know, Tess, the pleasure of having a good slap at yourself . . .' The 1891 convert insists that faith came to him 'like a shining light'; in 1902 it came 'like a jolly new idea'. The man who blames himself for the 'iniquity' at Trantridge in 1891 (XLVI) blames himself only for 'the whole unconventional business' in 1902. In 1891 when Alec breaks his engagement to preach to the 'poor drunken sinners' at Casterbridge Fair, he claims that it is the first time he has done 'such a monstrous thing'; in 1902, they are 'poor drunken boobies', and it has become 'a practical joke'.

In conclusion, a few words should be said about the development of the narrator and the narrative voice, and about changes in the use of dialect. The narrative voice in *Tess* is perplexing to many readers. It periodically engages in commentary, generalizations and stereotypes which are challenged by the narrative itself, and seems at other points to betray its author's emotional involvement with his heroine. The most conspicuous example of the latter may be found in Chapter XIV where the narrator unexpectedly intrudes into the scene of Sorrow's baptism, remarking that Tess's 'stopt-diapason' voice will 'never be forgotten by those who knew her'. This has been taken as evidence that Hardy had become too close to Tess and had begun to think of her as a real person (in a letter to Sir George Douglas, he admits that 'I . . . lost my heart to her as I went on with her history'[43]). Significantly, however, the intrusion enters the text in 'The Midnight Baptism' (Appendix V), not in the manuscript, where it might be expected if Hardy was becoming more attached to his heroine as he wrote. Its tone of narratorial familiarity with the world of the narrative echoes the tone of the narrators in *A Group of Noble Dames* (the local historian, the rural dean and so on), on which Hardy was also at work at this time. Considered with other dramatic shifts between past and present tense in *Tess*, and with other notable inconsistencies in the way the narrator positions himself in relation to the characters and events, this interjection in Chapter XIV cannot be attributed with any confidence to Hardy's 'involvement' with Tess.

Similarly, as Margaret Higonnet argues in the Introduction (pp. xxvii–xxviii), the conspicuous generalizing commentary about femininity in *Tess* – a commentary consistently ironized by the events – is in part a product of the MS. revisions Hardy made in the preparation of the 1891 *Tess*. Tess's 'feminine hope' that Angel will relent (XXXVI) was originally only her 'hope'; the adjective 'feminine' is added as an afterthought to the MS., as it is in describing her 'feminine loss of courage' in Chapter XLIV.

Another change after 1891 concerns the narrator's attitude towards the labouring poor. Much more could be said about this aspect of the novel, and about Hardy's sources both for it and 'The Dorsetshire Labourer', which is itself used as a 'source'. In Chapter X, in a narratorial aside on the conspicuous youth of the mothers among the workfolk, 1891 has: 'under pressure from matrons not much older than herself – for marriage before means was the rule here as elsewhere – Tess at length consented to go'. This betrays a certain 'Malthusian vexation' (v) on the part of the narrator with the labourers, who carelessly wed before they can afford to raise children, and it also betrays a certain patronizing and generalizing air which sits more than a little uneasily with the novel's castigation of the city-folk who can see only 'Hodge'. The revision of 1892 is sensitive to the inconsistency, and sympathetic towards the labourers' hardships: 'for a fieldman's wages being as high at twenty-one as at forty, marriage was early here'.

The most important alteration concerning dialect in the 1892 revisions is that of Chapter III: 'Mrs Durbeyfield still habitually spoke the dialect; her daughter, who had passed the Sixth Standard in the National School under a London-trained mistress, used it only when excited by joy, surprise, or grief.' In 1892 Tess no longer merely fell into dialect when emotional, but 'spoke two languages; the dialect at home, more or less; ordinary English abroad and to persons of quality'. After 1891, therefore, this marked discrimination between the two worlds of *Tess* bears a more important relation to the tragic events. Educated out of the dying world of her mother's language and culture (the dialect of the elder Durbeyfields is given greater emphasis in 1892 and later), and equally unfitted for the *déraciné* world into which she is propelled, Tess is the country-girl who is intelligent (she 'held a leading place' in the school – v) and profoundly receptive to modern inflections of language and ideas which nevertheless exclude her. Tess's speech is accordingly reduced somewhat in dialect in 1892, though it is also considerably simplified and rendered less educated (probably in response to the first reviews). In 1892, Chapter v, for example, she says she was 'in the mind' to come to The Slopes (in 1891 she was 'inclined' to come) and that the name D'Urberville has 'worn away' to Durbeyfield, not 'corrupted'; to her mother she says 'tending' fowls rather than 'managing' them (vi); likewise 'chance' replaces 'opportunity'.[44]

THE PENGUIN EDITION

This edition of *Tess of the D'Urbervilles* is based on the three-volume first edition, published in December 1891 by James R. Osgood, McIlvaine and Co., London. It has been collated with the following texts:

Holograph manuscript (British Library Additional MS. 38,182)
Graphic serial edition
Harper's Bazar serial edition (partly the basis of Harper's first
    American edition)
'The Midnight Baptism', *Fortnightly Review*, May 1891
'Saturday Night in Arcady', *National Observer*, 14 November 1891
1892 'Fifth Edition' (the first one-volume edition)
1895 Osgood, McIlvaine 'Wessex Novels' edition
1900 Harper Paperback Edition
1902 Macmillan Uniform Edition
1912 Macmillan Wessex Edition
Hardy's study-copy of the 1912 Wessex Edition with pencilled
    emendations destined for the 1920 Mellstock Edition

For this edition the *Nottinghamshire Guardian* and *Sydney Mail* serial editions, which began simultaneously with the *Graphic* on 4 July 1891, have also been consulted. Both are based on unrevised *Graphic* proof-sheets, representing an earlier stage of the serial which is useful where manuscript readings are missing.

This is not a critical edition with full textual apparatus. It does, however, aim to establish a correct and authoritative copy-text based on 1891 by eliminating compositorial errors and inconsistencies (see below). I have included only a fraction of the available textual variants: those which seem significant and of interest to the general reader. Where appropriate, I have tried above and in the explanatory notes to suggest what they tell us about aspects of the novel and its development.

I have silently corrected small errors in punctuation and spelling, and a number of other errors and inconsistencies, some of which were introduced in the typesetting of 1891, others of which originate in the manuscript. These include: in Chapter XI, Alec's '. . . often by love-making?' is missing a question mark; 'Velasquez' is printed as 'Valasquez' (XXV; Hardy has 'Velasquez' in the MS., and in 1892); Chapter XXXV contained an error of agreement ('eyes . . . was yet ever'), which has been corrected to 'were'; in XXXVII 'grey' has been corrected to 'gray' for consistency; in XLI 'well-to-door boor' is corrected to 'well-to-do boor'; 'bye-lanes' has been corrected to 'by-lanes' (L); 'the summit of the road' has been changed to 'the summit of the load' (LII; this misprint particularly annoyed Hardy because it was pointed out in the damning *Saturday Review* notice (Cox, 191), which remarked that 'Mr. Hardy would do well to look to his grammar'); and 'pony-chase' has been corrected to 'pony-chaise' (LIII). Hardy repeats in full Tess's short angry letter to Clare, and gives excerpts from her long impassioned first letter from Flintcomb-Ash and from the letter of the 'Two WELL-WISHERS': these have been made to match the originals in wording and punctuation. 'O' and 'Oh' are used interchangeably throughout in both exclamation and direct address, and they have not been standardized in this edition.

Tim Dolin

Notes

1. William Frederic Tillotson was proprietor of the *Bolton Weekly Journal*. Tillotson's 'purchased the serial rights to novels and stories and then distributed them, in proof or stereotyped form, to magazines and, more frequently, provincial newspapers both in England and abroad' (*Biography*, 284n).

2. The letter of offer is located in the Dorset County Museum, Dorchester.

3. 'Tillotson Fiction Agreements, 1885–1887', Bodleian Library MS., Eng. Misc. f.395/1, pp. 152–61.

4. In the letter to Tillotson's of 7 February declining the 'short paper of 3000 words', Hardy advises that he is 'now engaged' on the serial story (*Collected Letters*, I, 187).

5. 'The Valley of the Great Dairies' 'may have been used as an early working title for the manuscript as a whole' (*Biography*, 291).

6. Not only was Tess at one stage to be called Sue, but Hardy also briefly considered 'Bridehead' as her family name. See Chapter 1, note 2.

7. *Life*, 231.

8. 4 August 1889; *Collected Letters*, I, 196.

9. *Collected Letters*, I, 200. According to Millgate, Tillotson's received a manuscript completed 'to a point just prior to Tess's arrival at Talbothays' (*Biography*, 300), which would therefore have included both the seduction scene and the baptism scene.

10. Purdy, 72.

11. The American serial rights for *Tess*, negotiated between Tillotson's and Harper's, were presumably also affected. Harper's had originally arranged to publish in October 1889, and the date was pushed back to January 1890 at this time. After the contract with Tillotson's was cancelled, Hardy approached Harper's himself (on 10 January 1890), and *Tess* finally began in *Harper's Bazar* on 18 July 1891, two weeks after its début in the *Graphic*.

12. Grindle and Gatrell, 5.

13. Hardy learned to streamline the arduous and complicated process by using different coloured inks in his manuscripts to denote text to be removed from serial editions.

14. The 'restoration' of the text did not always occur, however.

15. Grindle and Gatrell, 5.

16. *Collected Letters*, I, 170.

17. Ibid., I, 173−4.

18. Ibid., I, 201.

19. 18 November 1889; *Collected Letters*, I, 202. Hardy offered Locker serial rights in the UK, Canada and Australia, and serial and book rights in the USA, all for £800. Locker accepted the UK serial rights, as well as the Australian and Indian rights, and suggested Hardy offer American rights to Harper's (see note 11 above).

20. Dorset County Museum; quoted Grindle and Gatrell, 7−8.

21. Dorset County Museum.

22. See *Life*, 105.

23. Laird argues that in these two sections of the manuscript. Alec's surname changes from 'Hawnferne' to 'D'Urberville' without reference to the intermediate version of his name, 'Turberville', as elsewhere in the manuscript because 'it was only after 25 November 1889 that ["Hawnferne"] became "Turberville"'. Thus, 'the manuscript version being written after [25] November 1889 was, in effect, the *serial* version' (Laird, 16).

24. *Life*, 232.

25. Dorset County Museum; quoted Grindle and Gatrell, 11. 'A Group of Noble Dames' was published at the end of May 1891.

26. Grindle and Gatrell, 11.

27. Ibid., 11–12.

28. According to the *Life* (p. 245) he was 'putting the finishing touches to *Tess*' during March. See also *Collected Letters*, I, 230 (to Thomas Bailey Aldrich): 'My own preoccupation at present is that of correcting a bundle of miserably small-typed proofs' (4 March 1891).

29. *Life*, 250. This is corroborated by two letters: 9 August to Louise Moulton: 'I shall get through the work in about ten days or a fortnight, I hope'; and 12 August to Sir George Douglas: 'At present, & all this month, I am and shall be getting ready what I have to publish in the autumn' (*Collected Letters*, I, 241, 242).

30. Grindle and Gatrell note that *Tess* sold 'between 2,000 and 2,500 copies in four months . . . , and this seems to have been regarded as a success beyond the expectations of author or publisher' (p. 17).

31. Grindle and Gatrell, 18.

32. Quoted in Purdy, 76.

33. Osgood, McIlvaine had approached Hardy about a collected edition some years before this, but earlier agreements with other publishers had not expired.

34. Grindle and Gatrell, 25.

35. Laird, 6.

36. Laird, 6.

37. Lionel Johnson, *The Art of Thomas Hardy* (London: Mathews and Lane, 1895), p. 232.

38. Laura Claridge, 'Tess: A Less than Pure Woman Ambivalently Presented', *Texas Studies in Literature and Language* 28 (1986), 332. See also, for example, Mary Jacobus, 'Tess: The Making of a Pure Woman', in *Tearing the Veil: Essays on Femininity*, ed. Susan Lipshitz (London, 1978), pp. 77–92; and Boumelha, *Thomas Hardy and Women* (in 'Further Reading').

39. Hardy's 1891 'Explanatory Note'.

40. Jacobus, 'Tess: The Making of a Pure Woman', p. 78.

41. Ibid., pp. 82, 81.

42. Cox, 215.

43. *Collected Letters*, I, 249.

44. Further discussion of dialect in the novel may be found in Patricia Ingham, 'Dialect in the Novels of Hardy and George Eliot', in George Watson (ed.), *Literary English Since Shakespeare* (Oxford: Oxford University Press, 1970). For an alternative discussion of the changes between the 1891 and the 1892 editions, see Gatrell, 97–110.

TESS
OF THE D'URBERVILLES

A PURE WOMAN

FAITHFULLY PRESENTED BY
THOMAS HARDY

IN THREE VOLUMES

VOL. I

'. . . Poor wounded name! My bosom as a bed
Shall lodge thee.'—W. SHAKSPEARE.

O.   M.

EXPLANATORY NOTE

The main portion of the following story appeared – with slight modifications – in the *Graphic* newspaper; other chapters, more especially addressed to adult readers, in the *Fortnightly Review* and the *National Observer*, as episodic sketches.[1] My thanks are tendered to the editors and proprietors of those periodicals for enabling me now to piece the trunk and limbs of the novel together, and print it complete, as originally written two years ago.[2]

I will just add that the story is sent out in all sincerity of purpose, as representing on the whole a true sequence of things;[3] and I would ask any too genteel reader who cannot endure to have it said what everybody thinks and feels, to remember a well-worn sentence of St. Jerome's: If an offence come out of the truth, better is it that the offence come than that the truth be concealed.[4]

T. H.
November, 1891.

CONTENTS

PHASE THE FIRST

The Maiden

I

On an evening in the latter part of May a middle-aged man was walking homeward from Shaston to the village of Marlott, in the adjoining Vale of Blakemore or Blackmoor. The pair of legs that carried him were rickety, and there was a bias in his gait which inclined him somewhat to the left of a straight line. He occasionally gave a smart nod, as if in confirmation of some opinion, though he was not thinking of anything in particular. An empty egg-basket was slung upon his arm, the nap of his hat was ruffled, a patch being quite worn away at its brim where his thumb came in taking it off. Presently he was met by an elderly parson astride on a gray mare, who, as he rode, hummed a wandering tune.

'Good night t'ye,' said the man with the basket.

'Good night, Sir John,' said the parson.

The pedestrian, after another pace or two, halted, and turned round.

'Now, sir, begging your pardon; we met last market-day on this road about this time, and I said "Good night," and you made reply *"Good night, Sir John,"* as now.'

'I did,' said the parson.

'And once before that – near a month ago.'

'I may have.'

'Then what might your meaning be in calling me "Sir John" these different times, when I be plain Jack Durbeyfield, the haggler?'

The parson rode a step or two nearer.

'It was only my whim,' he said; and, after a moment's hesitation: 'It was on account of a discovery I made some little time ago, whilst I was hunting up pedigrees for the new county history. I am Parson Tringham, the antiquary,[1] of Stagfoot Lane. Don't you really know,

7

Durbeyfield, that you are the direct lineal representative of the ancient and knightly family of the D'Urbervilles,[2] who derive their descent from Sir Pagan D'Urberville, that renowned knight who came from Normandy with William the Conqueror, as appears by Battle Abbey roll?'[3]

'Never heard it before.'[4]

'Well, it's true. Throw up your chin a moment, so that I may catch the profile of your face better. Yes, that's the D'Urberville nose and chin – a little debased. Your ancestor was one of the twelve knights who assisted the Lord of Estremavilla in Normandy in his conquest of Glamorganshire. Branches of your family held manors over all this part of England; their names appear in the Pipe Rolls in the time of King Stephen. In the reign of King John one of them was rich enough to give a manor to the Knights Hospitallers; and in Edward the Second's time your forefather Brian was summoned to Westminster to attend the great Council there. You declined a little in Oliver Cromwell's time, but to no serious extent, and in Charles the Second's reign you were made Knights of the Royal Oak[5] for your loyalty. There have been generations of Sir Johns among you, and if knighthood were hereditary, like a baronetcy,[6] as it practically was in old times, when men were knighted from father to son, you would be Sir John now.'

'You don't say so!' murmured Durbeyfield.

'In short,' concluded the parson, decisively smacking his leg with his switch, 'there's hardly such another family in England.'

'Daze my eyes, and isn't there?' said Durbeyfield. 'And here have I been knocking about, year after year, from pillar to post, as if I was no more than the commonest feller in the parish . . . And how long hev this news about me been knowed, Pa'son Tringham?'

The clergyman explained that, as far as he was aware, it had quite died out of knowledge, and could hardly be said to be known at all. His own investigations had begun on a day in the preceding spring when, having been engaged in tracing the vicissitudes of the D'Urberville family, he had observed Durbeyfield's name on his waggon, and had thereupon been led to make inquiries, till he had no doubt on the subject.

'At first I resolved not to disturb you with such a useless piece of information,' said he. 'However, our impulses are too strong for our judgment sometimes. I thought you might perhaps know something of it all the while.'

'Well, I have heard once or twice, 'tis true, that my family had seen better days afore they came to Blackmoor. But I took no notice o't, thinking it to mean that we had once kept two horses where we now keep only one. I've got a wold silver spoon, and a wold graven seal at home, too; but, Lord, what's a graven seal? . . . And to think that I and these noble D'Urbervilles was one flesh all the time. 'Twas said that my gr't-grandfer had secrets, and didn't care to talk of where he came from . . . And where do we raise our smoke, now, parson, if I may make so bold; I mean, where do we D'Urbervilles live?'

'You don't live anywhere. You are extinct – as a county family.'

'That's bad.'

'Yes – what the mendacious family chronicles call extinct in the male line – that is, gone down – gone under.'

'Then where do we lie?'

'At Kingsbere-sub-Greenhill: rows and rows of you in your vaults, with your effigies under Purbeck-marble canopies.'[7]

'And where be our family mansions and estates?'

'You haven't any.'

'Oh? No lands neither?'

'None; though you once had 'em in abundance, as I said, for your family consisted of numerous branches. In this county there was a seat of yours at Kingsbere, and another at Sherton, and another at Millpond, and another at Lullstead, and another at Wellbridge.'

'And shall we ever come into our own again?'

'Ah – that I can't tell!'

'And what had I better do about it, sir?' asked Durbeyfield, after a pause.

'Oh – nothing, nothing; except chasten yourself with the thought of "how are the mighty fallen."[8] It is a fact of some interest to the local historian and genealogist, nothing more. There are several families among the cottagers of this county of almost equal lustre.[9] Good-night.'

'But you'll turn back and have a quart of beer wi' me on the strength o't, Pa'son Tringham? There's a very pretty brew in tap at The Pure Drop – though, to be sure, not so good as at Rolliver's.'

'No, thank you – not this evening, Durbeyfield. You've had enough already.' Concluding thus, the parson rode on his way, with doubts as to his discretion in retailing this curious bit of lore.

When he was gone, Durbeyfield walked a few steps in a profound reverie, and then sat down upon the grassy bank by the roadside, depositing his basket before him. In a few minutes a youth appeared in the distance, walking in the same direction as that which had been pursued by Durbeyfield. The latter, on seeing him, held up his hand, and the lad quickened his pace, and came near.

'Boy, take up that basket! I want 'ee to go on an errand for me.'

The lath-like stripling frowned. 'Who be you, then, John Durbey-field, to order me about and call me "boy"? You know my name as well as I know yours!'

'Do you, do you? That's the secret – that's the secret! Now obey my orders, and take the message I'm going to charge 'ee wi' . . . Well, Fred, I don't mind telling you that the secret is that I'm one of a noble race – it has been just discovered by me this present afternoon, P.M.' And as he made the announcement, Durbeyfield, declining from his sitting position, luxuriously stretched himself out upon the bank among the daisies.

The lad stood before Durbeyfield, and contemplated his length from crown to toe.

'Sir John D'Urberville – that's who I am,' continued the prostrate man. 'That is if knights were baronets – which they be. 'Tis recorded in history all about me. Dost know of such a place, lad, as Kingsbere-sub-Greenhill?'

'Yes. I've been there to Greenhill Fair.'

'Well, under the church of that city there lie—'

''Tisn't a city, the place I mean; leastwise 'twasn't when I was there – 'twas a little one-eyed, blinking sort o' place.'

'Never you mind the place, boy, that's not the question before us. Under the church of that parish lie my ancestors – hundreds of 'em – in coats of mail and jewels, in great lead coffins weighing tons and tons. There's not a man in the county o' South-Wessex that's got grander and nobler skellingtons in his family than I.'

'Oh?'

'Now take up that basket, and go on to Marlott, and when you come to The Pure Drop Inn, tell 'em to send a horse and carriage to me immediately, to carry me home. And in the bottom o' the carriage they be to put a noggin o' rum in a small bottle, and chalk it up to my account. And when you've done that go on to my house with the basket, and tell my wife to put away that washing, because she needn't finish it, and wait till I come home, as I've news to tell her.'

As the lad stood in a dubious attitude, Durbeyfield put his hand in his pocket, and produced a shilling, one of the comparatively few that he possessed.

'Here's for your labour, lad.'

This made a difference in the young man's estimate of the position.

'Yes, Sir John. Thank you. Anything else I can do for 'ee, Sir John?'

'Tell 'em at home that I should like for supper, – well, lamb's fry if they can get it; and if they can't, black-pot; and if they can't get that, well, chitterlings will do.'

'Yes, Sir John.'

The boy took up the basket, and as he set out the notes of a brass band were heard from the direction of the village.

'What's that?' said Durbeyfield. 'Not on account o' I?'

''Tis the women's club-walking,[10] Sir John. Why, your daughter is one o' the members.'

'To be sure – I'd quite forgot it in my thoughts of greater things! Well, vamp on to Marlott, will 'ee, and order that carriage, and maybe I'll drive round and inspect the club.'

The lad departed, and Durbeyfield lay waiting on the grass and daisies in the evening sun. Not a soul passed that way for a long while, and the faint notes of the band were the only human sounds audible within the rim of blue hills.

II

The village of Marlott lay amid the north-eastern undulations of the beautiful Vale of Blakemore or Blackmoor aforesaid, an engirdled and secluded region, for the most part untrodden as yet by tourist or landscape painter, though within a four hours' journey from London.

It is a vale whose acquaintance is best made by viewing it from the summits of the hills that surround it – except perhaps during the droughts of summer. An unguided ramble into its recesses in bad weather is apt to engender dissatisfaction with its narrow, tortuous, and miry ways.

This fertile and sheltered tract of country, in which the fields are never brown and the springs never dry, is bounded on the south by the bold chalk ridge that embraces the prominences of Hambledon Hill, Bulbarrow, Nettlecombe-Tout, Dogbury, High-Stoy, and Bubb Down. The traveller from the coast, who, after plodding northward for a score of miles over calcareous downs and corn-lands, suddenly reaches the verge of one of these escarpments, is surprised and delighted to behold, extended like a map beneath him, a country differing absolutely from that which he has passed through. Behind him the hills are open, the sun blazes down upon fields so large as to give an unenclosed character to the landscape,[1] the lanes are white, the hedges low and plashed, the atmosphere colourless. Here, in the valley, the world seems to be constructed upon a smaller and more delicate scale; the fields are mere paddocks, so reduced that from this height their hedgerows appear a network of dark green threads overspreading the paler green of the grass. The atmosphere beneath is languorous, and is so tinged with azure that what artists call the middle distance partakes also of that hue, while the horizon beyond is of the deepest ultramarine. Arable lands are few and limited; with but slight exceptions the prospect is a broad rich mass of grass and trees, mantling minor hills and dales within the major. Such is the Vale of Blackmoor.

The district is of historic, no less than of topographical interest. The Vale was known in former times as the Forest of White Hart, from a curious legend of King Henry III.'s reign, in which the killing by a certain Thomas de la Lynd of a beautiful white hart which the king had run down and spared, was made the occasion of a heavy fine.[2] In those days, and till comparatively recent times, the country was densely wooded. Even now, traces of its earlier condition are to be found in the old oak copses and irregular belts of timber that yet survive upon its slopes, and the hollow-trunked trees that shade so many of its pastures.

The forests have departed, but some old customs of their shades remain. Many, however, linger only in a metamorphosed or disguised form. The May-Day dance, for instance, was to be discerned on the afternoon under notice, in the guise of the club revel, or 'club-walking,' as it was there called.

It was an interesting event to the younger inhabitants of Marlott, though its real interest was not observed by the participators in the ceremony. Its singularity lay less in the retention of a custom of walking in procession and dancing on each anniversary than in the members being solely women. In men's clubs such celebrations were, though expiring, less uncommon; but either the natural shyness of the softer sex, or a sarcastic attitude on the part of male relatives, had denuded such women's clubs as remained (if any other did) of this their glory and consummation. The club of Marlott alone lived to uphold the local Cerealia.[3] It had walked for hundreds of years,[4] and it walked still.

The banded ones were all dressed in white gowns – a gay survival from Old Style days,[5] when cheerfulness and May-time were synonyms – days before the habit of taking long views had reduced emotions to a monotonous average. Their first exhibition of themselves was in a processional march of two and two round the parish. Ideal and real clashed slightly as the sun lit up their figures against the green hedges and creeper-laced house-fronts; for, though the whole troop wore white garments, no two whites were alike among them. Some approached pure blanching; some had a bluish pallor; some worn by the older characters (which had possibly lain by folded for many a year) inclined to a cadaverous tint, and to a Georgian style.[6]

In addition to the distinction of a white frock, every woman and girl carried in her right hand a peeled willow-wand, and in her left a bunch of white flowers. The peeling of the former, and the selection of the latter, had been an operation of personal care.

There were a few middle-aged and even elderly women in the train, their silver-wiry hair and wrinkled faces, scourged by time and trouble, having almost a grotesque, certainly a pathetic, appearance in such a jaunty situation. In a true view, perhaps, there was more to be gathered and told of each anxious and experienced one, to whom the years were drawing nigh when she should say, 'I have no pleasure in them,'[7] than of her juvenile comrades. But let the elder be passed over here for those under whose bodices the life throbbed quick and warm.

The young girls formed, indeed, the majority of the band, and their heads of luxuriant hair reflected in the sunshine every tone of gold, and black, and brown. Some had beautiful eyes, others a beautiful nose, others a beautiful mouth and figure: few, if any, had all. A difficulty of arranging their lips in this crude exposure to public scrutiny, an inability to balance their heads, and to dissociate self-consciousness from their features, was apparent in them, and showed that they were genuine country girls, unaccustomed to many eyes.

And as each and all of them were warmed without by the sun, so each had a private little sun for her soul to bask in; some dream, some affection, some hobby, at least some remote and distant hope which, though perhaps starving to nothing, still lived on, as hopes will. Thus they were all cheerful, and many of them merry.

They came round by The Pure Drop Inn, and were turning out of the high road to pass through a wicket-gate into the meadows, when one of the women said –

'The Lord-a-Lord! Why, Tess Durbeyfield, if there isn't thy father riding home in a carriage!'

A young member of the band turned her head at the exclamation. She was a fine and handsome girl – not handsomer than some others, possibly – but her mobile peony mouth[8] and large innocent eyes added eloquence to colour and shape. She wore a red ribbon in her hair,[9] and was the only one of the white company who could boast of such a pronounced adornment. As she looked round Durbeyfield was seen moving along the road in a chaise belonging to The Pure Drop, driven

by a frizzle-headed brawny damsel, with her gown-sleeves rolled above
her elbows. This was the cheerful servant of that establishment, who,
in her part of factotum, turned groom and ostler at times. Durbeyfield,
leaning back, and with his eyes closed luxuriously, was waving his
hand above his head, and singing in a slow recitative –

'I've-got-a-great-family-vault-at-Kingsbere – and-knighted-fore-
fathers-in-lead-coffins-there!'

The clubbists tittered, except the girl called Tess – in whom a slow
heat seemed to rise at the sense that her father was making himself
foolish in their eyes.

'He's tired, that's all,' she said hastily, 'and he has got a lift home,
because our own horse has to rest to-day.'

'Bless thy simplicity, Tess,' said her companions. 'He's got his
market-nitch. Haw-haw!'

'Look here; I won't walk another inch with ye, if you say any jokes
about him!' Tess cried, and the colour upon her cheeks spread over
her face and neck. Her eyes grew moist, and her glance drooped to
the ground. Perceiving that they had really pained her they said no
more, and order again prevailed. Tess's pride would not allow her to
turn her head again, to learn what her father's meaning was, if he
had any; and thus she moved on with the whole body to the enclosure
where there was to be dancing on the green. By the time the spot was
reached she had recovered her equanimity, and tapped her neighbour
with her wand and talked as usual.

Tess Durbeyfield at this time of her life was a mere vessel of emotion
untinctured by experience. The dialect was on her tongue to some
extent, despite the village school:[10] the characteristic intonation of that
dialect for this district being the voicing approximately rendered by
the syllable UR, probably as rich an utterance as any to be found in
human speech. The pouted-up deep red mouth to which this syllable
was native had hardly as yet settled into its definitive shape, and her
lower lip had a way of thrusting the middle of her top one upward,
when they closed together after a word.

Phases of her childhood lurked in her aspect still.[11] As she walked
along to-day, for all her bouncing handsome womanliness, you could
sometimes see her twelfth year in her cheeks, or her ninth sparkling

from her eyes; and even her fifth would flit over the curves of her mouth now and then.

Yet few knew, and still fewer considered this.[12] A small minority, mainly strangers, would look long at her in casually passing by, and grow momentarily fascinated by her freshness, and wonder if they would ever see her again: but to almost everybody she was a fine and picturesque country girl, and no more.

Nothing was seen or heard further of Durbeyfield in his triumphal chariot under the conduct of the ostleress, and the club having entered the allotted space, dancing began. As there were no men in the company the girls danced at first with each other, but when the hour for the close of labour drew on, the masculine inhabitants of the village, together with other idlers and pedestrians, gathered round the spot, and appeared inclined to negotiate for a partner.

Among these on-lookers were three young men of a superior class, carrying small knapsacks strapped to their shoulders, and stout sticks in their hands. Their general likeness to each other, and their consecutive ages, would almost have suggested that they might be, what in fact they were, brothers. The eldest wore the white tie, high waistcoat, and thin-brimmed hat of the regulation curate;[13] the second was the normal undergraduate; the appearance of the third and youngest would hardly have been sufficient to characterize him; there was an uncribbed, uncabined aspect[14] in his eyes and attire, implying that he had hardly as yet found the entrance to his professional groove. That he was a desultory tentative student of something and everything might only have been predicated of him.

These three brethren told casual acquaintance that they were spending their Whitsun holidays in a walking tour through the Vale of Blackmoor, their course being south-westerly from the town of Shaston on the north-east.[15]

They leant over the gate by the highway, and inquired as to the meaning of the dance and the white-frocked maids. The two elder of the brothers were plainly not intending to linger more than a moment, but the spectacle of a bevy of girls dancing without male partners seemed to amuse the third, and make him in no hurry to move on.[16]

He unstrapped his knapsack, put it, with his stick, on the hedge-bank, and opened the gate.

'What are you going to do, Angel?' asked the eldest.

'I am inclined to go and have a fling with them. Why not all of us – just for a minute or two – it will not detain us long?'

'No – no; nonsense!' said the first. 'Dancing in public with a troop of country hoydens – suppose we should be seen! Come along, or it will be dark before we get to Stourcastle, and there's no place we can sleep at nearer than that; besides, we must get through another chapter of *A Counterblast to Agnosticism*[17] before we turn in, now I have taken the trouble to bring the book.'

'All right – I'll overtake you and Cuthbert in five minutes; don't stop; I give my word that I will, Felix.'

The two elder reluctantly left him and walked on, taking their brother's knapsack to relieve him in following, and the youngest entered the field.

'This is a thousand pities,' he said gallantly, to two or three of the girls nearest him, as soon as there was a pause in the dance. 'Where are your partners, my dears?'

'They've not left off work yet,' answered one of the boldest. 'They'll be here by and by. Till then, will you be one, sir?'

'Certainly. But what's one among so many!'

'Better than none. 'Tis melancholy work facing and footing it to one of your own sort, and no clasping and colling at all. Now, pick and choose.'

' 'Ssh – don't be so for'ard!' said a shyer girl.

The young man, thus invited, glanced them over, and attempted some discrimination; but, as the group were all so new to him, he could not very well exercise it. He took almost the first that came to hand, which was not the speaker, as she had expected; nor did it happen to be Tess Durbeyfield. Pedigree, ancestral skeletons, monumental record, the D'Urberville lineaments, did not help Tess in her life's battle as yet, even to the extent of attracting to her a dancing-partner over the heads of the commonest peasantry. So much for Norman blood unaided by Victorian lucre.

The name of the eclipsing girl, whatever it was, has not been handed down; but she was envied by all as the first who enjoyed the luxury of a masculine partner that evening. Yet such was the force of example that the village young men, who had not hastened to enter the gate while no intruder was in the way, now dropped in quickly, and soon the couples became leavened with rustic youths to a marked extent, till at length the plainest woman in the club was no longer compelled to foot it on the masculine side of the figure.

The church clock struck, when suddenly the student said that he must leave – he had been forgetting himself – he had to join his companions. As he fell out of the dance his eyes lighted on Tess Durbeyfield, whose own large orbs wore, to tell the truth, the faintest aspect of reproach that he had not chosen her. He, too, was sorry then that, owing to her backwardness, he had not observed her; and, with that in his mind, he left the pasture.

On account of his long delay he started in a flying-run down the lane westward, and had soon passed the hollow and mounted the next rise. He had not yet overtaken his brothers, but he paused to take breath, and looked back. He could see the white figures of the girls in the green enclosure whirling about as they had whirled when he was among them. They seemed to have quite forgotten him already.

All of them, except, perhaps, one. This white figure stood apart by the hedge alone. From her position he knew it to be the pretty maiden with whom he had not danced. Trifling as the matter was, he yet instinctively felt that she was hurt by his oversight. He wished that he had asked her; he wished that he had inquired her name. She was so modest, so expressive, she had looked so soft in her thin white gown that he felt he had acted stupidly.

However, it could not be helped, and turning, and bending himself to a rapid walk, he dismissed the subject from his mind.

III

As for Tess Durbeyfield, she did not so easily dislodge the incident from her consideration. She had no spirit to dance again for a long time, though she might have had plenty of partners; but, ah! they did not speak so nicely as the strange young man had done. It was not till the rays of the sun had absorbed the young stranger's retreating figure on the hill that she shook off her temporary sadness and answered her would-be partner in the affirmative.

She remained with her comrades till dusk, and participated with a certain zest in the dancing; though, being heart-whole as yet, she enjoyed treading a measure purely for its own sake; little divining when she saw 'the soft torments, the bitter sweets, the pleasing pains, and the agreeable distresses'[1] of those girls who had been wooed and won, what she herself was capable of in that kind. The struggles and wrangles of the lads for her hand in a jig were an excitement[2] to her no more; and when they became fierce she rebuked them.

She might have stayed even later, but the incident of her father's odd appearance and manner[3] returned upon the girl's mind to make her anxious, and wondering what had become of him she dropped away from the dancers and bent her steps towards the end of the village at which the parental cottage lay.

While yet many score yards off, other rhythmic sounds than those she had quitted became audible to her; sounds that she knew well – so well. They were a regular series of thumpings from the interior of the house, occasioned by the violent rocking of a cradle upon a stone floor, to which movement a feminine voice kept time by singing, in a vigorous gallopade, the favourite ditty of 'The Spotted Cow'[4] –

> I saw her lie do–own in yon–der green gro–ove;
> Come, love! and I'll tell you where!

The cradle-rocking and the song would cease simultaneously for a moment, and an exclamation at highest vocal pitch would take the place of the melody.

'God bless thy diment eyes! And thy waxen cheeks! And thy cherry mouth! And thy Cubit's lags! And every bit o' thy blessed body!'

After this invocation the rocking and the singing would recommence, and 'The Spotted Cow' proceed as before. So matters stood when Tess opened the door, and paused upon the mat within it surveying the scene.

The interior, in spite of the melody, struck upon the girl's senses with an unspeakable dreariness. From the holiday gaieties of the day – the white gowns, the nosegays, the willow-wands, the whirling movements on the green, the flash of gentle sentiment towards the stranger – to the yellow melancholy of this one-candled spectacle, what a step! Besides the jar of contrast there came to her a chill self-reproach that she had not returned sooner, to help her mother in these domesticities, instead of indulging herself out-of-doors.

There stood her mother amid the group of children, as Tess had left her, hanging over the Monday washing-tub, which had now, as always, lingered on to the end of the week. Out of that tub had come the day before – Tess felt it with a dreadful sting of remorse – the very white frock upon her back which she had so carelessly greened about the skirt on the damping grass – which had been wrung up and ironed by her mother's own hands.

As usual, Mrs Durbeyfield was balanced on one foot beside the tub, the other being engaged in the aforesaid business of rocking her youngest child. The cradle-rockers had done hard duty for so many years, under the weight of so many children, on that flagstone floor, that they were worn nearly flat, in consequence of which a huge jerk accompanied each swing of the cot, flinging the baby from side to side like a weaver's shuttle, as Mrs Durbeyfield, excited by her song, trod the rocker with all the spring that was left in her after a long day's seething in the suds.

Nick-knock, nick-knock, went the cradle; the candle-flame stretched itself tall, and began jigging up and down; the water dribbled from her mother's elbows, and the song galloped on to the end of the verse, Mrs Durbeyfield regarding her daughter the while. Even now, when burdened with a young family, Joan Durbeyfield was a passionate lover of tune. No ditty floated into Blackmoor Vale from the outer world but Tess's mother caught up its notation in a week.

There still faintly beamed from the woman's features something of the freshness, and even the prettiness, of her youth; rendering it evident that the personal charms which Tess could boast of were in main part her mother's gift, and therefore unknightly, unhistorical.

'I'll rock the cradle for 'ee, mother,' said the daughter gently. 'Or

I'll take off my best frock and help you wring up? I thought you had finished long ago.'

Her mother bore Tess no ill-will for leaving the housework to her single-handed efforts for so long; indeed, she seldom upbraided her thereon at any time, feeling but slightly the lack of Tess's assistance whilst her chief plan for relieving herself of her diurnal labours lay in postponing them. To-night, however, she was even in a blither mood than usual. There was a dreaminess, a preoccupation, an exaltation, in the maternal look which the girl could not understand.

'Well, I'm glad you've come,' her mother said, as soon as the last note had passed out of her. 'I want to go and fetch your father; but what's more'n that, I want to tell 'ee what have happened. You'll be fess enough, my poppet, when th'st know!' (Mrs Durbeyfield still habitually spoke the dialect; her daughter, who had passed the Sixth Standard in the National School[5] under a London-trained mistress, used it only when excited by joy, surprise, or grief.)[6]

'Since I've been away?' Tess asked.

'Ay!'

'Had it anything to do with father's making such a mommet of himself in the carriage this afternoon? Why did he? I felt inclined to sink into the ground with shame!'

'That was all a part of the larry! We've been found to be the greatest gentlefolk in the whole county – reaching all back long before Oliver Grumble's time – to the days of the Pagan Turks[7] – with monuments, and vaults, and crests, and 'scutcheons, and the Lord knows what all. In Charles's days we was made Knights o' the Royal Oak, our real name being D'Urberville! . . . Don't that make your bosom plim? 'Twas on this account that your father rode home in the carriage; not because he'd been drinking, as people supposed.'

'I'm glad of that. Will it do us any good, mother?'

'Oh yes! 'Tis thoughted that great things may come o't. No doubt a mampus of folk of our own rank will be down here in their carriages as soon as 'tis known. Your father learnt it on his way home from Stourcastle, and has been telling me the whole pedigree of the matter.'

'Where is father now?' asked Tess suddenly.

Her mother gave irrelevant information by way of answer.

'He called to see the doctor to-day in Stourcastle. It is not consumption at all, it seems. It is fat round his heart, he says. There, it is like this.' Joan Durbeyfield, as she spoke, curved a sodden thumb and forefinger to the shape of the letter C, and used the other forefinger as a pointer. ' "At the present moment," he says to your father, "your heart is enclosed all round there, and all round there; this space is still open," he says. "As soon as it meets, so," ' – Mrs Durbeyfield closed her fingers into a circle complete – ' "off you will go like a shadder, Mr Durbeyfield," he says. "You mid last ten years; you mid go off in ten months, or ten days." '

Tess looked alarmed. Her father possibly to go behind the eternal cloud so soon, notwithstanding this sudden greatness!

'But where *is* father?' she asked again.

Her mother put on a deprecating look. 'Now don't you be bursting out angry! The poor man – he felt so weak after his uplifting at the news – that he went up to Rolliver's half an hour ago. He do want to get up his strength for his journey to-morrow with that load of beehives, which must be delivered, family or no. He'll have to start shortly after twelve to-night, as the distance is so long.'

'Get up his strength!' said Tess impetuously, the tears welling to her eyes. 'O my God! Go to a public-house to get up his strength! And you as well agreed as he, mother!'

Her rebuke and her mood seemed to fill the whole room, and to impart a cowed look to the furniture, and candle, and children playing about, and to her mother's face.

'No,' said the latter touchily, 'I am not agreed. I have been waiting for 'ee to bide and keep house while I go to fetch him.'

'I'll go.'

'Oh no, Tess. You see, it would be no use.'

Tess did not expostulate. She knew what her mother's objection meant. Mrs Durbeyfield's jacket and bonnet were already hanging slily upon a chair by her side, in readiness for this contemplated jaunt, the reason for which the matron deplored more than its necessity.

'And take the *Complete Fortune-Teller*[8] to the outhouse,' she continued, rapidly wiping her hands, and donning the garments.

The *Complete Fortune-Teller* was an old thick volume, which lay on a table at her elbow, so worn by pocketing that the margins had reached the edge of the type. Tess took it up, and her mother started.

This going to hunt up her shiftless husband at the inn was one of Mrs Durbeyfield's still extant enjoyments in the muck and muddle of rearing children. To discover him at Rolliver's, to sit there for an hour or two by his side and dismiss all thought and care of the children during the interval, made her happy. A sort of halo, an occidental glow, came over life then. Troubles and other realities took on themselves a metaphysical impalpability, sinking to minor cerebral phenomena for quiet contemplation, in place of standing as pressing concretions which chafe body and soul. The youngsters, not immediately within sight, seemed rather bright and desirable appurtenances than otherwise; the incidents of daily life were not without humorousness and jollity in their aspect there. She felt a little as she had used to feel when she sat by her now wedded husband in the same spot during his wooing, shutting her eyes to his defects of character, and regarding him only in his ideal presentation as a lover.

Tess, being left alone with the younger children, went first to the outhouse with the fortune-telling book, and stuffed it into the thatch. A curious fetishistic fear of this grimy volume on the part of her mother prevented her ever allowing it to stay in the house all night, and hither it was brought back whenever it had been consulted. Between the mother, with her fast-perishing lumber of superstitions, folk-lore, dialect, and orally transmitted ballads, and the daughter, with her trained National teachings and Standard knowledge under an infinitely Revised Code,[9] there was a gap of two hundred years as ordinarily understood. When they were together the Jacobean and the Victorian ages[10] were juxtaposed.

Returning along the garden path Tess mused on what the mother could have wished to ascertain from the book on this particular day. She guessed the recent discovery to bear upon it, but did not divine that it solely concerned herself. Dismissing this, however, she busied herself with sprinkling the linen dried during the daytime, in company with her nine-year-old brother Abraham, and her sister Eliza-Louisa of twelve, called ''Liza-Lu,' the youngest ones being put to bed. There was an interval of four years between Tess and the next of the family, the two who had filled the gap having died in their infancy, and this lent her a deputy-maternal attitude when she was alone with her juniors. Next in juvenility to Abraham came two more girls, Hope and Modesty; then a boy of three, and then the baby, who had just completed his first year.

All these young souls were passengers in the Durbeyfield ship – entirely dependent on the judgment of the two Durbeyfield adults for their pleasures, their necessities, their health, even their existence. If the heads of the Durbeyfield household chose to sail into difficulty, disaster, starvation, disease, degradation, death, thither were these half-dozen little captives under hatches compelled to sail with them – six helpless creatures, who had never been asked if they wished for life on any terms, much less if they wished for it on such hard conditions as were involved in being of the shiftless house of Durbeyfield. Some people would like to know whence the poet whose philosophy is in these days deemed as profound and trustworthy as his verse is pure and breezy, gets his authority for speaking of 'Nature's holy plan.'[11]

It grew later, and neither father nor mother reappeared. Tess looked out of the door, and took a mental journey through Marlott. The village was shutting its eyes. Candles and lamps were being put out everywhere: she could inwardly behold the extinguisher and the extended hand.

Her mother's fetching simply meant one more to fetch. Tess began to perceive that a man in indifferent health, who proposed to start on a journey before one in the morning, ought not to be at an inn at this late hour celebrating his ancient blood.

'Abraham,' she said to her little brother, 'do you put on your hat – you baint afraid? – and go up to Rolliver's, and see what has become of father and mother.'

The boy jumped promptly from his seat, and opened the door, and the night swallowed him up. Half an hour passed yet again; neither man, woman, nor child returned. Abraham, like his parents, seemed to have been limed and caught by the ensnaring inn.

'I must go myself,' she said.

'Liza-Lu then went to bed, and Tess, locking them all in, started on her way up the dark and crooked lane or street not made for hasty progress; a street laid out before inches of land had value, and when one-handed clocks sufficiently subdivided the day.

IV

Rolliver's inn, the single alehouse at this end of the long and broken village, could only boast of an off-license; hence, as nobody could legally drink on the premises, the amount of overt accommodation for consumers was strictly limited to a little board about six inches wide and two yards long, fixed to the garden palings by pieces of wire, so as to form a ledge. On this board thirsty strangers deposited their cups as they stood in the road and drank, and threw the dregs on the dusty ground to the pattern of Polynesia,[1] and wished they could have a restful seat inside.

Thus the strangers. But there were also local customers who felt the same wish; and where there's a will there's a way.

In a large bedroom upstairs, the window of which was thickly curtained with a great woollen shawl lately discarded by the landlady Mrs Rolliver, were gathered on this evening nearly a dozen persons, all seeking vinous bliss; all old inhabitants of the nearer end of Marlott, and frequenters of this retreat. Not only did the distance to The Pure Drop, the fully-licensed tavern at the farther part of the dispersed village, render its accommodation practically unavailable for dwellers at this end; but the far more serious question, the quality of the liquor, confirmed the prevalent opinion that it was better to drink with Rolliver in a corner of the housetop than with the other landlord in a wide house.[2]

A gaunt four-post bedstead which stood in the room afforded sitting-space for several persons gathered round three of its sides; a couple more men had elevated themselves on a chest of drawers; another rested on the oak-carved 'cwoffer'; two on the wash-stand; another on the stool; and thus all were, somehow, seated at their ease. The stage of mental comfort to which they had arrived at this hour was one wherein their souls expanded beyond their skins, spreading their personalities warmly through the room. In this process the chamber and its furniture grew more and more dignified and luxurious; the shawl hanging at the window took upon itself the richness of tapestry; the brass handles of the chest of drawers were as golden knockers; and the carved bed-posts seemed to have some kinship with the magnificent pillars of Solomon's temple.[3]

Mrs Durbeyfield, having quickly walked hitherward after parting from Tess, opened the front door, crossed the downstairs room, which was in deep gloom, and then unfastened the stair-door like one whose fingers knew the tricks of the latches well. Her ascent of the crooked staircase was a slower process, and her face, as it rose into the light above the last stair, encountered the gaze of all the party assembled in the bedroom.

'—Being a few private friends I've asked in to keep up club-walking at my own expense,' the landlady exclaimed at the sound of footsteps, as glibly as a child repeating the Catechism, while she peered over the stairs. 'Oh, 'tis you, Mrs Durbeyfield – Lard – how you frightened me! – I thought it might be some gaffer sent by Gover'ment.'

Mrs Durbeyfield was welcomed with glances and nods by the remainder of the conclave, and turned to where her husband sat. He was humming absently to himself, in a low tone: 'I be as good as some folks here and there! I've got a great family vault at Kingsbere-sub-Greenhill, and finer skellingtons than any man in the counties o' Wessex!'

'I've something to tell 'ee that's come into my head about that – a grand project!' whispered his cheerful wife. 'Here, John, don't 'ee see me?' She nudged him, while he, looking through her as through a window-pane, went on with his recitative.

'Hush! Don't 'ee sing so loud, my good man,' said the landlady; 'in case any member of the Gover'ment should be passing, and take away my licends.'

'He's told 'ee what's happened to us, I suppose?' asked Mrs Durbeyfield.

'Yes – in a way. D'ye think there's any money hanging by it?'

'Ah, that's the secret,' said Joan Durbeyfield sagely. 'However, 'tis well to be kin to a coach, even if you don't ride in en.' She dropped her public voice, and continued in a low tone to her husband: 'I've been thinking since you brought the news that there's a great rich lady out by Trantridge, on the edge o' The Chase, of the name of D'Urberville.'

'Hey – what's that?' said Sir John.

She repeated the information. 'That lady must be our relation,' she said. 'And my project is to send Tess to claim kin.'

'There *is* a lady of the name, now you mention it,' said Durbeyfield. 'Pa'son Tringham didn't think of that. But she's nothing beside we – a junior branch of us, no doubt, long since King Norman's day.'[4]

While this question was being discussed neither of the pair noticed, in their preoccupation, that little Abraham had crept into the room, and was awaiting an opportunity of asking them to return.

'She is rich, and she'd be sure to take notice o' the maid,' continued Mrs Durbeyfield; 'and 'twill be a very good thing. I don't see why two branches of one family should not be on visiting terms.'

'Yes; and we'll all claim kin!' said Abraham brightly from under the bedstead. 'And we'll all go and see her when Tess has gone to live with her; and we'll ride in her coach and wear black clothes!'

'How do you come here, child? What nonsense be ye talking! Go away, and play on the stairs till father and mother be ready! . . . Well, Tess ought to go to this other member of our family. She'd be sure to win the lady – Tess would; and likely enough 'twould lead to some noble gentleman marrying her. In short, I know it.'

'How?'

'I tried her fate in the *Fortune-Teller*, and it brought out that very thing . . . You should ha' seen how pretty she looked to-day; her skin is as sumple as a duchess's.'

'What says the maid herself to going?'

'I've not asked her. She don't know there is any such lady relation yet. But it would certainly put her in the way of a grand marriage, and she won't refuse to go.'

'Tess is queer.'

'But she's tractable at bottom. Leave her to me.'

Though this conversation had been private, sufficient of its import reached the understandings of those around to suggest to them that the Durbeyfields had weightier concerns to talk of now than common folks had, and that Tess, their pretty eldest daughter, had fine prospects in store.

'Tess is a fine figure o' fun,[5] as I said to myself to-day when I zeed her vamping round parish with the rest,' observed one of the elderly boozers in an undertone. 'But Joan Durbeyfield must mind that she don't get green malt in flower.'[6] It was a local phrase which had a peculiar meaning, and there was no reply.

The conversation became inclusive, and presently other footsteps were heard crossing the room below.

'—Being a few private friends asked in to-night to keep up club-walking at my own expense.' The landlady had rapidly re-used the formula she kept on hand for intruders before she recognized that the newcomer was Tess.

Even to her mother's gaze the girl's young features looked sadly out of place amid the alcoholic vapours which floated here as no unsuitable medium for wrinkled middle-age; and hardly was a reproachful flash from Tess's dark eyes needed to make her father and mother rise from their seats, hastily finish their ale, and descend the stairs behind her, Mrs Rolliver's caution following their footsteps.

'No noise, please, if ye'll be so good, my dears; or I mid lose my licends, and be summons'd, and I don't know what all! 'Night t'ye!'

They went home together, Tess holding one arm of her father, and Mrs Durbeyfield the other. He had, in truth, drunk very little – not a fourth of the quantity which a systematic tippler could carry to church on a Sunday morning without a hitch in his eastings or genuflections; but the weakness of Sir John's constitution made mountains of his petty sins in this kind. On reaching the fresh air he was sufficiently unsteady to incline the row of three at one moment as if they were marching to London, and at another as if they were marching to Bath – which produced a comical effect, frequent enough in families on nocturnal homegoings; and, like most comical effects, not quite so comic after all. The two women valiantly disguised these forced excursions and countermarches as well as they could from Durbeyfield their cause, and from Abraham, and from themselves; and so they approached by degrees their own door, the head of the family bursting suddenly into his former refrain as he drew near, as if to fortify his soul at sight of the smallness of his present residence –

'I've got a fam – ily vault at Kingsbere!'

'Hush – don't be so silly, Jacky,' said his wife. 'Yours is not the only family that was of 'count in wold days. Look at the Anktells, and Horseys,[7] and the Tringhams themselves – gone to seed a'most as much as you – though you was bigger folks than they, that's true. Thank God, I was never of no family, and have nothing to be ashamed of in that way!'

'Don't you be so sure o' that. From your nater 'tis my belief you've disgraced yourselves more than any o' us, and was kings and queens outright at one time.'

Tess turned the subject by saying what was far more prominent in her own mind at the moment than thoughts of her ancestry –

'I am afraid father won't be able to take the journey with the beehives to-morrow so early.'

'I? I shall be all right in an hour or two,' said Durbeyfield.

It was eleven o'clock before the family were all in bed, and two o'clock next morning was the latest hour for starting with the beehives if they were to be delivered to the retailers in Casterbridge before the Saturday market began, the way thither lying by bad roads over a distance of between twenty and thirty miles, and the horse and wag-gon being of the slowest. At half-past one Mrs Durbeyfield came into the large bedroom where Tess and all her little brothers and sisters slept.

'The poor man can't go,' she said to her eldest daughter, whose great eyes had opened the moment her mother's hand touched the door.

Tess sat up in bed, lost in a vague interspace between a dream and this information.

'But somebody must go,' she replied. 'It is late for the hives already. Swarming will soon be over for the year;[8] and if we put off taking 'em till next week's market the call for 'em will be past, and they'll be thrown on our hands.'

Mrs Durbeyfield looked unequal to the emergency. 'Some young feller, perhaps, would go? One of them who were so much after dancing with 'ee yesterday,' she presently suggested.

'Oh no – I wouldn't have it for the world!' declared Tess proudly. 'And letting everybody know the reason – such a thing to be ashamed of! I think *I* could go if Abraham could go with me to keep me company.'

Her mother at length agreed to this arrangement. Little Abraham was aroused from his deep sleep in a corner of the same apartment, and made to put on his clothes while still mentally in the other world. Meanwhile Tess had hastily dressed herself; and the twain, lighting a lantern, went out to the stable. The rickety little waggon was already laden, and the girl led out the horse Prince, only a degree less rickety than the vehicle.

The poor creature looked wonderingly round at the night, at the lantern, at their two figures, as if he could not believe that at that hour, when every living thing was intended to be at shelter and at rest, he was called upon to go out and labour. They put a stock of candle-ends into the lantern, hung the latter to the off-side of the road, and directed the horse onward, walking at his shoulder at first during the uphill portion of the way, in order not to overload an animal of so little vigour. To cheer themselves as well as they could, they made an artificial morning with the lantern, some bread and butter, and their own conversation, the real morning being far from come. Abraham, as he more fully awoke (for he had moved in a sort of trance so far), began to talk of the strange shapes assumed by the various dark objects against the sky; of this tree that looked like a raging tiger springing from a lair; of that which resembled a giant's head.

When they had passed the little town of Stourcastle, dumbly somnolent under its thick brown thatch, they reached higher ground. Still higher, on their left, the elevation called Bulbarrow or Bealbarrow, well-nigh the highest in South Wessex, swelled into the sky, engirdled by its earthen trenches.[9] From hereabout the long road declined gently for a great distance onward. They mounted in front of the waggon, and Abraham grew reflective.

'Tess!' he said in a preparatory tone, after a silence.

'Yes, Abraham.'

'Bain't you glad that we've become gentlefolk?'

'Not particular glad.'

'But you be glad that you are going to marry a gentleman?'

'What?' said Tess, lifting her face.

'That our great relation will help 'ee to marry a gentleman.'

'I? Our great relation? We have no such relation. What has put that into your head?'

'I heard 'em talking about it up at Rolliver's when I went to find father. There's a rich lady of our family out at Trantridge, and mother said that if you claimed kin with the lady, she'd put 'ee in the way of marrying a gentleman.'

His sister became abruptly still, and lapsed into a pondering silence. Abraham talked on, rather for the pleasure of utterance than for audition, so that his sister's abstraction was of no account. He leant back against the hives, and with upturned face made observations on the stars, whose cold pulses were beating amid the black hollows above, in serene dissociation from these two wisps of human life. He asked how far away those twinklers were, and whether God was on the other side of them. But ever and anon his childish prattle recurred to what impressed his imagination even more deeply than the wonders of creation. If Tess were made rich by marrying a gentleman, would she have money enough to buy a spy-glass so large that it would draw the stars as near to her as Nettlecombe-Tout?

The renewed subject, which seemed to have impregnated the whole family, filled Tess with impatience.

'Never mind that now!' she exclaimed.

'Did you say the stars were worlds, Tess?'

'Yes.'

'All like ours?'

'I don't know; but I think so. They sometimes seem to be like the apples on our stubbard-tree. Most of them splendid and sound – a few blighted.'

'Which do we live on – a splendid one or a blighted one?'

'A blighted one.'

''Tis very unlucky that we didn't pitch on a sound one, when there were so many more of 'em!'

'Yes.'

'Is it like that *really*, Tess?' said Abraham, turning to her much impressed, on reconsideration of this rare information. 'How would it have been if we had pitched on a sound one?'

'Well, father wouldn't have coughed and creeped about as he does, and wouldn't have got too tipsy to go this journey; and mother wouldn't have been always washing, and never getting finished.'

'And you would have been a rich lady ready-made, and not have had to be made rich by marrying a gentleman?'

'Oh, Aby, don't – don't talk of that any more!'

Left to his reflections, Abraham soon grew drowsy. Tess was not skilful in the management of a horse, but she thought that she could take upon herself the entire conduct of the load for the present, and allow Abraham to go to sleep if he wished to do so. She made him a sort of nest in front of the hives, in such a manner that he could not fall, and, taking the rope-reins into her own hands, jogged on as before.

Prince required but slight attention, lacking energy for superfluous movements of any sort. With no longer a companion to distract her, Tess fell more deeply into reverie than ever, her back leaning against the hives. The mute procession past her of trees and hedges became attached to fantastic scenes outside reality, and the occasional heave of the wind became the sigh of some immense sad soul, conterminous with the universe in space, and with history in time.

Then, examining the mesh of events in her own life, she seemed to see the vanity of her father's pride; the gentlemanly match awaiting herself in her mother's fancy; to see him as a grimacing personage, laughing at her poverty, and her shrouded knightly ancestry.[10] Everything grew more and more extravagant, and she no longer knew how time passed. A sudden jerk shook her in her seat, and Tess awoke from the sleep into which she, too, had fallen.

They were a long way farther on than when she had lost consciousness, and the waggon had stopped. A hollow groan, unlike anything she had ever heard in her life, came from the front, followed by a shout of 'Hoi, there!'

The lantern hanging at her waggon had gone out, but another was shining in her face – much brighter than her own had been. Something terrible had happened. The harness was entangled with an object which blocked the way.

In consternation Tess jumped down, and discovered the dreadful truth. The groan had proceeded from her father's poor horse Prince. The morning mail-cart, with its two noiseless wheels, speeding along these lanes like an arrow, as it always did, had driven into her slow and unlighted equipage. The pointed shaft of the cart had entered the breast of the unhappy Prince like a sword, and from the wound his life's blood was spouting in a stream, and falling with a hiss into the road.[11]

In her despair Tess sprang forward and put her hand upon the hole, with the only result that she became splashed from face to skirt with the crimson drops. Then she stood helplessly looking on. Prince also stood firm and motionless as long as he could; till he suddenly sank down in a heap.

By this time the mail-cart man had joined her, and began dragging and unharnessing the hot form of Prince. But he was already dead, and seeing that nothing more could be done immediately the mail-cart man returned to his own animal, which was uninjured.

'You was on the wrong side,' he said. 'I am bound to go on with the mail-bags, so that the best thing for you to do is to bide here with your load. I'll send somebody to help you as soon as I can. It will soon be daylight, and you have nothing to fear.'

He mounted and sped on his way; while Tess stood and waited. The atmosphere turned pale, the birds shook themselves in the hedges, arose, and twittered; the lane showed all its white features, and Tess showed hers, still whiter. The huge pool of blood in front of her was already assuming the iridescence of coagulation; and when the sun rose a million prismatic hues were reflected from it. Prince lay alongside still and stark; his eyes half open, the hole in his chest looking scarcely large enough to have let out all that had animated him.

'Tis all my doing – all mine!' the distracted girl cried, gazing intently at the spectacle. 'No excuse for me – none. What will father and mother live on now? Aby, Aby!' She shook the child, who had slept soundly through the whole disaster. 'We can't go on with our load – Prince is killed!'

When Abraham realized all, the furrows of fifty years were extemporized on his young face.

'Why, I danced and laughed only yesterday!' she went on to herself. 'To think that I was such a fool!'

''Tis because we be on a blighted star, and not a sound one, isn't it, Tess?' murmured Abraham through his tears.

In stagnant blankness[12] they waited through an interval which seemed endless. At length a sound, and an approaching object, proved to them that the driver of the mail-cart had been as good as his word. A farmer's man from near Stourcastle came up, leading a strong cob. He was harnessed to the waggon of beehives in the place of Prince, and the load taken on towards Casterbridge.

The evening of the same day saw the empty waggon reach again the spot of the accident. Prince had lain there in the ditch since the morning; but the place of the blood-pool was still visible in the middle of the road, though scratched and scraped over by passing vehicles. All that was left of Prince was now hoisted into the waggon he had formerly hauled, and with his hoofs in the air, and his shoes shining in the setting sunlight, he retraced the dozen miles to Marlott.

Tess had gone back earlier. How to break the news was more than she could think. It was a relief to her tongue to find from the faces of her parents that they already knew of their loss, though this did not lessen the self-reproach which she continued to heap upon herself for her negligence in falling asleep.

But the very shiftlessness of the household rendered the misfortune a less terrifying one to them than it would have been to a striving family, though in the present case it meant ruin, and in the other it would only have meant inconvenience. In the Durbeyfield countenances there was nothing of the red wrath that would have burnt upon the girl from parents more ambitious for her welfare. Nobody blamed Tess as she blamed herself.

When it was discovered that the knacker and tanner would give only a very few shillings for Prince's carcase because of his decrepitude, Durbeyfield rose to the occasion.

'No,' said he stoically, 'I won't sell his old body. When we D'Urbervilles was knights in the land, we didn't sell our chargers for cat's meat.

Let 'em keep their shillings! He has served me well in his lifetime, and I won't part from him now.'

He worked harder the next day in digging a grave for Prince in the garden than he had worked for months to grow a crop for his family. When the hole was ready, Durbeyfield and his wife tied a rope round the horse and dragged him up the path towards it, the children following. Abraham and 'Liza-Lu sobbed, Hope and Modesty discharged their griefs in loud blares which echoed from the walls; and when Prince was tumbled in they gathered round the grave. The bread-winner had been taken away from them; what would they do?

'Is he gone to heaven?' asked Abraham, between the sobs.

Then Durbeyfield began to shovel in the earth, and the children cried anew. All except Tess. Her face was dry and pale, as though she regarded herself in the light of a murderess.

V

The higgling business, which had mainly depended on the horse, became disorganized forthwith. Distress, if not penury, loomed in the distance. Durbeyfield was what was locally called a slack-twisted fellow; he had good strength to work at times; but none of the times could be relied on to coincide with the hours of requirement; and, having been unaccustomed to the regular toil of the day-labourer, he was not particularly persistent when they did so coincide.

Tess, meanwhile, as the one who had dragged them into this quagmire, was silently wondering what she could do to help them out of it; and then her mother broached her scheme.

'We must take the ups wi' the downs, Tess,' said she; 'and never could your high blood have been discovered at a more necessary moment. You must try your friends. Do you know that there is a very rich Mrs D'Urberville living out on the edge of The Chase, who must be our relation? You must go to her and claim kin, and ask for some assistance in our trouble.'

'I shouldn't care to do that,' says Tess. 'If there is such a lady, 'twould be enough for us if she were friendly – not to expect her to give us help.'

'You could win her round to do anything, my dear. Besides, perhaps there's more in it than you know of. I've heard what I've heard.'

The oppressive sense of the harm she had done led Tess to be more deferential than she might otherwise have been to the maternal wish; but she could not understand why her mother should find such satisfaction in contemplating an enterprise of, to her, such doubtful profit. Her mother might have made inquiries, and have discovered that this Mrs D'Urberville was a lady of unequalled virtues and charity. But Tess's pride made the part of poor relation one of particular distaste to her.

'I'd rather try to get work,' she murmured.

'Durbeyfield, you can settle it,' said his wife, turning to where he sat in the background. 'If you say she ought to go, she will go.'

'I don't like my children going and making themselves beholden to strange kin,' murmured he. 'I'm the head of the noblest branch of the family, and I ought to keep myself up.'[1]

His reasons for staying away were worse to Tess than her own objection to going. 'Well, as I killed the horse, mother,' she said mournfully, 'I suppose I ought to do something. I don't mind going and seeing her, but you must leave it to me about asking for help. And don't go thinking about her making a match for me – it is silly.'

'Very well said, Tess!' observed her father sententiously.

'Who said I had such a thought?' asked Joan.

'I fancy it is in your mind, mother. But I'll go.'

Rising early next day, she walked to the hill-town called Shaston, and there took advantage of a van which twice in the week ran from Shaston eastward to Chaseborough, passing near Trantridge, the parish in which the vague and mysterious Mrs D'Urberville had her residence.

Tess Durbeyfield's route on this memorable morning lay amid the north-eastern undulations of the Vale in which she had been born, and in which her life had unfolded. The Vale of Blackmoor was to her the world, and its inhabitants the races thereof. From the gates and stiles of Marlott she had looked down its length in the wondering days of infancy, and what had been mystery to her then was not much less than mystery to her now. She had seen daily from her chamber-window towers, villages, faint white mansions; above all the town of Shaston standing majestically on its height; its windows shining like lamps in the evening sun. She had hardly ever visited it, only a small tract even of the Vale and its environs being known to her by close inspection. Much less had she been far outside the valley. Every contour of the surrounding hills was as personal to her as that of her relatives' faces; but for what lay beyond her judgment was dependent on the teaching of the village school, where she had held a leading place at the time of her leaving, a year or two before this date.

In those early days she had been much loved by others of her own sex and age, and had used to be seen about the village as one of three – all nearly of the same year – walking home from school side by side, Tess being the middle one – in a pink print pinafore, of a finely reticulated pattern, worn over a stuff frock that had lost its original colour for a nondescript tertiary – marching on upon long stalky legs, in tight stockings which had little ladder-like holes at the knees, torn by kneeling in the roads and banks in search of vegetable and mineral treasures; her then earth-coloured hair hanging like pot-hooks; the arms of the two outside girls resting round the waist of Tess; her arms on the shoulders of the two supporters.

As Tess grew older, and began to see how matters stood, she felt Malthusian vexation[2] with her mother for thoughtlessly giving her so many little sisters and brothers, when it was such a trouble to nurse those that had already come. Her mother's intelligence was that of a happy child: Joan Durbeyfield was simply an additional one, and that not the eldest, to her own long family of nine when all were living.[3]

However, Tess became humanely beneficent towards the small ones, and to help them as much as possible she used, as soon as she left school, to lend a hand at haymaking or harvesting on neighbouring farms; or, by preference, at milking or butter-making processes, which she had learnt when her father had owned cows; and being deft-fingered it was a kind of work in which she excelled.

Every day seemed to throw upon her young shoulders more of the family burdens, and that Tess should be the representative of the

Durbeyfields at the D'Urberville mansion came as a thing of course. In this instance it must be admitted that the Durbeyfields were putting their fairest side outward.

She alighted from the van at Trantridge Cross, and ascended on foot a hill in the direction of the district known as The Chase, on the borders of which, as she had been informed, Mrs D'Urberville's seat, The Slopes, would be found. It was not a manorial home in the ordinary sense, with fields, and pastures, and a grumbling farmer, out of which a living had to be dragged by the owner and his family by hook or by crook. It was more, far more; a country house, built for enjoyment pure and simple, with not an acre of troublesome land attached to it beyond what was required for residential purposes, and a little fancy farm kept in hand by the owner, and tended by a bailiff.[4]

The warm red brick lodge came first in sight, up to its eaves in dense evergreens. Tess thought this was the mansion itself till, passing through the side wicket with some trepidation, and onward to a point at which the drive took a turn, the house proper stood in full view. It was of recent erection – indeed almost new – and of the same rich crimson colour that formed such a contrast with the evergreens of the lodge. Far behind the bright brick corner of the house – which rose like a red geranium against the subdued colours around – stretched the soft azure landscape of The Chase – a truly venerable tract of forest land, one of the few remaining woodlands in England of undoubted primæval date, wherein Druidical mistletoe was still found on aged oaks, and where enormous yew-trees, not planted by the hand of man, grew as they had grown when they were pollarded for bows.[5] All this sylvan antiquity, however, though visible from The Slopes, was outside the immediate boundaries of the estate.

Everything on this snug property was bright, thriving, and well kept; acres of glass-houses stretched down the inclines to the copses at their feet. Everything looked like money – like the last coin issued from the Mint. The stables, partly screened by Austrian pines and evergreen oaks, and fitted with every late appliance, were as dignified as Chapels-of-Ease, and on the extensive lawn stood an ornamental tent,[6] its door being towards her.

Simple Tess Durbeyfield stood at gaze, in a half-paralyzed attitude,

38

on the edge of the gravel sweep. Her feet had brought her onward to this point before she had quite realized where she was; and now all was contrary to her expectation.

'I thought we were an old family; but this is all new!' she said, in her girlish artlessness.[7] She wished that she had not fallen in so readily with her mother's plans for 'claiming kin,' and had endeavoured to gain assistance nearer home.

The D'Urbervilles – or Stoke-D'Urbervilles,[8] as they at first called themselves – who owned all this, were a somewhat unusual family to find in such an old-fashioned part of the country. Parson Tringham had spoken truly when he said that our shambling John Durbeyfield was the only really lineal representative of the old D'Urberville family existing in the county, or near it; he might have added, what he knew very well, that the Stoke-D'Urbervilles were no more D'Urbervilles of the true tree than he was himself. Yet it must be admitted that this family formed a very good stock whereon to regraft a name which sadly wanted such renovation.

When old Mr Simon Stoke, latterly deceased, had made his fortune as an honest merchant (some said money-lender) in the North, he decided to settle as a county man in the South of England, out of hail of his business district; and in doing this he felt the necessity of recommencing with a name not quite so well remembered there, and less commonplace than the two original bald stark words.[9] Conning for an hour in the British Museum the pages of works devoted to extinct, half-extinct, obscured, and ruined families appertaining to the quarter of England in which he proposed to settle, he considered that *D'Urberville* looked and sounded as well as any of them: and D'Urberville accordingly was annexed to his own name for himself and his heirs eternally. Yet he was not an extravagant-minded man in this, and in constructing his family tree on the new basis was reasonable in framing his intermarriages and connecting links, never inserting a single title above a rank of strict moderation.

Of this work of imagination poor Tess and her parents were naturally in ignorance – much to their own discomfiture; indeed, the very possibility of such annexations was unknown to them; who supposed that, though to be well-favoured might be the gift of fortune, a family name came by nature.[10]

Tess still stood hesitating like a bather about to make his plunge, hardly knowing whether to retreat or to persevere, when a figure came forth from the dark triangular door of the tent. It was that of a tall young man, smoking.

He had an almost swarthy complexion, with full lips, badly moulded, though red and smooth, above which was a well-groomed black moustache with curled points, though his age could not be more than three- or four-and-twenty.[11] Despite the touches of barbarism in his contours, there was a singular force in the gentleman's face, and in his bold rolling eye.

'Well, my big Beauty,[12] what can I do for you?' said he, coming forward. And perceiving that she stood quite confounded: 'Never mind me. I am Mr D'Urberville. Have you come to see me or my mother?'

This embodiment of a D'Urberville and a namesake differed even more from what Tess had expected than the house and grounds had differed. She had dreamed of an aged and dignified face, the sublimation of all distinctively D'Urberville lineaments, furrowed with incarnated memories representing in hieroglyphic the centuries of her family and England's history.[13] But she screwed herself up to the work in hand, since she could not get out of it, and answered –

'I came to see your mother, sir.'

'I am afraid you cannot see her – she is an invalid,' replied the present representative of the spurious house; for this was Mr Alec, the only son of the lately deceased gentleman. 'Cannot I answer your purpose? What is the business you wish to see her about?'

'It isn't business – it is – I can hardly say what!'

'Pleasure?'

'Oh no. Why, sir, if I tell you, it will seem –'

Tess's sense of a certain ludicrousness in her errand was now so strong that, notwithstanding her awe of him, and her general discomfort at being here, her rosy lips curved towards a smile, much to the attraction of the swarthy Alexander.[14]

'It is so very foolish,' she stammered; 'I fear I can't tell you!'

'Never mind; I like foolish things. Try again, my dear,' said he kindly.

'Mother asked me to come,' Tess continued; 'and, indeed, I was inclined to do so myself likewise. But I did not think it would be like this. I came, sir, to tell you that we be of the same family as you.'

'Ho! Poor relations?'

'Yes.'

'Stokes?'

'No; D'Urbervilles.'

'Ay, ay; I mean D'Urbervilles.'

'Our names are corrupted to Durbeyfield; but we have several proofs that we be D'Urbervilles. Antiquarians say we are, – and – and we have an old seal, and a very old silver spoon, round in the bowl, like a little ladle, with a ramping lion on the handle, and a castle over him. But it is so old that mother uses it to stir the pea-soup.'

'A castle argent is certainly my crest,' said he blandly.[15]

'And so mother said we ought to make ourselves beknown to you – as we've lost our horse by a bad accident, and are the oldest branch o' the family.'

'Very kind of your mother, I'm sure. And I, for one, don't regret her step.' Alec looked at Tess as he spoke, in a way that made her blush a little. 'And so, my pretty girl, you've come on a friendly visit to us, as relations?'

'I suppose I have,' faltered Tess, looking uncomfortably at the mansion.

'Well – there's no harm in it. Where do you live? What are you?'

She gave him brief particulars; and, after further inquiries, told him that she was intending to go back by the same carrier who had brought her.

'It is a long while before he returns past Trantridge Cross. Supposing we walk round the grounds to pass the time, my pretty Coz?'[16]

Tess wished to abridge her visit as much as possible; but the young man was pressing, and she consented to accompany him. He conducted her about the lawns, and flower-beds, and conservatories; and thence to the fruit-garden,[17] where he asked her if she liked strawberries.

'Yes,' said Tess, 'when they come.'

'They are already here.' D'Urberville began gathering specimens of the fruit for her, handing them back to her as he stooped; and, presently, selecting a specially fine product of the 'British Queen'[18] variety, he stood up and held it by the stem to her mouth.

'No – no!' she said quickly, putting her fingers between his hand and her lips. 'I would rather take it in my own hand.'

'Nonsense!' he insisted; and in a slight distress she parted her lips and took it in.[19]

They had spent some time wandering desultorily thus, Tess eating in an abstracted half-hypnotized state whatever D'Urberville offered her. When she could consume no more of the strawberries he filled her little basket with them; and then the two passed round to the rose-trees, whence he gathered blossoms and gave her to put in her bosom. She obeyed, still like one in a dream, and when she could affix no more he himself tucked a bud or two into her hat, and heaped her basket with others in the prodigality of his bounty. At last, looking at his watch, he said, 'Now, by the time you have had something to eat, it will be time for you to leave, if you want to catch the carrier to Shaston. Come here, and I'll see what grub I can find.'

Stoke-D'Urberville took her back to the lawn and into the tent, where he left her, soon reappearing with a basket of light luncheon, which he put before her himself. It was evidently the gentleman's wish not to be disturbed in this pleasant *tête-à-tête* by the servantry.

'Do you mind my smoking?' he asked.

'Oh, not at all, sir.'

He watched her pretty and unconscious munching through the skeins of smoke that pervaded the tent, and Tess Durbeyfield did not divine, as she innocently looked down at the roses in her bosom, that there behind the blue narcotic haze sat the 'tragic mischief' of her drama – he who was to be the blood-red ray in the spectrum of her young life. She had an attribute which amounted to a disadvantage just now; and it was this that caused Alec D'Urberville's eyes to rivet themselves upon her. It was a luxuriance of aspect, a fulness of growth, which made her appear more of a woman than she really was. She had inherited the feature from her mother without the quality it denoted. It had troubled her mind occasionally, till her companions had said that it was a fault which time would cure.

She soon had finished her lunch. 'Now I am going home, sir,' she said, rising.

'And what do they call you?' he asked, as he accompanied her along the drive till they were out of sight of the house.

'Tess Durbeyfield, down at Marlott.'

'And you say your people have lost their horse?'

'I – killed him!' she answered, her eyes filling with tears as she gave particulars of Prince's death. 'And I don't know what to do for father on account of it!'

'I must think if I cannot do something. My mother must find a berth for you. But, Tess, no nonsense about "D'Urberville"; – "Durbeyfield" only, you know – quite another name.'

'I wish for no better, sir,' said she with something of dignity.

For a moment – only for a moment – when they were in the turning of the drive, between the tall rhododendrons and conifers, before the lodge became visible, he inclined his face towards her as if – but, no! he thought better of it, and let her go.

Thus the thing began. Had she perceived this meeting's import she might have asked why she was doomed to be seen and marked and coveted[20] that day by the wrong man, and not by a certain other man, the exact and true one in all respects – as nearly as human mutuality can be exact and true; yet to him at this time she[21] was but a transient impression, half forgotten.

In the ill-judged execution of the well-judged plan of things the call seldom produces the comer, the man to love rarely coincides with the hour for loving. Nature does not often say 'See!' to her poor creature at a time when seeing can lead to happy doing; or reply 'Here!' to a body's cry of 'Where?' till the hide-and-seek has become an irksome outworn game. We may wonder whether at the acme and summit of the human progress these anachronisms will become corrected by a finer intuition, a closer interaction of the social machinery than that which now jolts us round and along; but such completeness is not to be prophesied, or even conceived as possible. Enough that in the present case, as in millions, the two halves of an approximately perfect whole did not confront each other at the perfect moment; part and counterpart wandered independently about the earth in the stupidest manner for a while,[22] till the late time came. Out of which maladroit delay sprang anxieties, disappointments, shocks, catastrophes – what was called a strange destiny.[23]

When D'Urberville got back to the tent he sat down astride on a chair reflecting, with a pleased gleam in his face. Then he broke into a loud laugh.

'Well, I'm damned! What a funny thing! Ha-ha-ha! And what a charming[24] girl!'

VI

Tess went down the hill to Trantridge Cross, and inattentively waited to take her seat in the van returning from Chaseborough to Shaston. She did not know what the other occupants said to her as she entered, though she answered them; and when they had started anew she rode along with an inward and not an outward eye.

One among her fellow-travellers addressed her more pointedly than any had spoken before: 'Why, you be quite a posy! And such roses in early June!'

Then she became aware of the spectacle she presented to their surprised vision: roses at her breast; roses in her hat; roses and straw-berries in her basket to the brim. She blushed, and said confusedly that the flowers had been given to her. When the passengers were not looking she stealthily removed the more prominent blooms from her hat and placed them in the basket, where she covered them with her handkerchief. Then she fell to reflecting again, and in looking downwards a thorn of the rose remaining in her breast accidentally pricked her chin. Like all the cottagers of Blackmoor Vale, Tess was steeped in fancies and prefigurative superstitions; she thought this an ill omen – the first she had noticed that day.

The van travelled only so far as Shaston, and there were several miles of pedestrian descent from that mountain-town into the vale to Marlott. Her mother had advised her to stay here for the night, at the house of a cottage-woman they knew, if she should feel too tired to come on; and this Tess did, not descending to her home till the following afternoon.

When she entered the house she perceived in a moment from her mother's triumphant manner that something had occurred in the interim.

'Oh yes; I know all about it! I told 'ee it would be all right, and now 'tis proved!'

'Since I've been away? What has?' said Tess rather wearily.

Her mother surveyed the girl up and down with arch approval, and went on banteringly: 'So you've brought 'em round!'

'How do you know, mother?'

'I've had a letter.'

Tess then remembered that there would have been just time for this.

'They say – Mrs D'Urberville says – that she wants you to look after a little poultry-farm which is her hobby. But this is only her artful way of getting you there without raising your hopes. She's going to acknowledge 'ee as kin – that's the meaning o't.'

'But I didn't see her.'

'You zid somebody, I suppose?'

'I saw her son.'

'And did he acknowledge 'ee?'

'Well – he called me Coz.'

'An' I knew it! Jacky – he called her Coz!' cried Joan to her husband. 'Well, he spoke to his mother, of course, and she do want 'ee there.'

'But I don't know that I am apt at managing fowls,' said the dubious Tess.

'Then I don't know who is apt. You've be'n born in the business, and brought up in it. They that be born in a business always know more about it than any 'prentice. Besides, that's only just a show of something for you to do, that you midn't feel dependent.'

'I don't altogether think I ought to go,' said Tess thoughtfully. 'Who wrote the letter? Will you let me look at it?'

'Mrs D'Urberville wrote it. Here it is.'

The letter was in the third person, and briefly informed Mrs Durbey-field that her daughter's services would be useful to that lady in the management of her poultry-farm, that a comfortable room would be provided for her if she could come, and that the emolument would be on a liberal scale if they liked her.

'Oh – that's all!' said Tess.

'You couldn't expect her to throw her arms round 'ee, an' to kiss and to coll 'ee all at once.'

Tess looked out of the window.

'I would rather stay here with father and you,' she said, nervously reflecting.

'But why?'

'I'd rather not tell you why, mother; indeed, I don't quite know why.'

A week afterwards she came in one evening from an unavailing search for some light occupation in the immediate neighbourhood. Her idea had been to get together sufficient money during the summer to purchase another horse. Hardly had she crossed the threshold before one of the children danced across the room, saying, 'The gentleman has been here!'

Her mother hastened to explain, smiles breaking from every inch of her person. Mrs D'Urberville's son had called on horseback, having been riding by chance in the direction of Marlott. He had wished to know, finally, in the name of his mother, if Tess could really come to manage the old lady's fowl-farm or not; the lad who had hitherto superintended the birds having proved untrustworthy. 'Mr D'Urber-ville says you must be a good girl if you are at all as you appear; he knows you must be worth your weight in gold. He is very much interested in 'ee – truth to tell.'

Tess seemed for the moment really pleased to hear that she had won such high opinion from a stranger when, in her own esteem, she had sunk so low.

'It is very good of him to think that,' she murmured; 'and if I was quite sure how it would be living there, I would go in a moment.'

'He is a mighty handsome man!'

'I don't think so,' said Tess coldly.

'Well, there's your chance, whether or no; and I'm sure he wears a beautiful diamond ring!'

'Yes,' said little Abraham, brightly, from the window-bench; 'and I seed it! and it did twinkle when he put his hand up to his mistarshers. Mother, why did our noble relation keep on putting his hand up to his mistarshers?'

'Hark at that child!' cried Mrs Durbeyfield, with parenthetic admiration.

'Perhaps to show his diamond ring,' murmured Sir John, dreamily, from his chair.

'I'll think it over,' said Tess, leaving the room.

'Well, she's made a conquest o' the junior branch of us, straight off,' continued the matron to her husband, 'and she's a fool if she don't follow it up.'

'I don't quite like my children going away from home,' said the higgler. 'As the head of the family, the rest ought to come to me.'

'But do let her go, Jacky,' coaxed his poor witless wife. 'He's struck wi' her – you can see that. He called her Coz! He'll marry her, most likely, and make a lady of her; and then she'll be what her forefathers was.'

John Durbeyfield had more conceit than energy or health, and this supposition was pleasant to him.

'Well, perhaps, that's what young Mr D'Urberville means,' he admitted; 'and he really may have serious thoughts about improving his blood by linking on to the old line. Tess, the little rogue! And has she really paid 'em a visit to such an end as this?'

Meanwhile Tess was walking thoughtfully among the gooseberry-bushes[1] in the garden, and over Prince's grave. When she came in her mother pursued her advantage.

'Well, what be you going to do?' she asked.

'I wish I had seen Mrs D'Urberville,' said Tess.

'I think you mid as well settle it. Then you'll see her soon enough.'

Her father coughed in his chair.

'I don't know what to say!' answered the girl restlessly. 'It is for you to decide. I killed the old horse, and I suppose I ought to do something to get ye a new one. But – but – I don't quite like Mr D'Urberville!'

The children, who had made use of this idea of Tess being taken up by their wealthy kinsfolk (as they imagined the other family to be) as a species of dolorifuge[2] after the death of the horse, began to cry at Tess's reluctance, and teased and reproached her for hesitating.

'Tess won't go – o – o and be made a la – a – dy of! – no, she says she wo – o – on't!' they wailed, with square mouths. 'And we shan't have a nice new horse, and lots o' golden money to buy fairlings! And Tess won't look pretty in her best cloze no mo – o – ore!'

Her mother chimed in to the same tune: a certain way she had of making her labours in the house seem heavier than they were by prolonging them indefinitely, also weighed in the argument. Her father alone preserved an attitude of neutrality.

'I will go,' said Tess at last.

Her mother could not repress her consciousness of the nuptial Vision conjured up by the girl's consent.

'That's right! For such a pretty girl, it is a fine opportunity!'

Tess smiled crossly.

'I hope it is an opportunity for earning money. It is no other kind of opportunity. You had better say nothing of that silly sort to the neighbours.'

Mrs Durbeyfield did not promise. She was not quite sure that she did not feel proud enough, after the visitor's remarks, to say a good deal.

Thus it was arranged; and the young girl wrote, agreeing to be ready to set out on any day on which she might be required. She was duly informed that Mrs D'Urberville was glad of her decision, and that a spring-cart should be sent to meet her and her luggage at the top of the Vale on the day after the morrow, when she must hold herself prepared to start. Mrs D'Urberville's handwriting seemed rather masculine.

'A cart?' murmured Joan Durbeyfield doubtingly. 'It might have been a carriage for her own kin!'

Having at last taken her course, Tess was less restless and abstracted, going about her business with some self-assurance in the thought of acquiring another horse for her father by an occupation which would not be onerous. She had hoped to be a teacher at the school, but the fates seemed to decide otherwise. Being mentally older than her mother she did not regard Mrs Durbeyfield's matrimonial hopes for her in a serious aspect for a moment. The light-minded woman had been discovering good matches for her daughter almost from the year of her birth.

VII

On the morning appointed for her departure Tess was awake before dawn – at the marginal minute of the dark when the grove is still mute, save for one prophetic bird who sings with a clear-voiced conviction that he at least knows the correct time of day, the rest preserving silence as if equally convinced that he is mistaken. She remained upstairs packing till breakfast-time, and then came down in her ordinary weekday clothes, her Sunday apparel being carefully folded in her box.

Her mother expostulated. 'You will never set out to see your folks without dressing up more the dand than that?'

'But I am going to work!' said Tess.

'Well, yes,' said Mrs Durbeyfield; and, in a private tone, 'at first there may be a little pretence o't . . . But I think it will be wiser of 'ee to put your best side outward,' she added.

'Very well; I suppose you know best,' replied Tess with calm abandonment.

And to please her parent the girl put herself quite in Joan's hands, saying serenely – 'Do what you like with me, mother.'

Mrs Durbeyfield was only too delighted at this tractability. First she fetched a great basin, and washed Tess's hair with such thoroughness that when dried and brushed it looked twice as much as at other times. She tied it with a broader pink ribbon[1] than usual. Then she put upon her the white frock that Tess had worn at the club-walking, the airy fulness of which, supplementing her enlarged *coiffure*, imparted to her developing figure an amplitude which belied her age, and might cause her to be estimated as a woman when she was not much more than a child.

'I declare there's a hole in my stocking-heel!' said Tess.

'Never mind holes in your stockings – they don't speak! When I was a maid, so long as I had a pretty bonnet the devil might ha' found me in heels.'

Her mother's pride in the girl's appearance led her to step back, like a painter from his easel, and survey her work as a whole.

'You must see yourself!' she cried. 'It is much better than you was t'other day.'

As the looking-glass was only large enough to reflect a very small portion of Tess's person at one time, Mrs Durbeyfield hung a black cloak outside the casement, and so made a large reflector of the panes, as it is the wont of bedecking cottagers to do. After this she went downstairs to her husband, who was sitting in the lower room.

'I'll tell 'ee what 'tis, Durbeyfield,' said she exultingly; 'he'll never have the heart not to love her. But whatever you do, don't say too much to Tess of his fancy for her, and this chance she has got. She is such an odd maid that it mid set her against him, or against going there, even now. If all goes well, I shall certainly be for making some return to that pa'son at Stagfoot Lane for telling us – dear, good man!'

However, as the moment for the girl's setting out drew nigh, when the first excitement of the dressing had passed off, a slight misgiving found place in Joan Durbeyfield's mind. It prompted the matron to say that she would walk a little way – as far as to the point where the acclivity from the valley began its first steep ascent to the outer world. At the top Tess was going to be met with the spring-cart sent by the Stoke-D'Urbervilles, and her box had already been wheeled ahead towards this summit by a lad with trucks, to be in readiness.

Seeing their mother put on her bonnet the younger children clamoured to go with her.

'I do want to walk a little-ways wi' Sissy, now she's going to marry our gentleman-cousin, and wear fine cloze!'

'Now,' said Tess, flushing and turning quickly, 'I'll hear no more o' that! Mother, how could you ever put such stuff into their heads?'

'Going to work, my dears, for our rich relation, and help get enough money for a new horse,' said Mrs Durbeyfield pacifically.

'Good-bye, father,' said Tess, with a lumpy throat.

'Good-bye, my maid,' said Sir John, raising his head from his breast as he suspended his nap, induced by a slight excess this morning in honour of the occasion. 'Well, I hope my young friend will like such a comely specimen of his own blood. And tell'n, Tess, that being reduced, quite, from our former grandeur, I'll sell him the title – yes, sell it – and at no onreasonable figure.'

'Not for less than a thousand pound!' cried Lady Durbeyfield.

'Tell'n – I'll take a thousand pound. Well, I'll take less, when I come to think o't. He'll adorn it better than a poor broken-down feller like myself can. Tell'n he shall hae it for a hundred. But I won't stand upon trifles – tell'n he shall hae it for fifty – for twenty pound! Yes, twenty pound – that's the lowest. Dammy, family honour is family honour, and I won't take a penny less!'

Tess's eyes were too full and her voice too choked to utter the bitter sentiments that were in her. She turned quickly, and went out.

So the girls and their mother all walked together, a child on each side of Tess, holding her hand, and looking at her meditatively from time to time, as at one who was about to do great things; her mother just behind; the group forming a picture of honest beauty flanked by innocence, and backed by simple-souled vanity. They followed the way till they reached the beginning of the ascent, on the crest of which the vehicle from Trantridge was to receive her, this limit having been fixed to save the horse the labour of the last slope. Far away behind the first hills the cliff-like dwellings of Shaston broke the line of the ridge. Nobody was visible in the elevated road which skirted the ascent save the lad whom they had sent on before them, sitting on the handle of the barrow that contained all Tess's worldly possessions.

'Bide here a bit, and the cart will soon come, no doubt,' said Mrs Durbeyfield. 'Yes, I see it yonder!'

It had come – appearing suddenly from behind the forehead of the nearest upland, and stopping beside the boy with the barrow.[2] Her mother and the children thereupon decided to go no farther, and bidding them a hasty good-bye Tess bent her steps up the hill.

They saw her white shape draw near to the spring-cart, on which her box was already placed. But before she had quite reached it another vehicle shot out from a clump of trees on the summit, came round the bend of the road there, passed the luggage-cart, and halted beside Tess, who turned as if in great surprise.

Her mother perceived, for the first time, that the second vehicle was not a humble conveyance like the first, but a spick-and-span gig or dog-cart, highly varnished and equipped. The driver was a young man of three- or four-and-twenty, with a cigar between his teeth; wearing a dandy cap, drab jacket, breeches of the same hue, white neckcloth, stick-up collar, and brown driving-gloves – in short, he was the handsome, horsey young buck who had visited Joan a week or two before to get her answer about Tess.

Mrs Durbeyfield clapped her hands like a child. Then she looked down, then stared again. Could she be deceived as to the meaning of this?

'Is dat the gentleman-kinsman who'll make Sissy a lady?' asked the youngest child.

Meanwhile the muslined form of Tess could be seen standing still, undecided, beside this turn-out, whose owner was talking to her. Her seeming indecision was, in fact, more than indecision: it was misgiving. She would have preferred the humble cart. The young man dismounted, and appeared to urge her to ascend. She turned her face down the hill to her relatives, and regarded the little group. Something seemed to quicken her to a determination; possibly the thought that she had killed Prince. She suddenly stepped up; he mounted beside her, and immediately whipped on the horse. In a moment they had passed the slow cart with the box, and disappeared behind the shoulder of the hill.

Directly Tess was out of sight, and the interest of the matter as a drama was at an end, the little ones' eyes filled with tears. The youngest child said, 'I wish poor, poor Tess wasn't gone away to be a lady!' and, lowering the corners of his lips, burst out crying. The new point of view was infectious, and the next child did likewise, and then the next, till the whole three of them wailed loud.

There were tears also in Joan Durbeyfield's eyes as she turned to go home. But by the time she had got back to the village she was passively trusting to the favour of accident. However, in bed that night she sighed, and her husband asked her what was the matter.

'Oh, I don't know exactly,' she said. 'I was thinking that perhaps it would ha' been better if Tess had not gone.'

'Oughtn't ye to have thought of that before?'

'Well, 'tis a chance for the maid — Still, if 'twere the doing again, I wouldn't let her go till I had found out whether the gentleman is really a good-hearted young man and interested in her as his kinswoman.'

'Yes, you ought, perhaps, to ha' done that,' snored Sir John.

Joan Durbeyfield always managed to find consolation somewhere: 'Well, as one of the genuine stock, she ought to make her way with 'en, if she plays her trump card aright. And if he don't marry her afore he will after.[3] For that he's all afire wi' love for her any eye can see.'

'What's her trump card? Her D'Urberville blood, you mean?'

'No, stupid; her face – as 'twas mine.'

VIII

Having mounted beside her, Alec D'Urberville drove rapidly along the crest of the first hill, chatting compliments to Tess as they went, the cart with her box being left far behind. Rising still, an immense landscape stretched around them on every side; behind, the green valley of her birth, before, a gray country of which she knew nothing except from her first brief visit to Trantridge. Thus they reached the verge of an incline down which the road stretched in a long straight descent of nearly a mile.

Ever since the accident with her father's horse Tess Durbeyfield, courageous as she naturally was, had been exceedingly timid on wheels; the least irregularity of motion startled her. She began to get uneasy at a certain recklessness in her conductor's driving.

'You will go down slowly, sir, I suppose?' she said with attempted unconcern.

D'Urberville looked round upon her, nipped his cigar with the tips of his large white centre-teeth, and allowed his lips to smile slowly of themselves.

'Why, Tess,' he answered, after another whiff or two, 'it isn't a brave bouncing girl like you who asks that? Why, I always go down at full gallop. There's nothing like it for raising your spirits.'

'But perhaps you need not now?'

'Ah,' he said, shaking his head, 'there are two to be reckoned with. It is not me alone. Tib has to be considered, and she has a very queer temper.'

'Who?'

'Why, this mare. I fancy she looked round at me in a very grim way just then. Didn't you notice it?'

'Don't try to frighten me, sir,' said Tess stiffly.

'Well, I don't. If any living man can manage this horse I can: – I won't say any living man can do it – but if such has the power, I am he.'

'Why do you have such a horse?'

'Ah, well may you ask it! It was my fate, I suppose. Tib has killed one chap; and just after I bought her she nearly killed me. And then, take my word for it, I nearly killed her. But she's queer still, very queer; and one's life is hardly safe behind her sometimes.'

They were just beginning to descend; and it was evident that the horse, whether of her own will or of his (the latter being the more likely) knew so well the reckless performance expected of her that she hardly required a hint from behind.

Down, down, they sped, the wheels humming like a top, the dog-cart rocking right and left, its axis acquiring a slightly oblique set in relation to the line of progress; the figure of the horse rising and falling in undulations before them. Sometimes a wheel was off the ground, it seemed, for many yards; sometimes a stone was sent spinning over the hedge, and flinty sparks from the horse's hoofs outshone the daylight. The fore part of the straight road enlarged with their advance, the two banks dividing like a splitting stick; and one rushed past at each shoulder.

The wind blew through Tess's white muslin to her very skin, and her washed hair flew out behind. She was determined to show no open fear, but she clutched D'Urberville's rein-arm.

'Don't touch my arm! We shall be thrown out if you do! Hold on round my waist!'

She grasped his waist, and so they reached the bottom.

'Safe, thank God, in spite of your folly!' said she, her face on fire.

'Tess – fie! that's temper!' said D'Urberville.

"'Tis truth.'

'Well, you need not let go your hold of me so thanklessly the moment you feel yourself out of danger.'

She had not considered what she had been doing; whether he were man or woman, stick or stone, in her involuntary hold on him. Recovering her reserve she sat without replying, and thus they reached the summit of another declivity.

'Now then, again!' said D'Urberville.

'No, no!' said Tess. 'Show more sense, do, please.'

'But when people find themselves on one of the highest points in the county, they must get down again,' he retorted.

He loosened rein, and away they went a second time. D'Urberville turned his face to her as they rocked, and said, in playful raillery: 'Now then, put your arms round my waist again, as you did before, my beauty.'

'Never!' said Tess independently, holding on as well as she could without touching him.

'Let me put one little kiss on those holmberry lips, Tess; or even on that warmed cheek, and I'll stop – on my honour, I will!'

Tess, surprised beyond measure, slid farther back still on her seat, at which he urged the horse anew, and rocked her the more.

'Will nothing else do?' she cried at length, in desperation, her large eyes staring at him like those of a wild animal. This dressing her up so prettily by her mother had apparently been to lamentable purpose.

'Nothing, dear Tess,' he replied.

'Oh, I don't know – very well; I don't mind!' she panted miserably.

He drew rein, and as they slowed he was on the point of imprinting the desired salute, when, as if hardly yet aware of her own modesty, she dodged aside. His arms being occupied with the reins there was left him no power to prevent her manœuvre.

'Now, damn it – I'll break both our necks!' swore her capriciously passionate companion. 'So you can go from your word like that, you young witch, can you?'

'Very well,' said poor Tess, 'I'll not move since you be so determined! But I – thought you would be kind to me, and protect me, as my kinsman!'

'Kinsman be hanged! Now!'

'But I don't want anybody to kiss me, sir!' she implored, a big tear beginning to roll down her face, and the corners of her mouth trembling in her attempts not to cry. 'And I wouldn't ha' come if I had known!'

He was inexorable, and she sat still, and D'Urberville gave her the kiss of mastery. No sooner had he done so than she flushed with shame, took out her handkerchief, and wiped the spot on her cheek that had been touched by his lips. His ardour was nettled at the sight, for the act on her part had been unconsciously done.

'You are mighty sensitive for a farm girl!'[1] said the young man.

Tess made no reply to this remark, of which, indeed, she did not quite comprehend the drift, unheeding the snub she had administered by her instinctive rub upon her cheek. She had, in fact, undone the kiss, as far as such a thing was physically possible. With a dim sense that he was vexed she looked steadily ahead as they trotted on for a further half-hour, till she saw, to her consternation, that there was yet another descent to be undergone.

'You shall be made sorry for that!' he resumed, his injured tone still remaining, as he flourished the whip anew. 'Unless, that is, you agree willingly to let me do it again, and no handkerchief.'

She sighed. 'Very well, sir!' she said. 'Oh – let me get my hat!'

At the moment of speaking her hat had blown off into the road, their present speed on the upland being by no means slow. D'Urberville pulled up, and said he would get it for her, but Tess was down on the other side.

She turned back and picked up the article.

'You look prettier with it off, upon my soul, if that's possible,' he said, contemplating her over the back of the vehicle. 'Now then, up again! What's the matter?'

The hat was in place and tied, but Tess had not stepped forward.

'No, sir,' she said, revealing the red and ivory of her mouth in defiant triumph; 'not again, if I know it!'

'What – you won't get up beside me?'

'No; I shall walk.'

''Tis five or six miles yet to Trantridge.'

'I don't care if 'tis dozens. Besides, the cart is behind.'

'You artful hussy! Now, tell me – didn't you make that hat blow off on purpose? I'll swear you did!'

Her guarded silence[2] confirmed his suspicion.

Then D'Urberville cursed and swore at her, and called her everything he could think of for the trick. Turning the horse suddenly he tried to drive back upon her, and so hem her in between the gig and the hedge. But he could not do this short of injuring her.

'You ought to be ashamed of yourself for using such wicked words!' cried Tess with spirit, from the top of the hedge into which she had scrambled. 'I don't like you at all! I hate and detest you! I'll go back to mother, I will!'

D'Urberville's bad temper cleared up at sight of hers; and he laughed heartily.

'Well, I like you all the better,' he said. 'Come, let there be peace. I'll never do it again against your will.[3] My life upon it now!'

Still Tess could not be induced to remount. She did not, however, object to his keeping his gig alongside her; and in this manner, at a slow pace, they advanced towards the village of Trantridge. From time to time D'Urberville exhibited a sort of fierce distress at the sight of the tramping he had driven her to by his misdemeanour. She might in truth have safely trusted him now; but he had forfeited her confidence for the time, and she kept on the ground, progressing thoughtfully, as if wondering whether it would be wiser to return home. Her resolve, however, had been taken, and it seemed vacillating even to childishness to abandon it now, unless for graver reasons. How could she face her parents, get back her box, and disconcert the whole scheme for the rehabilitation of her family on such sentimental grounds?

A few minutes later the chimneys of The Slopes appeared in view, and in a snug nook to the right the poultry-farm and cottage of Tess's destination.

IX

The community of fowls to which Tess had been appointed as supervisor, purveyor, nurse, surgeon, and friend, made their headquarters in an old thatched cottage standing in an enclosure that had once been a garden, but was now a trampled and sanded square. The house was overrun with ivy, its chimney being enlarged by the boughs of the parasite to the aspect of a ruined tower. The lower rooms were entirely given over to the birds, who walked about them with a proprietary air, as though the place had been built by and for themselves, and not by and for certain dusty copyholders[1] who now lay east and west in the churchyard. The descendants of these bygone owners felt it almost as a slight to their family when the house which had so much of their affection, had cost so much of their forefathers' money, and had been in their possession for several generations before the D'Urbervilles came and built here, was indifferently turned into a fowl-house by Mrs Stoke-D'Urberville as soon as the property fell into hand according to law. ''Twas good enough for Christians in grandfather's time,' they said.

The rooms wherein dozens of infants had wailed at their nursing now resounded with the tapping of nascent chicks. Distracted hens in coops occupied spots where formerly stood chairs supporting sedate agriculturists. The chimney-corner and once blazing hearth was now filled with inverted beehives, in which the hens laid their eggs; while out of doors the plots that each succeeding householder had carefully shaped with his spade were torn by the cocks in wildest fashion.

The garden in which the cottage stood was surrounded by a wall, and could only be entered through a door.

When Tess had occupied herself about an hour the next morning in altering and improving the arrangements, according to her skilled ideas as the daughter of a professed poulterer, the door in the wall opened and a servant in white cap and apron entered. She had come from the manor-house.

'Mrs D'Urberville wants the fowls as usual,' she said; but perceiving that Tess did not quite understand, she explained, 'Mis'ess is a old lady, and blind.'

'Blind!' said Tess.

Almost before her misgiving at the news could find time to shape itself she took, under her companion's direction, two of the most beautiful of the Hamburghs in her arms, and followed the maidservant, who had likewise taken two, to the adjacent mansion, which, though ornate and imposing, showed traces everywhere on this side that some occupant of its chambers could bend to the love of dumb creatures – feathers floating within view of the front, and hen-coops standing on the grass.

In a sitting-room on the ground-floor, ensconced in an armchair with her back to the light, was the owner and mistress of the estate, a white-haired woman of not more than sixty, or even less, wearing a large cap. She had the mobile face frequent in those whose sight has decayed by stages, has been laboriously striven after, and reluctantly let go, rather than the stagnant mien apparent in persons long sightless or born blind. Tess walked up to this lady with her feathered charges – one sitting on each arm.

'Ah, you are the young woman come to look after my birds?' said Mrs D'Urberville, recognizing a new footstep. 'I hope you will be kind to them. My bailiff tells me you are quite the proper person. Well, where are they? Ah, this is Strut! But he is hardly so lively to-day, is he? He is alarmed at being handled by a stranger, I suppose. And Phena too – yes, they are a little frightened – aren't you, dears? But they will soon get used to you.'

While the old lady had been speaking Tess and the other maid, in obedience to her gestures, had placed the fowls severally in her lap, and she had felt them over from head to tail, examining their beaks, their combs, the manes of the cocks, their wings, and their claws. Her touch enabled her to recognize them in a moment, and to discover if a single feather were crippled or draggled. She handled their crops, and knew what they had eaten, and if too little or too much; her face enacting a vivid pantomime of the criticisms passing in her mind.

The birds that the two girls had brought in were duly returned to the yard, and the process was repeated till all the pet cocks and hens had been submitted to the old woman – Hamburghs, Bantams, Cochins, Brahmas, Dorkings, and such other sorts as were in fashion just then – her perception of each visitor being seldom at fault as she received the bird upon her knees.

It reminded Tess of a Confirmation, in which Mrs D'Urberville was the bishop, the fowls the young people presented, and herself and the maidservant the parson and curate of the parish bringing them up. At the end of the ceremony Mrs D'Urberville abruptly asked Tess, wrinkling and twitching her face into undulations, 'Can you whistle?'

'Whistle, ma'am?'

'Yes, whistle tunes.'

Tess could whistle, like most other country girls, though the accomplishment was one which she did not care to profess in genteel company. However, she blandly admitted that such was the fact.

'Then you will have to practise it every day. I had a lad who did it very well, but he has left. I want you to whistle to my bullfinches; as I cannot see them I like to hear them, and we teach 'em airs that way. Tell her where the cages are, Elizabeth. You must begin to-morrow, or they will go back in their piping. They have been neglected these several days.'

'Mr D'Urberville whistled to 'em this morning, ma'am,' said Elizabeth.

'He! Pooh!'

The old lady's face creased into furrows of repugnance, and she made no further reply.

Thus the reception of Tess by her fancied kinswoman terminated, and the birds were taken back to their quarters. The girl's surprise at Mrs D'Urberville's manner was not great; for since seeing the size of the house she had expected no more. But she was far from being aware that the old lady had never heard a word of the so-called kinship. She gathered that no great affection flowed between the blind woman and her son. But in that, too, she was mistaken. Mrs D'Urberville was not the first mother compelled to love her offspring resentfully, and to be bitterly fond.

In spite of the unpleasant initiation of the day before, Tess inclined to the freedom and novelty of her new position in the morning when the sun shone, now that she was once installed there; and she was curious to test her powers in the unexpected direction asked of her, so as to ascertain her chance of retaining her post. As soon as she was alone within the walled garden she sat herself down on a coop, and seriously screwed up her mouth for the long-neglected practice. She found her former ability to have degenerated to the production of a hollow sepulchral rush of wind through the lips, and no clear note at all.

She remained fruitlessly blowing and blowing,[2] wondering how she could have so grown out of the art which had come by nature, till she became aware of a movement among the ivy-boughs which cloaked the garden-wall no less than the cottage. Looking that way she beheld a form springing from the coping to the plot.[3] It was Alec D'Urberville, whom she had not set eyes on since he had conducted her the day before to the door of the gardener's cottage where she had lodgings.

'Upon my honour!' cried he, 'there was never before such a beautiful thing in Nature or Art[4] as you look, "Cousin" Tess ["Cousin" had a faint ring of mockery]. I have been watching you from over the wall – sitting like *Im*-patience on a monument,[5] and pouting up that pretty red mouth to whistling shape, and whooing and whooing, and privately swearing, and never being able to produce a note. Why, you are quite cross because you can't do it.'

'I am cross, but I didn't swear.'

'Ah! I understand why you are trying – those bullies! My mother wants you to carry on their musical education. How selfish of her! As if attending to these curst cocks and hens here were not enough work for any girl. I would flatly refuse, if I were you.'

'But she wants me particularly to do it, and to be ready by to-morrow morning.'

'Does she? Well then – I'll give you a lesson or two.'

'Oh no, you won't!' said Tess, withdrawing towards the door.

'Nonsense; I don't want to touch you. See – I'll stand on this side of the wire-netting, and you can keep on the other; so you may feel quite safe. Now, look here; you screw up your lips too harshly. There 'tis – so.'

He suited the action to the word, and whistled a line of 'Take, O take those lips away.'[6] But the allusion was lost upon Tess.

'Now try,' said D'Urberville.

She attempted to look reserved; her face put on its utmost phase of sculptural severity. But he persisted in his demand, and at last, to get rid of him, she did put up her lips as directed, laughing distressfully, however, before she could succeed in producing a clear note, and then blushing with vexation that she had laughed.

He encouraged her with 'Try again!'

Tess was quite serious, painfully serious by this time; and she tried – ultimately and unexpectedly emitting a real round sound. The momentary pleasure of success got the better of her; her eyes enlarged, and she involuntarily smiled in his face.[7]

'That's it! Now I have started you – you'll go on beautifully. There – I said I would not come near you; and, in spite of such temptation as never before fell to mortal man, I'll keep my word . . . Tess, do you think my mother a queer old soul?'

'I don't know much of her yet.'[8]

'You'll find her so; she must be, to make you learn to whistle to her bullfinches. I am rather out of her books just now, but you will be quite in favour if you treat her live-stock well. Good morning. If you meet with any difficulties and want help here, don't go to the bailiff, come to me.'

It was in the economy of this *régime* that Tess Durbeyfield had undertaken to fill a place. Her first day's experiences were fairly typical of those which followed through many succeeding days. A familiarity with Alec D'Urberville's presence – which that young man carefully cultivated in her by playful dialogue, and by jestingly calling her his cousin when they were alone – removed most of her original shyness of him, without, however, implanting any feeling which could engender shyness of a new and tenderer kind. But she was more pliable under his hands than a mere companionship would have made her, owing to her inevitable dependence upon his mother, and, through her comparative helplessness, upon him.[9]

She soon found that whistling to the bullfinches in Mrs D'Urberville's room was no such onerous business when she had regained the art, for she had caught from her musical mother numerous airs that suited those songsters admirably. A far more satisfactory time than when she practised in the garden was this whistling by the cages each morning. Unrestrained by the young man's presence she threw up her mouth, put her lips near the bars, and piped away in easeful grace to the attentive listeners.

Mrs D'Urberville slept in a large four-post bedstead hung with heavy damask curtains, and the bullfinches occupied the same apartment, where they flitted about freely at certain hours, and made little spots on the furniture. Once while Tess was at the window where the cages were ranged, giving her lesson as usual, she thought she heard a rustling behind the bed. The old lady was not present, and turning round the girl had an impression that the toes of a pair of boots were visible below the fringe of the curtains. Thereupon her whistling became so disjointed that the listener, if such there were, must have discovered her suspicion of his presence. She searched the curtains every morning after that, but never found anybody within them. Alec D'Urberville had evidently thought better of his freak to terrify her by an ambush of that kind.[10]

X

Every village has its idiosyncrasy, its constitution, its own code of morality. The levity of some of the younger women in and about Trantridge was marked, and was perhaps symptomatic of the choice spirit who ruled The Slopes in that vicinity. The place had also a more abiding defect; it drank hard. The staple conversation on the farms around was on the uselessness of saving money; and smockfrocked arithmeticians, leaning on their ploughs or hoes, would enter into calculations of great nicety to prove that parish relief was a fuller provision for a man in his old age than any which could result from savings out of their wages during a whole lifetime.

The chief pleasure of these philosophers lay in going every Saturday night, when work was done, to Chaseborough, a decayed market-town two or three miles distant; and, returning in the small hours of the next morning, to spend Sunday in sleeping off the dyspeptic effects of the curious compounds sold to them as beer by the monopolizers of the once independent inns.[1]

For a long time Tess did not join in the weekly pilgrimages. But under pressure from matrons not much older than herself – for marriage before means was the rule here as elsewhere – Tess at length consented to go. Her first experience of the journey afforded her more enjoyment than she had expected, the hilariousness of the others being quite contagious after her monotonous attention to the poultry-farm all the week. She went again and again. Being graceful and interesting, standing moreover on the momentary threshold of womanhood, her appearance drew down upon her some sly regards from loungers in the streets of Chaseborough; hence, though sometimes her journey to the town was made independently, she always searched for her fellows at nightfall, to have the protection of their companionship homeward.

This had gone on for a month or two when a Saturday came in early September, on which a fair and a market coincided; and the pilgrims from Trantridge sought double delights at the inns on that account.[2] It was long past sunset, and Tess waited for the troop till she was quite weary. While she stood at a corner by the tavern in which they sat she heard a footstep, and looking round saw the red coal of a cigar. D'Urberville was standing there also. He beckoned to her, and she reluctantly went to him.

'My Pretty, what are you doing here at this time of night?'

She was so tired after her long day and her walk that she confided her trouble to him.

'I have been waiting ever so long, sir, to have their company home, because the road is rather strange to me at night. But I really think I will wait no longer.'

'Do not. I have only a saddle-horse here to-day; but come to the "Flower-de-Luce," and I'll hire a trap, and drive you home with me.'[3]

Tess had never quite got over her original mistrust of him, and, with all their tardiness, she preferred to walk home with the workfolk. So she answered that she was much obliged to him, but on second thoughts would not trouble him. 'I have said that I will wait for 'em, and they will expect me to now.'

'Very well, silly![4] Please yourself.'

As soon as he had re-lit a cigar and walked away the Trantridge villagers within began also to recollect how time was flying, and prepared to leave in a body. Their bundles and baskets were gathered up, and half an hour later, when the clock-chime sounded a quarter past eleven, they were straggling along the lane which led up the hill towards their homes.

It was a three-mile walk, along a dry white road, made whiter to-night by the light of the moon.

Tess soon perceived as she walked in the flock, sometimes with this one, sometimes with that, that the fresh night air was producing staggerings and serpentine courses among the men who had partaken too freely; some of the more careless women also were wandering in their gait – to wit, a dark virago, Car Darch, dubbed Queen of Spades,[5] till lately a favourite of D'Urberville's; Nancy, her sister, nicknamed the Queen of Diamonds; and a young married woman who had already tumbled down. Yet however terrestrial and lumpy their appearance just now to the mean unglamoured eye, to themselves the case was different. They followed the road with a knowledge that they were soaring along in a supporting medium, possessed of original and profound thoughts, themselves and surrounding nature forming an organism of which all the parts harmoniously and joyously interpenetrated each other.[6] They were as sublime as the moon and stars above them, and the moon and stars were as ardent as they.

Tess, however, had undergone such painful experiences in this kind in her father's house, that the discovery of their condition spoilt the pleasure she was beginning to feel in the moonlight journey. Yet she stuck to the party, for reasons above given.

In the open highway they had progressed in scattered order; but now their route was through a field-gate, and the foremost finding a difficulty in opening it they closed up together.

This leading pedestrian was Car the Queen of Spades, who carried a wicker-basket containing her mother's groceries, her own draperies, and other purchases for the week. The basket being large and heavy, Car had placed it for convenience of porterage on the top of her head, where it rode on in jeopardized balance as she walked with arms akimbo.

'Well – whatever is that a-creeping down thy back, Car Darch?' said one of the group suddenly.

All looked at Car. Her gown was a light cotton print, and from the back of her head a kind of rope could be seen descending to some distance below her waist like a Chinaman's queue.

''Tis her hair falling down,' said another.

No; it was not her hair: it was a black stream of something oozing from her basket, and it glistened like a slimy snake in the cold still rays of the moon.

''Tis treacle,' said an observant matron.

Treacle it was.[7] Car's poor old grandmother had a weakness for the sweet stuff. Honey she had in plenty out of her own hives, but treacle was what her soul desired, and Car had been about to give her a treat of surprise. Hastily lowering the basket the dark girl found that the vessel containing the liquid had been smashed within.

By this time there had arisen a shout of laughter at the extraordinary appearance of Car's back, which irritated the dark queen into getting rid of the disfigurement by the first sudden means available, and independently of the help of the scoffers. She rushed excitedly into the field they were about to cross, and flinging herself flat on her back upon the grass, began to wipe her gown as well as she could by gyrating horizontally on the herbage and dragging herself over it upon her elbows.

The laughter rang louder; they clung to the gate, to the posts, rested on their staves, in the weakness engendered by their convulsions at the spectacle of Car. Our heroine, who had hitherto held her peace, at this wild moment could not help joining in with the rest.

It was a misfortune – in more ways than one. No sooner did the dark queen hear the soberer richer note of Tess among those of the other workpeople than a long smouldering sense of rivalry inflamed her to madness. She sprang to her feet and closely faced the object of her dislike.

'How darest th' laugh at me, hussy!' she cried.

'I couldn't really help it when t'others did,' apologized Tess, still tittering.

'Ah, th'st think th' beest everybody, dostn't, because th' beest first favourite with He just now! But stop a bit, my lady, stop a bit! I'm as good as two of such! Look here – here's at 'ee!'

To Tess's horror the dark queen began stripping off the bodice of her gown – which for the added reason of its ridiculed condition she was only too glad to be free of – till she had bared her plump neck, shoulders, and arms to the moonshine, under which they looked as luminous and beautiful as some Praxitelean creation,[8] in their possession of the faultless rotundities of a lusty country girl. She closed her fists and squared up at Tess.

'Indeed, then, I shall not fight!' said the latter majestically; 'and if I had known you was of that sort, I wouldn't have so let myself down as to come with such a whorage[9] as this is!'

The rather too inclusive speech brought down a torrent of vituperation from other quarters upon fair Tess's unlucky head, particularly from the Queen of Diamonds, who having stood in the relations to D'Urberville that Car had also been suspected of, united with the latter against the common enemy. Several other women also chimed in, with an animus which none of them would have been so fatuous as to show but for the rollicking evening they had passed. Thereupon, finding Tess unfairly browbeaten, the husbands and lovers tried to make peace by defending her; but the result of that attempt was directly to increase the war.

Tess was indignant and ashamed. She no longer minded the loneliness of the way and the lateness of the hour; her one object was to get away from the whole crew as soon as possible. She knew well enough that the better among them would repent of their passion next day. They were all now inside the field, and she was edging about to rush off alone when a horseman emerged almost silently from the corner of the hedge that screened the road, and Alec D'Urberville looked round upon them.

'What the devil is all this row about, workfolk?' he asked.

The explanation was not readily forthcoming; and, in truth, he did not require any. Having heard their voices while yet some way off he had ridden creepingly forward, and learnt enough to satisfy himself.

Tess was standing apart from the rest, near the gate. He bent over towards her. 'Jump up behind me,' he whispered, 'and we'll get shot of the screaming cats in a jiffy!'

She felt almost ready to faint, so vivid was her sense of the crisis. At almost any other moment of her life she would have refused such proffered aid and company, as she had refused them several times before; and now the loneliness would not of itself have forced her to do otherwise. But coming as the invitation did at the particular juncture when fear and indignation at these adversaries could be transformed by a spring of the foot into a triumph over them, she abandoned herself to her impulse, put her toe upon his instep, and leapt into the saddle behind him. The pair were speeding away into the distant gray by the time that the contentious revellers became aware of what had happened.

The Queen of Spades forgot the stain on her bodice, and stood beside the Queen of Diamonds and the new-married, staggering young woman – all with a gaze of fixity in the direction in which the horse's tramp was diminishing into silence on the road.

'What be ye looking at?' asked a man who had not observed the incident.

'Ho-ho-ho!' laughed dark Car.

'Hee-hee-hee!' laughed the tippling bride, as she steadied herself on the arm of her fond husband.

'Heu-heu-heu!' laughed dark Car's mother, stroking her moustache as she explained laconically: 'Out of the frying-pan into the fire!'

And then these children of the open air, whom even excess of alcohol could scarce injure permanently, betook themselves to the field-path; and as they went there moved onward with them, around the shadow of each one's head, an opalized circle of glory,[10] formed by the moon's rays upon the glistening sheet of dew. Each pedestrian could see no halo but his or her own, which never deserted the head-shadow, whatever its vulgar unsteadiness might be; but adhered to it, and persistently beautified it; till the erratic motions seemed an inherent part of the irradiation, and the fumes of their breathing a component of the night's mist; and the spirit of the scene, and of the moonlight, and of Nature, seemed harmoniously to mingle with the spirit of wine.

XI

The twain cantered along for some time without speech, Tess as she clung to him still panting in her triumph, yet in other respects dubious. She had perceived that the horse was not the spirited one he sometimes rode, and felt no alarm on that score, though her seat was precarious enough.[1] She asked him to slow the animal to a walk, which Alec accordingly did.

'Neatly done, was it not, dear Tess,' he said by and by.

'Yes!' said she. 'I am sure I ought to be much obliged to you.'

'And are you?'

She did not reply.

'Tess, why do you always dislike my kissing you?'

'I suppose —because I don't love you.'[2]

'You are quite sure?'

'I am angry with you sometimes!'

'Ah, I half feared as much.' Nevertheless, Alec did not object to that confession. He knew that anything was better than frigidity. 'Why haven't you told me when I have made you angry?'

'You know very well why. Because I cannot help myself here.'

'I haven't offended you often by love-making?'

'You have sometimes.'

'How many times?'

'You know as well as I – too many times.'

'Every time I have tried?'

She was silent, and the horse ambled along for a considerable distance, till a faint luminous fog, which had hung in the hollows all the evening, became general and enveloped them. It seemed to hold the moonlight in suspension, rendering it more pervasive than in clear air. Whether on this account, or from absent-mindedness, or from sleepiness, she did not perceive that they had long ago passed the point at which the lane to Trantridge branched from the highway, and that her conductor had not taken the Trantridge track.

She was inexpressibly weary.[3] She had risen at five o'clock every morning of that week, had been on foot the whole of each day, and on this evening had in addition walked the three miles to Chaseborough, waited three hours for her neighbours without eating or drinking, her impatience to start them preventing either; she had then walked a mile of the way home, and had undergone the excitement of the quarrel, till it was now nearly one o'clock.[4] Only once, however, was she overcome by actual drowsiness. In that moment of oblivion she sank gently against him.

D'Urberville withdrew his feet from the stirrups, turned sideways on the saddle, and enclosed her waist with his arm to support her.

This immediately put her on the defensive, and with one of those sudden impulses of reprisal to which she was liable she gave him a little push from her. In his ticklish position he nearly lost his balance and only just avoided rolling over into the road, the horse, though a powerful one, being fortunately the quietest he rode.[5]

'That is devilish unkind!' he said. 'I mean no harm – only to keep you from falling.'

She pondered suspiciously; till, thinking that this might after all be true, she relented, and said quite humbly, 'I beg your pardon, sir.'

'I won't pardon you unless you show some confidence in me. Good God!' he burst out, 'what am I, to be repulsed so by a mere chit like you? For near three mortal months have you trifled with my feelings, eluded me, and snubbed me; and I won't stand it!'

'I'll leave you to-morrow, sir.'

'No, you will not leave me to-morrow! Will you, I ask once more, show your belief in me by letting me encircle you with my arm? Come, between us two and nobody else, now. We know each other well; and you know that I love you, and think you are the prettiest girl in the world, which you are. May I treat you as a lover?'

She drew a quick pettish breath of objection, writhing uneasily on her seat, looked far ahead, and murmured, 'I don't know – I wish – how can I say yes or no when—'

He settled the matter by clasping his arm round her as he desired,

and Tess expressed no further negative. Thus they sidled onward till
it struck her they had been advancing for an unconscionable time –
far longer than was usually occupied by the short journey from
Chaseborough, even at this walking pace, and that they were no longer
on hard road, but in a mere trackway.

'Why, where be we?' she exclaimed.

'Passing by a wood.'

'A wood – what wood? Surely we are quite out of the road?'

'A bit of The Chase – the oldest wood in England.[6] It is a lovely
night, and why should we not prolong our ride a little?'

'How could you be so treacherous!' said Tess, between archness
and real dismay, and getting rid of his arm by pulling open his fingers
one by one, though at the risk of slipping off herself. 'Just when I've
been putting such trust in you, and obliging you to please you, because
I thought I had wronged you by that push! Please set me down, and
let me walk home.'

'You cannot walk home, even if the air were clear. We are miles
away from Trantridge, if I must tell you, and in this growing fog you
might wander for hours among these trees.'

'Never mind that,' she coaxed. 'Put me down, I beg you. I don't
mind where it is; only let me get down, sir, please!'

'Very well, then, I will – on one condition. Having brought you
here to this out-of-the-way place, I feel myself responsible for your
safe-conduct home, whatever you may yourself feel about it. As to
your getting to Trantridge without assistance, it is quite impossible;
for, to tell the truth, owing to this fog, which so disguises everything,
I don't quite know where we are myself. Now, if you will promise to
wait beside the horse while I walk through the bushes till I come to
some road or house, and ascertain exactly our whereabouts, I'll deposit
you here willingly. When I come back I'll give you full directions, and
if you insist upon walking you may; or you may ride – at your pleasure.'

She accepted these terms, and slid off on the near side, though not
till he had stolen a hearty kiss.[7] He sprang down on the other side.

'I suppose I must hold the horse?' said she.

'Oh no; it's not necessary,' replied Alec, patting the panting creature.
'He's had enough of it for to-night.'

He turned the horse's head into the bushes, hitched him on to a bough, and pulling off a light dust-coat that he wore, spread it upon the thick leaves.[8]

'Now, you sit there,' he said. 'That will keep away the damp. Just give an eye to the horse – it will be quite sufficient.'

He took a few steps away from her, but, returning, said, 'By the bye, Tess, your father has a new cob to-day. Somebody gave it to him.'

'Somebody? You!'

D'Urberville nodded.

'Oh how very good of you that is!' she exclaimed, with a painful sense of the awkwardness of having to thank him just then.

'And the children have some toys.'

'I didn't know – you ever sent them anything!' she murmured, much moved. 'I almost wish you had not – yes, I almost wish it!'

'Why, dear?'

'It – hampers me so.'

'Tessy – don't you love me ever so little now?'

'I'm grateful,' she reluctantly admitted. 'But I fear I do not—' The sudden vision of his passion for herself as a factor in this result so distressed her that, beginning with one slow tear, and then following with another, she wept outright.

'Don't cry, dear, dear one! Now sit down here, and wait till I come.' She passively sat down on the coat that he had spread, and shivered slightly. 'Are you cold?' he asked.

'Not very – a little.'

He touched her with his fingers, which sank into her as into a billow. 'You have only that puffy muslin dress on – how's that?'

'It's my best summer one. 'Twas very warm when I started, and I didn't know I was going to ride, and that it would be night.'

'Nights grow chilly in September. Let me see.' He went to the horse, took a druggist's bottle[9] from a parcel on the saddle, and after some trouble in opening it held it to her mouth unawares. Tess sputtered and coughed, and gasping 'It will go on my pretty frock!' swallowed as he poured, to prevent the catastrophe she feared.

'That's it – now you'll feel warmer,' said D'Urberville, as he restored the bottle to its place. 'It is only a well-known cordial that my mother ordered me to bring for household purposes, and she won't mind me using some of it medicinally. Now, my pretty, rest there; I shall soon be back again.'

He pulled the overcoat round her shoulders and plunged into the webs of vapour which by this time formed veils between the trees. She could hear the rustling of the branches as he ascended the adjoining slope, till his movements were no louder than the hopping of a bird, and finally died away. With the setting of the moon the pale light lessened, and Tess became invisible as she fell into reverie upon the leaves where he had left her.

In the meantime Alec D'Urberville had pushed on up the slope to clear his genuine doubt as to the quarter of the Chase they were in. He had, in fact, ridden quite at random for over an hour, taking any turning that came to hand in order to prolong companionship with her, and giving far more attention to Tess's moonlit person than to any wayside object. A little rest for the jaded animal being desirable, he did not hasten his search for landmarks. A clamber over the hill into the adjoining vale brought him to the fence of a highway whose aspect he recognized, which settled the question of their whereabouts. D'Urberville thereupon turned back; but by this time the moon had quite gone down, and partly on account of the fog the Chase was wrapped in thick darkness, although morning was not far off. He was obliged to advance with outstretched hands to avoid contact with the boughs, and discovered that to hit the exact spot from which he had started was at first entirely beyond him. Roaming up and down, round and round, he at length heard a slight movement of the horse close at hand; and the sleeve of his overcoat unexpectedly caught his foot.

'Tess!' said D'Urberville.

There was no answer. The obscurity was now so great that he could see absolutely nothing but a pale nebulousness at his feet, which represented the white muslin figure he had left upon the dead leaves. Everything else was blackness alike. D'Urberville stooped; and heard a gentle regular breathing. She was sleeping soundly.[10]

Darkness and silence ruled everywhere around. Above them rose the primæval yews and oaks of the Chase, in which were poised gentle roosting birds in their last nap; and around them the hopping rabbits and hares. But where was Tess's guardian angel? where was Providence?[11] Perhaps, like that other god of whom the ironical Tishbite[12] spoke, he was talking, or he was pursuing, or he was in a journey, or peradventure he was sleeping and was not to be awaked.

Already at that hour some sons of the forest were stirring and striking lights in not very distant cottages; good and sincere hearts among them, patterns of honesty and devotion and chivalry. And powerful horses were stamping in their stalls, ready to be let out into the morning air. But no dart or thread of intelligence inspired these men to harness and mount, or gave them by any means the least inkling that their sister was in the hands of the spoiler;[13] and they did not come that way.

Why it was that upon this beautiful feminine tissue, sensitive as gossamer, and practically blank as snow as yet, there should have been traced such a coarse pattern as it was doomed to receive; why so often the coarse appropriates the finer thus,[14] many thousand years of analytical philosophy have failed to explain to our sense of order. One may, indeed, admit the possibility of a retribution lurking in the catastrophe. Doubtless some of Tess D'Urberville's mailed ancestors rollicking home from a fray had dealt the same wrong even more ruthlessly upon peasant girls of their time. But though to visit the sins of the fathers upon the children may be a morality good enough for divinities, it is scorned by average human nature; and it therefore does not mend the matter.[15]

As Tess's own people down in those retreats are never tired of saying among each other in their fatalistic way: 'It was to be.' There lay the pity of it. An immeasurable chasm was to divide our heroine's personality thereafter from that previous self of hers who stepped from her mother's door to try her fortune at Trantridge poultry-farm.

END OF PHASE THE FIRST

Maiden no More

XII

The basket was heavy and the bundle was large, but she lugged them along like a person who did not find any especial burden in material things. Occasionally she stopped to rest in a mechanical way by some gate or post; and then, giving the baggage another hitch upon her full round arm, went steadily on again.

It was a Sunday morning in late October, about four months after Tess Durbeyfield's arrival at Trantridge. The time was not long past daybreak, and the yellow luminosity upon the horizon behind her back lighted the ridge towards which her face was set[1] – the barrier of the vale wherein she had of late been a stranger – which she would have to climb over to reach her birthplace. The ascent was gradual on this side, and the soil and scenery differed much from those within Blakemore Vale. Even the character and accent of the two peoples had shades of difference, despite the amalgamating effects of a roundabout railway;[2] so that, though less than twenty miles from the place of her sojourn at Trantridge, her native village had seemed a far-away spot. The field-folk shut in there traded northward and westward, travelled, courted, and married northward and westward, thought northward and westward; those on this side mainly directed their energies and attention to the east and south.

The incline was the same down which D'Urberville had driven with her so wildly on that day in June. Tess went up the remainder of its length without stopping, and on reaching the edge of the escarpment gazed over the familiar green world beyond, now half veiled in mist. It was always beautiful from here; it was terribly beautiful to Tess to-day, for since her eyes last fell upon it she had learnt that the serpent hisses where the sweet birds sing.[3] Life was totally changed for her forthwith.[4] Verily another girl than the one she had been at home was she who, bowed by the thought, stood still here, and turned to look behind her. She could not bear to look forward into the Vale.

Ascending by the long white road that Tess herself had just laboured up, she saw a two-wheeled vehicle, beside which walked a man, who held up his hand to attract her attention.

She obeyed the signal to wait for him with unspeculative repose, and in a few minutes man and horse stopped beside her.

'Why did you slip away by stealth like this?' said D'Urberville, with upbraiding breathlessness; 'on a Sunday morning, too, when people were all in bed! I only discovered it by accident, and I have been driving like the deuce to overtake you. Just look at the mare. Why go off like this? You know that nobody wished to hinder your going. And how unnecessary it has been for you to toil along on foot, and encumber yourself with this heavy load! I have followed like a madman, simply to drive you the rest of the distance, if you won't come back.'

'I shan't come back,' said she.

'I thought you wouldn't – I said so. Well, then, put up your baskets, and let me help you on.'

She listlessly placed her basket and bundle within the dog-cart, and stepped up, and they sat side by side. She had no fear of him now, and in the cause of her confidence her sorrow lay.

D'Urberville mechanically lit a cigar, and the journey was continued with broken unemotional conversation on the commonplace objects by the wayside. He had quite forgotten his struggle to kiss her when, in the early summer, they had driven in the opposite direction along the same road. She sat[5] now, like a puppet, replying to his remarks in monosyllables. After a space they came in view of the clump of trees beyond which the village of Marlott stood. It was only then that her still face showed the least emotion, a tear or two beginning to trickle down.

'What are you crying for?' he coldly asked.

'I was only thinking that I was born over there,' murmured Tess.

'Well – we must all be born somewhere.'

'I wish I had never been born – there or anywhere else!'

'Pooh! Well, if you didn't wish to come to Trantridge why did you come?'

She did not reply.

'You didn't come for love of me, that I'll swear.'

''Tis quite true. If I had gone for love o' you, if I had ever really loved 'ee, if I loved you still, I should not so loathe and hate myself for my weakness as I do now!'

He shrugged his shoulders. She resumed –

'I didn't understand your meaning till it was too late.'[6]

'That's what every woman says.'

'How can you dare to use those words!' she cried, turning impetuously upon him, her eyes flashing as the latent spirit (of which he was to see more some day) awoke in her. 'My God! I could knock you out of the gig! Did it never strike your mind that what every woman says some women may feel?'[7]

'Very well,' he said, laughing; 'I am sorry to wound you. I did wrong – I admit it.' He dropped into some little bitterness as he continued: 'Only you needn't be so everlastingly flinging it in my face. I am ready to pay to the uttermost farthing. You know you need not work in the fields or the dairies again. You know you may clothe yourself with the best, instead of in the bald plain way you have lately affected, as if you couldn't get a ribbon more than you earn.'

Her lip lifted slightly, though there was little scorn, as a rule, in her large and impulsive nature.

'I have said I will not take anything more from you, and I will not – I cannot! I *should* be your creature to go on doing that, and I won't!'

'One would think you were a princess from your manner, in addition to a true and original D'Urberville – ha! ha! Well, Tess, dear, I can say no more. I suppose I am a bad fellow – a damn bad fellow. I was born bad, and I have lived bad, and I shall die bad in all probability. But, upon my lost soul, I won't be bad towards you again, Tess. And if certain circumstances should arise – you understand – in which you are in the least need, the least difficulty, send me one line, and you shall have by return whatever you require. I may not be at Trantridge – I am going to London for a time – I can't stand the old woman. But all letters will be forwarded.'

She said that she did not wish him to drive her farther, and they stopped just under the clump of trees. D'Urberville alighted, and lifted her down bodily in his arms, afterwards placing her articles on the ground beside her. She bowed to him slightly, her eye just lingering in his; and then she turned to take the parcels for departure.

Alec D'Urberville removed his cigar, bent towards her, and said –

'You are not going to turn away like that, dear? Come!'

'If you wish,' she answered indifferently. 'See how you've mastered me!'

She thereupon turned round and lifted her face to his, and remained like a marble term while he imprinted a kiss upon her cheek – half perfunctorily, half as if zest had not yet quite died out. Her eyes vaguely rested upon the remotest trees in the lane while the kiss was given, as though she were nearly unconscious of what he did.

'Now the other side, for old acquaintance' sake.'

She turned her head in the same passive way, as one might turn at the request of a sketcher or hairdresser, and he kissed the other side, his lips touching cheeks that were damp and smoothly chill as the skin of the mushrooms growing around them.

'You don't give me your mouth and kiss me back.[8] You never willingly do that – you'll never love me, I fear.'

'I have said so, often. It is true. I have never really and truly loved you, and I think I never can.' She added mournfully, 'Perhaps, of all things, a lie on this thing would do the most good to me now; but I have honour enough left, little as 'tis, not to tell that lie. If I did love you I may have the best o' causes for letting you know it. But I don't.'

He emitted a laboured breath, as if the scene were getting rather oppressive to his heart, or to his conscience, or to his gentility.

'Well, you are absurdly melancholy, Tess. I have no reason for flattering you now, and I can say plainly that you need not be so sad. You can hold your own for beauty against any woman of these parts, gentle or simple; I say it to you as a practical man and well-wisher. If you are wise you will show it to the world more than you do before it fades . . . And yet, Tess, will you come back to me? Upon my soul I don't like to let you go like this!'

'Never, never! I made up my mind as soon as I saw – what I ought to have seen sooner;[9] and I won't come.'

'Then good-morning, my four months' cousin – good-bye!'

He leapt up lightly, arranged the reins, and was gone between the tall red-berried hedges.

Tess did not look after him, but slowly wound along the crooked lane. It was still early, and though the sun's lower limb was just free of the hill his rays, ungenial and peering, addressed the eye rather than the touch as yet. There was not a human soul near. Sad October and her sadder self seemed the only two existences haunting that lane.

As she walked, however, some footsteps approached behind her, the footsteps of a man; and owing to the briskness of his advance he was close at her heels and had said 'Good-morning' before she had been long aware of his propinquity. He appeared to be an artisan of some sort, and carried a tin pot of red paint in his hand. He asked in a business-like manner if he should take her basket, which she permitted him to do, walking beside him.

'It is early to be astir this Sabbath morn,' he said cheerfully.

'Yes,' said Tess.

'When most people are at rest from their week's work.'

She also assented to this.

'Though I do more real work to-day than all the week besides.'

'Do you?'

'All the week I work for the glory of man, and on Sunday for the glory of God. That's more real than the other – hey? I have a little to do here at this stile.' The man turned as he spoke to an opening at the roadside leading into a pasture. 'If you'll wait a moment,' he added, 'I shall not be long.'

As he had her basket she could not well do otherwise; and she waited, observing him. He set down her basket and the tin pot, and stirring the paint with the brush that was in it began painting large square letters on the middle board of the three composing the stile, placing a comma between each word, as if to give pause while that word was driven well home to the reader's heart –

THY, DAMNATION, SLUMBERETH, NOT.[10]

2 PET. ii. 3.

Against the peaceful landscape, the pale, decaying tints of the copses, the blue air of the horizon, and the lichened stile-boards, these staring vermilion words shone forth. They seemed to shout themselves out and make the atmosphere ring. Some people might have cried 'Alas, poor Theology!' at the hideous defacement – the last grotesque phase of a creed which had served mankind well in its time. But the words entered Tess with accusatory horror. It was as if this man had known her recent history; yet he was a total stranger.

Having finished his text he picked up her basket, and she mechanically resumed her walk beside him.

'Do you believe what you paint?' she asked in low tones.

'Believe that tex? Do I believe in my own existence!'

'But,' said she tremulously, 'suppose your sin was not of your own seeking?'

He shook his head.

'I cannot split hairs on that burning query,' he said. 'I have walked hundreds of miles during this past summer, painting these texes on every wall, gate, and stile in the length and breadth of this district. I leave their application to the hearts of the people who read 'em.'

'I think they are horrible,' said Tess. 'Crushing! killing!'

'That's what they are meant to be!' he replied in a trade voice. 'But you should read my hottest ones – them I kips for slums and seaports. They'd make ye wriggle! Not but what this is a very good tex for the rural districts . . . Ah – there's a nice bit of blank wall up by that barn standing to waste. I must put one there.[11] Will you wait, miss?'

'No,' said she; and taking her basket Tess trudged on. A little way forward she turned her head. The old gray wall began to advertise a similar fiery lettering to the first, with a strange and unwonted mien, as if distressed at duties it had never before been called upon to perform. It was with a sudden flush that she read and realized what was to be the inscription he was now half-way through –

THOU, SHALT, NOT, COMMIT —[12]

Her cheerful friend saw her looking, stopped his brush, and shouted –

'If you want to ask anything of the sort we was talking about, there's a very earnest good man going to preach a charity-sermon to-day in the parish you are going to – Mr Clare, of Emminster. I'm not of his persuasion now, but he's a good man, and he'll explain as well as any parson I know. 'Twas he began the work in me.'

But Tess did not answer; she throbbingly resumed her walk, her eyes fixed on the ground. 'Pooh – I don't believe any of it!'[13] she said contemptuously when her flush had died away.

A plume of smoke soared up suddenly from her father's chimney, the sight of which made her heart ache. The aspect of the interior, when she reached it, made her heart ache more. Her mother, who had just come down stairs, turned to greet her from the fireplace, where she was kindling barked-oak twigs under the breakfast kettle. The young children were still above, as was also her father, it being Sunday morning, when he felt justified in lying an additional half-hour.

'Well! – my dear Tess!' exclaimed her surprised mother, jumping up and kissing the girl. 'How be ye? I didn't see you till you was in upon me! Have you come home to be married?'

'No, I have not come for that, mother.'

'Then for a holiday?'

'Yes – for a holiday; for a long holiday,' said Tess.

'What, isn't your cousin going to do the handsome thing?'

'He's not my cousin, and he's not going to marry me.'

Her mother eyed her narrowly.

'Come, you have not told me all,' she said.

Then Tess told.[14]

'And yet th'st not got him to marry 'ee!' reiterated her mother. 'Any woman would have done it but you!'

'Perhaps any woman would except me.'

'It would have been something like a story to come back with, if you had!' continued Mrs Durbeyfield, ready to burst into tears of vexation. 'After all the talk about you and him which has reached us here, who would have expected it to end like this! Why didn't ye think of doing some good for your family instead o' thinking only of yourself? See how I've got to teave and slave, and your poor weak father with his heart clogged like a dripping-pan. I did hope for something to come out o' this! To see what a pretty pair you and he made that day when you drove away together four months ago! See what he has given us – all, as we thought, because we were his kin. But if he's not, it must have been done because of his love for 'ee. And yet you've not got him to marry!'

Get Alec D'Urberville in the mind to marry her! He marry *her*! On matrimony he had never once said a word. And what if he had? How she might have been impelled to answer him by a crude snatching at social salvation she could not say. But her poor foolish mother little knew her feeling towards this man. Perhaps it was unusual in the circumstances, unnatural, unaccountable; but there it was; and this, as she had said, was what made her detest herself. She had never cared for him, she did not care for him now. She had dreaded him, winced before him, succumbed to him, and that was all. Hate him she did not quite; but he was dust and ashes to her,[15] and even for her name's sake she scarcely wished to marry him.

'You ought to have been more careful if you didn't mean to get him to make you his wife!'

'O mother, my mother!' cried the agonized girl, turning passionately upon her parent as if her poor heart would break. 'How could I be expected to know? I was a child when I left this house four months ago. Why didn't you tell me there was danger? Why didn't you warn me? Ladies know what to guard against, because they read novels that tell them of these tricks; but I never had the chance of discovering in that way, and you did not help me!'

Her mother was subdued.

'I thought if I spoke of his fond feelings and what they might lead to, you would dislike him and lose your chance,' she murmured, wiping her eyes with her apron. 'Well, we must make the best of it, I suppose. 'Tis nater, after all, and what pleases God.'

XIII

The event of Tess Durbeyfield's return from the house of her rich kinsfolk[1] was rumoured abroad, if rumour be not too large a word for a space of a square mile. In the afternoon several young girls of

Marlott, former schoolfellows and acquaintances of Tess, called to see her, arriving dressed in their best starched and ironed, as became visitors to a person who had made a transcendent conquest (as they supposed), and sat round the room looking at her with great curiosity. For the fact that it was this said thirty-first cousin, Mr D'Urberville, who had fallen in love with her, a gentleman not altogether local, whose reputation as a reckless gallant and heart-breaker was beginning to spread beyond the immediate boundaries of Trantridge, lent Tess's supposed position, by its fearsomeness, a far higher fascination than it would have exercised if unhazardous.

Their interest was so deep that the younger ones whispered when her back was turned –

'How pretty she is; and how that best frock do set her off! I believe it cost an immense deal, and that it was a gift from him.'

Tess, who was reaching up to get the tea-things from the corner-cupboard, did not hear these commentaries. If she had heard them, she might soon have set her friends right on the matter. But her mother heard, and Joan's simple vanity, having been denied the hope of a dashing marriage, fed itself as well as it could upon the sensation of a dashing flirtation.[2] Upon the whole she felt gratified, even though such a limited and meretricious triumph should involve her daughter's reputation; it might end in marriage yet, and in the warmth of her responsiveness to their admiration she invited her visitors to stay to tea.[3]

Their chatter, their laughter, their good-humoured innuendoes, above all, their flashes and flickerings of envy, revived Tess's spirits also; and, as the evening wore on, she caught the infection of their excitement, and grew almost gay. The marble hardness left her face, she moved with something of her old bounding step, and flushed in all her young beauty.

At moments, in spite of thought, she would reply to their inquiries with a manner of superiority, as if recognizing that her experiences in the field of courtship had, indeed, been slightly enviable. But so far was she from being, in the words of Robert South, 'in love with her own ruin,'[4] that the illusion was transient as lightning; cold reason came back to mock her spasmodic weakness;[5] the ghastliness of her momentary pride would convict her, and recall her to reserved listlessness again.

And the despondency of the next morning's dawn, when it was no longer Sunday, but Monday; and no best clothes; and the laughing visitors were gone, and she awoke alone in her old bed, the innocent younger children breathing softly around her. In place of the excitement of her return, and the interest it had inspired, she saw before her a long and stony highway which she had to tread, without aid, and with little sympathy.[6] Her depression was then terrible, and she could have hidden herself in a tomb.

In the course of a few weeks Tess revived sufficiently to show herself so far as was necessary to get to church one Sunday morning. She liked to hear the chanting – such as it was – and the old Psalms, and to join in the Morning Hymn.[7] That innate love of melody, which she had inherited from her ballad-singing mother, gave the simplest music a power over her which could wellnigh drag her heart out of her bosom at times.

To be as much out of observation as possible for reasons of her own, and to escape the gallantries of the young men, she set out before the chiming began, and took a back seat under the gallery, close to the lumber, where only old men and women came, and where the bier stood on end among the churchyard tools.

Parishioners dropped in by twos and threes, deposited themselves in rows before her, rested three-quarters of a minute on their foreheads as if they were praying, though they were not; then sat up, and looked around. When the chants came on one of her favourites happened to be chosen among the rest – the double chant 'Langdon'[8] – but she did not know what it was called, though she would much have liked to know. She thought, without exactly wording the thought, how strange and godlike was a composer's power, who from the grave could lead through sequences of emotion, which he alone had felt at first, a girl like her who had never heard of his name, and never would have a clue to his personality.[9]

The people who had turned their heads turned them again as the service proceeded; and at last observing her they whispered to each other. She knew what their whispers were about, grew sick at heart, and felt that she could come to church no more.

The bedroom which she shared with some of the children formed her retreat more continually than ever. Here, under her few square yards of thatch, she watched winds, and snows, and rains, gorgeous sunsets, and successive moons at their full. So close kept she that at length almost everybody thought she had gone away.[10]

The only exercise that Tess took at this time was after dark; and it was then, when out in the woods, that she seemed least solitary. She knew how to hit to a hair's-breadth that moment of evening when the light and the darkness are so evenly balanced that the constraint of day and the suspense of night neutralize each other,[11] leaving absolute mental liberty. It is then that the plight of being alive becomes attenuated to its least possible dimensions. She had no fear of the shadows; her sole idea seemed to be to shun mankind – or rather that cold accretion called the world, which, so terrible in the mass, is so unformidable, even pitiable, in its units.

On these lonely hills and dales her quiescent glide was of a piece with the element she moved in. Her flexuous and stealthy figure became an integral part of the scene. At times her whimsical fancy would intensify natural processes around her till they seemed a part of her own story. Rather they became a part of it; for the world is only a psychological phenomenon, and what they seemed they were. The midnight airs and gusts, moaning amongst the tightly-wrapped buds and bark of the winter twigs, were formulæ of bitter reproach. A wet day was the expression of irremediable grief at her weakness in the mind of some vague ethical being whom she could not class definitely as the God[12] of her childhood, and could not comprehend as any other.

But this encompassment of her own characterization, based on shreds of convention, peopled by phantoms and voices antipathetic to her, was a sorry and mistaken creation of Tess's fancy – a cloud of moral hobgoblins by which she was terrified without reason. It was they that were out of harmony with the actual world, not she. Walking among the sleeping birds in the hedges, watching the skipping rabbits on a moonlit warren, or standing under a pheasant-laden bough, she looked upon herself as a figure of Guilt intruding into the haunts of Innocence. But all the while she was making a distinction where there was no difference. Feeling herself in antagonism she was quite in accord. She had been made to break a necessary social law, but no law known to the environment in which she fancied herself such an anomaly.

XIV[1]

It was a hazy sunrise in August. The denser nocturnal vapours, attacked by the warm beams, were dividing and shrinking into isolated fleeces within hollows and coverts, where they waited till they should be dried away to nothing.

The sun, on account of the mist, had a curious sentient, personal look, demanding the masculine pronoun for its adequate expression. His present aspect, coupled with the lack of all human forms in the scene, explained the old-time heliolatries[2] in a moment. One could feel that a saner religion had never prevailed under the sky. The luminary was a golden-haired, beaming-faced, mild-eyed, God-like creature, gazing down in the vigour and intentness of youth upon an earth that was brimming with interest for him.

His light, a little later, broke through chinks of cottage shutters, throwing stripes like red-hot pokers upon cupboards, chests of drawers, and other furniture within; and awakening harvesters who were not already astir.

But of all ruddy things that morning the brightest were two broad arms of painted wood, which rose from the margin of a yellow cornfield hard by Marlott village. They, with two others below, formed the revolving Maltese cross of the reaping-machine, which had been brought to the field on the previous evening to be ready for operations this day. The paint with which they were smeared, intensified in hue by the sunlight, imparted to them a look of having been dipped in liquid fire.

The field had already been 'opened'; that is to say, a lane a few feet wide had been hand-cut through the wheat along the whole circumference of the field, for the first passage of the horses and machine.

Two groups, one of men and lads, the other of women, had come down the lane just at the hour when the shadows of the eastern hedge-top struck the west hedge midway, so that the heads of the groups were enjoying sunrise while their feet were still in the dawn. They disappeared from the lane between the two stone posts which flanked the nearest field-gate.

Presently there arose from within a ticking like the love-making of the grasshopper. The machine had begun, and a moving concatenation was[3] visible over the gate, a driver sitting upon one of the hauling horses, and an attendant on the seat of the implement. Along one side of the field the whole wain went, the arms of the mechanical reaper revolving slowly, till it passed down the hill quite out of sight. In a minute it came up on the other side of the field at the same equable pace; the glistening brass star in the forehead of the fore horse catching the eye as it rose into view over the stubble, then the bright arms, and then the whole machine.

The narrow lane of stubble encompassing the field grew wider with each circuit, and the standing corn was reduced to smaller area as the morning wore on. Rabbits, hares, snakes, rats, mice, retreated inwards as into a fastness, unaware of the ephemeral nature of their refuge, and of the doom that awaited them later in the day when, their covert shrinking to a more and more horrible narrowness, they were huddled together, friends and foes, till the last few yards of upright wheat fell also under the teeth of the unerring reaper, and they were every one put to death by the sticks and stones of the harvesters.

The reaping-machine left the fallen corn behind it in little heaps, each heap being of the quantity for a sheaf; and upon these the active binders in the rear laid their hands – mainly women, but some of them men in print shirts, and trousers supported round their waists by leather straps, rendering useless the two buttons behind, which twinkled and bristled with sunbeams at every movement of each wearer, as if they were a pair of eyes in the small of his back.

But those of the other sex were the most interesting of this company of binders, by reason of the charm which is acquired by woman when she becomes part and parcel of outdoor nature, and is not merely an object set down therein as at ordinary times. A field-man is a personality afield; a field-woman is a portion of the field; she has somehow lost her own margin, imbibed the essence of her surrounding, and assimilated herself with it.

The women – or rather girls, for they were mostly young – wore drawn cotton bonnets[4] with great flapping curtains to keep off the sun, and gloves to prevent their hands being wounded by the stubble. There was one wearing a pale pink jacket, another in a cream-coloured tight-sleeved gown, another in a petticoat as red as the arms of the reaping-machine; and others, older, in the brown-rough 'wropper' or over-all – the old-established and most appropriate dress of the field-woman, which the young ones were abandoning. This morning the eye returns involuntarily to the girl in the pink cotton jacket, she being the most flexuous and finely-drawn figure of them all. But her bonnet is pulled so far over her brow that none of her face is disclosed while she binds, though her complexion may be guessed from a stray twine or two of dark brown hair which extends below the curtain of her bonnet. Perhaps one reason why she seduces casual attention is that she never courts it, though the other women often gaze around them.

Her binding proceeds with clock-like monotony. From the sheaf last finished she draws a handful of ears, patting their tips with her left palm to bring them even. Then stooping low she moves forward, gathering the corn with both hands against her knees, and pushing her left gloved hand under the bundle to meet the right on the other side, holding the corn in an embrace like that of a lover. She brings the ends of the bond together, and kneels on the sheaf while she ties it, beating back her skirts now and then when lifted by the breeze. A bit of her naked arm is visible between the buff leather of the gauntlet and the sleeve of her gown; and as the day wears on its feminine smoothness becomes scarified by the stubble, and bleeds.

At intervals she stands up to rest, and to retie her disarranged apron, or to pull her bonnet straight. Then one can see the oval face of a handsome young woman with deep dark eyes and long heavy clinging tresses, which seem to clasp in a beseeching way anything they fall against. The cheeks are paler, the teeth more regular, the red lips thinner than is usual in a country-bred girl.

It is Tess Durbeyfield, otherwise D'Urberville, somewhat changed – the same, but not the same; at the present stage of her existence living as a stranger and an alien here, though it was no strange land that she was in.[5] After a long seclusion she had come to a resolve, during the week under notice, to undertake outdoor work in her native village, the busiest season of the year in the agricultural world having arrived, and nothing that she could do within the house being so remunerative for the time as harvesting in the fields.

The movements of the other women were more or less similar to Tess's, the whole bevy of them drawing together like dancers in a quadrille at the completion of a sheaf by each, every one placing her sheaf on end against those of the rest, till a shock, or 'stitch' as it was here called, of ten or a dozen was formed.

They went to breakfast, and came again, and the work proceeded as before. As the hour of eleven drew near a person watching her might have noticed that Tess's glance flitted wistfully to the brow of the hill every now and then, though she did not pause in her sheafing. On the verge of the hour the heads of a group of children, of ages ranging from six to fourteen, rose above the stubbly convexity of the hill.

The face of Tess flushed slightly, but still she did not pause.

The eldest of the comers, a girl who wore a triangular shawl, its corner draggling on the stubble, carried in her arms what at first sight seemed to be a doll, but proved to be an infant in long clothes. Another brought some lunch. The harvesters ceased working, took their provisions, and sat down against one of the shocks. Here they fell to, the men plying a stone jar freely, and passing round a cup.

Tess Durbeyfield had been one of the last to suspend her labours. She sat down at the end of the shock, her face turned somewhat away from her companions. When she had deposited herself a man in a rabbit-skin cap and with a red handkerchief tucked into his belt, held the cup of ale over the top of the shock for her to drink. But she did not accept his offer. As soon as her lunch was spread she called up the big girl her sister, and took the baby of her, who, glad to be relieved of the burden, went away to the next shock and joined the other children playing there. Tess, with a curiously stealthy yet courageous movement, and with a still rising colour, unfastened her frock and began suckling the child.

The men who sat nearest considerately turned their faces towards the other end of the field, some of them beginning to smoke; one, with absent-minded fondness, regretfully stroking the jar that would no longer yield a stream. All the women but Tess fell into animated talk, and adjusted the disarranged knots of their hair.

When the infant had taken its fill the young mother sat it upright in her lap, and looking into the far distance dandled it with a gloomy indifference that was almost dislike; then all of a sudden she fell to violently kissing it some dozens of times, as if she could never leave off, the child crying at the vehemence of an onset which strangely combined passionateness with contempt.

'She's fond of that there child, though she mid pretend not to be, and say she wishes the baby and her too were in the churchyard,' observed the woman in the red petticoat.

'She'll soon leave off saying that,' replied the one in buff. 'Lord, 'tis wonderful what a body can get used to in time!'

''Twas a thousand pities that it should have happened to she, of all others. But 'tis always the comeliest! The plain ones be as safe as churches – hey, Jenny?' The speaker turned to one of the group who certainly was not ill-defined as plain.

It was a thousand pities, indeed; it was impossible for even an enemy to feel otherwise on looking at Tess as she sat there, with her flower-like mouth and large tender eyes, neither black nor blue nor gray nor violet; rather all those shades together, and a hundred others, which could be seen if one looked into their irises – shade behind shade – tint beyond tint – round depths that had no bottom; an almost typical woman, but for the slight incautiousness of character inherited from her race.

A resolution which had surprised herself had brought her into the fields this week for the first time during many months. After wearing and wasting her palpitating heart with every engine of regret that lonely inexperience could devise, common-sense had illumined her. She felt that she would do well to be useful again – to taste anew sweet independence at any price. The past was past; whatever it had been it was no more at hand. Whatever its consequences, time would close over them; they would all in a few years be as if they had never been, and she herself grassed down and forgotten. Meanwhile the trees were just as green as before; the birds sang and the sun shone as clearly now as ever. The familiar surroundings had not darkened because of her grief, nor sickened because of her pain.

She might have seen that what had bowed her head so profoundly – the thought of the world's concern at her situation – was founded on an illusion. She was not an existence, an experience, a passion, a structure of sensations, to anybody but herself. To all humankind besides Tess was only a passing thought. Even to friends she was no more than a frequently passing thought. If she made herself miserable the livelong night and day it was only this much to them – 'Ah, she makes herself unhappy.' If she tried to be cheerful, to dismiss all care, to take pleasure in the daylight, the flowers, the baby, she could only be this idea to them – 'Ah, she bears it very well.' Alone in a desert island would she have been wretched at what had happened to her? Not greatly. If she could have been but just created, to discover herself as a spouseless mother, with no experience of life except as the parent of a nameless child, would the position have caused her to despair? No, she would have taken it calmly, and found pleasures therein. Most of the misery had been generated by her conventional aspect, and not by her innate sensations.

Whatever Tess's reasoning, some spirit had induced her to dress herself up neatly as she had formerly done, and come out into the fields, harvest-hands being greatly in demand just then. This was why she had borne herself with dignity, and had looked people calmly in the face at times, even when holding the baby in her arms.

The harvest-men rose from the shock of corn, and stretched their limbs, and extinguished their pipes. The horses, which had been unharnessed and fed, were again attached to the scarlet machine. Tess, having quickly eaten her own meal, beckoned to her eldest sister to come and take away the baby, fastened her dress, put on the buff gloves again, and stooped anew to draw a bond from the last completed sheaf for the tying of the next.

In the afternoon and evening the proceedings of the morning were continued, Tess staying on till dusk with the body of harvesters. Then they all rode home in one of the largest waggons, in the company of a broad tarnished moon that had risen from the ground to the eastwards, its face resembling the outworn gold-leaf halo of some worm-eaten Tuscan saint.[6] Tess's female companions sang songs, and showed themselves very sympathetic and glad at her reappearance out of doors, though they could not refrain from mischievously throwing in a few verses of the ballad about the maid who went to the merry green wood and came back a changed person.[7] There are counterpoises and compensations in life; and the event which had made of her a social warning had also for the moment made her the most interesting personage in the village to many. Their friendliness won her still farther away from herself, their lively spirits were contagious, and she became almost gay.

But now that her moral sorrows were passing away a fresh one arose on the natural side of her which knew no social law. When she reached home it was to learn to her grief that the baby had been suddenly taken ill since the afternoon. Some such collapse had been probable, so tender and puny was its frame; but the event came as a shock nevertheless.

The baby's offence against society in coming into the world was forgotten by the girl-mother; her soul's desire was to continue that offence by preserving the life of the child. However, it soon grew clear that the hour of emancipation for that little prisoner of the flesh was to arrive earlier than her worst misgivings had conjectured. And when she had discovered this she was plunged into a misery which transcended that of the child's simple loss. Her baby had not been baptized.

Tess had drifted into a frame of mind which accepted passively the consideration that if she should have to burn for what she had done, burn she must, and there was an end of it. Like all village girls she was well grounded in the Holy Scriptures, and had dutifully studied the histories of Aholah and Aholibah,[8] and knew the inferences to be drawn therefrom. But when the same question arose with regard to the baby, it had a very different colour. Her darling was about to die, and no salvation.

It was nearly bedtime, but she rushed downstairs and asked if she might send for the parson. The moment happened to be one at which her father's sense of the antique nobility of his family was highest, and his sensitiveness to the smudge which Tess had set upon that nobility most pronounced, for he had just returned from his evening booze at Rolliver's Inn. No parson should come inside his door, he declared, prying into his affairs just then, when, by her shame, it had become more necessary than ever to hide them. He locked the door and put the key in his pocket.

The household went to bed, and, distressed beyond measure, Tess retired also. She was continually waking as she lay, and in the middle of the night found that the baby was still worse. It was obviously dying – quietly and painlessly, but none the less surely.

In her misery she rocked herself upon the bed. The clock struck the solemn hour of one, that hour when thought stalks outside reason, and malignant possibilities stand rock-firm as facts. She thought of the child consigned to the nethermost corner of hell, as its double doom for lack of baptism and lack of legitimacy; saw the arch-fiend tossing it with his three-pronged fork,[9] like the one they used for heating the oven on baking days; to which picture she added many other quaint and curious details of torment taught the young in this Christian country. The lurid presentment so powerfully affected her imagination in the silence of the sleeping house that her nightgown became damp with perspiration, and the bedstead shook with each throb of her heart.

The infant's breathing grew more difficult, and the mother's mental tension increased. It was useless to devour the little thing with kisses; she could stay in bed no longer, and walked feverishly about the room.

'O merciful God, have pity; have pity upon my poor baby!' she cried. 'Heap as much anger as you want to upon me, and welcome; but pity the child!'

She leant against the chest of drawers, and murmured incoherent supplications for a long while, till she suddenly started up.

'Ah! perhaps baby can be saved! Perhaps it will be just the same!'

She spoke so brightly that it seemed as though her face might have shone in the gloom surrounding her.

She lit a candle, and went to a second and a third bed under the wall, where she awoke her little sisters and brothers, all of whom occupied the same room. Pulling out the washing-stand so that she could get behind it, she poured some water from a jug, and made them kneel around, putting their hands together with fingers exactly vertical. While the children, scarcely awake, awe-stricken at her manner, their eyes growing larger and larger, remained in this position, she took the baby from her bed – a child's child – so immature as scarce to seem a sufficient personality to endow its producer with the maternal title. Tess then stood erect with the infant on her arm beside the basin, the next sister held the Prayer-Book open before her, as the clerk at church held it before the parson; and thus the emotional girl set about baptizing her child.

Her figure looked singularly tall and imposing as she stood in her long white nightgown, a thick cable of twisted dark hair hanging straight down her back to her waist. The kindly dimness of the weak candle abstracted from her form and features the little blemishes which sunlight might have revealed – the stubble scratches upon her wrists, and the weariness of her eyes – her high enthusiasm having a transfiguring effect upon the face which had been her undoing, showing it as a thing of immaculate beauty, with an impress of dignity which was almost regal.[10] The little ones kneeling round, their sleepy eyes blinking and red, awaited her preparations full of a suspended wonder which their physical heaviness at that hour would not allow to become active.

The eldest of them said:

'Be you really going to christen him, Tess?'

The girl-mother replied in a grave affirmative.

'What's his name going to be?'

She had not thought of that, but a name came into her head as she proceeded with the baptismal service, and now she pronounced it:

'Sorrow, I baptize thee in the name of the Father, and of the Son, and of the Holy Ghost.'

She sprinkled the water, and there was silence.

'Say "Amen," children.'

The tiny voices piped in obedient response: 'Amen!'

Tess went on:

'We receive this child' – and so forth – 'and do sign him with the sign of the Cross.'

Here she dipped her hand into the basin, and fervently drew an immense cross upon the baby with her forefinger, continuing with the customary sentences as to his manfully fighting against sin, the world, and the devil, and being a faithful soldier and servant unto his life's end.[11] She duly went on with the Lord's Prayer, the children lisping it after her in a thin gnat-like wail, till, at the conclusion, raising their voices to clerk's pitch, they again piped into the silence, 'Amen!'

Then their sister, with much augmented confidence in the efficacy of this sacrament, poured forth from the bottom of her heart the thanksgiving that follows, uttering it boldly and triumphantly in the stopt-diapason[12] note which her voice acquired when her heart was in her speech, and which will never be forgotten by those who knew her. The ecstasy of faith almost apotheosized her; it set upon her face a glowing irradiation, and brought a red spot into the middle of each cheek; while the miniature candle-flame inverted in her eye-pupils shone like a diamond. The children gazed up at her with more and more reverence, and no longer had a will for questioning. She did not look like Sissy to them now, but as a being large, towering, and awful – a divine personage with whom they had nothing in common.

Poor Sorrow's campaign against sin, the world, and the devil was doomed to be of limited brilliancy – luckily perhaps for himself, considering his beginnings. In the blue of the morning that fragile soldier and servant breathed his last, and when the other children awoke they cried bitterly, and begged Sissy to have another pretty baby.

The calmness which had possessed Tess since the christening remained with her in the infant's loss. In the daylight, indeed, she felt her terrors about his soul to have been somewhat exaggerated; whether well founded or not she had no uneasiness now, reasoning that if Providence would not ratify such an act of approximation she, for one, did not value the kind of heaven lost by the irregularity – either for herself or for her child.

So passed away Sorrow the Undesired – that intrusive creature, that bastard gift of shameless Nature who respects not the civil law; a waif to whom eternal Time had been a matter of days merely, who knew not that such things as years and centuries ever were; to whom the cottage interior was the universe, the week's weather climate, new-born babyhood human existence, and the instinct to suck human knowledge.

Tess, who mused on the christening a good deal, wondered if it were doctrinally sufficient to secure a Christian burial for the child. Nobody could tell this but the parson of the parish, and he was a new-comer, and a very reserved man. She went to his house after dusk, and stood by the gate, but could not summon courage to go in. The enterprise would have been abandoned if she had not by accident met him coming homeward as she turned away. In the gloom she did not mind speaking freely.

'I should like to ask you something, sir.'

He expressed his willingness to listen, and she told the story of the baby's illness and the extemporized ordinance.

'And now, sir,' she added earnestly, 'can you tell me this – will it be just the same for him as if you had baptized him?'

Having the natural feelings of a tradesman at finding that a job he should have been called in for had been unskilfully botched by his customers among themselves, he was disposed to say no. Yet the dignity of the girl, the strange tenderness in her voice, combined to affect his nobler impulses – or rather those that he had left in him after ten years of endeavour to graft technical belief on actual scepticism. The man and the ecclesiastic fought within him, and the victory fell to the man.

'My dear girl,' he said, 'it will be just the same.'

'Then will you give him a Christian burial?' she asked quickly.

The Vicar felt himself cornered.

Hearing of the baby's illness, he had conscientiously come to the house after nightfall to perform the rite, and, unaware that the refusal to admit him had come from Tess's father and not from Tess, he could not allow the plea of necessity.

'Ah – that's another matter,' he said.

'Another matter – why?' asked Tess rather warmly.

'Well – I would willingly do so if only we two were concerned. But I must not – for liturgical reasons.'

'Just for once, sir!'

'Really I must not.'

'O sir, for pity's sake!' She seized his hand as she spoke.

He withdrew it, shaking his head.

'Then I don't like you!' she burst out, 'and I'll never come to your church no more!'

'Don't talk so rashly, Tess.'

'Perhaps it will be just the same to him if you don't? . . . Will it be just the same? Don't for God's sake speak as saint to sinner, but as you yourself to me myself – poor me!'

How the Vicar reconciled his answer with the strict notions he supposed himself to hold on these subjects it is beyond a layman's power to tell, though not to excuse. Somewhat moved, he said in this case also –

'It will be just the same.'

So the baby was carried in a small deal box, under an ancient woman's shawl, to the churchyard that night, and buried by lantern-light, at the cost of a shilling and a pint of beer to the sexton, in that shabby corner of God's allotment where He lets the nettles grow, and where all unbaptized infants, notorious drunkards, suicides, and others of the conjecturally damned are laid. In spite of the untoward surroundings, however, Tess bravely made a little cross of two laths and a piece of string, and having bound it with flowers, she stuck it up at the head of the grave one evening when she could enter the churchyard without being seen, putting at the foot also a bunch of the same flowers in a little jar of water to keep them alive. What matter was it that on the outside of the jar the eye of mere observation noted the words 'Keelwell's Marmalade'? The eye of maternal affection did not see them in its vision of higher things.

XV

'By experience,' says Roger Ascham, 'we find out a short way by a long wandering.'[1] Not seldom that long wandering unfits us for farther travel, and of what use is our experience to us then? Tess Durbeyfield's experience was of this incapacitating kind. At last she had learned what to do; but who would now accept her doing?

If before going to the D'Urbervilles' she had rigorously moved under the guidance of sundry gnomic texts and phrases known to her and to the world in general, no doubt she would never have been imposed on. But it had not been in Tess's power – nor is it in anybody's power – to feel the whole truth of golden opinions when it is possible to profit by them. She – and how many more – might have ironically said to God with Saint Augustine, 'Thou hast counselled a better course than Thou hast permitted.'[2]

She remained in her father's house during the winter months, plucking fowls, or cramming turkeys and geese, or making clothes for her sisters and brothers out of some finery which D'Urberville had given her, and she had put by with contempt. Apply to him she would not. But she would often clasp her hands behind her head and muse when she was supposed to be working hard.

She philosophically noted dates as they came past in the revolution of the year; the disastrous night of her life at Trantridge with its dark background of The Chase; also the dates of the baby's birth and death; also her own birthday; and every other day individualized by incidents in which she had taken some share. She suddenly thought one afternoon, when looking in the glass at her fairness, that there was yet another date, of greater importance to her than those; that of her own death, when all these charms would have disappeared; a day which lay sly and unseen among all the other days of the year, giving no sign or sound when she annually passed over it; but not the less surely there. When was it? Why did she not feel the chill of each yearly encounter with such a cold relation? She had Jeremy Taylor's thought that some time in the future those who had known her would say, 'It is the –th, the day that poor Tess Durbeyfield died';[3] and there would be nothing singular to their minds in the statement. Of that day, doomed to be her terminus in time through all the ages, she did not know the place in month, week, season, or year.

Almost at a leap Tess thus changed from simple girl to complex woman. Symbols of reflectiveness passed into her face, and a note of tragedy at times into her voice. Her eyes grew larger and more eloquent. She became what would have been called a fine creature; her aspect was fair and arresting; her soul that of a woman whom the turbulent experiences of the last year or two had quite failed to demoralize. But for the world's opinion those experiences would have been simply a liberal education.

She had held so aloof of late that her trouble, never generally known, was nearly forgotten in Marlott. But it became evident to her that she could never be really comfortable again in a place which had seen the collapse of her family's attempt to 'claim kin' – and, through her, even closer union – with the rich D'Urbervilles. At least she could not be comfortable there till long years should have obliterated her keen consciousness of it. Yet even now Tess felt the pulse of hopeful life still warm within her; she might be happy in some nook which had no memories. To escape the past and all that appertained thereto was to annihilate it, and to do that she would have to get away.

Was once lost always lost really true of chastity? she would ask herself. She might prove it false if she could veil bygones. The recuperative power which pervaded organic nature was surely not denied to maidenhood alone.[4]

She waited a long time without finding opportunity for a new departure.[5] A particularly fine spring came round, and the stir of germination was almost audible in the buds; it moved her, as it moved the wild animals, and made her passionate to go. At last, one day in early May, a letter reached her from an old friend of her mother's, to whom she had addressed inquiries long before – a dairyman whom she had never seen – that a skilful milkmaid was required at his dairy-house, and that he would be glad to have her for the summer months, if she had found nothing to do in the interim.

It was not quite so far off as could have been wished; but it was probably far enough, her radius of movement and repute having been so small. To persons of limited spheres, miles are as geographical degrees, parishes as counties, counties as provinces and kingdoms.

On one point she was resolved: there should be no more D'Urberville air-castles in the dreams and deeds of her new life. She would be the dairymaid Tess, and nothing more. Her mother knew Tess's feeling on this point so well, though no words had passed between them on the subject, that she never alluded to the knightly ancestry now.[6]

Yet such is human inconsistency that one of the interests of the new place to her was the accidental virtue of its lying near her forefathers' country (for they were not Blakemore men, though her mother was Blakemore to the bone). The dairy called Talbothays,[7] for which she was bound, stood not remotely from some of the former estates of the D'Urbervilles, near the great family vaults of her granddames and their powerful husbands. She would be able to look at them, and think not only that D'Urberville, like Babylon, had fallen,[8] but that the individual innocence of a humble descendant could lapse as silently. All the while she wondered if any strange good thing might come of her being in her ancestral land; and some spirit within her rose automatically as the sap in the twigs. It was unexpended youth, surging up anew after its temporary check, and bringing with it hope, and the invincible instinct towards self-delight.

END OF PHASE THE SECOND

PHASE THE THIRD

The Rally

XVI

On a thyme-scented, bird-singing morning in May, between two and three years after the return from Trantridge – two silent reconstructive years for Tess Durbeyfield – she left her home for the second time.

Having packed up her luggage so that it could be sent to her later, she started in a hired trap for the little town of Stourcastle, through which it was necessary to pass on her journey, now in a direction almost opposite to that of her first adventuring. On the curve of the nearest hill she looked back regretfully at Marlott and her father's house, although she had been so anxious to get away.[1]

Her kindred dwelling there would probably continue their daily lives as heretofore, with no great diminution of pleasure in their consciousness, although she would be far off, and they deprived of her smile. In a few days the children would engage in their games as merrily as ever without the sense of any gap left by her departure. This leaving of the younger children she had decided was for the best;[2] were she to remain they would probably gain less good by her precepts than harm by her example.

She went through Stourcastle without pausing, and onward to a junction of highways, where she could await a carrier's van that ran to the south-west; for the railways which engirdled this interior tract of country had never yet struck across it. While waiting, however, there came along a farmer in his spring-cart, driving approximately in the direction that she wished to pursue; though he was a stranger to her she accepted his offer of a seat beside him, ignoring that its motive was a mere tribute to her countenance. He was going to Weatherbury, and by accompanying him thither she could walk the remainder of the distance instead of travelling in the van by way of Casterbridge.

Tess did not stop at Weatherbury, after this long drive, further than to make a slight nondescript meal at noon at a cottage to which the farmer recommended her. Thence she started on foot, basket in hand, to reach the wide upland of heath dividing this district from the low-lying meads of a farther valley in which the dairy stood that was the aim and end of her day's pilgrimage.[3]

Tess had never before visited this part of the country, and yet she felt akin to the landscape. Not so very far to the left of her she could discern a dark patch in the scenery, which inquiry confirmed her in supposing to be trees, marking the environs of Kingsbere – in the church of which parish the bones of her ancestors – her useless ancestors – lay entombed.

She had no admiration for them now; she almost hated them for the dance they had led her; not a thing of all that had been theirs did she retain but the old seal and spoon. 'Pooh – I have as much of mother as father in me!' she said. 'All my prettiness comes from her, and she was only a dairymaid.'[4]

The journey over the intervening uplands and lowlands of Egdon, when she reached them, was a more troublesome walk than she had anticipated, the distance being actually but a few miles. In two hours, after sundry wrong turnings, she found herself on a summit commanding the long-sought-for vale, the valley of the Great Dairies, the valley in which milk and butter grew to rankness, and were produced more profusely, if less delicately, than at her home – the verdant plain so well watered by the river Var or Froom.

It was intrinsically different from the Vale of Little Dairies, Blackmoor Vale, which, save during her disastrous sojourn at Trantridge, she had exclusively known till now. The world was drawn to a larger pattern here. The enclosures numbered fifty acres instead of ten, the farmsteads were more extended, the groups of cattle formed tribes here about; there only families. These myriads of cows stretching under her eyes from the far east to the far west outnumbered any she had ever seen at one glance before. The green lea was speckled as thickly with them as a canvas by Van Alsloot or Sallaert with burghers.[5] The ripe hue of the red and dun kine absorbed the evening sunlight, which the white-coated animals returned to the eye in rays almost dazzling, even at the distant elevation on which she stood.

The bird's-eye perspective before her was not so luxuriantly beautiful, perhaps, as that other one which she knew so well; yet it was more cheering. It lacked the intensely blue atmosphere of the rival vale, and its heavy soils and scents; the new air was clear, bracing, ethereal. The river itself, which nourished the grass and cows of these renowned dairies, flowed not like the streams in Blackmoor. Those were slow, silent, often turbid; flowing over beds of mud into which the incautious wader might sink and vanish unawares. The Var waters were clear as the pure River of Life shown to the Evangelist,[6] rapid as the shadow of a cloud, with pebbly shallows that prattled to the sky all day long. There the water-flower was the lily; the crowfoot here.

Either the change in the quality of the air from heavy to light, or the sense of being amid new scenes where there were no invidious eyes upon her, sent up her spirits wonderfully. Her hopes mingled with the sunshine in an ideal photosphere[7] which surrounded her as she bounded along against the soft south wind. She heard a pleasant voice in every breeze, and in every bird's note seemed to lurk a joy.

Her face had latterly changed with changing states of mind, continually fluctuating between beauty and ordinariness, according as the thoughts were gay or grave. One day she was pink and flawless; another pale and tragical. When she was pink she was feeling less than when pale; her more perfect beauty accorded with her less elevated mood; her more perfect mood with her less perfect beauty. It was her best face physically that was now set against the south wind.

The irresistible, universal, automatic tendency to find sweet pleasure somewhere, which pervades all life, from the meanest to the highest, had at length mastered Tess.[8] Being even now only a young woman of twenty, one who mentally and sentimentally had not finished growing, it was impossible that any event should have left upon her an impression that was not at least capable of transmutation.

And thus her spirits, and her thankfulness, and her hopes, rose higher and higher. She tried several ballads, but found them inadequate; till, recollecting the psalter that her eyes had so often wandered over of a Sunday morning before she had eaten of the tree of knowledge,[9] she chanted: 'O ye Sun and Moon . . . O ye Stars . . . ye Green Things upon the Earth . . . ye Fowls of the Air . . . Beasts and Cattle . . . Children of Men . . . bless ye the Lord, praise Him and magnify Him for ever!'[10]

She suddenly stopped and murmured: 'But perhaps I don't quite know the Lord as yet.'

And probably the half-unconscious rhapsody was a Fetichistic utterance in a Monotheistic falsetto; women whose chief companions are the forms and forces of outdoor Nature retain in their souls far more of the Pagan fantasy of their remote forefathers than of the systematized religion taught their race at later date. However, Tess found at least approximate expression for her feelings in the old *Benedicite* that she had lisped from infancy; and it was enough. Such high contentment with such a slight and initial performance as that of having started towards a means of independent living was a part of the Durbeyfield temperament. Tess really wished to walk uprightly, while her father did nothing of the kind; but she resembled him in being content with immediate and small achievements, and in having no mind for laborious effort towards such petty social advancement as could alone be effected by a family so heavily handicapped as the once powerful D'Urbervilles were now.

There was, of course, the energy of her mother's unexpended family, as well as the natural energy of Tess's years, rekindled after the experience which had so overwhelmed her for the time. Let the truth be told – women do as a rule live through such humiliations, and regain their spirits, and again look about them with an interested eye. While there's life there's hope is a conviction not so entirely unknown to the 'betrayed' as some amiable theorists would have us believe.

Tess Durbeyfield, then, in good heart, and full of zest for life, descended the Egdon slopes lower and lower towards the dairy of her pilgrimage.

The marked difference, in the final particular, between the rival vales now showed itself. The secret of Blackmoor was best discovered from the heights around; to read aright the valley before her it was necessary to descend into its midst. When Tess had accomplished this feat she found herself to be standing on a carpeted level, which stretched to the east and west as far as the eye could reach.

The river had stolen from the higher tracts and brought in particles to the vale all this horizontal land; and now, exhausted, aged, and attenuated, lay serpentining along through the midst of its former spoils.

Not quite sure of her direction Tess stood still upon the hemmed expanse of verdant flatness, like a fly on a billiard-table of indefinite length, and of no more consequence to the surroundings than that fly. The sole effect of her presence upon the placid valley so far had been to excite the mind of a solitary heron, which, after descending to the ground not far from her path, stood with neck erect, looking at her.

Suddenly there arose from all parts of the lowland a prolonged and repeated call –

'Waow! waow! waow!'

From the farthest east to the farthest west the cries spread as if by contagion, accompanied in some cases by the barking of a dog. It was not the expression of the valley's consciousness that beautiful Tess had arrived, but the ordinary announcement of milking-time – half-past four o'clock, when the dairymen set about getting in the cows.

The red and white herd nearest at hand, which had been phlegmatically waiting for the call, now trooped towards the steading in the background, their great bags of milk swinging under them as they walked. Tess followed slowly in their rear, and entered the barton by the open gate through which they had entered before her. Long thatched sheds stretched round the enclosure, their slopes encrusted with vivid green moss, and their eaves supported by wooden posts rubbed to a glossy smoothness by the flanks of infinite cows and calves of bygone years, now passed to an oblivion almost inconceivable in its profundity. Between the posts were ranged the milchers, each exhibiting herself at the present moment to an eye in the rear as a circle on two stalks, down the centre of which a switch moved pendulum-wise; while the sun, lowering itself behind this patient row, threw their shadows accurately inwards upon the wall. Thus it threw shadows of these obscure and unstudied figures every evening with as much care over each contour as if it had been the profile of a Court beauty on a palace wall; copied them as diligently as it had copied Olympian shapes on marble *façades* long ago, or the outline of Alexander, Cæsar, and the Pharaohs.

They were the less restful cows that were stalled. Those that would stand still of their own free will were milked in the middle of the yard, where many of such better behaved ones stood waiting now – all prime milchers, such as were seldom seen out of this valley, and not always within it; nourished by the succulent feed which the water-meads supplied at this prime season of the year. Those of them that were spotted with white reflected the sunshine in dazzling brilliancy, and the polished brass knobs on their horns[11] glittered with something of military display. Their large-veined udders hung ponderous as sandbags, the teats sticking out like the legs of a gipsy's crock; and as each animal lingered for her turn to arrive the milk oozed forth and fell in drops to the ground.

XVII

The dairymaids and men had flocked down from their cottages and out of the dairy-house with the arrival of the cows from the meads; the maids walking in pattens, not on account of the weather, but to keep their shoes above the mulch of the barton. Each girl sat down on her three-legged stool, her face sideways, her right cheek resting against the cow, and looked musingly along the animal's flank at Tess as she approached. The male milkers, with hat-brims turned down, resting on their foreheads and gazing on the ground, did not observe her.

One of these was a sturdy middle-aged man – whose long white 'pinner' was somewhat finer and cleaner than the wraps of the others, and whose jacket underneath had a presentable marketing aspect – the master-dairyman, of whom she was in quest, his double character as a working milker and butter-maker here during six days, and on the seventh as a man in shining broad-cloth in his family pew at church, being so marked as to have inspired a rhyme –

Dairyman Dick
All the week: –
On Sundays Mister Richard Crick.

Seeing Tess standing at gaze he went across to her.

The majority of dairymen have a cross manner at milking-time, but it happened that Mr Crick was glad to get a new hand – for the days were busy ones now – and he received her warmly; inquiring for her mother and the rest of the family – (though this as a matter of form mainly, for in reality he had quite forgotten Mrs Durbeyfield's existence till reminded of the fact by her daughter's letter).

'Oh – ay, I knowed yer mother very well,' he said terminatively. 'And I heard of her marriage.[1] And a aged woman of ninety that used to live nigh here, but is dead and gone long ago, once told me that the family yer mother married into in Blackmoor Vale came originally from these parts, and that 'twere a old ancient race that had all but perished off the earth – though the new generations didn't know it. But, Lord, I took no notice of the old woman's ramblings, not I.'

'Oh no – it is nothing,' said Tess.

Then the talk was of business only.

'You can milk 'em clean, my maidy? I don't want my cows going azew at this time o' year.'

She reassured him on that point, and he surveyed her up and down. She had been staying indoors since the autumn, and her complexion had grown delicate.

'Quite sure you can stand it? 'Tis comfortable enough here for rough folk; but we don't live in a cowcumber frame.'

She declared that she could stand it, and her zest and willingness seemed to win him over.

'Well, I suppose you'll want a dish o' tay, or victuals of some sort, hey? Not yet? Well, do as ye like about it. But faith, if 'twas I, I should be as dry as a kex wi' travelling so far.'

'I'll begin milking now, to get my hand in,' said Tess.

She drank a little milk as temporary refreshment – to the surprise – indeed, slight contempt – of Dairyman Crick, to whose mind it had apparently never occurred that milk was good as a beverage.

'Oh, if ye can swaller that, be it so,' he said indifferently, while holding up the pail that she sipped from. ''Tis what I haint touched for years – not I. Rot the stuff; it would lie in my innerds like lead. You can try your hand upon she,' he pursued, nodding to the nearest cow. 'Not but what she do milk rather hard. We've hard ones and we've easy ones, like other folks. However, you'll find out that soon enough.'

When Tess had changed her bonnet for a hood, and was really on her stool under the cow, and the milk was squirting from her fists into the pail, she appeared to feel that she really had laid a new foundation for her future. The conviction bred serenity, her pulse slowed, and she was able to look about her.

The milkers formed quite a little battalion of men and maids, the men operating on the hard-teated animals, the maids on the kindlier natures. It was a large dairy. There were more than a hundred milchers under Crick's management, all told; and of the herd the master-dairyman milked six or eight with his own hands, unless away from home. These were the cows that milked hardest of all; for his journey-milkmen being more or less casually hired, he would not entrust this half-dozen to their treatment, lest, from indifference, they should not milk them clean; nor to the maids, lest they should fail in the same way for lack of finger-grip; with the result that in course of time the cows would 'go azew' – that is, dry up. It was not the loss for the moment that made slack milking so serious, but that with the decline of demand there came decline, and ultimately cessation, of supply.

After Tess had settled down to her cow there was for a time no talk in the barton, and not a sound interfered with the purr of the milk-jets into the numerous pails, except a momentary exclamation to one of the beasts requesting her to turn round or stand still. The only move-ments were those of the milkers' hands up and down, and the swing of the cows' tails. Thus they all worked on, encompassed by the vast flat mead which extended to either slope of the valley – a level landscape compounded of old landscapes long forgotten, and, no doubt, differing in character very greatly from the landscape they composed now.

'To my thinking,' said the dairyman, rising suddenly from a cow he had just finished off, snatching up his three-legged stool in one hand and the pail in the other, and moving on to the next hard-yielder in his vicinity; 'to my thinking, the cows don't gie down their milk to-day as usual. Upon my life, if Winker do begin keeping back like this, she'll not be worth going under by midsummer.'

"Tis because there's a new hand come among us,' said Jonathan Kail. 'I've noticed such things afore.'

'To be sure. It may be so. I didn't think o't.'

'I've been told that it goes up into their horns at such times,' said a dairymaid.

'Well, as to going up into their horns,' replied Dairyman Crick dubiously, as though even witchcraft might be limited by anatomical possibilities, 'I couldn't say; I certainly could not. But as nott cows will keep it back as well as the horned ones, I don't quite agree to it. Do ye know that riddle about the nott cows, Jonathan? Why do nott cows give less milk in a year than horned?'

'I don't!' interposed the milkmaid. 'Why do they?'

'Because there baint so many of 'em,' said the dairyman. 'Howsom-ever, these gam'sters do certainly keep back their milk to-day. Folks, we must lift up a stave or two – that's the only cure for't.'

Songs were often resorted to in dairies hereabout as an enticement to the cows when they showed signs of withholding their usual yield; and the band of milkers at this request burst into melody – in purely business-like tones, it is true, and with no great spontaneity; the result, according to their own belief, being a decided improvement during the song's continuance. When they had gone through fourteen or fifteen verses of a cheerful ballad about a murderer who was afraid to go to bed in the dark because he saw certain brimstone flames around him, one of the male milkers said –

'I wish singing on the stoop didn't use up so much of a man's wind!'

'You should get your harp, sir; not but what a fiddle is best.'

Tess, who had given ear to this, thought the words were addressed to the dairyman, but she was wrong. A reply, in the shape of 'Why?' came as it were out of the belly of a dun cow in the stalls; it had been spoken by a milker behind the animal, whom she had not hitherto perceived.

'Oh yes; there's nothing like a fiddle,' said the dairyman. 'Though I do think that bulls are more moved by a tune than cows – at least that's my experience. Once there was a old aged man over at Mellstock – William Dewy by name[2] – one of the family that used to do a good deal of business as tranters over there, Jonathan, do ye mind? – I knowed the man by sight as well as I know my own brother, in a manner of speaking. Well, this man was a coming home along from a wedding where he had been playing his fiddle, one fine moonlight night, and for shortness' sake he took a cut across Forty-acres, a field lying that way, where a bull was out to grass. The bull seed William, and took after him, horns aground, begad; and though William runned his best, and hadn't much drink in him (considering 'twas a wedding, and the folks well off), he found he'd never reach the fence and get over in time to save himself. Well, as a last thought, he pulled out his fiddle as he runned, and struck up a jig, turning to the bull, and backing towards the corner. The bull softened down, and stood still, looking hard at William Dewy, who fiddled on and on; till a sort of a smile stole over the bull's face. But no sooner did William stop his playing and turn to get over hedge than the bull would stop his smiling and lower his horns to the seat of William's breeches. Well, William had to turn about and play on, willy-nilly; and 'twas only three o'clock in the world, and 'a knowed that nobody would come that way for hours, and he so leery and tired that 'a didn't know what to do. When he had scraped till about four o'clock he felt that he verily would have to give over soon, and he said to himself, "There's only this last tune between me and eternal welfare! Heaven save me, or I'm a done man." Well, then he called to mind how he'd seed the cattle kneel o' Christmas Eves in the dead o' the night. It was not Christmas Eve then, but it came into his head to play a trick upon the bull. So he broke into the 'Tivity Hymn,[3] just as at Christmas carol-singing; when, lo and behold, down went the bull on his bended knees, in his ignorance, just as if 'twere the true 'Tivity night and hour. As soon as his horned friend were down, William turned, clinked off like a long-dog, and jumped safe over hedge, before the praying bull had got on his feet again to take after him. William used to say that he'd seen a man look a fool a good many times, but never such a fool as that bull looked when he found his pious feelings had been played upon, and 'twas not Christmas Eve . . . Yes, William Dewy, that was the man's name; and I can tell ye to a foot where he's a-lying in Mellstock Churchyard at this very moment – just between the second yew-tree and the north aisle.'

'It's a curious story; it carries us back to mediæval times, when faith was a living thing!'

The remark, singular for a dairy-yard, was murmured by the voice behind the dun cow; but as nobody understood the reference no notice was taken, except that the narrator seemed to think it might imply scepticism as to his tale.

'Well, 'tis quite true, sir, whether or no. I knowed the man well.'

'Oh yes; I have no doubt of it,' said the person behind the dun cow.

Tess's attention was thus attracted to the dairyman's interlocutor, of whom she could see but the merest patch, owing to his burying his head so persistently in the flank of the milcher. She could not understand why he should be addressed as 'sir' even by the dairyman himself. But no explanation was discernible; he remained under the cow long enough to have milked three, uttering a private ejaculation now and then, as if he could not get on.

'Take it gentle, sir; take it gentle,' said the dairyman. ''Tis knack, not strength, that does it.'

'So I find,' said the other, standing up at last and stretching his arms. 'I think I have finished her, however, though she made my fingers ache.'

Tess could then see him at full length. He wore the ordinary white pinner and leather leggings of a dairy-farmer when milking, and his boots were clogged with the mulch of the yard; but this was all his local livery. Beneath it was something educated, reserved, subtle, sad, differing.

But the details of his aspect were temporarily thrust aside by the discovery that he was one whom she had seen before. Such vicissitudes had Tess passed through since that time that for a moment she could not remember where she had met him; and then it flashed upon her that he was the pedestrian who had joined in the club-dance at Marlott – the passing stranger who had come she knew not whence, had danced with others but not with her, had slightingly left her, and gone on his way with his friends.

The flood of memories brought back by this revival of an incident anterior to her troubles produced a momentary dismay lest, recognizing her also, he should by some means discover her story. But it passed away when she found no sign of remembrance in him. She saw by degrees that since their first and only encounter his mobile face had grown more thoughtful, and had acquired a young man's shapely moustache and beard – the latter of the palest straw colour where it began upon his cheeks, and deepening to a warm brown farther from its root. Under his linen milking-pinner he wore a dark velveteen jacket, cord breeches and gaiters, and a starched white shirt. Without the milking-gear nobody could have guessed what he was. He might with equal probability have been an eccentric landowner or a gentlemanly ploughman. That he was but a novice at dairy-work she had realized in a moment, from the time he had spent upon the milking of one cow.[4]

Meanwhile many of the milkmaids had said to one another of the new-comer, 'How pretty she is!' with something of real generosity and admiration, though with a half hope that the auditors would deny the assertion – which, strictly speaking, they might have done, prettiness being an inexact definition of what struck the eye in Tess. When the milking was finished for the evening they straggled indoors, where Mrs Crick, the dairyman's wife – who was too respectable to go out milking herself, and wore a hot stuff gown in warm weather because the dairymaids wore prints – was giving an eye to the leads and things.

Only two or three of the maids, Tess learnt, slept in the dairy-house besides herself; most of the helpers going to their homes. She saw nothing at supper-time of the superior milker who had commented on the story, and asked no questions about him, the remainder of the evening being occupied in arranging her place in the bedchamber. It was a large room over the milk-house, some thirty feet long; the sleeping-cots of the other three indoor milkmaids being in the same apartment. They were blooming young women, and, except one, rather older than herself. By bedtime Tess was thoroughly tired, and fell asleep immediately.

But one of the girls who occupied an adjoining bed was more wakeful than Tess, and would insist upon relating to the latter various particulars of the homestead into which she had just entered. The girl's whispered words mingled with the shades, and, to Tess's drowsy mind, they seemed to be generated by the darkness in which they floated.

'Mr Angel Clare – he that is learning milking, and that plays the harp – never says much to us. He is a pa'son's son, and is too much taken up wi' his own thoughts to notice girls. He is the dairyman's pupil – learning farming in all its branches. He has learnt sheep-farming at another place, and he's now mastering dairy-work . . . Yes, he is quite the gentleman-born. His father is the Reverent Mr Clare at Emminster – a good many miles from here.'

'Oh – I have heard of him,' said her companion, now awake. 'A very earnest clergyman, is he not?'

'Yes – that he is – the earnestest man in all Wessex, they say – the last of the old Low Church sort, they tell me – for all about here be what they call High.[5] All his sons, except our Mr Clare, be made pa'sons too.'

Tess had not at this hour the curiosity to ask why the present Mr Clare was not made a parson like his brethren, and gradually fell asleep again, the words of her informant coming to her along with the smell of the cheeses in the adjoining cheese-loft, and the measured dripping of the whey from the wrings downstairs.

XVIII

Angel Clare rises out of the past not altogether as a distinct figure, but as an appreciative voice, a long regard of fixed, abstracted eyes, and a mobility of mouth somewhat too small and delicately lined for a man's, though with an unexpectedly firm close of the lower lip now and then; enough to do away with any suggestion of indecision. Nevertheless, something nebulous, preoccupied, vague, in his bearing and regard, marked him as one who probably had no very definite aim or concern about his material future. Yet as a lad people had said of him that he was one who might do anything if he tried.

He was the youngest son of his father, a poor parson at the other end of the county, and had arrived at Talbothays Dairy as a six months' pupil, after going the round of some other farms, his object being to acquire a practical skill in the various processes of farming, with a view either to the Colonies, or the tenure of a home-farm, as circumstances might decide.

His entry into the ranks of the agriculturists and breeders was a step in the young man's career which had been anticipated neither by himself nor by others.

Mr Clare the elder, whose first wife had died and left him a daughter, married a second late in life. This lady had somewhat unexpectedly brought him three sons, so that between Angel, the youngest, and his father the vicar there seemed to be almost a missing generation. Of these boys the aforesaid Angel, the child of his old age,[1] was the only son who had not taken a University degree, though he was the single one of them whose early promise might have done full justice to an academical training.

Some three years before Angel's appearance at the Marlott dance, on a day when he had left school and was pursuing his studies at home, a parcel came to the vicarage from the local bookseller's, directed to the Reverend James Clare. The vicar having opened it and found it to contain a book, read a few pages; whereupon he jumped up from his seat and went straight to the shop with the book under his arm.

'Why has this been sent to my house?' he asked peremptorily, holding up the volume.

'It was ordered, sir.'

'Not by me, or any one belonging to me, I am happy to say.'

The shopkeeper looked into his order-book.

'Oh, it has been misdirected, sir,' he said. 'It was ordered by Mr Angel Clare, and should have been sent to him.'

Mr Clare winced as if he had been struck. He went home pale and dejected, and called Angel into his study.

'Look into this book, my boy,' he said. 'What do you know about it?'

'I ordered it,' said Angel simply.

'What for?'

'To read.'

'How can you think of reading it?'

'How can I? Why – it is a system of philosophy. There is no more moral, or even religious, work published.'

'Yes – moral enough; I don't deny that. But religious! – and for *you*, who intend to be a minister of the Gospel!'[2]

'Since you have alluded to the matter, father,' said the son, with anxious thought upon his face, 'I should like to say, once for all, that I should prefer not to take Orders. I fear I could not conscientiously do so. I love the Church as one loves a parent. I shall always have the warmest affection for her. There is no institution for whose history I have a deeper admiration; but I cannot honestly be ordained her minister, as my brothers are, while she refuses to liberate her mind from an untenable redemptive theolatry.'[3]

It had never occurred to the straightforward and simple-minded Vicar that one of his own flesh and blood could come to this! He was stultified, shocked, paralyzed. And if Angel were not going to enter the Church, what was the use of sending him to Cambridge? The University as a step to anything but ordination seemed, to this man of fixed ideas, a preface without a volume. He was a man not merely religious, but devout; a firm believer – not as the phrase is now elusively construed by theological thimble-riggers[4] in the Church and out of it, but in the old and ardent sense of the Evangelical school: one who could

> Indeed opine
> That the Eternal and Divine
> Did, eighteen centuries ago
> In very truth . . . [5]

Angel's father tried argument, persuasion, entreaty.

'No, father; I cannot underwrite Article Four (leave alone the rest), taking it "in the literal and grammatical sense" as required by the Declaration;[6] and, therefore, I can't be a parson in the present state of affairs,' said Angel. 'My whole instinct in matters of religion is towards reconstruction; to quote your favourite Epistle to the Hebrews, "the removing of those things that are shaken, as of things that are made, that those things which cannot be shaken may remain." '[7]

His father grieved so deeply that it made Angel quite ill to see him.

'What is the good of your mother and me economizing and stinting ourselves to give you a University education, if it is not to be used for the honour and glory of God?' his father repeated.

'Why, that it may be used for the honour and glory of man, father.'[8]

Perhaps if Angel had persevered he might have gone to Cambridge like his brothers. But the Vicar's view of that seat of learning as a stepping-stone to Orders alone was quite a family tradition; and so rooted was the idea in his mind that perseverance began to appear to the sensitive son akin to an intent to misappropriate a trust, and wrong the pious heads of the household, who had been and were, as his father had hinted, compelled to exercise much thrift to carry out this uniform plan of education for the three young men.

'I will do without Cambridge,' said Angel at last. 'I feel that I have no right to go there in the circumstances.'

The effects of this decisive debate were not long in showing themselves. He spent years and years in desultory studies, undertakings, and meditations; he began to evince considerable indifference to social forms and observances. The material distinctions of rank and wealth he increasingly despised. Even the 'good old family' (to use a favourite phrase of a late local worthy) had no aroma for him unless there were good new resolutions in its representatives. As a balance to these austerities, when he went to London to see what the world was like, he was carried off his head, and nearly entrapped by a woman much older than himself, though luckily he returned not greatly the worse for the experience.

Early association with country solitudes had bred in him an unconquerable, and almost unreasonable, aversion to modern town life, and shut him out from such success as he might have aspired to by entering a mundane profession in the impracticability of the spiritual one. But something had to be done; and having an acquaintance who was starting on a thriving life as a Colonial farmer, it occurred to Angel that this might be a lead in the right direction. Farming, either in the Colonies, America, or at home – farming, at any rate, after becoming well qualified for the business by a careful apprenticeship – that was a calling which would probably afford an independence without the sacrifice of what he valued even more than a competency – intellectual liberty.

So we find Angel Clare at six-and-twenty here at Talbothays as a student of kine, and, as there were no houses near at hand in which he could get a comfortable lodging, a boarder at the dairyman's.

His room was an immense attic which ran the whole length of the dairy-house. It could only be reached by a ladder from the cheese-loft, and had been closed up for a long time till he arrived and selected it as his retreat. Here Clare had plenty of space, and could often be heard by the dairy-folk pacing up and down when the household had gone to rest. A portion was divided off at one end by a curtain, behind which was his bed, the outer part being furnished as a homely sitting-room.

At first he lived up above entirely, reading a good deal, and strumming upon an old harp which he had bought at a sale. But he soon preferred to read human nature by taking his meals downstairs in the general dining-kitchen, with the dairyman and his wife, and the maids and men, who all together formed a lively assembly; for though but few milking hands slept in the house, several joined the family at meals. The longer Clare resided here the less objection had he to his company, and the more did he like to share quarters with them in common.

Much to his surprise he took, indeed, a real delight in their companionship. The conventional farm-folk of his imagination – personified by the pitiable dummy known as Hodge[9] – were obliterated after a few days' residence. At close quarters no Hodge was to be seen. At first, it is true, when Clare's intelligence was fresh from a contrasting society, these friends with whom he now hobnobbed seemed a little strange. Sitting down as a level member of the dairyman's household seemed at the outset an undignified proceeding. The ideas, the modes, the surroundings, appeared retrogressive and unmeaning. But with living on there, day after day, the acute sojourner became conscious of a new aspect in the spectacle. Without any objective change whatever, variety had taken the place of monotonousness. His host and his host's household, his men and his maids, as they became intimately known to Clare began to differentiate themselves as in a chemical process. The thought of Pascal's was brought home to him: 'A mesure qu'on a plus d'esprit, on trouve qu'il y a plus d'hommes originaux. Les gens du commun ne trouvent pas de différence entre les hommes.'[10] The typical and unvarying Hodge ceased to exist. He had been disintegrated into a number of varied fellow-creatures – beings of many minds, beings infinite in difference; some happy, many serene, a few depressed, one here and there bright even to genius, some stupid, others wanton, others austere; some mutely Miltonic, some potentially Cromwellian;[11] into men who had private views of each other, as he had of his friends; who could applaud or condemn each other, amuse or sadden themselves by the contemplation of each other's foibles or vices; men every one of whom walked in his own individual way the road to dusty death.[12]

Unexpectedly he began to like the outdoor life for its own sake, and for what it brought, apart from its bearing on his own proposed career. Considering his position he became wonderfully free from the chronic melancholy which is taking hold of the civilized races with the decline of belief in a beneficent Power. For the first time of late years he could read as his musings inclined him, without any eye to cramming for a profession, since the few farming handbooks which he deemed it desirable to master occupied him but little time.

He grew away from old associations, and saw something new in life and humanity. Secondarily, he made close acquaintance with phenomena which he had before known but darkly – the seasons in their moods, morning and evening, night and noon in their temperaments, winds in their several dispositions, trees, waters, and clouds, shades and silences, *ignes-fatui*,[13] constellations, and the voices of inanimate things.

The early mornings were still sufficiently cool to render a fire acceptable in the large room wherein they breakfasted; and, by Mrs Crick's orders, who insisted that he was too genteel to mess at their table, it was Angel Clare's custom to sit in the yawning chimney-corner during the meal, his cup-and-saucer and plate being placed on a hinged bracket at his elbow. The light from the long, wide, mullioned window opposite shone in upon his nook, and, assisted by a secondary light of cold blue quality which shone down the chimney, enabled him to read there easily whenever disposed to do so. Between Clare and the window was the table at which his companions sat, their munching profiles rising sharp against the panes; while to the rear was the milk-house door, through which were visible the rectangular leads in rows, full to the brim with the morning's milk. At the farther end the great churn could be seen revolving, and its slip-slopping heard – the moving power being discernible through the window in the form of a spiritless horse walking in a circle and driven by a boy.

For several days after Tess's arrival Clare, sitting abstractedly reading from some book, periodical, or piece of music just come by post, hardly noticed that she was present at table. She talked so little, and the other maids talked so much, that the babble did not strike him as possessing a new note, and he was ever in the habit of neglecting the particulars of an outward scene for the general impression. One day, however, when he had been conning one of his music-scores, and by force of imagination was hearing the tune in his head, he lapsed into listlessness, and the music-sheet rolled to the hearth. He looked at the fire of logs, with its one flame pirouetting on the top in a dying dance after the breakfast-cooking and boiling, and it seemed to jig to his inward tune; also at the two chimney crooks dangling down from the cross-bar, plumed with soot which quivered to the same melody; also at the half-empty kettle whining an accompaniment. The conversation at the table mixed in with his phantasmal orchestra till he thought: 'What a fluty voice one of those milkmaids has! I suppose it is the new one.'

Clare looked round upon her, seated with the others.

She was not looking towards him. Indeed, owing to his long silence, his presence in the room was almost forgotten.

'I don't know about ghosts,' she was saying; 'but I do know that our souls can be made to go outside our bodies when we are alive.'

The dairyman turned to her with his mouth full, his eyes charged with serious inquiry, and his great knife and fork (breakfasts were breakfasts here) planted erect on the table, like the beginning of a gallows.

'What – really now? And is it so, maidy?' he said.

'A very easy way to feel 'em go,' continued Tess, 'is to lie on the grass at night and look straight up at some big bright star; and, by fixing your mind upon it, you will soon find that you are hundreds and hundreds o' miles away from your body, which you don't seem to want at all.'

The dairyman removed his hard gaze from Tess, and fixed it on his wife.

'Now that's a rum thing, Christianner – hey? To think o' the miles I've vamped o' nights these last thirty year, courting, or trading, or for doctor, or for nurse, and yet never had the least notion o' that till now.'

The general attention being drawn to her, including that of the dairyman's pupil, Tess flushed, and remarking indifferently that it was only a fancy, resumed her breakfast.

Clare continued to observe her. She soon finished her eating, and having a consciousness that Clare was regarding her, began to trace imaginary patterns on the table-cloth with her forefinger with the constraint of a domestic animal that perceives itself to be watched.[14]

'What a genuine daughter of Nature that milkmaid is!' he said to himself.

And then he seemed to discern in her something that was familiar, something which carried him back into a joyous and unforeseeing past, before the necessity of taking thought had made the heavens gray. He concluded that he had beheld her before; where he could not tell. A casual encounter during some country ramble it certainly had been, and he was not greatly curious about it. But the circumstance was sufficient to lead him to select Tess in preference to the other pretty milkmaids when he wished to contemplate contiguous womankind.

XIX

In general the cows were milked as they presented themselves, without fancy or choice. But certain cows will show a fondness for a particular pair of hands, sometimes carrying this predilection so far as to refuse to stand at all except to their favourite, the pail of a stranger being unceremoniously kicked over.

It was Dairyman Crick's rule to insist on breaking down these partialities and aversions by constant interchange, since, in the event of a milkman or maid going away from the dairy, he was otherwise placed in a difficulty. The maids' private aims, however, were the reverse of the dairyman's rule, the daily selection by each damsel of the eight or ten cows to which she had grown accustomed rendering the operation on their willing udders surprisingly easy and effortless.

Tess, like her compeers, soon discovered which of the cows had a predilection for her style of manipulation, and her fingers having become delicate from the long domiciliary imprisonments to which she had subjected herself at intervals during the last two or three years, she would have been glad to meet the milchers' views in this respect. Out of the whole hundred-and-five there were eight in particular – Dumpling, Fancy, Lofty, Mist, Old Pretty, Young Pretty, Tidy, and Loud – who, though the teats of one or two were as hard as carrots, gave down to her with a readiness that made her work on them a mere touch of the fingers. Knowing, however, the dairyman's wish, she endeavoured conscientiously to take the animals just as they came, excepting the very hard yielders which she could not yet manage.

But she soon found a curious correspondence between the ostensibly chance position of the cows and her wishes in this matter, till at length she felt that their order could not be the result of accident. The dairyman's pupil had lent a hand in getting the cows together of late, and at the fifth or sixth time she turned her eyes, as she rested against the cow, full of sly inquiry upon him.

'Mr Clare, you have ranged the cows!' she said, blushing; and in making the accusation symptoms of a smile lifted her upper lip gently in the middle, in spite of her, so as to show the tips of her teeth, the lower lip remaining severely still.

'Well, it makes no difference,' said he. 'You will always be here to milk them.'

'Do you think so? I *hope* I shall! But I don't *know*.'

She was angry with herself afterwards, thinking that he, unaware of her grave reasons for liking this seclusion, might have mistaken her meaning. She had spoken so earnestly to him, as if his presence were somehow a factor in her wish. Her misgiving was such that at dusk, when the milking was over, she walked in the garden alone to continue her regrets that she had disclosed to him her discovery of his considerateness.

It was a typical summer evening in June, the atmosphere being in such delicate equilibrium and so transmissive that inanimate objects seemed endowed with two or three senses, if not five. There was no distinction between the near and the far, and an auditor felt close to everything within the horizon. The soundlessness impressed her as a positive entity rather than as the mere negation of noise. It was broken by the notes of a harp.

Tess had heard those notes in the attic above her head. Dim, flattened, constrained by their confinement, they had never appealed to her as now, when they wandered in the still air with a stark quality like that of nudity. To speak absolutely, both instrument and execution were poor; but the relative is all, and as she listened Tess, like a fascinated bird, could not leave the spot. Far from leaving she drew up towards the performer, keeping behind the hedge that he might not guess her presence.

The outskirt of the garden in which Tess found herself had been left uncultivated for some years, and was now damp and rank with juicy grass which sent up mists of pollen at a touch; and with tall blooming weeds emitting offensive smells – weeds whose red and yellow and purple hues formed a polychrome as dazzling as that of cultivated flowers. She went stealthily as a cat through this profusion of growth, gathering cuckoo-spittle on her skirts, cracking snails that were underfoot, staining her hands with thistle-milk and slug-slime, and rubbing off upon her naked arms sticky blights which, though snow-white on the apple-tree trunks, made blood-red stains on her skin; thus she drew quite near to Clare, still unobserved of him.

Tess was conscious of neither time nor space. The exaltation which she had described as being producible at will by gazing at a star, came now without any determination of hers; she undulated upon the thin notes as upon billows, and their harmonies passed like breezes through her, bringing tears into her eyes. The floating pollen seemed to be his notes made visible, and the dampness of the garden the weeping of the garden's sensibility. Though near nightfall, the rank-smelling weed-flowers glowed as if they would not close for intentness, and the waves of colour mixed with the waves of sound.

The light which still shone was derived entirely from a large hole in the western bank of cloud; it was like a piece of day left behind by accident, dusk having closed in elsewhere. He concluded his plaintive melody, a very simple performance, demanding no great skill; and she waited, thinking another might be begun. But, tired of playing, he had desultorily come round the fence, and was rambling up behind her. Tess, her cheeks on fire, moved away furtively, as if hardly moving at all.

Angel, however, saw her light summer gown, and he spoke; his low tones quite reaching her, though he was some distance off.

'What makes you draw off in that way, Tess?' said he. 'Are you afraid?'

'Oh no, sir . . . not of outdoor things; especially just now when the apple-blooth is falling, and everything so green.'

'But you have your indoor fears – eh?'

'Well – yes, sir.'

'What of?'

'I couldn't quite say.'

'The milk turning sour?'

'No.'

'Life in general?'

'Yes, sir.'[1]

'Ah – so am I, very often. This hobble of being alive is rather serious, don't you think so?'

'It is – now you put it that way, sir.'

'All the same, I shouldn't have expected a young girl like you to see it so just yet. How is it you do?'

She maintained a hesitating silence.

'Come, Tess, tell me in confidence.'

She thought that he meant what were the aspects of things to her, and replied shyly –

'The trees have inquisitive eyes, haven't they? – that is, seem as if they had. And the river says, – "Why do ye trouble me with your looks?" And you seem to see numbers of to-morrows just all in a line, the first of 'em the biggest and clearest, the others getting smaller and smaller as they stand farther away; but they all seem very fierce and cruel and as if they said, "I'm coming! Beware o' me! Beware o' me!" . . . But *you* can raise up dreams with your music, and drive all such horrid fancies away!'

He was surprised to find this young woman – who though but a milkmaid had just that touch of rarity about her which might make her the envied of her housemates – shaping such sad imaginings. She was expressing in her own native phrases – assisted a little by her Sixth Standard training – feelings which might almost have been called those of the age – the ache of modernism.[2] The perception arrested him less when he reflected that what are called advanced ideas are really in great part but the latest fashion in definition – a more accurate expression, by words in *logy* and *ism*, of sensations which men and women have vaguely grasped for centuries.[3]

Still, it was strange that they should have come to her while yet so young; more than strange; it was impressive, interesting, pathetic. Not guessing the cause, there was nothing to remind him that experience is as to intensity, and not as to duration. Tess's passing corporeal blight had been her mental harvest.

Tess, on her part, could not understand why a man of clerical family and good education, and above physical want, should look upon it as a plight to be alive. For the unhappy pilgrim herself there was very good reason. But how could this admirable and poetic man ever have descended into the Valley of Humiliation,[4] have felt with the man of Uz – as she herself had felt many a day and night two or three years ago – 'My soul chooseth strangling and death rather than my life. I loathe it; I would not live alway.'[5]

It was true that he was at present out of his class. But she knew that was only because, like Peter the Great in a shipwright's yard,[6] he was studying what he wanted to know. He did not milk cows because he was obliged to milk cows, but because he was learning how to be a rich and prosperous dairyman, landowner, agriculturist, and breeder of cattle. He would become an American or Australian Abraham, commanding like a monarch his flocks and his herds, his spotted and his ring-straked,[7] his men-servants and his maids. At times, nevertheless, it did seem unaccountable to her that a decidedly bookish, musical, thinking young man should have chosen deliberately to be a farmer, and not a clergyman, like his father and brothers.

Thus, neither having the clue to either's secret, they were respectively puzzled at what each revealed, and awaited new knowledge of each other's character and moods without attempting to pry into each other's history.

Every day, every hour, brought to him one more little stroke of her nature, and to her one more of his. Tess was trying to lead a repressed life, but she little recked the strength of her own vitality.

At first Tess seemed to regard Angel Clare as an intelligence rather than as a man. As such she compared him with herself; and at every discovery of the abundance of his illuminations, of the distance between her own modest mental standpoint and the unmeasurable, Andean altitude of his, she became quite dejected, disheartened from all further effort on her own part whatever.

He observed her dejection one day, when he had casually mentioned something to her about pastoral life in ancient Greece. She was gathering the buds called 'lords and ladies' from the bank while he spoke.

'Why do you look so woebegone all of a sudden?' he asked.

'Oh, 'tis only – about my own self,' she said, with a frail laugh of sadness, fitfully beginning to peel 'a lady' meanwhile. 'Just a sense of what might have been with me! My life looks as if it had been wasted for want of chances! When I see what you know, what you have read, and seen, and thought, I feel what a nothing I am! I'm like the poor Queen of Sheba who lived in the Bible. There is no more spirit in me.'[8]

'Bless my soul, don't go troubling about that! Why,' he said, with some enthusiasm, 'I should be only too glad, my dear Tess, to help you to anything in the way of history, or any line of reading you would like to take up—'

'It is a lady again,' interrupted she, holding out the bud she had peeled.

'What?'

'I meant that there are always more ladies than lords when you come to peel them.'

'Never mind about the lords and ladies. Would you like to take up any course of study – history, for example?'

'Well, sometimes I feel I don't want to know anything more about it than I know already.'

'Why not?'

'Because what's the use of learning that I am one of a long row only – finding out that there is set down in some old book somebody just like me, and to know that I shall only act her part; making me sad, that's all. The best is not to remember that your nature and your past doings have been just like thousands' and thousands', and that your coming life and doings 'll be like thousands' and thousands'.'

'What, really, then, you don't want to learn anything?'

'I shouldn't mind learning why – why the sun shines on the just and on the unjust alike,'[9] she answered, with a slight quaver in her voice. 'But that is what books will not tell me.'

'Tess, fie for such bitterness!' Of course he spoke with a conventional sense of duty only, for that sort of wondering had not been unknown to himself in bygone days. And as he looked at the unpractised mouth and lips, he thought that such a daughter of the soil could only have caught up the sentiment by rote. She went on peeling the lords and ladies till Clare, regarding for a moment the wave-like curl of her lashes as they drooped with her bent gaze, lingeringly went away. When he was gone she stood awhile, thoughtfully peeling the last bud;

and then, awakening from her reverie, flung it and all the crowd of floral nobility impatiently on the ground, in an ebullition of displeasure with herself for her *niaiseries*, and with a quickening warmth in her heart of hearts.

How stupid he must think her! In an access of hunger for his good opinion she bethought herself of what she had latterly endeavoured to forget, so unpleasant had been its issues – the identity of her family with that of the knightly D'Urbervilles. Barren attribute as it was, disastrous as its discovery had been in many ways to her, perhaps Mr Clare, as a gentleman and a student of history, would respect her sufficiently to forget her childish conduct with the lords and ladies if he knew that those Purbeck-marble and alabaster people in Kingsbere Church really represented her own lineal forefathers; that she was no spurious D'Urberville, compounded of money and ambition like those at Trantridge, but true D'Urberville to the bone.

But before venturing to make the revelation dubious Tess indirectly sounded the dairyman as to its possible effect upon Mr Clare, by asking the former if Mr Clare had any great respect for old county families when they had lost all their money and land.

'Mr Clare,' said the dairyman emphatically, 'is one of the most rebellest rozums you ever knowed – not a bit like the rest of his family; and if there's one thing that he do hate more than another 'tis the notion of what's called an old family. He says that it stands to reason that old families have done their spurt of work in past days, and can't have anything left in 'em now. There's the Billetts and the Drenkhards and the Greys and the St Quintins and the Hardys and the Goulds, who used to own the lands for miles down this valley; you could buy 'em all up now for an old song a'most.[10] Why, our little Retty Priddle here, you know, is one of the Paridelles[11] – the old family that used to own lots o' the lands out by King's-Hintock now owned by the Earl o' Wessex, afore even he or his was heard of. Well, Mr Clare found this out, and spoke quite scornful to the poor girl for days. "Ah!" he says to her, "you'll never make a good dairymaid! All your skill was used up ages ago in Palestine,[12] and you must lie fallow for a thousand years to git strength for more deeds!" A boy came here t'other day asking for a job, and said his name was Matt, and when we asked him his surname he said he'd never heard that 'a had any surname, and when we asked why, he said he supposed his folks hadn't been 'stablished long enough. "Ah! you're the very boy I want!" says Mr Clare, jumping up and shaking hands wi'en; "I've great hopes of you;" and gave him half-a-crown. Oh no! he can't stomach old families!'

After hearing this caricature of Clare's opinions, poor Tess was glad that she had not said a word in a weak moment – even though her family was so unusually old as almost to have gone round the circle and become a new one. Besides, another dairy-girl was as good as she, it seemed, in that respect. She held her tongue about the D'Urberville vault, and the Knight of the Conqueror whose name she bore. The insight afforded into Clare's character suggested to her that it was largely owing to her supposed untraditional newness that she had won interest in his eyes.

XX

The season developed and matured. Another year's instalment of flowers, leaves, nightingales, thrushes, finches, and such ephemeral creatures, took up their positions where only a year ago others had stood in their place when these were nothing more than germs and inorganic particles.[1] Rays from the sunrise drew forth the buds and stretched them into long stalks, lifted up sap in noiseless streams, opened petals, and sucked out scents in invisible jets and breathings.

Dairyman Crick's household of maids and men lived on comfortably, placidly, even merrily. Their position was perhaps the happiest of all positions in the social scale, being above the line at which neediness ends, and below the line at which the *convenances* begin to cramp natural feeling, and the stress of threadbare modishness makes too little of enough.

Thus passed the leafy time when arborescence seems to be the one thing aimed at out of doors. Tess and Clare unconsciously studied each other, ever balanced on the edge of a passion, yet apparently keeping out of it. All the while they were converging, under an irresistible law, as surely as two streams in one vale.

Tess had never in her recent life been so happy as she was now, possibly never would be so happy again. She was, for one thing, physically and mentally suited among these new surroundings. The sapling which had rooted down to a poisonous stratum on the spot of its sowing had been transplanted to a deeper soil. Moreover she, and Clare also, stood as yet on the debatable land between predilection and love; where no profundities have been reached; no reflections have set in, awkwardly inquiring, 'Whither does this new current tend to carry me? What does it mean to my future? How does it stand towards my past?'

Tess was the merest stray phenomenon[2] to Angel Clare as yet – a rosy warming apparition, which had only just acquired the attribute of persistence in his consciousness. So he allowed his mind to be occupied with her, deeming his preoccupation to be no more than a philosopher's regard of an exceedingly novel, fresh, and interesting specimen of womankind.

They met continually; they could not help it. They met daily in that strange and solemn interval, the twilight of the morning, in the violet or pink dawn; for it was necessary to rise early, so very early, here. Milking was done betimes; and before the milking came the skimming, which began at a little past three. It usually fell to the lot of some one or other of them to wake the rest, the first being aroused by an alarm clock; and, as Tess was the latest arrival, and they soon discovered that she could be depended upon not to sleep through the alarm as the others did, this task was thrust most frequently upon her. No sooner had the hour of three struck and whizzed, than she left her room and ran to the dairyman's door; then up the ladder to Angel's, calling him in a loud whisper; then woke her fellow-milkmaids. By the time that Tess was dressed Clare was downstairs and out in the humid air. The remaining maids and the dairyman usually gave themselves another turn on the pillow, and did not appear till a quarter of an hour later.

The gray half-tones of daybreak are not the gray half-tones of the day's close, though the degree of their shade may be the same. In the twilight of the morning light seems active, darkness passive; in the twilight of evening it is the darkness which is active and crescent, and the light which is the drowsy reverse.

Being so often – possibly not always by chance – the first two persons to get up at the dairy-house, they seemed to themselves the first persons up of all the world. In these early days of her residence here Tess did not skim, going out of doors at once after rising, where he was generally awaiting her. The spectral, half-compounded, aqueous light which pervaded the open mead, impressed them with a feeling of isolation, as if they were Adam and Eve. At this dim inceptive stage of the day Tess seemed to Clare to exhibit a dignified largeness both of disposition and physique, an almost regnant power, possibly because he knew that at that preternatural time hardly any woman so well endowed in person as she was likely to be walking in the open air within the boundaries of his horizon; very few in all England. Fair women are usually asleep at midsummer dawns. She was close at hand, and the rest were nowhere.

The mixed, singular, luminous gloom in which they walked along together to the spot where the cows lay, often made him think of the Resurrection hour. He little thought that the Magdalen[3] might be at his side. Whilst all the landscape was in neutral shade his companion's face, which was the focus of his eyes, rising above the mist stratum, seemed to have a sort of phosphorescence[4] upon it. She looked ghostly, as if she were merely a soul at large. In reality her face, without appearing to do so, had caught the cold gleam of day from the north-east; his own face, though he did not think of it, wore the same aspect to her.

It was then, as has been said, that she impressed him most deeply. She was no longer the milkmaid, but a visionary essence of woman – a whole sex condensed into one typical form. He called her Artemis, Demeter,[5] and other fanciful names half teasingly, which she did not like because she did not understand them.

'Call me Tess,' she would say askance; and he did.

Then it would grow lighter, and her features would become simply feminine; they had changed from those of a divinity who could confer bliss to those of a being who craved it.

At these non-human hours they could get quite close to the water-fowl. Herons came, with a great bold noise as of opening doors and shutters, out of the boughs of a plantation which they frequented at the side of the mead; or, if already on the spot, hardily maintained their standing in the water as the pair walked by, watching them by moving their heads round in a slow, horizontal, passionless wheel, like the turn of puppets by clockwork.

They could then see the faint summer fogs in layers, woolly, level, and apparently no thicker than counterpanes, spread about the meadows in detached remnants of small extent. On the gray moisture of the grass were marks where the cows had lain through the night – dark-green islands of dry herbage the size of their carcases, in the general sea of dew. From each island proceeded a serpentine trail, by which the cow had rambled away to feed after getting up, at the end of which trail they found her; the snoring breath from her nostrils, when she recognized them, making an intenser little fog of her own amid the prevailing one. Then they drove the animals back to the barton, or sat down to milk them on the spot, as the case might require.

Or perhaps the summer fog was more general, and the meadows lay like a white sea, out of which the scattered trees rose like dangerous rocks. Birds would soar through it into the upper radiance, and hang on the wing sunning themselves, or alight on the wet rails subdividing the mead, which now shone like glass rods. Minute diamonds of moisture from the mist hung, too, upon Tess's eyelashes, and drops upon her hair, like seed pearls. When the day grew quite strong and commonplace these dried off her; moreover, Tess then lost her strange and ethereal beauty; her teeth, lips, and eyes scintillated in the sun-beams, and she was again the dazzlingly fair dairymaid only, who had to hold her own against the other women of the world.

About this time they would hear Dairyman Crick's voice, lecturing the non-resident milkers for arriving late, and speaking sharply to old Deborah Fyander for not washing her hands.

'For Heaven's sake, pop thy hands under the pump, Deb! Upon my soul, if the London folk only knowed of thee and thy slovenly ways, they'd swaller their milk and butter more mincing than they do a'ready; and that's saying a good deal.'

The milking progressed, till towards the end Tess and Clare, in common with the rest, could hear the heavy breakfast-table dragged out from the wall in the kitchen by Mrs Crick, this being the invariable preliminary to each meal; the same horrible scrape accompanying its return journey when the table had been cleared.

END OF VOL. I

There was a great stir in the milk-house just after breakfast. The churn revolved as usual, but the butter would not come. Whenever this happened the dairy was paralyzed. Squish, squash, echoed the milk in the great cylinder, but never arose the sound they waited for.

Dairyman Crick and his wife, the milkmaids Tess, Marian,[1] Retty Priddle, Izz Huett, and the married ones from the cottages; also Mr Clare, Jonathan Kail, old Deborah, and the rest, stood gazing hopelessly at the churn; and the boy who kept the horse going outside put on moon-like eyes to show his sense of the situation. Even the melancholy horse himself seemed to look in at the window in inquiring despair at each walk round.

''Tis years since I went to Conjuror Trendle's son in Egdon[2] – years,' said the dairyman bitterly. 'And he was nothing to what his father had been. I have said fifty times, if I have said once, that I don't believe in him. And I don't believe in him. But I shall have to go to him if he's alive. Oh yes, I shall have to go to him, if this sort of thing continnys!'

Even Mr Clare began to feel tragical at the dairyman's desperation.

'Conjuror Fall, 'tother side of Casterbridge, that they used to call "Wide-O," was a very good man when I was a boy,'[3] said Jonathan Kail. 'But he's rotten as touchwood by now.'

'My grandfather used to go to Conjuror Mynterne, out at Owls-combe, and a clever man a' were, so I've heard grandfather say,' continued Mr Crick. 'But there's no such genuine folk about nowa-days!'

Mrs Crick's mind kept nearer to the matter in hand.

'Perhaps somebody in the house is in love,' she said tentatively. 'I've heard tell in my younger days that that will cause it. Why, Crick

– that maid we had years ago, do ye mind, and how the butter didn't come then—'

'Ah yes, yes! – but that isn't the rights o't. It had nothing to do with the love-making. I remember all about it – 'twas the damage to the churn.'

He turned to Clare.

'Jack Dollop, a 'hor's-bird of a fellow we had here as milker at one time, sir, courted a young woman over at Mellstock, and deceived her as he had deceived many afore. But he had another sort o' woman to reckon with this time, and it was not the girl herself. One Holy Thursday,[4] of all days in the almanack, we was here as we mid be now, only there was no churning in hand, when we saw the girl's mother coming up to the door, with a great brass-mounted umbrella in her hand that would have felled an ox, and saying "Do Jack Dollop work here? – because I want him! I have a big bone to pick with he, I can assure 'n!" And some way behind her mother walked Jack's young woman, crying bitterly into her handkercher. "O, Lard, here's a time!" said Jack, looking out o' winder at 'em. "She'll murder me! Where shall I get – where shall I—? Don't tell her where I be!" And with that he scrambled into the churn through the trap-door, and shut himself inside, just as the young woman's mother busted into the milk-house. "The villain – where is he?" says she, "I'll claw his face for'n, let me only catch him!" Well, she hunted about everywhere, ballyragging Jack by side and by seam, Jack lying a'most stifled inside the churn, and the poor maid – or young woman rather – standing at the door crying her eyes out. I shall never forget it, never! 'Twould have melted a marble stone! But she couldn't find him nowhere at all.'

The dairyman paused, and one or two words of comment came from the listeners.

Dairyman Crick's stories had the peculiarity of seeming to be ended when they were not really so, and strangers were often betrayed into premature interjections of finality; though old friends knew better.

The narrator went on –

'Well, how the old woman should have had the wit to guess it I

134

could never tell, but she found out that he was inside that there churn. Without saying a word she took hold of the winch (it was turned by hand-power then), and round she swung him, and Jack began to flop about inside. "Oh, Lard! stop the churn! let me out!" says he, popping out his head, "I shall be churned into a pummy!" (he was a cowardly chap in his heart, as such men mostly be). "Not till you make amends for ravaging her trustful innocence!"[5] says the old woman. "Stop the churn, you old witch!" screams he. "You call me old witch, do ye, you deceiver!" says she, "when ye ought to ha' been calling me mother-law these last five months!" And on went the churn, and Jack's bones rattled round again. Well, none of us ventured to interfere; and at last 'a promised to make it right wi' her. "Yes – I'll be as good as my word!" he said. And so it ended that day.'

While the listeners were smiling and commenting there was a quick movement behind their backs, and they looked round. Tess, pale-faced, had gone to the door.

'How warm it is to-day!' she said, almost inaudibly.

It was warm, and none of them connected her withdrawal with the reminiscences of the dairyman. He went forward, and opened the door for her, saying with tender raillery –

'Why, maidy' (he frequently, with unconscious irony, gave her this pet name), 'the prettiest milker I've got in my dairy; you mustn't get so fagged as this at the first breath of summer weather, or we shall be finely put to for want of 'ee by dog-days, shan't we, Mr Clare?'

'I was faint – and – I think I am better out of doors,' she said mechanically; and disappeared outside.

Fortunately for her the milk in the revolving churn at that moment changed its squashing for a decided flick-flack.

''Tis coming!' cried Mrs Crick, and the attention of all was called off from Tess.

That fair sufferer soon recovered herself externally; but she remained much depressed all the afternoon. When the evening milking was done she did not care to be with the rest of them, and went out of doors, wandering along she knew not whither. She was wretched – O so wretched – at the perception that to her companions the dairyman's story had been rather a humorous narration than otherwise; none of them but herself seemed to see the sorrow of it; to a certainty, not one knew how cruelly it touched the tender place in her experience. The evening sun was now ugly to her, like a great inflamed wound in the sky. Only a solitary cracked-voiced reed-sparrow greeted her from the bushes by the river, in a sad, machine-made tone, resembling that of a past friend whose friendship she had outworn.

In these long June days the milkmaids, and, indeed, most of the household, went to bed at sunset or sooner, the morning work before milking being so early and heavy at a time of full pails. Tess usually accompanied her fellows upstairs. To-night, however, she was the first to go to their common chamber; and she had dozed when the other girls came in. She saw them undressing in the orange light of the vanished sun, which flushed their forms with its colour; she dozed again, but she was reawakened by their voices, and quietly turned her eyes towards them.

Neither of her three chamber-companions had got into bed. They were standing in a group, in their nightgowns, barefooted, at the window, the last red rays of the west still warming their faces and necks, and the walls around them. All were watching somebody in the garden with deep interest, their three faces close together: a jovial and round one, a pale one with dark hair, and a fair one whose tresses were auburn.

'Don't push! You can see as well as I,' said Retty, the auburn-haired and youngest girl, without removing her eyes from the window.

''Tis no use for you to be in love with him any more than me, Retty Priddle,' said jolly-faced Marian, the eldest, slily. 'His thoughts be of other cheeks than thine!'

Retty Priddle still looked, and the others looked again.

'There he is again!' cried Izz Huett, the pale girl, with dark damp hair, and keenly cut lips.

'You needn't say anything, Izz,' answered Retty. 'For I saw you kissing his shade.'

'*What* did you see her doing?' asked Marian.

'Why – he was standing over the whey-tub to let off the whey, and the shade of his face came upon the wall behind, close to Izz, who was standing there filling a vat. She put her mouth against the wall and kissed the shade of his mouth; I saw her, though he didn't.'

'O Izz Huett!' said Marian.

A rosy spot came into the middle of Izz Huett's cheek.

'Well, there was no harm in it,' she declared, with attempted coolness. 'And if I be in love with him, so is Retty, too; and so be you, Marian, come to that.'

Marian's full face could not blush past its chronic pinkness.

'I!' she said. 'What a tale! Ah, there he is again! Dear eyes – dear face – dear Mr Clare!'

'There – you've owned it!'

'So have you – so have we all,' said Marian, with the dry frankness of complete indifference to opinion. 'It is silly to pretend otherwise amongst ourselves, though we need not own it to other folks. I would just marry him to-morrow!'

'So would I – and more,'[6] murmured Izz Huett.

'And I too,' whispered the more timid Retty.

The listener grew warm.

'We can't all marry him,' said Izz.

'We shan't, either of us; which is worse still,' said the eldest. 'There he is again!'

They all three blew him a silent kiss.

'Why?' asked Retty quickly.

'Because he likes Tess Durbeyfield best,' said Marian, lowering her voice. 'I have watched him every day, and have found it out.'

There was a reflective silence.

'But she don't care anything for him?' at length breathed Retty.

'Well – I sometimes think that too.'

'But how silly all this is!' said Izz Huett impatiently. 'Of course he won't marry any one of us, or Tess either – a gentleman's son, who's going to be a great landowner and farmer abroad! More likely to ask us to come with him as farm-hands at so much a year!'

One sighed, and another sighed, and Marian's plump figure sighed biggest of all. Somebody in bed hard by sighed too. Tears came into the eyes of Retty Priddle, the pretty red-haired youngest – the last bud of the Paridelles, so important in the county annals. They watched silently a little longer, their three faces still close together as before, and the triple hues of their hair mingling. But the unconscious Mr Clare had gone indoors, and they saw him no more; and, the shades beginning to deepen, they crept into their beds. In a few minutes they heard him ascend the ladder to his own room. Marian was soon snoring, but Izz did not drop into forgetfulness for a long time. Retty Priddle cried herself to sleep.

The deeper-passioned Tess was very far from sleeping even then. This conversation was another of the bitter pills she had been obliged to swallow that day. Scarce the least feeling of jealousy arose in her breast. For that matter she knew herself to have the preference. Being more finely formed, better educated, and, though the youngest except Retty, more woman than either,[7] she perceived that only the slightest ordinary care was necessary for holding her own in Angel Clare's heart against these her candid friends. But the grave question was, ought she to do this? There was, to be sure, hardly a ghost of a chance for either of them, in a serious sense; but there was, or had been, a chance of one or the other inspiring him with a passing fancy for her, and enjoying the pleasure of his attentions while he stayed here. Such unequal attachments had led to marriage; and she had heard from Mrs Crick that Mr Clare had one day asked, in a laughing way, what would be the use of his marrying a fine lady, and all the while a thousand acres of Colonial pasture to feed, and cattle to rear, and corn to reap. A farm-woman would be the only sensible kind of wife for him. But whether Mr Clare had spoken seriously or not, why should she, who could never conscientiously allow any man to marry her now, and who had religiously determined that she never would be tempted to do so, draw off Mr Clare's attention from other women, for the brief happiness of sunning herself in his eyes while he remained at Talbothays?

XXII

They came downstairs yawning next morning; but skimming and milking were proceeded with as usual, and they went indoors to breakfast. Dairyman Crick was discovered stamping about the house.

He had received a letter, in which a customer had complained that the butter had a twang.

'And begad, so 't have!' said the dairyman, who held in his left hand a wooden slice on which a lump of butter was stuck. 'Yes – taste for yourself!'

Several of them gathered round him; and Mr Clare tasted, Tess tasted, also the other indoor milkmaids, one or two of the milking-men, and last of all Mrs Crick, who came out from the waiting breakfast-table. There certainly was a twang.

The dairyman, who had thrown himself into abstraction to better realize the taste, and so divine the particular species of noxious weed to which it appertained, suddenly exclaimed –

''Tis garlic! and I thought there wasn't a blade left in that mead!'

Then all the old hands remembered that a certain dry mead, into which a few of the cows had been admitted of late, had, in years gone by, spoilt the butter in the same way. The dairyman had not recognized the taste at that time, and thought the butter bewitched.

'We must overhaul that mead,' he resumed; 'this mustn't continny!'

All having armed themselves with old pointed knives they went out together. As the inimical plant could only be present in very microscopic dimensions to have escaped ordinary observation, to find it seemed rather a hopeless attempt in the stretch of rich grass before them. However, they formed themselves into line, all assisting, owing to the importance of the search; the dairyman at the upper end with Mr Clare, who had volunteered to help; then Tess, Marian, Izz Huett, and Retty; then Bill Lewell, Jonathan, and the married dairywomen – namely, Beck Nibbs, with her woolly black hair and rolling eyes; and flaxen Frances, consumptive from the winter damps of the water-meads – who lived in their respective cottages.

With eyes fixed upon the ground they crept slowly across a strip of the field, returning a little farther down in such a manner that, when they should have finished, not a single inch of the pasture but would have fallen under the eye of some one of them. It was a most tedious business, not more than half a dozen shoots of garlic being discoverable in the whole field; yet such was the herb's pungency that probably one bite of it by one cow had been sufficient to season the whole dairy's produce for the day.

Differing one from another in natures and moods so greatly as they did, they yet formed, bending, a curiously uniform row – automatic, noiseless; and an alien observer passing down the neighbouring lane might well have been excused for massing them as 'Hodge.' As they crept along, stooping low to discern the plant, a soft yellow gleam was reflected from the buttercups into their shaded faces, giving them an elfish, moonlit aspect, though the sun was pouring upon their backs in all the strength of noon.

Angel Clare, who communistically stuck to his rule of taking part with the rest in everything, glanced up now and then. It was not, of course, by accident that he walked next to Tess.

'Well, how are you?' he murmured.

'Very well, thank you, sir,' she replied demurely.

As they had been discussing a score of personal matters only half-an-hour before, the introductory style seemed a little superfluous. But they got no further in speech just then. They crept and crept, the hem of her petticoat just touching his gaiter, and his elbow sometimes brushing hers. At last the dairyman, who came next, could stand it no longer.

'Upon my soul and body, this here stooping do fairly make my back open and shut!' he exclaimed, straightening himself slowly with an excruciated look till quite upright. 'And you, maidy Tess, you wasn't well a day or two ago – this will make your head ache finely! Don't do any more, if you feel fainty; leave the rest to finish it.'

Dairyman Crick withdrew, and Tess dropped behind. Mr Clare also stepped out of line, and began privateering about for the weed. When she found him near her, her very tension at what she had heard the night before made her the first to speak.

'Don't they look pretty?' she said.

'Who?'

'Izzy Huett and Retty.'

Tess had moodily decided that either of these maidens would make a good farmer's wife, and that she ought to recommend them, and obscure her own wretched charms.

'Pretty? Well, yes – they are pretty girls – fresh-looking. I have often thought so.'

'Though, poor dears, prettiness won't last long!'

'Oh no, unfortunately.'

'They be excellent dairywomen.'

'Yes; though not better than you.'

'They skim better than I.'

'Do they?'

Clare remained observing them – not without their observing him.

'She is colouring up,' continued Tess heroically.

'Who?'

'Retty Priddle.'

'Oh! Why is that?'

'Because you are looking at her.'

Self-sacrificing as her mood might be Tess could not well go further and cry, 'Marry one of them, if you really do want a dairywoman and not a lady; and don't think of marrying me!' She followed Dairyman Crick, and had the mournful satisfaction of seeing that Clare remained behind.

From this day she forced herself to take pains to avoid him – never allowing herself, as formerly, to remain long in his company, even if their juxtaposition were purely accidental. She gave the other three every chance.

Tess was woman enough to realize from their avowals to herself that Angel Clare had the honour of all the dairymaids in his keeping, and her perception of his care to avoid compromising the happiness of either in the least degree bred a tender respect in Tess for what she deemed the self-controlling sense of duty shown by him,[1] a quality which she had never expected to find in one of the opposite sex, and in the absence of which more than one of the simple hearts who were his housemates might have gone weeping on her pilgrimage.

XXIII

The hot weather of July had crept upon them unawares, and the atmosphere of the flat vale hung heavy as an opiate over the dairy-folk, the cows, and the trees. Hot steaming rains fell frequently, making the grass where the cows fed yet more rank, and hindering the late haymaking in the other meads.

It was Sunday morning; the milking was done; the outdoor milkers had gone home. Tess and the other three were dressing themselves rapidly, the whole bevy having agreed to go together to Mellstock Church, which lay some three or four miles distant from the dairy-house. She had now been two months at Talbothays, and this was her first excursion.[1]

All the preceding afternoon and night heavy thunderstorms had hissed down upon the meads, and washed some of the hay into the river; but this morning the sun shone out all the more brilliantly for the deluge, and the air was balmy and clear.

The crooked lane leading from their own parish to Mellstock ran along the lowest levels in a portion of its length, and when the girls reached the most depressed spot they found that the result of the rain had been to flood the lane over-shoe to a distance of some fifty yards. This would have been no serious hindrance on a weekday; they would have clicked through it in their high pattens and boots quite unconcerned; but on this day of vanity, this Sun's-day,[2] when flesh went forth to coquet with flesh while hypocritically affecting business with spiritual things; on this occasion for wearing their white stockings and thin shoes, and their pink, white, and buff gowns, on which every mud spot would be visible, the pool was an awkward impediment. They could hear the church-bell calling – as yet nearly a mile off.

'Who would have expected such a rise in the river in summer-time!' said Marian, from the top of the roadside bank on which they had climbed, and were maintaining a precarious footing in the hope of creeping along its slope till they were past the pool.

'We can't get there anyhow, without walking right through it, or else going round Stone Bridge way; and that would make us so very late!' said Retty, pausing hopelessly.

'And I do colour up so hot, walking into church late, and all the people staring round,' said Marian, 'that I hardly cool down again till we get into the That-it-may-please-Thees.'[3]

While they stood clinging to the bank they heard a splashing round the bend of the road, and presently appeared Angel Clare, advancing along the lane towards them through the water.

Four hearts gave a big throb simultaneously.

His aspect was probably as un-Sabbatarian[4] a one as a dogmatic parson's son often presented; his attire being his dairy clothes, long wading boots, a cabbage-leaf inside his hat to keep his head cool, with a thistle-spud to finish him off.

'He's not going to church,' said Marian.

'No—I wish he was!' murmured Tess.

Angel, in fact, rightly or wrongly (to adopt the safe phrase of evasive controversialists), preferred sermons in stones[5] to sermons in churches and chapels on fine summer days. This morning, moreover, he had gone out to see if the damage to the hay by the flood was considerable or not. On his walk he observed the girls from a long distance, though they had been so occupied with their difficulties of passage as not to notice him. He knew that the water had risen at that spot, and that it would quite check their progress. So he had hastened on, with a dim idea of how he could help them – one of them in particular.

The rosy-cheeked, bright-eyed quartet looked so charming in their light summer attire, clinging to the roadside bank like pigeons on a roof-slope, that he stopped a moment to regard them before coming close. Their gauzy skirts had brushed up from the grass innumerable flies and butterflies which, unable to escape, remained caged in the transparent tissue as in an aviary. Angel's eye at last fell upon Tess, the hindmost of the four; she, being full of suppressed laughter at their dilemma, could not help meeting his glance radiantly.

He came beneath them in the water, which did not rise over his long boots; and stood looking at the entrapped flies and butterflies.

'Are you trying to get to church?' he said to Marian, who was in front, including the next two in his remark, but avoiding Tess.

'Yes, sir; and 'tis getting late; and my colour do come up so—'

'I'll carry you through the pool – every Jill of you.'[6]

The whole four flushed as if one heart beat through them.

'I think you can't, sir,' said Marian.

'It is the only way for you to get past. Stand still. Nonsense – you are not too heavy! I'd carry you all four together. Now, Marian, attend,' he continued, 'and put your arms round my shoulders, so. Now! Hold on. That's well done.'

Marian had lowered herself upon his arm and shoulder as directed, and Angel strode off with her, his slim figure, as viewed from behind, looking like the mere stem to the great nosegay suggested by hers. They disappeared round the curve of the road, and only his sousing footsteps and the top ribbon of Marian's bonnet told where they were. In a few minutes he reappeared. Izz Huett was the next in order upon the bank.

'Here he comes,' she murmured, and they could hear that her lips were dry with emotion. 'And I have to put my arms round his neck and look into his face as Marian did.'

'There's nothing in that,' said Tess quickly.

'There's a time for everything,' continued Izz, unheeding. 'A time to embrace, and a time to refrain from embracing;[7] the first is now going to be mine.'

'Fie – it is Scripture, Izz!'

'Yes,' said Izz, 'I've always a' ear at church for pretty verses.'

Angel Clare, to whom three-quarters of this performance was a commonplace act of kindness, now approached Izz. She quietly and dreamily lowered herself into his arms, and Angel methodically marched off with her. When he was heard returning for the third time Retty's throbbing heart could be almost seen to shake her. He went up to the red-haired girl, and while he was seizing her he glanced at Tess. His lips could not have pronounced more plainly, 'It will soon be you and I.' Her comprehension appeared in her face; she could not help it. There was an understanding between them.

Poor little Retty, though by far the lightest weight, was the most troublesome of Clare's burdens. Marian had been like a sack of meal, a dead weight of plumpness under which he had literally staggered. Izz had ridden sensibly and calmly. Retty was a bunch of hysterics.

However, he got through with the disquieted creature, deposited her, and returned. Tess could see over the hedge the distant three in a group, standing as he had placed them on the next rising ground. It was now her turn. She was embarrassed to discover that excitement at the proximity of Mr Clare's breath and eyes, which she had contemned in her companions, was intensified in herself; and as if fearful of betraying her secret she paltered with him at the last moment.

'I may be able to clim' along the bank perhaps – I can clim' better than they. You must be so tired, Mr Clare!'

'No, no, Tess,' said he quickly. And almost before she was aware she was seated in his arms and resting against his shoulder.

'Three Leahs to get one Rachel,'[8] he whispered.

'They are better women than I,' she replied, magnanimously sticking to her resolve.

'Not to me,' said Angel.

He saw her grow warm at this; and they went some steps in silence.

'I hope I am not too heavy?' she said timidly.

'Oh no. You should lift Marian! Such a lump. You are like an undulating billow warmed by the sun. And all this fluff of muslin about you is the froth.'

'It is very pretty – if I seem like that to you.'

'Do you know that I have undergone three-quarters of this labour entirely for the sake of the fourth quarter?'

'No.'

'I did not expect such an event to-day.'

'Nor I . . . The water came up so sudden.'

That the rise in the water was what she understood him to refer to, the state of her breathing belied. Clare stood still, and inclined his face towards hers.

'O Tessy!' he exclaimed.

The girl's cheeks burned to the breeze, and she could not look into his eyes for her emotion. It reminded Angel that he was somewhat unfairly taking advantage of an accidental position; and he went no further with it. No definite words of love had crossed their lips as yet, and suspension at this point was desirable now. However, he walked slowly, to make the remainder of the distance as long as possible; but at last they came to the bend, and the rest of their progress was in full view of the other three. The dry land was reached, and he set her down.

Her friends were looking with round thoughtful eyes at her and him, and she could see that they had been talking of her. He hastily bade them farewell, and splashed back along the stretch of submerged road.

The four moved on together as before, till Marian broke the silence by saying –

'No – in all truth; we have no chance against her!' She looked joylessly at Tess.

'What do you mean?' asked the latter.

'He likes 'ee best – the very best! We could see it as he brought 'ee. He would have kissed 'ee, if you had encouraged him to do it, ever so little.'

'No, no,' said she.

The gaiety with which they had set out had somehow vanished; and yet there was no enmity or malice between them. They were generous young souls; they had been reared in the lonely country nooks where fatalism is a strong sentiment, and they did not blame her. Such supplanting was to be.

Tess's heart ached. There was no concealing from herself the fact that she loved Angel Clare, perhaps all the more passionately from knowing that the others had also lost their hearts to him. There is contagion in this sentiment, especially among women. And yet that same hungry heart of hers compassionated her friends. Tess's honest nature had fought against this, but too feebly, and the natural result had followed.

'I will never stand in your way, nor in the way of either of 'ee!' she declared to Retty that night in the bedroom (her tears running down). 'I can't help this, my dear! I don't think marrying is in his mind at all; but if he were even to ask me I should refuse him, as I should refuse any man.'

'Oh! would you? Why?' said wondering Retty.

'It cannot be! But I will be plain. Putting myself quite on one side, I don't think he will choose either of you.'

'I have never expected it – thought of it!' moaned Retty. 'But O! I wish I was dead!'

The poor child, torn by a feeling which she hardly understood, turned to the two other girls who came upstairs just then.

'We be friends with her again,' she said to them. 'She thinks no more of his choosing her than we do.'

So the reserve went off, and they were confiding and warm.

'I don't seem to care what I do now,' said Marian, whose mood was tuned to its lowest bass. 'I was going to marry a dairyman at Stickleford, who's asked me twice; but – my soul – I would put an end to myself rather'n be his wife now! Why don't ye speak, Izz?'

'To confess, then,' said Izz, 'I made sure to-day that he was going to kiss me as he held me; and I stayed still against his breast, hoping and hoping, and never moved at all. But he did not. I don't like biding here at Talbothays any longer! I shall go home.'

The air of the sleeping-chamber seemed to palpitate with the hopeless passion of the girls. They writhed feverishly under the oppressiveness of an emotion thrust on them by cruel Nature's law – an emotion which they had neither expected nor desired. The incident of the day had fanned the flame that was burning the inside of their hearts out, and the torture was almost more than they could endure. The differences which distinguished them as individuals were abstracted by this passion, and each was but portion of one organism called sex. There was little jealousy because there was no hope. Each one was a girl of fair common-sense, and she did not delude herself with any vain conceits, or dress herself up,[9] or give herself airs, in the idea of outshining the others. The full recognition of the futility of their infatuation, from a social point of view; its purposeless beginning; its self-bounded outlook; its lack of everything to justify its existence in the eye of civilization (while lacking nothing in the eye of Nature); the one fact that it did exist, ecstasizing them to a killing joy; all this imparted to them a resignation, a dignity, which a practical and sordid expectation of winning him as a husband would have destroyed.

They tossed and turned on their little beds, and the cheese-wring dripped monotonously downstairs.

'B' you awake, Tess?' whispered one, half-an-hour later.

It was Izz Huett's voice.

Tess replied in the affirmative, whereupon also Retty and Marian suddenly flung the bed-clothes off them, and sighed –

'So be we!'

'I wonder what she is like – the lady they say his family have looked out for him!'

'I wonder,' said Izz.

'Some lady looked out for him?' gasped Tess, starting. 'I have never heard o' that!'

'Oh yes – 'tis whispered; a young lady of his own rank, chosen by his family; a Doctor of Divinity's daughter near his father's parish of Emminster; he don't much care for her, they say. But he is sure to marry her.'

They had heard so very little of this; yet it was enough to build up wretched dolorous dreams upon, there in the shade of the night. They pictured all the details of his being won round to consent, of the wedding preparations, of the bride's happiness, of her dress and veil, of her blissful home with him, when oblivion would have fallen upon themselves as far as he and their love were concerned. Thus they talked, and ached, and wept till sleep charmed their sorrow away.

After this disclosure Tess nourished no further foolish thought that there lurked any grave and deliberate import in Clare's attentions to her. It was a passing summer love of her face, for love's own temporary sake – nothing more. And the thorny crown of this sad conception was that she whom he really did prefer in a cursory way to the rest, she who knew herself to be more impassioned in nature, cleverer, more beautiful than they, was in the eyes of propriety far less worthy of him than the homelier ones whom he ignored.

XXIV

Amid the oozing fatness and warm ferments of the Var Vale, at a season when the rush of juices could almost be heard below the hiss of fertilization, it was impossible that the most fanciful love should not grow passionate. The ready bosoms existing there were impregnated by their surroundings.

July passed over their heads, and the Thermidorean weather[1] which came in its wake seemed an effort on the part of Nature to match the state of hearts at Talbothays Dairy. The air of the place, so fresh in the spring and early summer, was stagnant and enervating now. Its heavy scents weighed upon them, and at mid-day the landscape seemed lying in a swoon. Ethiopic scorchings browned the upper slopes of the pastures, but there was still bright green herbage here where the watercourses purled. And as Clare was oppressed by the outward heats, so was he burdened inwardly by a waxing fervour of passion for the soft and silent Tess.[2]

The rains having passed the uplands were dry. The wheels of the dairyman's spring-cart, as he sped home from market, licked up the pulverized surface of the highway, and were followed by white ribands of dust, as if they had set a thin powder-train on fire. The cows jumped wildly over the five-barred barton-gate, maddened by the gad-fly; Dairyman Crick kept his shirt-sleeves permanently rolled up past his elbows: open windows produced no effect in ventilation without open doors, and in the dairy-garden the blackbirds and thrushes crept about under the currant-bushes, rather in the manner of quadrupeds than of winged creatures. The flies in the kitchen were lazy, teasing, and familiar, crawling about in unwonted places, on the floor, into drawers, and over the backs of the milkmaids' hands. Conversations were concerning sunstroke; while butter-making, and still more butter-keeping, was a despair.

They milked entirely in the meads for coolness and convenience, without driving in the cows. During the day the animals obsequiously followed the shadow of the smallest tree as it moved round the stem with the diurnal roll; and when the milkers came they could hardly stand still for the flies.

On one of these afternoons four or five unmilked cows chanced to stand apart from the general herd, behind the corner of a hedge, among them being Dumpling and Old Pretty, who loved Tess's hands above those of any other maid. When she rose from her stool under a finished cow Angel Clare, who had been observing her for some time, asked her if she would take the aforesaid creatures next. She silently assented, and with her stool at arm's length, and the pail against her knee, went round to where they stood. Soon the sound of Old Pretty's milk fizzing into the pail came through the hedge, and then Angel felt inclined to go round the corner also, to finish off a hard-yielding milcher who had strayed there, he being now as capable of this as the dairyman himself.

All the men, and some of the women, when milking, dug their foreheads into the cows and gazed into the pail. But a few – mainly the younger ones – rested their heads sideways. This was Tess Durbeyfield's habit, her temple pressing the milcher's flank, her eyes fixed on the far end of the meadow with the gaze of one lost in meditation. She was milking Old Pretty thus, and the sun chancing to be on the milking-side it shone flat upon her pink-gowned form, and her white curtain-bonnet, and upon her profile, rendering it dazzlingly keen as a cameo cut from the dun background of the cow.

She did not know that Clare had followed her round, and that he sat under his cow watching her. The absolute stillness of her head and features was remarkable; she might have been in a trance, her eyes open, yet unseeing. Nothing in the picture moved but Old Pretty's tail and Tess's pink hands, the latter so gently as to be a rhythmic pulsation only, as if they were obeying a reflex stimulus, like a beating heart.

How very lovable her face was to him. Yet there was nothing ethereal about it; all was real vitality, real warmth, real incarnation. And it was in her mouth that this culminated. Eyes almost as deep and speaking he had seen before, and cheeks perhaps as fair; brows as arched, a chin and throat almost as shapely; her mouth he had seen nothing to equal on the face of the earth. To a young man with the least fire in him that little upward lift in the middle of her red top lip was distracting, infatuating, maddening. He had never before seen a woman's lips and teeth which forced upon his mind with such persistent iteration the old Elizabethan simile of roses filled with snow.[3] Perfect, he, as a lover, might have called them off-hand. But no – they were not perfect. And it was the touch of the imperfect upon the would-be perfect that gave the sweetness, because it was that which gave the humanity.

Clare had studied the curves of those lips so many times that he could reproduce them mentally with ease; and now, as they again confronted him, clothed with colour and life, they sent an *aura*[4] over his flesh, a cold breeze through his nerves, which wellnigh produced a qualm; and actually produced, by some mysterious physiological process, a prosaic sneeze.

She then became conscious that he was observing her; but she would not show it by any change of position, though the curious dream-like fixity disappeared, and a close eye might easily have discerned that the rosiness of her face slowly deepened, and then faded till only a tinge of it was left.

The stimulus that had passed into Clare like an annunciation from the sky did not die down. Resolutions, reticences, prudences, fears, fell back like a defeated battalion. He jumped up from his seat, and, leaving his pail to be kicked over if the milcher had such a mind, went quickly towards the desire of his eyes, and, kneeling down beside her, clasped her in his arms.

Tess was taken completely by surprise, and she yielded to his embrace with unreflecting inevitableness. Having seen that it was really her lover who had advanced, and no one else, her lips parted, and she sank upon him in her momentary joy, with something very like an ecstatic cry.

He had been on the point of kissing that too tempting mouth, but he checked himself, for tender conscience' sake.[5]

'Forgive me, Tess dear!' he whispered. 'I ought to have asked. I – did not know what I was doing. I do not mean it as a liberty. I am devoted to you, Tessy, dearest, in all sincerity!'

Old Pretty by this time had looked round, puzzled; and seeing two people crouching under her where, by immemorial custom, there should have been only one, lifted her hind leg crossly.

'She is angry – she doesn't know what we mean – she'll kick over the milk!' exclaimed Tess, gently striving to free herself, her eyes concerned with the quadruped's actions, her heart more deeply concerned with herself and Clare.

She slipped up from her seat, and they stood together, his arm still encircling her. Tess's eyes, fixed on distance, began to fill.

'Why do you cry, my darling?' he said.

'O – I don't know!' she murmured regretfully.

As she saw and felt more clearly the position she was in she became agitated, looked askance, and tried to withdraw.

'Well, I have betrayed my feeling, Tess, at last,' said he, with a curious sigh of desperation, signifying unconsciously that his heart had outrun his judgment. 'That I love you dearly and truly I need not say. But I – it shall go no farther now – it distresses you – I am as surprised as you are. You will not think I have presumed upon your defencelessness – been too quick and unreflecting, will you?'

'I cannot tell.'

He had allowed her to free herself; and in a minute or two the milking of each was resumed. Nobody had beheld the gravitation of the two into one; and when the dairyman came round by that screened nook a few minutes later there was not a sign to reveal that the markedly-sundered pair were more to each other than mere acquaintance. Yet in the interval since Crick's last view of them something had occurred which changed the pivot of the universe for their two natures – whilst it should last; something which, had he known its quality, the dairyman would have despised, as a practical man; yet which was based upon a more stubborn and resistless tendency than a whole heap of so-called practicalities. A veil had been whisked aside; the tract of each one's outlook was to have a new horizon thenceforward – for a short time or for a long.

END OF PHASE THE THIRD

PHASE THE FOURTH

The Consequence

XXV

Clare, restless, went out into the dusk when evening drew on, she who had won him having retired to her chamber.

The night was as sultry as the day. There was no coolness after dark unless on the grass. Roads, garden-paths, the house fronts, the barton walls were warm as hearths, and reflected the noontide temperature into the noctambulist's face.[1]

He sat on the east gate of the dairy-yard, and knew not what to think of himself. Feeling had indeed smothered judgment that day.

Since the sudden embrace, three hours before, the twain had kept apart. She seemed fevered, almost alarmed, at what had occurred, while the novelty, unpremeditation, mastery of circumstance disquieted him – palpitating, contemplative being that he was. He could hardly realize their true relations to each other as yet, and what their mutual bearing should be before third parties thenceforward.

Angel had come as pupil to this dairy in the idea that his temporary existence here was to be the merest episode in his life, soon passed through and early forgotten; he had come as to a place from which as from a screened alcove he could calmly view the absorbing world without, and, apostrophizing it with Walt Whitman –

> Crowds of men and women attired in the usual costumes,
> How curious you are to me! –[2]

resolve upon a plan for plunging into that world anew. But, behold, the absorbing scene had been imported hither. What had been the engrossing world had dissolved into an uninteresting outer dumb-show; while here, in this apparently dim and unimpassioned place, novelty had volcanically started up, as it had never, for him, started up elsewhere.[3]

Every window of the house being open Clare could hear across the yard each trivial sound of the retiring household. That dairy-house, so humble, so insignificant, so purely to him a place of constrained sojourn that he had never hitherto deemed it of sufficient importance to be reconnoitred as an object of any quality whatever in the landscape; what was it now? The aged and lichened brick gables breathed forth 'Stay!' The windows smiled, the door coaxed and beckoned, the creeper blushed confederacy. A personality within it was so far-reaching in her influence as to spread into and make the bricks, mortar, and whole overhanging sky throb with a burning sensibility. Whose was this mighty personality? A milkmaid's.

It was amazing, indeed, to find how great a matter the life of the obscure dairy had become to him. And though new love was to be held partly responsible for this it was not solely so. Many besides Angel have learnt that the magnitude of lives is not as to their external displacements, but as to their subjective experiences. The impressionable peasant leads a larger, fuller, more dramatic life than the pachydermatous king. Looking at it thus he found that life was to be seen of the same magnitude here as elsewhere.

Despite his heterodoxy Clare was a man with a conscience. Tess was no insignificant creature to toy with and dismiss; but a woman living her precious life – a life which, to herself who endured or enjoyed it, possessed as great a dimension as the life of the mightiest to himself. Upon her sensations the whole world depended to Tess; through her existence all her fellow-creatures existed, to her. The universe itself only came into being for Tess on the particular day in the particular year in which she was born.

This consciousness upon which he had intruded was the single opportunity of existence ever vouchsafed to Tess by an unsympathetic First Cause[4] – her all; her every and only chance. How then should he look upon her as of less consequence than himself; as a pretty trifle to caress and grow weary of; and not deal in the greatest seriousness with the affection which he knew that he had awakened in her – so fervid and so impressionable as she was under her reserve; in order that it might not agonize and wreck her?

To encounter her daily in the accustomed manner would be to

develop what had begun. Living in such close relations, to meet meant to fall into endearment; flesh and blood could not resist it; and, having arrived at no conclusion as to the issue of such a tendency, he decided to hold aloof for the present from occupations in which they would be mutually engaged. As yet the harm done was small.

But it was not easy to carry out the resolution never to approach her. He was driven towards her by every heave of his pulse.

He thought he would go and see his friends. It might be possible to sound them upon this. In less than six months his term here would have ended, and after a few additional months spent upon other farms he would be fully equipped in agricultural knowledge, and in a position to start on his own account. Would not a farmer want a wife, and should a farmer's wife be a drawing-room wax-figure, or a woman who understood farming? Notwithstanding the pleasing answer returned to him by the silence he resolved to go his journey.

One morning when they sat down to breakfast at Talbothays Dairy some maid observed that she had not seen anything of Mr Clare that day.

'Oh no,' said Dairyman Crick. 'Mr Clare has gone home to Emmin-ster to spend a few days wi' his kinsfolk.'

For four impassioned ones around that table the sunshine of the morning went out at a stroke, and the birds muffled their song. But neither girl by word or gesture revealed her blankness.

'He's getting on towards the end of his time wi' me,' added the dairyman, with a phlegm which unconsciously was brutal; 'and so I suppose he is beginning to see about his plans elsewhere.'

'How much longer is he to bide here?' asked Izz Huett, the only one of the gloom-stricken bevy who could trust her voice with the question.

The others waited for the dairyman's answer as if their lives hung upon it; Retty, with parted lips, gazing on the table-cloth, Marian with heat added to her redness, Tess throbbing and looking out at the meads.

'Well, I can't mind the exact day without looking at my memor-andum-book,' replied Crick, with the same intolerable unconcern. 'But even that may be altered a bit. He'll bide to get a little practice in the calving out at the straw-yard, for certain. He'll hang on till the end of the year I should say.'

Four months and more of torturing ecstasy in his society – of 'pleasure girdled about with pain.'[5] After that the blackness of unutterable night.

At this moment of the morning Angel Clare was riding along a narrow lane ten miles distant from the breakfasters, in the direction of his father's vicarage at Emminster, carrying, as well as he could, a little basket which contained some black-puddings and a bottle of mead, sent by Mrs Crick, with her kind respects, to his parents. The white lane stretched before him, and his eyes were upon it; but they were staring into next year, and not at the lane. He loved her; ought he to marry her? Dared he to marry her? What would his mother and his brothers say? What would he himself say a couple of years after the event? That would depend upon whether the germs of staunch comradeship underlay the temporary emotion, or whether it were a sensuous joy in her form only, with no substratum of everlastingness.

His father's hill-surrounded little town, the Tudor church-tower of red stone, the clump of trees near the vicarage, came at last into view beneath him, and he rode down towards the well-known gate. Casting a glance in the direction of the church before entering his home, he beheld standing by the vestry-door a group of girls, of ages between twelve and sixteen, apparently awaiting the arrival of some other one, who in a moment became visible; a figure somewhat older than the school-girls, wearing a broad-brimmed hat and highly-starched cambric morning-gown, with a couple of books in her hand.

Clare knew her well. He could not be sure that she observed him; he hoped she did not, so as to render it unnecessary that he should go and speak to her, blameless creature that she was. An overpowering reluctance to greet her made him decide that she had not seen him. The young lady was Miss Mercy Chant, the only daughter of his father's neighbour and friend, whom it was his parents' quiet hope that he might wed some day. She was great at Antinomianism[6] and Bible-classes, and was plainly going to hold a class now in the vestry. Clare's mind for a moment flew back to the impassioned, summer-saturated heathens in the Var Vale, and to the most living, intensest[7] of them all.

It was on the impulse of the moment that he had resolved to trot over to Emminster, and hence had not written to apprise his mother and father, aiming, however, to arrive about the breakfast hour, before they should have gone out to their parish duties. He was a little late, and they had already sat down to the morning meal. The group at table jumped up to welcome him as soon as he entered. They were his father and mother, his brother the Reverend Felix – curate at a town in the adjoining county, home for the inside of a fortnight – and his other brother, the Reverend Cuthbert, the classical scholar, and Fellow and Dean of his College, down from Cambridge for the long vacation. His mother appeared in a cap and silver spectacles, and his father looked what in fact he was – an earnest, God-fearing man, somewhat gaunt, in years about sixty-five, his pale face lined with thought and purpose. Over their heads hung the picture of Angel's sister, the eldest of the family, sixteen years his senior, who had married a missionary and gone out to Africa.

Old Mr Clare was a clergyman of a type which, within the last twenty years, has well-nigh dropped out of contemporary life. A spiritual descendant in the direct line from Wycliff, Huss, Luther, Calvin; an Evangelical of the Evangelicals, a Conversionist, a man of Apostolic simplicity in life and thought,[8] he had in his raw youth made up his mind once for all on the deeper questions of existence, and admitted no further reasoning on them thenceforward. He was regarded even by those of his own date and school of thinking as extreme; while, on the other hand, those totally opposed to him were unwillingly won to admiration for his thoroughness, and for the remarkable power he showed in dismissing all question as to principles in his energy for applying them. He loved Paul of Tarsus, liked St John, hated St James as much as he dared, and regarded Timothy and Titus with mixed feelings. The New Testament was less a Christiad than a Pauliad[9] to his intelligence – less an argument than an intoxication. His creed of determinism was such that it almost amounted to a vice, and quite amounted, on its negative side, to a renunciative philosophy which had cousinship with that of Schopenhauer and Leopardi.[10] He despised the Canons and Rubric,[11] swore by the Articles, and deemed himself consistent through the whole category – which in a way he might have been. One thing he certainly was – sincere.

To the æsthetic, sensuous, pagan pleasure in natural life and lush womanhood which his son Angel had lately been experiencing in Var Vale, his temper would have been antipathetic in a high degree, had he either by inquiry or imagination been able to apprehend it. Once upon a time Angel had been so unlucky as to say to his father, in a moment of irritation, that it might have resulted far better for mankind if Greece had been the source of the religion of modern civilization, and not Palestine;[12] and his father's grief was of that blank description which could not realize that there might lurk a thousandth part of a truth, much less a half truth or a whole truth, in such a proposition. He had simply preached austerely at Angel for a long time after. But the kindness of his heart was such that he never resented anything for long, and welcomed his son to-day with a smile which was as candidly sweet as a child's.

Angel sat down, and the place felt like home; yet he did not so much as formerly feel himself one of the family gathered there. Every time that he returned hither he was conscious of this divergence, and since he had last shared in the Vicarage life it had grown even more distinctly foreign to his own than usual. Its transcendental aspirations – still unconsciously based on the geocentric view of things, a zenithal paradise, a nadiral hell – were as foreign to his own as if they had been the dreams of people on another planet.[13] Latterly he had seen only Life, felt only the great passionate pulse of existence, unwarped, uncontorted, untrammelled by those creeds which futilely attempt to check what wisdom would be content to regulate.

On their part they saw a great difference in him, a growing divergence from the Angel Clare of former times. It was chiefly a difference in his manner that they noticed just now, particularly his brothers. He was getting to behave like a farmer; he flung his legs about; the muscles of his face had grown more expressive; his eyes looked as much information as his tongue spoke, and more. The manner of the scholar had nearly disappeared; still more the manner of the drawing-room young man. A prig would have said that he had lost culture, and a prude that he had become coarse. Such was the contagion of domiciliary fellowship with the Talbothays nymphs and swains.[14]

After breakfast he walked with his two brothers, non-evangelical,[15] well-educated, hall-marked young men, correct to their remotest fibre; such unimpeachable models as are turned out yearly by the lathe of a systematic tuition. They were both somewhat short-sighted, and when it was the custom to wear a single eyeglass and string they wore a single eyeglass and string; when it was the custom to wear a double glass they wore a double glass; when it was the custom to wear spectacles they wore spectacles straightway, all without reference to the particular variety of defect in their own vision. When Wordsworth was enthroned they carried pocket copies; and when Shelley was belittled they allowed him to grow dusty on their shelves. When Correggio's Holy Families were admired, they admired Correggio's Holy Families; when he was decried in favour of Velasquez, they sedulously followed suit without any personal objection.[16]

If these two noticed Angel's growing social ineptness, he noticed their growing mental limitations. Felix seemed to him all Church; Cuthbert all College. His Diocesan Synod and Visitations[17] were the mainsprings of the world to the one; Cambridge to the other. Each brother candidly recognized that there were a few unimportant scores of millions of outsiders in civilized society, persons who were neither University men nor churchmen; but they were to be tolerated rather than reckoned with and respected.

They were both dutiful and attentive sons, and were regular in their visits to their parents. Felix, though an offshoot from a far more recent point in the devolution of theology than his father, was less self-sacrificing and disinterested. More tolerant than his father of a contradictory opinion, in its aspect as a danger to its holder, he was less ready than his father to pardon it as a slight to his own teaching. Cuthbert was, upon the whole, the more liberal-minded, though, with greater subtlety, he had not so much heart.

As they walked along the hillside Angel's former feeling revived in him – that whatever their advantages by comparison with himself, neither set forth life as it really was lived. Perhaps, as with many men, their opportunities of observation were not so good as their opportunities of expression. Neither had an adequate conception of the complicated forces at work outside the smooth and gentle current in which they and their associates floated. Neither saw the difference between local truth and universal truth; that what the inner world said in their clerical and academic hearing was quite a different thing from what the outer world was thinking.

'I suppose it is farming or nothing for you now, my dear fellow,' Felix was saying, among other things, to his youngest brother, as he looked through his spectacles at the distant fields with sad austerity. 'And, therefore, we must make the best of it. But I do entreat you to endeavour to keep as much as possible in touch with moral ideals. Farming, of course, means roughing it externally; but high thinking may go with plain living,[18] nevertheless.'

'Of course it may,' said Angel. 'Was it not proved nineteen hundred years ago – if I may trespass upon your domain a little? Why should you think, Felix, that I am likely to drop my high thinking and my moral ideals?'

'Well, I fancied, from the tone of your letters and our conversation – it may be fancy only – that you were somehow losing intellectual grasp. Hasn't it struck you, Cuthbert?'

'Now, Felix,' said Angel drily, 'we are very good friends, you know; each of us treading our allotted circles; but if it comes to intellectual grasp, I think you, as a contented dogmatist, had better leave mine alone, and inquire what has become of yours.'

They returned down the hill to dinner, which was fixed at any time at which their father's and mother's morning work in the parish usually concluded. Convenience as regarded afternoon callers was the last thing to enter into the consideration of unselfish Mr and Mrs Clare; though the three sons were sufficiently in unison on this matter to wish that their parents would conform a little to modern notions.

The walk had made them hungry, Angel in particular, who was now an outdoor man, accustomed to the profuse *dapes inemptæ*[19] of the dairyman's somewhat coarsely-laden table. But neither of the old people had arrived, and it was not till the sons were almost tired of waiting that their parents entered. The self-denying pair had been occupied in coaxing the appetites of some of their sick parishioners, whom they, somewhat inconsistently, tried to keep imprisoned in the flesh, their own appetites being quite forgotten.

The family sat down to table, and a frugal meal of cold viands was deposited before them. Angel looked round for Mrs Crick's black-puddings, which he had directed to be nicely grilled, as they did them at the dairy, and of which he wished his father and mother to appreciate the marvellous herbal savours as highly as he did himself.

'Ah! you are looking for the black-puddings, my dear boy,' observed Clare's mother. 'But I am sure you will not mind doing without them, as I am sure your father and I shall not, when you know the reason. I suggested to him that we should take Mrs Crick's kind present to the children of the man who can earn nothing just now because of his attacks of delirium tremens; and he agreed that it would be a great pleasure to them; so we did.'

'Of course,' said Angel cheerfully, looking round for the mead.

'I found the mead so extremely alcoholic,' continued his mother, 'that it was quite unfit for use as a beverage, but as valuable as rum or brandy in emergency; so I have put it in my medicine-chest.'

'We never drink spirits at this table, on principle,' added his father.

'But what shall I tell the dairyman's wife?' said Angel.

'The truth, of course,' said his father.

'I rather wanted to say we enjoyed the mead and the black-puddings very much. She is a kind, jolly sort of body, and is sure to ask me directly I return.'

'You cannot, if we did not,' Mr Clare answered lucidly.

'Ah – no; though that mead was a drop of pretty tipple.'

'A what?' said Cuthbert and Felix both.

'Oh – 'tis an expression they use down at Talbothays,' replied Angel, blushing. He felt that his parents were right in their practice if wrong in their want of sentiment, and said no more.

XXVI

It was not till the evening, after family prayers, that Angel found opportunity of broaching to his father one or two subjects near his heart. He had strung himself up to the purpose while kneeling behind his brothers on the carpet, studying the soles of their walking boots, and the little nails in their heels. When the service was over they went out of the room with their mother, and Mr Clare and himself were left alone.

The young man first discussed with the elder his plans for the attainment of his position as a farmer on an extensive scale – either in England or in the Colonies. His father then told him that, as he had not been put to the expense of sending Angel up to Cambridge, he had felt it his duty to set by a sum of money every year towards the purchase or lease of land for him some day, that he might not feel himself unduly slighted.

'As far as worldly wealth goes,' continued his father, 'you will no doubt stand far superior to your brothers in a few years.'

This considerateness on old Mr Clare's part led Angel onward to the other and dearer subject. He observed to his father that he was then six-and-twenty, and that when he should start in the farming business he would require eyes in the back of his head to see to all matters – some one would be necessary to superintend the domestic labours of his establishment whilst he was afield. Would it not be well, therefore, for him to marry?

His father seemed to think this idea not unreasonable; and then Angel put the question –

'What kind of wife do you think would be best for me as a thrifty hard-working farmer?'

'A truly Christian woman, who will be a help and a comfort to you in your goings-out and your comings-in.[1] Beyond that, it really matters little. Such an one can be found; indeed, my earnest-minded friend and neighbour, Dr Chant—'

'But ought she not primarily to be able to milk cows, churn good butter, make immense cheeses; know how to sit hens and turkeys and rear chickens, to direct a field of labourers in an emergency, and estimate the value of sheep and calves?'

'Yes; a farmer's wife; yes, certainly. It would be desirable.' Mr Clare, the elder, had plainly never thought of these points before. 'I was going to add,' he said, 'that for a pure and saintly woman you will not find one more to your true advantage, and certainly not more to your mother's mind and my own, than your friend Mercy, whom you used to show a certain interest in. It is true that my neighbour Chant's daughter has lately caught up the fashion of the younger clergy round about us for decorating the Communion-table – altar, as I was shocked to hear her call it one day[2] – with flowers and other stuff on festival occasions. But her father, who is quite as opposed to such flummery as I, says that can be cured. It is a mere girlish outbreak which, I am sure, will not be permanent.'

'Yes, yes; Mercy is good and devout, I know. But, father, don't you think that a young woman equally pure and virtuous as Miss Chant, but one who, in place of that lady's ecclesiastical accomplishments, understands the duties of farm life as well as a farmer himself, would suit me infinitely better?'

His father persisted in his conviction that a knowledge of a farmer's wife's duties came second to a Pauline view of humanity;[3] and the impulsive Angel, wishing to honour his father's feelings and to advance the cause of his heart at the same time, grew specious. He said that fate or Providence had thrown in his way a woman who possessed every qualification to be the helpmate of an agriculturist, and was decidedly of a serious turn of mind. He would not say whether or not she had attached herself to the sound Low Church School of his father; but she would probably be open to conviction on that point; she was a regular church-goer of simple faith; honest-hearted, receptive, intelligent, graceful to a degree, virtuous as a vestal, and, in personal appearance, exceptionally beautiful.

'Is she of a family such as you would care to marry into – a lady, in short?' asked his startled mother, who had come softly into the study during the conversation.

'She is not what in common parlance is called a lady,' said Angel unflinchingly, 'for she is a cottager's daughter, as I am proud to say. But she *is* a lady, nevertheless – in feeling and nature.'

'Mercy Chant is of a very good family.'

'Pooh! – what's the advantage of that, mother?' said Angel quickly. 'How is family to avail the wife of a man who has to rough it as I have, and shall have to do?'

'Mercy is accomplished. And accomplishments have their charm,' returned his mother, looking at him through her silver spectacles.

'As to external accomplishments, what will be the use of them in the life I am going to lead? – while as to her reading, I can take that in hand. She'll be apt pupil enough, as you would say if you knew her. She's brim full of poetry – actualized poetry, if I may use the expression. She *lives* what paper-poets only write[4]. . . And she is an unimpeachable Christian, I am sure; perhaps of the very tribe, genus, and species you desire to propagate.'

'O Angel, you are mocking!'

'Mother, I beg pardon. But as she really does attend Church almost every Sunday morning, and is a good Christian girl, I am sure you will tolerate any social shortcomings for the sake of that quality, and feel that I may do worse than choose her.' Angel waxed quite earnest on that rather automatic orthodoxy in his beloved Tess which (never dreaming that it might stand him in such good stead) he had been prone to slight when observing it practised by her and the other milkmaids, because of its obvious unreality amid beliefs essentially demonistic.

In their sad doubts as to whether their son had himself any right whatever to the title he claimed for the unknown young woman, Mr and Mrs Clare began to feel it as an advantage not to be overlooked that she at least was sound in her views; especially as the conjunction of the pair must have arisen by chance or Providence; for Angel never would have made orthodoxy a condition of his choice. They said finally that it was better not to act in a hurry, but that they would not object to see her.

Angel therefore refrained from declaring more particulars now. He felt that, single-minded and self-sacrificing as his parents were, there yet existed certain latent prejudices of theirs, as middle-class people, which would require some tact to overcome. For though legally at liberty to do as he chose, and though their daughter-in-law's qualifications could make no practical difference to their lives, in the probability of her living far away from them, he wished for affection's sake not to wound their sentiment in the most important decision of his life.

He observed his own inconsistencies in dwelling upon accidents in Tess's life as if they were vital features. It was for herself that he loved Tess; her soul, her heart, her substance – not for her skill in the dairy, her aptness as his scholar, and certainly not for her simple formal faith-profession. Her unsophisticated open-air existence required no varnish of conventionality to make it palatable to him. He held that education had as yet but little affected the beats of emotion and impulse on which domestic happiness depends. It was probable that, in the lapse of ages, improved systems of moral and intellectual training would appreciably, perhaps considerably, elevate the involuntary and even the unconscious instincts of human nature; but up to the present day culture, as far as he could see, might be said to have affected only the mental epiderm of those lives which had been brought under its influence. This belief was confirmed by his experience of women, which, having latterly been extended from the cultivated middle-class into the rural community, had taught him how much less was the intrinsic difference between the good and wise woman of one social stratum and the good and wise woman of another social stratum, than between the good and bad, the wise and the foolish, of the same stratum or class.

It was the morning of his departure. His brothers had already left the vicarage to proceed on a walking tour in the north, whence one was to return to his college, and the other to his curacy. Angel might have accompanied them, but preferred to rejoin his sweetheart at Talbothays. He would have been an awkward member of the party; for, though the most appreciative humanist, the most ideal religionist, even the best-versed Christologist[5] of the three, there was an alienation in the standing consciousness that his squareness would not fit the round hole that had been prepared for him. To neither Felix nor Cuthbert had he ventured to mention Tess.

His mother made him sandwiches, and his father accompanied him, on his own mare, a little way along the road. Having fairly well advanced his own affairs Angel listened in a willing silence, as they jogged on together through the shady lanes, to his father's account of his parish difficulties, and the coldness of brother clergymen whom he loved, because of his strict interpretations of the New Testament by the light of what they deemed a pernicious Calvinistic doctrine.

'Pernicious!' said Mr Clare, with genial scorn; and he proceeded to recount experiences which would show the absurdity of that idea. He told of wondrous conversions of evil livers of which he had been the instrument, not only amongst the poor, but amongst the rich and well-to-do; and he also candidly admitted many failures.

As an instance of the latter, he mentioned the case of a young upstart squire named D'Urberville, living some forty miles off, in the neighbourhood of Trantridge.

'Not one of the ancient D'Urbervilles of Kingsbere and other places?' asked his son. 'That curiously historic worn-out family, with its ghostly legend of the coach-and-four?'[6]

'Oh no. The original D'Urbervilles decayed and disappeared sixty or eighty years ago – at least, I believe so. This seems to be a new family which has taken the name; for the credit of the former knightly line I hope they are spurious, I'm sure. But it is odd to hear you express interest in old families. I thought you set less store by them even than I.'

'You misapprehend me, father; you often do,' said Angel with a little impatience. 'Politically I am sceptical as to the virtue of their being old. Some of the wise even among themselves "exclaim against their own succession,"[7] as Hamlet puts it; but lyrically, dramatically, and even historically, I am tenderly attached to them.'

This distinction, though by no means a subtle one, was yet too subtle for Mr Clare the elder, and he went on with the story he had been about to relate; which was that after the death of the senior so-called D'Urberville the young man developed the most reckless passions, though he had a blind mother, whose condition should have made him know better. A knowledge of his career having come to the ears of Mr Clare, when he was in that part of the country preaching missionary sermons, he boldly took occasion to speak to him point-blank on his spiritual state. Though he was a stranger, occupying another's pulpit, he had felt this to be his duty, and took for his text the words from St Luke, 'Thou fool, this night thy soul shall be required of thee!'[8] The young man much resented this directness of attack, and in the war of words which followed when they met he did not scruple publicly to insult Mr Clare, without respect for his gray hairs.

Angel flushed with distress.

'Dear father,' he said sadly, 'I wish you would not expose yourself to such gratuitous pain from scoundrels!'

'Pain?' said his father, his rugged face shining in the ardour of self-abnegation. 'The only pain to me was pain on his account, poor, foolish young man. Do you suppose his incensed words could give me any pain, or even his blows? "Being reviled we bless; being persecuted we suffer it; being defamed we entreat; we are made as the filth of the world, and as the offscouring of all things unto this day."[9] Those ancient and noble words to the Corinthians are strictly true at this present hour.'

'Not blows, father? He did not proceed to blows?'

'No, he did not. Though I have borne blows from men in a mad state of intoxication.'

'No!'

'A dozen times, my boy. What then? I have saved them from the guilt of murdering their own flesh and blood thereby; and they have lived to thank me, and praise God.'

'May this young man do the same!' said Angel fervently. 'But I fear otherwise, from what you say.'

'We'll hope, nevertheless,' said Mr Clare. 'And I continue to pray for him, though on this side of the grave we shall probably never meet again. But, after all, one of those poor words of mine may spring up in his heart as a good seed some day.'[10]

Now, as always, Clare's father was sanguine as a child; and though the younger could not accept his parent's narrow dogma he revered his practice and recognized the hero under the pietist. Perhaps he revered his father's practice even more now than ever, seeing that, in the question of making Tessy his wife, his father had not once thought of inquiring whether she were well provided or penniless. The same unworldliness was what had necessitated Angel's getting a living as a farmer, and would probably keep his brothers in the position of poor parsons for the term of their activities; yet Angel admired it none the less. Indeed, despite his own heterodoxy, Angel often felt that he was nearer to his father on the human side than to either of his brethren.

XXVII

An up-hill and down-dale ride of twenty-odd miles through a garish mid-day atmosphere brought him in the afternoon to a detached knoll a mile or two west of Talbothays, whence he again looked into that green trough of sappiness and humidity, the valley of the River Var. Immediately he began to descend from the upland to the fat alluvial soil below the atmosphere grew heavier; the languid perfume of the summer fruits, the mists, and hay, and flowers formed therein a vast pool of odour which at this hour seemed to make the animals, the very bees and butterflies, drowsy. Clare was now so familiar with the spot that he knew the individual cows by their names when, a long distance off, he saw them dotted about the meads. It was with a sense of luxury that he recognized his power of viewing life here from its inner side, in a way that had been quite foreign to him in his student-days; and, much as he loved his parents, he could not help being aware that to come here, as now, after an experience of home-life, affected him like throwing off splints and bandages; even the one customary curb on the humours of English rural societies being absent in this place, Talbothays having no resident landlord.[1]

Not a human being was out of doors at the dairy. The denizens were all enjoying the usual afternoon nap of an hour or so which the exceedingly early hours kept in summer-time rendered a necessity. At the door the wood-hooped pails, sodden and bleached by infinite scrubbings, hung like hats on a stand upon the forked and peeled limb of an oak fixed there for that purpose; all of them ready and dry for the evening milking. Angel entered, and went through the silent passages of the house to the back quarters, where he listened for a moment. Sustained snores came from the cart-house, where some of the men were lying down; the grunt and squeal of sweltering pigs arose from the still farther distance. The large-leaved rhubarb and cabbage plants slept too, their broad limp surfaces hanging in the sun like half-closed umbrellas.

He unbridled and fed his horse, and as he re-entered the house the clock struck three. Three was the afternoon skimming-hour; and, with the stroke, Clare heard the creaking of the floor-boards above, and then the touch of a descending foot on the stairs. It was Tess's, who in another moment came down before his eyes.

She had not heard him enter, and hardly realized his presence there. She was yawning, and he saw the red interior of her mouth as if it had been a snake's. She had stretched one arm so high above her coiled-up cable of hair that he could see its satin delicacy above the sunburn; her face was flushed with sleep, and her eyelids hung heavy over their pupils. The brimfulness of her nature breathed from her. It was a moment when a woman's soul is more incarnate than at any other time; when the most spiritual beauty bespeaks itself flesh; and sex takes the outside place in the presentation.

Then those eyes flashed brightly through their filmy heaviness, before the remainder of her face was well awake. With an oddly compounded look of gladness, shyness, and surprise, she exclaimed –

'O Mr Clare! How you frightened me – I—'

There had not at first been time for her to think of the changed relations which his declaration had introduced; but the full sense of the matter rose up in her face when she encountered Clare's tender look as he stepped forward to the bottom stair.

'Dear, darling Tessy!' he whispered, putting his arm round her, and his face to her flushed cheek. 'Don't, for Heaven's sake, Mister me any more. I have hastened back so soon because of you!'

Tess's excitable heart beat against his by way of reply; and there they stood upon the red-brick floor of the entry, the sun slanting in by the window upon his back, as he held her tightly to his breast; upon her inclining face, upon the blue veins of her temple, upon her naked arm, and her neck, and into the depths of her hair. Having been lying down in her clothes she was warm as a sunned cat. At first she would not look straight up at him, but her eyes soon lifted, and his plumbed the deepness of the ever-varying pupils, with their radiating fibrils of blue, and black, and gray, and violet, while she regarded him as Eve at her second waking might have regarded Adam.[2]

'I've got to go a-skimming,' she pleaded, 'and I have on'y old Deb to help me to-day. Mrs Crick is gone to market wi' Mr Crick, and Retty is not well, and the others are gone out somewhere, and won't be home till milking.'

As they retreated to the milk-house Deborah Fyander appeared on the stairs.

'I have come back, Deborah,' said Mr Clare, upwards. 'So I can help Tess with the skimming; and, as you are very tired, I am sure, you needn't come down till milking-time.'

Possibly the Talbothays milk was not very thoroughly skimmed that afternoon. Tess was in a dream wherein familiar objects appeared as having light and shade and position, but no particular outline. Every time she held the skimmer under the pump to cool it for the work her hand trembled, the ardour of his affection being so palpable that she seemed to flinch under it like a plant in too burning a sun.

Then he pressed her again to his side, and when she had done running her forefinger round the leads to cut off the cream-edge he cleaned it in nature's way; for the unconstrained manners of Talbothays dairy came convenient now.

'I may as well say it now as later, dearest,' he resumed gently. 'I wish to ask you something of a very practical nature, which I have been thinking of ever since that day last week in the meads. I shall soon want to marry, and, being a farmer, you see I shall require for my wife a woman who knows all about the management of farms. Will you be that woman, Tessy?'

He put it in that way that she might not think he had yielded to an impulse of which his head would disapprove.

She turned quite pale. She had bowed to the inevitable result of proximity, the necessity of loving him; but she had not calculated upon this sudden corollary, which, indeed, Clare had put before her without quite meaning himself to do it so soon. With pain that was like the bitterness of dissolution she murmured the words of her indispensable and sworn answer as an honourable woman.

'Oh, Mr Clare – I cannot be your wife – I cannot be!'

The sound of her own decision seemed to break Tess's very heart, and she bowed her face in her grief.

'But, Tess!' he said, amazed at her reply, and holding her still more greedily close. 'Do you say no? Surely you love me?'

'O yes, yes! And I would rather marry you than anybody in the world,' returned the honest voice of the distressed girl. 'But I *cannot* marry you!'

'Tess,' he said, holding her at arm's length, 'you are engaged to marry some one else!'

'No, no!'

'Then why do you refuse me?'

'I don't want to marry. I have not thought o' doing it. I cannot. I only want to love you.'

'But why?'

Driven to subterfuge, she stammered –

'Your father is a parson, and your mother wouldn' like you to marry such as me. She will want you to marry a lady.'

'Nonsense – I have spoken to them both. That was partly why I went home.'

'I feel I cannot – never, never!' she echoed.[3]

'Is it too sudden to be asked thus, my Pretty?'

'Yes – I did not expect it.'

'If you will let it pass, please, Tessy, I will give you time,' he said. 'It was very abrupt to come home and speak to you all at once. I'll not allude to it again for a while.'

She again took up the shining skimmer, held it beneath the pump, and began anew. But she could not, as at other times, hit the exact under-surface of the cream with the delicate dexterity required, try as she might: sometimes she was cutting down into the milk, sometimes in the air. She could hardly see, her eyes having filled with two blurring tears drawn forth by a grief which, to this her best friend and dear advocate, she could never explain.

'I can't skim – I can't!' she said, turning away from him.

Not to agitate and hinder her longer the gentle Clare began talking in a more general way:

'You quite misapprehend my parents. They are the most simple-mannered people alive, and quite unambitious. They are two of the few remaining Evangelical school. Tessy, are you an Evangelical?'

'I don't know.'

'You go to church very regularly, and our parson here is not very High, they tell me.'

Tess's ideas on the views of the parish clergyman, whom she heard every week, seemed to be rather more vague than Clare's, who had never heard him at all.

'I wish I could fix my mind on what I hear there more firmly than I do,' she remarked as a safe generality. 'It is often a great sorrow to me.'

She spoke so unaffectedly that Angel was sure in his heart that his father could not object to her on religious grounds, even though she did not know whether her principles were High, Low, or Broad. He himself knew that, in reality, the confused beliefs which she held, apparently imbibed in childhood, were, if anything, Tractarian as to phraseology, and Pantheistic as to essence.[4] Confused or otherwise, to disturb them was his last desire:

> Leave thou thy sister when she prays,
>   Her early Heaven, her happy views;
>   Nor thou with shadow'd hint confuse
> A life that leads melodious days.[5]

He had occasionally thought the counsel less honest than musical; but he gladly conformed to it now.

He spoke further of the incidents of his visit, of his father's mode of life, of his zeal for his principles; she grew serener, and the undulations disappeared from her skimming; as she finished one lead after another he followed her, and drew the plugs for letting down the milk.

'I fancied you looked a little downcast when you came in,' she ventured to observe, anxious to keep away from the subject of herself.

'Yes – well, my father has been talking a good deal to me of his

troubles and difficulties, and the subject always tends to depress me.
He is so zealous that he gets many snubs and buffetings from people
of a different way of thinking from himself, and I don't like to hear of
such humiliations to a man of his age, the more particularly as I don't
think earnestness does any good when carried so far. He has been
telling me of a very unpleasant scene in which he took part quite
recently. He went as the deputy of some missionary society to preach
in the neighbourhood of Trantridge, a place forty miles from here,
and made it his business to expostulate with a young rake-hell he met
with somewhere about there – son of some landowner up that way –
and who has a mother afflicted with blindness. My father addressed
himself to the gentleman point-blank, and there was quite a disturbance. It was very foolish of my father, I must say, to intrude his
conversation upon a stranger when the probabilities were so obvious
that it would be useless. But whatever he thinks to be his duty, that
he'll do, in season or out of season;[6] and, of course, he makes many
enemies, not only among the absolutely vicious, but among the easy-
going, who hate being bothered. He says he glories in what happened,
and that good may be done indirectly; but I wish he would not so
wear himself out now he is getting old, and would leave such pigs to
their wallowing.'

Tess's look had grown hard and worn, and her ripe mouth tragical;
but she no longer showed any tremulousness. Clare's revived thoughts
of his father prevented his noticing her particularly; and so they went
on down the white row of liquid rectangles till they had finished and
drained them off, when the other maids returned, and took their pails,
and Deb came to scald out the leads for the new milk. As Tess withdrew
to go afield to the cows he said to her softly –

'And my question, Tessy?'

'O no – no!' replied she with grave firmness, as one who heard
anew the turmoil of her own past. 'It *can't* be!'

She went out towards the mead, joining the other milkmaids with
a bound, as if trying to make the open air drive away her sad constraint.
All the girls drew onward to the spot where the cows were grazing in
the farther mead, the bevy advancing with the bold grace of wild
animals – the reckless unchastened motion of women accustomed to

unlimited space – in which they abandoned themselves to the air as a swimmer to the wave. It seemed natural enough to him now that Tess was again in sight to choose a mate from unconstrained Nature, and not from the abodes of Art.

XXVIII

Her refusal, though unexpected, did not permanently daunt Clare. His experience of women was great enough for him to be aware that the negative often meant nothing more than the preface to the affirmative; and it was little enough for him not to know that in the manner of the present negative there lay a great exception to the dallyings of coyness. That she had already permitted him to make love to her he read as an additional assurance, not fully trowing that in the fields and pastures to 'sigh gratis'[1] is by no means deemed waste; love-making being here more often accepted inconsiderately and for its own sweet sake than in the carking anxious homes of the ambitious, where a girl's craving for an establishment paralyzes her healthy thought of a passion as an end.

'Tess, why did you say "no" in such a positive way?' he asked her in the course of a few days.

She started.

'Don't ask me. I told you – partly. I am not good enough – not worthy enough.'

'How? Not fine lady enough?'

'Yes – something like that,' murmured she. 'Your friends would scorn me.'

'Indeed, you mistake them – my father and mother. As for my brothers, I don't care—' He clasped his fingers behind her back to keep her from slipping away. 'Now – you did not mean it, sweet? – I am sure you did not! You have made me so restless that I cannot read, or play, or do anything. I am in no hurry, Tess, but I want to know – to hear from your own warm lips – that you will some day be mine – any time you may choose; but some day?'

She could only shake her head and look away from him.

Clare regarded her attentively, conned the characters of her face as if they had been hieroglyphics. The denial seemed real.

'Then I ought not to hold you in this way – ought I? I have no right to you – no right to seek out where you are, or to walk with you! Honestly, Tess, do you love any other man?'

'How can you ask?' she said, with continued self-suppression.

'I almost know that you do not. But then, why do you repulse me?'

'I don't repulse you. I like you to – tell me you love me; and you may always tell me so as you go about with me – and never offend me.'

'But you will not accept me as a husband?'

'Ah – that's different – it is for your good, indeed my dearest! O, believe me, it is only for your sake! I don't like to give myself the great happiness o' promising to be yours in that way – because – because I am *sure* I ought not to do it.'

'But you will make me happy!'

'Ah – you think so, but you don't know.'

At such times as this, apprehending the grounds of her refusal to be her sense of incompetence for the position of wife to a man like himself,[2] he would say that she was wonderfully well-informed and versatile – which was certainly true, her natural quickness, and her admiration for him, having led her to pick up his vocabulary, his accent, and fragments of his knowledge, to a surprising extent. After these tender contests and her victory she would go away by herself under the remotest cow, if at milking-time, or into the sedge, or into her room, if at a leisure interval, and mourn silently, not a minute after an apparently phlegmatic negative.[3]

The struggle was so fearful; her own heart was so strongly on the side of his – two ardent hearts against one poor little conscience – that she tried to fortify her resolution by every means in her power. She had come to Talbothays with a made-up mind. On no account could she agree to a step which might afterwards cause bitter rueing to her husband for his blindness in wedding her. And she held that what her conscience had decided for her when her mind was unbiassed ought not to be overruled now.

'Why don't somebody tell him all about me?' she said. 'It was only forty miles off – why hasn't it reached here? Somebody must know!'

Yet nobody seemed to know; nobody told him.

For two or three days no more was said. She guessed from the sad countenances of her chamber companions that they regarded her not only as the favourite, but as the chosen; but they could see for themselves that she did not put herself in his way.

Tess had never before known a time in which the thread of her life was so distinctly twisted of two strands, positive pleasure and positive pain. At the next cheese-making the pair were again left alone together. The dairyman himself had been lending a hand; but Mr Crick, as well as his wife, seemed latterly to have acquired a suspicion of mutual interest between these two; though they walked so circumspectly that suspicion was but of the faintest. Anyhow, the dairyman left them to themselves.

They were breaking up the masses of curd before putting them into the vats. The operation resembled the act of crumbling bread on a large scale; and amid the immaculate whiteness of the curds Tess Durbeyfield's hands showed themselves of the pinkness of the rose. Angel, who was filling the vats with his handfuls, suddenly ceased, and laid his hands flat upon hers. Her sleeves were rolled far above the elbow, and bending lower he kissed the inside vein of her soft arm.[4]

Although the early September weather was sultry, her arm, from her dabbling in the curds, was as cold and damp to his mouth as a new-gathered mushroom, and tasted of the whey. But she was such a sheaf of susceptibilities that her pulse was accelerated by the touch, her blood driven to her finger-ends, and the cool arms flushed hot. Then, as though her heart had said, 'Is coyness longer necessary? Truth is truth between man and woman, as between man and man,' she lifted her eyes, and they beamed devotedly into his, as her lip rose in a tender half-smile.

'Do you know why I did that, Tess?' he said.

'Because you love me very much!'

'Yes, and as a preliminary to a new entreaty.'

'Not *again*!'

She looked a sudden fear that her resistance might break down under her own desire.

'O, Tessy!' he went on, 'I *cannot* think why you are so tantalizing. Why do you disappoint me so? You seem almost like a coquette, upon my life you do – a coquette of the first urban water![5] They blow hot and blow cold, just as you do; and it is the very last sort of thing to expect to find in a retreat like Talbothays ... And yet, dearest,' he quickly added, observing how the remark had cut her, 'I know you to be the most honest, spotless creature that ever lived. So how can I suppose you a flirt? Tess, why don't you like the idea of being my wife, if you love me as you seem to do?'

'I have never said I don't like the idea, and I never could say it; because – it isn't true!'

The stress now getting beyond endurance her lip quivered, and she was obliged to go away. Clare was so pained and perplexed that he ran after and caught her in the passage.

'Tell me, tell me!' he said, passionately clasping her, in forgetfulness of his curdy hands, 'do tell me that you won't belong to anybody but me!'

'I will, I will tell you!' she exclaimed. 'And I will give you a complete answer, if you will let me go now. I will tell you my experiences – all about myself – all!'

'Your experiences, dear; yes, certainly; any number.' He expressed assent in loving satire, looking into her face. 'My Tess has, no doubt, almost as many experiences as that wild convolvulus out there on the garden hedge, that opened itself this morning for the first time. Tell me anything, but don't use that wretched expression any more about not being worthy of me.'

'I will try – not! And I'll give you my reasons to-morrow – next week.'

'Say on Sunday?'

'Yes, on Sunday.'

At last she got away, and did not stop in her retreat till she was in the thicket of pollard willows at the lower side of the barton, where she could be quite unseen. Here Tess flung herself down upon the rustling undergrowth of spear-grass, as upon a bed, and remained crouching in palpitating misery broken by momentary shoots of joy, which her fears about the ending could not altogether suppress.

In reality, she was drifting into acquiescence. Every see-saw of her breath, every wave of her blood, every pulse singing in her ears, was a voice that joined with nature in revolt against her scrupulousness. Reckless, inconsiderate acceptance of him; to close with him at the altar, revealing nothing, and chancing discovery; to snatch ripe pleasure before the iron teeth of pain could have time to shut upon her:[6] that was what love counselled; and in almost a terror of ecstasy Tess divined that, despite her many months of lonely self-chastisement, wrestlings, communings, schemes to lead a future of austere isolation, love's counsel would prevail.[7]

The afternoon advanced, and still she remained among the willows. She heard the rattle of taking down the pails from the forked stands; the 'waow-waow!' which accompanied the getting together of the cows. But she did not go to the milking. They would see her agitation; and the dairyman, thinking the cause to be love alone, would good-naturedly tease her; and that harassment could not be borne.

Her lover must have guessed her overwrought state, and invented some excuse for her non-appearance, for no inquiries were made or calls given. At half-past six the sun settled down upon the levels, with the aspect of a great forge in the heavens, and presently a monstrous pumpkin-like moon arose on the other hand. The pollard willows, tortured out of their natural shape by incessant choppings, became spiny-haired monsters as they stood up against it. She went in, and upstairs without a light.

It was now Wednesday. Thursday came, and Angel looked thoughtfully at her from a distance, but intruded in no way upon her. The indoor milkmaids, Marian and the rest, seemed to guess that something definite was afoot, for they did not force any remarks upon her in the bedchamber. Friday passed; Saturday. To-morrow was the day.

'I shall gie way – I shall say yes – I shall let myself marry him – I cannot help it!' she jealously panted, with her hot face to the pillow that night, on hearing one of the other girls sigh his name in her sleep. 'I can't bear to let anybody have him but me! Yet it is a wrong to him, and may kill him when he knows! O my heart – O – O – O!'

XXIX

'Now, who mid ye think I've heard news o' this morning?' said Dairyman Crick, as he sat down to breakfast next day, with a riddling gaze round upon the munching men and maids. 'Now just who mid ye think?'

One guessed, and another guessed. Mrs Crick did not guess, because she knew already.

'Well,' said the dairyman, ''tis that slack-twisted 'hor's-bird of a feller, Jack Dollop. He's lately got married to a widow-woman.'

'Not Jack Dollop? A villain – to think o' that!' said a milker.

The name entered quickly into Tess Durbeyfield's consciousness, for it was the name of the lover who had wronged his sweetheart, and had afterwards been so roughly used by the young woman's mother in the butter-churn.

'And has he married the valiant matron's daughter, as he promised?' asked Angel Clare absently, as he turned over the newspaper he was reading at the little table to which he was always banished by Mrs Crick, in her sense of his gentility.

'Not he, sir. Never meant to,' replied the dairyman. 'As I say, 'tis a widow-woman, and she had money, it seems – fifty poun' a year or so; and that was all he was after. They were married in a great hurry; and then she told him that by marrying she had lost her fifty poun' a year. Just fancy the state o' my gentleman's mind at that news! Never such a cat-and-dog life as they've been leading ever since! Serves him well beright. But unluckily the poor woman gets the worst o't.'

'Well, the silly body should have told him sooner that the ghost of her first man would trouble him,' said Mrs Crick.

'Yes, yes,' responded the dairyman indecisively. 'Still, you can see exactly how it was. She wanted a home, and didn't like to run the risk of losing him. Don't ye think that was something like it, maidens?'

He glanced towards the row of girls.

'She ought to ha' told him just before they went to church, when he could hardly have backed out,' exclaimed Marian.

'Yes, she ought,' agreed Izz.

'She must have seen what he was after, and should ha' refused him,' cried Retty spasmodically.

'And what do you say, my dear?' asked the dairyman of Tess.

'I think she ought – to have told him the true state of things – or else refused him – I don't know,' replied Tess, the bread and butter choking her.

'Be cust if I'd have done either o't,' said Beck Nibbs, a married helper from one of the cottages. 'All's fair in love and war. I'd ha' married en just as she did, and if he'd said two words to me about not telling him beforehand anything whatsomdever about my first chap that I hadn't chose to tell, I'd ha' knocked him down wi' the rolling-pin – a scram little feller like he! Any woman could do it.'

The laughter which followed this sally was supplemented only by a sorry smile, for form's sake, from Tess. What was comedy to them was tragedy to her; and she could hardly bear their mirth. She soon rose from table, and with an impression that Clare would follow her, went along a little wriggling path, now stepping to one side of the irrigating channels, and now to the other, till she stood by the main stream of the Var. Men had been cutting the water-weeds higher up the river, and masses of them were floating past her – moving islands of green crowfoot, on which she might almost have ridden; long locks of which weed had lodged against the piles driven to keep the cows from crossing.

Yes, there was the pain of it. This question of a woman telling her story – the heaviest of crosses to herself – seemed but amusement to others.[1] It was as if people should laugh at martyrdom.

'Tessy!' came from behind her, and Clare sprang across the gully, alighting beside her feet. 'My wife – soon – I may say?'

'No, no; I cannot. For your sake, O Mr Clare; for your sake, I say no!'

'Tess!'

'Still I say no!' she repeated.

Not expecting this he had put his arm lightly round her waist the moment after speaking, beneath her hanging tail of hair. (The younger dairymaids, including Tess, breakfasted with their hair loose on Sunday mornings before building it up extra high for attending church, a style they could not adopt when milking with their heads against the cows.) If she had said 'Yes' instead of 'No' he would have kissed her; it had evidently been his intention; but her determined negative deterred his scrupulous heart. Their condition of domiciliary comradeship put her, as the woman, to such disadvantage by its enforced intercourse, that he felt it unfair to her to exercise any pressure of blandishment which he might have honestly employed had she been better able to avoid him. He released her momentarily-imprisoned waist, and withheld the kiss.

It all turned on that release. What had given her strength to refuse him this time was solely the tale of the widow told by the dairyman; and that would have been overcome in another moment. But Angel said no more; his face was perplexed; he went away.

Day after day they met – somewhat less constantly than before; and thus two or three weeks went by. The end of September drew near, and she could see in his eye that he might ask her again.

His plan of procedure was different now – as though he had made up his mind that her negatives were, after all, only coyness and youth startled by the novelty of the proposal. The fitful evasiveness of her manner when the subject was under discussion countenanced the idea. So he played a more coaxing game; and while never going beyond words, or attempting the renewal of caresses, he did his utmost orally.

In this way Clare persistently wooed her in undertones like that of the purling milk – at the cow's side, at skimmings, at butter-makings, at cheese-makings, among broody poultry, and among farrowing pigs – as no milkmaid was ever wooed before by such a man.

Tess knew that she must break down. Neither a religious sense of a certain moral validity in the previous union nor a conscientious wish for candour could hold out against it much longer.[2] She loved him so passionately, and he was so godlike in her eyes; and being, though untrained, instinctively refined, her nature cried for his tutelary guidance. And thus, though Tess kept repeating to herself, 'I can never be his wife,' the words were vain. A proof of her weakness lay in the very utterance of what calm strength would not have taken the trouble to formulate. Every sound of his voice beginning on the old subject stirred her with a terrifying bliss, and she coveted the recantation she feared.

His manner was – what man's is not? – so much that of one who would love and cherish and defend her under any conditions, changes, charges, or revelations, that her gloom lessened as she basked in it. The season meanwhile was drawing onward to the equinox, and though it was still fine, the days were much shorter. The dairy had again worked by morning candle-light for a long time; and a fresh renewal of Clare's pleading occurred one morning between three and four.

She had run up in her bedgown to his door to call him as usual; then had gone back to dress and call the others; and in ten minutes was walking to the head of the stairs with the candle in her hand. At the same moment he came down his steps from above in his shirt-sleeves and put his arm across the stair-way.

'Now, Miss Flirt, before you go down,' he said peremptorily. 'It is a fortnight since I spoke, and this won't do any longer. You *must* tell me what you mean, or I shall have to leave this house. My door was ajar just now, and I saw you. For your own safety I must go. You don't know. Well? Is it to be yes at last?'

'I am only just up, Mr Clare, and it is too early to take me to task!' she pouted. 'You need not call me Flirt. 'Tis cruel and untrue. Wait till by and by. Please wait till by and by! I will really think seriously about it between now and then. Let me go downstairs!'

She looked a shade like what he said she was as, holding the candle sideways, she tried to smile away the seriousness of her words.

'Call me Angel, then, and not Mr Clare.'

'Angel.'

'Angel, dearest – why not?'

''Twould mean that I agree, wouldn't it?'

'It would only mean that you love me, even if you cannot marry me; and you were so good as to own that long ago.'

'Very well, then, "Angel, dearest," if I *must*,' she murmured, looking at her candle, a roguish curl coming upon her mouth, notwithstanding her suspense.

Clare had resolved never to kiss her until he had obtained her promise; but somehow, as Tess stood there in her prettily tucked-up milking-gown, her hair carelessly heaped upon her head till there should be leisure to arrange it when skimming and milking were done, he broke his resolve, and brought his lips to her cheek for one moment. She passed downstairs very quickly, never looking back at him, or saying another word. The other maids were already down, and the subject was not pursued. Except Marian they all looked wistfully and suspiciously at the pair, in the sad yellow rays which the morning candles emitted in contrast with the first cold signals of the dawn without.

When skimming was done – which, as the milk diminished with the approach of autumn, was a lessening process day by day – Retty and the rest went out. The lovers followed them.

'Our tremulous lives are so different from theirs, are they not?' he musingly observed to her, as he regarded the three figures tripping before him through the frigid pallor of opening day.

'Not so very different, I think,' she said.

'Why do you think that?'

'There be very few women's lives that are not – tremulous,' Tess replied, pausing over the new word as if it impressed her. 'There's more in those three than you think.'

'What is in them?'

'Almost – either of 'em,' she began, 'would make – perhaps would make – a properer wife than I. And perhaps they love you as well as I – almost.'

'O, Tessy!'

There were signs that it was an exquisite relief to her to hear the impatient exclamation, though she had resolved so intrepidly to let generosity make one bid against herself. That was now done, and she had not the power to attempt self-immolation a second time then. They were joined by a milker from one of the cottages, and no more was said on that which concerned them so deeply. But Tess knew that this day would decide it.[3]

In the afternoon several of the dairyman's household and assistants went down to the meads as usual, a long way from the dairy, where many of the cows were milked without being driven home. The supply was getting less as the animals were advancing in calf, and the supernumerary milkers of the lush green season had been dismissed.

The work progressed leisurely. Each pailful was poured into tall cans that stood in a large spring-waggon which had been brought upon the scene; and when they were milked the cows trailed away.

Dairyman Crick, who was there with the rest, his wrapper gleaming miraculously white against a leaden evening sky, suddenly looked at his heavy watch.

'Why, 'tis later than I thought,' he said. 'Begad! We shan't be soon enough with this milk at the station, if we don't mind. There's no time to-day to take it home and mix it with the bulk afore sending off. It must go to station straight from here. Who'll drive it across?'

Mr Clare volunteered to do so, though it was none of his business, asking Tess to accompany him. The evening, though sunless, had been warm and muggy for the season, and Tess had come out with her milking-hood only, naked-armed and jacketless; certainly not dressed for a drive. She therefore replied by glancing over her scant habiliments; but Clare gently urged her. She assented by relinquishing her pail and stool to the dairyman to take home; and mounted the spring-waggon beside Clare.

XXX

In the diminishing daylight they went along the level roadway through the meads, which stretched away into gray miles, and were backed in the extreme edge of distance by the swarthy abrupt slopes of Egdon Heath. On its summit stood clumps and stretches of fir-trees, whose notched tips appeared like battlemented towers crowning black-fronted castles of enchantment.

They were so absorbed in the sense of being close to each other that they did not begin talking for a long while, the silence being broken only by the clucking of the milk in the tall cans behind them. The lane they followed was so solitary that the hazel nuts had remained on the boughs till they slipped from their shells, and the blackberries hung in heavy clusters. Every now and then Angel would fling the lash of his whip round one of these, pluck it off, and give it to his companion.

The dull sky soon began to tell its meaning by sending down herald-drops of rain, and the stagnant air of the day changed into a fitful breeze which played about their faces. The quicksilvery glaze on the rivers and pools vanished; from broad mirrors of light they changed to lustreless sheets of lead, with a surface like a rasp. But that spectacle did not affect her preoccupation. Her countenance, a natural carnation, slightly embrowned by the season, deepened on the cheeks with the beating of the rain-drops, and a portion of her hair, which the pressure of the cows' flanks had, as usual, caused to tumble down from its fastenings, hung below the curtain of her calico bonnet; the rain began to make it clammy, till it hardly was better than seaweed.

'I ought not to have come, I suppose,' she murmured, looking at the sky.

'I am sorry for the rain,' said he. 'But how glad I am to have you here!'

Remote Egdon disappeared by degrees behind the liquid gauze. The evening grew darker, and the roads being crossed by gates it was not safe to drive faster than at a walking pace. The air was rather chill.

'I am so afraid you will get cold, with nothing upon your arms and shoulders,' he said. 'Creep close to me, and perhaps the drizzle won't hurt you much. I should be sorrier still if I did not think that the rain might be helping me.'

She imperceptibly crept closer, and he wrapped round them both a large piece of sail-cloth, which was sometimes used to keep the sun off the milk-cans. Tess held it from slipping off him as well as herself, Clare's hands being occupied.

'Now we are all right again. Ah – no we are not! It runs down into my neck a little, and it must still more into yours. That's better. Your arms are like wet marble, Tess. Wipe them in the cloth. Now, if you stay quiet, you will not get another drop. Well, dear – about that question of mine – that long-standing question?'

The only reply that he could hear for a little while was the smack of the horse's hoofs on the moistening road, and the cluck of the milk in the cans behind them.

'Do you remember what you said?'

'I do,' she replied.

'Before we get home, mind.'

'I'll try.'

He said no more then. As they drove the fragment of an old manor-house of Caroline date[1] rose against the sky, and was in due course passed and left behind.

'That,' he observed, to entertain her, 'is an interesting old place – one of the several seats which belonged to an ancient Norman family formerly of great influence in this county, the D'Urbervilles. I never pass one of their residences without thinking of them. There is something very sad in the extinction of a family of renown, even if it was fierce, domineering, feudal renown.'

'Yes,' said Tess.

They crept along towards a point in the expanse of shade before them at which a feeble light was beginning to assert its presence, a spot where, by day, a fitful white streak of steam at intervals upon the dark green background denoted intermittent moments of contact between their secluded world and modern life. Modern life stretched out its steam feeler to this point three or four times a day, touched the native existences, and quickly withdrew its feeler again, as if what it touched had been uncongenial.

They reached the feeble light, which came from the smoky lamp of a little railway-station; a poor enough terrestrial star,[2] yet in one sense of more importance to Talbothays Dairy[3] and mankind than the celestial ones to which it stood in such humiliating contrast. The cans of new milk were unladen in the rain, Tess getting a little shelter from a neighbouring holly tree.

Then there was the hissing of a train, which drew up almost silently upon the wet rails, and the milk was rapidly swung can by can into the truck. The light of the engine flashed for a second upon Tess Durbeyfield's figure, motionless under the great holly tree. No object could have looked more foreign to the gleaming cranks and wheels than this unsophisticated girl, with the round bare arms, the rainy face and hair, the suspended attitude of a friendly leopard at pause, the print gown of no date or fashion, and the cotton bonnet drooping on her brow.

She mounted again beside her lover, with a mute obedience characteristic of impassioned natures at times, and when they had wrapped themselves up over head and ears in the sail-cloth again, they plunged back into the now thick night. Tess was so susceptible that the few minutes of contact with the whirl of material progress lingered in her thought.

'Londoners will drink it at their breakfasts to-morrow, won't they?' she asked. 'Strange people that we have never seen.'

'Yes – I suppose they will. Though not as we send it. When its strength has been lowered, so that it may not get up into their heads.'

'Noble men and noble women, ambassadors and centurions, ladies and tradeswomen, and babies who have never seen a cow.'

'Well, yes; perhaps; particularly centurions.'

'Who don't know anything of us, and where it comes from; or think how we two drove miles across the moor to-night in the rain that it might reach 'em in time?'

'We did not drive entirely on account of these precious Londoners; we drove a little on our own – on account of that anxious matter which you will, I am sure, set at rest, dear Tess. Now, permit me to put it in this way. You belong to me already, you know; your heart, I mean. Does it not?'

'You know as well as I. O yes – yes!'

'Then, if your heart does, why not your hand?'

'My only reason was on account of you – on account of a question. I have something to tell you—'

'But suppose it to be entirely for my happiness, and my worldly convenience also?'

'O yes; if it is for your happiness and worldly convenience. But my last experiences, I want—'

'Well, it is for my convenience as well as my happiness. If I have a very large farm, either English or Colonial, you will be invaluable as a wife to me; better than a woman out of the largest mansion in the country. So please – please, dear Tessy, disabuse your mind of the feeling that you will stand in my way.'

'But my history. I want you to know it – you must let me tell you – you will not like me so well!'

'Tell it if you wish to, dearest. This precious history then. Yes, I was born at so and so, Anno Domini—'

'I was born at Marlott,' she said, catching at his words as a help, lightly as they were spoken. 'And I grew up there. And I was in the Sixth Standard when I left school, and they said I had great aptness, and should make a good teacher, so it was settled that I should be one. But there was trouble in my family; my father was not very industrious, and he drank a little.'

'Yes, yes. Poor child! Nothing new.' He pressed her more closely to his side.

'And then – there is something very peculiar about it – about me.'
Tess's breath quickened.

'Yes, dearest. Never mind.'

'I – I – am not a Durbeyfield, but a D'Urberville – a descendant of the same family as those who owned the old house we passed. And – we are all gone to nothing!'

'A D'Urberville! – Indeed! And is that all the trouble, dear Tess?'

'Yes,' she answered faintly.

'Well – why should I love you less after knowing this?'

'I was told by the dairyman that you hated old families.'

He laughed.

'Well, it is true, in one sense. I do hate the aristocratic principle of blood before everything, and do think that as reasoners the only pedigrees we ought to respect are those spiritual ones of the wise and virtuous, without regard to corporeal paternity. But I am extremely interested in this news – you can have no idea how interested I am. Are not you interested yourself in being one of that well-known line?'

'No. I have thought it sad – especially since coming here, and knowing that many of the hills and fields I see once belonged to my father's people. But other hills and fields belonged to Retty's people, and perhaps others to Marian's, so that I don't value it particularly.'

'Yes – it is surprising how many of the present tillers of the soil were once owners of it, and I sometimes wonder that a certain school of politicians don't make capital of the circumstance;[4] but they don't seem to know it ... I wonder that I did not see the resemblance of your name to D'Urberville, and trace the manifest corruption. And this was the carking secret!'

She had not told. At the last moment her courage had failed her, she feared his blame for not telling him sooner; and her instinct of self-preservation was stronger than her candour.

'Of course,' continued the unwitting Clare, 'I should have been glad to know you to be descended exclusively from the long-suffering, dumb, unrecorded rank and file of the English nation, and not from the self-seeking few who made themselves powerful at the expense of the rest. But I am corrupted away from that by my affection for you, Tess [he laughed as he spoke], and made selfish likewise. For your own sake I rejoice in your descent. Society is hopelessly snobbish, and this fact of your extraction may make an appreciable difference to its acceptance of you as my wife, after I have made you the well-read woman that I mean to make you. My mother too, poor soul, will think so much better of you on account of it. Tess, you must spell your name correctly – D'Urberville – from this very day.'

'I like the other way rather best.'

'But you *must*, dearest! Good heavens, why dozens of mushroom millionaires would jump at such a possession! By the bye, there's one of that kidney who has taken the name – where have I heard of him? – Up in the neighbourhood of The Chase, I think. Why, he is the very man who had that rumpus with my father I told you of. What an odd coincidence!'

'Angel, I think I would rather not take the name! It is unlucky, perhaps!'

She was agitated.

'Now then, Mistress Teresa D'Urberville, I have you. Take my name, and so you will escape yours! The secret is out, so why should you any longer refuse me?'

'If it is *sure* to make you happy to have me as your wife, and you feel that you do wish to marry me, *very, very* much—'

'I do, dearest, of course!'

'I mean, that it is only your wanting me very much, and being hardly able to keep alive without me, whatever my offences, that would make me feel I ought to say I will.'

'You will – you do say it, I know! You will be mine for ever and ever.'

He clasped her close and kissed her.

'Yes.'

She had no sooner said it than she burst into a dry hard sobbing, so violent that it seemed to rend her. Tess was not a hysterical girl by any means, and he was surprised.

'Why do you cry, dearest?'

'I can't tell – quite! – I am so glad to think – of being yours, and making you happy!'

'But this does not seem very much like gladness, my Tessy!'

'I mean – I cry because I have broken down in my vow! I said I would die unmarried.'

'But, if you love me you would like me to be your husband?'

'Yes, yes, yes! But O, I sometimes wish I had never been born!'[5]

'Now, my dear Tess, if I did not know that you are very much excited, and very inexperienced, I should say that remark was not very complimentary. How came you to wish that if you care for me? Do you care for me? I wish you would prove it in some way.'

'How can I prove it more than I have done?' she cried, in a distraction of tenderness. 'Will this prove it more?'

She clasped his neck, and for the first time Clare learnt what an impassioned woman's kisses were like upon the lips of one whom she loved with all her heart and soul, as Tess loved him.

'There – now do you believe?' she asked, flushed, and wiping her eyes.

'Yes. I never really doubted – never, never!'

So they drove on through the gloom, forming one bundle inside the sail-cloth, the horse going as he would, and the rain driving against them. She had consented. She might as well have agreed at first. The 'appetite for joy'[6] which pervades all creation, that tremendous force which sways humanity to its purpose, as the tide sways the helpless weed, was not to be controlled by vague lucubrations over the social rubric.[7]

'I must write to my mother,' she said. 'You don't mind my doing that?'

'Of course not, dear child. You are a child to me, Tess, not to know how very proper it is to write to your mother at such a time, and how wrong it would be in me to object. Where does she live?'

'At the same place – Marlott. On the farther side of Blackmoor Vale.'

'Ah, then I *have* seen you before this summer—'

'Yes; at that dance on the green; but you would not dance with me. O, I hope that is of no ill-omen for us now!'

XXXI

Tess wrote a most touching and urgent letter to her mother the very next day, and by the end of the week a response to her communication arrived in Joan Durbeyfield's wandering last-century hand.[1]

DEAR TESS, – J write these few lines Hoping they will find you well, as they leave me at present, thank God for it. Dear Tess, we are all glad to Hear that you are going really to be married soon. But with respect to your question, Tess, J say between ourselves, quite private but very strong, that on no account do you say a word of your Bygone Trouble to him. J did not tell everything to your Father, he being so proud on account of his Respectability, which, perhaps, your Intended is the same. Many a woman – some of the Highest in the Land – have had a Trouble in their time; and why should you Trumpet yours when others don't Trumpet theirs? No girl would be such a Fool, especially as it is so long ago, and not your Fault at all. J shall answer the same if you ask me fifty times. Besides, you must bear in mind that, knowing it to be your Childish Nature to tell all that's in your heart – so simple! – J made you promise me never to let it out by Word or Deed, having your welfare in my Mind; and you solemnly did promise going from this Door. J have not mentioned either that Question or your coming Marriage to your Father, as he would blab it everywhere, poor Simple Man.

Dear Tess, keep up your Spirits, and we mean to send you a Hogshead of Cider for your Wedding, knowing there is not much in your parts, and thin Sour Stuff what there is. So no more at present, and with kind love to your Young Man. – From your affectte. Mother,

J. DURBEYFIELD.

'O mother, mother!' murmured Tess.

She was recognizing how light was the touch of events the most oppressive upon Mrs Durbeyfield's elastic spirit. Her mother did not see life as Tess saw it. That haunting episode of bygone days[2] was to her mother but a passing accident. But perhaps her mother was right as to the course to be followed, whatever she might be in her reasons. Silence seemed, on the face of it, best for her adored one's happiness: silence it should be.

Thus steadied by a command from the only person in the world who had any shadow of right to control her action, Tess grew calmer. The responsibility was shifted, and her heart was lighter than it had been for weeks. The days of declining autumn which followed her assent, beginning with the month of October, formed a season through which she lived in spiritual altitudes more nearly approaching ecstasy than any other period of her life.

There was hardly a touch of earth[3] in her love for Clare. To her sublime trustfulness he was all that goodness could be – knew all that a guide, philosopher, and friend should know.[4] She thought every line in the contour of his person the perfection of masculine beauty, his soul the soul of a saint, his intellect that of a seer. The wisdom of her love for him, as love, sustained her dignity; she seemed to be wearing a crown. The compassion of his love for her, by comparison, made her lift up her heart to him in devotion. He would sometimes catch her large, worshipful eyes, that had no bottom to them, looking at him from their depths, as if she saw something immortal before her.

She dismissed the past – trod upon it and put it out, as one treads on a coal that is smouldering and dangerous.

She had not known that men could be so disinterested, chivalrous, protective, in their love for women as he. Angel Clare was far from all that she thought him in this respect; but he was, in truth, more spiritual than animal; he had himself well in hand, and was singularly free from grossness.[5] Though not cold-natured, he was rather bright than hot – less Byronic than Shelleyan;[6] could love desperately, but his love more especially inclined to the imaginative and ethereal; it was an emotion which could jealously guard the loved one against his very self. This amazed and enraptured Tess, whose slight experiences had been so infelicitous till now; and in her reaction from indignation against the male sex she swerved to excess of honour for Clare.

They unaffectedly sought each other's company; in her honest faith she did not disguise her desire to be with him. The sum of her instincts on this matter, if clearly stated, would have been that the elusive quality in her sex which attracts men in general might be distasteful to so perfect a man after an avowal of love, since it must in its very nature carry with it a suspicion of art.

The country custom of unreserved comradeship out of doors during betrothal was the only custom she knew, and to her it had no strangeness; though it seemed oddly anticipative to Clare till he saw how normal a thing she, in common with all the other dairyfolk, regarded it. Thus, during this October month of wonderful afternoons they roved along the meads by creeping paths which followed the brinks of trickling tributary brooks, hopping across by little wooden bridges to the other side, and back again. They were never out of the sound of some purling weir, whose buzz accompanied their own murmuring, while the beams of the sun, almost as horizontal as the mead itself, formed a pollen of radiance over the landscape. They saw tiny blue fogs in the shadows of trees and hedges, all the time that there was bright sunshine elsewhere. The sun was so near the ground, and the sward so flat, that the shadows of Clare and Tess would stretch a quarter of a mile ahead of them, like two long fingers pointing afar to where the green alluvial reaches abutted against the sloping sides of the vale.

Men were at work here and there – for it was the season for 'taking up' the meadows, or digging the little waterways clear for the winter irrigation, and mending their banks where trodden down by the cows. The shovelfuls of loam, black as jet, brought there by the river when it was as wide as the whole valley, were an essence of soils, pounded champaigns of the past, steeped, refined, and subtilized to extraordinary richness, out of which came all the fertility of the mead, and of the cattle grazing there.

Clare hardily kept his arm round her waist in sight of these watermen, with the air of a man who was accustomed to public dalliance, though actually as shy as she who, with lips parted and eyes askance on the labourers, wore the look of a wary animal the while.

'You are not ashamed of owning me as yours before them!' she said gladly.

'O no!'

'But if it should reach the ears of your friends at Emminster that you are walking about like this with me, a milkmaid—'

'The most bewitching ever seen.'

'They might feel it a hurt to their dignity.'

'My dear girl – a D'Urberville hurt the dignity of a Clare! It is a grand card to play – that of your belonging to such a family, and I am reserving it for a grand effect when we are married, and have the proofs of your descent from Parson Tringham. Apart from that, my future is to be totally foreign to my family – it will not affect even the periphery[7] of their lives. We shall leave this part of England – perhaps England itself – and what does it matter how people regard us here? You will like going, will you not?'

She could answer no more than a bare affirmative, so great was the emotion aroused in her at the thought of going through the world with him as his own familiar friend. Her feelings almost filled her ears like a babble of waves, and surged up to her eyes. She put her hand in his, and thus they went on, to a place where the reflected sun glared up from the river, under a bridge, with a molten-metallic glow that dazzled their eyes, though the sun itself was hidden by the bridge. They stood still, whereupon little furred and feathered heads popped up from the smooth surface of the water; but, finding that the disturbing presences had paused, and not passed by, they disappeared again. Upon this river-brink they lingered till the fog began to close round them – which was very early in the evening at this time of the year – settling on the lashes of her eyes, where it rested like crystals, and on his brows and hair.

They walked later on Sundays, when it was quite dark. Some of the dairy-people, who were also out of doors on the first Sunday evening after their engagement, heard her impulsive speeches, ecstasized to fragments, though they were too far off to hear the words discoursed; noted the spasmodic catch in her remarks, broken into syllables by the leapings of her heart, as she walked leaning on his arm; her contented pauses, the occasional little laugh upon which her soul seemed to ride – the laugh of a woman in company with the man she loves and has won from all other women – unlike anything else in nature. They saw the buoyancy of her tread, like the skim of a bird which has not quite alighted.

Her affection for him was now the breath and life of Tess's being; it enveloped her as a photosphere, irradiated her into forgetfulness of her past sorrows, keeping back the gloomy spectres that would persist in their attempts to touch her – doubt, fear, moodiness, care, shame. She knew that they were waiting like wolves just outside the circum-scribing light, but she had long spells of power to keep them in hungry subjection there.

A spiritual forgetfulness co-existed with an intellectual remem-brance. She walked in brightness, but she knew that in the back-ground those shapes of darkness were always spread. They might be receding, or they might be approaching, one or the other, a little every day.

One evening Tess and Clare were obliged to sit indoors keeping house, all the other occupants of the domicile being away. As they talked she looked thoughtfully up at him, and met his two appreciative eyes.

'I am not worthy of you – no, I am not!' she burst out, jumping up from her low stool as though appalled at his homage, and the fulness of her own joy thereat.

Clare, deeming the whole basis of her excitement to be that which was only the smaller part of it, said –

'I won't have you speak like it, dear Tess! Distinction does not consist in the facile use of a contemptible set of conventions, but in being numbered among those who are true, and honest, and just, and pure, and lovely, and of good report[8] – as you are, my Tess.'

She struggled with the sob in her throat. How often had that string of excellencies made her young heart ache in church of late years, and how strange that he should have cited them now.

'Why didn't you stay and love me when I – was sixteen; living with my little sisters and brothers, and you danced on the green? O, why didn't you, why didn't you!' she said, impetuously clasping her hands.

Angel began to comfort and reassure her, thinking to himself, truly enough, what a creature of moods she was, and how careful he would have to be of her when she depended for her happiness entirely on him.

'Ah – why didn't I come!' he said. 'That is just what I feel. If I had only known! But you must not be so bitter in your regret – why should you be?'

With the woman's instinct to hide she diverged hastily –

'I should have had three years more of your heart than I can ever have now. Then I should not have wasted my time as I have done – I should have had so much longer happiness!'

It was no mature woman with a long dark vista of intrigue behind her who was tormented thus; but a girl of simple life, not yet one-and-twenty, who had been caught during her days of immaturity like a bird in a springe. To calm herself the more completely she rose from her little stool and left the room, overturning the stool with her skirts as she went.

He sat on by the cheerful firelight thrown from a bundle of green ash-sticks laid across the dogs; the sticks snapped pleasantly, and hissed out bubbles of sap from their ends. When she came back she was herself again.

'Do you not think you are just a wee bit capricious, fitful, Tess?' he said, good-humouredly, as he spread a cushion for her on the stool, and seated himself in the settle beside her. 'I wanted to ask you something, and just then you ran away.'

'Yes, perhaps I am capricious,' she murmured. She suddenly approached him, and put a hand upon each of his arms. 'No, Angel, I be not really so – by Nature, I mean!' The more particularly to assure him that she was not, she placed herself close to him in the settle, and allowed her head to find a resting-place against Clare's shoulder. 'What did you want to ask me – I am sure I will answer it,' she continued humbly.

'Well, you love me, and have agreed to marry me, and hence there follows a thirdly, "When shall the day be?"'[9]

'I like living like this.'

'But I must think of starting in business on my own hook with the new year, or a little later. And before I get involved in the multifarious details of my new position, I should like to have secured my partner.'

'But,' she timidly answered, 'to speak quite practically, wouldn't it be best not to marry till after all that? – Though I can't bear the thought o' your going away and leaving me here!'

'Of course you cannot – and it is not best in this case. I want you to help me in many ways in making my start. When shall it be? Why not a fortnight from now?'

'No,' she said, becoming grave; 'I have so many things to think of first.'

'But—'

He drew her gently nearer to him.

The reality of marriage was startling when it loomed so near. Before discussion of the question had proceeded further there walked round the corner of the settle into the full firelight of the apartment Mr Dairyman Crick, Mrs Crick, and two of the milkmaids.

Tess sprang like an elastic ball from his side to her feet, while her face flushed and her eyes shone in the fire-light.

'I knew how it would be if I sat so close to him!' she cried, with vexation. 'I said to myself, they are sure to come and catch us! But I wasn't really sitting on his knee, though it might have seemed as if I was almost.'

'Well – if so be you hadn't told us, I am sure we shouldn' ha' noticed that you had been sitting anywhere at all in this light,' replied the dairyman. He continued to his wife, with the stolid mien of a man who understood nothing of the emotions relating to matrimony – 'Now, Christianer, that shows that folks should never fancy other folks be supposing things when they bain't. Oh no, I should never ha' thought a word of where she was a sitting if she hadn't told me – not I.'

'We are going to be married soon,' said Clare, with improvised phlegm.

'Ah – and be ye! Well, I am truly glad to hear it, sir. I've thought you mid do such a thing for some time. She's too good for a dairymaid – I said so the very first day I saw her – and a prize for any man; and what's more, a wonderful woman for a gentleman-farmer's wife; he won't be at the mercy of his baily wi' her at his side.'

Somehow Tess disappeared. She had been even more struck with the look of the girls who followed Crick than abashed by Crick's blunt praise.

After supper, when she reached her bedroom, they were all present. A light was burning, and each girl was sitting up whitely in her bed, awaiting Tess, like a row of avenging ghosts.

But she saw in a few moments that there was no malice in their mood. They could scarcely feel as a loss what they had never expected to have. Their condition was objective, contemplative.

'He's going to marry her!' murmured Retty, never taking eyes off Tess. 'How her face shows it!'

'You *be* going to marry him?' asked Marian.

'Yes,' said Tess.

'When?'

'Some day.'

They thought that this was evasiveness only.

'*Yes* – going to *marry* him – a gentleman!' repeated Izz Huett.

And by a sort of fascination the three girls, one after another, crept out of their beds, and came and stood barefooted round Tess. Retty put her hands upon Tess's shoulders, as if to realize her friend's corporeality after such a miracle, and the other two laid their arms round her waist, all looking into her face.

'How it do seem! Almost more than I can think of!' said Izz Huett.

Marian kissed Tess. 'Yes,' she murmured as she withdrew her lips.

'Was that because of love for her, or because other lips have touched there by now?' continued Izz drily to Marian.

'I wasn't thinking o' that,' said Marian simply. 'I was on'y feeling all the strangeness o't – that she is to be his wife, and nobody else. I don't say nay to it, nor either of us, because we did not think of it – only loved him. Still, nobody else is to marry him in the world – no fine lady, nobody in jewels and gold, in silks and satins; but she who do live like we.'

'Are you sure you don't dislike me for it?' said Tess in a low voice.

They hung about her in their scant white nightgowns, before replying, as if they considered their answer might lie in her look.

'I don't know – I don't know,' murmured Retty Priddle. 'I want to hate 'ee; but I cannot!'

'That's how I feel,' echoed Izz and Marian. 'I can't hate her. Somehow she hinders me!'

'He ought to marry one of you,' murmured Tess.

'Why?'

'You are all better than I.'

'We better than you?' said the girls in a low, slow whisper. 'No, no, dear Tess!'

'You are!' she contradicted impetuously. And suddenly tearing away from their clinging arms she burst into a hysterical fit of tears, bowing herself on the chest of drawers and repeating incessantly, 'O yes, yes, yes!'

Having once given way she could not stop her weeping.

'He ought to have had one of you!' she cried. 'I think I ought to make him even now! You would be better for him than – I don't know what I am saying! O! O!'

They went up to her and clasped her round, but still her sobs tore her.

'Get some water,' said Marian. 'She's upset by us, poor thing, poor thing!'

They gently led her back to the side of her bed, where they kissed her warmly.

'You are best for'n,' said Marian. 'More ladylike, and a better scholar than we, especially since he has taught 'ee so much. But even you ought to be proud. You *be* proud, I'm sure!'

'Yes, I am,' she said; 'and I am ashamed at so breaking down!'

When they were all in bed, and the light was out, Marian whispered across to her –

'You will think of us when you be his wife, Tess, and of how we told 'ee that we loved him, and how we tried not to hate you, and did not hate you, and could not hate you, because you were his choice, and we never hoped to be chose by him.'

They were not aware that, at these words, salt, stinging tears trickled down upon Tess's pillow anew, and how she resolved, with a bursting heart, to tell all her history to Angel Clare, despite her mother's command – to let him for whom she lived and breathed despise her if he would, and her mother regard her as a fool, rather than preserve a silence which might be deemed a treachery to him, and which somehow seemed a wrong to these.

XXXII

This penitential mood kept her from naming the wedding-day. The beginning of November found its date still in abeyance, though he asked her at the most tempting times. But Tess's desire seemed to be for a perpetual betrothal in which everything should remain as it was then.

The meads were changing now; but it was still warm enough in early afternoons before milking to idle there awhile, and the state of dairy-work at this time of year allowed a spare hour for idling. Looking over the damp sod in the direction of the sun, a glistening ripple of gossamer webs was visible to their eyes under the luminary, like the track of moonlight on the sea. Gnats, knowing nothing of their brief glorification, wandered across the air in this pathway, irradiated as if they bore fire within them, then passed out of its line, and were quite extinct. In the presence of these things he would remind her that the date was still the question.

Or he would ask her at night, when he accompanied her on some mission invented by Mrs Crick to give him the opportunity. This was mostly a journey to the farmhouse on the slopes above the vale, to inquire how the advanced cows were getting on in the straw-barton to which they were relegated. For it was a time of the year that brought great changes to the world of kine. Batches of the animals were sent away daily to this lying-in hospital, where they lived on straw till their calves were born, after which event, and as soon as the calf could walk, mother and offspring were driven back to the dairy. In the interval which elapsed before the calves were sold there was, of course, little milking to be done, but as soon as the calf had been taken away the milkmaids would have to set to work as usual.

Returning from one of these dark walks they reached a great gravel-cliff immediately over the levels, where they stood still and listened. The water was now high in the streams, squirting through the weirs, and tinkling under culverts; the smallest gulleys were all full; there was no taking short cuts anywhere, and foot passengers were compelled to follow the permanent ways. From the whole extent of the invisible vale came a multitudinous intonation; it forced upon their fancy that a great city lay below them, and that the murmur was the vociferation of its populace.

'It seems like tens of thousands of them,' said Tess; 'holding public meetings in their market-places, arguing, preaching, quarrelling, sob-bing, groaning, praying, and cursing.'

Clare was not particularly heeding.

'Did Crick speak to you to-day, dear, about his not wanting much assistance during the winter months?'

'No.'

'The cows are going dry rapidly.'

'Yes,' she answered. 'Six or seven went to the straw-barton yesterday, and three the day before, making nearly twenty in the straw already. Ah – is it that the farmer don't want my help for the calving? O, I am not wanted here any more! And I have tried so hard to—'

'Crick didn't exactly say that he would no longer require you. But, knowing what our relations were, he said in the most good-natured and respectful manner possible that he supposed on my leaving at Christmas I should take you with me, and on my asking what he would do without you he merely observed that, as a matter of fact, it was a time of year when he could do with a very little female help. I am afraid I was sinner enough to feel rather glad that he was in this way forcing your hand.'

'I don't think you ought to have felt glad, Angel. Because 'tis always mournful not to be wanted, even if at the same time 'tis convenient.'

'Well, it is convenient – you have admitted that.' He put his finger upon her cheek. 'Ah!' he said.

'What?'

'I feel the red rising up at her having been caught! But why should I trifle so! We will not trifle – life is too serious.'

'It is – I saw that before you did.'

She was seeing it then. To decline to marry him after all – in obedience to her emotion of last night – and leave the dairy, meant to go to some strange place, not a dairy; for milkmaids were not in request now calving-time was coming on; to go to some arable farm where no divine being like Angel Clare was. She hated the thought, and she hated more the thought of going home.

'So that, seriously, dearest Tess,' he continued, 'since you will probably have to leave at Christmas, it is in every way desirable and convenient that I should carry you off then as my property. Besides, if you were not the most uncalculating girl in the world you would know that we could not go on like this for ever.'

'I wish we could. That it would always be summer and autumn, and you always courting me, and always thinking as much of me as you have done through the past summer-time!'

'I always shall.'

'O, I know you will!' she cried, with a sudden fervour of faith in him. 'Angel, I will fix the day when I will become yours for always!'

Thus at last it was arranged between them, during that dark walk home, amid the myriads of liquid voices on the right and left.

When they reached the dairy Mr and Mrs Crick were promptly told – with injunctions to secrecy; for each of the lovers was desirous that the marriage should be kept as private as possible. The dairyman, though he had thought of dismissing her soon, now made a great concern about losing her. What should he do about his skimming? Who would make the ornamental butter-pats for the Anglebury and Sandbourne ladies? Mrs Crick congratulated Tess on the shilly-shallying having at last come to an end, and said that directly she set eyes on Tess she divined that she was to be the chosen one of somebody who was no common outdoor man; Tess had looked so superior as she walked across the barton on that afternoon of her arrival; that she was of a good family she could have sworn. In point of fact Mrs Crick did remember thinking that Tess was graceful and good-looking as she approached; but the superiority might have been a growth of the imagination aided by subsequent knowledge.

Tess was now carried along upon the wings of the hours, without the sense of a will. The word had been given; the number of the day written down. Her naturally bright intelligence had begun to admit the fatalistic convictions common to field-folk and those who associate more extensively with natural phenomena than with their fellow-creatures; and she accordingly drifted into that passive responsiveness to all things her lover suggested, characteristic of the frame of mind.

But she wrote anew to her mother, ostensibly to notify the wedding-day; really to again implore her advice. It was a gentleman who had chosen her, which perhaps her mother had not sufficiently considered. A post-nuptial explanation, which might be accepted with a light heart by a rougher man, might not be received with the same feeling by him. But this communication brought no reply from Mrs Durbeyfield.

Despite Angel Clare's plausible representations to himself and to Tess of the practical need for their immediate marriage, there was in truth an element of precipitancy in the step, as became apparent at a later date. He loved her dearly, though perhaps rather ideally than with the impassioned thoroughness of her feeling for him. He had entertained no notion, when doomed as he had thought to an unintellectual bucolic life, that such charms as he beheld in this idyllic creature would be found behind the scenes. Unsophistication was a thing to talk of; but he had not known how it really struck one until he came here. But he was very far from seeing his future track clearly, and it might be a year or two before he would be able to consider himself fairly started in life. The secret lay in the tinge of recklessness imparted to his career and character by the sense that he had been made to miss his true destiny through the prejudices of his family.

'Don't you think 'twould ha' been better for us to wait till you were quite settled in your midland farm?' she once asked timidly. (A midland farm was the idea just then.)

'To tell the truth, my Tess, I don't like you to be left anywhere away from my influence and sympathy.'

The reason was a good one, so far as it went. His influence over her had been so marked that she had caught his manner and habits, his speech and phrases, his likings and his aversions. And to leave her in farm-land would be to let her slip back again out of accord with him. He wished to have her under his charge for another reason. His parents had naturally desired to see her once at least before he carried her off to a distant settlement, English or Colonial; and as no opinion of theirs was to be allowed to change his intention, he judged that a couple of months' life with him in lodgings whilst seeking for an advantageous opening would be of some social assistance to her at what she might feel to be a trying ordeal – her presentation to his mother at the Vicarage.

Next, he wished to see a little of the working of a flour-mill, having an idea that he might combine the use of one with corn-growing. The proprietor of a large old water-mill at Wellbridge – once the mill of an Abbey – had offered him the inspection of his time-honoured mode of procedure, and a hand in the operations for a few days, whenever he should choose to come. Clare paid a visit to the place, some few miles distant, one day at this time, to inquire particulars, and returned to Talbothays in the evening. She found him determined to spend a short time at the Wellbridge flour-mills. And what had determined him? Less the opportunity of an insight into grinding and bolting than the casual fact that lodgings were to be obtained in that very farm-house which, before its mutilation, had been the mansion of a branch of the D'Urberville family. This was always how Clare decided practical questions; by a sentiment which had nothing to do with them. They decided to go immediately after the wedding, and remain for a fort-night, instead of journeying to towns and inns.

'Then we will start off to examine some farms on the other side of London that I have heard of,' he said, 'and by March or April we will pay a visit to my father and mother.'

Questions of procedure such as these arose and passed, and the day, the incredible day, on which she was to become his, loomed large in the near future. The thirty-first of December, New Year's Eve, was the date. His wife, she said to herself. Could it ever be? Their two selves together, nothing to divide them, every incident shared by them; why not? And yet why?

One Sunday morning Izz Huett returned from church, and spoke privately to Tess.

'You was not called home* this morning.'

'What?'

'It should ha' been the first time of asking to-day,' she answered, looking quietly at Tess. 'You meant to be married New Year's Eve, deary?'

The other returned a quick affirmative.

'And there must be three times of asking. And now there be only two Sundays left between.'

Tess felt her cheek paling; Izz was right; of course there must be three. Perhaps he had forgotten! If so, there must be a week's postponement, and that was unlucky. How could she remind her lover? She who had been so backward was suddenly fired with impatience and alarm lest she should lose her dear prize.

A natural incident relieved her anxiety. Izz mentioned the omission of the banns to Mrs Crick, and Mrs Crick assumed a matron's privilege of speaking to Angel on the point.

'Have ye forgot 'em, Mr Clare? The banns I mean.'

'No, I have not forgot 'em,' says Clare.

As soon as he caught Tess alone he assured her:

'Don't let them tease you about the banns. A licence will be quieter for us, and I have decided on a licence.¹ So if you go to church on Sunday morning you will not hear your own name if you wished to.'

'I didn't wish to go and hear it, dearest,' she said proudly.

But to know that things were in train was an immense relief to Tess notwithstanding, who had well-nigh feared that somebody would stand up and forbid the banns on the ground of her history. How events were favouring her!

'I don't quite feel easy,' she said to herself. 'All this good fortune may be scourged out o' me afterwards by a lot of ill. That's how Heaven mostly does. I wish I could have had common banns!'

But everything went smoothly. She wondered whether he would like her to be married in her present best white frock, or if she ought

* 'Called home' – local phrase for publication of banns.

to buy a new one. The question was set at rest by his forethought, disclosed by the arrival of some large packages addressed to her. Inside them she found a whole stock of clothing, from bonnet to shoes, including a perfect morning costume, such as would well suit the simple wedding they planned. He entered the house shortly after the arrival of the packages, and heard her upstairs undoing them.

A minute later she came down with a flush on her face and tears in her eyes.

'How thoughtful you've been!' she murmured, her cheek upon his shoulder. 'Even to the gloves and handkerchief! My own love – how good, how kind!'

'No, no, Tess; just an order to a tradeswoman in London – nothing more.'

And to divert her from thinking too highly of him he told her to go upstairs, and take her time, and see if it all fitted; and, if not, to get the village seampstress to make a few alterations.

She did return upstairs, and put on the gown. Alone, she stood for a moment before the glass looking at the effect of her silk attire; and then there came into her head her mother's ballad of the mystic robe –

> That never would become that wife
> That had once done amiss,[2]

which Mrs Durbeyfield had used to sing to her as a child, so blithely and so archly, her foot on the cradle, which she rocked to the tune. Suppose this robe should betray her by changing colour, as her robe had betrayed Queen Guénever. Since she had been at the dairy she had not once thought of the lines till now.

XXXIII

Angel felt that he would like to spend a day with her before the wedding, somewhere away from the dairy, as a last jaunt in her company while they were yet mere lover and mistress; a romantic day, in circumstances that would never be repeated; with that other and greater day beaming close ahead of them. During the preceding week, therefore, he suggested making a few purchases in the nearest town, and they started together.

Clare's life at the dairy had been that of a recluse in respect to the world of his own class. For months he had never gone near a town, and, requiring no vehicle, had never kept one, hiring the dairyman's cob or gig if he rode or drove. They went in the gig that day.

And then for the first time in their lives they shopped as partners in one concern. It was Christmas Eve, with its loads of holly and mistletoe, and the town was very full of strangers who had come in from all parts of the country on account of the day. Tess paid the penalty of walking about with happiness superadded to beauty on her countenance by being much stared at as she moved amid them on his arm.[1]

In the evening they returned to the inn at which they had put up, and Tess waited in the entry while Angel went to see the horse and gig brought to the door. The general sitting-room was full of guests, who were continually going in and out. As the door opened and shut each time for the passage of these, the light within the parlour fell full upon Tess's face. Two men came out and passed by her among the rest. One of them had stared her up and down in surprise, and she fancied he was a Trantridge man, though that village lay so many miles off that Trantridge folk were rarities here.

'A comely maid that,' said the other.

'True, comely enough. But unless I make a great mistake[2]—' And he negatived the remainder of the remark forthwith.

Clare had just returned from the stable-yard, and, confronting the man on the threshold, heard the words, and saw the shrinking of Tess. The insult to her stung him to the quick, and before he had considered anything at all he struck the man on the chin with the full force of his fist, sending him staggering backwards into the passage.

The man recovered himself, and seemed inclined to come on, and Clare, stepping outside the door, put himself in a posture of defence. But his opponent began to think better of the matter. He looked anew at Tess as he passed her, and said to Clare –

'I beg pardon, sir; 'twas a complete mistake. I thought she was another woman, forty miles from here.'

Clare, feeling then that he had been too hasty, and that he was, moreover, to blame for leaving her standing in an inn-passage, did what he usually did in such cases, gave the man five shillings to plaster the blow; and thus they parted, bidding each other a pacific good-night. As soon as Clare had taken the reins from the ostler, and the young couple had driven off, the two men went in the other direction.

'And was it a mistake?' said the second one.

'Not a bit of it. But I didn't want to hurt the gentleman's feelings – not I.'

In the meantime the lovers were driving onward.

'Could we put off our wedding till a little later?' Tess asked, in a dry dull voice. 'I mean, if we wished?'

'No, my love. Calm yourself. Do you mean that the fellow may have time to summon me for assault?' he asked good-humouredly.

'No – I only meant – if it should have to be put off.'

What she meant was not very clear, and he directed her to dismiss such fancies from her mind, which she obediently did as well as she could. But she was grave, very grave, all the way home; till she thought, 'We shall go away, a very long distance, hundreds of miles from these parts, and such as this can never happen again, and no ghost of the past reach there.'

They parted tenderly that night on the landing, and Clare ascended to his attic. Tess sat up getting on with some little requisites, lest the few remaining days should not afford sufficient time. While she sat she heard a noise in Angel's room overhead, a sound of thumping and struggling. Everybody else in the house was asleep, and in her anxiety lest Clare should be ill she ran up and knocked at his door, and asked him what was the matter.

'Oh, nothing, dear,' he said from within. 'I am so sorry I disturbed you! But the reason is rather an amusing one: I fell asleep and dreamt that I was fighting that fellow again who insulted you, and the noise you heard was my pummelling away with my fists at my portmanteau, which I pulled out to-day for packing. I am occasionally liable to these freaks in my sleep. Go to bed and think of it no more.'

This[3] was the last drachm required to turn the scale of her indecision. Declare the past to him by word of mouth she could not; but there was another way. She sat down and wrote on the four pages of a note-sheet a succinct narrative of those events of three years ago, put it into an envelope, and directed it to Clare. Then, lest the flesh should again be weak, she crept upstairs without any shoes and slipped the note under his door.

Her night was a broken one, as it well might be, and she listened for the first faint noise overhead. It came, as usual; he descended, as usual. She descended. He met her at the bottom of the stairs and kissed her. Surely it was as warmly as ever!

He looked a little disturbed and worn, she thought. But he said not a word to her about her revelation, even when they were alone. Could he have had it? Unless he began the subject she felt that she could say nothing. So the day passed, and it was evident that, whatever he thought, he meant to keep to himself. Yet he was frank and affectionate as before. Could it be that her doubts were childish? that he forgave her; that he loved her for what she was, just as she was, and smiled at her disquiet as at a foolish nightmare? Had he really received her note? She glanced into his room, and could see nothing of it. It must be that he forgave her.

Every morning and night he was the same, and thus New Year's Eve broke – the wedding-day.

The lovers did not rise at milking-time, having through the whole of this last week of their sojourn at the dairy been accorded something of the position of guests, Tess being honoured with a room of her own. When they arrived downstairs at breakfast-time they were surprised to see what effects had been produced in the large kitchen to their glory since they had last beheld it. At some unnatural hour of the morning the dairyman had caused the yawning chimney-corner to be whitened, and the brick hearth reddened, and a blazing yellow damask blower to be hung across the arch in place of the old grimy blue cotton one with a black sprig pattern which had formerly done duty here. This renovated aspect of what was the focus indeed of the room on a dull winter morning, threw a smiling demeanour over the whole apartment.

'I was determined to do summat in honour o't,' said the dairyman.

'And as you wouldn't hear of my gieing a rattling good randy wi' fiddles and bass-viols complete, as we should ha' done in old times, this was all I could think o' as a noiseless thing.'

Tess's friends lived so far off that none could conveniently have been present at the ceremony, even had any been asked; but as a fact nobody was invited from Marlott. As for Angel's family, he had written and duly informed them of the time, and assured them that he would be glad to see one at least of them there for the day if he would like to come. His brothers had not replied at all, seeming to be indignant with him; while his father and mother had written a rather sad letter, deploring his precipitancy in rushing into marriage, but making the best of the matter by saying that, though a dairywoman was the last daughter-in-law they could have expected, their son had arrived at an age at which he might be supposed to be the best judge.

This coolness in his relations distressed Clare less than it would have done had he been without the grand card with which he meant to surprise them ere long. To produce Tess, fresh from the dairy, as a D'Urberville and a lady he had felt to be temerarious and risky; hence he had concealed her lineage till such time as, familiarized with worldly ways by a few months' travel and reading with him, he could take her on a visit to his parents, and impart the knowledge while triumphantly producing her as worthy of such an ancient line. It was a pretty lover's dream, if no more. Perhaps Tess's lineage had more value for himself than for anybody in the world besides.

Her perception that Angel's bearing towards her still remained in no whit altered by her own communication rendered Tess still doubtful if he could have received it.[4] She rose from breakfast before he had finished, and hastened upstairs. It had occurred to her to look once more into the queer gaunt room which had been Clare's den, or rather eyrie, for so long, and climbing the ladder, she stood at the open door of the apartment, regarding and pondering. She stooped to the threshold of the doorway, where she had pushed in the note two or three days earlier in such excitement. The carpet reached close to the sill, and under the edge of the carpet she discerned the faint white margin of the envelope containing her letter to him, which he obviously had never seen, owing to her having in her haste thrust it beneath the carpet as well as beneath the door.

With a feeling of faintness she withdrew the letter. There it was – sealed up, just as it had left her hands. The mountain had not yet been removed. She could not let him read it now, the house being in full bustle of preparation; and descending to her own room she destroyed the letter there.

She was so pale when he saw her again that he felt quite anxious. The incident of the misplaced letter overwhelmed her; what could she do at this late moment?[5] Everything was in a stir; there was coming and going; all had to dress, the dairyman and Mrs Crick having been asked to accompany them as witnesses; and reflection or deliberate talk were well-nigh impossible. The only minute Tess could get to be alone with Clare was when they met upon the landing.

'I am so anxious to talk to you – I want to confess all my faults and blunders!' she said with attempted lightness.

'No, no – we can't have faults talked of – you must be deemed perfect to-day at least, Sweet!' he cried. 'We shall have plenty of time, hereafter, I hope, to talk over our failings. I will confess mine at the same time.'

'But it would be better for me to do it now, I think, so that you could not say—'

'Well, you shall tell me anything – say, as soon as we are settled in our lodging; not now. I, too, will tell you my faults then. But do not let us spoil the day with them; they will be excellent matter for a dull time.'

'Then you don't wish me to, dearest?'

'I do not, Tessy, really.'

The hurry of dressing and starting left no time for more than this. Those words of his seemed to reassure her on further reflection. She was whirled onward through the next couple of critical hours by the mastering tide of her devotion to him, which closed up further meditation. Her one desire, so long resisted, to make herself his, to call him her lord, her own – then, if necessary, to die – had at last lifted her up from her plodding reflective pathway. In dressing, she moved about in a mental cloud of many-coloured idealities, which eclipsed all sinister contingencies by its brightness.

The church was a long way off, and they were obliged to drive, particularly as it was winter. A close carriage was ordered from a roadside inn, a vehicle which had been kept there ever since the old days of post-chaise travelling. It had stout wheel-spokes, and heavy felloes, a great curved bed, immense straps and springs, and a pole like a battering-ram. The postilion was a venerable 'boy' of sixty – a martyr to rheumatic gout, the result of excessive exposure in youth, counteracted by strong liquors – who had stood at inn-doors doing nothing for the whole five-and-twenty years that had elapsed since he had no longer been required to ride professionally, as if expecting the old times to come back again. He had a permanent running wound on the outside of his right leg, originated by the constant bruisings of aristocratic carriage-poles during the many years that he had been in regular employ at the Golden Crown, Casterbridge.

Inside this cumbrous and creaking structure, and behind this decayed conductor, the *partie carrée* took their seats – the bride and bridegroom and Mr and Mrs Crick. Angel would have liked one at least of his brothers to be present as groomsman, but their silence after his gentle hint to that effect by letter had signified that they did not care to come. They disapproved of the marriage, and could not be expected to countenance it. Perhaps it was as well that they could not be present. They were not worldly young fellows, but fraternizing with dairy-folk would have struck unpleasantly upon their biassed niceness, apart from their views of the match.

Upheld by the momentum of the time Tess knew nothing of this; did not see anything; did not know the road they were taking to the church. She knew that Angel was close to her; all the rest was a luminous mist. She was a sort of celestial person, who owed her being to poetry – one of those classical divinities Clare was accustomed to talk to her about when they took their walks together.

The marriage being by licence there were only a dozen or so of people in the church; had there been a thousand they would have produced no more effect upon her. They were at stellar distances from her present world. In the ecstatic solemnity with which she swore her faith to him the ordinary sensibilities of sex seemed a flippancy. At a pause in the service, while they were kneeling together, she unconsciously inclined herself towards him, so that her shoulder touched his arm; she had been frightened by a passing thought, and the movement had been automatic, to assure herself that he was really there, and to fortify her belief that his fidelity would be proof against all things.

Clare knew that she loved him – every curve of her form showed that – but he did not know at that time the full depth of her devotion, its single-mindedness, its meekness; what long-suffering it guaranteed, what honesty, what endurance, what good faith.

As they came out of church the ringers swung the bells off their rests, and a limited peal of three notes broke forth – the power of expressing joy in such a small parish ranging no further. Passing by the tower with her husband on the path to the gate she could feel the vibrant air humming round them from the louvred belfry in a circle of sound, and it matched the highly-charged mental atmosphere in which she was living.

This condition of exaltation, wherein she felt glorified by an irradiation not her own, like the Angel whom St John saw in the sun,[6] lasted till the sound of the church bells had died away, and the emotions of the wedding-service had calmed down.[7] Her eyes could dwell upon details more clearly now, and Mr and Mrs Crick having directed their own gig to be sent for them, to leave the carriage to the young couple, she observed the build and character of that conveyance for the first time. Sitting in silence she regarded it long.

'I fancy you seem oppressed, Tessy,' said Clare.

'Yes,' she answered, putting her hand to her brow. 'I tremble at many things. It is all so serious, Angel. Among other things I seem to have seen this carriage before, to be very well acquainted with it. It is very odd – I must have seen it in a dream.'

'Oh – you have heard the legend of the D'Urberville Coach – that well-known superstition of this county about your family when they were very popular here; and this lumbering old thing reminds you of it.'

'I have never heard of it to my knowledge,' said she. 'What is the legend – may I know it?'

'Well – I would rather not tell it in detail just now. A certain D'Urberville of the sixteenth or seventeenth century committed a dreadful crime in his family coach; and since that time members of the family see or hear the old coach whenever—But I'll tell you another day – it is rather gloomy. Evidently some dim knowledge of it has been brought back to your mind by the sight of this venerable caravan.'

'I don't remember hearing it before,' she murmured. 'Is it when we are going to die, Angel, that members of my family see it, or is it when we have committed a crime?'

'Now Tess!'

He silenced her by a kiss.

By the time they reached home she was contrite and spiritless. She was Mrs Angel Clare, indeed, but had she any moral right to the name? Was she not more truly Mrs Alexander D'Urberville? Had intensity of love any power to justify what might possibly be considered in upright souls as culpable reticence? She knew not what was expected of women in such cases; and she had no counsellor.

However, when she found herself alone in her room for a few minutes – the last day this on which she was ever to enter it – she knelt down and prayed. She tried to pray to God, but it was her husband who really had her supplication. Her idolatry of this man was such that she herself almost feared it to be ill-omened. She was conscious of the notion expressed by Friar Laurence, 'These violent delights have violent ends.'[8] It might be too desperate for human conditions – too rank, too wild, too deadly.

'O my love, my love, why do I love you so?' she whispered there alone; 'for she you love is not my real self, but one in my image; the one I might have been!'

Afternoon came, and with it the hour for departure. They had decided to fulfil the plan of going for a few days to the lodgings in the old farmhouse near Wellbridge Mill, at which he meant to reside during his investigation of flour-processes. At two o'clock there was nothing left to do but to start. All the servantry of the dairy were standing in the red-brick entry to see them go out, the dairyman and his wife following to the door. Tess saw her three chamber-mates in a row against the wall, pensively inclining their heads. She had much questioned if they would appear at the parting moment; but there they were, stoical and staunch to the last. She knew why the delicate Retty looked so fragile, and Izz so tragically sorrowful, and Marian so blank; and she forgot her own dogging shadow for a moment in contemplating theirs.

She impulsively whispered to him –

'Will you kiss 'em all, once, poor things, for the first and last time?'

Clare had not the least objection to such a farewell formality – which was all that it was to him – and as he passed them he kissed them in succession where they stood, saying 'Good-bye' to each as he did so. When they reached the door Tess femininely glanced back to discern the effect of that kiss of charity; there was no triumph in her glance, as there might have been. If there had it would have disappeared when she saw how moved the girls all were. The kiss had obviously done harm by awakening feelings they were trying to subdue.

Of all this Clare was unconscious. Passing on to the wicket-gate he shook hands with the dairyman and his wife, and expressed his last thanks to them for their attentions; after which there was a moment of silence before they had moved off. It was interrupted by the crowing of a cock. The white one with the rose comb had come and settled on the palings in front of the house, within a few yards of them, and his notes thrilled their ears through, dwindling away like echoes down a valley of rocks.

'Oh?' said Mrs Crick. 'An afternoon crow?'

Two men were standing by the yard gate, holding it open.

'That's bad,'[9] one murmured to the other, not thinking that the words could be heard by the group at the door-wicket.

The cock crew again – straight towards Clare.

'Well!' said the dairyman.

'I don't like to hear him!' said Tess to her husband. 'Tell the man to drive on. Good-bye, good-bye!'

The cock crew again.

'Hoosh! Just you be off, sir, or I'll twist your neck!' said the dairyman with some irritation, turning to the bird and driving him away. And to his wife as they went indoors: 'Now, to think o' that just to-day! I've not heard his crow of an afternoon all the year afore.'

'It only means a change in the weather,' said she; 'not what you think: 'tis impossible!'

XXXIV

They drove by the level road along the valley to a distance of a few miles, and, reaching Wellbridge, turned away from the village to the left, and over the great Elizabethan bridge which gives the place half its name. Immediately behind it stood the house wherein they had engaged lodgings, whose exterior features are so well known to all travellers through the Froom Valley; once portion of a fine manorial residence, and the property and seat of a D'Urberville, but since its partial demolition a farm-house.

'Welcome to one of your ancestral mansions!' said Clare as he handed her down. But he regretted the pleasantry; it was too near a satire.

On entering they found that, though they had only engaged a couple of rooms, the farmer had taken advantage of their proposed presence during the coming days to pay a New Year's visit to some friends, leaving a woman from a neighbouring cottage to minister to their few wants. The absoluteness of possession pleased them, and they realized it as the first moment of their experience under their own exclusive roof-tree.

But he found that the mouldy old habitation somewhat depressed his bride. When the carriage was gone they ascended the stairs to wash their hands, the charwoman showing the way. On the landing Tess stopped and started.

'What's the matter?' said he.

'Those horrid women!' she answered, with a smile. 'How they frightened me.'

He looked up, and perceived two life-size portraits on panels built into the masonry. As all visitors to the mansion are aware, these paintings represent women of middle age, of a date some two hundred years ago, whose lineaments once seen can never be forgotten. The long pointed features, narrow eye, and smirk of the one, so suggestive of merciless treachery; the bill-hook nose, large teeth, and bold eye of the other, suggesting arrogance to the point of ferocity, haunt the beholder afterwards in his dreams.[1]

'Whose portraits are those?' asked Clare of the charwoman.

'I've been told by old folk that they were ladies of the D'Urberville family, the ancient lords of this manor,' she said. 'Owing to their being builded into the wall they can't be removed.'

The unpleasantness of the matter was that, in addition to their effect upon Tess, her fine features were unquestionably traceable in these exaggerated forms. He said nothing of this, however, and, regretting that he had gone out of his way to choose the house for their bridal time, went on into the adjoining room. The place having been rather hastily prepared for them they washed their hands in one basin. Clare touched hers under the water.[2]

'Which are my fingers and which are yours?' he said, looking up. 'They are very much mixed.'

'They are all yours,' said she, very prettily, and endeavoured to be gayer than she was. He had not been displeased with her thoughtfulness on such an occasion; it was what every sensible woman would show; but Tess knew that she had been thoughtful to excess, and struggled against it.

The sun was so low on that short last afternoon of the year that it shone in through a small opening and formed a golden staff which stretched across to her skirt, where it made a spot like a paint-mark set upon her. They went into the ancient parlour to tea, and here they shared their first common meal alone. Such was their childishness, or rather his, that he found it interesting to use the same bread-and-butter plate as herself, and to brush crumbs from her lips with his own. He wondered a little that she did not enter into these frivolities with his own zest.

Looking at her silently for a long time: 'She is a dear dear Tess,' he thought to himself, as one deciding on the true construction of a difficult passage. 'Do I realize solemnly enough how utterly and irretrievably this little womanly thing is the creature of my good or bad faith and fortune? I think not. I think I could not, unless I were a woman myself. What I am, she is. What I become she must become. What I cannot be she cannot be. And shall I ever neglect her, or hurt her, or even forget to consider her? God forbid such a crime!'

They sat on over the tea-table, waiting for their luggage, which the dairyman had promised to send before it grew dark. But evening began to close in, and the luggage did not arrive, and they had brought nothing more than they stood in. With the departure of the sun the calm mood of the winter day changed. Out of doors there began noises as of silk smartly rubbed; the restful dead leaves of the preceding autumn were stirred to irritated resurrection, and whirled about unwillingly, and tapped against the shutters. It soon began to rain.

'That cock knew the weather was going to change,' said Clare.

The woman who had attended upon them had gone home for the night, but she had placed candles upon the table, and now they lit them. Each candle-flame drew towards the fireplace.

'These old houses are so draughty,' continued Angel, looking at the flames, and at the grease guttering down the sides. 'I wonder where that luggage is. We haven't even a brush and comb.'

'I don't know,' she answered, absent-minded.

'Tess, you are not a bit cheerful this evening – not at all as you used to be. Those harridans on the panels upstairs have unsettled you. I am sorry I brought you here. I wonder if you really love me, after all?'

He knew that she did, and the words had no serious intent; but she was surcharged with emotion, and winced like a wounded animal. Though she tried not to shed tears she could not help showing one or two.

'I did not mean it!' said he, sorry. 'You are worried at not having your things, I know. I cannot think why old Jonathan has not come with them. Why, it is seven o'clock! Ah, there he is!'

A knock had come to the door, and, there being nobody else to answer it Clare went out. He returned to the room with a small package in his hand.

'It is not Jonathan, after all,' he said.

'How vexing!' said Tess.

The packet had been brought by a special messenger, who had arrived at Talbothays from Emminster Vicarage immediately after the departure of the married couple, and had followed them hither, being under injunction to deliver it into nobody's hands but theirs. Clare brought it to the light. It was less than a foot long, sewed up in canvas, sealed in red wax with his father's seal, and directed in his father's hand to 'Mrs Angel Clare.'

'It is a little wedding-present for you, Tess,' said he, handing it to her. 'How thoughtful they are!'

Tess looked a little flustered as she took it.

'I think I would rather have you open it, dearest,' said she, turning over the parcel. 'I don't like to break those great seals; they look so serious. Please open it for me!'

He undid the parcel. Inside was a case of morocco leather, on the top of which lay a note and a key.

The note was for Clare, in the following words:

> MY DEAR SON, – Possibly you have forgotten that on the death of your godmother, Mrs Pitney, when you were a lad, she – vain kind woman that she was – left to me a portion of the contents of her jewel-case in trust for your wife, if you should ever have one, as a mark of her affection for you and whomsoever you should choose. This trust I have fulfilled, and the diamonds have been locked up at my banker's ever since. Though I feel it to be a somewhat incongruous act in the circumstances, I am, as you will see, bound to hand over the articles to the woman to whom the use of them for her lifetime will now rightly belong,[3] and they are therefore promptly sent. They become, I believe, heirlooms, strictly speaking, according to the terms of your godmother's will. The precise words of the clause that refers to this matter are enclosed.

'I do remember,' said Clare; 'but I had quite forgotten.'

Unlocking the case, they found it to contain a necklace, with pendant, bracelets, and ear-rings; and also some other small ornaments.

Tess seemed afraid to touch them at first, but her eyes sparkled for a moment as much as the stones when Clare spread out the set.

'Are they mine?' she asked incredulously.

'They are, certainly,' said he.

He looked into the fire. He remembered how, when he was a lad of fifteen, his godmother, the Squire's wife – the only rich person with whom he had ever come in contact – had pinned her faith to his success; had prophesied a wondrous career for him. There had seemed nothing at all out of keeping with such a conjectured career in the storing up of these showy ornaments for his wife and the wives of her descendants. They gleamed somewhat ironically now. 'Yet why?' he asked himself. It was but a question of vanity throughout; and if that were admitted into one side of the equation it should be admitted into the other. His wife was a D'Urberville: whom could they become better than her?

Suddenly he said with enthusiasm –

'Tess, put them on – put them on!' And he turned from the fire to help her.

As if by magic she had already donned them – necklace, ear-rings, bracelets, and all.

'But the gown isn't right, Tess,' said Clare. 'It ought to be a low one for a set of brilliants like that.'

'Ought it?' said Tess.

'Yes,' said he.

He suggested to her how to tuck in the upper edge of her bodice, so as to make it roughly approximate to the cut for evening wear; and when she had done this, and the pendant to the necklace hung isolated amid the whiteness of her throat, as it was designed to do, he stepped back to survey her.

'My heavens,' said Clare, 'how beautiful you are!'

As everybody knows, fine feathers make fine birds; a peasant girl but very moderately prepossessing to the casual observer in her simple condition and attire, will bloom as an amazing beauty if clothed as a woman of fashion with the aids that Art can render; while the beauty of the midnight crush would often cut but a sorry figure if placed inside the field-woman's wrapper upon a monotonous acreage of turnips on a dull day. He had never till now estimated the artistic excellence of Tess's limbs and features.

'If you were only to appear in a ball-room!' he said. 'But no – no, dearest; I think I love you best in the wing-bonnet and cotton-frock – yes, better than in this, well as you support these dignities.'

Tess's sense of her striking appearance had given her a flush of excitement, which was yet not happiness.

'I'll take them off!' she said, 'in case Jonathan should see me. They are not fit for me, are they? They must be sold, I suppose?'

'Let them stay a few minutes longer. Sell them? Never. It would be a breach of faith.'

Influenced by a second thought, she readily obeyed. She had something to tell, and there might be help in these. She sat down with the jewels upon her; and they again indulged in conjectures as to where Jonathan could possibly be with their baggage. The ale they had poured out for his consumption when he came had gone flat with long standing.

Shortly after this they began supper, which was already laid on a side-table. Ere they had finished there was a jerk in the fire-smoke, the rising skein of which bulged out into the room, as if some giant had laid his hand on the chimney-top for a moment. It had been caused by the opening of the outer door. A heavy step was now heard in the passage, and Angel went out.

'I couldn'' make nobody hear at all by knocking,' apologized Jonathan Kail, for it was he at last; 'and as't was raining out I opened the door. I've brought the things, sir.'

'I am very glad to see them. But you are very late.'

'Well, yes, sir.'

There was something subdued in Jonathan Kail's tone which had not been there in the day, and lines of concern were ploughed upon his forehead in addition to the lines of years. He continued –

'We've all been gallied at the dairy at what might ha' been a most terrible affliction since you and your Mis'ess – so to name her now – left us this a'ternoon. Perhaps you ha'nt forgot the cock's afternoon crow?'

'Dear me; – what—'

'Well, some says it do mane one thing, and some another; but what's happened is that poor little Retty Priddle hev tried to drown herself.'

'No! Really! Why, she bade us good-bye with the rest—'

'Yes. Well, sir, when you and your Mis'ess – so to name what she lawful is – when you two drove away, as I say, Retty and Marian put on their bonnets and went out; and as there is not much doing now, being New Year's Eve, and folks mops and brooms[4] from what's inside 'em, nobody took much notice. They went on to Lew-Everard, where they had sommat to drink, and then on they vamped to Dree-armed Cross, and there they seemed to have parted, Retty striking across the water-meads as if for home, and Marian going on to the next village, where there's another public-house. Nothing more was seed or heard o' Retty till the waterman, on his way home, noticed something by the Great Pool; 'twas her bonnet and shawl packed up. In the water he found her. He and another man brought her home, thinking a' was dead; but she came round by degrees.'

Angel, suddenly recollecting that Tess was overhearing this gloomy tale, went to shut the door between the passage and the parlour; but his wife, flinging a shawl round her, had approached and listened to the man's narrative, her eyes resting absently on the luggage and the drops of rain glistening upon it.

'And, more than this, there's Marian; she's been found dead drunk by the withy-bed – a girl who hev never been known to touch anything before except shilling ale; though, to be sure, a' was always a good trencher-woman, as her face showed. It seems as if the maids had all gone out o' their minds!'

'And Izz?' asked Tess.

'Izz is about house as usual; but a' do say a' can guess how it happened; and she seems to be very low in mind about it, poor maid, as well she mid be. And so you see, sir, as all this happened just when we was packing your few traps and your Mis'ess's night-rail and dressing things into the cart, why, it belated me.'

'Yes. Well, Jonathan, will you get the trunks upstairs, and drink a cup of ale, and hasten back as soon as you can, in case you should be wanted?'

Tess had gone back to the parlour, and sat down by the fire, looking wistfully into it. She heard Jonathan Kail's heavy footsteps up and down the stairs till he had done placing the luggage, and heard him express his thanks for the ale her husband took out to him, and for

222

the gratuity he received. Jonathan's footsteps then died from the door, and his cart creaked away.

Angel slid forward the massive oak bar which secured the door, and coming in to where she sat over the hearth, pressed her cheeks between his hands from behind. He expected her to jump up gaily and unpack the toilet-gear that she had been so anxious about, but as she did not rise he sat down with her in the firelight, the candles on the supper-table being too thin and glimmering to interfere with its glow.

'I am so sorry you should have heard this sad story about the girls,' he said. 'Still, don't let it depress you. Retty was naturally morbid, you know.'

'Without the least cause,' said Tess. 'While they who have cause to be, hide it, and pretend they are not.'

This incident had turned the scale for her. They were simple and innocent girls on whom the unhappiness of unrequited love had fallen; they had deserved better at the hands of Fate. She had deserved worse – yet she was the chosen one. It was wicked of her to take all without paying. She would pay to the uttermost farthing; she would tell, there and then. This final determination she came to when she looked into the fire, he holding her hand.

A steady crimson glare from the now flameless embers painted the sides and back of the fireplace with its colour, and the well-polished andirons, and the old brass tongs that would not meet. The underside of the mantel-shelf was flushed with the blood-coloured light, and the legs of the table nearest the fire. Tess's face and neck reflected the same warmth, which each gem turned into an Aldebaran or a Sirius[5] – a constellation of white, red, and green flashes, that interchanged their hues with her every pulsation.

'Do you remember what we said to each other this morning about telling our faults?' he asked abruptly, finding that she still remained immovable. 'We spoke lightly perhaps, and you may well have done so. But for me it was no light promise. I want to make a confession to you, Love.'

This, from him, so unexpectedly apposite, had the effect upon her of a Providential interposition.

'You have to confess something?' she said quickly, and even with gladness and relief.

'You did not expect it? Ah – you thought too highly of me. Now listen. Put your head there, because I want you to forgive me, and not to be indignant with me for not telling you before, as perhaps I ought to have done.'

How strange it was! He seemed to be her double. She did not speak, and Clare went on –

'I did not mention it because I was afraid of endangering my chance of you, darling, the great prize of my life – my Fellowship I call you. My brother's Fellowship was won at his college, mine at Talbothays Dairy. Well, I would not risk it. I was going to tell you a month ago – at the time you agreed to be mine, but I could not; I thought it might frighten you away from me. I put it off; then I thought I would tell you yesterday, to give you a chance at least of escaping me. But I did not. And I did not this morning, when you proposed our confessing our faults on the landing – the sinner that I was! But I must, now I see you sitting there so solemnly. I wonder if you will forgive me?'

'O yes! I am sure that—'

'Well, I hope so. But wait a minute. You don't know. To begin[6] at the beginning. Though I believe my poor father fears that I am one of the eternally lost for my doctrines, I am a stickler for good morals, Tess. I used to wish to be a teacher of men, and it was a great disappointment to me when I found I could not enter the Church. I loved spotlessness, and hated impurity, as I do now.[7] Whatever I may think of plenary inspiration,[8] I heartily subscribe to these words of Paul: "Be thou an example – in word, in conversation, in charity, in spirit, in faith, in purity."[9] It is the only safeguard for us poor human beings. "Integer vitæ,"[10] says a Roman poet, who is strange company for St Paul –

> The man of upright life, from frailties free,
> Stands not in need of Moorish spear or bow.

Well, having felt this so strongly, you will see what a terrible remorse it bred in me when I, my very self, fell.'[11]

He then told her of that time of his life to which allusion has been made when, tossed about by doubts and difficulties like a cork on the waves, he went to London and plunged into eight-and-forty hours' dissipation with a stranger.

'Happily I awoke almost immediately to a sense of my folly,' he continued. 'I would have no more to say to her, and I came home. I have never repeated the offence. But I felt I should like to treat you with perfect frankness and honour, and I could not do so without telling this. Do you forgive me?'

She pressed his hand tightly for an answer.

'Then we will dismiss it at once and for ever – too painful as it is for the occasion – and talk of something lighter.'

'Oh, Angel – I am almost glad – because now *you* can forgive *me*! I have not made my confession. I have a confession, too – remember, I said so.'

'Ah, to be sure! Now then for it, wicked little one.'

'Perhaps, although you smile, it is as serious as yours, or more so.'

'It can hardly be more serious, dearest.'

'It cannot – O no, it cannot!' She jumped up joyfully at the hope. 'No, it cannot be more serious, certainly,' she cried. 'I will tell you now.'

She sat down again.

Their hands were still joined. The ashes under the grate were lit by the fire vertically, like a torrid waste. Her imagination beheld a Last Day luridness[12] in this red-coaled glow, which fell on his face and hand, and on hers, peering into the loose hair about her brow, and firing the delicate skin underneath. A large shadow of her shape rose upon the wall and ceiling. She bent forward, at which each diamond on her neck gave a sinister wink like a toad's; and pressing her forehead against his temple she entered on her story of her acquaintance with Alec D'Urberville and its results, murmuring the words without flinching, and with her eyelids drooping down.[13]

END OF PHASE THE FOURTH

The Woman Pays

XXXV

Her narrative ended; even its re-assertions and secondary explanations were done. Tess's voice throughout had hardly risen higher than its opening tone; there had been no exculpatory phrase of any kind, and she had not wept.

But the complexion even of external things seemed to suffer transmutation as her announcement progressed. The fire in the grate looked impish – demoniacally funny, as if it did not care in the least about her strait. The fender grinned idly, as if it too did not care. The light from the water-bottle was merely engaged in a chromatic problem. All material objects around announced their irresponsibility with terrible iteration. And yet nothing had changed since the moments when he had been kissing her; or rather, nothing in the substance of things. But the essence of things had changed.

When she ceased the auricular impressions[1] from their previous endearments seemed to hustle away into the corners of their brains, repeating themselves as echoes from a time of supremely purblind foolishness.

Clare performed the irrelevant act of stirring the fire; the intelligence had not even yet got to the bottom of him. After stirring the embers he rose to his feet; all the force of her disclosure had imparted itself now. His face had withered. In the strenuousness of his concentration he treadled fitfully on the floor. He could not, by any contrivance, think closely enough; that was the meaning of his vague movement. When he spoke it was in the most inadequate, commonplace voice of the many varied tones she had heard from him.

'Tess, am I to believe this? From your manner I am to take it as true. You cannot be out of your mind, though you ought to be. Yet you are not. I see nothing in you to warrant such a supposition as that.' He stopped; to resume sharply, 'Why didn't you tell me before? Ah, yes, you would have told me, in a way – but I hindered you, I remember!'

These and other of his words were nothing but the perfunctory babble of the surface while the depths remained paralyzed. He turned away, bent over a chair, and stood up again. She followed him to the middle of the room where he was, standing there with one hand on a chair-back, staring at him with eyes that did not weep.[2] Presently she slid down upon her knees beside his foot, and from this position she crouched in a heap.

'In the name of our love, forgive me!' she whispered with a dry mouth. 'I have forgiven you for the same.'

And, as he did not answer, she said again –

'Forgive me as you are forgiven! *I* forgive *you*, Angel.'

'You – yes, you do.'

'But you do not forgive me?'

'Forgiveness does not apply to the case. You were one person; now you are another. How can forgiveness meet such a grotesque prestidigitation as that?'[3]

He paused; then suddenly broke into horrible introspective laughter – as unnatural and ghastly as a laugh in hell.

'Don't – don't! It kills me quite, that!' she shrieked. 'Have mercy upon me – have mercy!'

He did not answer; and, sickly white, she jumped up.[4]

'Angel, Angel! what do you mean?' she cried out. 'Do you know what this is to me?'

He shook his head in uncomprehensive reverie.

'I have been hoping, longing, praying, to make you happy! I have thought what joy it will be to do it, what an unworthy wife I shall be if I do not! That's what I have felt, Angel!'

'I know that.'

'I thought, Angel, that you loved me – me, my very self! If it is I you do love, O how can it be that you look and speak so? It frightens me! Having begun to love 'ee, I love 'ee for ever – in all changes, in all disgraces, because you are yourself. I ask no more. Then how can you, O my own husband, stop loving me?'

'I repeat, the woman I have been loving is not you.'

'But who?'

'Another woman in your shape.'

She perceived in his words the realization of her own apprehensive foreboding in former times. He looked upon her as a species of impostor; a guilty woman in the guise of an innocent one. Terror was upon her white face as she saw it; her cheek was flaccid, and her mouth had the aspect of a round little hole. The horrible sense of his view of her so deadened her that she staggered; and he stepped forward, thinking she was going to fall.

'Sit down, sit down,' he said in pure pity. 'You are ill; and it is natural that you should be.'

She did sit down, without knowing where she was, that vacant look still upon her face, and her eyes such as to make his flesh creep.

'I don't belong to you any more, then; do I, Angel?' she asked helplessly. 'It is not me, but another woman like me that he loved, he says.'

The image raised caused her to take pity upon herself as one who was ill-used. Her eyes filled as she regarded her position further; she turned round and burst into a flood of self-sympathetic tears.

Angel Clare was relieved at this change, for the effect on her of what had happened was beginning to be a trouble to him only less than the woe of the disclosure itself. He waited patiently, apathetically, till the violence of her grief had worn itself out, and her rush of weeping had lessened to a catching gasp at intervals.

'Angel,' she said suddenly, in her natural tones, the insane, dry voice of terror having left her now. 'Angel, am I too wicked for you and me to live together?'

'I have not been able to think what we can do.'

'I shan't ask you to let me live with you, Angel, because I have no right to! I shall not write to mother and sisters to say we be married, as I said I would do; and I shan't finish the good hussif' I cut out and meant to make while we were in lodgings.'

'Shan't you?'

'No, I shan't do anything, unless you order me to; and if you go away from me I shall not follow 'ee; and if you never speak to me any more I shall not ask why, unless you tell me I may.'

'And if I do order you to do anything?'

'I will obey you like your wretched slave, even if it is to lie down and die.'

'You are very good. But it strikes me that there is a want of harmony between your present mood of self-sacrifice and your past mood of self-preservation.'

To[5] fling elaborate sarcasms at Tess, however, was much like flinging them at a dog or cat. The charms of their subtlety passed by her unappreciated, and she only received them as inimical sounds which meant that anger ruled. She remained mute, not knowing that he was desperately smothering his affection for her. She did not observe that a tear came out upon his cheek, descending slowly, a tear so large that it magnified the pores of the skin over which it rolled, like the object-lens of a microscope. But reillumination as to the terrible and total change that her confession had wrought in his life, in his universe, returned to him, and he tried desperately to advance among the new conditions in which he stood. Some consequent action was necessary; yet what?

'Tess,' he said, as gently and as civilly as he could speak, 'I cannot stay – in this room with you. I will walk out a little way.'

He quietly left the room, and the two glasses of wine that he had poured out for their supper – one for her, one for him – remained on the table untasted. This was what their *Agape* had come to. At tea, two or three hours earlier, they had, in the freakishness of affection, drunk from one cup.

The closing of the door behind him, gently as it had been pulled to, roused Tess from her stupor. He was gone; she could not stay. Hastily flinging her cloak around her she opened the door and followed, putting out the candles as if she were never coming back. The rain was over and the night was now clear.

She was soon close at his heels, for Clare walked slowly and without purpose. His form beside her light gray figure looked black, sinister, and forbidding, and she had forgotten to take off the jewels of which she had been momentarily so proud. Clare turned at hearing her footsteps, but his recognition of her presence seemed to make no difference in him, and he went on over the five yawning arches of the great bridge in front of the house.

The cow and horse-tracks in the road were full of water, the rain having been enough to charge them, but not enough to wash them away. Across these minute pools the reflected stars flitted in a quick transit as she passed; she would not have known they were shining overhead if she had not seen them there – the vastest things of the universe imaged in objects so mean.

The place to which they had travelled to-day was in the same valley as Talbothays, but some miles lower down the river; and the surroundings being open she kept easily in sight of him. Away from the house the road wound through the meads, and along these she followed Clare without any attempt to come up with him or to attract him, but with dumb and vacant fidelity.

At last, however, her listless walk brought her up alongside him, and still he said nothing. The cruelty of fooled honesty is often great after enlightenment, and it was mighty in Clare now. The outdoor air had apparently taken away from him all tendency to act on impulse; she knew that he saw her without irradiation – in all her bareness.

Time was chanting his satiric psalm at Tess then –

Behold, when thy face is made bare, he that loved thee shall hate;
Thy face shall be no more fair at the fall of thy fate.
For thy life shall fall as a leaf and be shed as the rain;
And the veil of thine head shall be grief, and the crown shall be pain.[6]

He was still intently thinking, and her companionship had now insufficient power to break or divert the strain of thought. What a weak thing her presence must have become to him! She could not help addressing Clare.

'What have I done – what *have* I done? I have not told of anything that interferes with or belies my love for you. You don't think I planned it, do you? It is in your own mind what you are angry at, Angel; it is not in me. O, it is not in me, and I am not that deceitful woman you think me!'

'H'm – well. Not deceitful; but not the same. No, not the same. But do not make me reproach you. I have sworn that I will not; and I do everything to avoid it.'

But she went on pleading in her distraction; and perhaps said things that would have been better left to silence.

'Angel! – Angel! I was a child – a child when it happened! I knew nothing of men.'

'You were more sinned against than sinning,[7] that I admit.'

'Then will you not forgive me?'

'I do forgive you. But forgiveness is not all.'

'And love me?'

To this question he did not answer.

'O Angel – my mother says that it sometimes happens so! – she knows several cases where they were worse than I, and the husband has not minded it much – has forgiven her at least. And yet the woman has not loved him as I do you!'

'Don't, Tess; don't argue. Different societies, different manners. You are an unapprehending peasant woman, who have never been initiated into the proportions of social things. You don't know what you say.'

'I am only a peasant by position, not by nature!'

She spoke with an impulse to anger, but it went as it came.

'So much the worse for you. I think that parson who unearthed your pedigree would have done better if he had held his tongue. I cannot help associating your decline as a family with this other fact – of your want of firmness.[8] Decrepit families postulate decrepit wills, decrepit conduct. Heaven, why did you give me a handle for despising you more by informing me of your descent! Here was I thinking you a new-sprung child of nature; there were you, the exhausted seedling of an effete aristocracy!'

'Lots o' families are as bad as mine in that! Retty's family were once large landowners, and so were Dairyman Billett's. And the Debbyhouses, who now be carters, were once the De Bayeux family. You find such as I everywhere; 'tis a feature of our county, and I can't help it.'

'So much the worse for the county.'

She took these reproaches in their bulk simply, not in their particulars; he did not love her as he had loved her hitherto, and to all else she was indifferent.

They wandered on again in silence. It was said afterwards that a cottager of Wellbridge, who went out late that night for a doctor, met two lovers in the pastures, walking very slowly, without converse, one behind the other, as in a funeral procession, and the glimpse that he obtained of their faces seemed to denote that they were anxious and sad. Returning later, he passed them again in the same field, progressing just as slowly, and as regardless of the hour and of the cheerless night as before. It was only on account of his preoccupation with his own affairs, and the illness in his house, that he did not bear in mind the curious incident, which, however, he recalled a long while after.[9]

During the interval of the cottager's going and coming she had said to her husband –

'I don't see how I can help being the cause of much misery to you all your life. The river is down there. I can put an end to myself in it. I am not afraid.'

'I don't wish to add murder to my other follies,' he said.

'I will leave something to show that I did it myself – on account of my shame. They will not blame you then.'

'Don't speak so – I wish not to hear it. It is absurd to have such thoughts in this kind of case, which is rather one for satirical laughter than for tragedy. You don't in the least understand the quality of the mishap. It would be viewed in the light of a joke by nine-tenths of the world if it were known. Please oblige me by returning to the house, and going to bed.'

'I will,' said she dutifully.

They had rambled round by a road which led to the well-known ruins of the Cistercian abbey[10] behind the mill, the latter having, in centuries past, been attached to the monastic establishment. The mill still worked on, food being a perennial necessity; the abbey had perished, creeds being transient. One continually sees the ministration of the temporary outlasting the ministration of the eternal. Their walk having been circuitous they were still not far from the house, and in obeying his direction she only had to reach the large stone bridge across the main river, and follow the road for a hundred yards. When she got back everything remained as she had left it, the fire being still burning. She did not stay downstairs for more than a few moments, but proceeded to her chamber, whither the luggage had been taken. Here she sat down on the edge of the bed, looking vacantly around, and presently began to undress. In removing the light towards the bedstead its rays fell upon the tester of white dimity; something was hanging beneath it, and she lighted the candle to see what it was. A bough of mistletoe.[11] Angel had put it there; she knew that in an instant. This was the explanation of that mysterious parcel which it had been so difficult to pack and bring; whose contents he would not explain to her, saying that time would soon show her the purpose thereof. In his zest and his gaiety he had hung it there. How foolish and inopportune that mistletoe looked now.

Having nothing more to fear, having scarce anything to hope, for that he would relent there seemed no promise whatever, she lay down dully. When sorrow ceases to be speculative sleep sees her opportunity. Among so many happier moods which forbid repose this was a mood which welcomed it, and in a few minutes the lonely Tess forgot existence, surrounded by the aromatic stillness of the chamber that had once, possibly, been the bride-chamber of her own ancestry.

Later on that night Clare also retraced his steps to the house. Entering softly to the sitting-room he obtained a light, and with the manner of one who had considered his course he spread his rugs upon the old horse-hair sofa which stood there, and roughly shaped it to a sleeping-couch. Before lying down he crept shoeless upstairs, and listened at the door of her apartment. Her measured breathing told that she was sleeping profoundly.

'Thank God!' murmured Clare; and yet he was conscious of a pang of bitterness at the thought – approximately true, though not wholly so – that having shifted the burden of her life to his shoulders she was now reposing without care.

He turned away to descend; then, irresolute, faced round to her door again. In the act he caught sight of one of the D'Urberville dames, whose portrait was immediately over the entrance to Tess's bedchamber. In the candlelight the painting was more than unpleasant. Sinister design lurked in the woman's features, a concentrated purpose of revenge on the other sex – so it seemed to him then. The Caroline bodice of the portrait was low – precisely as Tess's had been when he tucked it in to show the necklace; and again he experienced the distressing sensation of a resemblance between them.

The check was sufficient. He resumed his retreat and descended.

His air remained calm and cold, his small compressed mouth indexing his powers of self-control; his face wearing still that terribly sterile expression which had spread thereon since her disclosure. It was the face of a man who was no longer passion's slave,[12] yet who found no advantage in his enfranchisement. He was simply regarding the harrowing contingencies of human experience, the unexpectedness of things. Nothing so pure, so sweet, so virginal as Tess had seemed possible all the long while that he had adored her, up to an hour ago; but

> The little less, and what worlds away![13]

He argued erroneously when he said to himself that her heart was not indexed in the honest freshness of her face; but Tess had no advocate to set him right. Could it be possible, he continued, that eyes which as they gazed never expressed any divergence from what the tongue was telling, were yet ever seeing another world behind her ostensible one, discordant and contrasting?

He reclined on his couch in the sitting-room, and extinguished the light. The night came in, and took up its place there, unconcerned and indifferent; the night which had already swallowed up his happiness, and was now digesting it listlessly; and was ready to swallow up the happiness of a thousand other people with as little disturbance or change of mien.

XXXVI

Clare arose in the light of a dawn that was ashy and furtive, as though associated with crime. The fireplace confronted him with its extinct embers; the spread supper-table, whereon stood the two full glasses of untasted wine, now flat and filmy; her vacated seat and his own; the other articles of furniture, with their eternal look of not being able to help it, their intolerable inquiry what was to be done? From above there was no sound; but in a few minutes there came a knock at the door. He remembered that it would be the neighbouring cottager's wife, who was to minister to their wants while they remained here.

The presence of a third person in the house would be extremely awkward just now, and, being already dressed, he opened the window and informed her that they could manage to shift for themselves that morning. She had a milk-can in her hand, which he told her to leave at the door. When the dame had gone away he searched in the back quarters of the house for fuel, and speedily lit a fire. There was plenty of eggs, butter, bread, and so on in the larder, and Clare soon had breakfast laid, his experiences at the dairy having rendered him facile in domestic preparations. The smoke of the kindled wood rose from the chimney without like a lotus-headed column;[1] local people who were passing by saw it, and thought of the newly-married couple, and envied their happiness.

Angel cast a final glance round, and then going to the foot of the stairs, said in a clear note –

'Breakfast is ready!'

He opened the front door, and took a few steps in the morning air. When, after a short space, he came back she was already in the sitting-room, mechanically readjusting the breakfast things. As she was fully attired, and the interval since his calling her had been but two or three minutes, she must have been dressed or nearly so before he went to summon her. Her hair was twisted up in a large round mass at the back of her head, and she had put on one of the new frocks – a pale blue woollen garment with neck-frillings of white. Her hands and face appeared to be cold, and she had possibly been sitting dressed in the bedroom a long time without any fire. The marked civility of Clare's tone in calling her seemed to have inspired her, for the moment, with a new glimmer of hope. But it soon died when she looked at him.

The pair were, in truth, but the ashes of their former fires.[2] To the hot sorrow of the previous night had succeeded heaviness; it seemed as if nothing could kindle either of them to fervour of sensation any more.

He spoke gently to her, and she replied with a like undemonstrativeness. At last she came up to him, looking in his sharply-defined face as one who had no consciousness that her own formed a visible object also.

'Angel!' she said, and paused, touching him with her fingers lightly as a breeze, as though she could hardly believe to be there in the flesh the man who was once her lover. Her eyes were bright, her pale cheek still showed its wonted roundness, though half-dried tears had left glistening traces thereon; and the usually ripe red mouth was almost as pale as her cheek. Throbbingly alive as she was still, under the stress of her mental grief, the life beat so brokenly that a little further pull upon it would cause real illness, dull her characteristic eyes, and make her mouth thin.

She looked absolutely pure. Nature, in her fantastic trickery, had set such a seal of maidenhood upon Tess's countenance that he gazed at her with a stupefied air.

'Tess! Say it is not true! No, it is not true!'

'It is true.'

'Every word?'

'Every word.'

He looked at her imploringly, as if he would willingly have taken a lie from her lips, knowing it to be one, and have made of it, by some sort of sophistry, a valid denial. However, she only repeated –

'It is true.'

'Is he living?' Angel then asked.

'The baby died.'

'But the man?'

'He is alive.'

A last despair passed over Clare's face.

'Is he in England?'

'Yes.'

He took a few steps in a circle.

'My position – is this,' he said abruptly. 'I thought – any man would have thought – that by giving up all ambition to win a wife with social standing, with fortune, with knowledge of the world, I should secure rustic unsophistication as surely as I should secure pink cheeks; but— However, I am no man to reproach you, and I will not.'

Tess felt his position so entirely that the remainder had not been needed. Therein lay just the distress of it; she saw that he had lost all round.

'Angel – I should not have let it go on to marriage with 'ee if I had not known that, after all, there was a last way out of it for you; though I hoped you would never—'

Her voice grew husky.

'A last way?'

'I mean, to get rid of me. You *can* get rid of me.'

'How?'

'By divorcing me.'

'Good heavens – how can you be so simple! How can I divorce you?'

'Can't you – now I have told you this? I thought my confession would give you grounds for that.'

'O, Tess – you are too, too – childish – unformed – crude, I suppose! I don't know what you are. You don't understand the law – you don't understand!'

'What – you cannot?'

'Indeed I cannot.'[3]

A quick shame mixed with the misery upon his listener's face.

'I thought – I thought,' she whispered. 'O, now I see how wicked I seem to you! Believe me – believe me, on my soul, Mr Clare, I never thought but that you could! I hoped you would not; yet I believed, without a doubt, that you could cast me off if you were determined, and didn't love me at – at – all!'

'You were mistaken,' he said coldly.

'O, then I ought to have done it, to have done it last night! But I hadn't the courage. That's just like me!'

'The courage to do what?'

As she did not answer he took her by the hand.

'What were you thinking of doing?' he inquired.

'Of putting an end to myself.'

'When?'

She writhed under this inquisitorial manner of his. 'Last night,' she answered.

'Where?'

'Under your mistletoe.'

'My good –! how?' he asked sternly.

'I'll tell you, if you won't be angry with me!' she said shrinking. 'It was with the cord of my box. But I could not – do the last thing! I was afraid that it might cause a scandal to your name.'

The unexpected quality of this confession, wrung from her, and not volunteered, shook him indescribably. But he still held her, and, letting his glance fall from her face downwards, he said –

'Now, listen to this. If you do not want to sink still lower in my esteem you will promise me to⁴ attempt that no more.'

'I am ready to promise. I saw how wicked it was.'

'Wicked! I am shocked at the idea beyond description.'

'But, Angel,' she pleaded, enlarging her eyes in calm unconcern upon him, 'it was thought of entirely on your account – to set you free without the scandal of the divorce that I thought you would have to get. I should never have dreamt of doing it on mine. However, to do it with my own hand is too good for me, after all. It is you, my ruined husband, who ought to strike the blow. I think I should love you more, if that were possible, if you could bring yourself to do it, since there's no other way of escape for 'ee. I feel I am so utterly worthless! So very greatly in the way!'

'Ssh!'

'Well, since you say no, I won't. I have no wish opposed to yours.'

He knew this to be true enough. Since the desperation of the night her activities had dropped to zero, and there was no further rashness to be feared.

Tess tried to busy herself again with the breakfast-table with more or less success, and they sat down both on the same side, so that their glances did not meet. There was at first something awkward in hearing each other eat and drink, but this could not be escaped; moreover, the amount of eating done was small on both sides. Breakfast over he rose, and telling her the hour at which he might be expected to dinner, went off to the miller's in a mechanical pursuance of the plan of studying that business, which had been his only practical reason for coming here.

When he was gone Tess stood at the window, and presently saw his form crossing the great stone bridge which conducted to the mill premises. He sank behind it, crossed the railway beyond, and disappeared. Then, without a sigh, she turned her attention to the room, and began clearing the table and setting it in order.

The charwoman soon came. Her presence was at first a strain upon Tess, but afterwards an alleviation. At half-past twelve she left her assistant alone in the kitchen, and, returning to the front room, waited for the reappearance of Angel's form behind the bridge.

About one he showed himself. Her face flushed, although he was a quarter of a mile off. She ran to the kitchen to get the dinner served by the time he should enter. He went first to the room where they had washed their hands together the day before, and as he entered the sitting-room the dish-covers rose from the dishes as if by his own motion.

'How punctual!' he said.

'Yes. I saw you coming over the bridge,' said she.

The meal was passed in commonplace talk of what he had been doing during the morning at the Abbey Mill, of the methods of bolting and the old-fashioned machinery, which he feared would not enlighten him greatly on modern improved methods, some of it seeming to have been in use ever since the days it ground for the monks in the adjoining conventual buildings – now a heap of ruins. He left the house again in the course of an hour, coming home at dusk, and occupying himself through the evening with his papers. She feared she was in the way, and, when the old woman was gone, retired to the kitchen, where she made herself busy as well as she could for more than an hour.

Clare's shape appeared at the door.

'You must not work like this,' he said. 'You are not my servant; you are my wife.'

She did not raise her eyes,[5] but she brightened. 'I may think myself that – indeed?' she murmured, in piteous raillery. 'You mean in name! Well, I don't want to be anything more.'

'You *may* think so, Tess! You are. What do you mean?'

'I don't know,' she said hastily, with tears in her glance. 'I thought I – because I am not respectable, I mean. I told you I thought I was not respectable enough long ago – and I didn't want to marry you, on that account – only you urged me!'

She broke into sobs, and turned her back to him. It would almost have won round any man but Angel Clare. Within the remote depths of his constitution, so gentle and affectionate as he was in general, there lay hidden a hard logical deposit, like a vein of metal in a soft loam, which turned the edge of everything that attempted to traverse it. It had blocked his way with the Church; it blocked his way with Tess. Moreover, his affection itself was less fire than radiance, and, with regard to the other sex, when he ceased to believe he ceased to follow: contrasting in this with many impressionable natures, who remain sensuously infatuated with what they intellectually despise. He waited till her sobbing ceased.

'I wish half the women in England were as respectable as you,' he said, in an ebullition of bitterness against womankind in general. 'It isn't a question of respectability, but one of principle.'

He spoke such things as these and more of a kindred sort to her, being still swayed by the antipathetic wave which warps direct souls with such persistence when once their vision finds itself mocked by appearances. There was, it is true, underneath, a back current of sympathy through which a woman of the world might have conquered him. But Tess did not think of this; she took everything as her deserts, and hardly opened her mouth. The firmness of her devotion to him was indeed almost pitiful; quick-tempered as she naturally was, nothing that he could say made her unseemly; she sought not her own; was not provoked – thought no evil of his treatment of her. She might just now have been Apostolic Charity[6] herself returned to a self-seeking modern world.

This evening, night, and morning were passed precisely as the preceding ones had been passed. On one, and only one, occasion did she – the formerly free and independent Tess – venture to make any advances. It was on the third occasion of his starting after a meal to go out to the flour-mill. As he was leaving the table he said 'Good-bye,' and she replied in the same words, at the same time inclining her mouth in the way of his. He did not avail himself of the invitation, saying, as he turned hastily aside –

'I shall be home punctually.'

Tess shrank into herself as if she had been struck. Often enough had he tried to reach those lips against her consent – often had he said gaily that her mouth and breath tasted of the butter and eggs and milk and honey on which she mainly lived, that he drew sustenance from them, and other follies of that sort. But he did not care for them now. He observed her sudden shrinking, and said gently –

'You know, I have to think of a course. It was imperative that we should stay together a little while, to avoid the scandal to you that would have resulted from our immediate parting. But you must see it is only for form's sake.'

'Yes,' said Tess absently.

He went out, and on his way to the mill stood still, and wished for a moment that he had responded yet more kindly, and kissed her once at least.

Thus they lived through this despairing day or two; in the same house, truly; but more widely apart than before they were lovers. It was evident to her that he was, as he had said, living with paralyzed activities, in his endeavour to think of a plan of procedure. She was awe-stricken to discover such determination under such apparent flexibility. She no longer expected forgiveness now. More than once she thought of going away from him during his absence at the mill; but she feared that this, instead of benefiting him, might be the means of hampering and humiliating him yet more if it should become known.

Meanwhile Clare was meditating, verily. His thought had been unsuspended; he was becoming ill with thinking; eaten out with thinking, withered by thinking; scourged out of all his former pulsating flexuous domesticity. He walked about saying to himself, 'What's to be done – what's to be done?' and by chance she overheard him. It caused her to break the reserve about their future which had hitherto prevailed.

'I suppose – you are not going to live wi' me – long, are you, Angel?'

she asked, the sunk corners of her mouth betraying how purely mechanical were the means by which she retained that expression of chastened calm upon her face.

'I cannot,' he said, 'without despising myself, and what is worse, perhaps, despising you. I mean, of course, cannot live with you in the ordinary sense. At present, whatever I feel, I do not despise you. And, since we have begun to speak, Tess, let me speak plainly, otherwise you may not perceive all my difficulties. How can we live together while that man lives?'[7]. . . Now I put it to you. Don't think of me or of yourself, my feelings or your feelings. That's not all the difficulty; it lies in another consideration – one bearing upon the future of other people than ourselves. Think of years to come, and children being brought to us, and this past matter getting known – for it must get known. There is not an uttermost part of the earth but somebody comes from it or goes to it from elsewhere. Well, think of wretches of our flesh and blood growing up under a taunt which they will gradually get to feel the full force of with their expanding years. What an awakening for them! What a prospect! Can you honestly say Remain, after contemplating this contingency? Don't you think we had better endure the ills we have than fly to others?'[8]

Her eyelids, weighted with trouble, continued drooping as before.

'I cannot say Remain,' she answered. 'I cannot; I had not thought so far.'

Tess's feminine hope – shall we confess it – had been so obstinately recuperative as to revive in her surreptitious visions of a domiciliary intimacy continued long enough to break down his coldness even against his judgment. Though unsophisticated in the usual sense, she was not incomplete; and it would have denoted deficiency of womanhood if she had not instinctively known what an argument lies in propinquity. Nothing else would serve her, she knew, if this failed. It was wrong to hope in what was of the nature of strategy, she said to herself: yet that sort of hope she could not extinguish. His last representation had now been made, and it was, as she said, a new view. She had truly never thought so far as that, and his lucid picture of possible offspring who would scorn her was one that brought deadly conviction to an honest heart which was humanitarian to its centre.

Sheer experience had already taught her that, in some circumstances, there was one thing better than to lead a good life, and that was to be saved from leading any life whatever. Like all who have been previsioned by suffering, she could, in the words of M. Sully-Prudhomme, hear a penal sentence in the fiat, 'You shall be born,'[9] particularly if addressed to potential issue of hers.

Yet such is the vulpine slyness of Dame Nature, that, till now, Tess had been hoodwinked by her love for Clare into forgetting it might result in vitalizations[10] that would inflict upon others what she had bewailed as a misfortune to herself.

She therefore could not withstand his argument. But with the self-combating proclivity of the supersensitive, an answer thereto arose in Clare's own mind, and he almost feared it. It was based on her exceptional physical nature; and she might have used it promisingly. She might have added besides: 'On an Australian upland or Texan plain, who is to know or care about my misfortunes, or to reproach me or you?' Yet, like the majority of women, she accepted the momentary presentment as if it were the inevitable. And she may have been right. The heart of woman knoweth not only its own bitterness,[11] but its husband's, and even if these assumed reproaches were not likely to be addressed to him or to his by strangers, they might have reached his ears from his own fastidious brain.

It was the third day of the estrangement. Clare's love was ethereal to a fault, imaginative to impracticability. With these natures, corporeal presence is sometimes less appealing than corporeal absence; the latter creating an ideal presence that conveniently drops the defects of the real. She found that her personality did not plead her cause so forcibly as she had anticipated. The figurative phrase was true: she was another woman than the one he had desired.

'I have thought over what you say,' she remarked to him, moving her forefinger over the table-cloth, her other hand, which bore the ring that mocked them both, supporting her forehead. 'It is quite true, all of it; it must be. You must go away from me.'

'But what can you do?'

'I can go home.'

Clare had not thought of that.

'Are you sure?' he said.

'Quite sure. We ought to part, and we may as well get it past and done. You once said that I was apt to win men against their better judgment; and if I am constantly before your eyes I may cause you to change your plans in opposition to your reason and wish; and afterwards your repentance and my sorrow will be terrible.'

'And you would like to go home?' he asked.

'I want to leave you, and go home.'

'Then it shall be so.'

Though she did not look up at him, she started. There was a difference between the proposition and the covenant, which she had felt only too quickly.

'I feared it would come to this,' she murmured, her countenance fixed in meek vacuity. 'I don't complain, Angel. I – I think it best. What you said has quite convinced me. And though nobody else should reproach me if we should stay together, and you should ever, years hence, get angry with me for any ordinary matter, knowing what you do of my bygones, you yourself might be tempted to say words, and they might be overheard, perhaps by my own children. O, what only hurts me now would torture and kill me then! I will go – to-morrow.'

'And I shall not stay here. Though I didn't like to initiate it, I have seen that it was advisable we should part – at least for a while, till I can better see the shape that things have taken, and can write to you.'

Tess stole a glance at her husband. He was pale, even tremulous; but, as before, she was appalled by the determination revealed in the depths of this gentle being she had married – the will to subdue the grosser to the subtler emotion, the substance to the conception, the flesh to the spirit. Propensities, tendencies, habits, were as dead leaves upon the tyrannous wind of his imaginative ascendency.

He may have observed her look, for he explained –

'I think of people more kindly when I am away from them;' adding cynically, 'God knows; perhaps we shall shake down together some day, for weariness; thousands have done it!'

That day he began to pack up, and she went upstairs and began to pack also. Both knew that it was in their two minds that they might part the next morning for ever, despite the gloss of assuaging conjectures thrown over their proceeding because they were of the sort to whom any parting which has an air of finality is a torture. He knew, and she knew, that, though the fascination which each had exercised over the other – on her part independently of accomplishments – would probably in the first days of their separation be even more potent than ever, time must attenuate that effect; the practical arguments against accepting her as a housemate might pronounce themselves more strongly in the cold boreal light of a remoter time. Moreover, when two people are once parted – have abandoned a common domicile and a common environment – new growths insensibly bud upward to fill each vacated place; unforeseen accidents hinder intentions, and old plans are forgotten.

XXXVII

Midnight came and passed silently, for there was nothing to announce it in the Valley of the Var.

Not long after one o'clock there was a slight creak in the darkened farm-house once the mansion of the D'Urbervilles. Tess, who used the upper chamber, heard it and awoke. It had come from the corner step of the staircase, which, as usual was loosely nailed.[1] She saw the door of her bedroom open, and the figure of her husband crossed the stream of moonlight with a curiously careful tread. He was in his shirt and trousers only, and her first flush of joy died when she perceived that his eyes were fixed in an unnatural stare on vacancy. When he reached the middle of the room he stood still and murmured, in tones of indescribable sadness –

'Dead! dead! dead!'

Under the influence of any strongly-disturbing force Clare would occasionally walk in his sleep, and even perform strange feats, such as he had done on the night of their return from market just before their marriage, when he re-enacted in his bedroom his combat with the man who had insulted her. Tess saw that continued mental distress had wrought him into that somnambulistic state now.

Her loyal confidence in him lay so deep down in her heart that, awake or asleep, he inspired her with no sort of personal fear. If he had entered with a pistol in his hand he would scarcely have disturbed her trust in his protectiveness.

Clare came close, and bent over her. 'Dead, dead, dead!' he murmured.

After fixedly regarding her for some moments with the same gaze of unmeasurable woe he bent lower, enclosed her in his arms, and rolled her in the sheet as in a shroud. Then lifting her from the bed with as much respect as one would show to a dead body in such circumstances, he carried her across the room, murmuring –

'My poor, poor Tess – my dearest, darling Tess! So sweet, so good, so true!'

The words of endearment, withheld so severely in his waking hours, were inexpressibly sweet to her forlorn and hungry heart. If it had been to save her weary life she would not, by moving or struggling, have put an end to the position she found herself in. Thus she lay in absolute stillness, scarcely venturing to breathe, and, wondering what he was going to do with her, suffered herself to be borne out upon the landing.

'My wife – dead, dead!' he said.

He paused in his labours for a moment to lean with her against the bannister, over which her feet hung ominously. Was he going to throw her down? Self-solicitude was near extinction in her, and in the sickening knowledge that he had planned to depart on the morrow, possibly for always, she lay in his arms in this precarious position with a sense rather of luxury than of terror. If they could only fall together, and both be dashed to pieces, how fit, how desirable. She did not wish to save herself.

However, he did not let her fall, but took advantage of the support of the handrail to imprint a kiss upon her lips – lips in the daytime scorned. Then he clasped her with a renewed firmness of hold, and descended the staircase. The creak of the loose stair did not awaken him, and they reached the ground-floor safely. Freeing one of his hands from its grasp of her for a moment, he slid back the door-bar and passed out, slightly striking his stockinged toe against the edge of the door. But this he seemed not to mind, and, bearing her off the premises, turned in the direction of the river a few yards off.

His ultimate intention, if he had any, she had not yet divined; and she found herself conjecturing on the matter as a third person might have done. So easefully had she delivered her whole being up to him that it pleased her to think he was regarding her as his absolute possession, to dispose of as he should choose. It was consoling, under the hovering terror of to-morrow's separation, to feel that he really recognized her now as his wife Tess, and did not cast her off, even if in that recognition he went so far as to arrogate to himself the right of harming her.

Ah! now she knew what he was dreaming of – that Sunday morning when he had borne her along through the water with the other dairymaids, who had loved him nearly as much as she, if that were possible, which Tess could hardly admit. Clare did not cross the bridge with her, but proceeding several paces on the same side till he was drawing towards the mill, at length stood still on the brink of the river.

Its waters, in creeping down these miles of meadow-land, frequently divided, serpentining in purposeless curves, looping themselves around little islands that had no name, returning, and re-embodying themselves as a broad main stream further on. Opposite the spot to which he had arrived with her was such a general confluence, and the river was proportionately voluminous and deep. Across it was a narrow foot-bridge; but now the autumn rains had washed the handrail away, leaving the bare plank only, which, lying a few inches above the speeding current, formed a giddy pathway for all but steady heads;[2] and Tess had noticed from the window of the house in the daytime young men walking across upon it as a feat in balancing. Her husband had possibly observed the same performance; anyhow, he now mounted the plank, and, sliding one foot forward, advanced along it.

Was he going to drown her? Probably he was. The spot was lonely, the river deep and wide enough to make such a purpose easy of accomplishment. He might drown her if he would; it would be better than parting to-morrow to lead severed lives.

The swift stream raced and gyrated under them, tossing, distorting, and splitting the moon's reflected face. Spots of froth travelled past, and intercepted weeds waved behind the piles. If they could both fall together into the current now, their arms would be so tightly clasped together that they could not be saved; they would go out of the world almost painlessly, and there would be no more reproach to her, or to him for marrying her. His last half-hour with her would have been a loving one, while if they lived till he awoke his daytime aversion would return, and this hour would remain to be contemplated only as a transient dream.

The impulse stirred in her, yet she dared not indulge it, to make a movement that would have precipitated them both into the gulf. How she valued her own life had been proved; but his – she had no right to tamper with it. He reached the other side with her in safety.

Here the ground led up to a plantation, and close to it was a fence which had formed the margin of the Abbey grounds. He paused at this spot, clambered over, and, taking a new hold of her, went onward a few steps till they reached the ruined choir of the Abbey-church. Against the north wall was the empty stone coffin of an abbot, without a lid.[3] In this he carefully laid her. Having kissed her lips a second time, he breathed deeply, as if a greatly desired end were attained. Clare then lay down on the ground alongside,[4] when he immediately fell into the deep dead slumber of exhaustion, and remained motionless as a log. The spurt of mental excitement which had produced the effort was now over.

Tess sat up in the coffin. The night, though dry and mild for the season, was more than sufficiently cold to make it dangerous for him to remain here long, in his half-clothed state. If he were left to himself he would in all probability stay there till the morning, and be chilled to certain death. She had heard of such deaths after sleep-walking. But how could she dare to awaken him, and let him know what he had been doing, when it would mortify him to discover his folly in respect of her? Tess, however, stepping out of her stone confine, shook him slightly, but was unable to arouse him without being violent. It was indispensable to do something, for she was beginning to shiver, the sheet being but a poor protection. Her excitement had in a measure kept her warm during the adventure; but that beatific interval was over.

It suddenly occurred to her to try persuasion; and accordingly she whispered in his ear, with as much firmness and decision as she could summon –

'Let us walk on darling,' at the same time taking him suggestively by the arm. To her relief, he unresistingly acquiesced; her words had apparently thrown him back into his dream, which thenceforward seemed to enter on a new phase, wherein he fancied she had risen as a spirit, and was leading him to Heaven. Thus she conducted him by the arm, by the track away from the ruins, and along to the outskirts of their residence where they reached the stone bridge over the stream, crossing which they stood at the manor-house door. Tess's feet were quite bare, and the stones hurt her, and chilled her to the bone; but Clare was in his woollen stockings, and appeared to feel no discomfort.

There was no further difficulty. She induced him to lie down on his own sofa bed, and covered him up warmly, lighting a temporary fire of wood, to dry any dampness out of him. The noise of these attentions she thought might awaken him, and secretly wished that they might. But the exhaustion of his mind and body was such that he remained undisturbed.

As soon as they met the next morning Tess divined that Angel knew nothing of how far she had been concerned in the night's excursion, though as regarded himself, he may have had an inkling that he had not lain still. In truth, he had awakened that morning from a sleep deep as annihilation; and during those first few moments in which the brain, like a Samson shaking himself,[5] is trying its strength, had waited in expectancy to discern its pointing; he knew that if any intention of his, concluded over-night, did not vanish in the light of morning, it stood on a basis approximating to one of pure reason, even if initiated by impulse of feeling; that it was so far, therefore, to be trusted.

He had thus beheld in the pale morning light the resolve to separate from her; not as a hot and indignant instinct, but denuded of the passionateness which had made it scorch and burn; standing in its bones; nothing but a skeleton, but none the less there. Clare no longer hesitated.

At breakfast, and while they were packing the few remaining articles, he showed his weariness from the night's effort so unmistakably that

Tess was on the point of revealing all that had happened; but the reflection that it would anger him, grieve him, stultify him, to know that he had instinctively manifested a fondness for her of which his common-sense did not approve; that his inclination had compromised his dignity when reason slept, again deterred her. It was too much like laughing at a man when sober for his erratic deeds during intoxication.

It just crossed her mind, too, that he might have a faint recollection of his tender vagary, and was disinclined to allude to it from a conviction that she would take advantage of the undoubted opportunity it gave her of appealing to him anew not to go.

He had ordered by letter a vehicle from the nearest town, and soon after breakfast it arrived. She saw in it the beginning of the end – the temporary end, at least, for the revelation of his tenderness by the incident of the night raised dreams of a possible future with him. The luggage was put on the top, and the man drove them off, the miller and the old waiting-woman expressing some surprise at their precipitate departure, which Clare attributed to his discovery that the mill-work was not of the modern kind which he wished to investigate, a statement that was true so far as it went. Beyond this there was nothing in the manner of their leaving to suggest a *fiasco*, or that they were not going together to visit friends.

Their route lay near the dairy from which they had started with such solemn joy in each other a few days back, and, as Clare wished to wind up his business with Mr Crick, Tess could hardly avoid paying Mrs Crick a call at the same time, unless she would excite suspicion of their unhappy state.

To make the call as unobtrusive as possible they left the carriage by the wicket leading down from the high road to the dairy-house, and descended the track on foot, side by side. The withy-bed had been cut, and they could see over the stumps the spot to which Clare had followed her when he pressed her to be his wife; to the left the enclosure in which she had been fascinated by his harp; and far away behind the cowstalls the mead which had been the scene of their first embrace. The gold of the summer picture was now gray, the colours mean, the rich soil mud, and the river cold.

Over the barton-gate the dairyman saw them, and came forward, throwing into his face the kind of joviality deemed appropriate in Talbothays and its vicinity on the reappearance of the newly-married. Then Mrs Crick emerged from the house, and several others of their old acquaintance, though Marian and Retty did not appear to be there.

Tess valiantly bore their sly attacks and friendly humours, which affected her far otherwise than they supposed. In the tacit agreement of husband and wife to keep their estrangement a secret they behaved as would have been ordinary. And then, although she would rather there had been no word spoken on the subject, Tess had to hear in detail the story of Marian and Retty. The latter had gone home to her father's, and Marian had left to look for employment elsewhere. They feared she would come to no good.

To dissipate the sadness of this recital Tess went and bade all her favourite cows good-bye, touching each of them with her hand, and as she and Clare stood side by side at leaving, as if united body and soul, there would have been something peculiarly sorry in their aspect to one who should have seen it truly; two limbs of one life, as they outwardly were, his arm touching hers, her skirts touching him, facing one way, as against all the dairy facing the other, speaking in their adieux as 'we,' and yet sundered like the poles. Perhaps something unusually stiff and embarrassed in their attitude, some awkwardness in acting up to their profession of unity, different from the natural shyness of young couples, may have been apparent, for when they were gone Mrs Crick said to her husband—

'How onnatural the brightness of her eyes did seem, and how they stood like waxen images and talked as if they were in a dream! Didn't it strike 'ee that 'twas so? Tess had always sommat strange in her, and she's not now quite like the proud young bride of a well-be-doing man.'

They re-entered the vehicle, and were driven along the roads to distant Weatherbury and Stagfoot Lane, till they reached Nuzzlebury, where Clare dismissed the fly and man. They rested here a while, and entering the Vale were next driven onward towards her home by a stranger who did not know their relations. At a midway point, when many miles had been passed over, and where there were cross-roads,

Clare stopped the conveyance and said to Tess that if she meant to return to her mother's house it was here that he would leave her. As they could not talk with freedom in the driver's presence he asked her to accompany him for a few steps on foot along one of the branch roads; she assented, and directing the man to wait a few minutes they strolled away.

'Now, let us understand each other,' he said gently. 'There is no anger between us, though there is that which I cannot endure at present. I will try to bring myself to endure it. I will let you know where I go to as soon as I know myself. And if I can bring myself to bear it – if it is desirable, possible – I will come to you. But until I come to you it will be better that you should not try to come to me.'

The severity of the decree seemed deadly to Tess; she saw his view of her clearly enough; he could regard her in no other light than that of one who had practised gross deceit upon him. Yet could a woman who had done even what she had done deserve all this? But she could contest the point with him no further. She simply repeated after him his own words.

'Until you come to me I must not try to come to you?'

'Just so.'

'May I write to you?'

'Oh yes – if you are ill, or want anything at all. I hope that will not be the case; so that it may happen that I write first to you.'

'I agree to the conditions, Angel; because you know best what my punishment ought to be; only – only – don't make it more than I can bear!'

That was all she said on the matter. If Tess had been artful, had she made a scene, fainted, wept hysterically, in that lonely lane, notwithstanding the fury of fastidiousness with which he was possessed, he would probably not have withstood her.[6] But her mood of long-suffering made his way easy for him, and she herself was his best advocate. In her submission – which perhaps was a symptom of that acquiescence[7] in chance too apparent in the whole D'Urberville family – the many effective chords which she could have stirred by an appeal were left untouched.

The remainder of their discourse was on practical matters only. He now handed her a packet containing a fairly good sum of money, which he had obtained from his bankers for the purpose. The brilliants, the interest in which seemed to be Tess's for her life only (if he understood the wording of the will), he advised her to let him send to a bank for safety; and to this she readily agreed.[8]

These things arranged he walked with Tess back to the carriage, and handed her in. The coachman was paid and told where to drive her. Taking then his own bag and umbrella – the sole articles he had brought with him hitherwards – he bade her good-bye; and they parted there and then.

The fly moved creepingly up the hill, and Clare watched it go with an unpremeditated hope that Tess would look out of the window for one moment. But that she never thought of doing, would not have ventured to do, lying in a half-dead faint inside. Thus he beheld her recede, and in the anguish of his heart quoted a line from a poet, with peculiar emendations of his own –

God's *not* in his heaven: all's *wrong* with the world![9]

When Tess had passed over the crest of the hill he turned to go his own way, and did not know that he loved her still.

XXXVIII

As she drove on through Blackmoor Vale, and the landscape of her youth began to open around her, Tess aroused herself from her stupor. Her first thought was how would she be able to face her parents?

She reached the turnpike-gate which stood near the entrance to the village. It was thrown open by a stranger, not by the old man who had kept it for many years, and to whom she had been known; he had probably left on New Year's Day, the date when such changes were made.[1] Having received no intelligence lately from her home, she asked the turnpike-keeper for news.

'Oh – nothing, miss,' he answered. 'Marlott is Marlott still. Folks

254

have died and that. John Durbeyfield, too, hev had a daughter married this week to a gentleman-farmer; not from John's own house, you know; they was married elsewhere; the gentleman being of that high standing that John's own folk was not considered well-be-doing enough to have any part in it, the bridegroom seeming not to know how't have been discovered that John is a old and ancient nobleman himself by blood, with family skellingtons in their own vaults to this day, but done out of his property in the time o' the Romans. However, Sir John, as we call 'n now, kept up the wedding-day as well as he could, and stood treat to everybody in the parish; and John's wife sung songs at The Pure Drop till past eleven o'clock.'

Hearing this, Tess felt so sick at heart that she could not decide to go home publicly in the fly with her luggage and belongings. She asked the turnpike-keeper if she might deposit her things at his house for a while, and, on his offering no objection, she dismissed her carriage, and went on to the village alone by a back lane.

At sight of her father's chimney she asked herself how she could possibly enter the house? Inside that cottage her relations were calmly supposing her far away on a wedding tour with a comparatively rich man, who was to conduct her to bouncing prosperity; while here she was, friendless, creeping up to the old door quite by herself, with no better place to go to in the world.

She did not reach the house unobserved. Just by the garden-hedge she was met by a girl who knew her – one of the two or three with whom she had been intimate at school. After making a few inquiries as to how Tess came there, her friend, unheeding her tragic look, interrupted with –

'But where's thy gentleman, Tess?'

Tess hastily explained that he had been called away on business, and, leaving her interlocutor, clambered over the garden-hedge, and thus made her way to the house.

As she went up the garden-path she heard her mother singing by the back door, coming in sight of which she perceived Mrs Durbeyfield on the doorstep in the act of wringing a sheet. Having performed this without observing Tess, she went indoors, and her daughter followed her.

The washing-tub stood in the same old place on the same old quarter-hogshead, and her mother, having thrown the sheet aside, was about to plunge her arms in anew.

'Why – Tess! – my chil' – I thought you was married! – married really and truly this time – we sent the cider—'

'Yes, mother; so I am.'

'Going to be?'

'I mean – I am married.'

'Married! Then where's thy husband?'

'Oh, he's gone away for a time.'

'Gone away! When was you married, then? The day you said?'

'Yes, Tuesday, mother.'

'And now 'tis on'y Saturday, and he gone away?'

'Yes; he's gone.'

'What's the meaning o' that? 'Nation seize such husbands as you seem to get, say I!'

'Mother!' Tess went across to Joan Durbeyfield, laid her face upon the matron's bosom, and burst into sobs. 'I don't know how to tell 'ee, mother! You said to me, and wrote to me, that I was not to tell him. But I did tell him – I couldn't help it – and he went away!'

'O you little fool – you little fool!' burst out Mrs Durbeyfield, splashing Tess and herself in her agitation. 'My heaven! that ever I should ha' lived to say it, but I say it again, you little fool!'

Tess was convulsed with weeping, the tension of so many days having relaxed at last.

'I know it – I know – I know!' she gasped through her sobs. 'But, O my mother, I could not help it! He was so good – and I felt the wickedness of trying to blind him as to what had happened! If – if – it were to be done again – I should do the same. I could not – I dared not – so sin – against him.'

'But you sinned enough to marry him first!'

'Yes, yes; that's where my misery do lie! But I thought he could get rid of me by law if he were determined not to overlook it. And oh, if you knew – if you could only half know how I loved him – how anxious I was to have him – and how distressed I was between caring so much for him and my wish to be fair to him!'

Tess was so shaken that she could get no further, and sank a helpless heap into a chair.

'Well, well; what's done can't be undone! I'm sure I don't know why children o' my bringing forth should all be bigger simpletons than other people's – not to know better than to blab such a thing as that, when he couldn't ha' found it out till too late!' Here Mrs Durbeyfield began shedding tears on her own account as a mother to be pitied. 'What your father will say I don't know,' she continued; 'for he's been talking about the wedding up at Rolliver's and The Pure Drop every day since, and about his family getting back to their rightful position through you – poor silly man! – and now you've made this mess of it! The Lord-a-Lord!'

As if to bring matters to a focus, Tess's father was heard approaching at that moment. He did not, however, enter immediately, and Mrs Durbeyfield said that she would break the bad news to him herself, Tess keeping out of sight for the present. After her first burst of disappointment Joan began to take the mishap as she had taken Tess's original trouble, as she would have taken a wet holiday or failure in the potato-crop; as a thing which had come upon them irrespective of desert or folly; an external impingement to be borne with; not a lesson.[2]

Tess retreated upstairs, and beheld casually that the beds had been shifted, and new arrangements made. Her old bed had been adapted for two younger children. There was no place here for her now.

The room below being unceiled she could hear most of what went on there. Presently her father entered, apparently carrying a live hen. He was a foot-higgler now, having been obliged to sell his second horse, and he travelled with his basket on his arm. The hen had been carried about this morning as it was often carried, to show people that he was in his work, though it had lain, with its legs tied, under the table at Rolliver's for more than an hour.

'We've just had up a story about—' Durbeyfield began, and thereupon related in detail to his wife a discussion which had arisen at the inn about the clergy, originated by the fact of his daughter having married into a clerical family. 'They was formerly styled "sir," like my own ancestry,' he said, 'though nowadays their true style, strictly speaking, is "clerk" only.' As Tess had wished that no great publicity should be given to the event, he had mentioned no name. He hoped she would remove that prohibition soon. He proposed that the couple should take Tess's own name, D'Urberville, as uncorrupted. It was better than her husband's. He asked if any letter had come from her that day.

Then Mrs Durbeyfield informed him that no letter had come, but Tess unfortunately had come herself.

When at length the collapse was explained to him a sullen mortification, not usual with Durbeyfield, overpowered the effect of the cheering glass. Yet the intrinsic quality of the event affected his touchy sensitiveness less than its conjectured effect upon the minds of others.

'To think, now, that this was to be the end o't!' said Sir John. 'And I with a family vault under that there church of Kingsbere as big as Squire Jollard's ale-cellar, and my folk lying there in sixes and sevens, as genuine county bones and marrow as any recorded in history. And now to be sure what they fellers at Rolliver's and The Pure Drop will say to me! How they'll squint and glane, and say, "This is yer mighty match is it; this is yer getting back to the true level of yer forefathers in King Norman's time!" I feel this too much, Joan; I shall put an end to myself, title and all – I can bear it no longer! . . . But she can make him keep her if he's married her?'

'Why, yes. But she won't think o' doing that.'

'D'ye think he really have married her? – or is it like the first—'

Poor Tess, who had heard as far as this, could not bear to hear more. The perception that her word could be doubted even here, in her own parental house, set her mind against the spot as nothing else could have done. How unexpected were the attacks of destiny! And if her father doubted her a little, would not strangers and acquaintance doubt her much? O, she could not live long at home!

A few days, accordingly, were all that she allowed herself here, at the end of which time she received a short note from Clare, informing her that he had gone to the North of England to look at a farm. In her craving for the lustre of her true position as his wife, and to hide from her parents the vast extent of the division between them, she made use of this letter as her reason for again departing, leaving them under the impression that she was setting out to join him. Still further to screen her husband from any imputation of unkindness to her, she took twenty-five of the fifty pounds Clare had given her, and handed the sum over to her mother, as if the wife of a man like Angel Clare could well afford it, saying that it was a slight return for the trouble and humiliation she had brought upon them in years past. With this assertion of her dignity she bade them farewell; and after that there were lively doings in the Durbeyfield household for some time on the strength of Tess's bounty, her mother saying, and, indeed, believing, that the rupture which had arisen between the young husband and wife had adjusted itself under their strong feeling that they could not live apart from each other.

XXXIX

It was three weeks after the marriage that Clare found himself descending the hill which led to the well-known parsonage of his father. With his downward course the tower of the church rose into the evening sky in a manner of inquiry as to why he had come; and no living person in the twilighted town seemed to notice him, still less to expect him. He was arriving like a ghost, and the sound of his own footsteps was almost an encumbrance to be got rid of.

The picture of life had changed for him. Before this time he had known it but speculatively; now he thought he knew it as a practical man; though perhaps he did not, even yet. Nevertheless humanity stood before him no longer in the pensive sweetness of Italian art, but in the staring and ghastly attitudes of a Wiertz Museum, and with the leer of a study by Van Beers.[1]

His conduct during these first weeks had been desultory beyond description. After mechanically attempting to pursue his agricultural plans as though nothing unusual had happened, in the manner recommended by the great and wise men of all ages, he concluded that not one of those great and wise men had ever gone so far outside themselves as to test the feasibility of his own counsel. 'This is the chief thing: be not perturbed,' said the Pagan moralist.[2] That was just Clare's own opinion. But he was perturbed. 'Let not your heart be troubled, neither let it be afraid,' said the Nazarene.[3] Clare chimed in cordially; but his heart was troubled all the same. How he would have liked to confront those two thinkers, and earnestly appeal to them as fellow-man to fellow-men, and ask them to tell him their method!

His mood transmuted itself into a dogged indifference till at length he fancied he was looking on his own existence with the passive interest of an outsider.

He was embittered by the conviction that all this desolation had been brought about by the accident of her being a D'Urberville. When he found that Tess came of that exhausted ancient line, and was not of the new tribes from below, as he had fondly dreamed, why had he not stoically abandoned her, in fidelity to his principles? This was what he had got by apostacy, and his punishment was deserved.

Then he became weary and anxious, and his anxiety increased. He wondered if he had treated her unfairly. He ate without knowing that he ate, and drank without tasting. As the hours dropped past, as the motive of each act in the long series of bygone days presented itself to his view, he perceived how intimately the notion of having Tess as a dear possession was mixed up with all schemes and words and ways.

In going hither and thither he observed in the outskirts of a small town a red-and-blue placard setting forth the great advantages of the Empire of Brazil[4] as a field for the emigrating agriculturist. Land was offered there on exceptionally advantageous terms. Brazil somewhat attracted him as a new idea. Tess could eventually join him there, and perhaps in that country of contrasting scenes and notions and habits the conventions would not be so operative which made life with her seem impracticable to him here. In brief he was strongly inclined to try Brazil, especially as the season for going thither was just at hand.

With this view he was returning to Emminster to disclose his plan to his parents, and to make the best explanation he could make of arriving without Tess, short of revealing what had actually separated them. As he reached the door the new moon shone upon his face, just as the old one had done in the small hours of that morning when he had carried his wife in his arms across the river to the graveyard of the monks; but his face was thinner now.

Clare had given his parents no warning of his visit, and his arrival stirred the atmosphere of the Vicarage as the dive of the kingfisher stirs a quiet pool. His father and mother were both in the drawing-room, but neither of his brothers was now at home. Angel entered, and closed the door quietly behind him.

'But – where's your wife, dear Angel?' cried his mother. 'How you surprise us!'

'She is at her mother's – temporarily. I have come home rather in a hurry because I've decided to go to Brazil.'

'Brazil! Why they are all Roman Catholics there, surely!'

'Are they? I hadn't thought of that.'

But even the novelty and painfulness of his going to a Papistical land could not displace for long Mr and Mrs Clare's natural interest in their son's marriage.

'We had your brief note three weeks ago announcing that it had taken place,' said Mrs Clare, 'and your father sent your godmother's gift to her, as you know. Of course it was best that none of us should be present, especially as you preferred to marry her from the dairy, and not at her home, wherever that may be. It would have embarrassed you, and given us no pleasure. Your brothers felt that very strongly. Now it is done we do not complain, particularly if she suits you for the business you have chosen to follow, instead of the ministry of the Gospel . . . Yet I wish I could have seen her first, Angel, or have known a little more about her. We sent her no present of our own, not knowing what would best give her pleasure, but you must suppose it only delayed. Angel, there is no irritation in my mind or your father's against you for this marriage; but we have thought it much better to reserve our liking for your wife till we could see her. And now you have not brought her. It seems strange. What has happened?'

He replied that it had been thought best by them that she should go to her parents' home for the present, whilst he came there.

'I don't mind telling you, dear mother,' he said, 'that I always meant to keep her away from this house till I should feel she could come with credit to you. But this idea of Brazil is quite a recent one. If I do go it will be unadvisable for me to take her on this my first journey. She will remain at her mother's till I come back.'

'And I shall not see her before you start?'

He was afraid they would not. His original plan had been, as he had said, to refrain from bringing her there for some little while – not to wound their prejudices – feelings – in any way; and for other reasons he had adhered to it. He would have to visit home in the course of a year, if he went out at once; and it would be possible for them to see her before he started a second time – with her.

A hastily prepared supper was brought in, and Clare gave further explanation of his plans. His mother's disappointment at not seeing the bride still remained with her. Clare's late enthusiasm for Tess had infected her through her maternal sympathies, till she had almost fancied that a good thing could come out of Nazareth[5] – a charming woman out of Talbothays Dairy. She watched her son as he ate.

'Cannot you describe her! I am sure she is very pretty, Angel.'

'Of that there can be no question!' he said, with a zest which covered its bitterness.

'And that she is pure and virtuous goes without question?'

'Pure and virtuous, of course, she is.'

'I can see her quite distinctly. You said the other day that she was fine in figure; roundly built; had deep red lips with keen corners; dark eyelashes and brows, an immense rope of hair like a ship's cable; and large eyes violety-bluey-blackish.'

'I did, mother.'

'I quite see her. And living in such seclusion she naturally had scarce ever seen any young man from the world without till she saw you.'

'Scarcely.'

'You were her first love?'

'Of course.'

'There are worse wives than these simple, rosy-mouthed, robust girls of the farm. Certainly I could have wished – well, since my son is to be an agriculturist, it is perhaps but proper that his wife should have been accustomed to an outdoor life.'

His father was less inquisitive; but when the time came for the chapter from the Bible which was always read before evening prayers, the Vicar observed to Mrs Clare –

'I think, since Angel has come, that it will be more appropriate to read the thirty-first of Proverbs than the chapter which we should have had in the usual course of our reading?'

'Yes, certainly,' said Mrs Clare. 'The words of King Lemuel' (she could cite chapter and verse as well as her husband). 'My dear son, your father has decided to read us the chapter in Proverbs in praise of a virtuous wife. We shall not need to be reminded to apply the words to the absent one. May Heaven shield her in all her ways!'

A lump rose in Clare's throat. The portable lectern was taken out from the corner and set in the middle of the fireplace, the two old servants came in, and Angel's father began to read at the tenth verse of the aforesaid chapter –

' "Who can find a virtuous woman? for her price is far above rubies. She riseth while it is yet night, and giveth meat to her household. She girdeth her loins with strength and strengtheneth her arms. She perceiveth that her merchandise is good; her candle goeth not out by night. She looketh well to the ways of her household, and eateth not the bread of idleness. Her children arise up and call her blessed; her husband also, and he praiseth her. Many daughters have done virtuously, but thou excellest them all." '[6]

When prayers were over, his mother said –

'I could not help thinking how very aptly that chapter your dear father read applied, in some of its particulars, to the woman you have chosen. The perfect woman, you see, was a working woman; not an idler; not a fine lady; but one who used her hands and her head and her heart for the good of others. "Her children arise up and call her blessed; her husband also, and he praiseth her. Many daughters have done virtuously, but she excelleth them all." Well, I wish I could have seen her, Angel. Since she is pure and chaste she would have been refined enough for me.'

Clare could bear this no longer. His eyes were full of tears, which seemed like drops of molten lead. He bade a quick good-night to these sincere and simple souls whom he loved so well; who knew neither the world, the flesh, nor the devil in their own hearts;[7] only as something vague and external to themselves. He went to his own chamber.

His mother followed him, and tapped at his door. Clare opened it to discover her standing without, with anxious eyes.

'Angel,' she asked, 'is there something wrong that you go away so soon? I am quite sure you are not yourself.'

'I am not, quite, mother,' said he.

'About her? Now, my son, I know it is that – I know it is about her! Have you quarrelled in these three weeks?'

'We have not exactly quarrelled,' he said. 'But we have had a difference—'

'Angel – is she a young woman whose history will bear investigation?'

With a mother's instinct Mrs Clare had put her finger on the kind of trouble that would cause such a disquiet as seemed to agitate her son.

'She is spotless!' he replied; and felt that if it had sent him to eternal hell there and then he would have told that lie.

'Then never mind the rest. After all, there are few purer things in nature than an unsullied country maid. Any crudeness of manner which may offend your more educated sense at first, will, I am sure, disappear under the influence of your companionship and tuition.'

Such terrible sarcasm of blind magnanimity brought home to Clare the secondary perception that he had utterly wrecked his career by this marriage, which had not been among his early thoughts after the disclosure. True, on his own account he cared very little about his career; but he had wished to make it at least a respectable one on account of his parents and brothers. And now as he looked into the candle its flame dumbly expressed to him that it was made to shine on sensible people, and that it abhorred lighting the face of a dupe and a failure.[8]

When his agitation had cooled he would be at moments incensed with his poor wife for causing a situation in which he was obliged to practise deception on his parents. He almost talked to her in his anger, as if she had been in the room. And then her cooing voice, plaintive in expostulation, disturbed the darkness, the velvet touch of her lips passed over his brow, and he could distinguish in the air the warmth of her breath.

This night the woman of his belittling deprecations was thinking how great and good her husband was. But over them both there hung a deeper shade than the shade which Angel Clare perceived, namely, the shade of his own limitations. With all his attempted independence of judgment this advanced man was yet the slave to custom and conventionality[9] when surprised back into his early teachings. No prophet had told him, and he was not prophet enough to tell himself, that essentially this young wife of his was as deserving of the praise of King Lemuel as any other woman endowed with the same dislike of evil, her moral value having to be reckoned not by achievement but by tendency. Moreover, the figure near at hand suffers on such occasions, because it shows up its sorriness without shade; while vague figures afar off are honoured, in that their distance makes artistic virtues of their stains. In considering what Tess was not, he overlooked what she was, and forgot that the defective can be more than the entire.

END OF VOL. II

At breakfast Brazil was the topic, and all endeavoured to take a hopeful view of Clare's proposed experiment with that country's soil, notwithstanding the discouraging reports of some farm-labourers who had emigrated thither and returned home within the twelve months. After breakfast Clare went into the little town to wind up such trifling matters as he was concerned with there, and to get from the local bank all the money he possessed. On his way back he encountered Miss Mercy Chant by the church, from whose walls she seemed to be a sort of emanation. She was carrying an armful of Bibles for her class, and such was her view of life that events which produced heartache in others wrought beatific smiles upon her – an enviable result, although, in the opinion of Angel, it was obtained by a curiously unnatural sacrifice of humanity to mysticism.

She had learnt that he was about to leave England, and observed what an excellent and promising scheme it seemed to be.

'Yes; it is a likely scheme enough in a commercial sense, no doubt,' he replied. 'But, my dear Mercy, it snaps the continuity of existence. Perhaps a cloister would be preferable.'

'A cloister! O, Angel Clare!'

'Well?'

'Why, you wicked man, a cloister implies a monk, and a monk Roman Catholicism.'

'And Roman Catholicism sin, and sin damnation. Thou art in a parlous state, Angel Clare.'[1]

'*I* glory in my Protestantism,' she said severely.

Then Clare, thrown by sheer misery into one of the demoniacal moods in which a man does despite to his true principles, called her close to him, and fiendishly whispered in her ear the most heterodox ideas he could think of. His momentary laughter at the horror which appeared on her fair face ceased when it merged in pain and anxiety for his welfare.

'Dear Mercy,' he said, 'you must forgive me. I think I am going crazy!'

She thought that he was; and thus the interview ended, and Clare re-entered the Vicarage. With the local banker he deposited the jewels till happier days should arise. He also paid into the bank thirty pounds – to be sent to Tess in a few months as she might require; and wrote to her at her parents' home in Blackmoor Vale to inform her of what he had done. This amount, with the sum he had already placed in her hands – about fifty pounds – he hoped would be amply sufficient for her wants just at present, particularly as in an emergency she had been directed to apply to his father.

He deemed it best not to put his parents into communication with her by informing them of her address; and, being unaware of what had really happened to estrange the two, neither his father nor his mother suggested that he should do so. During the day he left the parsonage, for what he had to complete he wished to get done quickly.

As the last duty before leaving this part of England it was necessary for him to call at the Wellbridge farmhouse, in which he had spent with Tess the first three days of their marriage, the trifle of rent having to be paid, the key given up of the two rooms they had occupied, and two or three small articles fetched away that they had left behind. It was under this roof that the deepest shadow ever thrown upon his life had stretched its gloom over him. Yet when he had unlocked the door of the sitting-room and looked into it, the memory which returned first upon him was that of their happy arrival on a similar afternoon, the first fresh sense of sharing a habitation conjointly, the first meal together, the chatting by the fire with joined hands.

The farmer and his wife were in the fields at the moment of his visit, and Clare was in the rooms alone for some time. Inwardly swollen with a renewal of sentiments that he had not quite reckoned with, he went upstairs to her chamber, which had never been his. The bed was smooth as she had made it with her own hands on the morning of leaving. The mistletoe hung under the tester just as he had placed it. Having been there three or four weeks it was turning colour, and the leaves and berries were wrinkled. Angel took it down and crushed it into the grate. Standing there he for the first time doubted whether his course in this conjuncture had been a wise, much less a generous, one. But had he not been cruelly blinded? In the incoherent multitude of his emotions he knelt down at the bedside and wept. 'O Tess! If you had only told me sooner, I would have forgiven you,' he said.

Hearing a footstep below he rose and went to the top of the stairs. At the bottom of the flight he saw a woman standing, and on her turning up her face recognized the pale, dark-eyed Izz Huett.

'Mr Clare,' she said, 'I've called to see you and Mrs Clare, and to inquire if ye be as well as can be expected.'

This was a girl whose secret he had guessed, but who had not yet guessed his; an honest girl who loved him – one who would have made as good, or nearly as good, a practical farmer's wife as Tess.

'I am here alone,' he said; 'we are not living here now.' Explaining why he had come, he asked, 'Which way are you going home, Izz?'

'I have no home at Talbothays Dairy now, sir,' she said.

'Why is that?'

Izz looked down.

'It was so dismal there that I left! I am staying out this way.' She pointed in a contrary direction, the direction in which he was journeying.

'Well – are you going there now? I can take you if you wish for a lift.'

Her olive complexion grew richer in hue.

'Thank 'ee, Mr Clare,' she said.

He soon found the farmer, and settled the account for his rent and the few other items which had to be considered by reason of the sudden abandonment of the lodgings. On Clare's return to his horse and gig Izz jumped up beside him.

'I am going to leave England, Izz,' he said, as they drove on. 'Going to Brazil.'

'And do Mrs Clare like the notion of such a journey?' she asked.

'She is not going at present – say for a year or so. I am going out to reconnoitre – to see what life there is like.'

They sped along eastward for some considerable distance, Izz making no observation.

'How are the others?' he inquired. 'How is Retty?'

'She is in a sort of nervous state; and so thin and hollow-cheeked that 'a do seem in a decline. Nobody will ever fall in love wi' her any more,' said Izz absently.

'And Marian?'

Izz lowered her voice.

'Marian drinks.'

'Indeed!'

'Yes. The dairyman says he must get rid of her.'[2]

'And you?'

'I don't drink, and I am not in a decline. But – I am no great things at singing afore breakfast now!'

'How is that? Do you remember how neatly you used to turn "'Twas down in Cupid's Gardens" and "The Tailor's Breeches"[3] at morning milking?'

'Ah, yes! When you first came, sir, that was. Not when you had been there a bit.'

'Why was that falling-off?'

Her black eyes flashed up to his face for one moment by way of answer.

'Izz – yes, I understand,' he said kindly, and fell into reverie. 'Then – suppose I had asked *you* to marry me?'

'If you had I should have said "Yes," and you would have married a woman who loved 'ee!'

'Really!'

'Down to the ground!' she whispered. 'O my God! did you never guess it till now?'

By-and-by they reached a branch road to a village.

'I must get down. I live out there,' said Izz abruptly, never having spoken since her avowal.

Clare slowed the horse. He was incensed against his fate, bitterly disposed towards social ordinances; for they had cooped him up in a corner, out of which there was no legitimate pathway. Why not be revenged on society by ruling his future domesticities himself, instead of kissing the pedagogic rod[4] of convention in this lonely manner?

'I am going to Brazil alone, Izz,' said he. 'I have separated from my wife for personal, not voyaging, reasons. I may never live with her again. Will you go with me instead of her?'

'Do you truly wish me to go?'

'I do. I have been badly used enough to wish for relief. And you at least love me disinterestedly.'

'Yes – I will go,' said Izz, after a pause.

'You will? You know what it means, Izz?'

'It means that I shall be with you for the time you are over there – that's good enough for me.'

'Remember, you are not to trust me in morals now. But I ought to remind you that it will be wrong-doing in the eyes of civilization – Western civilization, that is to say.'

'I don't mind that; no woman do when it comes to agony-point, and there's no other way!'

'Then don't get down, but sit where you are.'

He drove past the cross-roads, one mile, two miles, without showing any signs of affection.[5]

'You love me very, very much, Izz?' he suddenly asked.

'I do – I have said I do! I loved you all the time we was at the dairy together.'

'More than Tess?'

She shook her head.

'No,' she murmured, 'not more than she.'

'How's that?'

'Because nobody could love 'ee more than Tess did! . . . She would have laid down her life for 'ee.[6] I could do no more.'

Like the prophet on the top of Peor[7] Izz Huett would fain have spoken perversely at such a moment, but the fascination exercised over her rougher nature by Tess's character compelled her to grace.

Clare was silent; his heart had risen at these straightforward words from such an unexpected, unimpeachable quarter. In his throat was something as if a sob had solidified there. His ears repeated, '*She would have laid down her life for 'ee. I could do no more!*'

'Forget our idle talk, Izz,' he said, turning the horse's head suddenly.

'I don't know what I've been saying! I will now drive you back to where your lane branches off.'

'So much for honesty towards 'ee! O – how can I bear it – how can I – how can I!'

Izz Huett burst into wild tears, and beat her forehead as she saw what she had done.

'Do you regret that poor little act of justice to an absent one? O, Izz, don't spoil it by regret!'

She stilled herself by degrees.

'Very well, sir. Perhaps I didn't know what I was saying, either, when I agreed to go. I wish – what cannot be!'

'Because I have a loving wife already.'

'Yes, yes. You have.'

They reached the corner of the lane which they had passed half an hour earlier, and she hopped down.

'You will forget my momentary levity?' he said. 'It was ill-considered, ill-advised.'

'Forget it? Never, never! O, it was no levity to me!'

He felt how richly he deserved the reproach that the wounded cry conveyed, and, in a sorrow that was inexpressible, leapt down and took her hand.

'Well, but, Izz, we'll part friends, anyhow? You don't know what I've had to bear!'

She was a really generous girl, and allowed no further bitterness to mar their adieux.

'I forgive 'ee, sir,' she said.

'Now, Izz,' he said solemnly, while she stood beside him there; 'I want you to tell Marian when you see her that she is to be a good woman, and not to give way to folly. Promise that, and tell Retty that there are more worthy men than I in the world, that for my sake she is to act wisely and well[8] – remember the words – wisely and well – for my sake. I send this message to them as a dying man to the dying;[9] for I shall never see them more. And you, Izzy, you have saved me by your honest words about my wife from an incredible impulse towards folly and treachery. Women may be bad, but they are not so bad as men in these things! On that one account I can never forget you. Be always the good and sincere girl you have hitherto been; and think of me as a worthless lover, but a true friend. Promise.'

She gave the promise gravely.

'Heaven bless and keep you, sir. Good-bye!'

He drove on; but no sooner had Izz turned into the lane, and Clare was out of sight, than she flung herself down on the bank in a fit of racking anguish; and it was with a strained unnatural face that she entered her mother's cottage late that night. Nobody ever knew how Izz spent the dark hours that intervened between Angel Clare's parting from her and her arrival home.

Clare, too, after bidding the girl farewell, was wrought to aching thoughts and quivering lips. But his sorrow was not for Izz. That evening he was within a feather-weight's turn of abandoning his road to the nearest station, and driving across the elevated dorsal line of South Wessex towards his Tess's home. It was neither a contempt for her nature, nor the probable state of her heart, which deterred him.

No; it was a sense that, despite her love, as corroborated by Izz's admission, the facts had not changed. If he was right at first, he was right now. And the momentum of the course on which he had embarked tended to keep him going in it, unless diverted by a stronger, more sudden force than had played upon him this afternoon. He could soon come back to her. He took the train that night for London, and five days after shook hands in farewell of his brothers at the port of embarkation.

XLI

From the foregoing events of the winter-time let us press on to an October day, more than eight months subsequent to the parting of Clare and Tess. We discover the latter in changed conditions; instead of a bride with boxes and trunks which others bore, we see her a lonely woman with a basket and a bundle in her own porterage, as at an earlier time when she was no bride; instead of the ample means that were anticipated by her husband for her comfort through this probationary period, she can produce only a flattened purse.

After again leaving Marlott, her home, she had got through the spring and summer without any great stress upon her physical powers, the time being mainly spent in rendering light irregular service at dairy-work near Port Bredy to the west of the Blackmoor Valley, equally remote from her native place and from Talbothays. She preferred this to living on his allowance. Mentally she remained in utter stagnation, a condition which the mechanical occupation rather fostered than checked. Her consciousness was at that other dairy, at that other season, in the presence of the tender lover who had confronted her there – he who, the moment she had grasped him to keep him for her own, had disappeared like a shape in a vision.

The dairy-work lasted only till the milk began to lessen, for she had not met with a second regular engagement as at Talbothays, but had done duty as a supernumerary only. However, as harvest was now beginning, she had simply to remove from the pasture to the stubble to find plenty of further occupation, and this continued till harvest was done.

Of the five-and-twenty pounds which had remained to her of Clare's allowance, after deducting the other half of the fifty as a contribution to her parents for the trouble and expense to which she had put them, she had as yet spent but little. But there now followed an unfortunate interval of wet weather, during which she was obliged to fall back upon her sovereigns.

She could not bear to let them go. Angel had put them into her hand, had obtained them bright and new from his bank for her; his touch had consecrated them to souvenirs of himself – they appeared to have had as yet no other history than such as was created by his and her own experiences – and to disperse them was like giving away relics. But she had to do it, and one by one they left her hands.

She had been compelled to send her mother her address from time to time, but she concealed her circumstances. When her money had almost gone a letter from her mother reached her. Joan stated that they were in dreadful difficulty; the autumn rains had gone through the thatch of the house, which required entire renewal; but this could not be done because the previous thatching had never been paid for. New rafters and a new ceiling upstairs also were required, which, with the previous bill, would amount to a sum of twenty pounds. As her husband was a man of means, and had doubtless returned by this time, could she not send them the money?

Tess had thirty pounds coming to her almost immediately from Angel's bankers, and, the case being so deplorable, as soon as the sum was received she sent the twenty as requested. Part of the remainder she was obliged to expend in winter clothing, leaving only a nominal sum for the whole inclement season at hand. When the last pound had gone, a remark of Angel's that whenever she required further resources she was to apply to his father, remained to be considered.

But the more Tess thought of the step the more reluctant was she to take it. The same delicacy, pride, false shame, whatever it may be called, on Clare's account, which had led her to hide from her own parents the prolongation of the estrangement, hindered her in owning to his that she was in want after the fair allowance he had left her. They probably despised her already; how much more they would despise her in the character of a mendicant. The consequence was that by no effort could the parson's daughter-in-law bring herself to let him know her state.

Her reluctance to communicate with her husband's parents might, she thought, lessen with the lapse of time; but with her own the reverse obtained. On her leaving their house after the short visit subsequent to her marriage they were under the impression that she was ultimately going to join her husband; and from that time to the present she had done nothing to disturb their belief that she was awaiting his return in comfort, hoping against hope that his journey to Brazil would result in a short stay only, after which he would come to fetch her, or that he would write for her to join him; in any case that they would soon present a united front to their families and the world. This hope she still fostered. To let her parents know that she was a deserted wife, dependent, now that she had relieved their necessities, on her own hands for a living, after the *éclat* of a marriage which was to nullify the collapse of the first attempt, would be too much indeed.

The set of brilliants returned to her mind. Where Clare had deposited them she did not know, and it mattered little, if it were true that she could only use and not sell them. Even were they absolutely hers it would be passing mean to enrich herself by a legal title to them which was not essentially hers at all.[1]

Meanwhile her husband's days had been by no means free from trial. At this moment he was lying ill of fever in the clay lands near Curitiba in Brazil, having been drenched with thunderstorms and persecuted by other hardships, in common with all the English farmers and farm-labourers who, just at this time, were deluded into going thither by the promises of the Brazilian Government, and by the baseless assumption that those frames which, ploughing and sowing on English uplands, had resisted all the weathers to whose moods they had been born, could resist equally well all the weathers by which they were surprised on Brazilian plains.[2]

To return. Thus it happened that when the last of Tess's sovereigns had been spent she was unprovided with others to take their place, while on account of the season she found it increasingly difficult to get employment. Not being aware of the rarity of intelligence, energy, health, and willingness in any sphere of life, she refrained from seeking an indoor occupation; fearing towns, large houses, people of means and social sophistication, and of manners other than rural. From that direction of gentility Black Care[3] had come.[4] Society might be better than she supposed from her slight experience of it. But she had no proof of this, and her instinct in the circumstances was to avoid its purlieus.

The small dairies in which she had served as supernumerary milk-maid during the spring and summer required no further aid. The harvest was over. Room would probably have been made for her at Talbothays, if only out of sheer compassion; but comfortable as her life had been there she could not go back. The anti-climax would be too intolerable; and her return might bring reproach upon her idolized husband. She could not have borne their pity, and their whispered remarks to one another upon her strange situation; though she would almost have faced a knowledge of her circumstances by every individual there, so long as her story had remained isolated in the mind of each. It was the interchange of ideas about her that made her sensitiveness wince. Tess could not account for this distinction; she simply knew that she felt it.

She was now on her way to an upland farm in the centre of the county, to which she had been recommended by a wandering letter which had reached her from Marian. Marian had somehow heard that Tess was separated from her husband – probably through Izz Huett – and the good-natured and now tippling girl, deeming Tess in trouble, had hastened to notify to her former friend that she herself had gone to this upland spot after leaving the dairy, and would like to see her there, where there was room for other hands, if it was really true that she worked again as of old.

With the shortening of the days all hope of obtaining her husband's forgiveness began to leave her; and there was something of the habitude of the wild animal in the unreflecting instinct with which she rambled on – disconnecting herself by littles from her eventful past at every step, obliterating her identity, giving no thought to accidents or contingencies which might make a quick discovery of her whereabouts by others of importance to her own happiness, if not to theirs.

Among the difficulties of her lonely position not the least was the attention she excited by her appearance, a certain bearing of distinction, which she had caught from Clare, being superadded to her natural attractiveness. Whilst the clothes lasted which had been prepared for her marriage, these casual glances of interest caused her no inconvenience, but as soon as she was compelled to don the wrapper of a field-woman, rude words were addressed to her more than once; but nothing occurred to cause her bodily fear till a particular November afternoon.

She had preferred the fertile country of the south-west to the upland farm for which she was now bound, because, for one thing, it was nearer to the home of her husband's father; and to hover about that region unrecognized, with the notion that she might decide to call at the Vicarage some day, gave her pleasure. But having once decided to try the higher and drier levels, she pressed on, marching afoot towards the village of Chalk-Newton, where she meant to pass the night.

The lane was long and unvaried, and, owing to the rapid shortening of the days, dusk came upon her before she was aware. She had reached the top of a hill down which the lane stretched its serpentine length in glimpses, when she heard footsteps behind her back, and, in a few moments, she was overtaken by a man. He stepped up alongside Tess and said –

'Good-night, my pretty maid,' to which she civilly replied.

The light still remaining in the sky lit up her face, though the landscape was nearly dark. The man turned and stared hard at her.

'Why, surely, it is the young wench who was at Trantridge awhile – young Squire D'Urberville's friend? I was there at that time, though I don't live there now.'

She recognized in him the well-to-do boor whom Angel had knocked down at the inn for addressing her coarsely. A spasm of anguish shot through her, and she returned him no answer.

'Be honest enough to own it, and that what I said in the town was true, though your fancy-man was so up about it – hey, my sly one? You ought to beg my pardon for that blow of his, considering.'

Still no answer came from Tess.[5] There seemed only one escape for her hunted soul. She suddenly took to her heels with the speed of the wind, and, without looking behind her, ran along the road till she came to a gate which opened directly into a plantation. Into this she plunged, and did not pause till she was deep enough in its shade to be safe against any possibility of discovery.

Underfoot the leaves were dry, and the foliage of some holly bushes which grew among the deciduous trees was dense enough to keep off draughts. She scraped together the dead leaves till she had formed them into a large heap, making a sort of nest in the middle. Into this Tess crept.

Such sleep as she got was naturally fitful; she fancied she heard strange noises, but persuaded herself that they were caused by the breeze. She thought of her husband in some vague warm clime on the other side of the globe, while she was here in the cold. Was there another such a wretched being as she in the world? Tess asked herself; and, thinking of her wasted life, said, 'All is vanity.'[6] She repeated the words mechanically, till she reflected that this was a most inadequate thought for modern days. Solomon had thought as far as that more than two thousand years ago; she herself, though not in the van of thinkers, had got much farther. If all were only vanity, who would

277

mind it? All was, alas, worse than vanity.[7] The wife of Angel Clare put her hand to her brow, and felt its curve, and the edges of her eye-sockets as perceptible under the soft skin, and thought as she did so that a time would come when that bone would be bare. 'I wish it were now,' she said.

In the midst of these whimsical fancies she heard a new strange sound among the leaves. It might be the wind; yet there was scarcely any wind. Sometimes it was a palpitation, sometimes a flutter; sometimes it was a sort of gasp or gurgle. Soon she was certain that the noises came from wild creatures of some kind, the more so when, originating in the boughs overhead, they were followed by the fall of a heavy body upon the ground. Had she been ensconced here under other and more pleasant conditions she would have become alarmed; but, outside humanity, she had at present no fear.

Day at length broke in the sky. When it had been day aloft for some little while it became day in the wood.

Directly the assuring and prosaic light of the world's active hours had grown strong she crept from under her hillock of leaves, and looked around boldly. Then she perceived what had been going on to disturb her. The plantation wherein she had taken shelter ran down at this spot into a peak, which ended it hitherward, outside the hedge being arable ground. Under the trees several pheasants lay about, their rich plumage dabbled with blood; some were dead, some feebly moving their wings, some staring up at the sky, some pulsating feebly, some contorted, some stretched out – all of them writhing in agony, except the fortunate ones whose tortures had ended during the night by the inability of nature to bear more.

Tess guessed at once the meaning of this. The birds had been driven down into this corner the day before by some shooting-party; and while those that had dropped dead under the shot, or had died before nightfall, had been searched for and carried off, many slightly wounded birds had escaped and hidden themselves away, or risen among the thick boughs, where they had maintained their position till they grew weaker with loss of blood in the night-time, when they had fallen one by one as she had heard them.[8]

She had occasionally caught glimpses of these men in girlhood,

THE WOMAN PAYS, XLII

looking over hedges, or peering through bushes, and pointing their guns, strangely accoutred, a bloodthirsty light in their eyes. She had been told that, rough and brutal as they seemed just then, they were not like this all the year round, but were, in fact, quite civil persons save during certain weeks of autumn and winter, when, like the inhabitants of the Malay Peninsula, they ran amuck, and made it their purpose to destroy life – in this case harmless feathered creatures, brought into being by artificial means solely to gratify these propensities – at once so unmannerly and so unchivalrous towards their weaker fellows in Nature's teeming family.

With the impulse of a soul who could feel for kindred sufferers as much as for herself, Tess's first thought was to put the still-living birds out of their torture, and to this end with her own hands she broke the necks of as many as she could find, leaving them to lie where she had found them till the gamekeepers should come – as they probably would come – to look for them a second time.

'Poor darlings – to suppose myself the most miserable being on earth in the presence of such misery as this!' she exclaimed, her tears running down as she killed the birds tenderly. 'And not a twinge of bodily pain about me! I am not mangled, and I am not bleeding, and I have two hands to feed and clothe me.' She was ashamed of herself for her gloom of the night, based on nothing more tangible than a sense of condemnation under an arbitrary law of society which had no foundation in Nature.[9]

XLII

It was now broad day, and she started again, emerging cautiously upon the highway. But there was no need for caution; not a soul was at hand, and Tess went onward with fortitude, her recollection of the birds' silent endurance of their night of agony impressing upon her the relativity of sorrows and the tolerable nature of her own, if she could once rise high enough to despise opinion. But that she could not do so long as it was held by Clare.

She reached Chalk-Newton, and breakfasted at an inn, where

several young men were troublesomely complimentary to her good looks. Somehow she felt hopeful, for was it not possible that her husband might claim her even yet? But she was bound to take care of herself on the chance of it, and keep off lovers. To this end Tess resolved to run no further risks from her appearance. As soon as she got out of the village she entered a thicket and took from her basket one of the old field-gowns which she had never put on even at the dairy – never since she had worked among the stubble at Marlott. She also, by a felicitous thought, took a handkerchief from her bundle and tied it round her face under her bonnet, covering her chin and half her cheeks and temples, as if she were suffering from toothache. Then with her little scissors, by the aid of a pocket looking-glass, she mercilessly nipped her eyebrows off, and thus insured against aggressive admiration she went on her uneven way.

'What a mommet of a maid!' said the next man who met her to a companion.

Tears came into her eyes for very pity of herself as she heard him.

'But I don't care!' she said. 'Oh no – I don't care! I'll always be ugly now, because Angel is not here, and I have nobody to take care of me. My husband that was is gone away, and never will love me any more; but I love him just the same, and hate all other men, and like to make 'em think scornful o' me!'

Thus Tess walks on; a figure which is part of the landscape; a field-woman pure and simple, in winter guise; a gray serge cape, a red woollen cravat, a stuff skirt covered by a whitey-brown rough wrapper, and buff-leather gloves. Every thread of that old attire has become wire-drawn and thin under the stroke of rain-drops, the burn of sunbeams, and the stress of winds. There is no sign of young passion in her now –

> The maiden's mouth is cold.
>
> .   .   .   .   .
>
> Fold over simple fold
> Binding her head.[1]

Inside this exterior, over which the eye might have roved as over a thing scarcely percipient, almost inorganic, there was the record of a pulsing life which had learnt too well, for its years, of the dust and ashes of things, of the cruelty of lust and the fragility of love.

Next day the weather was bad, but she trudged on, the honesty, directness, and impartiality of elemental enmity disconcerting her but little. Her object being a winter's occupation and a winter's home, there was no time to lose. Her experience of short hirings had been such that she determined to accept no more.

Thus she went forward from farm to farm in the direction of the place whence Marian had written to her, which she determined to make use of as a last shift only, its rumoured stringencies being the reverse of tempting. First she inquired for the lighter kinds of employment, and, as acceptance in any variety of these grew hopeless, applied next for the less light, till, beginning with the dairy and poultry tendance that she liked best, she ended with the heavy and coarse pursuits which she liked least – work on arable land: work of such roughness, indeed, as she would never have deliberately volunteered for.

Towards the second evening she reached the irregular chalk table-land or plateau, bosomed with semi-globular tumuli,[2] which stretched between the valley of her birth and the valley of her love.

Here the air was dry and cold, and the long cart-roads were blown white and dusty again within a few hours after rain. There were few trees, or none, those that would have grown in the hedges being mercilessly plashed down with the quickset by the tenant-farmers, the natural enemies of tree, bush, and brake. In the middle distance ahead of her she could see the summits of Bulbarrow and of Nettlecombe-Tout, and they seemed friendly. They had a low and unassuming aspect from this upland, though as approached on the other side from Blackmoor in her childhood they were as lofty bastions against the sky. Southerly, at many miles' distance, and over the hills and ridges coastward, she could discern a surface like polished steel: it was the English Channel at a point far out towards France.

Before her, in a slight depression, were the remains of a village. She had, in fact, reached Flintcomb-Ash, the place of Marian's sojourn. There seemed to be no help for it; hither she was doomed to come.

The stubborn soil around her showed plainly enough that the kind of labour in demand here was of the roughest kind; but it was time to rest from searching, and she resolved to stay, particularly as it began to rain. At the entrance to the village was a cottage whose gable jutted into the road, and before applying for a lodging she stood under its shelter, and watched the evening close in.

'Who would think I was Mrs Angel Clare!' she said.

The wall felt warm to her back and shoulders, and she found that immediately within the gable was the cottage fireplace, the heat of which came through the bricks. She warmed her hands upon them, and also put her cheek – red and moist with the drizzle – against their comforting surface. The wall seemed to be the only friend she had. She had so little wish to leave it that she could have stayed there all night.

Tess could hear the occupants of the cottage – gathered together after their day's labour – talking to each other within, and the rattle of their supper-plates was also audible. But in the village-street she had seen no soul as yet. The solitude was at last broken by the approach of one feminine figure, who, though the evening was cold, wore the print gown and the tilt-bonnet of summer-time. Tess instinctively thought it might be Marian, and when she came near enough to be distinguishable in the gloom surely enough it was she. Marian was even stouter and redder in the face than formerly, and decidedly shabbier in attire. At any previous period of her existence Tess would hardly have cared to renew the acquaintance in such conditions; but her loneliness was excessive, and she responded readily to Marian's greeting.

Marian was quite respectful in her inquiries, but seemed much moved by the fact that Tess should still continue in no better condition than at first; though she had dimly heard of the separation.

'Tess – Mrs Clare – the dear wife of dear he! And is it really so bad as this, my child? Why is your comely face tied up in such a way? Anybody been beating 'ee? Not *he*?'

'No, no, no! I merely did it not to be molested,[3] Marian.'

She pulled off in disgust a bandage which could suggest such wild thoughts.

'And you've got no collar on' (Tess had been accustomed to wear a little white collar at the dairy).

'I know it, Marian.'

'You've lost it travelling.'

'I've not lost it. The truth is, I don't care anything about my appearance; and so I didn't put it on.'

'And you don't wear your wedding-ring?'

'Yes, I do; but not publicly. I wear it round my neck on a ribbon. I don't wish people to suspect who I am by marriage, or that I am married at all; it would be so awkward while I lead my present life.'

Marian paused.

'But you *be* a gentleman's wife; and it seems hardly fair that you should live like this!'

'Oh, yes it is, quite fair; though I am very unhappy.'

'Well, well. *He* married you – and you can be unhappy!'

'Wives are unhappy sometimes; from no fault of their husbands – from their own.'

'You've no faults, deary; that I'm sure of. And he's none. So it must be something outside ye both.'

'Marian, dear Marian, will you do me a good turn without asking questions? My husband has gone abroad, and somehow I have overrun my allowance, so that I have to fall back upon my old work for a time. Do not call me Mrs Clare, but Tess, as before. Do they want a hand here?'

'Oh yes; they'll take one always, because few care to come. 'Tis a starve-acre place. Corn and swedes are all they grow. Though I be here myself, I feel 'tis a pity for such as you to come.'

'But you used to be as good a dairywoman as I.'

'Yes; but I've got out o' that since I took to drink. Lord, that's the only happiness I've got now. If you engage, you'll be set swede-hacking. That's what I am doing; but you won't like it.'

'Oh – anything! Will you speak for me?'

'You will do better by speaking for yourself.'

'Very well. Now, Marian, remember – nothing about *him*, if I get the place. I don't wish to bring his name down to the dirt.'

Marian, who was really a trustworthy girl, though of coarser grain than Tess, promised anything she asked.

'This is pay-night,' she said, 'and if you were to come with me you would know at once. I be real sorry that you are not happy; but 'tis because he's away, I know. You couldn't be unhappy if he were here, even if he gave you no money – even if he used you like a drudge.'

'That's true; I could not!'

They walked on together, and soon reached the farmhouse, which was almost sublime in its dreariness. There was not a tree within sight; there was not, at this season, a green pasture – nothing but fallow and turnips everywhere; in large fields divided by hedges plashed to unrelieved levels.

Tess waited outside the door of the farmhouse till the group of workfolk had received their wages, and then Marian introduced her. The farmer himself, it appeared, was not at home, but his wife, who represented him this evening, made no objection to hiring Tess, on her agreeing to remain till Old Lady-Day.[4] Female field-labour was seldom offered now, and its cheapness made it profitable for tasks which women could perform as readily as men.

Having signed the agreement, there was nothing more for Tess to do at present than to get a lodging, and she found one in the house at whose gable-wall she had warmed herself. It was a poor subsistence that she had ensured, but it would afford a shelter for the winter at any rate.

That night she wrote to inform her parents of her new address, in case a letter should arrive at Marlott from her husband. But she did not tell them of the sorriness of her situation: it might have brought reproach upon him.

XLIII

There was no exaggeration in Marian's definition of Flintcomb-Ash Farm as a starve-acre place. The single fat thing on the soil was Marian herself: and she was an importation. Of the three classes of village, the village cared for by its lord, the village cared for by itself, and the village uncared for either by itself or by its lord – (in other words, the village of a resident squire's tenantry, the village of free or copyholders, and the absentee-owner's village, farmed with the land) – this place, Flintcomb-Ash, was the third.

But Tess set to work. Patience, that blending of moral courage with physical timidity, was now no longer a minor feature in Mrs Angel Clare; and it sustained her.

The swede-field in which she and her companion were set hacking[1] was a stretch of a hundred-odd acres, in one patch, on the highest ground of the farm, rising above stony lanchets or lynchets – the outcrop of siliceous veins in the chalk formation, composed of myriads of loose white flints in bulbous, cusped, and phallic shapes. The upper half of each swede-turnip had been eaten-off by the live-stock, and it was the business of the two women to grab out the lower or earthy half of the root with a hooked fork called a hacker, that it might be eaten also. Every leaf of the vegetable having already been consumed, the whole field was in colour a desolate drab; it was a complexion without features, as if a face, from chin to brow, should be only an expanse of skin. The sky wore, in another colour, the same likeness; a white vacuity of countenance with the lineaments gone. So these two upper and nether visages confronted each other all day long, the white face looking down on the brown face, and the brown face looking up at the white face, without anything standing between them but the two girls crawling over the surface of the former like flies.

Nobody came near them, and their movements showed a mechanical regularity; their forms enshrouded in Hessian 'wroppers' – sleeved brown pinafores, tied behind to the bottom, to keep their gowns from blowing about – short skirts revealing boots that reached high up the ankles, and yellow sheepskin gloves with gauntlets. The pensive character which the curtained hood lent to their bent heads would have reminded the observer of some early Italian conception of the two Marys.[2]

They worked on hour after hour, unconscious of the forlorn aspect they bore in the landscape, not thinking of the justice or injustice of their lot. Even in such a position as theirs it was possible to exist in a dream. In the afternoon the rain came on again, and Marian said that they need not work any more. But if they did not work they would not be paid; so they worked on. It was so high a situation, this field, that the rain had no occasion to fall, but raced along horizontally upon the yelling wind, sticking into them like glass splinters till they were wet through. Tess had not known till now what was really meant by that. There are degrees of dampness, and a very little is called being wet through in common talk. But to stand working slowly in a field, and feel the creep of rain-water, first in legs and shoulders, then on hips and head, then at back, front, and sides, and yet to work on till the leaden light diminishes and marks that the sun is down, demands a distinct modicum of stoicism, even of valour.

Yet they did not feel the wetness so much as might be supposed. They were both young, and they were talking of the time when they lived and loved together at Talbothays Dairy, that happy green tract of land where summer had been liberal in her gifts; in substance to all, emotionally to these. Tess would fain not have conversed with Marian of the man who was legally, if not obviously, her husband; but the irresistible fascination of the subject betrayed her into reciprocating Marian's remarks. And thus, as has been said, though the damp curtains of their bonnets flapped smartly into their faces, and their wrappers clung about them to wearisomeness, they lived all this afternoon in memories of green, sunny, romantic Talbothays.

'You can see a gleam of a hill within a few miles of Froom Valley from here when it is fine,' said Marian.

'Ah! Can you?' said Tess, awake to the new value of this locality.

So the two forces were at work here as everywhere, the inherent will to enjoy, and the circumstantial will against enjoyment. Marian's will had a method of assisting itself by taking from her pocket as the afternoon wore on a pint bottle corked with white rag, from which she invited Tess to drink. Tess's unassisted power of dreaming, however, being enough for her sublimation at present, she declined except the merest sip, and then Marian took a pull herself from the spirits.

'I've got used to it,' she said, 'and can't leave it off now. 'Tis my only comfort—You see I lost him: you didn't; and you can do without it perhaps.'

Tess thought her loss as great as Marian's, but upheld by the dignity of being Angel's wife, in the letter at least, she accepted Marian's differentiation.

Amid this scene Tess slaved in the morning frosts and in the afternoon rains. When it was not swede-hacking it was swede-trimming, in which process they sliced off the earth and the fibres with a bill-hook before storing the roots for future use. At this occupation they could shelter themselves by a thatched hurdle if it rained; but if it was frosty even their thick leather gloves could not prevent the frozen masses they handled from biting their fingers. Still Tess hoped. She had a conviction that sooner or later the magnanimity which she persisted in reckoning as a chief ingredient of Clare's character would lead him to rejoin her; and what would a winter of swede-trimming matter if it resulted in such a consummation?[3]

They often looked across the country to where the Var or Froom was known to stretch, even though they might not be able to see it; and, fixing their eyes on the cloaking gray mist, imagined the old times they had spent out there.

'Ah,' said Marian, 'how I should like another or two of our old set to come here! Then we could bring up Talbothays every day here afield, and talk of he, and of what nice times we had there, and o' the old things we used to know, and make it all come back again a'most, in seeming!' Marian's eyes softened, and her voice grew vague as the visions returned. 'I'll write to Izz Huett,' she said. 'She's biding at home doing nothing now, I know, and I'll tell her we be here, and ask her to come; and perhaps Retty is well enough now.'

Tess had nothing to say against the proposal, and the next she heard of this plan for importing old Talbothays' joys was two or three days later, when Marian informed her that Izz had replied to her inquiry, and had promised to come if she could.

There had not been such a winter for years. It came on in stealthy and measured glides, like the moves of a chess-player. One morning the few lonely trees and the thorns of the hedgerows appeared as if they had put off a vegetable for an animal integument. Every twig was covered with a white nap as of fur grown from the rind during the night, giving it four times its usual dimensions; the whole bush or tree forming a staring sketch in white lines on the mournful gray of the sky and horizon. Cobwebs revealed their presence on sheds and walls where none had ever been observed till brought out into visibility by the crystallizing atmosphere, hanging like loops of white worsted from salient points of the out-houses, posts, and gates.

After this season of congealed dampness came a spell of dry frost, when strange birds from behind the North Pole began to arrive silently on the upland of Flintcomb-Ash; gaunt spectral creatures with tragical eyes – eyes which had witnessed scenes of cataclysmal horror in inaccessible polar regions of a magnitude such as no human being had ever conceived, in curdling temperatures that no man could endure; which had beheld the crash of icebergs and the slide of snow-hills by the shooting light of the Aurora; been half blinded by the whirl of colossal storms and terraqueous distortions; and re-tained the expression of feature that such scenes had engendered. These nameless birds came quite near to Tess and Marian, but of all they had seen which humanity would never see, they brought no account. The traveller's ambition to tell was not theirs, and, with dumb impassivity, they dismissed experiences which they did not value for the immediate incidents of this homely upland – the trivial movements of the two girls in disturbing the clods with their hackers so as to uncover something or other that these visitants relished as food.

Then one day a peculiar quality invaded the air of this open country. There came a moisture which was not of rain, and a cold which was not of frost. It chilled the eyeballs of the twain, made their brows ache, penetrated to their skeletons, affecting the surface of the body less than its core. They knew that it meant snow, and in the night the snow came. Tess, who continued to live at the cottage with the warm gable that cheered the lonely pedestrian who paused beside it, awoke in the night, and heard above the thatch noises which seemed to signify that the roof had turned itself into a gymnasium of all the winds. When she lit her lamp to get up in the morning she found that the snow had blown through a chink in the casement, forming a white cone of the finest powder against the inside, and had also come down the chimney, so that it lay sole-deep upon the floor, on which her shoes left tracks when she moved about. Without, the storm drove so fast as to create a snow-mist in the kitchen; but as yet it was too dark out of doors to see anything.

Tess knew that it was impossible to go on with the swedes; and by the time she had finished breakfast beside the solitary little lamp, Marian arrived to tell her that they were to join the rest of the women at reed-drawing in the barn till the weather changed. As soon, therefore, as the uniform cloak of darkness without began to turn to a disordered medley of grays, they blew out the lamp, wrapped themselves up in their thickest pinners, tied their woollen cravats round their necks and across their chests, and started for the barn. The snow had followed the birds from the polar basin as a white pillar of a cloud, and individual flakes could not be seen. The blast smelt of icebergs, arctic seas, whales, and white bears, carrying the snow so that it licked the land but did not deepen on it. They trudged onwards with slanted bodies through the flossy fields, keeping as well as they could in the shelter of hedges, which, however, acted as strainers rather than screens. The air, afflicted to pallor with the hoary multitudes that infested it, twisted and spun them eccentrically, suggesting an achromatic chaos of things. But both the young women were fairly cheerful; such weather on a dry upland is not in itself dispiriting.

'Ha-ha! the cunning northern birds knew this was coming,' said Marian. 'Depend upon 't, they kept just in front of it all the way from the North Star. Your husband, my dear, is, I make no doubt, having scorching weather all this time. Lord, if he could only see his pretty wife now! Not that this weather hurts your beauty at all – in fact, it rather does it good.'

'You mustn't talk about him to me, Marian,' said Tess severely.

'Well, but – surely you care for him. Do you?'

Instead of answering, Tess, with tears in her eyes, impulsively faced in the direction in which she imagined South America to lie, and, putting up her lips, blew out a passionate kiss upon the snowy wind.

'Well, well, I know you do. But 'pon my body, it is a rum life for a married couple! There – I won't say another word! Well, as for the weather, it won't hurt us in the wheat-barn; but reed-drawing is fearful hard work – worse than swede-hacking. I can stand it because I'm stout; but you be slimmer than I. I can't think why maister should have set 'ee at it.'

They reached the wheat-barn and entered it. One end of the long structure was full of corn; the middle was where the reed-drawing was carried on, and there had already been placed in the reed-press the evening before as many sheaves of wheat as would be sufficient for the women to draw from during the day.

'Why, here's Izz!' said Marian.

Izz it was, and she came forward. She had walked all the way from her mother's home on the previous afternoon, and, not deeming the distance so great, had been belated, arriving, however, just before the snow began, and sleeping at the ale-house. The farmer had agreed with her mother at market to take her on if she came to-day, and she had been afraid to disappoint him by delay.

In addition to Tess, Marian, and Izz, there were two women from a neighbouring village; two Amazonian sisters, whom Tess with a start remembered as Dark Car the Queen of Spades and her sister the Queen of Diamonds – those who had tried to fight with her in the midnight quarrel at Trantridge. They showed no recognition of her, and possibly had none, for they had been under the influence of liquor on that occasion, and were only temporary sojourners there as here. They did all kinds of men's work by preference, including well-sinking, hedging, ditching, and excavating, without any sense of fatigue. Noted reed-drawers were they too, and looked round upon the other three with some superciliousness.

Putting on their gloves all set to work in a row in front of the press, an erection formed of two posts connected by a cross-beam, under which the sheaves to be drawn from were laid ears outward, the beam being pegged down by pins in the uprights, and lowered as the sheaves diminished.

The day hardened in colour, the light coming in at the barn-doors upwards from the ground instead of downwards from the sky. The girls pulled handful after handful from the press; but by reason of the presence of the strange women who were recounting scandals, Marian and Izz could not at first talk of old times as they wished to do.

Presently they heard the muffled tread of a horse, and the farmer rode up to the barn-door. When he had dismounted he came close to Tess, and remained looking musingly at the side of her face. She had not turned at first, but his fixed attitude led her to look round, when she perceived that her employer was the native of Trantridge from whom she had taken flight on the high-road because of his allusion to her history.

He waited till she had carried the drawn bundles to the pile outside, when he said, 'So you be the young woman who took my civility in such ill part? Be drowned if I didn't think you might be as soon as I heard of your being hired! Well, you thought you had got the better of me the first time at the inn with your fancy-man, and the second time on the road, when you bolted; but now I think I've got the better of you.' He concluded with a hard laugh.

Tess, between the Amazons and the farmer like a bird caught in a springe, returned no answer, continuing to pull the straw. She could read character sufficiently well to know by this time that she had nothing to fear from her employer's gallantry; it was rather the tyranny induced by his mortification at Clare's treatment of him. Upon the whole she preferred that sentiment in man, and felt brave enough to endure it.

'You thought I was in love with 'ee I suppose? Some women are such fools, to take every look as serious earnest. But there's nothing like a winter afield for taking that nonsense out o' young women's heads; and you've signed and agreed till Lady-Day. Now, are you going to beg my pardon?'

'I think you ought to beg mine.'

'Very well – as you like. But we'll see which is master here. Be they all the sheaves you've done to-day?'

'Yes, sir.'

''Tis a very poor show. Just see what they've done over there' (pointing to the two stalwart women). 'The rest, too, have done better than you.'

'They've all practised it before, and I have not. And I thought it made no difference to you as it is task work, and we are only paid for what we do.'

'Oh, but it does. I want the barn cleared.'

'I am going to work all the afternoon instead of leaving at two as the others will do.'

He looked sullenly at her and went away. Tess felt that she could not have come to a much worse place; but anything was better than gallantry. When two o'clock arrived the professional reed-drawers tossed off the last half-pint in their flagon, put down their hooks, tied their last sheaves, and went away. Marian and Izz would have done likewise, but on hearing that Tess meant to stay, to make up by longer hours for her lack of skill, they would not leave her. Looking out at the snow, which still fell, Marian exclaimed, 'Now we've got it all to ourselves.' And so at last the conversation turned to their old experiences at the dairy; and, of course, the incidents of their affection for Angel Clare.

'Izz and Marian,' said Mrs Angel Clare, with a dignity which was extremely touching, seeing how very little of a wife she was: 'I can't join in talk with you now, as I used to do, about Mr Clare; you will see that I cannot; because, although he is gone away from me for the present, he is my husband.'

Izz was by nature the sauciest and most caustic of all the four girls who had loved Clare. 'He was a very splendid lover, no doubt,' she said; 'but I don't think he is a too fond husband to go away from you so soon.'

'He had to go – he was obliged to go, to see about the land over there,' pleaded Tess.

'He might have tided 'ee over the winter.'

'Ah – that's owing to an accident – a misunderstanding; and we won't argue it,' Tess answered, with tearfulness in her words. 'Perhaps there's a good deal to be said for him! He did not go away, like some husbands, without telling me; and I can always find out where he is.'

After this they continued for some long time in a reverie, as they went on seizing the ears of corn, drawing out the straw, gathering it under their arms, and cutting off the ears with their bill-hooks, nothing sounding in the barn but the swish of the straw and the crunch of the hook. Then Tess suddenly flagged, and sank down upon the heap of wheat-ears at her feet.

'I knew you wouldn't be able to stand it!' cried Marian. 'It wants harder flesh than yours for this work.'

Just then the farmer entered. 'Oh, that's how you get on when I am away,' he said to her.

'But it is my own loss,' she pleaded. 'Not yours.'

'I want it finished,' he said doggedly, as he crossed the barn and went out at the other door.

'Don't 'ee mind him, there's a dear,' said Marian. 'I've worked here before. Now you go and lie down there, and Izz and I will make up your number.'

'I don't like to let you do that. I'm taller than you, too.'

However, she was so overcome that she consented to lie down awhile, and reclined on a heap of pull-tails – the refuse after the straight straw had been drawn – thrown up at the further side of the barn. Her succumbing had been as largely owing to agitation at re-opening the subject of her separation from her husband as to the hard work. She lay in a state of percipience without volition, and the rustle of the straw and the cutting of the ears by the others had the weight of bodily touches.

She could hear from her corner, in addition to these noises, the murmur of their voices. She felt certain that they were continuing the subject already broached, but their voices were so low that she could not catch the words. At last Tess grew more and more anxious to know what they were saying, and, persuading herself that she felt better, she got up and resumed work.

Then Izz Huett broke down. She had walked more than a dozen miles the previous evening, had gone to bed at midnight, and had risen again at five o'clock. Marian alone, thanks to her bottle of liquor and her stoutness of build, stood the strain upon back and arms without suffering. Tess urged Izz to leave off, agreeing, as she felt better, to finish the day without her, and make equal division of the number of sheaves.

Izz accepted the offer gratefully, and disappeared through the great door into the snowy track to her lodging. Marian, as was the case every afternoon at this time on account of the bottle, began to feel in a romantic vein.

'I should not have thought it of him – never!' she said in a dreamy tone. 'And I loved him so! I didn't mind his having you. But this about Izz is too bad!'

Tess, in her start at the words, narrowly missed cutting off a finger with the bill-hook.

'Is it about my husband?' she stammered.

'Oh, yes. Izz said, "Don't 'ee tell her;" but I am sure I can't help it! It was what he wanted Izz to do. He wanted her to go off to Brazil with him.'

Tess's face faded as white as the scene without, and its curves straightened. 'And did Izz refuse to go?' she asked.

'I don't know. Anyhow he changed his mind.'

'Pooh – then he didn't mean it. 'Twas just a man's jest!'

'Yes he did; for he drove her a good way towards the station.'

'He didn't take her!'

They pulled on in silence till Tess, without any premonitory symptoms, burst out crying.

'There!' said Marian. 'Now I wish I hadn't told 'ee!'

'No. It is a very good thing that you have done! I have been living on in a thirtover, lackadaisical way, and have not seen what it may lead to! I ought to have sent him a letter oftener. He said I could not go to him, but he didn't say I was not to write as often as I liked. I won't stay like this any longer! I have been very wrong and neglectful in leaving everything to be done by him!'

The dim light in the barn grew dimmer, and they could see to work no longer. When Tess had reached home that evening, and had entered into the privacy of her little white-washed chamber, she began impetuously writing a letter to Clare. But falling into doubt she could not finish it. Afterwards she took the ring from the ribbon on which she wore it next her heart, and retained it on her finger all night, as if to fortify herself in the sensation that she was really the wife of this elusive love of hers, who could propose that Izz should go with him abroad, so shortly after he had left her. Knowing that, how could she write entreaties to him, or show that she cared for him any more?

XLIV

By the disclosure in the barn her thoughts were led anew in the direction which they had taken more than once of late – to the distant Emminster Vicarage. It was through her husband's parents that she had been charged to send a letter to Clare if she desired; and to write to them direct if in difficulty. But that sense of her having morally no claim upon him had always led Tess to suspend her impulses to send these notes; and to the family at the Vicarage, therefore, as to her own parents since her marriage, she was virtually non-existent. This self-effacement in both directions had been quite in consonance with her independent character of desiring nothing by way of favour or pity to which she was not entitled on a fair consideration of her deserts. She had set herself to stand or fall by her qualities, and to waive such merely technical claims upon a strange family as had been established for her by the flimsy fact of a member of that family, in a moment of impulse, writing his name in a church-book beside hers.

But now that she was stung to a fever by Izz's tale there was a limit to her powers of renunciation.[1] Why had her husband not written to her? He had distinctly implied that he would at least let her know of the locality to which he had journeyed; but he had not sent a line to notify his address. Was he really indifferent? But was he ill? Was it for her to make some advance? Surely she might summon the courage of solicitude, call at the Vicarage for intelligence, and express her grief at his silence. If Angel's father were the good man she had heard him represented to be, he would be able to enter into her heart-starved situation. Her social hardships she could conceal.

To leave the farm on a week-day was not in her power; Sunday was the only possible opportunity. Flintcomb-Ash being in the middle of the cretaceous tableland over which no railway had climbed as yet, it would be necessary to walk. And the distance being fifteen miles each way, she would have to allow herself a long day for the undertaking by rising early.

A fortnight later, when the snow had gone, and had been followed by a hard black frost, she took advantage of the state of the roads to try the experiment. At three o'clock that Sunday morning she came downstairs and stept out into the starlight. The weather was still favourable, the ground ringing under her feet like an anvil.

Marian and Izz were much interested in her excursion, knowing that the journey concerned her husband. Their lodgings were in a cottage a little farther along the lane, but they came and assisted Tess in her departure, and argued that she should dress up in her very prettiest guise to captivate the hearts of her parents-in-law; though she, knowing of the austere and Calvinistic tenets of old Mr Clare, was indifferent, and even doubtful. A year had now elapsed since her sad marriage, but she had preserved sufficient draperies from the wreck of her then full wardrobe to clothe her very charmingly as a simple country girl with no pretensions to recent fashion; a soft gray woollen gown, with white crape quilling against the pink skin of her face and neck, and a black velvet jacket and hat.

''Tis a thousand pities your husband can't see 'ee now – you do look a real beauty!' said Izz Huett, regarding Tess as she stood on the threshold between the steely starlight without and the yellow candlelight within. Izz spoke with a magnanimous abandonment of herself to the situation; she could not be – no woman with a heart bigger than a hazel-nut could be – antagonistic to Tess in her presence, the influence which she exercised over those of her own sex being of a warmth and strength quite unusual, curiously overpowering the less worthy feminine feelings of spite and rivalry.

With a final tug and touch here, and a slight brush there, they let her go; and she was absorbed into the pearly air of the fore-dawn. They heard her footsteps tap along the hard road as she stepped out to her full pace. Even Izz hoped she would win, and, though without any particular respect for her own virtue, felt glad that she had been prevented wronging her friend when momentarily tempted by Clare.

It was a year ago, all but a day, that Clare had married Tess, and only a few days less than a year that he had been absent from her. Still, to start on a brisk walk, and on such an errand as hers, on a dry clear wintry morning, through the rarefied air of these chalky hogs'-backs, was not depressing; and there is no doubt that her dream at starting was to win the heart of her mother-in-law, tell her whole history to that lady, enlist her on her side, and so gain back the truant.

She soon reached the edge of the vast escarpment below which stretched the loamy Vale of Blackmoor, now lying misty and still in the dawn. Instead of the colourless air of the uplands the atmosphere down there was a deep blue. Instead of the great enclosures of a hundred acres in which she was now accustomed to toil there were little fields below her of less than half-a-dozen acres, so numerous that they looked from this height like the meshes of a net. Here the landscape was whitey-brown; down there, as in Froom Valley, it was always green. Yet it was in that vale that her sorrow had taken shape, and she did not love it as formerly. Beauty to her, as to all who have felt, lay not in the thing, but in what the thing symbolized.

Keeping the Vale on her right she steered steadily westward; passing above the Hintocks, crossing at right-angles the high-road from Sherton-Abbas to Casterbridge, and skirting High-Stoy or Rubdon Hill. Still following the elevated way she reached Cross-in-Hand, where the stone pillar stands desolate and silent, to mark the site of a miracle, or murder, or both.[2] Three miles farther she cut across the straight deserted Roman road called Long-Ash Lane; leaving which as soon as she reached it she dipped down the hill by a transverse lane into the small town or village of Evershead, being now about half-way over the distance. She made a halt here, and breakfasted a second time, heartily enough – not at the Sow-and-Acorn, for she avoided inns, but at a cottage by the church.

The second half of her journey was through a more gentle country, by way of Benvill Lane. But as the mileage lessened between her and the spot of her pilgrimage, so did Tess's confidence decrease, and her enterprise loom out more formidably. She saw her purpose in such staring lines, and the landscape so faintly, that she was sometimes in danger of losing her way. However, about noon she paused by a gate on the edge of the basin in which Emminster and its Vicarage lay.

The square tower, beneath which she knew that at that moment the Vicar and his congregation were gathered, had a severe look in her eyes. She wished that she had somehow contrived to come on a week-day. Such a good man might be prejudiced against a woman who had chosen Sunday, never realizing the necessities of her case.

But it was incumbent upon her to go on now. She took off the thick boots in which she had walked thus far, put on her pretty thin ones of patent leather, and, stuffing the former into the hedge by the gate-post where she might readily find them again, descended the hill; the freshness of colour she had derived from the keen air thinning away in spite of her as she drew near the parsonage.

Tess hoped for some accident that might favour her, but nothing favoured her. The shrubs on the Vicarage lawn rustled uncomfortably in the frosty breeze; she could not feel by any stretch of imagination, dressed to her highest as she was, that the house was the residence of near relations; and yet nothing essential, in nature or emotion, divided her from them: in pains, pleasures, thoughts, birth, death, and after-death, they were the same.

She nerved herself by an effort, entered the swing-gate, and rang the door-bell. The thing was done; there could be no retreat. No; the thing was not done. Nobody answered to her ringing. The effort had to be risen to, and made again. She rang a second time, and the agitation of the act, coupled with her weariness after the fifteen miles' walk, led her to support herself while she waited by resting her hand on her hip, and her elbow against the wall of the porch. The wind was so drying that the ivy-leaves had become wizened and gray, each tapping incessantly upon its neighbour with a disquieting stir of her nerves. A piece of blood-stained paper, caught up from some meat-buyer's dust-heap, beat up and down the road without the gate; too flimsy to rest, too heavy to fly away; and a few straws kept it company.

The second peal had been louder, and still nobody came. Then she walked out of the porch, opened the gate, and passed through. And though she looked dubiously at the house-front as if inclined to return, it was with a breath of relief that she closed the gate. A feeling haunted her that she might have been recognized (though how she could not tell), and orders been given not to admit her.

Tess went as far as the corner. She had done all she could do; but determined not to escape present trepidation at the expense of future distress, she walked back again quite past the house, looking up at all the windows.

Ah – the explanation was that they were all at church, every one.

She remembered her husband saying that his father always insisted upon the household, servants included, going to morning-service, and, as a consequence, eating cold food when they came home. It was, therefore, only necessary to wait till the service was over. She would not make herself conspicuous by waiting on the spot, and she started to get past the church into the lane. But as she reached the churchyard-gate the people began pouring out, and Tess found herself in the midst of them.

The Emminster congregation looked at her as only a congregation of small country-townsfolk walking home at its leisure can look at a woman out of the common whom it perceives to be a stranger. She quickened her pace, and ascended the road by which she had come, to find a retreat between its hedges till the Vicar's family should have lunched, and it might be convenient for them to receive her. She soon distanced the churchgoers, except two youngish men, who, linked arm-in-arm, were beating up behind her at a quick step.

As they drew nearer she could hear their voices engaged in earnest discourse, and, with the natural quickness of a woman in her situation, did not fail to recognize in those voices the quality of her husband's tones. The pedestrians were his two brothers. Forgetting all her plans, Tess's one dread was lest they should overtake her now, in her disorganized condition, before she was prepared to confront them; for though she felt that they could not identify her she instinctively dreaded their scrutiny. The more quickly they walked the more quickly walked she. They were plainly bent upon taking a short quick stroll before going indoors to lunch or dinner, to restore warmth to limbs chilled with sitting through a long service.

Only one person had preceded Tess up the hill – a ladylike young woman, somewhat interesting, though, perhaps, a trifle *guindée* and prudish. Tess had nearly overtaken her when the speed of her brothers-in-law brought them so nearly behind her back that she could hear every word of their conversation. They said nothing, however, which particularly interested her till, observing the young lady still farther in front, one of them remarked, 'There is Mercy Chant. Let us overtake her.'

Tess knew the name. It was the woman who had been destined for

Angel's life-companion by his and her parents, and whom he probably would have married but for her intrusive self. She would have known as much without previous information if she had waited a moment, for one of the brothers proceeded to say: 'Ah! poor Angel, poor Angel! I never see that nice girl without more and more regretting his precipitancy in throwing himself away upon a dairymaid, or whatever she may be. It is a queer business, apparently. Whether she has joined him yet or not I don't know; but she had not done so some months ago when I heard from him.'

'I can't say. He never tells me anything nowadays. His ill-considered marriage seems to have completed that estrangement from me which was begun by his extraordinary opinions.'

Tess beat up the long hill still faster; but she could not outwalk them without exciting notice. At last they outsped her altogether, and passed her by. The young lady still farther ahead heard their footsteps and turned. Then there was a greeting and a shaking of hands, and the three went on together.

They soon reached the summit of the hill, and, evidently intending this point to be the limit of their promenade, slackened pace and turned all three aside to the gate whereat Tess had paused an hour before that time to reconnoitre the town before descending into it. During their discourse one of the clerical brothers probed the hedge carefully with his umbrella, and dragged something to light.

'Here's a pair of old boots,' he said. 'Thrown away, I suppose, by some tramp or other.'

'Some impostor who wished to come into the town barefoot, perhaps, and so excite our sympathies,' said Miss Chant. 'Yes, it must have been, for they are excellent walking-boots – by no means worn out. What a wicked thing to do! I'll carry them home for some poor person.'

Cuthbert Clare, who had been the one to find them, picked them up for her with the crook of his stick; and Tess's boots were appropriated.

She, who had heard this, walked past under the screen of her woollen veil, till, presently looking back, she perceived that the church party had left the gate with her boots and retreated down the hill.

Thereupon our heroine resumed her walk. Tears, blinding tears, were running down her face. She knew that it was all sentiment, all baseless impressibility, which had caused her to read the scene as her own condemnation; nevertheless she could not get over it; she could not contravene in her own defenceless person all these untoward omens. It was impossible to think of returning to the Vicarage. Angel's wife felt almost as if she had been hounded up that hill like a scorned thing by those – to her – superfine clerics. Innocently as the slight had been inflicted, it was somewhat unfortunate that she had encountered the sons and not the father, who, despite his narrowness, was far less starched and ironed than they, and had to the full the gift of charity. As she again thought of her dusty boots she almost pitied those habiliments for the scorn to which they had been subjected, and felt how hopeless life was for their owner.

'Ah!' she said, still weeping in pity of herself, '*they* didn't know that I wore those over the roughest part of the road to save these pretty ones *he* bought for me – no – they did not know it! And they didn't think that *he* chose the colour o' my pretty frock – no – how could they? If they had known perhaps they would not have cared, for they don't care much for him, poor thing!'

Then she wept for the beloved man whose conventional standard of judgment had caused her all these latter sorrows; and she went her way without knowing that the greatest misfortune of her life was this feminine loss of courage at the last and critical moment through her estimating her father-in-law by his sons. Her present condition was precisely one which would have enlisted the sympathies of old Mr and Mrs Clare. Their hearts went out of them at a bound towards extreme cases, when the subtle mental troubles of the less desperate among mankind failed to win their interest or regard. In jumping at Publicans and Sinners they would forget that a word might be said for the worries of Scribes and Pharisees;[3] and this defect or limitation might have recommended their own daughter-in-law to them at this moment as a fairly choice sort of lost person for their love.

Thereupon she began to plod back along the road by which she had come not altogether full of hope, but full of a conviction that a crisis in her life was approaching. No crisis, apparently, had supervened; and there was nothing left for her to do but to continue for the remainder of the winter upon that starve-acre farm.[4] She did, indeed, take sufficient interest in herself to throw up her veil on this return journey, as if to let the world see that she could at least exhibit a face such as Mercy Chant could not show. But it was done with a sorry shake of the head. 'It is nothing – it is nothing!' she said. 'Nobody loves it; nobody sees it. Who cares about the looks of a castaway like me!'

Her journey back was rather a meander than a march. It had no sprightliness, no purpose; only a tendency. Along the tedious length of Benvill Lane she began to grow tired, and she leant upon gates and paused by milestones.

She did not enter any house till, at the seventh or eighth mile, she descended the steep long hill below which lay the village or townlet of Evershead, where in the morning she had breakfasted with such contrasting expectations. The cottage by the church, in which she again sat down, was almost the first at that end of the village, and while the woman fetched her some milk from the pantry, Tess, looking down the street, perceived that the place seemed quite deserted.

'The people are gone to afternoon service, I suppose?' she said.

'No, my dear,' said the old woman. ''Tis too soon for that; the bells haint strook out yet. They be all gone to hear the preaching in Spring Barn. A ranter[5] preaches there between the services – a excellent, fiery, Christian man, they say. But, Lord, I don't go to hear'n! What comes in the regular way over the pulpit is hot enough for I.'

Tess soon went onward into the village, her footsteps echoing against the houses as though it were a place of the dead. Nearing the central part her echoes were intruded on by other sounds; and seeing the barn before her, she guessed these to be the utterances of the preacher.

His voice became so distinct in the still clear air that she could soon catch his sentences, though she was on the closed side of the barn. The sermon, as might be expected, was of the extremest antinomian type; on justification by faith, as expounded in the theology of St Paul. This fixed idea of the rhapsodist was delivered with animated enthusiasm, in a manner entirely declamatory, for he had plainly no skill as a dialectician.[6] Although Tess had not heard the beginning of the address, she learnt what the text had been from its constant iteration —

'*O foolish Galatians, who hath bewitched you, that ye should not obey the truth, before whose eyes Jesus Christ hath been evidently set forth, crucified among you?'* [7]

Tess was all the more interested, as she stood listening behind, in finding that the preacher's doctrine was a vehement form of the views of Angel's father, and her interest intensified when the speaker began to detail his own spiritual experiences of how he had come by those views. He had, he said, been the greatest of sinners. He had scoffed; he had wantonly associated with the reckless and the lewd. But a day of awakening had come, and, in a human sense, it had been brought about mainly by the influence of a certain clergyman, whom he had at first grossly insulted; but whose parting words had sunk into his heart, and had remained there, till by the grace of Heaven they had worked this change in him, and made him what they saw him.

But more startling to Tess than the doctrine had been the voice, which, impossible as it seemed, was precisely that of Alec D'Urberville. Her face fixed in painful suspense she came round to the front of the barn, and passed before it. The low winter sun beamed directly upon the great double-doored entrance on this side; one of the doors being open, so that the rays stretched far in over the threshing-floor to the preacher and his audience, all snugly sheltered from the northern breeze. The listeners were entirely villagers, among them being the man whom she had seen carrying the red paint-pot on a former memorable occasion. But her attention was given to the central figure, who stood upon some sacks of corn, facing the people and the door. The three o'clock sun shone full upon him, and the strange enervating conviction that her seducer confronted her, which had been gaining ground in Tess ever since she had heard his words distinctly, was at last established as a fact indeed.

END OF PHASE THE FIFTH

PHASE THE SIXTH

The Convert

XLV

Till this moment she had never seen or heard from D'Urberville since her departure from Trantridge.

The rencounter came at a heavy moment, one of all moments calculated to permit its impact with the least emotional shock. But such was unreasoning memory that, though he stood there openly and palpably a converted man, who was sorrowing for his past irregularities, a fear overcame her, paralyzing her movement so that she neither retreated nor advanced.

To think of what emanated from that countenance when she saw it last, and to behold it now! ... There was the same handsome unpleasantness of mien, but now he wore neatly-trimmed, old-fashioned whiskers, the sable moustache having disappeared; and his dress was half clerical, a modification which had changed his expression sufficiently to abstract the dandyism from his features, and to hinder for a second her belief in his identity.

To Tess's sense there was, just at first, a ghastly *bizarrerie*, a grim incongruity, in the march of these solemn words of Scripture out of such a mouth. This too familiar intonation, less than four years earlier, had brought to her ears expressions of such divergent purpose that her heart became quite sick at the irony of the contrast. Yet he was in earnest, unmistakably.

It was less a reform than a transfiguration. The former curves of sensuousness were now modulated to lines of devotional passion. The lip-shapes that had meant seductiveness were now made to express supplication; the glow on the cheek that yesterday could be translated as riotousness was evangelized to-day into the splendour of pious enthusiasm; animalism had become fanaticism; Paganism Paulinism; the bold rolling eye that had flashed upon her form in the old time with such mastery now beamed with the rude energy of a theolatry that was almost ferocious.[1] Those black angularities which his face had used to put on when his wishes were thwarted now did duty in picturing the incorrigible backslider who would insist upon turning again to his wallowing in the mire.

The lineaments, as such, seemed to complain. They had been diverted from their hereditary connotation to signify impressions for which nature did not intend them. Strange that their very elevation was a misapplication, that to raise seemed to falsify.

Yet could it be so? She would admit the ungenerous sentiment no longer. D'Urberville was not the first wicked man who had turned away from his wickedness to save his soul alive, and why should she deem it unnatural in him? It was but the usage of thought which had been jarred in her at hearing good new words in bad old notes. The greater the sinner the greater the saint; it was not necessary to dive far into Christian history to discover that.

Such impressions as these moved her vaguely, and without strict definiteness. As soon as the nerveless pause of her surprise would allow her to stir, her impulse was to pass on out of his sight. He had obviously not discerned her yet in her position against the sun.

But the moment that she moved again he recognized her. The effect upon her old lover was electric, far stronger than the effect of his presence upon her. His fire, the tumultuous ring of his eloquence, seemed to go out of him. His lip struggled and trembled under the words that lay upon it; but deliver them it could not as long as she faced him. His eyes, after their first glance upon her face, hung determinedly in every other direction but hers, but came back in a desperate leap every few seconds. This paralysis lasted, however, but a short time; for Tess's energies returned with the atrophy of his,[2] and she walked as fast as she was able past the barn and onward.

As soon as she could reflect it appalled her, this change in their relative platforms. He who had wrought her undoing was now on the side of the Spirit, while she remained unregenerate. And, as in the legend, it had resulted that her Cyprian image had suddenly appeared upon his altar, and the fire of the priest had been well-nigh extinguished.[3]

She went on without turning her head. Her back seemed to be endowed with a sensitiveness to ocular beams – even her clothing – so alive was she to a fancied gaze which might be resting upon her from the outside of that barn. All the way along to this point her heart had been heavy with an inactive sorrow; now there was a change in the quality of its trouble. That hunger for affection too long withheld was for the time displaced by an almost physical sense of an implacable past which still engirdled her. It intensified her consciousness of error to a practical despair; the break of continuity between her earlier and present existence, which she had hoped for, had not, after all, taken place. Bygones would never be complete bygones till she was a bygone herself.

Thus absorbed she recrossed the northern half of Long-Ash Lane at right angles, and presently saw before her the road ascending whitely to the upland along whose margin the remainder of her journey lay. Its dry pale surface stretched mercilessly onward, unbroken by a single figure, vehicle, or mark, save some occasional horse-droppings which dotted its cold aridity here and there. While slowly breasting this ascent Tess became conscious of footsteps behind her, and, turning quickly, she saw approaching that well-known form, so strangely accoutred as the Methodist – the one personage in all the world she wished not to encounter alone on this side of the grave.

There was not much time, however, for thought or elusion, and she yielded as calmly as she could to the necessity of letting him overtake her. She saw that he was excited, less by the speed of his walk than by the feelings within him.

'Tess!' he said.

She slackened speed without looking round.

'Tess!' he repeated. 'It is I – Alec D'Urberville.'

She then looked back at him, and he came up.

'I see it is,' she answered coldly.

'Well – is that all? Yet I deserve no more! . . . I heard you had gone away, nobody knew where. Tess, you wonder why I have followed you?'

'I do, rather; and I would that you had not with all my heart!'

'Yes – you may well say it,' he returned gravely, as they moved

307

onward together, she with unwilling tread. 'But don't mistake me; and
I beg this because you may have been led to do so in noticing – if you
did notice it – how your sudden appearance unnerved me down there.
It was but a momentary spasm; and considering what you had been
to me, it was natural enough. But God helped me through it, and
immediately afterwards I felt that, of all persons in the world whom
it was my duty and desire to save from the wrath to come, the woman
whom I had so grievously wronged was that person. I have come with
that sole purpose in view – nothing more.'

There was the smallest vein of scorn in her words of rejoinder:
'Have you saved yourself? Charity begins at home, they say.'

'*I* have done nothing!' said he impetuously. 'Heaven, as I have been
telling my hearers, has done all. No amount of contempt that you can
pour upon me, Tess, will equal what I have poured upon myself – the
old Adam of my former years! But I can tell you the means by which
my conversion was brought about, and I hope you will be interested
enough in me to listen. Have you ever heard the name of the parson
of Emminster – you must have done so? – old Mr Clare; one of the
most earnest of his school; one of the few intense men left in the
Church; not so intense as the extreme wing of Christian believers to
which I belong, but quite an exception among the Established clergy,
the younger of whom are gradually attenuating the true doctrines by
their sophistries, till they are but the shadow of what they were. I only
differ from him on the question of Church and State – the interpretation
of the text, "Come out from among them and be ye separate, saith
the Lord"[4] – that's all. He is one who, I firmly believe, has been the
humble means of saving more souls in this country than any other
man you can name. You have heard of him?'

'I have,' she said.

'He came to Trantridge two or three years ago to preach on behalf
of some missionary society; and I, wretched man that I was, insulted
him when, in his disinterestedness, he tried to reason with me and
show me the way. He did not resent my conduct, he simply said that
some day I should receive the first-fruits of the Spirit[5] – that those
who came to scoff sometimes remained to pray.[6] There was a strange
magic in his words. They sank into my mind, though I did not know

it at the time, nor did he; and by degrees I was brought to the light. Since then my one desire has been to hand on the good news to others, and that is what I was trying to do to-day; though it is only lately that I have preached hereabout. The first months of my ministry have been spent in the North of England among strangers, where I preferred to make my earliest clumsy attempts, so as to acquire courage before undergoing that severest of all tests of one's sincerity, addressing those who have known one, and have been one's companions in the days of darkness. If you could only know, Tess, the sense of security, the certainty, you would, I am sure—'

'Don't go on with it!' she cried passionately, as she turned away from him to a stile by the wayside, on which she bent herself. 'I can't believe in such sudden things! I feel indignant with you for talking to me like this, when you know – when you know what harm you've done me! You, and those like you, take your fill of pleasure on earth by making the life of such as me bitter and black with sorrow; and then it is a fine thing, when you have had enough of that, to think of securing your pleasure in heaven by becoming converted! Out upon such – I don't believe in you – I hate it!'

'Tess,' he insisted; 'don't speak so! It came to me like a shining light! And you don't believe me? What don't you believe?'

'Your conversion. Your scheme of religion.'

'Why?'

She dropped her voice. 'Because a better man than you does not believe in such.'

'What a woman's reason! Who is this better man?'

'I cannot tell you.'

'Well,' he declared, a resentment beneath his words seeming ready to spring out at a moment's notice, 'God forbid that I should say I am a good man – and you know I don't say any such thing. I am new to goodness, truly; but new comers see farthest sometimes.'

'Yes,' she replied sadly. 'But I cannot believe in your conversion to a new spirit. Such flashes as you feel, Alec, I fear don't last!'

Thus speaking she turned from the stile over which she had been leaning, and faced him; whereupon his eyes, falling casually upon the familiar countenance and form, remained contemplating her. The inferior man was quiet in him now; but it was surely not extracted, nor even entirely subdued.

'Don't look at me like that!' he said abruptly.

Tess, who had been quite unconscious of her action and mien, instantly withdrew the large dark gaze of her eyes, stammering with a flush, 'I beg your pardon!' And there was revived in her the wretched sentiment which had often come to her before, that in inhabiting the fleshly tabernacle[7] with which nature had endowed her she was somehow doing wrong.

'No, no! Don't beg my pardon. But since you wear a veil to hide your good looks, why don't you keep it down?'

She pulled down the veil, saying hastily, 'It was to keep off the wind.'

'It may seem harsh of me to dictate like this,' he went on; 'but it is better that I should not look too often on you. It might be dangerous.'

'Ssh!' said Tess.

'Well, women's faces have had too much power over me already for me not to fear them! An evangelist has nothing to do with such as they; and it reminds me of the old times that I would forget!'

After this their conversation dwindled to a cursory remark now and then as they rambled onward, Tess inwardly wondering how far he was going with her, and not liking to send him back by positive mandate. Frequently when they came to a gate or stile they found painted thereon in red letters some text of Scripture, and she asked him if he knew who had been at the pains to blazon these announcements. He told her that the man was employed by himself and others who were working with him in that district, to paint these reminders that no means might be left untried which might move the hearts of a wicked generation.

At length the road touched the spot called 'Cross-in-Hand.' Of all spots on this bleached and desolate upland this was the most forlorn. It was so far removed from the charm which is sought in landscape by artists and view-lovers as to reach a new kind of beauty, a negative beauty of tragic blackness.[8] The place took its name from a stone pillar which stood there, a strange rude monolith, from a stratum unknown in any local quarry, on which was roughly carved a human hand.

Differing accounts were given of its history and purport. Some author-
ities stated that a devotional cross had once formed the complete
erection thereon, of which the present relic was but the stump; others
that the stone as it stood was entire, and that it had been fixed there
to mark a boundary or place of meeting. Anyhow, whatever the origin
of the relic, there was and is something sinister, or solemn, according
to mood, in the scene amid which it stands; something tending to
impress the most phlegmatic passer-by.

'I think I must leave you now,' he remarked, as they drew near to
this spot. 'I have to preach at Abbot's Cernel at six this evening, and
my way lies across to the right from here. And you upset me somewhat
too, Tessy – I cannot, will not, say why. I must go away and get
strength . . . How is it that you speak so fluently now? Who has taught
you such good English?'

'I have learnt things in my troubles,' she said evasively.

'What troubles have you had?'

She told him of the first one – the only one that related to him.

'Heaven!' said D'Urberville. 'I knew nothing of this till now! Why
didn't you write to me?'

She did not reply; and he broke the silence by adding: 'Well – you
will see me again.'

'No,' she answered. 'Do not again come near me!'

'I will think. But before we part, come here.' He stepped up to the
pillar. 'This was once a Holy Cross. Relics are not in my creed; but I
fear you at moments – far more than you need fear me; and to lessen
my fear, put your hand upon that stone hand, and swear that you will
never tempt me – by your charms or ways.'

'Good God – how can you ask what is so unnecessary! All that is
furthest from my thought!'

'Yes – but swear it, swear it!' he pleaded desperately.

Tess, half frightened, gave way to his importunity; placed her hand
upon the stone and swore.

'I am sorry you are not a believer,' he continued; 'that some
unbeliever should have got hold of you and unsettled your mind. But
no more now. At home at least I can pray for you; and I will; and
who knows what may not happen? I'm off. Good-bye!'

He turned to a gap in the hedge, and without letting his eyes again rest upon her leapt over, and struck out across the down in the direction of Abbot's Cernel. As he walked his pace showed perturbation, and by and by, as if instigated by a bracing thought, he drew from his pocket a small Bible, between the leaves of which was folded a letter, worn and soiled, as from much re-reading. D'Urberville opened the letter. It was dated several months before this time, and was signed by Parson Clare.

The letter began by expressing the writer's unfeigned joy at D'Urberville's conversion, and thanked him for his kindness in communicating with the parson on the subject. It expressed Mr Clare's warm assurance of forgiveness for D'Urberville's former conduct, and his interest in the young man's plans for the future. He, Mr Clare, would much have liked to see D'Urberville in the Church to whose ministry he had devoted so many years of his own life, and would have helped him to enter a theological college to that end;[9] but since his correspondent had possibly not cared to do this on account of the delay it would have entailed, he was not the man to insist upon its paramount importance. Every man must work as he could best work, and in the method towards which he felt impelled by the Spirit.

D'Urberville read and re-read this letter, and seemed to fortify himself thereby. He also read some passages from his Bible as he walked till his face assumed a calm, and apparently the image of Tess no longer troubled his mind.

She meanwhile had kept along the edge of the hill by which lay her nearest way home. Within the distance of a mile she met a solitary shepherd.

'What is the meaning of that old stone I have passed?' she asked of him. 'Was it ever a Holy Cross?'

'Cross – no; 'twer not a cross! 'Tis a thing of ill-omen, Miss. It was put up in wuld times by the relations of a malefactor who was tortured there by nailing his hand to a post, and afterwards hung. The bones lie underneath. They say he sold his soul to the devil, and that he walks at times.'

She felt the *petite mort* at this unexpectedly gruesome information, and left the solitary man behind her. It was dusk when she drew near to Flintcomb-Ash, and in the lane at the entrance to the hamlet she approached a girl and her lover without their observing her. They were talking no secrets, and the clear unconcerned voice of the young woman, in response to the warmer accents of the man, spread into the chilly air as the one soothing thing within the dusky horizon, full of a stagnant obscurity upon which nothing else intruded. For a moment the voices cheered the heart of Tess, till she reasoned that this interview had its origin, on one side or the other, in the same attraction which had been the prelude to her own tribulation. When she came close the girl turned serenely and recognized her, the young man walking off in embarrassment. The woman was Izz Huett, whose interest in Tess's excursion immediately superseded her own proceedings. Tess did not explain very clearly its results, and Izz, who was a girl of tact, began to speak of her own little affair, a phase of which Tess had just witnessed.

'He is Amby Seedling, the chap who used to sometimes come and help at Talbothays,' she explained indifferently. 'He actually inquired and found out that I had come here, and has followed me. He says he's been in love wi' me these two years. But I've hardly answered him.'

XLVI

Several days had passed since her futile journey, and Tess was afield. The dry winter wind still blew, but a screen of thatched hurdles erected in the eye of the blast kept its force away from her. On the sheltered side was a turnip-slicing machine, whose bright blue hue of new paint seemed almost vocal in the otherwise subdued scene. Opposite its front was a long mound or 'grave,' in which the roots had been preserved since early winter. Tess was standing at the uncovered end, chopping off with a bill-hook the fibres and earth from each root, and throwing it after the operation into the slicer. A man was turning the handle of the machine, and from its trough came the newly-cut swedes, the fresh smell of whose yellow chips was accompanied by the sounds of the snuffling wind, the smart swish of the slicing-blades, and the choppings of the hook in Tess's leather-gloved hand.

The wide acreage of blank agricultural brownness, apparent where the swedes had been pulled, was beginning to be striped in wales of darker brown, gradually broadening to ribands. Along the edge of each of these something crept upon ten legs, moving without haste and without rest up and down the whole length of the field; it was two horses and a man, the plough going between them, turning up the cleared ground for a spring sowing.

For hours nothing relieved the joyless monotony of things. Then, far beyond the ploughing-teams, a black speck was seen. It had come from the corner of a fence, where there was a gap, and its tendency was up the incline, towards the swede-cutters. From the proportions of a mere point it advanced to the shape of a ninepin, and was soon perceived to be a man in black, arriving from the direction of Flintcomb-Ash. The man at the slicer, having nothing else to do with his eyes, continually observed the comer, but Tess, who was occupied, did not perceive him till her companion directed her attention to his approach.

It was not her hard taskmaster, Farmer Groby; it was one in a semi-clerical costume, who now represented what had once been the dare-devil Alec D'Urberville. Not being hot at his preaching there was less enthusiasm about him now, and the presence of the grinder seemed to embarrass him. A pale distress was already on Tess's face, and she pulled her curtained hood further over it.

D'Urberville came up and said quietly –

'I want to speak to you, Tess.'

'You have refused my last request, not to come near me!' said she.

'Yes, but I have a good reason.'

'Well, tell it.'

'It is more serious than you may think.'

He glanced round to see if he were overheard. They were at some distance from the man who turned the slicer, and the movement of the machine, too, sufficiently prevented Alec's words reaching other ears. D'Urberville placed himself so as to screen Tess from the labourer, turning his back to the latter.

'It is this,' he continued, with impetuous compunction. 'In thinking of your soul and mine when we last met, I neglected to inquire as to your worldly condition. You were well dressed, and I did not think of it. But I see now that it is hard – harder than it used to be when I – knew you – harder than you deserve. Perhaps a good deal of it is owing to me!'

She did not answer, and he watched her inquiringly as, with bent head, her face completely screened by the hood, she resumed her trimming of the swedes. By going on with her work she felt better able to keep him outside her emotions.

'Tess,' he added, with a sigh that verged on a groan, 'yours was the very worst case I ever was concerned in! I had no idea of what had resulted till you told me. Wretch that I was to foul that innocent life! The whole blame was mine – the whole blackness of the sin, the awful, awful iniquity. You, too, the real blood of which I am but the base imitation, what a blind young thing you were as to possibilities! I say in all earnestness that it is a shame for parents to bring up their girls in such dangerous ignorance of the gins and nets that the wicked may set for them, whether their motive be a good one or the result of simple indifference.'

Tess still did no more than listen, throwing down one globular root and taking up another with automatic regularity, the pensive contour of the mere field-woman alone marking her.

'But it is not that I came to say,' D'Urberville went on. 'My circumstances are these. I have lost my mother since you were at Trantridge, and the place is my own. But I intend to sell it, and devote myself to missionary work in Africa, either as an ordained deacon or as an outside worker – I care very little which. Now, what I want to ask you is, will you put it in my power to do my duty – to make the only reparation I can make for the wrong I did you: that is, will you be my wife, and go with me? . . . I have already obtained this, to save time.'[1]

He drew a piece of parchment from his pocket.

'What is it?' said she.

'A marriage licence.'

'O no, sir – no!' she said quickly, starting back.

'You will not? Why is that?'

And as he asked the question a disappointment which was not entirely the disappointment of thwarted duty crossed D'Urberville's face. It was unmistakably a symptom that something of his old passion for her had been revived; duty and desire ran hand-in-hand.

'Surely,' he began again, in more impassioned tones, and then looked round at the labourer who turned the slicer.

Tess, too, felt that the argument could not be ended there. Informing the man that a gentleman had come to see her, with whom she wished to walk a little way, she moved off with D'Urberville across the zebra-striped field. When they reached the first newly-ploughed section he held out his hand to help her over it; but she stepped forward on the summits of the earth-rolls as if she did not see him.

'You will not marry me, Tess, and make me a self-respecting man?' he repeated, as soon as they were over the furrows.

'I cannot.'

'But why?'

'You know I have no affection for you.'

'But you would get to feel that in time, perhaps – as soon as you really could forgive me?'

'Never!'

'Why so positive?'

'I love somebody else.'

The words seemed to stupefy him.

'You do?' he cried. 'Somebody else? But has not a sense of what is morally right and proper any weight with you?'

'No, no, no – don't say that!'

'Anyhow, then, your love for this other man may be only a passing feeling which you will overcome—'

'No – no.'

'Yes, yes! Why not?'

'I cannot tell you.'

'You must in honour!'

'Well then . . . I have married him.'

'Ah!' he exclaimed; and he stopped dead and gazed at her.

'I did not wish to tell – I did not mean to!' she pleaded. 'It is a secret here, or at any rate but dimly known. So will you, *please* will you, keep from questioning me? You must remember that we are now strangers.'

'Strangers – are we? Strangers!'

For a moment a flash of his old irony marked his face; but he determinedly chastened it down.

'Is that man your husband?' he asked mechanically, denoting by a sign the labourer who turned the machine.

'That man!' she said proudly. 'I should think not!'

'Who, then?'

'Do not ask what I do not wish to tell!' she begged, and in her eagerness flashed an appeal to him from her upturned face and lash-shadowed eyes.

D'Urberville was disturbed.

'But I only asked for your sake!' he retorted hotly. 'Thunder of heaven – God forgive me for such an expression – I came here, I swear, as I thought for your good. Tess – don't look at me so – I cannot stand your looks![2] There never were such eyes, surely, before Christianity or since! There – I won't lose my head; I dare not. I own that the sight of you has revived my love for you, which, I believed, was extinguished with all such feelings. But I thought that our marriage might be a sanctification for us both. "The unbelieving husband is sanctified by the wife, and the unbelieving wife is sanctified by the husband,"[3] I said to myself. But my plan is dashed from me; and I must bear the disappointment!'

He moodily reflected with his eyes on the ground.

'Married! Married! . . . Well, that being so,' he added, quite calmly, tearing the licence slowly into halves and putting them in his pocket; 'that being prevented, I should like to do some good to you and your husband, whoever he may be. There are many questions that I am tempted to ask, but I will not do so, of course, in opposition to your wishes. Though, if I could know your husband, I might more easily benefit him and you. Is he on this farm?'

'No,' she murmured. 'He is far away.'

'Far away? From *you*? What sort of husband can he be?'

'O, do not speak against him! It was through you. He found out—'

'Ah, is it so! . . . That's sad, Tess!'

'Yes.'

'But to stay away from you – to leave you to work like this!'

'He does not leave me to work!' she cried, springing to the defence of the absent one with all her fervour. 'He don't know it! It is by my own arrangement.'

'Then, does he write?'

'I – I cannot tell you. There are things which are private to ourselves.'

'Of course that means that he does not. You are a deserted wife, my poor Tess!'

In an impulse he turned suddenly to take her hand; the buff-glove was on it, and he seized only the rough leather fingers which did not express the life or shape of those within.

'You must not – you must not!' she cried fearfully, slipping her hand from the glove as from a pocket, and leaving it in his grasp. 'O, will you go away – for the sake of me – my husband – go, in the name of your own Christianity!'

'Yes, yes; I will,' he said hastily, and thrusting the glove back to her turned to leave. Facing round, however, he said, 'Tess, as God is my judge, I meant no sin in taking your hand!'

A pattering of hoofs on the soil of the field, which they had not noticed in their preoccupation, ceased close behind them; and a voice reached her ear:

'What the devil are ye doing away from your work at this time o' day?'

Farmer Groby had espied the two figures from the distance, and had inquisitively ridden across, to learn what was their business in his field.

'Don't speak like that to her!' said D'Urberville, his face blackening with something that was not Christianity.

'Indeed, Mister! And what mid Methodist pa'sons have to do with she?'

'Who is the fellow?' asked D'Urberville, turning to Tess.

She went close up to him.

'Go – I do beg you!' she said.

'What? And leave you to that tyrant? I can see in his face what a churl he is.'

'He won't hurt me. *He's* not in love with me. I can leave at Lady-Day.'

'Well, I have no right but to obey, I suppose. But – well, good-bye!'

Her defender, whom she dreaded more than her assailant, having reluctantly disappeared, the farmer continued his reprimand, which Tess took with the greatest coolness, that sort of attack being independent of sex. To have as a master this man of stone, who would have cuffed her if he had dared, was almost a relief after her former experiences. She silently walked back towards the summit of the field that was the scene of her labour, so absorbed in the interview which had just taken place that she was hardly aware that the nose of Groby's horse almost touched her shoulders.

'If so be you make an agreement to work for me till Lady-Day, I'll see that you carry it out,' he growled. ''Od rot the women – now 'tis one thing, and then 'tis another! But I'll put up with it no longer!'

Knowing very well that he did not harass the other women of the farm as he harassed her out of spite for the flooring he had once received, she did for one moment picture what might have been the result if she had been free to accept the offer just made her of being the monied Alec's wife. It would have lifted her completely out of subjection, not only to her present oppressive employer, but to a whole world who seemed to despise her. 'But no, no!' she said breathlessly; 'I could not have married him now! He is so unpleasant to me.'

That very night she began an appealing letter to Clare, concealing from him her hardships, and assuring him of her undying affection. Any one who had been in a position to read between the lines would have seen that at the back of her great love was some monstrous fear – almost a desperation – as to some secret circumstances which were not disclosed. But again she did not finish her effusion; he had asked Izz to go with him, and perhaps did not care for her at all. She put the letter in her box, and wondered if it would ever reach Angel's hands.

After this her daily tasks were gone through heavily enough, and brought on the day which was of great import to agriculturists – the day of the Candlemas Fair.[4] It was at this fair that new engagements were entered into for the twelve months following the ensuing Lady-Day, and those of the farming population who thought of changing their places duly attended at the county-town where the fair was held. Nearly all the labourers on Flintcomb-Ash Farm intended flight, and early in the morning there was a general exodus in the direction of the town, which lay at a distance of from ten to a dozen miles over hilly country. Though Tess also meant to leave at the quarter-day she was one of the few who did not go to the fair, having a vaguely-shaped hope that something would happen to render another outdoor engagement unnecessary.

It was a peaceful February day, of wonderful softness for the time, and one would almost have thought that winter was over. She had hardly finished her dinner when D'Urberville's figure darkened the window of the cottage wherein she was a lodger, which she had all to herself to-day.

Tess jumped up, but her visitor had knocked at the door, and she could hardly in reason run away. D'Urberville's knock, his walk up to the door, had some indescribable quality of difference from his air when she last saw him. They seemed to be acts of which the doer was ashamed. She thought that she would not open the door; but, as there was no sense in that either, she arose, and having lifted the latch stepped back quickly. He came in, saw her, and flung himself down into a chair before speaking.

'Tess – I couldn't help it!' he began desperately, as he wiped his heated face which had also a superimposed flush of excitement. 'I felt that I must call to at least ask how you are. I assure you I had not been thinking of you at all till I saw you that Sunday; now I cannot get rid of your image, try how I may! It is hard that a good woman should do harm to a bad man; yet so it is. If you would only pray for me, Tess!'

The suppressed distraction of his manner was almost pitiable, and yet Tess did not pity him.

'How can I pray for you,' she said, 'when I am forbidden to believe that the great Power who moves the world would alter His plans on my account?'

'You really think that?'

'Yes. I have been cured of the presumption of thinking otherwise.'

'Cured? By whom?'

'By my husband, if I must tell.'

'Ah – your husband – your husband! How strange it seems! I remember you hinted something of the sort the other day. What do you really believe in these matters, Tess?' he asked. 'You seem to have no religion – perhaps owing to me.'

'But I have. Though I don't believe in anything supernatural.'

D'Urberville looked at her with misgiving.

'Then do you think that the line I take is all wrong?'

'A good deal of it.'

'H'm – and yet I've felt so sure about it,' he said uneasily.

'I believe in the *spirit* of the Sermon on the Mount, and so did my dear husband[5]. . . But I don't believe—'

Here she gave her negations.[6]

'The fact is,' said D'Urberville drily, 'whatever your dear husband believed you accept, and whatever he rejected you reject, without the least inquiry or reasoning on your own part. That's just like you women. Your mind is enslaved to his.'

'Ah, because he knew everything!' said she, with a triumphant simplicity of faith in Angel Clare that the most perfect man could hardly have deserved, much less her husband.

'Yes, but you should not take negative opinions wholesale from another person like that. A pretty fellow he must be to teach you such scepticism!'

'He never forced my judgment! He would never argue on the subject wi' me! But I looked at it in this way; what he believed, after inquiring deeply into doctrines, was much more likely to be right than what I might believe, who hadn't looked into doctrines at all.'

'What used he to say? He must have said something?'

She reflected; and with her acute memory for the letter of Angel Clare's remarks, even when she did not comprehend their spirit, she recalled a merciless polemical syllogism that she had heard him use when, as it occasionally happened, he indulged in a species of thinking aloud with her at his side. In delivering it she gave also Clare's accent and manner with reverential faithfulness.

'Say that again,' asked D'Urberville, who had listened with the greatest attention.

She repeated the argument, and D'Urberville thoughtfully murmured the words after her.

'Anything else?' he presently asked.

'He said at another time something like this;' and she gave another, which might possibly have been paralleled in many a work of the pedigree ranging from the *Dictionnaire Philosophique* to Huxley's essays.[7]

'Ah – ha! How do you remember them?'

'I wanted to believe what he believed, though he didn't wish me to; and I managed to coax him to tell me a few of his thoughts. I can't say I quite understand that one; but I know it is right.'

'H'm. Fancy your being able to teach me what you don't know yourself.'

He fell into thought.

'And so I threw in my spiritual lot wi' his,' she resumed. 'I didn't wish it to be different. What's good enough for him is good enough for me.'

'Does he know that you are as big a sceptic as he?'

'No – I never told him – if I am a sceptic.'

'Well – you are better off to-day than I am, Tess, after all! You don't believe that you ought to preach my doctrine, and, therefore, do no despite to your conscience in abstaining. I do believe I ought to preach it, but like the devils I believe and tremble,[8] for I suddenly leave off preaching it, and give way to my passion for you.'

'How?'

'Why,' he said wearily; 'I have come all the way here to see you to-day! But I started from home to go to Casterbridge Fair, where I have undertaken to preach the Word from a waggon at half-past two this afternoon, and where all the brethren are expecting me this minute. Here's the announcement.'

He drew from his breast-pocket a poster whereon was printed the day, hour, and place of meeting, at which he, D'Urberville, would preach the Gospel as aforesaid.

'But how can you get there?' said Tess, looking at the clock.

'I cannot get there. I have come here.'

'But, you have really arranged to preach the—'

'I have arranged to preach, and I shall not be there – by reason of

322

my burning desire to see a woman whom I once despised! – No, by my word and truth, I never despised you; if I had I should not love you now! Why I did not despise you was on account of your intrinsic purity in spite of all; you withdrew yourself from me so quickly and resolutely when you saw the situation; you did not remain at my pleasure; so there was one victim[9] in the world for whom I had no contempt, and you are she. But you may well despise me now! I thought I worshipped on the mountains, but I find I still serve in the groves.[10] Ha! ha!'

'O Alec D'Urberville! what does this mean? What have I done!'

'Done?' he said, with a soulless sneer at himself. 'Nothing intentionally. But you have been the means – the innocent means – of my backsliding, as they call it. I ask myself, am I, indeed, one of those "servants of corruption" who, "after they have escaped the pollutions of the world, are again entangled therein and overcome" – whose latter end is worse than their beginning?"[11] He laid his hand on her shoulder. 'Tess, Tess, I was on the way to salvation till I saw you again!' he said, feverishly shaking her, as if she were a child. 'And why then have you tempted me? I was firm as a man could be till I saw those eyes and that mouth again – surely there never was such a maddening mouth since Eve's!' His voice sank, and a hot archness shot from his own black eyes. 'You temptress, Tess; you dear witch of Babylon[12] – I could not resist you as soon as I met you again!'

'I couldn't help your seeing me again!' said Tess recoiling.

'I know it – I repeat that I do not blame you. But the fact remains. When I saw you ill-used on the farm that day I was nearly mad to think that I had no legal right to protect you – that I could not have it; whilst he who has it seems to neglect you utterly!'

'Don't speak against him – he is absent!' she cried excitedly. 'Treat him honourably – he has never wronged you! Oh, leave his wife before any scandal spreads that may do grievous harm to his honest name!'

'I will – I will,' he said, like a man awakening from a lurid dream. 'I have broken my engagement to preach Christ to those poor drunken sinners at the fair – it is the first time I have done such a monstrous thing! A month ago I should have been horrified at such a possibility.

I'll go away – to hide – and – ah, can I! – pray.' Then, suddenly, 'One clasp, Tessy – one! Only for old friendship—'

'I am defenceless, Alec! A good man's honour is in my keeping – think – and be ashamed!'

'O yes – yes! My God!'

He clenched his lips, mortified with himself for his weakness. His eyes were equally barren of amatory and religious hope. The corpses of those old black passions which had lain inanimate amid the lines of his face ever since his reformation seemed to wake and come together as in a resurrection. He went out indeterminately, hardly responsible for his acts.

Though D'Urberville had declared that this breach of his engagement to-day was the simple backsliding of a believer, Tess's words, as echoed from Angel Clare, had made a deep impression upon him, and continued to do so after he had left her. He moved on in silence, as if his energies were benumbed by the hitherto undreamt-of possibility that his position was untenable. Reason had had nothing to do with his conversion,[13] and the drops of logic that Tess had let fall into the sea of his enthusiasm served to chill its effervescence to stagnation. He said to himself, as he pondered again and again over the crystallized phrases that she had handed on to him, 'That clever fellow little thought that, by telling her those things, he might be paving my way back to her!'

XLVII

It is the threshing of the last wheat-rick at Flintcomb-Ash Farm. The dawn of the March morning is singularly inexpressive, and there is nothing to show where the eastern horizon lies. Against the twilight rises the trapezoidal top of the stack, which has stood forlornly here through the washing and bleaching of the wintry weather.

When Izz Huett and Tess arrived at the scene of operations only a rustling denoted that others had preceded them; to which, as the light increased, there were presently added the silhouettes of two men on the summit. They were busily 'unhaling' the rick, that is, stripping off the thatch before beginning to throw down the sheaves; and while this was in progress Izz and Tess, with the other women-workers, in their whitey-brown pinners, stood waiting and shivering, Farmer Groby having insisted upon their being on the spot thus early to get the job over if possible by the end of the day. Close under the eaves of the stack, and as yet barely visible, was the red tyrant that the women had come to serve – a timber-framed construction, with straps and wheels apper-taining – the threshing-machine which, whilst it was going, kept up a despotic demand upon the endurance of their muscles and nerves.

A little way off there was another indistinct figure; this one black, with a sustained hiss that spoke of strength very much in reserve. The long chimney running up beside an ash-tree, and the warmth which radiated from the spot, explained without the necessity of much daylight that here was the engine which was to act as the *primum mobile*[1] of this little world. By the engine stood a dark motionless being, a sooty and grimy embodiment of tallness, in a sort of trance, with a heap of coals by his side: it was the engineman. The isolation of his manner and colour lent him the appearance of a creature from Tophet,[2] who had strayed into the pellucid smokelessness of this region of yellow grain and pale soil, with which he had nothing in common, to amaze and to discompose its aborigines.

What he looked he felt. He was in the agricultural world, but not of it. He served fire and smoke; these denizens of the fields served vegetation, weather, frost, and sun. He travelled with this engine from farm to farm, from county to county, for as yet the steam-threshing machine was itinerant in this part of Wessex. He spoke in a strange northern accent;[3] his thoughts being turned inwards upon himself, his eye on his iron charge, hardly perceiving the scenes around him, and caring for them not at all: holding only strictly necessary intercourse with the natives, as if some ancient doom compelled him to wander here against his will in the service of his Plutonic master.[4] The long strap which ran from the driving-wheel of his engine to the red thresher under the rick was the sole tie-line between agriculture and him.

While they uncovered the sheaves he stood apathetic beside his portable repository of force, round whose hot blackness the morning air quivered. He had nothing to do with preparatory labour. His fire was waiting incandescent, his steam was at high pressure, in a few seconds he could make the long strap move at an invisible velocity. Beyond its extent the environment might be corn, straw, or chaos; it was all the same to him. If any of the autochthonous idlers asked him what he called himself, he replied shortly, 'an engineer.'

The rick was unhaled by full daylight; the men then took their places, the women mounted, and the work began. Farmer Groby – or, as they called him, 'he' – had arrived ere this, and by his orders Tess was placed on the platform of the machine, close to the man who fed it, her business being to untie every sheaf of corn handed on to her by Izz Huett, who stood next, but on the rick; so that the feeder could seize it and spread it over the revolving drum, which whisked out every grain in one moment.

They were soon in full progress, after a preparatory hitch or two, which rejoiced the hearts of those who hated machinery. The work sped on till breakfast-time, when the thresher was stopped for half an hour; and on starting again after the meal the whole supplementary strength of the farm was thrown into the labour of constructing the straw-rick, which began to grow beside the stack of corn. A hasty lunch was eaten as they stood, without leaving their positions, and then another couple of hours brought them near to dinner-time; the inexorable wheels continuing to spin, and the penetrating hum of the thresher to thrill to the very marrow all who were near the revolving wire-cage.

The old men on the rising straw-rick talked of the past days when they had been accustomed to thresh with flails on the oaken barn-floor; when everything, even to winnowing, was effected by hand-labour, which, to their thinking, though slow, produced better results. Those, too, on the corn-rick talked a little; but the perspiring ones at the machine, including Tess, could not lighten their duties by the exchange of many words. It was the ceaselessness of the work which tried her so severely, and began to make her wish that she had never come to Flintcomb-Ash. The women on the corn-rick – Marian, who was one of them, in particular – could stop to drink ale or cold tea from the flagon now and then, or to exchange a few gossiping remarks while they wiped their faces or cleared the fragments of straw and husk from their clothing; but for Tess there was no respite; for, as the drum never stopped, the man who fed it could not stop, and she, who had to supply the man with untied sheaves, could not stop either.[5]

For some probably economical reason[6] it was usually a woman who was chosen for this particular duty, and Groby gave as his motive in selecting Tess that she was one of those who best combined strength with quickness in untying, and both with staying power, and this may have been true. The hum of the thresher, which prevented speech, increased to a raving whenever the supply of corn fell short of the regular quantity. As Tess and the man who fed could never turn their heads she did not know that just before the dinner-hour a person had come silently into the field by the gate, and had been standing under a second rick watching the scene, and Tess in particular. He was dressed in a tweed suit of fashionable pattern, and he twirled a gay walking-cane.

'Who is that?' said Izz Huett to Marian. She had at first addressed the inquiry to Tess, but the latter could not hear it.

'Somebody's fancy-man, I s'pose,' said Marian laconically.

'I'll lay a guinea he's after Tess.'

'O no. 'Tis a ranter pa'son who's been sniffing after her lately; not a dandy like this.'

'Well – this is the same man.'

'The same man as the preacher? But he's quite different!'

'He hev left off his black coat and white neckercher, and hev cut off his whiskers; but he's the same man for all that.'

'D'ye really think so? Then I'll tell her,' said Marian.

'Don't. She'll see him soon enough.'

'Well, I don't think it at all right for him to join his preaching to courting a married woman, even though her husband mid be abroad, and she, in a sense, a widow.'

'Oh – he can do her no harm,' said Izz drily. 'Her mind can no more be heaved from that one place where it do bide than a stooded waggon from the hole he's in. Lord love 'ee, neither court-paying, nor preaching, nor the seven thunders[7] themselves, can shake a woman when 'twould be better for her that she should be shaken.'

Dinner-time came, and the whirling ceased; whereupon Tess left her post, her knees trembling so wretchedly with the shaking of the machine that she could scarcely walk.

'You ought to het a quart o' drink into 'ee, as I've done,' said Marian. 'You wouldn't look so white then. Why, souls above us, your face is as if you'd been hag-rode!'

It occurred to the good-natured Marian that, as Tess was so tired, her discovery of her visitor's presence might have the bad effect of taking away her appetite; and Marian was thinking of inducing Tess to descend by a ladder on the farther side of the stack when the gentleman came forward and looked up.

Tess uttered a short little 'Oh!' And a moment after she said, quickly, 'I shall eat my dinner here – right on the rick.'

Sometimes, when they were so far from their cottages, they all did this; but as there was rather a keen wind going to-day, Marian and the rest descended, and sat under the straw-stack.

The new-comer was, indeed, Alec D'Urberville, the late Evangelist, despite his changed attire and aspect. It was obvious at a glance that the original *Weltlust*[8] had come back; that he had restored himself, as nearly as a man could do who had grown three or four years older, to the old jaunty, slap-dash guise under which Tess had first known her admirer, and cousin so-called. Having decided to remain where she was, Tess sat down among the bundles, out of sight of the ground, and began her meal; till, by and by, she heard footsteps on the ladder, and immediately after Alec appeared upon the stack – now an oblong and level platform of sheaves. He strode across them, and sat down opposite to her without a word.

Tess continued to eat her modest dinner, a slice of thick pancake which she had brought with her. The other workfolk were by this time all gathered under the rick, where the loose straw formed a comfortable retreat.

'I am here again, as you see,' said D'Urberville.

'Why do you trouble me so?' she cried, reproach flashing from her very finger-ends.

'*I* trouble *you*? I think I may ask, why do you trouble me?'

'Indeed I don't trouble you.'

'You say you don't? But you do! You haunt me. Those very eyes that you turned upon me with such a bitter flash a moment ago, they come to me just as you showed them then, in the night and in the day! Tess, ever since you told me of the child, it is just as if my emotions, which have been flowing in a strong stream heavenward, had suddenly found a sluice open in the direction of you, through which they have at once gushed. The Gospel channel is left dry forthwith; and it is you who have done it – *you!*'

She gazed with parted lips.

'What – you have given up your preaching entirely?' she asked.

She had gathered from Angel sufficient of the incredulity of modern thought to despise flash enthusiasms; but, as a woman, she was somewhat appalled.

In affected lightness D'Urberville continued –

'Entirely. I have broken every engagement since that afternoon I was to address the drunkards at Casterbridge Fair. The deuce only knows what I am thought of by the brethren. Ah-ha! The brethren! No doubt they pray for me – weep for me; for they are kind people in their way. But what do I care? How could I go on with the thing when I had lost my faith in it? – it would have been hypocrisy of the basest kind! Among them I should have stood like Hymenæus and Alexander, who were delivered over to Satan that they might learn not to blaspheme.[9] What a grand revenge you have taken! I saw you innocent, and I deceived you. Three-and-a-half years after, you find me a Christian enthusiast; you then work upon me, perhaps to my complete perdition! But Tess, my coz, as I used to call you, this is only my way of talking, and you must not look so horribly concerned. Of course you have done nothing except retain your pretty face and shapely figure. I saw it on the rick before you saw me – that tight pinafore-thing sets it off, and that wing-bonnet – you field-girls should never wear those bonnets if you wish to keep out of danger.' He regarded her silently for a few moments, and with a short cynical laugh resumed: 'I believe that if the bachelor-apostle,[10] whose deputy I thought I was, had been tempted by such a pretty face, he would have let go the plough[11] for her sake as I do!'

Tess attempted to expostulate, but at this juncture all her fluency failed her, and without heeding he added:

'Well, this paradise that you supply is perhaps as good as any other, after all. But to speak seriously, Tess.' D'Urberville rose and came nearer, reclining sideways amid the sheaves, and resting upon his elbow. 'Since I last saw you, I have been thinking of what you said that *he* said. I have come to the conclusion that there does seem rather a want of common-sense in these threadbare old propositions; how I could have been so fired by poor Parson Clare's enthusiasm, and have gone so madly to work, transcending even him, I cannot make out! As for what you said last time, on the strength of your wonderful husband's intelligence – whose name you have never told me – about having what they call an ethical system without any dogma, I don't see my way to that at all.'

'Why, you can have the religion of loving-kindness and purity at least, if you can't have – what do they call it – dogma.'[12]

'O no! I'm a different sort of fellow from that! If there's nobody to say, "Do this, and it will be a good thing for you after you are dead; do that, and it will be a bad thing for you," I can't warm up. Hang it, I am not going to feel responsible for my deeds and passions if there's nobody to be responsible to; and if I were you, my dear, I wouldn't either!'

She tried to argue, and tell him that he had mixed in his dull brain two matters, theology and morals, which in the primitive days of mankind had been quite distinct. But owing to Angel Clare's reticence, to her absolute want of training, and to her being a vessel of emotions rather than reasons, she could not get on.

'Well, never mind,' he resumed. 'Here I am, my love, as in the old times!'

'Not as then – never as then – it is different!' she entreated. 'And there was never warmth with me. O why didn't you retain your faith, if the loss of it have brought 'ee to speak to me like this!'

'Because you've knocked it out of me; so the evil be upon your sweet head! Your husband little thought how his teaching would recoil upon him! Ha-ha – I'm awfully glad you have made an apostate of me all the same! Tess, I am more taken with you than ever, and I pity you too. For all your closeness, I see you are in a bad way – neglected by one who ought to cherish you.'

She could not get her morsels of food down her throat; her lips were dry, and she was ready to choke. The voices and laughs of the workfolk eating and drinking under the rick came to her as if they were a quarter of a mile off.

'It is cruelty to me!' she said. 'How – how can you treat me to this talk, if you care ever so little for me?'

'True, true,' he said, wincing a little. 'I did not come to reproach you for my fall. I came, Tess, to say that I don't like you to be working like this, and I have come on purpose for you. You say you have a husband who is not I. Well, perhaps you have; but I've never seen him, and you've not told me his name; and altogether he seems rather a mythological personage. However, even if you have one, I think I am nearer to you than he is. I, at any rate, try to help you out of trouble, but he does not, bless his invisible face! The words of the stern prophet Hosea that I used to read come back to me. Don't you know them, Tess? – "And she shall follow after her lover, but she shall not overtake him; and she shall seek him, but shall not find him: then shall she say, I will go and return to my first husband; for then was it better with me than now!"[13] ... Tess, my trap is waiting just under the hill, and – darling mine, not his! – you know the rest.'

Her face had been rising to a dull crimson fire while he spoke; but she did not answer.

'You have been the cause of my backsliding,' he continued jauntily; 'you should be willing to share it, and leave that mule you call husband for ever!'

One of her leather gloves, which she had taken off to eat her skimmer-cake, lay in her lap, and without the slightest warning she passionately swung the glove by the gauntlet directly in his face. It was heavy and thick as a warrior's, and it struck him flat on the mouth. Fancy might have regarded the act as the recrudescence of a trick in which her mailed progenitors were not unpractised. Alec fiercely started up from his reclining position. A scarlet oozing appeared where her blow had alighted, and in a moment the blood began dropping from his mouth upon the straw. But he soon controlled himself, calmly drew his handkerchief from his pocket, and mopped his bleeding lips.

She too had sprung up, but she sank down again.

'Now punish me!' she said, turning up her eyes to him with the hopeless defiance of the sparrow's gaze before its captor twists its neck. 'Whip me, crush me; you need not mind those people under the rick! I shall not cry out. Once victim, always victim – that's the law!'

'Oh no, no, Tess,' he said blandly. 'I can make full allowance for this. Yet you most unjustly forget one thing, that I would have married you if you had not put it out of my power to do so. Did I not ask you flatly to be my wife – hey? Answer me.'

'You did.'

'And you cannot be. But remember one thing!' His voice hardened as his temper got the better of him with the recollection of his sincerity in asking her and her present ingratitude, and he stepped across to her side and held her by the shoulders, so that she shook under his grasp. 'Remember, I was your master once! I will be your master again. If you are any man's wife you are mine!'

The threshers now began to stir below.

'So much for our quarrel,' he said, letting her go. 'Now I shall leave you, and shall come again for your answer during the afternoon. You don't know me yet! But I know you.'

She had not spoken again, remaining as if stunned. D'Urberville retreated over the sheaves, and descended the ladder, while the workers below rose and stretched their arms, and shook down the beer they had drunk. Then the threshing-machine started afresh; and amid the renewed rustle of the straw Tess resumed her position by the buzzing drum as one in a dream, untying sheaf after sheaf in endless succession.

XLVIII

In the afternoon the farmer made it known that the rick was to be finished that night, since there was a moon by which they could see to work, and the man with the engine was engaged for another farm on the morrow. Hence the twanging and humming and rustling proceeded with even less intermission than usual.

It was not till 'nammet'-time, about three o'clock, that Tess raised her eyes and gave a momentary glance round. She felt but little surprise at seeing that Alec D'Urberville had come back, and was standing under the hedge by the gate. He had seen her lift her eyes, and waved his hand urbanely to her, while he blew her a kiss. It meant that their quarrel was over. Tess at once looked down again, and carefully abstained from gazing in that direction.

Thus the afternoon dragged on. The wheat-rick shrank lower, and the straw-rick grew higher, and the corn-sacks were carted away. At six o'clock the wheat-rick was about shoulder-high from the ground. But the unthreshed sheaves remaining untouched seemed countless still, notwithstanding the enormous numbers that had been gulped down by the insatiable swallower, fed by the man and Tess, through whose two young hands every sheaf of them had passed. And the immense stack of straw where in the morning there had been nothing appeared as the *fæces* of the same buzzing red glutton. From the west sky a wrathful shine – all that wild March could afford in the way of sunset – had burst forth after the cloudy day, flooding the tired and sticky faces of the threshers and dyeing them with a coppery light, as also the flapping garments of the women, which clung to them like dull flames.

A panting ache ran through the rick. The man who fed was weary, and Tess could see that the red nape of his neck was covered with husks. She still stood at her post, her flushed and perspiring face coated with the corn-dust, and her white bonnet embrowned by it. She was the only woman whose place was upon the machine, so as to be shaken bodily by its spinning, and this incessant quivering, in which every fibre of her body participated, had thrown her into a stupefied reverie in which her arms worked on independently of her consciousness. She hardly knew where she was, and did not hear Izz Huett – who with the sinking of the rick had necessarily moved farther down from her side – offer to change places with her.

By degrees the freshest among them began to grow cadaverous and saucer-eyed. Whenever Tess lifted her head she beheld always the great upgrown straw-stack, with the men in shirt-sleeves upon it, against the gray north sky; in front of it the long red elevator like a Jacob's ladder,[1] on which a perpetual stream of threshed straw ascended, a yellow river running up-hill, and spouting out on the top of the rick.

She knew that Alec D'Urberville was still on the scene, observing her from some point or other, though she could not say where. There was an excuse for his remaining, for when the threshed rick drew near its final sheaves a little ratting was always done, and men unconnected with the threshing sometimes dropped in for that performance – sporting characters of all descriptions, gents with terriers and facetious pipes, roughs with sticks and stones.

But there was another hour's work before the layer of live rats at the base of the stack would be reached; and as the evening light in the direction of the Giant's Hill by Abbot's Cernel[2] dissolved away, the white-faced moon of the season arose from the horizon that lay towards Middleton Abbey and Shottsford on the other side. For the last hour or two Marian had felt uneasy about Tess, whom she could not get near enough to speak to, the other women having kept up their strength by drinking ale, and Tess having done without it through traditionary dread, owing to its results at her home in childhood. But Tess still kept going: if she could not fill her part she would have to leave; and this contingency, which she would have regarded with equanimity and even with relief a month or two earlier, had become a terror since D'Urberville had begun to hover round her.

The sheaf-pitchers and feeders had now worked the rick so low that people on the ground could talk to them. To Tess's surprise Farmer Groby came up on the machine to her, and said that if she desired to join her friend he did not wish her to keep on any longer, and would send somebody else to take her place. The 'friend' was D'Urberville, she knew, and also that this concession had been granted in obedience to the request of that friend, or enemy. She shook her head and toiled on.

The time for the rat-catching arrived at last, and the hunt began. The creatures had crept downwards with the subsidence of the rick till they were all together at the bottom, and being now uncovered from their last refuge they ran across the open ground in all directions, a loud shriek from the by this time half-tipsy Marian informing her companions that one of the rats had invaded her person – a terror which the rest of the women had guarded against by various schemes of skirt-tucking and self-elevation. The rat was at last dislodged, and, amid the barking of the dogs, masculine shouts, feminine screams, oaths, stampings, and confusion as of Pandemonium,[3] Tess untied her last sheaf; the drum slowed, the whizzing ceased, and she stepped from the bedding to the ground.

Her lover, who had only looked on at the rat-catching, was promptly at her side.

'What – after all – my insulting slap, too!' said she in an underbreath. She was so utterly exhausted that she had not strength to speak louder.

'I should indeed be foolish to feel offended at anything you say or do,' he answered, in the seductive voice of the Trantridge time. 'How the little limbs tremble! You are as weak as a bled calf,[4] you know you are; and yet you need have done nothing since I arrived. How could you be so obstinate? However, I have told the farmer that he has no right to employ women at steam-threshing. It is not proper work for them; and on all the better class of farms it has been given up, as he knows very well. I will walk with you as far as your home.'

'O yes,' she answered with a jaded gait. 'Walk with me if you will! I do bear in mind that you came to marry me before you knew of my state. Perhaps – perhaps you be a little better and kinder than I have been thinking you were. Whatever is meant as kindness I am grateful for; whatever is meant in any other way I am angry at. I cannot sense your meaning sometimes.'

'If I cannot legitimize our former relations at least I can assist you. And I will do it with much more regard for your feelings than I formerly showed. My religious mania, or whatever it was, is over. But I retain a little good nature; I hope I do. Now Tess, by all that's tender and strong between man and woman, trust me! I have enough and more than enough to put you out of anxiety, both for yourself and your parents and sisters. I can make them all comfortable if you will only show confidence in me.'

'Have you seen them lately?' she quickly inquired.

'Yes. They didn't know where you were. It was only by chance that I found you here.'

The cold moon looked aslant upon Tess's fagged face between the twigs of the garden-hedge as she paused outside the cottage which was her temporary home, D'Urberville pausing beside her.

'Don't mention my little brothers and sisters – don't make me break down quite!' she said. 'If you want to help them – God knows they need it – do it without telling me. But no, no!' she cried. 'I will accept nothing from you, either for them or for me!'

He did not accompany her farther since, as she lived with the household, all was public indoors. No sooner had she herself entered and mechanically shared supper with the family than she fell into thought, and withdrawing to the table under the wall, by the light of her own little lamp wrote in a passionate mood –

MY OWN HUSBAND, – Let me call you so – I must – even if it makes you angry to think of such an unworthy wife as I. I must cry to you in my trouble – I have no one else! I am so exposed to temptation, Angel. I fear to say who it is, and I do not like to write about it all. But I cling to you in a way you cannot think! Can you not come to me now, at once, before anything terrible happens? O, I know you cannot, because you are so far away! I think I must die if you do not come soon, or tell me to come to you. The punishment you have measured out to me is deserved – I do know that – well deserved – and you are right and just to be angry with me. But, Angel, please, please, not to be just – only a little kind to me, even if I do not deserve it, and come to me! If you would come, I could die in your arms! I would be well content to do that if so be you had forgiven me!

Angel, I live entirely for you. I love you too much to blame you for going away, and I know it was necessary you should find a farm. Do not think I shall say a word of sting or bitterness. Only come back to me. I am desolate without you, my darling, O, so desolate! I do not mind having to work; but if you will send me one little line, and say, '*I am coming soon*,' I will bide on, Angel – O, so cheerfully!

It have been so much my religion ever since we were married to be faithful to you in every thought and look, that even when a man speaks a compliment to me before I am aware, it seems wronging you. Have you never felt one little bit of what you used to feel when we were at the dairy? If you have, how can you keep away from me? I am the same woman, Angel, as she you fell in love with; yes, the very same! – not the one you disliked but never saw. What was the past to me as soon as I met you? It was a dead thing altogether. I became another woman, filled full of new life from you. How could I be the early one? Why do you not see this? Dear, if you would only be a little more conceited, and believe in yourself so far as to see that you was strong enough to work this change in me, you would perhaps be in a mind to come to me, your poor wife.

How silly I was in my happiness when I thought I could trust you always to love me! I ought to have known that such as that was not for poor me. But I am sick at heart, not only for old times, but for the present. Think – think how it do hurt my heart not to see you ever – ever! Ah, if I could only make your dear heart ache one little minute of each day as mine does every day and all day long, it might lead you to show pity to your poor lonely one.

People still say that I am rather pretty, Angel (handsome is the word they use, since I wish to be truthful). Perhaps I am what they say. But I do not value my good looks; I only like to have them because they belong to you, my dear, and that there may be at least one thing about me worth your having. So much have I felt this, that when I met with annoyance on account of the same I tied up my face in a bandage as long as people would believe in it. O Angel, I tell you all this not from vanity – you will certainly know I do not – but only that you may come to me.

If you really cannot come to me will you let me come to you? I am as I say, worried, pressed to do what I will not do. It cannot be that I shall yield one inch, yet I am in terror as to what an accident might lead to, and I so defenceless on account of my first error. I cannot say more about this – it makes me too miserable. But if I break down by falling into some fearful snare, my last state will be worse than my first.[5] O God, I cannot think of it! Let me come at once, or at once come to me!

I would be content, ay, glad, to live with you as your servant, if I may not as your wife; so that I could only be near you, and get glimpses of you, and think of you as mine.

The daylight has nothing to show me, since you be not here, and I don't like to see the rooks and starlings in the fields, because I grieve and grieve to miss you who used to see them with me. I long for only one thing in heaven or earth or under the earth, to meet you, my own dear! Come to me – come to me, and save me from what threatens me!
– Your faithful heartbroken

TESS.

XLIX

The appeal duly found its way to the breakfast-table of the quiet Vicarage to the westward, in that valley where the air is so soft and the soil so rich that the effort of growth requires but superficial aid by comparison with the tillage at Flintcomb-Ash, and where to Tess the human world seemed so different (though it was much the same). It was purely for security that she had been requested by Angel to send her communications through his father, whom he kept pretty well informed of his changing addresses in the country he had gone to exploit for himself with a heavy heart.

'Now,' said old Mr Clare to his wife, when he had read the envelope, 'if Angel proposes leaving Rio for a visit home at the end of this month, as he suggested to us that he would do, I think this may hasten his plans; for I believe it to be from his wife.' He breathed deeply; and the letter was redirected to be promptly sent on to Angel.[1]

'Dear fellow, I hope he will get home safely,' murmured Mrs Clare. 'To my dying day I shall feel that he has been ill-used. You should have sent him to Cambridge in spite of his heterodoxy, and given him the same chance as the other boys had. He would have grown out of it under proper influence, and perhaps would have taken Orders after all. Church or no Church, it would have been fairer to him.'

This was the only wail with which Mrs Clare ever disturbed her husband's peace in respect of their sons. And she did not vent this often; for she was as considerate as she was devout, and knew that his mind too was troubled by doubts as to his justice in this matter. Only too often had she heard him lying awake at night, stifling sighs for Angel with prayers. But the uncompromising Evangelical did not even now hold that he would have been justified in giving his son, an unbeliever, the same academic advantages that he had given to the two others, when it was possible, if not probable, that those very advantages might have been used to decry the doctrines which he had made it his life's mission and desire to propagate, and the mission of his ordained sons likewise. To put with one hand a pedestal under the feet of the two faithful ones, and with the other to exalt the unfaithful by the same artificial means, he deemed to be alike inconsistent with his convictions, his position, and his hopes. Nevertheless, he loved his misnamed Angel, and in secret mourned over this treatment of him as Abraham might have mourned over the doomed Isaac while they went up the hill together.[2] His silent self-generated regrets were far bitterer than the reproaches which his wife rendered audible.

They blamed themselves for this unlucky marriage. If Angel had never been destined for a farmer he would never have been thrown with agricultural girls. They did not distinctly know what had separated him and his wife, nor the date on which the separation had taken place. At first they had supposed it must be something of the nature of a serious dislike. But in his later letters he occasionally alluded to the intention of coming home to fetch her; from which expressions they hoped the division might not owe its origin to anything so hopelessly permanent as that. He had told them that she was with her relatives, and in their doubts they had decided not to intrude into a situation which they knew no way of bettering.

The eyes for which Tess's letter was intended were gazing at this time on a limitless expanse of country from the back of a mule which was bearing him from the interior of the South-American Continent towards the coast. His experiences of this strange land had been sad. The severe illness from which he had suffered shortly after his arrival had never wholly left him, and he had by degrees almost decided to relinquish his hope of farming here, though, as long as the bare possibility existed of his remaining, he kept this change of view a secret from his parents.

The crowds of agricultural labourers who had come out to the country in his wake, dazzled by representations of easy independence, had suffered, died, and wasted away. He would see mothers from English farms trudging along with their infants in their arms, when the child would be stricken with fever and would die; the mother would pause to dig a hole in the loose earth with her bare hands, would bury the babe therein with the same natural grave-tools, shed one tear, and again trudge on.

Angel's original intention had not been emigration to Brazil, but a northern or eastern farm in his own country. He had come to this place in a fit of desperation, the Brazil movement among the English agriculturists having by chance coincided with his desire to escape from his past existence.

During this time of absence he had mentally aged a dozen years. What arrested him now as of value in life was less its beauty than its pathos. Having long discredited the old systems of mysticism, he now began to discredit the old appraisements of morality. He thought they wanted re-adjusting. Who was the moral man? Still more pertinently, who was the moral woman? The beauty or ugliness of a character lay not only in its achievements, but in its aims and impulses; its true history lay, not among things done, but among things willed.[3]

How, then, about Tess?

Viewing her in these lights, a regret for his hasty judgment began to oppress him. Did he reject her eternally, or did he not? He could no longer say that he would always reject her, and not to say that was in spirit to accept her now.

This growing fondness for her memory coincided in point of time with her residence at Flintcomb-Ash, but it was before she had felt herself at liberty to trouble him with a word about her circumstances or her feelings.[4] He was greatly perplexed; and in his perplexity as to her motives in withholding intelligence he did not inquire. Thus her silence of docility was misinterpreted. How much it really said if he had understood! – that she adhered to the letter to orders which he had given and forgotten; that despite her natural fearlessness she asserted no rights, admitted his judgment to be in every respect the true one, and bent her head dumbly thereto.

In the before-mentioned journey by mules through the interior of the country, another man rode beside him. Angel's companion was also an Englishman, bent on the same errand, though he came from another part of the island. They were both in a state of mental depression, and they spoke of home affairs. Confidence begat confidence. With that curious tendency evinced by men, more especially when in distant lands, to entrust to strangers details of their lives which they would on no account mention to friends, Angel admitted to this man as they rode along the sorrowful facts of his marriage.

The stranger had sojourned in many more lands and among many more peoples than Angel; to his cosmopolitan mind such deviations from the social norm, so immense to domesticity, were no more than are the irregularities of vale and mountain-chain to the whole terrestrial curve. He viewed the matter in quite a different light from Angel; thought that what Tess had been was of no importance beside what she would be, and plainly told Clare that he was wrong in coming away from her.

The next day they were drenched in a thunderstorm. Angel's companion was struck down with fever, and died by the week's end. Clare waited a few hours to bury him, and then went on his way.

The cursory remarks of the stranger, of whom he knew absolutely nothing beyond a commonplace name, were sublimed by his death, and influenced Clare more than all the reasoned ethics of the philosophers. A remorse struck into him. The words of Izz Huett, never quite stilled in his memory, came back to him. He had asked Izz if she loved him, and she had replied in the affirmative. Did she love him more than Tess did? No, she had replied; Tess would lay down her life for him, and she herself could do no more.

He thought of Tess as she had appeared on the day of the wedding. How her eyes had lingered upon him; how she had hung upon his words as if they were a god's! And during the terrible evening over the hearth, when her simple soul uncovered itself to his, how pitiful her face had looked by the rays of the fire, in her inability to realize that his love and protection could possibly be withdrawn.

Thus from being her critic he grew to be her advocate. Cynical things he had uttered to himself about her; but no man can be a cynic and live; and he withdrew them. The mistake of expressing them had arisen from his allowing himself to be influenced by general principles to the disregard of the particular instance.

But the reasoning is somewhat musty; lovers and husbands have gone over the ground before to-day. Clare had been harsh towards her; there is no doubt of it. Men are too often harsh with women they love or have loved; women with men. And yet these harshnesses are tenderness itself when compared with the universal harshness out of which they grow; the harshness of the position towards the temperament, of the means towards the aims, of to-day towards yesterday, of hereafter towards to-day.

The historic interest of her family – that masterful line of D'Urbervilles – whom he had despised as a spent force, touched his sentiments now. Why had he not known the difference between the political value and the imaginative value of these things? In the latter quality her D'Urberville descent was a fact of great dimensions; worthless to economics, it was a most useful ingredient to the dreamer, to the moralizer on declines and falls. It was a fact that would soon be forgotten – that little curiosity about poor Tess's blood and name, and oblivion would fall upon her hereditary link with the marble monuments and leaded skeletons at Kingsbere. So does Time ruthlessly destroy his own romances. In recalling her face again and again, he thought now that he could see therein a flash of the dignity which must have graced her grand-dames; and the vision sent that *aura* through his veins which he had formerly felt, and which left behind it a sense of sickness.

Despite her not inviolate past, what still abode in such a woman as Tess outvalued the freshness of her fellows. Was not the gleaning of the grapes of Ephraim better than the vintage of Abi-ezer?[5] So spoke love renascent, preparing the way for Tess's devoted outpouring, which was then just being forwarded to him by his father.

Meanwhile the writer, with an enlarging conviction that Angel would come soon in response to the entreaty,[6] addressed her mind to the tender question of what she could do to please him best when he should arrive. Sighs were expended on the wish that she had taken more notice of the tunes he played on his harp, that she had inquired more curiously of him which were his favourite ballads among those the country-girls sang. She indirectly inquired of Amby Seedling, who had followed Izz from Talbothays, and by chance Amby remembered that, amongst the snatches of melody in which they had indulged at the dairyman's, to induce the cows to let down their milk, Clare had seemed to like 'Cupid's Gardens,' 'I have parks, I have hounds,' and 'The break o' the day;' and had seemed not to care for 'The Tailor's Breeches,' and 'Such a beauty I did grow,'[7] excellent ditties as they were.

To perfect the ballads was now her deep desire.[8] She practised them privately at odd moments, especially 'The break o' the day':

> Arise, arise, arise!
> And pick your love a posy,
> All o' the sweetest flowers
> That in the garden grow.
> The turtle doves and sma' birds
> In every bough a building,
> So early in the spring-time,
> At the break o' the day!

It would have melted the heart of a stone to hear her singing these ditties, whenever she worked apart from the rest of the girls in this cold dry time; the tears running down her cheeks all the while at the thought that perhaps he would not, after all, come to hear her, and the simple silly words of the songs resounding in painful mockery of the aching heart of the singer.

Tess was so wrapt up in this fanciful dream that she seemed not to know how the season was advancing; that the days had lengthened, that Lady-Day was at hand, and would soon be followed by Old Lady-Day, the end of her term here.

But before the quarter-day had quite come something happened which made Tess think of far different matters. She was at her lodging as usual one evening, sitting in the downstairs room with the rest of the family, when somebody knocked at the door and inquired for Tess. Through the doorway she saw against the declining light a figure with the height of a woman and the breadth of a child, a tall, thin, girlish creature whom she did not recognize in the twilight till the girl said 'Tess!'

'What – is it 'Liza-Lu?' asked Tess, in startled accents. Her sister, whom a little over a year ago she had left at home as a child, had sprung up by a sudden shoot to a form of this presentation, of which as yet Lu seemed herself scarce able to understand the meaning. Her thin legs, visible below her once long frock, now short by her growing, and her uncomfortable hands and arms, revealed her youth and inexperience.

'Yes, I have been traipsing about all day, Tess,' said Lu, with unemotional gravity, 'a trying to find 'ee; and I'm very tired.'

'What is the matter at home?'

'Mother is took very bad, and the doctor says she's dying, and as father is not very well neither, and says 'tis wrong for a man of such a high family as his to slave and drave at common labouring work, we don't know what to do.'

Tess stood in reverie a long time before she thought of asking 'Liza-Lu to come in and sit down. When she had done so, and 'Liza-Lu was having some tea, she came to a decision. It was imperative that she should go home. Her agreement did not end till Old Lady-Day, the sixth of April, but as the interval thereto was not a long one she resolved to run the risk of starting at once.

To go that night would be a gain of twelve hours; but her sister was too tired to undertake such a distance till the morrow. Tess ran down to where Marian and Izz lived, informed them of what had happened, and begged them to make the best of her case to the farmer. Returning, she got Lu a supper, and after that, having tucked the younger into her own bed, packed up as many of her belongings as would go into a withy basket, and started, directing Lu to follow her next morning.

L

She plunged into the chilly equinoctial darkness as the clock struck ten, for her fifteen miles' walk under the steely stars. In lonely districts night is a protection rather than a danger to a noiseless pedestrian, and knowing this Tess pursued the nearest course along by-lanes that she would almost have feared in the day time; but marauders were wanting now, and spectral fears were driven out of her mind by thoughts of her mother. Thus she proceeded mile after mile, ascending and descending till she came to Bulbarrow, and about midnight looked from that height into the abyss of chaotic shade which was all that revealed itself of the vale on whose farther side she was born. Having already traversed about five miles on the upland she had now some ten or eleven in the lowland before her journey would be finished.

The winding road downwards became just visible to her under the wan starlight as she followed it, and soon she paced a soil so contrasting with that above it that the difference was perceptible to the tread and to the smell. It was the heavy clay land of Blackmoor Vale, and a part of the Vale to which turnpike-roads had never penetrated. Superstitions linger longest on these heavy soils. Having once been forest, at this shadowy time it seemed to assert something of its old character, the far and the near being blended, and every tree and tall hedge making the most of its presence. The harts that had been hunted here, the witches that had been pricked and ducked,[1] the green-spangled fairies that 'whickered' at you as you passed; – the place teemed with beliefs in them still, and they formed an impish multitude now.

At Nuzzlebury she passed the village inn, whose sign creaked in response to the greeting of her footsteps, which not a human soul heard but herself. Under the thatched roofs her mind's eye beheld relaxed tendons and flaccid muscles, spread out in the darkness beneath coverlets made of little purple patchwork squares, and undergoing a bracing process at the hands of sleep for renewed labour on the morrow, as soon as a hint of pink nebulosity appeared on Hambledon Hill.

At three she turned the last corner of the maze of lanes she had threaded, and entered Marlott, passing the field in which, as a club-girl, she had first seen Angel Clare, when he had not danced with her; the sense of disappointment remained with her yet. In the direction of her mother's house she saw a light. It came from the bedroom window, and a branch waved in front of it and made it wink at her. As soon as she could discern the outline of the house – newly thatched with her money – it had all its old effect upon Tess's imagination. Part of her body and life it ever seemed to be; the slope of its dormers, the finish of its gables, the broken courses of brick which topped the chimney, all had something in common with her personal character. A stupefaction had come into these features, to her regard; it meant the illness of her mother.

She opened the door so softly as to disturb nobody; the lower room was vacant, but the neighbour who was sitting up with her mother came to the top of the stairs, and whispered that Mrs Durbeyfield was no better, though she was sleeping just then. Tess prepared herself a breakfast, and then took her place as nurse in her mother's chamber.

In the morning, when she contemplated the children, they had all a curiously elongated look; although she had been away little more than a year their growth was astounding; and the necessity of applying herself heart and soul to their needs took her out of her own cares.

Her father's ill-health was of the same indefinite kind, and he sat in his chair as usual. But the day after her arrival he was unusually bright. He had a rational scheme for living, and Tess asked him what it was.

'I'm thinking of sending round to all the old antiquarians in this part of England,' he said, 'asking them to subscribe to a fund to maintain me. I'm sure they'd see it as a romantical, artistical, and proper thing to do. They spend lots o' money in keeping up old ruins, and finding the bones o' things, and such like; and living remains must be more interesting to 'em still, if they only knowed o' me. Would that somebody would go round and tell 'em what there is living among 'em, and they thinking nothing of him! If Pa'son Tringham, who discovered me, had lived, he'd ha' done it, I'm sure.'

Tess postponed her arguments on this high project till she had grappled with pressing matters in hand, which seemed little improved by her remittances. When indoor necessities had been eased she turned her attention to external things. It was now the season for planting and sowing; many gardens and allotments of the villagers had already received their spring tillage; but the garden and the allotment of the Durbeyfields were behindhand. She found, to her dismay, that this was owing to their having eaten all the seed-potatoes, – that last lapse of the improvident. At the earliest moment she obtained what others she could procure, and in a few days her father was well enough to see to the garden, under Tess's persuasive efforts: while she herself undertook the allotment-plot which they rented in a field a couple of hundred yards out of the village.

She liked doing it after the confinement of the sick chamber, where she was not now required by reason of her mother's improvement. Violent motion relieved thought. The plot of ground was in a high, dry, open enclosure, where there were forty or fifty such pieces, and where labour was at its briskest when the hired labour of the day had ended. Digging began usually at six o'clock, and extended indefinitely into the dusk or moonlight. Just now heaps of dead weeds and refuse were burning on many of the plots, the dry weather favouring their combustion.

One fine day Tess and 'Liza-Lu worked on here with their neighbours till the last rays of the sun smote flat upon the white pegs that divided the plots. As soon as twilight succeeded to sunset the flare of the couch-grass and cabbage-stalk fires began to light up the allotments fitfully, their outlines appearing and disappearing under the dense smoke as wafted by the wind. When a fire glowed, banks of smoke, blown level along the ground, would themselves become illuminated to an opaque lustre, screening the workpeople from one another; and the meaning of the 'pillar of a cloud,' which was a wall by day and a light by night,[2] could be understood.

As evening thickened some of the gardening men and women gave over for the night, but the greater number remained to get their planting done, Tess being among them, though she sent her sister home. It was on one of the couch-burning plots that she laboured with her fork, its four shining prongs resounding against the stones and dry clods in little clicks. Sometimes she was completely involved in the smoke of her fire; then it would leave her figure free, irradiated by the brassy glare from the heap. She was oddly dressed to-night, and presented a somewhat staring aspect, her attire being a gown bleached by many washings, with a short black jacket over it, the effect of the whole being that of a wedding and funeral guest in one. The women further back wore white aprons, which, with their pale faces, were all that could be seen of them in the gloom, except when at moments they caught a flash from the flames.

Westward, the wiry boughs of the bare thorn hedge which formed the boundary of the field rose against the pale opalescence of the lower sky. Above, Jupiter hung like a full-blown daffodil, so bright as almost to throw a shade. A few small nondescript stars were appearing elsewhere. In the distance a dog barked, and wheels occasionally rattled along the dry road.

Still the prongs continued to click assiduously, for it was not late;

and though the air was fresh and keen there was a whisper of spring in it that cheered the workers on. Something in the place, the hour, the crackling fires, the fantastic mysteries of light and shade, made others as well as Tess enjoy being there. Nightfall, which in the frost of winter comes as a fiend and in the warmth of summer as a lover, came as a tranquillizer on this March day.

Nobody looked at his or her companions. The eyes of all were on the soil as its turned surface was revealed by the fires. Hence as Tess stirred the clods, and sang her foolish little songs with scarce now a hope that Clare would ever hear them, she did not for a long time notice the person who worked nearest to her – a man in a long smockfrock who, she found, was forking the same plot as herself, and whom she supposed her father had sent there to advance the work. She became more conscious of him when the direction of his digging brought him closer. Sometimes the smoke divided them; then it swerved, and the two were visible to each other but divided from all the rest.

Tess did not speak to her fellow-worker, nor did he speak to her. Nor did she think of him further than to recollect that he had not been there when it was broad daylight, and that she did not know him as any one of the Marlott labourers, which was no wonder, her absences having been so long and frequent of late years. By and by he dug so close to her that the fire-beams were reflected as distinctly from the steel prongs of his fork as from her own. On going up to the fire to throw a pitch of dead weeds upon it, she found that he did the same on the other side. The fire flared up, and she beheld the face of D'Urberville.

The unexpectedness of his presence, the grotesqueness of his appearance in a gathered smockfrock, such as was now worn only by the most old-fashioned of the labourers, had a ghastly comicality that chilled her as to its bearing. D'Urberville emitted a low long laugh.

'If I were inclined to joke I should say, How much this seems like Paradise!' he remarked whimsically, looking at her with an inclined head.

'What do you say?' she weakly asked.

'A jester might say this is just like Paradise. You are Eve, and I am

348

the old Other One[3] come to tempt you in the disguise of an inferior animal. I used to be quite up in that scene of Milton's when I was theological. Some of it goes –

> "Empress, the way is ready, and not long,
> Beyond a row of myrtles, on a flat
> Fast by a fountain, one small thicket past
> Of blowing myrrh and balm; if thou accept
> My conduct, I can bring thee thither soon."
> "Lead then," said Eve.[4]

And so on. My dear, dear Tess, I am only putting this to you as a thing that you might have supposed or said quite untruly, because you think so badly of me.'

'I never said you were Satan, or thought it. I don't think of you in that way at all. My thoughts of you are quite cold, except when you affront me. What, did you come digging here in such a dress entirely because of me?'

'Entirely. To see you; nothing more. To protest against your working like this.'

'But I like doing it – it is for my father.'

'Your engagement at the other place is ended?'

'Yes.'

'Where are you going to next? To join your dear husband?'

She could not bear the humiliating reminder.

'Oh – I don't know,' she said bitterly. 'I have no husband!'

'It is quite true – in the sense you mean. But you have a friend, and I have determined that you shall be comfortable in spite of yourself. When you get down to your house you will see what I have sent there for you.'

'O, Alec, I wish you wouldn't give me anything at all! I cannot take it from you! I don't like – it is not right!'

'It *is* right!' he cried firmly. 'I am not going to see a woman whom I feel so tenderly for, as I do for you, in trouble without trying to help her.'

'But I am very well off! I am only in trouble about – about – not about living at all!'

She turned, and desperately resumed her digging, tears dripping upon the fork-handle and upon the clods.

'About the children – your brothers and sisters,' he resumed. 'I've been thinking of them.'

Tess's heart quivered – he was touching her in a weak place. He had divined her chief anxiety. Since returning home her soul had gone out to those children with an affection that was passionate.

'If your mother does not recover, somebody ought to do something for them; since your father will not be able to do much, I suppose.'

'He can with my assistance. He must!'

'And mine.'

'No, sir!'

'How damned foolish this is!' burst out D'Urberville. 'Why, he thinks we are the same family; and will be quite satisfied!'

'He don't. I've undeceived him.'

'The more fool you!'

D'Urberville in anger retreated from her to the hedge, where he pulled off the long smockfrock and red neckerchief which had mainly disguised him; and rolling them up and pushing them into the couch-fire, went away.

Tess could not get on with her digging after this; she felt restless; she wondered if he had gone back to her father's house; and taking the fork in her hand proceeded homewards.

Some twenty yards from the house she was met by one of her sisters.

'O, Tessy – what do you think! 'Liza-Lu is a crying and there's a lot of folk in the house, and mother is a good deal better, but they think father is dead!'

The child realized the grandeur of the news; but not as yet its sadness; and stood looking at Tess with round-eyed importance, till, beholding the effect it produced upon her, she said –

'What, Tess, shan't we talk to father never no more?'

'But father was only a little bit ill!' exclaimed Tess distractedly.

'Liza-Lu came up.

'He dropped down just now, and the doctor who was there for mother said there was no chance for him, because his heart was growed in.'

Yes; the Durbeyfield couple had changed places; the dying one was out of danger, and the indisposed one was dead. The news meant even more than it sounded. Her father's life had a value apart from his personal achievements, or perhaps it would not have had much. It was the last of the three lives for whose duration the house and premises were held under a lease; and it had long been coveted by the tenant-farmer for his regular labourers, who were stinted in cottage accommodation. Moreover, 'liviers' were disapproved of in villages almost as much as little freeholders, because of their independence of manner, and when a lease determined it was never renewed.[5]

Thus the Durbeyfields, once D'Urbervilles, saw descending upon them the destiny which, no doubt, when they were among the Olympians of the county, they had caused to descend many a time, and severely enough, upon the heads of such landless ones as they themselves were now. So do flux and reflux – the rhythm of change – alternate and persist in everything under the sky.

LI

At length it was the eve of Old Lady-Day, and the agricultural world was in a fever of mobility such as only occurs at that particular date of the year. It is a day of fulfilment; agreements for outdoor service during the ensuing year, entered into at Candlemas, are to be now carried out. The labourers – or 'workfolk,' as they used to call themselves immemorially till the other word was introduced from without[1] – who wish to remain no longer in old places are removing to the new farms.

These annual migrations from farm to farm were on the increase here.[2] When Tess's mother was a child the majority of the field-folk about Marlott had remained all their lives on one farm, which had been the home also of their fathers and grandfathers; but latterly the desire for yearly removal had risen to a high pitch. With the younger families it was a pleasant excitement which might possibly be an advantage. The Egypt of one family was the Land of Promise to the family who saw it from a distance, till by residence there it became in turn their Egypt also; and so they changed and changed.[3]

However, all the mutations so increasingly discernible in village life did not originate entirely in the agricultural unrest. A depopulation was also going on. The village had formerly contained, side by side with the agricultural labourers, an interesting and better-informed class, ranking distinctly above the former – the class to which Tess's father and mother had belonged – and including the carpenter, the smith, the shoemaker, the huckster, together with nondescript workers other than farm-labourers; a set of people who owed a certain stability of aim and conduct to the fact of their being life-holders like Tess's father, or copyholders, or, occasionally, small freeholders. But as the long holdings fell in they were seldom again let to similar tenants, and were mostly pulled down, if not absolutely required by the farmer for his hands. Cottagers who were not directly employed on the land were looked upon with disfavour, and the banishment of some starved the trade of others, who were thus obliged to follow. These families, who had formed the backbone of the village life in the past, had to seek refuge in the large centres; the process, humorously designated by statisticians as 'the tendency of the rural population towards the large towns,' being really the tendency of water to flow uphill when forced by machinery.[4]

The cottage accommodation at Marlott having been in this manner considerably curtailed by demolitions, every house which remained standing was required by the agriculturist for his workpeople. Ever since the occurrence of the event which had cast such a shadow over Tess's life the Durbeyfield family (whose descent was not credited) had been tacitly looked on as one which would have to go when their lease ended, if only in the interests of morality. It was, indeed, quite true that the household had not been shining examples either of temperance, soberness, or chastity. The father, and even the mother, had got drunk at times, the younger children seldom had gone to church, and the eldest daughter had made queer unions. By some means the village had to be kept pure. So on this, the first Lady-Day on which the Durbeyfields were expellable, the house, being roomy, was required for a carter with a large family; and Widow Joan, her daughters Tess and 'Liza-Lu, the boy Abraham and the younger children, had to go elsewhere.

On the evening preceding their removal it was getting dark betimes by reason of a drizzling rain which blurred the sky. As it was the last night they would spend in the village which had been their home and birthplace, Mrs Durbeyfield, 'Liza-Lu, and Abraham had gone out to bid some friends good-bye, and Tess was keeping house till they should return.

She was kneeling in the window-bench, her face close to the casement, where an outer pane of rain-water was sliding down the inner pane of glass. Her eyes rested on the web of a spider, probably starved long ago, which had been mistakenly placed in a corner where no flies ever came, and shivered in the slight draught through the casement. Tess was reflecting on the position of the household, in which she perceived her own evil influence. Had she not come home her mother and the children might probably have been allowed to stay on as weekly tenants. But she had been observed almost immediately on her return by some people of scrupulous character and great influence: they had seen her idling in the churchyard, restoring as well as she could with a little trowel a baby's obliterated grave. By this means they had found that she was living here again; her mother was scolded for 'harbouring' her; sharp words had ensued from Joan, who had independently offered to leave at once; she had been taken at her word; and here was the result.

'I ought never to have come home,' said Tess to herself, bitterly.

A sudden rebellious sense of injustice caused the region of her eyes to swell with the rush of hot tears thither; but they did not fall. Even her husband, Angel Clare himself, had dealt out hard measure to her, surely he had! She had never before admitted such a thought; but he had surely! Never in her life – she could swear it from the bottom of her soul – had she ever intended to do wrong; yet these hard judgments had come. Whatever her sins, they were not sins of intention, but of inadvertence, and why should she have been punished so persistently?

She passionately seized the first piece of paper that came to hand, and scribbled the following lines:

O why have you treated me so monstrously, Angel! I do not deserve it. I have thought it all over carefully, and I can never, never forgive you! You know that I did not intend to wrong you – why have you so wronged me? You are cruel, cruel indeed! I will try to forget you. It is all injustice I have received at your hands! – T.

She watched till the postman passed by, ran out to him with her epistle, and then again took her listless place inside the window-panes.[5]

She was so intent upon reproachful thoughts that she hardly at first took note of a man in a white mackintosh whom she saw riding down the street. Possibly it was owing to her face being near to the pane that he saw her so quickly, and directed his horse so close to the cottage-front that his hoofs were almost upon the narrow border for plants growing under the wall. It was not till he touched the window with his riding-crop that she observed him. The rain had nearly ceased, and she opened the casement in obedience to his gesture.

'Didn't you see me?' asked D'Urberville.

'I was not attending,' she said. 'I heard you, I believe, though I fancied it was a carriage and horses. I was in a sort of dream.'

'Ah! you heard the D'Urberville Coach, perhaps. You know the legend, I suppose?'

'No. My – somebody was going to tell it me once, but didn't.'

'If you are a genuine D'Urberville I ought not to tell you either, I suppose. As for me, I'm a spurious one, so it doesn't matter. It is rather dismal. It is that this sound of a non-existent coach can only be heard by one of D'Urberville blood, and it is held to be of ill-omen to the one who hears it. It has to do with a murder, committed by one of the family, centuries ago.'

'Now you have begun it, finish it.'

'Very well. One of the family is said to have abducted some beautiful woman, who tried to escape from the coach in which he was carrying her off, and in the struggle he killed her – or she killed him – I forget which. Such is the tale. I see that your tubs and buckets are packed together. Going away, aren't you?'

'Yes, to-morrow – Old Lady-Day.'

'I heard you were, but could hardly believe it; it seems so sudden. Why is it?'

'Father's was the last life on the property, and when that dropped we had no further right to bide. Though we might, perhaps, have stayed as weekly tenants – if it had not been for me.'

'What about you?'

'I am not a – proper woman.'

D'Urberville's face flushed.

'What an infernal shame! Miserable snobs! May their dirty souls be burnt to cinders!' he exclaimed in tones of fierce resentment. 'That's why you are going, is it? Turned out!'

'We are not turned out exactly; but as they said we should have to go soon, it was best to go now everybody was moving, because there are better chances.'

'Where are you going to?'

'Kingsbere. We have taken rooms there. Mother is so foolish about father's people that she will go there.'

'But your mother's family are not fit for lodgings, and in a little hole of a town like that. Now why not come to my garden-house at Trantridge? There are hardly any poultry now, since my mother's death; but there's the house, as you know it, and the garden. It can be whitewashed in a day, and your mother can live there quite comfortably; and I will put the children to a good school. Really I ought to do something for you!'

'But we have already taken the rooms at Kingsbere!' she declared.

'Now, though I have been your enemy, I am your friend, even if you won't believe it. Come to this cottage of mine. We'll get up a regular colony of fowls, and your mother can attend to them excellently; and the children can go to school.'

Tess breathed more and more quickly, and at length she said –

'How do I know that you would do all this? Your views may change – and then – we should be – my mother would be – homeless again.'

'Oh no – no. I would guarantee you against such as that in writing, if necessary. Think it over.'

Tess shook her head. But D'Urberville persisted; she had seldom seen him so determined; he would not take a negative.

'Please just tell your mother,' he said, in emphatic tones. 'It is her business to judge – not yours. I shall get the house swept out and whitened to-morrow morning, and fires lit; and it will be dry by the evening, so that you can come straight there. Now mind, I shall expect you.'

Tess again shook her head; her throat swelling with complicated emotion. She could not look up at D'Urberville.

'I owe you something for the past, you know,' he resumed. 'And you cured me, too, of that craze; so I am glad—'

'I would rather you had kept the craze, so that you had kept the practice which went with it!'

'I am glad of this opportunity of repaying you a little. To-morrow I shall expect to hear your mother's goods unloading . . . Give me your hand on it now – dear, beautiful Tess!'

With the last sentence he had dropped his voice to a murmur, and put his hand in at the half-open casement. With stormy eyes she pulled the stay-bar quickly, and, in doing so, caught his arm between the casement and the stone mullion.

'Damnation – you are very cruel!' he said, snatching out his arm. 'No, no! – I know you didn't do it on purpose. Well, I shall expect you, or your mother and the children at least.'

'I shall not come – I have plenty of money!' she cried.

'Where?'

'At my father-in-law's, if I ask for it.'

'*If* you ask for it. But you won't, Tess; I know you; you'll never ask for it – you'll starve first!'

With these words he rode off. Just at the corner of the street he met the man with the paint-pot, who asked him if he had deserted the brethren.

'You go to the devil!' said D'Urberville.

Tess remained where she was a long while, and it grew darker, the fire-light shining over the room. The two biggest of the younger children had gone out with their mother; the four smallest, their ages ranging from three-and-a-half years to eleven, all in black frocks, were gathered round the hearth babbling their own little subjects. Tess at length joined them, without lighting a candle.

'This is the last night that we shall sleep here, dears, in the house where we were born,' she said quickly. 'We ought to think of it, oughtn't we?'

They all became silent; with the impressibility of their age they were ready to burst into tears at the picture of finality she had conjured up, though all the day hitherto they had been rejoicing in the idea of a new place. Tess changed the subject.

'Sing to me, dears,' she said.

'What shall we sing?'

'Anything you know; I don't mind what.'

There was a momentary pause; it was broken, first, by one little tentative note; then a second voice strengthened it, and a third and a fourth chimed in in unison, with words they had learnt at the Sunday-school –

> Here we suffer grief and pain,
> Here we meet to part again;
> In Heaven we part no more;[6]

The four sang on with the phlegmatic passivity of persons who had long ago settled the question, and there being no mistake about it, felt that further thought was not required. With features strained hard to enunciate the syllables they continued to regard the centre of the flickering fire, the notes of the youngest straying over into the pauses of the rest.

Tess turned from them, and went to the window again. Darkness had now fallen without, but she put her face to the pane as though to peer into the gloom. It was really to hide her tears. If she could only believe what the children were singing; if she were only sure, how different all would now be; how confidently she would leave them to Providence and their future kingdom! But, in default of that, it behoved her to do something; to be their Providence; for to Tess, as to some few millions of others, there was ghastly satire in the poet's lines –

> Not in utter nakedness
> But trailing clouds of glory do we come.[7]

To her and her like, birth itself was an ordeal of degrading personal compulsion, whose gratuitousness nothing in the result seemed to justify, and at best could only palliate.

In the shades of the wet road she soon discerned her mother with tall 'Liza-Lu and Abraham. Mrs Durbeyfield's pattens clicked up to the door, and Tess opened it.

'I see the tracks of a horse outside the window,' said Joan. 'Hev somebody called?'

'No,' said Tess.

The children by the fire looked gravely at her, and one murmured –

'Why, Tess, the gentleman a-horseback!'

'He didn't call,' said Tess. 'He spoke to me in passing.'

'Who was the gentleman?' asked her mother.[8]

'Oh, you needn't ask,' Tess answered. 'You've seen him before, and so have I.'

'Ah! What did he say?' said Joan curiously.

'I will tell you when we are settled in our lodgings at Kingsbere to-morrow – every word.'

LII

During the small hours of the next morning, while it was still dark, dwellers near the highways were conscious of a disturbance of their night's rest by rumbling noises, intermittently continuing till daylight – noises as certain to recur in this particular first week of the month as the voice of the cuckoo in the third week of the same. They were the preliminaries of the general removal, the passing of the empty waggons and teams to fetch the goods of the migrating families; for it was always by the vehicle of the farmer who required his services that the hired man was conveyed to his destination. That this might be accomplished within the day was the explanation of the reverberation occurring so soon after midnight, the aim of the carters being to reach the door of the outgoing households by six o'clock, when the loading of their movables at once began.

But to Tess and her mother's household no such anxious farmer sent his team. They were only women; they were not regular labourers; they were not particularly required anywhere; hence they had to hire a waggon at their own expense, and got nothing sent gratuitously.

It was a relief to Tess, when she looked out of the window that morning, to find that though the weather was windy and louring, it did not rain, and that the waggon had come. A wet Lady-Day was a spectre which removing families never forgot; damp furniture, damp bedding, damp clothing accompanied it, and left a train of ills.

Her mother, 'Liza-Lu, and Abraham were also awake, but the younger children were let sleep on. The four breakfasted by the thin light, and the 'house-ridding' was taken in hand.

It proceeded with some cheerfulness, a friendly neighbour or two assisting. When the large articles of furniture had been packed in position a circular nest was made of the beds and bedding, in which Joan Durbeyfield and the young children were to sit through the journey. After loading there was a long delay before the horses were brought, these having been unharnessed during the ridding; but at length, about two o'clock, the whole was under way, the cooking-pot swinging from the axle of the waggon, Mrs Durbeyfield and family at the top, the matron having in her lap, to prevent injury to its works, the head of the clock, which, at any exceptional lurch of the waggon, struck one, or one-and-a-half, in thin tones. Tess and the next eldest girl walked alongside till they were out of the village.

They had called on a few neighbours that morning and the previous evening, and some came to see them off, all wishing them well, though, in their secret hearts, hardly expecting welfare possible to such a family, harmless as the Durbeyfields were to all except themselves. Soon the equipage began to ascend to higher ground, and the wind grew keener with the change of level and soil.

The day being the sixth of April, the Durbeyfield waggon met many other waggons with families on the summit of the load, which was built on a well-nigh unvarying principle, as peculiar, probably, to the rural labourer as the hexagon to the bee.[1] The groundwork of the arrangement was the family dresser, which, with its shining handles, and finger-marks, and domestic evidences thick upon it, stood importantly in front, over the tails of the shaft horses, in its erect and natural position, like some Ark of the Covenant[2] that they were bound to carry reverently.

Some of the households were lively, some mournful; some were stopping at the doors of wayside inns; where, in due time, the Durbeyfield menagerie also drew up to bait horses and refresh the travellers.

During the halt Tess's eyes fell upon a three-pint blue mug, which was ascending and descending through the air to and from the feminine section of a household, sitting on the summit of a load that had also drawn up at a little distance from the same inn. She followed one of the mug's journeys upward, and perceived it to be clasped by hands whose owner she well knew. Tess went towards the waggon.

'Marian and Izz!' she cried to the girls, for it was they, sitting with the moving family at whose house they had lodged. 'Are you house-ridding to-day, like everybody else?'

They were, they said. It had been too rough a life for them at Flintcomb-Ash, and they had come away, almost without notice, leaving Groby to prosecute them if he chose. They told Tess their destination, and Tess told them hers.

Marian leant over the load, and lowered her voice. 'Do you know that the gentleman who follows 'ee – you'll guess who I mean – came to ask for 'ee at Flintcomb after you had gone? We didn't tell'n where you was, knowing you wouldn't wish to see him.'

'Ah – but I did see him,' Tess murmured. 'He found me.'

'And do he know where you be going?'

'I think so.'

'Husband come back?'

'No.'

She bade her acquaintance good-bye – for the respective carters had now come out from the inn – and the two waggons resumed their journey in opposite directions; the vehicle whereon sat Marian, Izz, and the ploughman's family with whom they had thrown in their lot, being brightly painted, and drawn by three powerful horses with shining brass ornaments on their harness; while the waggon on which Mrs Durbeyfield and her family rode was a creaking erection that would scarcely bear the weight of the superincumbent load; one which had known no paint since it was made, and drawn by two horses only. The contrast well marked the difference between being fetched by a thriving farmer and conveying oneself whither no hirer waited one's coming.

The distance was great, and though they had started so early it was quite late in the day when they turned the flank of an eminence which formed part of the upland called Greenhill. While the horses stood to stale and breathe themselves Tess looked around. Under the hill, and just ahead of them, was the half-dead townlet of their pilgrimage, Kingsbere, where lay those ancestors of whom her father had spoken and sung to painfulness: Kingsbere, the spot of all spots in the world which could be considered the D'Urberville's home, since they had resided there full five hundred years.

A man could be seen advancing from the outskirts towards them, and when he beheld the nature of their waggon-load he quickened his steps.

'You be the woman they call Mrs Durbeyfield, I reckon?' he said to Tess's mother, who had descended to walk the remainder of the way.

She nodded. 'Though widow of the late Sir John D'Urberville, poor nobleman, if I cared for my rights; and returning to the domain of my knight's forefathers.'

'Oh? Well, I know nothing about that; but if you be Mrs Durbeyfield, I am sent to tell 'ee that the rooms you wanted be let. We didn't know you was coming till we got your letter this morning – when 'twas too late. But no doubt you can get other lodgings somewhere.'[3]

The man had noticed the face of Tess, which had become ash-pale at his intelligence. Her mother looked hopelessly at fault. 'What shall we do now, Tess?' she said bitterly. 'Here's a welcome to your ancestors' lands! However, let's try farther.'

They moved on into the town, and tried with all their might, Tess remaining with the waggon to take care of the children whilst her mother and 'Liza-Lu made inquiries. At the last return of Joan to the vehicle, an hour later, when her search for accommodation had still been fruitless, the driver of the waggon said the goods must be unloaded, as he was bound to return that night.

'Very well – unload it here,' said Joan recklessly. 'I'll get shelter somewhere.'

The waggon had drawn up under the churchyard wall, in a spot screened from view, and the driver, nothing loth, soon hauled down the poor battered heap of household goods. This done he moved off and left them, only too glad to get out of further dealings with such a family. It was a dry night, and he guessed that they would come to no harm.

Tess gazed desperately at the pile of furniture. The cold sunlight of this spring evening peered invidiously upon the crocks and kettles, upon the bunches of dried herbs shivering in the breeze, upon the brass handles of the dresser, upon the wicker-cradle they had all been rocked in, and upon the well-rubbed clock-case, all of which gave out the reproachful gleam of indoor articles exposed to the vicissitudes of a roofless exposure for which they were never made. Round about were deparked hills and slopes – now cut up into little paddocks – and the green foundations that showed where the D'Urberville mansion once had stood; also an outlying stretch of Egdon Heath that had always belonged to the estate. Hard by, the aisle of the church called the D'Urberville Aisle looked on imperturbably.

'Isn't your family vault your own freehold?' said Tess's mother, as she returned from a reconnoitre of the church and graveyard. 'Why of course 'tis, and that's where we will camp, girls, till the place of your ancestors finds us a roof! Now Tess and 'Liza and Abraham, you help me. We'll make a nest for these children, and then we'll have another look round.'

Tess listlessly lent a hand, and in a quarter of an hour the old four-post bedstead was dissociated from the heap of goods, and erected under the south wall of the church, the part of the building known as the D'Urberville Aisle, beneath which the huge vaults lay. Over the tester of the bedstead was a beautifully traceried window, of many lights, its date being the fifteenth century. It was called the D'Urberville Window, and in the upper part could be discerned heraldic emblems like those on Durbeyfield's old seal and spoon.

Joan drew the curtains round the bed so as to make an excellent tent of it, and put the smaller children inside. 'If it comes to the worst we can sleep there too, for one night,' she said. 'But let us try farther on, and get something for the dears to eat! O, Tess, what's the use of your playing at marrying gentlemen, if it leaves us like this!'

Accompanied by 'Liza-Lu and the boy she again ascended the little lane which secluded the church from the townlet. As soon as they got into the street they beheld a man on horseback gazing up and down. 'Ah – I'm looking for you,' he said riding up to them. 'This is indeed a family gathering on the historic spot!'

It was Alec D'Urberville. 'Where is Tess?' he asked.

Personally Joan had no liking for Alec. She cursorily signified the direction of the church, and went on, D'Urberville saying that he would see them again, in case they should be again unsuccessful in their search for a house, of which he had just heard. When they had gone D'Urberville rode to the inn, and shortly after came out on foot.

In the interim Tess, left with the children inside the bedstead, remained talking with them awhile, till, seeing that no more could be done to make them comfortable just then, she walked about the churchyard, now beginning to be embrowned by the shades of nightfall. The door of the church was unfastened, and she entered it for the first time in her life.

Within the window under which the bedstead stood were the tombs of the family, covering in their dates several centuries. They were canopied, altar-shaped, and plain; their carvings being defaced and broken; their brasses torn from the matrices, the rivet-holes remaining like marten-holes in a sand-cliff. Of all the reminders that she had ever received that her people were socially extinct there was none so forcible as this spoliation.

She drew near to a dark stone on which was inscribed:[4]

Ostium sepulchri antiquæ familiæ Đ'Urberville.

Tess did not read Church-Latin like a Cardinal, but she knew that this was the door of her ancestral sepulchre, and that the tall knights of whom her father had chanted in his cups lay inside.

She musingly turned to withdraw, passing near an altar-tomb, the oldest of them all, on which was a recumbent figure. In the dusk she had not noticed it before, and would hardly have noticed it now but for an odd fancy that the effigy moved. As soon as she drew close to it she discovered all in a moment that the figure was a living person; and the shock to her sense of not having been alone was so violent that she was quite overcome, and sank down nigh to fainting, not however till she had recognized Alec d'Urberville in the form.

363

He leapt off the slab and supported her.

'I saw you come in,' he said gently, 'and would not interrupt your meditations. A family gathering, is it not, with these old fellows under us here? Listen.'

He stamped with his heel heavily on the floor; whereupon there arose a hollow echo from below.

'That shook them a bit, I'll warrant!' he continued. 'And you thought I was the mere stone reproduction of one of them. But no. The old order changeth.[5] The little finger of the sham D'Urberville can do more for you than the whole dynasty of the real underneath . . . Now command me. What shall I do?'

'Go away!' she murmured.

'I will – I'll look for your mother,' said he blandly. But in passing her he whispered: 'Mark me; you'll be civil yet!'

When he was gone she bent down upon the entrance to the vaults, and said –

'Why am I on the wrong side of this door!'

In the meantime Marian and Izz Huett had journeyed onward with the chattels of the ploughman in the direction of their land of Canaan – the Egypt of some other family who had left it only that morning. But the girls did not for a long time think of where they were going. Their talk was of Angel Clare and Tess, and her persistent lover, whose connection with Tess's previous history they had partly heard and partly guessed ere this.

"Tisn't as though she had never known him afore,' said Marian. 'His having won her once makes all the difference in the world. 'Twould be a thousand pities if he were to tole her away again. Mr Clare can never be anything to us, Izz; and why should we grudge him to her, and not try to mend this quarrel? If he could on'y know what straits she's put to, and what's hovering round, he might come to take care of his own.'

'Could we let him know?'

They thought of this all the way to their destination; but the bustle of re-establishment in their new place took up all their attention then. But when they were settled, a month later, they heard of Clare's approaching return, though they had learnt nothing more of Tess. Upon that, agitated anew by their attachment to him, yet honourably disposed to her, Marian uncorked the penny ink-bottle they shared, and a few lines were concocted between the two girls.

> HONOUR'D SIR – Look to your Wife if you do love her as much as she do love you. For she is sore put to by an Enemy in the shape of a Friend. Sir, there is one near her who ought to be Away. A woman should not be try'd beyond her Strength, and continual dropping will wear away a Stone – ay, more – a Diamond.
>
> FROM TWO WELL-WISHERS.

This they addressed to Angel Clare at the only place they had ever heard him to be connected with, Emminster Vicarage; after which they continued in a mood of emotional exaltation at their own generosity, which made them sing in hysterical snatches and weep at the same time.

END OF PHASE THE SIXTH

Fulfilment

LIII

It was evening at Emminster Vicarage. The two customary candles were burning under their green shades in the Vicar's study, but he had not been sitting there. Occasionally he came in, stirred the small fire which sufficed for the increasing mildness of spring, and went out again; sometimes pausing at the front door, going on to the drawing-room, then returning again to the front door.

It faced westward, and though gloom prevailed inside there was still light enough without to see with distinctness. Mrs Clare, who had been sitting in the drawing-room, followed him hither.

'Plenty of time yet,' said the Vicar. 'He doesn't reach Chalk-Newton till six, even if the train should be punctual, and ten miles of country-road, five of them in Crimmercrock Lane, are not jogged over in a hurry by our old horse.'

'But he has done it in an hour with us, my dear.'

'Years ago.'

Thus they passed the minutes, each well knowing that this was only waste of breath, the one essential being simply to wait.

At length there was a slight noise in the lane, and the old pony-chaise appeared indeed outside the railings. They saw alight therefrom a form which they affected to recognize, but would actually have passed by in the street without identifying had he not got out of their carriage at the particular moment when a particular person was due.

Mrs Clare rushed through the dark passage to the door, and her husband came more slowly after.

The new arrival, who was just about to enter, saw their anxious faces in the doorway and the gleam of the west in their spectacles because they confronted the last rays of day, but they could only see his shape against the light.

'O, my boy, my boy – home again at last!' cried Mrs Clare, who cared no more at that moment for the stains of heterodoxy which had caused all this separation than for the dust upon his clothes. What woman, indeed, among the most faithful adherents of the truth, believes the promises and threats of the Word in the sense in which she believes in her own children, or would not throw her theology to the wind if weighed against their happiness? As soon as they reached the room where the candles were lighted she looked at his face.

'O, it is not Angel – not my son – the Angel who went away!' she cried in all the irony of sorrow, as she turned herself away.

His father, too, was shocked to see him, so reduced was that figure from its former contours by worry and the bad season that Clare had experienced, in the climate to which he had so rashly hurried in his first aversion to the mockery of events at home. You could see the skeleton behind the man, and almost the ghost behind the skeleton. He was Crivelli's dead *Christus*.[1] His sunken eye-pits were of morbid hue, and the light in his eyes had waned. The angular hollows and lines of his aged ancestors had succeeded to their reign in his face twenty years before their time.

'I was ill over there, you know,' he said. 'I am all right now.'

As if, however, to falsify this assertion, his legs seemed to give way, and he suddenly sat down to save himself from falling. It was only a slight attack of faintness, resulting from the tedious day's journey, and the excitement of arrival.

'Has any letter come for me lately?' he asked.[2]

Only one had recently come. Others, which had arrived a few weeks earlier they had sent on to him, not knowing he would start for home so soon.

He hastily opened the letter produced, and was much disturbed to read in Tess's handwriting the sentiments expressed in her last hurried scrawl to him.

O why have you treated me so monstrously, Angel! I do not deserve it. I have thought it all over carefully, and I can never, never forgive you! You know that I did not intend to wrong you – why have you so wronged me? You are cruel, cruel indeed! I will try to forget you. It is all injustice I have received at your hands! – T.[3]

'It is quite true!' said Angel, throwing down the letter. 'Perhaps she will never be reconciled to me!'

'Don't, Angel, be so anxious about a mere child of the soil!' said his mother.

'Child of the soil! Well, we all are children of the soil. I wish she were so in the sense you mean; but let me now explain to you what I have never explained before, that her father is a descendant in the male line of one of the oldest Norman houses, like a good many others who lead obscure agricultural lives in our villages, and are dubbed "sons of the soil." '

He soon retired to bed; and the next morning, feeling exceedingly unwell, he remained in his room pondering. The circumstances amid which he had left Tess were such that though, while on the south of the Equator, it had seemed the easiest thing in the world to rush back into her arms, now that he had arrived it was not so easy as it had seemed. She was passionate, and her letter[4] made him ask himself if it would be wise to confront her unannounced in the presence of her parents. Supposing that her love had indeed turned to dislike during the separation, a sudden meeting might lead to bitter words.

Clare therefore thought it would be best to prepare Tess and her family by sending a line to Marlott announcing his return, and his hope that she was still living with them there, as he had arranged for her to do when he left England. He despatched the inquiry that very day, and before the week was out there came a short reply from Mrs Durbeyfield which did not remove his embarrassment, for it bore no address, though to his surprise it was not written from Marlott.

SIR – J write these few lines to say that my Daughter is away from me at present, and J am not sure when she will return, but J will let you know as Soon as she do. J do not feel at liberty to tell you Where she is temporarily biding. J should say that me and my Family have left Marlott for some Time. – Yours,

J. DURBEYFIELD.

It was such a relief to Clare to learn that Tess was at least apparently well that her mother's stiff reticence as to her whereabouts did not long distress him. They were all angry with him, evidently. He would wait till Mrs Durbeyfield could inform him of Tess's return, which her letter implied to be soon. He deserved no more. His had been a love 'which alters when it alteration finds.'[5] He had undergone some strange experiences in his absence; he had seen the virtual Faustina in the literal Cornelia, a spiritual Lucretia in a corporeal Phryne; he had thought of the woman taken and set in the midst as one deserving to be stoned, and of the wife of Uriah being made a queen;[6] and he had asked himself why had he not judged Tess constructively rather than biographically, by the will rather than by the deed?

Day after day passed while he waited at his father's house for the promised second note from Joan Durbeyfield, and indirectly to recover a little more strength. The strength showed signs of coming back, but there was no sign of the letter. Then the letters that had been sent on to him in Brazil were returned, and he read the one from Tess which she had written from Flintcomb-Ash. The unexpected sentences unmanned him quite.[7]

'I must cry to you in my trouble – I have no one else! . . . I think I must die if you do not come soon, or tell me to come to you . . . please, please, not to be just – only a little kind to me . . . If you would come, I could die in your arms! I would be well content to do that if so be you had forgiven me! . . . if you will send me one little line, and say, "*I am coming soon*," I will bide on, Angel – O, so cheerfully! . . . think how it do hurt my heart not to see you ever – ever! Ah, if I could only make your dear heart ache one little minute of each day as mine does every day and all day long, it might lead you to show pity to your poor lonely one . . . I would be content, ay, glad, to live with you as your servant, if I may not as your wife; so that I could only be near you, and get glimpses of you, and think of you as mine . . . I long for only one thing in heaven or earth or under the earth, to meet you, my own dear! Come to me – come to me, and save me from what threatens me!'

Clare's eyes were blinded with tears as, springing wildly up to go and find her immediately, he asked his father if she had applied for any money during his absence. His father returned a negative, and then for the first time it occurred to Angel that her pride had stood in her way. From his remarks his parents now for the first time gathered the real reason of the separation; and their Christianity was such that, reprobates being their especial care, the tenderness towards Tess which her blood, her simplicity, even her poverty, had not engendered, was instantly excited by her sin.

Whilst he was hastily packing together a few articles for his journey he glanced over a poor plain missive also lately come to hand – the one from Marian and Izz Huett, beginning –

'HONOUR'D SIR – Look to your Wife if you do love her as much as she do love you,' and signed, 'FROM TWO WELL-WISHERS.'

LIV

In a quarter of an hour Clare was leaving the house, whence his mother watched his thin figure as it disappeared into the street. He had declined to borrow his father's old mare, well knowing of its necessity to the household. He went to the inn, where he hired a trap, and could hardly wait during the harnessing. In a very few minutes after he was driving up the hill out of the town which, three months earlier in the year, Tess had descended with such hopes and ascended with such shattered purposes.

Benvill Lane soon stretched before him, its hedges and trees purple with buds; but he was looking at other things, and only recalled himself to the scene sufficiently to enable him to keep the way. In something less than an hour-and-a-half he had skirted the south of the King's Hintock estates and ascended to the untoward solitude of Cross-in-Hand, the unholy stone whereon Tess had been compelled by Alec D'Urberville, in his converted character, to swear the strange oath that she would never wilfully tempt him again. The pale and blasted nettle-stems of the preceding year even now lingered nakedly in the banks, young green nettles of the present spring growing from their roots.

Thence he went along the verge of the upland overhanging the other Hintocks, and turning to the right, plunged into the bracing calcareous region of Flintcomb-Ash, the address from which she had written to him in one of the letters, and which he supposed to be the place of sojourn referred to by her mother. Here, of course, he did not find her; and what added to his depression was the discovery that no 'Mrs Clare' had ever been heard of by the cottagers or by the farmer himself, though Tess was remembered well enough by her Christian name. His name she had obviously never used during their separation, and her dignified sense of their total severance was shown not much less by this abstention than by the hardships she had chosen to undergo (of which he now learnt for the first time) rather than apply to his father for more funds.

From this place they told him Tess Durbeyfield had gone, without due notice, to the home of her parents on the other side of Blackmoor, and it therefore became necessary to find Mrs Durbeyfield. She had told him she was not now at Marlott, but had been curiously reticent as to her actual address, and the only course was to go to Marlott and inquire for it. The farmer who had been so churlish with Tess was quite smooth-tongued to Clare, and lent him a horse and man to drive him to Marlott, the gig he had arrived in being sent back to Emminster; for the limit of a day's journey with that horse was reached.

Clare would not accept the loan of the farmer's vehicle for a further distance than to the outskirts of Marlott, and, sending it back with the man who had driven him, he entered on foot the village which was the spot of his dear Tess's birth. It was as yet too early in the year for much colour to appear in the gardens and foliage; the so-called spring was but winter overlaid with a thin coat of greenness, and it was of a parcel with his expectations.

The house in which Tess had passed the years of her childhood was now inhabited by another family who had never known her. The new residents were in the garden, taking as much interest in their own doings as if the homestead had never passed its primal time in conjunction with the histories of others, beside which the histories of these were but as a tale that is told.[1] They walked about the garden paths with thoughts of their own concerns entirely uppermost, bringing their actions at every moment into jarring collision with the dim figures behind them, talking as though the time when Tess lived there were not one whit intenser in story than now. Even the spring birds sang over their heads as if they thought there was nobody missing in particular.

372

On inquiry of these precious innocents, to whom even the name of their predecessors was a failing memory, Clare learned that John Durbeyfield was dead; that his widow and children had left Marlott, declaring they were going to live at Kingsbere, but instead of doing so had gone on to another place they named. By this time Clare abhorred the house for ceasing to contain Tess, and hastened away from its hated presence without once looking back.

His way was by the field in which he had first beheld her at the dance. It was as bad as the house – even worse. He passed on through the churchyard, where, amongst the new headstones, he saw one of a somewhat superior design to the rest. The inscription ran thus:

In Memory of John Durbeyfield, rightly D'Urberville, of the once powerful family of that Name, and Direct Descendant through an Illustrious Line from Sir Bryan D'Urberville, one of the Knights of the Conqueror. Died March 10th, 18—

HOW ARE THE MIGHTY FALLEN.

Some man, apparently the sexton, had observed Clare standing there, and drew nigh. 'Ah, sir, now that's a man who didn't want to lie here, but wished to be carried to Kingsbere, where his ancestors be.'

'And why didn't they respect his wish?'

'Oh – no money. Bless your soul, sir, why – there, I wouldn't wish to say it everywhere, but – even this headstone, for all the flourish wrote upon en, is not paid for.'

'Ah, who put it up?'

The man told the name of a mason in the village, and, on leaving the churchyard, Clare called at the mason's house. He found that the statement was true, and paid the bill. This done he turned in the direction of the migrants.

The distance was too long for a walk, but Clare felt such a strong desire for isolation that at first he would neither hire a conveyance nor go to a circuitous line of railway by which he might eventually reach the place. At Shaston, however, he found he must hire; but the way was such that he did not enter Joan's place till about seven o'clock in the evening, having traversed a distance of over twenty miles since leaving Marlott.

The village being small he had little difficulty in finding Mrs Durbey-field's tenement, which was a house in a walled garden, remote from the main street, where she had stowed away her awkward old furniture as best she could. It was plain that for some reason or other she had not wished him to visit her, and he felt his call to be somewhat of an intrusion. She came to the door herself, and the light from the evening sky fell upon her face.

This was the first time that Clare had ever met her, but he was too preoccupied to observe more than that she was still a handsome woman, in the garb of a respectable widow. He was obliged to explain that he was Tess's husband, and his object in coming there, and he did it awkwardly enough. 'I want to see her at once,' he added. 'You said you would write to me again, but you have not done so.'

'Because she 've not come home,' said Joan.

'Do you know if she is well?'

'I don't. But you ought to, sir,' said she.

'I admit it. Where is she staying?'

From the beginning of the interview Joan had disclosed her embarrassment by keeping her hand to the side of her cheek.

'I – don't know exactly where she is staying,' she answered. 'She was – but—'

'Where was she?'

'Well, she is not there now.'

In her evasiveness she paused again, and the younger children had by this time crept to the door, where, pulling at his mother's skirts, the youngest murmured –

'Is this the gentleman who is going to marry Tess?'

'He has married her,' Joan whispered. 'Go inside.'

Clare saw her efforts for reticence, and asked –

'Do you think Tess would wish me to try and find her? If not, of course—'

'I don't think she would.'

'Are you sure?'

'I am sure she wouldn't.'

He was turning away; and then he thought of Tess's tender letter.

'I am sure she would!' he retorted passionately. 'I know her better than you do.'

'That's very likely, sir; for I have never really known her.'

'Please tell me her address, Mrs Durbeyfield, in kindness to a lonely wretched man!'

Tess's mother again restlessly swept her cheek with her vertical hand, and seeing that he suffered, she at last said, in a low voice –

'She is at Sandbourne.'

'Ah – where there? Sandbourne has become a large place, they say.'

'I don't know more particularly than I have said – Sandbourne. For myself, I was never there.'

It was apparent that Joan spoke the truth in this, and he pressed her no further.

'Are you in want of anything?' he said gently.

'No, sir,' she replied. 'We are fairly well provided for.'

Without entering the house Clare turned away. There was a station three miles ahead, and paying off his coachman, he walked thither. The last train to Sandbourne left shortly after, and it bore Clare on its wheels.

LV

At eleven o'clock that night, having secured a bed at one of the hotels and telegraphed his address to his father immediately on his arrival, he walked out into the streets of Sandbourne. It was too late to call on or inquire for any one, and he reluctantly postponed his purpose till the morning. But he could not retire to rest just yet.

This fashionable watering-place, with its eastern and its western stations, its piers, its groves of pines, its promenades, and its covered gardens was, to Angel Clare, like a fairy place suddenly created by the stroke of a wand, and allowed to get a little dusty. An outlying eastern tract of the enormous Egdon Waste was close at hand, yet on the very verge of that tawny piece of antiquity such a glittering novelty as this pleasure city had chosen to spring up. Within the space of a mile from its outskirts every irregularity of the soil was prehistoric, every channel an undisturbed British trackway; not a sod having been turned there since the days of the Cæsars. Yet the exotic had grown here, suddenly as the prophet's gourd;[1] and had drawn hither Tess.

By the midnight lamps he went up and down the winding ways of this new world in an old one, and could discern between the trees and against the stars the lofty roofs, chimneys, gazebos, and towers, of the numerous fanciful residences of which the place was composed. It was a city of detached mansions; a Mediterranean lounging-place on the English Channel; and as seen now by night it seemed even more imposing than it was.

The sea was near at hand, but not intrusive; it murmured, and he thought it was the pines; the pines murmured in precisely the same tones, and he thought they were the sea.

Where could Tess possibly be, a cottage-girl, his young wife, amidst all this wealth and fashion? The more he pondered the more was he puzzled. Were there any cows to milk here? There certainly were no fields to till. She was most probably engaged to do something in one of these large houses; and he sauntered along, looking at the chamber-windows and their lights going out one by one; and wondered which of them might be hers.

Conjecture was useless, and just after twelve o'clock he entered and went to bed. Before putting out his light he re-read Tess's impassioned letter. Sleep, however, he could not, – so near her, yet so far from her – and he continually lifted the window-blind and regarded the backs of opposite houses, and wondered behind which of the sashes she reposed at that moment.

He might almost as well have sat up all night. In the morning he arose at seven, and shortly after went out, taking the direction of the chief post-office. At the door he met an intelligent postman coming out with letters for the morning delivery.

'Do you know the address of a Mrs Clare?' asked Angel.

The postman shook his head.

Then, remembering that she would have been likely to continue the use of her maiden name, Clare said –

'Or a Miss Durbeyfield?'

'Durbeyfield?'

This also was strange to the postman addressed.

'There's visitors coming and going every day, as you know, sir,' he said; 'and without the name of the house 'tis impossible to find 'em.'

One of his comrades hastening out at that moment, the name was repeated to him.

'I know no name of Durbeyfield; but there is the name of D'Urberville at The Herons,' said the second.

'That's it!' cried Clare, pleased to think that she had reverted to the real pronunciation. 'What place is The Herons?'

'A stylish lodging-house. 'Tis all lodging-houses here, bless 'ee.'

Clare received directions how to find the house, and hastened thither, arriving with the milkman. The Herons, though an ordinary villa, stood in its own grounds, and was certainly the last place in which one would have expected to find lodgings, so private was its appearance. If poor Tess was a servant here, as he feared, she would go to the back-door to that milkman, and he was inclined to go thither also. However, in his doubts he turned to the front, and rang.

The hour being early the landlady herself opened the door. Clare inquired for Teresa D'Urberville or Durbeyfield.

'Mrs D'Urberville?'

'Yes.'

Tess, then, passed as a married woman,[2] and he felt glad, even though she had not adopted his name.

'Will you kindly tell her that a relative is anxious to see her.'

'It is rather early. What name shall I give, sir?'

'Angel.'

'Mr Angel?'

'No; Angel. It is my Christian name. She'll understand.'

'I'll see if she is awake.'

He was shown into the front room – the dining-room – and looked out through the spring curtains at the little lawn, and the rhododendrons and other shrubs upon it. Obviously her position was by no means so bad as he had feared, and it crossed his mind that she must somehow have claimed and sold the jewels to attain it. He did not blame her for one moment. Soon his sharpened ear detected footsteps upon the stairs, at which his heart thumped so painfully that he could hardly stand firm. 'Dear me! what will she think of me, so altered as I am!' he said to himself; and the door opened.

Tess appeared on the threshold – not at all as he had expected to see her – bewilderingly otherwise, indeed. Her great natural beauty was at last rendered full justice by her attire. She was loosely wrapped in a rich cashmere dressing-gown of gray-white, embroidered in half-mourning tints, and she wore slippers of the same hue. Her neck rose out of a frill of down, and her well-known cable of dark-brown hair was partially coiled up in a mass at the back of her head and partly hanging on her shoulder – the evident result of haste.

He had held out his arms, but they had fallen again to his side; for she had not come forward, remaining still in the opening of the doorway. Mere yellow skeleton that he was now he felt the contrast between them, and thought his appearance distasteful to her.

'Tessy!' he said huskily, 'can you forgive me for going away? Can't you – come to me? How do you get to be – like this?'

'It is too late!' said she, her voice being so hard that it echoed in the room, her eye glittering unnaturally.

'I did not think rightly of you – I did not see you as you were!' he continued to plead. 'I do now, dearest Tessy, mine!'

'Too late, too late!'[3] she said rapidly, waving her hand in the impatience of a person whose tortures cause every instant to seem an hour. 'Don't come close to me, Angel! No – you must not. Keep away!'

'But don't you love me, my dear wife, because I have been so pulled down by illness? You are not so fickle – I am come on purpose for you – my mother and father will welcome you now!'

'Yes – O, yes, yes! But I say, I say it is too late!' she almost shrieked. She seemed to feel like a fugitive in a dream, who tried to move away, but could not. 'Don't you know all – don't you know it? Yet how do you come here if you do not know?'

'I inquired here and there, and I found the way.'

'I waited and waited for you!' she went on, her tones suddenly resuming their old fluty pathos. 'But you did not come. And I wrote to you, and you did not come! He kept on saying you would never come any more, and that I was a foolish woman. He was very kind to me, and mother, and to all of us after father's death. He —'

'I don't understand.'

'He has won me back to him.'

Clare looked at her keenly, then, gathering her meaning, flagged like one plague-stricken, and his glance sank; it fell on her hands, which, once rosy, were now white and delicate.

She continued—

'He is upstairs. I hate him now, because he told me a lie – that you would not come again; and you *have* come![4] But – will you go away, Angel, please, and never come any more?'

They stood fixed, their baffled hearts looking out of their eyes with a joylessness pitiful to see. Both seemed to implore something to shelter them from reality.

'Ah – it is my fault!' said Clare.

But he could not get on. Speech was as inexpressive as silence.[5]

A few instants passed, and he found that Tess was gone. His face grew colder and more shrunken as he stood concentrated on the moment, and a minute or two after he found himself in the street, walking along he did not know whither.

LVI

Mrs Brooks, the lady who was the householder at The Herons, and owner of all the handsome furniture, was not a person of an unusually curious turn of mind. She was too deeply materialized, poor woman, by her long and enforced bondage to that arithmetical demon Profit-and-Loss, to retain much curiosity for its own sake, and apart from possible lodgers' pockets. Nevertheless, the visit of Angel Clare to her well-paying tenants, Mr and Mrs D'Urberville, as she deemed them, was sufficiently exceptional in point of time and manner to reinvigorate the feminine proclivity which had been stifled down as useless save in its bearings on the letting trade.

Tess had spoken to her husband from the doorway, without entering the dining-room, and Mrs Brooks, who stood within the partly-closed door of her own sitting-room at the back of the passage, could hear fragments of the conversation – if conversation it could be called – between those two wretched souls. She heard Tess re-ascend the stairs to the first floor, and the departure of Clare, and the closing of the front door behind him. Then the door of the room above was shut, and Mrs Brooks knew that Tess had re-entered her apartment. As the young lady was not fully dressed Mrs Brooks knew that she would not emerge again for some time.

She accordingly ascended the stairs softly, and stood at the door of the front room – a drawing-room, connected with the room immediately behind it (which was a bedroom) by folding-doors in the common manner. This first floor, containing Mrs Brooks's best apartments, had been taken by the week by the D'Urbervilles. The back room was now in silence; but from the drawing-room there came sounds.

All that she could at first distinguish of them was one syllable, continually repeated in a low note of moaning, as if it came from a soul bound to some Ixionian wheel[1] –

'O – O – O!'

Then a silence, then a heavy sigh, and again –

'O – O – O!'

The landlady looked through the keyhole. Only a small space of the room inside was visible, but within that space came a corner of the breakfast-table, which was already spread for the meal, and also a chair beside. Over the seat of the chair Tess's face was bowed, her posture being a kneeling one in front of it; her hands were clasped over her head, the skirts of her dressing-gown and the embroidery of her nightgown flowed upon the floor behind her, and her stockingless feet, from which the slippers had fallen, protruded upon the carpet. It was from her lips that came the murmur of unspeakable despair.

Then a man's voice from the adjoining room –

'What's the matter?'

She did not answer, but went on, in a tone which was a soliloquy rather than an exclamation, and a dirge rather than a soliloquy. Mrs Brooks could only catch a portion:

'And then my dear, dear husband came home to me . . . and I did not know it . . . And you had used your cruel persuasion upon me . . . you did not stop using it – no – you did not stop! My little sisters and brothers and my mother's needs – they were the things you moved me by . . . and you said my husband would never come back – never; and you taunted me, and said what a simpleton I was to expect him . . . And at last I believed you and gave way! . . . And then he came back! Now he is gone. Gone a second time, and I have lost him now for ever . . . and he will not love me the littlest bit ever any more – only hate me . . . O yes, I have lost him now – again because of – you!' In writhing, with her head on the chair, she turned her face towards the door, and Mrs Brooks could see the pain upon it; and that her lips were bleeding from the clench of her teeth upon them, and that the long lashes of her closed eyes stuck in wet tags to her cheeks. She continued: 'And he is dying – he looks as if he is dying! . . . And my sin will kill him and not kill me! . . . O, you have torn my life all to pieces . . . made me a victim, a caged bird! . . . My own true husband will never, never – O God – I can't bear this! – I cannot!'

There were more words from the man; then a sudden rustle; she had sprung to her feet. Mrs Brooks, thinking that the speaker was coming to rush out of the door, hastily retreated down the stairs.

She need not have done so, however, for the door of the sitting-room was not opened. But Mrs Brooks felt it unsafe to watch on the landing again, and entered her own parlour below.

She could hear nothing through the floor, although she listened intently, and thereupon went to the kitchen to finish her interrupted breakfast. Coming up presently to the front room on the ground floor she took up some sewing, waiting for her lodgers to ring that she might take away the breakfast, which she meant to do herself, to discover what was the matter if possible. Overhead, as she sat, she could now hear the floorboards slightly creak, as if some one were walking about, and presently the movement was explained by the rustle of garments against the banisters, the opening and the closing of the front door, and the form of Tess passing to the gate on her way into the street. She was fully dressed now in the walking costume of a well-to-do young lady in which she had arrived, with the sole addition that over her hat and black feathers a veil was drawn.

Mrs Brooks had not been able to catch any word of farewell, temporary or otherwise, between her tenants at the door above. They might have quarrelled, or Mr D'Urberville might still be asleep, for he was not an early riser.

She went into the back room, which was more especially her own apartment, and continued her sewing there. The lady lodger did not return, nor did the gentleman ring his bell. Mrs Brooks pondered on the delay, and on what probable relation the visitor who had called so early bore to the couple upstairs. In reflecting she leant back in her chair.

As she did so her eyes glanced casually over the ceiling till they were arrested by a spot in the middle of its white surface which she had never noticed there before. It was about the size of a wafer when she first observed it, but it speedily grew as large as the palm of her hand, and then she could perceive that it was red. The oblong white ceiling, with this scarlet blot in the midst, had the appearance of a gigantic ace of hearts.

Mrs Brooks had strange qualms of misgiving. She got upon the table, and touched the spot in the ceiling with her fingers. It was damp, and she fancied that it was a blood stain.

Descending from the table, she left the parlour, and went upstairs, intending to enter the room overhead, which was the bedchamber at the back of the drawing-room. But, nerveless woman as she had now become, she could not bring herself to attempt the handle. She listened. The dead silence within was broken only by a regular beat.

Drip, drip, drip.

Mrs Brooks hastened downstairs, opened the front door, and ran into the street. A man she knew, one of the workmen employed at an adjoining villa, was passing by, and she begged him to come in and go upstairs with her; she feared something had happened to one of her lodgers. The workman assented, and followed her to the landing.

She opened the door of the drawing-room, and stood back for him to pass in, entering herself behind him. The room was empty; the breakfast – a substantial repast of coffee, eggs, and a cold ham – lay spread upon the table untouched, as when she had taken it up, excepting that the carving knife was missing. She asked the man to go through the folding-doors into the adjoining room.

He opened the doors, entered a step or two, and came back almost instantly with a rigid face. 'My good God, the gentleman in bed is dead! I think he has been hurt with a knife – a lot of blood has run down upon the floor!'

The alarm was soon given, and the house which had lately been so quiet resounded with the tramp of many footsteps, a surgeon among the rest. The wound was small, but the point of the blade had touched the heart of the victim, who lay on his back, pale, fixed, dead, as if he had scarcely moved after the infliction of the blow. In a quarter of an hour the news that a gentleman who was a temporary visitor to the town had been stabbed in his bed, spread through every street and villa of the popular watering-place.

LVII

Meanwhile Angel Clare had walked automatically along the way by which he had come, and, entering his hotel, sat down over the breakfast, staring at nothingness. He went on eating and drinking unconsciously till on a sudden he demanded his bill; having paid which he took his dressing-bag in his hand, the only luggage he had brought with him, and went out.

At the moment of his departure a telegram was handed to him – a few words from his mother, stating that they were glad to know his address, and informing him that his brother Cuthbert had proposed to and been accepted by Mercy Chant.

Clare crumpled up the paper, and followed the route to the station; reaching it, he found that there would be no train leaving for an hour and more. He sat down to wait, and having waited a quarter of an hour felt that he could wait there no longer. Broken in heart and numbed, he had nothing to hurry for, but he wished to get out of a town which had been the scene of such an experience, and turned to walk to the first station onward, and let the train pick him up there.

The highway that he followed was open, and at a little distance dipped into a valley, across which it could be seen running from edge to edge. He had traversed the greater part of this depression, and was climbing the western acclivity, when, pausing for breath, he unconsciously looked back. Why he did so he could not say, but something seemed to impel him to the act. The tape-like surface of the road diminished in his rear as far as he could see, and as he gazed a moving spot intruded on the white vacuity of its perspective.

It was a human figure running. Clare waited, with a dim sense that somebody was trying to overtake him.

The form descending the incline was a woman's, yet so entirely was his mind blinded to the idea of his wife's following him that even when she came nearer he did not recognize her under the totally changed attire in which he now beheld her. It was not till she was quite close that he could believe her to be Tess.

'I saw you – turn away from the station – just before I got there – and I have been following you all this way!'

She was so pale, so breathless, so quivering in every muscle, that he did not ask her a single question, but seizing her hand, and pulling it within his arm, he led her along. To avoid meeting any possible wayfarers he left the high road, and took a footpath under some fir-trees. When they were deep among the moaning boughs he stopped and looked at her inquiringly.

'Angel,' she said, as if waiting for this, 'do you know what I have been running after you for? To tell you that I have killed him!' A pitiful white smile lit her face as she spoke.

'What!' said he, thinking from the strangeness of her manner that she was in some delirium.

'I have done it – I don't know how,' she continued. 'Still, I owed it to 'ee, and to myself, Angel. I feared long ago, when I struck him on the mouth with my glove, that I might do it some day for the wrong he did me in my simple youth, and to you through me. He has come between us and ruined us, and now he can never do it any more. I never loved him at all, Angel, as I loved you. You know it, don't you? You believe it? You didn't come back to me, and I was obliged to go back to him. Why did you go away – why did you – when I loved you so? I can't think why you did it. But I don't blame you; only, Angel, will you forgive me my sin against you, now I have killed him? I thought as I ran along that you would be sure to forgive me now I have done that. It came to me as an enlightenment[1] that I should get you back that way. I could not bear the loss of 'ee any longer – you don't know how entirely I was unable to bear your not loving me! Say you do now, dear, dear husband; say you do, now I have killed him!'

'I do love you, Tess – O, I do – it is all come back!' he said, tightening his arms round her with fevered pressure. 'But how do you mean – you have killed him?'

'I mean that I have,' she murmured in a reverie.

'What, bodily? Is he dead?'

'Yes. He heard me crying about you, and he bitterly taunted me; and called you by a foul name; and then I did it. My heart could not bear it. He had taunted me about you before. And then I dressed myself and came away to find you.'

By degrees he was inclined to believe that she had faintly attempted, at least, what she said she had done; and his horror at her impulse was mixed with amazement at the strength of her affection for himself, and at the strangeness of its quality, which had apparently extinguished her moral sense altogether. Unable to realize the gravity of her conduct she seemed at last content; and he looked at her as she lay upon his shoulder, weeping with happiness, and wondered what obscure strain in the D'Urberville blood had led to this aberration – if it were an aberration. There momentarily flashed through his mind that the family tradition might have arisen because the D'Urbervilles had been known to do these things. As well as his confused and excited ideas could reason, he supposed that in the moment of mad grief of which she spoke her mind had lost its balance, and plunged her into this abyss.

It was very terrible if true; if a temporary hallucination sad. But, anyhow, here was this deserted wife of his, this passionately-fond woman, clinging to him without a suspicion that he would be anything to her but a protector. He saw that for him to be otherwise was not, in her mind, within the region of the possible. Tenderness was absolutely dominant in Clare at last. He kissed her endlessly with his white lips, and held her hand, and said –

'I will not desert you! I will protect you by every means in my power, dearest love, whatever you may have done or not have done!'

They then walked on under the trees, Tess turning her head every now and then to look at him. Worn and unhandsome as he had become, it was plain that she did not discern the least fault in his appearance. To her he was, as of old, all that was perfection, personally and mentally. He was still her Antinous, her Apollo even;[2] his sickly face was beautiful as the morning to her affectionate regard on this day no less than when she first beheld him; for was it not the face of the one man on earth who had loved her purely, and who had believed in her as pure.

With an instinct as to possibilities he did not now, as he had intended, make for the first station beyond the town, but plunged still farther under the firs, which here abounded for miles. Each clasping the other round the waist they promenaded over the dry bed of fir-needles, thrown into a vague intoxicating atmosphere at the consciousness of being together at last, with no living soul between them; ignoring that there was a corpse. Thus they proceeded for several miles till Tess, arousing herself, looked about her, and said, timidly –

'Are we going anywhere in particular?'

'I don't know, dearest. Why?'

'I don't know.'

'Well, we might walk a few miles farther, and when it is evening find lodgings somewhere or other – in a lonely cottage, perhaps. Can you walk well, Tessy?'

'O yes! I could walk for ever and ever with your arm round me!'

Upon the whole it seemed a good thing to do. Thereupon they quickened their pace, avoiding high roads, and following obscure paths tending more or less northward. But there was an unpractical vagueness in their movements throughout the day; neither one of them seemed to consider any question of effectual escape, disguise, or long concealment. Their every idea was temporary and unforefending, like the plans of two children.

At mid-day they drew near to a roadside inn, and Tess would have entered it with him to get something to eat, but he persuaded her to remain among the trees and bushes of this half-woodland, halfmoorland part of the country, till he should come back. Her clothes were of the latest fashion, even to the dainty ivory-handled parasol that she carried, a fashion unknown in the retired spot to which they had now wandered; and the cut of such articles would have attracted attention in the settle of a tavern. He soon returned, with food enough for half-a-dozen people and two bottles of wine – enough to last them for a day or more, should any emergency arise.

They sat down upon some dead boughs and shared their meal. Between one and two o'clock they packed up the remainder and went on again.

'I feel strong enough to walk any distance,' said she.

'I think we may as well steer in a general northerly direction, and perhaps get to London by degrees,' remarked Clare. 'Vessels go thence to every part of the world, if we wish to leave; and we are less likely to be seen there than at the ports on the Channel.'[3]

She made no reply to this beyond that of clasping him more tightly. Though the season was an English May the weather was serenely bright, and during the afternoon it was quite warm. Through the latter miles of their walk their footpath had taken them into the depths of the New Forest, and towards evening, turning the corner of a lane, they perceived behind an ornamental gate a large board on which was painted in white letters, 'This desirable Mansion to be Let Furnished;' particulars following, with directions to apply to some London agents. Passing through the gate they could see the house, a dignified building of regular design and large accommodation.

'I know it,' said Clare. 'It is Bramshurst Manor-house.[4] You can see that it is shut up, and grass is growing on the drive.'

'Some of the windows are open,' said Tess.

'Just to air the rooms, I suppose.'

'All these rooms empty, and we without a roof to our heads!'

'You are getting tired, my Tessy,' he said. 'We'll stop soon.' And kissing her sad mouth he again led her onwards.

He was growing weary likewise, for they had walked not less than twenty miles, and it became necessary to consider what they should do for rest. They looked from afar at isolated cottages and little inns, and were inclined to approach one of the latter, when their hearts failed them, and they sheered off. At length their gait dragged, and they stood still.

'Could we sleep under the trees?' she asked.

He thought the season insufficiently advanced.

'I have been thinking of that empty mansion we passed,' he said. 'Let us go back towards it again.'

They retraced their steps, but it was half an hour before they stood without the entrance-gate as earlier. He then requested her to stay where she was, whilst he went to see who was within.

She sat down among the bushes within the gate, and Clare crept towards the house. His absence lasted some considerable time, and when he returned Tess was wildly anxious, not for herself, but for him. He had found out from a boy that there was only an old woman in charge as caretaker, and she only came there on fine days, from the hamlet near, to open and shut the windows. She would come to shut them at sunset. 'Now, we can get in through one of the lower windows, and rest there,' said he.

Under his escort she went tardily forward to the main front, whose shuttered windows, like sightless eyeballs, excluded the possibility of watchers. The door was reached by a flight of steps, and one of the windows beside it was open. Clare clambered in, and pulled Tess in after him.

Except the hall the rooms were all in darkness, and they ascended the staircase. Up here also the shutters were tightly closed, the ventilation being perfunctorily done, for this day at least, by opening the hall-window in front and an upper window behind. Clare unlatched the door of a large chamber, felt his way across it, and parted the shutters to the width of two or three inches. A shaft of dazzling sunlight glanced into the room, revealing heavy, old-fashioned furniture, crimson damask hangings, and an enormous four-post bedstead, along the head of which were carved running figures, apparently Atalanta's race.[5]

'Rest at last!' said he, setting down his bag and the parcel of viands.

They remained in great quietness till the caretaker should have come to shut the windows: as a precaution, putting themselves in total darkness by barring the shutters as before, lest the woman should open the door of their chamber for any casual reason. Between six and seven o'clock she came, but did not approach the wing they were in. They heard her close the windows, fasten them, lock the door, and go away. Then Clare again stole a chink of light from the window, and they shared another meal, till by and by they were enveloped in the shades of night which they had no candle to disperse.

LVIII

The night was strangely solemn and still. In the small hours she whispered to him the whole story of how he had walked in his sleep with her in his arms across the Froom stream, at the imminent risk of both their lives, and laid her down in the stone coffin at the ruined abbey. He had never known of that till now.

'Why didn't you tell me next day!' he said. 'It might have prevented much misunderstanding and woe.'

'Don't think of what's past!' said she. 'I am not going to think outside of now. Why should we! Who knows what to-morrow has in store?'

But it apparently had no sorrow. The morning was wet and foggy, and Clare, rightly informed that the caretaker only opened the windows on fine days, ventured to creep out of their chamber, and explore the house, leaving Tess asleep. There was no food on the premises, but there was water, and he took advantage of the fog to emerge from the mansion, and fetch tea, bread, and butter, from a shop in the little town two miles beyond.[1] His re-entry awoke her; and they breakfasted on what he had brought.

They were indisposed to stir abroad, and the day passed, and the night following, and the next, and next; till, almost without their being aware, five days had slipped by in absolute seclusion, not a sight or sound of a human being disturbing their reposefulness, such as it was. The changes of the weather were their only events, the birds of the New Forest their only company. By tacit consent they hardly once spoke of any incident of the past subsequent to their wedding-day. The gloomy intervening time seemed to sink into chaos, over which the present and prior times closed as if it never had been. Whenever he suggested that they should leave their shelter, and go forwards towards Southampton or London, she showed a strange unwillingness to move.

'Why should we put an end to all that's sweet and lovely!' she deprecated. 'What must come will come.' And, looking through the shutter-chink: 'All is trouble outside there; inside here content.'

He peeped out also. It was quite true; within was affection, pity, error forgiven: outside was the inexorable.

'And – and,' she said, pressing her cheek against his; 'I fear that what you think of me now may not last. I do not wish to outlive your present feeling for me. I would rather not. I would rather be dead and buried when the time comes for you to despise me, so that it may never be known to me that you despised me.'

'I cannot ever despise you.'

'I also hope that. But considering what my life has been I cannot see why any man should, sooner or later, be able to help despising me . . . How wickedly mad I was! Yet formerly I never could bear to hurt a fly or a worm, and the sight of a bird in a cage used often to make me cry.'

They remained yet another day. In the night the dull sky cleared, and the result was that the old caretaker at the cottage awoke early. The brilliant sunrise made her unusually brisk; she decided to open the contiguous mansion immediately, and to air it thoroughly on such a day. Thus it occurred that, having arrived and opened the lower rooms before six o'clock, she ascended to the bedchambers, and was about to turn the handle of the one wherein they lay. At that moment she fancied she could hear the breathing of persons within. Her slippers and her antiquity had rendered her progress a noiseless one so far, and she made for instant retreat; then, deeming that her hearing might have deceived her, she turned anew to the door and softly tried the handle. The lock was out of order, but a piece of furniture had been moved forward on the inside, which prevented her opening the door more than an inch or two. A stream of morning light through the shutter-chink fell upon the faces of the pair, wrapped in profound slumber, Tess's lips being parted like a half-opened flower near his cheek. The caretaker was so struck with their innocent appearance, and with the elegance of Tess's gown hanging across a chair, her silk stockings beside it, the ivory parasol, and the other dainty habits in which she had arrived, that her first indignation at the effrontery of tramps and vagabonds gave way to a momentary sentimentality over this genteel elopement, as it seemed. She closed the door, and withdrew as softly as she had come, to go and consult with her neighbours on the odd discovery.

Not more than a minute had elapsed after her withdrawal when Tess woke, and then Clare. Both had a sense that something had disturbed them, though they could not say what; and the uneasy feeling which it engendered grew stronger. As soon as he was dressed he narrowly scanned the lawn through the two or three inches of shutter-chink.

'I think we will leave at once,' said he. 'It is a fine day. And I cannot help fancying somebody is about the house. At any rate, the woman will be sure to come to-day.'

She passively assented, and, putting the room in order they took up the few articles that belonged to them, and departed noiselessly. When they had got into the Forest she turned to take a last look at the house.

'Ah, happy house – good-bye!' she said. 'My life can only be a question of a few weeks. Why should we not have stayed there?'

'Don't say it, Tess! We shall get to some port in two or three days. But perhaps it will be best to avoid London after all; and Southampton too, although it is near. Suppose we try Bristol?'

Having thus desultorily thought of a new course he adopted it, bearing approximately towards the last-named port. Their long repose at the manor-house lent them walking power now; and towards mid-day they approached the steepled city of Melchester, which lay directly in their way. He decided to rest her in a clump of trees during the afternoon, and push onward under cover of darkness. At dusk Clare purchased food as usual, and their night march began, the boundary between Upper and Mid-Wessex being crossed about eight o'clock.

Their course bowed to the right of a direct line, by reason of the intervening city. To walk across country without much regard to roads was not new to Tess, and she showed her old agility in the performance. One townlet, ancient Ambresbury, they were obliged to pass through in order to take advantage of the town bridge for crossing a large river. It was between two and three in the morning when they went along the deserted street, lighted by an oil lamp here and there, and bordered by no pavement to echo their footsteps. The massive church-tower rose on their right hand, and beyond it was the stone bridge they sought. Once over this they followed the turnpike road, which plunged across an open plain.

Though the sky was dense with cloud a diffused light from some fragment of a moon had hitherto helped them a little. But the moon had now sunk, the clouds seemed to settle almost on their heads, and the night grew as dark as a cave. However, they found their way along, keeping as much on the turf as possible that their tread might not resound, which it was easy to do, there being no hedge or fence of any kind. All around was open loneliness and black solitude over which a stiff breeze blew.

They had proceeded thus gropingly two or three miles when on a sudden Clare became conscious of some vast erection close in his front, rising sheer from the grass. They had almost struck themselves against it.

'What monstrous place is this?' said Angel.

'It hums,' said she. 'Hearken!'

He listened. The wind, playing upon the edifice, produced a booming tune, like the note of some gigantic one-stringed harp. No other sound came from it, and lifting his hand and advancing a step or two, Clare felt the vertical surface of the wall. It seemed to be of solid stone, without joint or moulding. Carrying his fingers onward he found that what he had come in contact with was a colossal rectangular pillar; by stretching out his left hand he could feel a similar one adjoining. At an indefinite height overhead something made the black sky blacker, which had the semblance of a vast architrave uniting the pillars horizontally. They carefully entered beneath and between; the surfaces echoed their soft rustle; but they seemed to be still out of doors.

The place was roofless. Tess drew her breath fearfully, and Angel, perplexed, said –

'What can it be?'

Feeling sideways they encountered another tower-like pillar, square and uncompromising as the first; beyond it another and another. The place was all doors and pillars, some connected above by continuous architraves.

'A very Temple of the Winds,' he said.

The next pillar was isolated; others composed a trilithon; others were prostrate, their flanks forming a causeway wide enough for a carriage; and it was soon obvious that they made up a forest of monoliths grouped upon the grassy expanse of the plain. The couple advanced farther into this pavilion of the night till they stood in its midst.

'It is Stonehenge!' said Clare.

'The heathen temple, you mean?'

'Yes. Older than the centuries; older than the D'Urbervilles! Well, what shall we do, darling? We may find shelter farther on.'

But Tess, really tired by this time, flung herself upon an oblong slab that lay close at hand, and was sheltered from the wind by a pillar. Owing to the action of the sun during the preceding day the stone was warm and dry, in comforting contrast to the rough and chill grass around, which had damped her skirts and shoes.

'I don't want to go any farther, Angel,' she said stretching out her hand for his. 'Can't we bide here?'

'I fear not. This spot is visible for miles by day, although it does not seem so now.'

'One of my mother's people was a shepherd hereabouts, now I think of it. And you used to say at Talbothays that I was a heathen. So now I am at home.'

He knelt down beside her outstretched form, and put his lips upon hers.

'Sleepy are you, dear? I think you are lying on an altar.'

'I like very much to be here,' she murmured. 'It is so solemn and lonely – after my great happiness – with nothing but the sky above my face. It seems as if there were no folk in the world but we two; and I wish there were not – except 'Liza-Lu.'

Clare thought she might as well rest here till it should get a little lighter, and he flung his overcoat upon her, and sat down by her side.

'Angel, if anything happens to me, will you watch over 'Liza-Lu for my sake?' she asked, when they had listened a long time to the wind among the pillars.

'I will.'

'She is so good and simple and pure. O, Angel – I wish you would marry her if you lose me, as you will do shortly. O, if you would!'

'If I lose you I lose all! And she is my sister-in-law.'[2]

'That's nothing, dearest. People marry sisters-in-law continually about Marlott; and 'Liza-Lu is so gentle and sweet, and she is growing so beautiful. O I could share you with her willingly when we are spirits! If you would train her and teach her, Angel, and bring her up for your own self! . . . She has all the best of me without the bad of me; and if she were to become yours it would almost seem as if death had not divided us[3] . . . Well, I have said it. I won't mention it again.'

She ceased, and he fell into thought. In the far north-east sky he could see between the pillars a level streak of light. The uniform concavity of black cloud was lifting bodily like the lid of a pot, letting in at the earth's edge the coming day, against which the towering monoliths and trilithons began to be blackly defined.

'Did they sacrifice to God here?' asked she.

'No,' said he.

'Who to?'

'I believe to the sun. That lofty stone set away by itself is in the direction of the sun, which will presently rise behind it.'[4]

'This reminds me, dear,' she said. 'You remember you never would interfere with any belief o' mine before we were married? But I knew your mind all the same, and I thought as you thought – not from any reasons o' my own, but because you thought so. Tell me now, Angel, do you think we shall meet again after we are dead? I want to know.'

He kissed her to avoid a reply at such a time.

'O, Angel – I fear that means no!' said she, with a suppressed sob.

'And I wanted so to see you again – so much, so much! What – not even you and I, Angel, who love each other so well?'

Like a greater than himself, to the critical question at the critical time he did not answer;[5] and they were again silent. In a minute or two her breathing became more regular, her clasp of his hand relaxed, and she fell asleep. The band of silver paleness along the east horizon made even the distant parts of the Great Plain appear dark and near; and the whole enormous landscape bore that impress of reserve, taciturnity, and hesitation which is usual just before day. The eastward pillars and their architraves stood up blackly against the light, and the great flame-shaped Sun-stone beyond them; and the Stone of Sacrifice midway. Presently the night wind died out, and the quivering little pools in the cup-like hollows of the stones lay still. At the same time something seemed to move on the verge of the dip eastward – a mere dot. It was the head of a man approaching them from the hollow beyond the Sun-stone. Clare wished they had gone onward, but in the circumstances decided to remain quiet. The figure came straight towards the circle of pillars in which they were.

He heard something behind him, the brush of feet. Turning, he saw over the prostrate columns another figure; then, before he was aware, another was at hand on the right, under a trilithon, and another on the left. The dawn shone full on the front of the man westward, and Clare could discern from this that he was tall, and walked as if trained. They all closed in with evident purpose. Her story then was true! Springing to his feet, he looked around for a weapon, means of escape, anything. By this time the nearest man was upon him.

'It is no use, sir,' he said. 'There are sixteen of us on the Plain, and the whole county is reared.'

'Let her finish her sleep!' he implored in a whisper of the men, as they gathered round.

When they saw where she lay, which they had not done till then, they showed no objection, and stood watching her, as still as the pillars around. He went to the stone and bent over her, holding one poor little hand; her breathing now was quick and small, like that of a lesser creature than a woman. All waited in the growing light, their faces and hands as if they were silvered, the remainder of their figures dark, the stones glistening green-gray, the Plain still a mass of shade. Soon the light was strong, and a ray shone upon her unconscious form, peering under her eyelids and waking her.

'What is it, Angel?' she said, starting up. 'Have they come for me?'

'Yes, dearest,' he said. 'They have come.'

'It is as it should be,' she murmured. 'Angel, I am almost glad – yes, glad! This happiness could not have lasted. It was too much. I have had enough; and now I shall not live for you to despise me!'

She stood up, shook herself, and went forward, neither of the men having moved.

'I am ready,' she said quietly.

LIX

The city of Wintoncester, that fine old city, aforetime capital of Wessex, lay amidst its convex and concave downlands in all the brightness and warmth of a July morning. The gabled brick, tile, and freestone houses had almost dried off for the season their integument of lichen, the streams in the meadows were low, and in the sloping High Street, from the West Gateway to the mediæval cross, and from the mediæval cross to the bridge, that leisurely dusting and sweeping was in progress which usually ushers in an old-fashioned market-day.

From the western gate aforesaid the highway, as every Wintonces-trian knows, ascends a long and regular incline of the exact length of a measured mile, leaving the houses gradually behind. Up this road from the precincts of the city two persons were walking rapidly, as if unconscious of the trying ascent – unconscious through preoccupation and not through buoyancy. They seemed anxious to get out of the sight of the houses and of their kind, and this road appeared to offer the quickest means of doing so. Though they were young they walked with bowed heads, which gait of grief the sun's rays smiled on piteously.

One of the pair was Angel Clare, the other a tall budding creature – half girl, half woman – a spiritualized image of Tess, slighter than she, but with the same beautiful eyes – Clare's sister-in-law, 'Liza-Lu. Their pale faces seemed to have shrunk to half their natural size. They moved on hand in hand, and never spoke a word, the drooping of their heads being that of Giotto's 'Two Apostles.'[1]

When they had nearly reached the top of the great West Hill the clocks in the town struck eight. Each gave a start at the notes, and, walking onward yet a few steps, they reached the first milestone, standing whitely on the green margin of the grass, and backed by the down, which here was open to the road. They entered upon the turf, and, impelled by an irresistible force, slackened their speed, stood still, turned, and waited beside the stone.

The prospect from this summit was almost unlimited. In the valley beneath lay the city they had just left, its more prominent buildings showing as in an isometric drawing – among them the broad cathedral tower, with its Norman windows and immense length of aisle and nave, the spires of St Thomas's, the pinnacled tower of the College, and, more to the right, the tower and gables of the ancient hospice, where to this day the pilgrim may receive his dole of bread and ale. Behind the city swept the rotund upland of St Catherine's Hill; farther off, landscape beyond landscape, till the horizon was lost in the radiance of the sun hanging above it.

Against these far stretches of country rose, in front of the other city edifices, a large red-brick building, with level gray roofs, and rows of short barred windows bespeaking captivity, the whole contrasting greatly by its formalism with the quaint irregularities of the Gothic erections. It was somewhat disguised from the road in passing it by yews and evergreen oaks, but it was visible enough up here. From the middle of the building an ugly flat-topped octagonal tower ascended against the east horizon, and viewed from this spot, on its shady side and against the light, it seemed the one blot on the city's beauty. Yet it was with this blot, and not with the beauty, that the two gazers were concerned.

Upon the cornice of the tower a tall staff was fixed. Their eyes were riveted on it. A few minutes after the hour had struck something moved slowly up the staff, and extended itself upon the breeze. It was a black flag.

'Justice' was done, and the President of the Immortals (in Æschylean phrase) had ended his sport with Tess.[2] And the D'Urberville knights slept on in their tombs unknowing. The two speechless gazers bent themselves down to the earth, as if in prayer, and remained thus a long time, absolutely motionless: the flag continued to wave silently. As soon as they had strength they arose, joined hands again, and went on.[3]

THE END

NOTES

Tess of the D'Urbervilles has been well served by its editors and textual critics. In compiling these notes I have been deeply indebted to two indispensable works, Grindle and Gatrell's critical edition and Laird's *The Shaping of 'Tess of the d'Urbervilles'*, and to the editors of the reader's editions listed below.

The following abbreviations are used for variant texts and editions cited in the notes (see also Bibliographical Note):

MS.	Manuscript (the 1889 manuscript foliation is distinguished as the 'Ur-*Tess*')
Graphic	*Graphic* edition
1891	Three-volume first edition, published by Osgood, McIlvaine and Co.
1892	One-volume 'Fifth Edition'
1895	Osgood, McIlvaine Wessex Novels Edition
1900	Harper Paperback Edition
1902	Macmillan Uniform Edition
1912	Macmillan Wessex Edition
Barrineau	Explanatory Notes to World's Classics Edition (ed. Juliet Grindle and Simon Gatrell) by Nancy Barrineau (1988)
Furbank	New Wessex Edition, ed. P. N. Furbank (1974)
Gibson	Everyman Edition, ed. James Gibson (1993)

NB: Throughout the notes the spelling of 'D'Urberville' follows the text of this edition – with a capital 'D' – except where quotations come from sources which use the later 'd'Urberville'.

Place-names have not been included in the explanatory notes; the common association of Hardy's location and its 'original', sketched in the 1895 Preface (Appendix I), is given in Appendix II.

TITLE-PAGE

A PURE WOMAN FAITHFULLY PRESENTED BY THOMAS HARDY: Hardy appended this controversial subtitle just as 1891 was going to print, possibly as an oblique retort to Mowbray Morris, who read and criticized the Ur-*Tess* (see 'A History of the Text'). Writing to Roden Noel in May 1892, Hardy claimed: 'Reading over the story after it was finished, the conviction was thrust upon me . . . that the heroine was essentially pure – purer than many a so-called unsullied virgin: therefore I called her so . . . But the parochial British understanding knocks itself against this word like a humblebee against a wall, not seeing that "paradoxical morality" may have a very great deal to say for itself, especially in a work of fiction' (*Collected Letters*, I, 267). Hardy also made important changes in the MS. in an attempt to establish Tess's purity: see Chapter x, note 3 and Chapter xxviii, note 7.

Poor wounded name . . . lodge thee: *The Two Gentlemen of Verona*, I.ii.115–16, which continues: 'till thy wound be thoroughly healed' (quotations from Alfred Harbage (ed.), *William Shakespeare: The Complete Works* (New York: Viking, 1975)). The strikingly personal tone of this epigraph, and the identity of its implied speaker, have puzzled readers since it first appeared in 1891.

EXPLANATORY NOTE

1. *The main portion . . . as episodic sketches*: These chapters are reproduced in Appendix V.

2. *as originally written two years ago*: Laird (pp. 17–20) observes that Hardy is being disingenuous here: the MS. as it was written in November 1889 (the Ur-*Tess*) is very different from 1891 (see 'A History of the Text').

3. *as representing on the whole . . . things*: For 1892 Hardy emended this to the now well-known explanation of his aims and intentions: 'an attempt to give artistic form to a true sequence of things'.

4. *a well-worn sentence . . . be concealed*: This has not been identified. John Goode notes that Hardy could have read an account of St Jerome, who was 'notorious for his violent adherence to chastity', in F. W. Farrar, *Lives of the Fathers: Sketches of Church History and Biography* (London, 1889), II, pp. 203–402 (*Thomas Hardy: The Offensive Truth* (Oxford: Basil Blackwell, 1988), p. 177n).

PHASE THE FIRST

The Maiden

PHASE THE FIRST: In the MS. and earlier editions Hardy labelled the part divisions more conventionally as 'Books', and there are five. Dividing the heroine's life into 'phases' has the effect of stressing both the discontinuities in the narrative (many of the events in the plot in fact fall between phases) and its tragic necessity (as inevitable as the phases of the moon).

CHAPTER I

1. *the antiquary*: The amateur antiquary was an often scorned figure in the nineteenth century, despite the growing popularity of antiquarian clubs (Hardy was a member of Dorset Natural History and Antiquarian Field Club) which, as Philippa Levine points out, 'did little to temper the vulgar view of the antiquarian as a man so transported by past delights as to be almost wholly unaware of, or at least indifferent to, the age in which he lived' (*The Amateur and the Professional: Antiquarians, Historians, Archaeologists in Victorian England, 1838–1885* (Cambridge: Cambridge University Press, 1986), p. 17). Parson Tringham is a sententious figure in this tradition, whose mildly comic self-importance and indifference to his own age ironically motivates the tragedy.

2. *the D'Urbervilles*: Hardy based the ancestral name of the Durbeyfields on the Turbervilles of Bere Regis, which he derived from his copy of the third edition of *The History and Antiquities of the County of Dorset* (1861–70) by John Hutchins (1698–1733): 'The Turberviles . . . derived their descent from sir *Pagon* or *Payne de Turbervile* who came out of France with William the Conqueror, as appears by Battel-Abby Roll. He was one of the twelve knights who assisted Robert Fitz-Haman, lord of Estremavilla in Normandy . . . in his conquest of Glamorganshire . . . This family of Turbervile . . . appear very early in the pipe or great rolls . . . *William* de Turbevile . . . gave the manor of Ansty, C. Wilts, to the knights hospitalers' (Furbank, 422).

Hardy tried several corruptions of D'Urberville, including Turbeyfield, Troublefield and Troublewell. (In the novel's earliest form in the MS., before he had settled on D'Urberville as the ancestral name, 'Bridehead' and 'Pride' also occur as the family name.)

According to Sydney Cockerell's recollection of a conversation, moreover, Hardy had once considered calling the novel *Tess of the Hardys*, in light of his deep interest in his own fallen family. In *Life* Hardy records notes from a preparatory journey to the country of *Tess* in September 1888:

The decline and fall of the Hardys much in evidence hereabout [i.e. the Vale of Blackmoor]. An instance: Becky S.'s mother's sister married one of the Hardys of this branch, who was considered to have demeaned himself by the marriage. 'All Woolcombe and Froom Quintin belonged to them at one time,' Becky used to say proudly. She might have added Up-Sydling and Toller Welme. This particular couple had an enormous lot of children. I remember when young seeing the man – tall and thin – walking beside a horse and common spring-trap, and my mother pointing him out to me and saying he represented what was once the leading branch of the family. So we go down, down, down. (p. 224)

The ancient Hardys are mentioned in Chapter XIX.

3. *Battle Abbey roll*: The Abbey of St Martin's in Battle is near Hastings in Sussex, and commemorates the victory of William the Conqueror in 1066. The Abbey Roll is said to contain the names of the knights and men who formed William's army, though this is doubtful. Its authenticity was first claimed by Holinshed in 1577, who published 629 names.

4. *Never heard it before*: In the Ur-*Tess*, the family has always known about their ancestry. When the heroine visits the 'Turberville' tombs, she beholds the figures she has known about 'since her infancy'. The discovery of the D'Urberville ancestry therefore originally played no part in motivating the tragedy.

5. *the Pipe Rolls . . . Royal Oak*: From King Stephen's time (1135–54) until the nineteenth century, the Pipe Rolls were the annual records of revenue kept by the British Exchequer. King John ruled 1199–1216. The Order of Knights Hospitaller of St John of Jerusalem was founded in the eleventh century, and along with the Knights Templar, they were the most formidable military order in the Holy Land. Edward II ruled 1307–27. Oliver Cromwell was Lord Protector of the republican Commonwealth of England, Scotland and Ireland, 1653–8. Charles II ruled 1660–85, and the Knights of the Royal Oak were 'a fictitious order of knights based by Hardy on the story of Charles II's hiding in an oak tree after the battle of Worcester (1651)' (Gibson, 377).

6. *if knighthood were hereditary, like a baronetcy*: The rank of baronet is the lowest hereditary rank in Britain. It was, however, only introduced in 1611 (by James I).

7. *Purbeck-marble canopies*: Purbeck marble is a fine form of the hard limestone quarried on the isle of Purbeck, the peninsula on the Dorset coast. It was used extensively in building.

8. *how are the mighty fallen*: Parson Tringham's cliché comes from the refrain of David's lamentation over Saul and his son Jonathan in 2 Samuel 1: 19, 25 and 27. See also Chapter LIV.

9. *There are several . . . lustre*: Many of the references to other noble families fallen to cottagers and labourers were added to 1891. In Hardy's fiction, and in his 1883 article in *Longman's Magazine* 'The Dorsetshire Labourer' (used extensively in *Tess*: see Chapters XVIII, note 9; LI, notes 1 and 4; and LII, note 1), he took considerable pains to correct urban stereotypes of rural social life. In the Wessex village, dependent agricultural labourers, such as Tess later mixes with, were sharply distinguished from the cottagers, the families of Durbeyfield's class who were self-employed in small-scale enterprises such as tranting (delivering goods or conveying passengers by cart, as the Dewys do in *Under the Greenwood Tree*) or haggling. The cottager's superior status was sustained by his modest dwelling, held either by freehold or, more typically in Hardy's fiction, by the tenuous copyhold (which must be renewed by each generation), or lifehold (see Chapter L, note 5). Hardy wrote in 'The Dorsetshire Labourer' that 'there is no more comfortable or serene being than the cottager who is sure of his roof'.

10. *club-walking*: During Whitsuntide (which begins on the seventh Sunday after Easter), members of parish clubs, or friendly societies, walked in procession around the village soliciting contributions for their members.

CHAPTER II

1. *an unenclosed character to the landscape*: Enclosure, which transformed communal fields, meadows and pastures into individually owned farm plots, began in England in the twelfth century. Although it proceeded rapidly during the early modern period, its most extensive impact was during the industrial age (from about 1750 to 1860), when it was pursued mainly for the sake of agricultural efficiency. The effects are felt most distinctly in *Tess* in later chapters, which focus on modern agricultural practices, and draw the reader's attention to the invisible presence of urban modernity in rural England. See Raymond Williams, *The Country and the City* (London: Chatto and Windus, 1973), and Keith Snell, *Annals of the Labouring Poor: Social Change and Agrarian England, 1660–1900* (Cambridge: Cambridge University Press, 1985), which points out that Dorset was one of the last counties to see the spread of parliamentary enclosure.

2. *The Vale was known . . . a heavy fine*: John Udal, in his *Dorsetshire Folk-Lore* (Hertford: Stephen Austin, 1922), records the legend of Henry III and the white hart he spared in the Vale of Blackmoor. When the hart was killed by other hunters, Henry punished them and taxed the land.

3. *Cerealia*: A festival in honour of Ceres, the Roman goddess of agriculture.

4. *It had walked for hundreds of years*: In 1892 Hardy expanded on the survival of women's club-walking in Marlott, adding that if it no longer walked as a 'benefit-club', it did so as a 'votive sisterhood of some sort'. The sisterhood of Tess's loyal friends at Crick's dairy will be significant.

5. *Old Style days*: From the fourteenth century until September 1752, the Julian Old Style calendar set the beginning of the year at 25 March. The 'Old Style days' were therefore more than a century earlier. See also Chapter XLII, note 4. (The Gregorian calendar, established by Pope Gregory XIII in October 1582, set 1 January as the beginning of the year, and was widely referred to as the New Style calendar.)

6. *a Georgian style*: It is likely that Hardy has in mind styles from the early nineteenth century, although 'Georgian' may refer to the fashions of the entire Hanoverian reign (from the accession of George I in 1714 to the death of George IV in 1830).

7. *I have no pleasure in them*: 'Remember now thy Creator in the days of thy youth, while the evil days come not, nor the years draw nigh, when thou shalt say, I have no pleasure in them' (Ecclesiastes 12: 1, Authorized Version). In the Ur-*Tess*, Tess's mother was among the elder women attending the club-walking.

8. *mobile peony mouth*: Tess has 'soft peony cheeks' in the toned-down *Graphic* version. Compare the 'peony lips' in Hardy's poem 'Julie-Jane' (in *Time's Laughingstocks* (1909)).

9. *She wore a red ribbon in her hair*: Tony Tanner traces uses of red and white in 'Colour and Movement in Hardy's *Tess of the d'Urbervilles*', *Critical Quarterly* 10 (1968), 219–39.

10. *The dialect . . . despite the village school*: See Chapter III, note 6.

11. *Phases of her childhood . . . still*: The novel repeatedly stresses that Tess is physically a woman, but in character and experience a child ('on the momentary threshold of womanhood' (Chapter X)). As the novel developed in MS., Tess grew more womanly (in the earlier stages, she is younger and less self-possessed). See also Chapter VII.

12. *Yet few knew, and still fewer considered this*: An echo of William Wordsworth's Lucy, who 'lived unknown' and whom 'few could know' ('She Dwelt Among the Untrodden Ways' (1799)). Hardy uses Wordsworth's Lucy poems elsewhere as points of reference for his heroines: see for example *Under the Greenwood Tree*.

13. *white tie . . . of the regulation curate*: 'Early in the period a "curate" commonly was a clergyman serving in a parish whose incumbent was not resident . . . By the middle of the nineteenth century, after reforms had reduced the incidence of multiple livings, the curate was more likely to be an assistant serving under a resident parson' (Mitchell, 157). In Victorian fiction the curate is often the object of ridicule.

14. *uncribbed, uncabined aspect*: In *Macbeth*, III.iv.24–5, Macbeth feels himself 'cabined, cribbed, confined, bound in/To saucy doubts and fears' after the first murderer informs him that, while Banquo has been killed, Banquo's son has escaped. This allusion suggests Angel's openness of mind and spirit, but also foreshadows a time when he will be beset by doubts and fears.

15. *north-east*: MS. and *Graphic* add a premonitory turn: 'Their presence at Marlott at this hour, though it had no bearing upon the nearer events which followed, was regarded as singular in after years, when viewed by the light of subsequent incidents.' Touches of narrative self-consciousness in MS. were removed later (see for example Chapter v, note 23).

16. *the spectacle of a bevy . . . no hurry to move on*: The Whitsun celebrations in Marlott are a survival from pagan May rites, and are associated with the May-time custom of choosing brides. Clare's sudden appearance as the one young man among the bevy of maidens looks forward to his odd situation in Crick's dairy.

17. *A Counterblast to Agnosticism*: In MS., the Clare brothers are reading 'Answers to *Essays and Reviews*', and in the *Harper's Bazar* edition, *A Counterblast to Essays and Reviews*. The Broad Church *Essays and Reviews* (1860) attempted to introduce the critical and historical study of the Bible into the Church of England. Among its contributors were Benjamin Jowett (1817–1893), Mark Pattison (1813–1884) and Frederick Temple (1821–1902). (For 'Broad Church', see Chapter XVII, note 5.)

CHAPTER III

1. *the soft torments . . . the agreeable distresses*: This quotation, untraced, echoes a later quotation from Swinburne: see Chapter XXV, note 5.

2. *excitement*: In 1892, Hardy, intent on creating a more exceptional heroine, plays this down: The lads are an 'amusement' no more.

3. *She might have . . . and manner*: *Graphic* accentuates Tess's feelings of duty: she hurries home in 'the knowledge that her mother was longing to come out, and was unable to leave the house till Tess returned'.

4. *'The Spotted Cow'*: In this song a young man offers to help a maid find her lost cow and leads her to a grove: instead they become lovers and spend the day there. The song foreshadows the events in The Chase (a kind of grove) and in the Valley of the Great Dairies. A version is reproduced in Peter Kennedy, *Folksongs of Britain and Ireland* (New York: Schirmer Books, 1975). See also *The Woodlanders*, Chapter XLVIII.

5. *National School*: The National School was instituted in 1811 by the 'National Society for Promoting the Education of the Poor in the Principles of the Established Church in England and Wales'.

6. *used it only . . . or grief*: Dennis Taylor notes: 'The Education Act of 1870 helped promote the spread of a standardized English idiom, so that by the 1890s non-standard dialect was little tolerated in the schools' (*Hardy's Literary Language and Victorian Philology* (Oxford: Clarendon Press, 1993), p. 83). See also Patricia Ingham, 'Thomas Hardy and the Dorset Dialect', in *Five Hundred Years of Words and Sounds*, ed. E. G. Stanley and D. Gray (Cambridge: Cambridge University Press, 1983); and Jean-Jacques Lecercle, *The Violence of Language* (London: Routledge, 1990). See also 'A History of the Text'.

7. *Oliver Grumble's time . . . Pagan Turks*: Oliver Cromwell's time and the Crusades, respectively. 'Pagan Turks' also echoes the name of the family scion, Sir Pagan D'Urberville (p. 8).

8. *Complete Fortune-Teller*: According to Firor, this book is based on the *Universal Fortune-Teller*, a compendium of folk magic which was 'still very popular in England' in the nineteenth century (p. 99).

9. *an infinitely Revised Code*: The Revised Code was introduced in 1862. It 'tied government grants to annual examination results in [reading, writing and arithmetic]. The system, popularly known as "payment by results", standardized previously varied elementary curricula' (Mitchell, 242).

10. *Jacobean and the Victorian ages*: The Jacobean age is that of the rule of James I (1603–25) (*Graphic* has 'Elizabethan'); Victorian that of Victoria (1837–1901).

11. *Nature's holy plan*: Wordsworth's 'Lines Written in Early Spring' (1798) concludes:

> If this belief from heaven be sent,
> If such be Nature's holy plan,
> Have I not reason to lament
> What man has made of man?

CHAPTER IV

1. *the pattern of Polynesia*: The droplets form into a pattern of tiny islands. Barrineau (p. 388) points out a similar usage noted in *OED*, from the *Cornhill Magazine*, July 1889: 'On the floor a polynesia of spittoons in a sea of sawdust'.

2. *it was better to drink . . . in a wide house*: Compare Proverbs 21: 9 and 25: 24: 'It is better to dwell in a corner of the housetop, than with a brawling woman in a wide house.'

3. *the magnificent pillars of Solomon's temple*: 1 Kings 6–7 records the building of

Solomon's temple with its 'four rows of cedar pillars, with cedar beams upon the pillars' (7:2).

4. *King Norman's day*: Durbeyfield's name for William I of Normandy ('William the Emperor' in *Graphic*).

5. *figure o' fun*: Not, as the phrase now suggests, a grotesque figure, but one ripe for courtship. Fancy Day is so described in *Under the Greenwood Tree* (I.111).

6. *don't get green malt in flower*: Altered to 'green malt in floor' in 1892, which Hardy explained in a letter to Macmillans of 24 February 1926: 'To have "green malt in floor" means to have a daughter in childbed before she is married – green malt meaning immature malt, and a floor of malt meaning the outspread malt for steeping' (*Collected Letters*, VII, 8). Presumably Hardy misremembered the exact expression in 1891.

7. *Anktells, and Horseys*: Furbank notes: 'The name of Anketell occurs in England as far back as 833, and landowners of this name in nineteen counties are recorded in Domesday Book. The Horseys of Clifton Maybank in Dorset were descended from lords of Horsey in Somersetshire, an ancient knightly family of Henry II's day' (p. 423). These references were added in 1891.

8. *Swarming will soon be over for the year*: When beehives become so crowded with adult bees that there is insufficient room for the queen to lay eggs, she leads the colony in a swarm to new hives, leaving behind new queens. This usually occurs in warm weather, and is associated in folklore with good luck in marriage (see *Under the Greenwood Tree*, V.1).

9. *engirdled by its earthen trenches*: The Neolithic or Bronze Age barrows (burial mounds) overlooking the Vale of Blackmoor also served as Iron Age fortresses.

10. *Then, examining . . . ancestry*: In the Ur-*Tess*, Mrs Durbeyfield (then Mrs Woodrow) meets and takes a fancy to 'Alec Hawnferne' at the club-dancing (Hawnferne is a younger man and a yeoman-farmer, not the layabout son of a *nouveau riche* – see Chapter v, note 11; Angel is not in the story at all at this stage). Tess's drowsy vision of things accordingly takes a nightmarish turn, transforming 'the young man who had so greatly taken her mother's fancy . . . but as yet unbeheld by herself' into a 'grimacing personage whose gig was a part of his body'.

11. *The pointed shaft . . . into the road*: In his unpublished 'Facts' notebook (Dorset County Museum), which comprises historical notes and some cuttings from local newspapers, Hardy records an incident from an old copy of the *Dorset County Chronicle*: '*Dark night*. Shaft of waggon enters breast of ridden horse, when latter was passing between former and a gig passing it'. Beside this entry Hardy has pencilled 'used Tess'.

12. *stagnant blankness*: Changed to the more effective 'silence' in 1892.

CHAPTER V

1. *I ought to keep myself up*: Durbeyfield's meaning is clarified in an alteration in 1892: '. . . I ought to live up to it.'

2. *Malthusian vexation*: In *Essay on the Principle of Population*, 2nd edn. (1803), Thomas Malthus argued that population growth must be kept in check by moral restraint – adults should delay marriage and remain celibate until they could support their children – if population were not to exceed the supply of food and be checked by war, famine and disease. Tess was merely 'somewhat vexed with' her mother in *Graphic*.

3. *her own . . . all were living*: In 1892 Joan is an addition to 'her own long family of waiters on Providence', which lays greater emphasis on the congenital passivity of the family and accords more closely with Tess's 'Malthusian' vexation.

4. *It was not a manorial home . . . tended by a bailiff*: Mark Girouard, in *The Victorian Country House* (Oxford: Clarendon Press, 1971), p. 4, observes:
Once a Victorian merchant, manufacturer or professional man had made a sufficient fortune he was faced with the dilemma of whether or not to set out to establish his family in the landed gentry. Not all who had the means took the plunge; it was, after all, a debatable advancement to cease being a great man in Manchester, Halifax or Newcastle and to take up a doubtful position as one of the new rich knocking at the door of county society. A socially ambitious wife, or a son educated at public school, often effected the change . . . If no country house property was available an estate had to be built up from scratch, and a completely new house built.

5. *Druidical mistletoe . . . pollarded for bows*: Mistletoe is a parasitic plant worshipped by the Druids as 'the plant sacred to the god of the oak . . . an all-heal and bringer of luck' (Firor, 155); see Chapter xxxv (and note 11). Yew-trees were polled (cut off at the top to encourage the growth of long uniform limbs) to make bows.

6. *an ornamental tent*: The tent, with its suggestion of the medieval tournament, contributes to the manifold ironies present in D'Urberville's appropriation of the name, in which the brand-new parades in imitation of old England.

7. *girlish artlessness*: In 1892 Tess is no longer 'girlish', a deletion that shifts the emphasis from her age to her nature.

8. *Stoke-D'Urbervilles*: In *Graphic*, they are the 'Smith-D'Urbervilles' (see following note). As Michael Millgate points out, the D'Urberville/Durbeyfield name is so fitting because the 'Norman-sounding d'Urberville . . . also manages to suggest the urban origins of the *nouveau riche* family by whom the name has been appropriated', while 'the uncompromisingly rural and plebeian

Durbeyfield . . . none the less sounds like an authentic "corruption" ' (*Biography*, 294).

9. *out of hail . . . stark words*: Hardy's satire on the name is less subtle in *Graphic*: as a Smith, the old man settled 'within hail of his native Vale; and in doing this he felt the necessity of recommencing with a name not quite so well remembered there as the two original bald stark words; one, moreover, that could show a little more definiteness than the patronymic which had hitherto served him but indifferently well, and had been the cause of endless mistakes in letters, visitors, clients, and friends from his youth up'. He was a stockbroker, not a merchant, in earlier stages of the MS.

10. *to be well-favoured . . . came by nature*: In *Much Ado About Nothing*, III.iii.13–16, the constable Dogberry says: 'God hath blessed you with a good name. To be a well-favored man is the gift of fortune, but to write and read comes by nature.'

11. *black moustache . . . four-and-twenty*: Alec's stage villain's moustache appears in 1891 for the first time. In MS. and *Graphic*, he is less physically mature (he is 'one- or two-and-twenty' in Chapter VII of *Graphic*): he sports 'a sooty fur' which 'represented for the present the dense black moustache that was to be'. All traces of callowness are removed, however, as Alec takes shape as the unscrupulous rake.

12. *my big Beauty*: In 1892 Hardy emended Alec's greeting to 'my Beauty', thereby removing its immediate overtones of casual sexual conquest. If, as Kaja Silverman and other critics have argued, Tess's mouth 'is consistently the most privileged feature of her physical appearance' ('History, Figuration, and Female Subjectivity, *Novel* 18 (1984), 8), her breasts are the most consistently euphemized one. This physical 'attribute which amounted to a disadvantage' (p. 42; Alec's eyes 'rivet themselves' to 'it'), is alluded to repeatedly. Referring to this passage, the reviewer for the *Saturday Review* (16 January 1892) objected that 'the story gains nothing by the reader being let into the secret of the physical attributes which especially fascinated him [Hardy] in Tess. Most people can fill in blanks for themselves, without its being necessary to put the dots on the i's so very plainly; but Mr. Hardy leaves little unsaid' (Cox, 189). See also Chapter XX, in which Angel, too, perceives Tess as a woman of 'dignified largeness . . . well endowed in person'. Significantly, the heroine who is seduced in 'Saturday Night in Arcady' is named 'Big Beauty' (see Appendix V).

13. *representing in hieroglyphic . . . family and England's history*: This convergence in Tess's mind of the D'Urberville family history and England's history hints at the novel's satirical subtext: the critique of contemporary society contained within the tragedy of a 'pure woman'. Compare Angel conning Tess's face in Chapter XXVIII.

14. *the swarthy Alexander*: Linking the dark-featured Alec with the Macedonian hero Alexander the Great (356–323 BC) is presumably meant to suggest his penchant for sexual conquest.

15. *said he blandly*: In 1892, Hardy has Alec correct Tess's 'ramping': 'And my arms a lion rampant.'

16. *my pretty Coz*: Alec's ironic Shakespearian archaism – a term of endearment from 'Cousin' – adds to the mock-courtly atmosphere of this chapter.

17. *fruit-garden*: In 1895, Hardy added 'and green-houses', to suggest that the strawberries, like the family name, are artifically cultivated.

18. *'British Queen'*: Hardy's allusion to this variety neatly encapsulates the pseudo-Elizabethan aspects of the scene, Tess's queenliness and the congruity between the D'Urberville family and the history of England.

19. *she parted her lips and took it in*: On similarities between this scene and Christina Rossetti's *Goblin Market* (1862), see Laura Claridge, 'Tess: A Less than Pure Woman Ambivalently Presented', *Texas Studies in Literature and Language* 28 (1986), 324–38.

20. *seen and marked and coveted*: In 1892, 'seen and coveted', to make Alec's motives seem less consciously mercenary.

21. *a certain other man . . . this time she*: This suggests that Tess is already half in love with Angel, and in 1892, to cloud this, Hardy emended it so that Tess might have asked why it was not 'some other man, the right and desired one in all respects – as nearly as humanity can supply the right and desired; yet to him who amongst her acquaintance might have approximated to this kind, she . . .'

22. *part and counterpart wandered . . . for a while*: An ironic reference to the belief expressed in Plato's *Symposium* that we are separated from our other half and spend our lives seeking it out; 'stupidest manner' became 'crass obtuseness' in 1895 and later.

23. *– what was called a strange destiny*: In MS. and *Graphic* this read '– and a story'. Hardy remained dissatisfied with the phrasing, tinkering with it in 1892 and again in 1895, when it read: 'and passing-strange destinies'.

24. *charming*: In MS. and *Graphic*, where the relationship is more that of social equals, Alec thinks of Tess as a 'nice' girl; in 1895, on the contrary, he thinks of her as a 'crumby', or delectable, girl.

CHAPTER VI

1. *gooseberry-bushes*: Firor (p. 218) notes that 'to be in the gooseberry bushes' euphemistically refers to being pregnant.

2. *dolorifuge*: Pain-killer or solace – Hardy's own invention, which infuriated the novel's early reviewers: 'Mr. Hardy continually delights in those long Latin and Greek words that seem to be made of springs rather than vowels. Think how absolutely out of colour in Arcadia are such words as "dolorifuge", "photosphere", "heliolatries", "arborescence", "concatenation", "noctambulist"' (Richard le Gallienne, *Star*, 23 December 1891; Cox, 179).

CHAPTER VII

1. *pink ribbon*: Tess wears a red ribbon in *Graphic*.

2. *It had come . . . with the barrow*: The Ur-*Tess* quotes 1 Kings 18: 27 here: 'the special providence tarried; and a voice from the sky might have exclaimed with the mocking Elijah, "Cry aloud: for he is a god; either he is talking, or he is pursuing; or he is in a journey, or peradventure he sleepeth, and must be awaked."' For 1891 Hardy employs the allusion in a dramatically different context: see Chapter XI and note 12.

3. *And if he don't marry . . . he will after*: This placidly pragmatic opinion, which caused some controversy when the novel was first reviewed, was omitted from *Graphic*.

CHAPTER VIII

1. *a farm girl*: Corrected in 1892 to 'a cottage girl'. See Chapter I, note 9.

2. *guarded silence*: Hardy characterized Tess's silence as 'guarded archness' and then 'arch wariness' in MS.; he settled on 'strategic silence' in 1892.

3. *I'll never do it again against your will*: The novel has already established the pattern of what might be termed Tess's involuntary consent to Alec's advances, at the first meeting (see also Chapter IX, note 7). In this scene, however, Hardy counterbalances Tess's fateful acquiescence with her angry resistance to Alec's advances, and this placatory speech of Alec's raises the vexed question of Tess's will.

CHAPTER IX

1. *copyholders*: One who holds land only at the will of the lord of the manor and on terms set down in the manorial court-roll, of which the copyholder holds a copy. See *The Woodlanders*, in which the plot turns in part on the fate of Giles Winterborne's property holdings.

2. *blowing and blowing*: MS. and *Graphic* have Tess also 'uttering impatient expletives' in frustration. This deletion removes any possible implication of hoydenishness.

3. *Looking that way . . . coping to the plot*: F. B. Pinion argues that in this scene Alec is associated with the Satan of Milton's *Paradise Lost* (1667): see *Thomas Hardy: Art and Thought* (London: Macmillan, 1977), p. 116. See also Chapter L, note 4.

4. *such a beautiful . . . Nature or Art*: Compare Angel's decision about a mate at the end of Chapter XXVII.

5. *sitting like Im-patience on a monument*: In *Twelfth Night*, II.iv.109–14, Viola, disguised as Cesario, tells Duke Orsino (whom she secretly loves) that her father's daughter loved a man:

> . . . She never told her love,
> But let concealment, like a worm i' the bud,
> Feed on her damask cheek. She pined in thought;
> And, with a green and yellow melancholy,
> She sat like Patience on a monument,
> Smiling at grief.

This allusion suggests Alec's mocking concealment of his obvious sexual intentions, and his sly intimation that she will not admit that she is attracted to him.

6. *Take, O take those lips away*: *Measure for Measure*, IV.i.1–6:

> Take, O take those lips away,
> That so sweetly were forsworn;
> And those eyes, the break of day,
> Lights that do mislead the morn;
> But my kisses bring again, bring again,
> Seals of love, but sealed in vain, sealed in vain.

7. *she involuntarily smiled in his face*: One of the suggestions that Tess leads Alec on without meaning to. In the Ur-*Tess*, the less sophisticated and more naïve Sue (i.e. Tess) smiled in his face 'like a child'; its removal scotches the hints of easy intimacy between Sue and Alec.

8. *her yet*: Hardy added 'sir' to the end of Tess's reply in 1892, to remove the impression of familiarity from this exchange.

9. *A familiarity . . . upon him*: This reflection on Tess's inevitable dependence upon Alec occurs in MS. at the beginning of Chapter XI.

10. *She soon found . . . ambush of that kind*: These two paragraphs, all of Chapter X and most of Chapter XI were cut from *Graphic*. It moves directly from the account of Tess's dependence on Alec to the famous question, 'But where was Tess's guardian angel?', near the end of Chapter XI (see 'A History of the Text'). Chapter X was separately published as 'Saturday Night in Arcady' (Appendix V). The substitute plot, in which Tess is tricked into 'marrying' Alec, is summarized in Chapter XII, note 14.

CHAPTER X

1. *the curious compounds . . . once independent inns*: For Hardy the adulteration of beer, taken up again in *Jude the Obscure*, symbolized the corruption of traditional rural life by the competitive capitalism already entrenched in those communities.

2. *on that account*: When Hardy removed this chapter from *Graphic* it included a long dance scene at this point. It was retained when the chapter was published separately, but was not restored to *Tess* until 1912. Appendix V reproduces both versions.

3. *Do not . . . drive you home with me*: The Alec of the Ur-*Tess* is not the domineering, socially superior stage villain of 1891, and accordingly he says: 'I am driving home. Come to *The Stag* and you shall ride with me. Do, Sue! I will start as soon as ever you like – say in a few minutes?' As Tess develops into the 'pure woman', Alec is correspondingly altered to invite the hostility of readers.

'Flower-de-luce' is an anglicization of *fleur-de-lys*, the lily emblem of the French crown.

4. *Very well, silly*: MS. cancels Alec's affectionate 'silly' and has him exclaim with rather more exasperation and scorn: 'Very well, Miss Independence; Please yourself. Then I shall not hurry'. Interestingly, though, Hardy reverted in 1891 to the MS. cancellation, which emphasizes Alec's genuine affection for Tess. 'Miss Independence' was, however, restored in 1912.

5. *dubbed Queen of Spades*: Tess's queenliness is repeatedly adverted to (see, for example, Chapter XXXI, in which she 'seemed to be wearing a crown') and the figure of Car the 'dark queen' shadows her (Car appears again in Chapter XLIII).

6. *They followed the road . . . each other*: These drunken revels foreshadow (and to some extent ironize) Tess's summer in the Vale of the Great Dairies. Hardy explores there the relationship between women and nature; and the idea of the world as on the one hand a 'psychological phenomenon' (Chapter XIII), and on the other an indifferent force.

7. *Treacle it was*: This image hints at Tess's own dark waist-length braids of hair, and the later images of blood.

8. *Praxitelean creation*: Praxiteles' (*fl.* 370–330 BC) *Aphrodite of Cnidus* boldly depicted the goddess naked. Hardy is drawing an ironic comparison between Car and Aphrodite, and an implicit comparison between Tess's body and Car's.

9. *whorage*: In response to the reviewer R. H. Hutton's claim that this 'coarse expression . . . betrays perfectly well [Tess's] knowledge of the dangers before her' in the *Spectator* (23 January 1892; Cox, 192), Emma Hardy wrote to the magazine: 'In the interest of dictionary-makers, may I be allowed to state that the apparently coarse word . . . has ceased in Somerset, Dorset, &c., to carry with it the coarse idea of its root-meaning, being spoken by the most modest to imply simply a company of slatternly, bickering and generally unpleasant women' (pasted into Hardy's 'Personal Reviews' scrapbook, Dorset County Museum). The more timid heroine of the Ur-*Tess* does not use this word.

10. *an opalized circle of glory*: This abstraction is emended in 1892 to 'a circle of opalized light'.

CHAPTER XI

1. *The twain . . . her seat was precarious enough*: To highlight Tess's dependence upon Alec, and emphasize that he exploits it, 1892 continues: 'despite her tight hold of him'. This, and Tess's request to slow the animal to a walk (she begs him in 1892), connects the scene with the earlier reckless journey to Trantridge. In MS. Tess is not 'dubious' about clinging on to him but 'indifferent', so she is more trusting and less guarded. MS. also explicitly refers to Tess's feelings of economic dependency, but Hardy shifted this passage to Chapter IX (see note 9), thereby establishing Tess's economic and sexual vulnerability much earlier.

2. *Tess, why do you . . . I don't love you*: In the Ur-*Tess* Alec asks Sue:
'. . . how many times have I kissed you since you have been here?'
    'You know as well as I.'
    'Not many.'
    'Too many.'
    'Only about four times, and never once on the lips, because you turn away so.'

3. *She was inexpressibly weary*: Many readers have noticed that *Tess*'s 'determining

scenes . . . are articulated in terms of sleep' (Philip Weinstein, *The Semantics of Desire: Changing Models of Identity from Dickens to Joyce* (Princeton: Princeton University Press, 1984), p. 112).

4. *now nearly one o'clock*: Since the revellers leave Chaseborough at a quarter to eleven, Hardy felt obliged to explain the lapse of time in 1892, and added a reference to 'the slow progress of their steed'.

5. *This immediately . . . the quietest he rode*: In MS., Tess pushes Alec right out of the gig and into the road, making it more plausible that she should apologetically consent to his placing his arm around her again.

6. *the oldest wood in England*: J. Hillis Miller points out that these scenes parallel the description of the Vale of Blackmoor 'known in former times' as the Forest of the White Hart (*Fiction and Repetition: Seven English Novels* (Cambridge, Mass.: Harvard University Press, 1982), p. 129).

7. *a hearty kiss*: He steals only a 'cursory' kiss from 1892.

8. *and pulling off . . . upon the thick leaves*: In 1892, Alec makes 'a sort of couch or nest for her in the deep mass of dead leaves', leaving his overcoat on until Tess confesses she is cold.

9. *a druggist's bottle*: In MS. Alec forces Tess to drink from a 'large wicker-cased jar' (which he takes from under the seat of the gig); it contains spirits, which Alec's mother wanted for 'household purposes'. Hardy's source (and in part for the mock marriage in *Graphic*) was a report in a newspaper of 29 July 1881, recorded in his 'Facts' notebook: '*Husband, to induce* wife to marry without settlement insists on her drinking some liquid – ceremony of marriage gone through – she does not know what she is doing.' The device of the druggist's bottle owes much to gothic melodrama and stage villainy, and is removed in 1892; in its place, Alec gets up to offer Tess the light overcoat he is wearing, so the narrative no longer explicitly represents the incident as rape, and relies instead on hearsay and implication.

10. *She was sleeping soundly*: In all layers of MS. Alec detects tears on Tess's eyelashes, and in 1892 this sign of her helplessness and fear is restored: 'He knelt, and bent lower, till her breath warmed his face, and in a moment his cheek was in contact with hers. She was sleeping soundly, and upon her eyelashes there lingered tears.' On the legal premise that a 'sleeping woman is incapable of consenting to sexual intercourse', see William A. Davis, Jr, 'The Rape of Tess: Hardy, English Law, and the Case for Sexual Assault', *Nineteenth-Century Literature* 52 (1997), 229 and ff.

11. *But where . . . was Providence*: In later editions Hardy emphasizes the narrator's religious scepticism by distancing these questions: in 1892, 'Providence' becomes 'the Providence of her simple faith'; and in 1895 'But where was Tess's guardian angel?' becomes 'But, might some say, where was . . .'

12. *the ironical Tishbite*: In 1 Kings 18, the prophet Elijah (called 'Elijah the Tishbite') challenges the followers of Baal to dress a sacrificial bullock and pray to their god to ignite the fire beneath it. When their prayers are not answered, Elijah mocks them. Hardy shifted this allusion from its position in the Ur-*Tess*, where, quoted in full, it heralds the arrival of Alec (the false god) (see Chapter VII, note 2). It also foreshadows Angel's later actions. This and the reference to Judges (see next note) form part of a sequence of Old Testament allusions to God's anger at the worship of false gods.

13. *the hands of the spoiler*: Judges 2: 14: 'the anger of the Lord was hot against Israel, and he delivered them into the hands of spoilers that spoiled them, and he sold them into the hands of their enemies round about, so that they could not any longer stand before their enemies.' The phrase simultaneously damns Alec and Tess's negligent guardian angel. See 'A History of the Text'.

14. *the coarse appropriates the finer thus*: In 1895, with this problem uppermost in his mind as he wrote *Jude the Obscure*, Hardy made it clear that the 'coarse' was not necessarily the man nor the 'finer' the woman, adding: 'the wrong man the woman, the wrong woman the man'.

15. *the sins of the fathers . . . mend the matter*: The implication is not that the innocent are punished because of the guilty: rather the ironical allusion to the second commandment (in which God threatens to visit 'the iniquity of the fathers upon the children' – Exodus 20: 5) only stresses that no meaning, even anger or Godly vengeance, can be reclaimed to explain Tess's fate.

PHASE THE SECOND

Maiden No More

CHAPTER XII

1. *the ridge towards . . . set*: *Graphic* adds: 'with marmorean hardness' (i.e. with the hardness of marble); the conjunction of the ridge and Tess's 'set' face casts such a quality upon Tess herself in this version (but see the description of her as a 'marble term' later in this chapter).

2. *the amalgamating effects . . . railway*: Not in *Graphic*. The roundabout railway is indicated on the map in Appendix II. Hardy used *Cruchley's Railway and Telegraphic County Map of Dorset* to sketch out Tess's wanderings.

3. *the serpent hisses . . . birds sing*: Shakespeare, 'The Rape of Lucrece', ll. 869–72:

> Unruly blasts wait on the tender spring;
> Unwholesome weeds take root with precious flow'rs;
> The adder hisses where the sweet birds sing;
> What Virtue breeds Iniquity devours.

4. *Life was totally . . . forthwith*: From 1892, Tess's 'views of life had been totally changed for her by the lesson'.

5. *She sat*: In 1892 Hardy makes it clear that Tess has not forgotten Alec's struggle: 'But she had not, and she sat'.

6. *I didn't understand . . . too late*: An echo of the novel's original title, *Too Late, Beloved!* – (itself an echo of a line in Shelley's 'Epipsychidion' (1821), ll. 131–2; or perhaps of Robert Browning's 'Too Late' (1864); or perhaps of Christina Rossetti's 'The Prince's Progress' (1861–5), ll. 481–2 (see also Chapter LV, note 3). *Graphic* has Tess exclaim: 'I didn't understand that it was not real until it was too late', to which Alec replies: 'I thought by your smiling that you quite understood.'

7. *Did it never . . . may feel*: This retort is altered in *Graphic* to: 'Did it never strike your mind that a woman might smile innocently?', and the allusion to pregnancy below (i.e. 'certain circumstances') is omitted.

8. *You don't give . . . me back*: Compare the ending of 'Saturday Night in Arcady', in which Big Beauty 'gave him her mouth to kiss, not her cheek as at one time'. In *Graphic*, Alec only protests that 'You don't kiss me back.'

9. *I made up my mind . . . seen sooner*: The text does not say what Tess saw: whether in the month (at least) since the rape she has been living as Alec's mistress and has 'seen the light'; or whether she realized that she was pregnant.

10. *THY, DAMNATION, SLUMBERETH, NOT*: In MS., the text is 'THE, WAGES, OF, SIN, IS, DEATH'. *Graphic* omits this encounter.

11. *I must put one there*: The text-writer's banter plagues Tess's conscience even more in 1892, where he adds: 'one that it will be good for dangerous young females like yerself to heed'.

12. *THOU, SHALT, NOT, COMMIT*: The seventh commandment ends '. . . commit adultery'.

13. *I don't . . . any of it*: Tess has not turned disbeliever: in 1892, Hardy emends her exclamation to 'I don't believe God said such things!' The change looks forward to later Phases in which Tess discovers that one tradition of Western thought coincides with her instinctual mistrust of Christian orthodoxy.

14. *Then Tess told*: All reference to Alec doing 'the handsome thing' is omitted from *Graphic*, where Tess tells an entirely different story:

'He made love to me, as you said he would do; and he asked me to marry me, also just as you declared he would. I never have liked him; but at last I agreed, knowing you'd be angry if I didn't. He said it must be private, even from you, on account of his mother; and by special licence; and foolish I agreed to that likewise, to get rid of his pestering. I drove with him to Melchester, and there in a private room I went through the form of marriage with him as before a registrar. A few weeks after, I found out that it was not the registrar's house we had gone to, as I had supposed, but the house of a friend of his, who had played the part of the registrar. I then came away from Trantridge instantly, though he wished me to stay; and here I am.'

'But he can be prosecuted for this,' said Joan.

'O, no – say nothing!' answered Tess. 'It will do me more harm than leaving it alone.'

Joan thought so too, 'as it was all in their own family', and silence was accordingly determined on and kept. Moreover, she could not help asking herself if it might not be a legal marriage after all? Stranger things had been known.

On the legal questions surrounding the mock marriage, see William A. Davis, Jr, '"But he can be prosecuted for this": Legal and Sociological Backgrounds to the Mock Marriage in Hardy's Serial *Tess*', *Colby Library Quarterly* 25 (1989), 28–41.

15. *he was dust and ashes to her*: As Abraham is to God in Genesis 18: 27, when he questions God's plan to destroy the righteous as well as the wicked in Sodom. The Old Testament links between promiscuity, idolatry and the implied guilt of the innocents are suggested elsewhere, e.g. Chapter XI and note 15, Chapter XIV and note 8.

CHAPTER XIII

1. *the house of her rich kinsfolk*: The 'manor of her bogus kinsfolk' in 1892.

2. *a dashing flirtation*: A 'just possible private' marriage in *Graphic*.

3. *she felt gratified . . . stay to tea*: Perhaps because 'meretricious' suggests prostitution, Hardy emended Joan's triumph to a limited and 'evanescent' triumph in 1912. In *Graphic*, only 'the discovery that her hopes [of a genuine marriage] were vain would involve her daughter's reputation', and there is of course no mention of it all ending in marriage.

4. *in love with her own ruin*: From a sermon by the English divine Robert South (1634–1716). Omitted from *Graphic*.

5. *cold reason came back . . . weakness*: Compare Shelley, 'When the Lamp is Shattered' (1822): 'Bright reason will mock thee,/Like the sun from a wintry sky' (ll. 27–8).

6. *to tread . . . little sympathy*: *Graphic* adds: 'for it was impossible to think the marriage valid'.

7. *the Morning Hymn*: By Bishop Ken (1637–1711), it begins 'Awake, my soul, and with the sun . . .'

8. *the double chant 'Langdon'*: A setting of Psalm 102 by Richard Langdon (1730–1803).

9. *She thought, without exactly wording . . . to his personality*: Jude Fawley is likewise moved by a hymn to muse on the composer as a 'man of sympathies', but he is profoundly disillusioned upon meeting him (*Jude the Obscure*, III.x).

10. *The bedroom . . . had gone away*: In *Graphic*, Tess (who is not pregnant) instead desultorily tries to keep herself occupied:

How should she occupy herself in this prison? There was a good deal of sewing-work to be done; but even when all that had been got through she had spare time on her hands. There were in the house a number of snuffy old volumes, many of which she had never before been sufficiently experienced in life to appreciate. She tried to read them now, but could not give her mind to the contents, and abandoned the attempt.

11. *that moment of evening . . . neutralize each other*: Hardy had explored the particular qualities of this 'transitional point' between day and night in the opening of *The Return of the Native*, and he further explores it in *Tess*: see, for example, the 'delicate equilibrium' in Chapter XIX.

12. *the God*: Altered to 'the Providence' for *Graphic*. In Chapter XV Hardy repeats this emendation (see note 2).

CHAPTER XIV

1. *XIV*: This chapter is omitted from *Graphic*. Hardy published it separately in the *Fortnightly Review* (May 1891) as 'The Midnight Baptism: A Study in Christianity' (reproduced in Appendix V). Tess is renamed Sis. All subsequent references to the night in The Chase, and the birth and death of Sorrow are omitted or altered in *Graphic*.

2. *the old-time heliolatries*: Rituals of sun worship; Helios was the Greek sun god. See J. B. Bullen, 'The Gods in Wessex Exile: Thomas Hardy and Mythology', in Bullen (ed.), *The Sun is God: Painting, Literature and Mythology in the Nineteenth Century* (Oxford: Clarendon Press, 1989), pp. 181–98.

3. *a moving concatenation was*: Hardy clarifies in 1892: 'a moving concatenation of three horses and the aforesaid long rickety machine was'.

4. *drawn cotton bonnets*: Gibson explains that these are 'cotton bonnets decorated by drawing out some of the threads to form a pattern' (p. 381).

5. *no strange land that she was in*: Moses is a 'stranger in a strange land' in Exodus 2: 22. For further allusions to the flight from Egypt, see Chapter L. An 'alien' amidst the corn, Tess is also likened here to Ruth (see Ruth 2).

6. *the outworn gold-leaf halo . . . Tuscan saint*: Hardy probably has in mind the Byzantine-influenced styles of the early Sienese and Florentine Renaissance: he knew the work of Cimabue (1240–1302) and Giotto (?1266–1337), for example, from visits to Italy and from his familiarity with the collections in the National Gallery, London (see his 'Schools of Painting' notebook, *Personal Notebooks*, 105).

7. *the ballad about . . . person*: A popular subject for ballads: compare 'The Spotted Cow' (Chapter III).

8. *Aholah and Aholibah*: In Ezekiel 23, the promiscuous Aholah and Aholibah are figures for the unfaithfulness of the chosen people of Samaria and Jerusalem. Ezekiel prophesies their stoning, and the slaying of their children.

9. *the arch-fiend . . . three-pronged fork*: In *Blackwood's Magazine* (March 1892), Margaret Oliphant protested: 'so far as we are aware, except, perhaps, in some quaint piece of medieval divinity still less likely to have fallen under Tess's notice than ours, the arch-fiend with the three-pronged toasting fork . . . occurs in certain grim passages of the *Inferno*, but in no more popular reading' (Cox, 208). Hardy responded in the Preface to the 'Fifth Edition' (Appendix I).

10. *which was almost regal*: Hardy goes further in MS. and *Graphic*, in which Tess exhibits 'Cleopatra's majesty and Atalanta's better part interfused' (on Atalanta, see Chapter LVII, note 5).

11. *manfully fighting . . . his life's end*: From the 'Ministration of Publick Baptism of Infants' in *The Book of Common Prayer*. The Ur-*Tess* quotes this passage almost in full: 'in token that hereafter he shall not be ashamed to confess the faith of Christ crucified, and manfully to fight under his banner against sin, the world, and the devil; and to continue Christ's faithful soldier and servant unto his life's end.'

12. *stopt-diapason*: Musical term for the muffled, higher note when an organ pipe is stopped.

CHAPTER XV

1. *By experience . . . wandering*: Roger Ascham (1515–68) was a scholar, author and private tutor to Elizabeth I. In *The Scholemaster* (1570), he wrote: 'We know by experience it selfe, that it is a maruelous paine, to find oute but a shorte waie, by long wandering.'

2. *Thou hast . . . hast permitted*: Book X.29 of the *Confessions* of Augustine (354–430). In *Graphic*, Hardy has 'Providence' in place of 'God'.

3. *Jeremy Taylor's thought . . . died*: In *The Rule and Exercises of Holy Dying* (1651).

4. *Was once lost . . . alone*: In *Graphic*, in place of these reflections, Hardy reworked a paragraph from Chapter XIV to mark her re-emergence: 'Meanwhile the trees were just as green as before; the birds sang, and the sun shone as clearly now as ever. The familiar surroundings had not darkened because of her mistake, nor sickened because of her regret. Time went on, and she dressed herself up picturesquely, as she had formerly done, and came out into the fields.'

5. *She waited . . . a new departure*: In M S. and *Graphic*, Tess then reflects that 'to carry out her once fond idea of teaching in a village school was now impossible'.

6. *she never alluded . . . ancestry now*: *Graphic* continues: 'Tess wished that her corrupted Marlott name were not quite so much like D'Urberville; but she consoled herself with the thought that none but a genealogist would observe or think of the resemblance.'

7. *Talbothays*: Hardy recalled that this name 'was based on that of a farm belonging to his father, which, however, had no house on it at that time' (*Life*, 250).

8. *D'Urberville, like Babylon, had fallen*: An ironical reference to the once powerful D'Urbervilles, suggesting the decadence at the root of their decline; one of many biblical allusions to God's revenge upon idolatry and sexual laxity in *Tess*. The phrase 'Babylon is fallen, is fallen' appears several times, e.g. Isaiah 21: 9 and Revelation 14: 8.

PHASE THE THIRD

The Rally

CHAPTER XVI

1. *although . . . anxious to get away*: *Graphic* continues:
It was somewhat stultifying to find a place suddenly becoming so dear in her contemplation when it was not so in her experience. Her foolish soul sent back tendrils of yearning towards it; the spirit of the spot thrilled her as it had never done before; its placid outlines, tinted with mellow lights and genial shades that were not those of the hour, but the accomplished impressions of the best moments of childhood.

2. *This leaving . . . for the best*: Tess's attachment to the children is given greater weight in M S. and *Graphic*, in which leaving them 'had been her great regret'.

3. *pilgrimage*: Hardy repeatedly figures Tess's journeys as pilgrimages (see Chapters XXII, XLIV and LII): ironical journeys to sacred places to redeem the family name and the fallen woman; and as a metaphor for the wandering journey that is Tess's life.

4. *Tess had never . . . only a dairymaid*: In *Graphic*, Tess does visit the tombs: 'to diverge from the direct route in order to glance at their resting-place was a passing courtesy to which they were entitled, and no serious task for so active a walker'.

5. *a canvas by Van Alsloot or Sallaert with burghers*: Denis van Alsloot (1570?–1626) and Antoon Sallaert (1590–1657) were minor Flemish genre painters in the manner of Bruegel. Their favourite subjects – crowded village scenes – are described in *The Return of the Native* (III.iii): 'vast masses of beings, jostling, zigzagging, and processioning in definite directions, but whose features are indistinguishable by the very comprehensiveness of the view.'

6. *the pure River of Life shown to the Evangelist*: In Revelation 22: 1, John the Evangelist has a vision of 'a pure river of water of life, clear as crystal'.

7. *photosphere*: Hardy's usage combines an archaic meaning (a sphere of light: Taylor, in *Hardy's Literary Language and Victorian Philology*, p. 176, notes that *OED* cites this as the last of three citations since 1664) and a precise contemporary astronomical meaning (the luminous envelope of the sun or star, from which its light and heat radiate). See also Chapter XXXI.

8. *mastered Tess*: In *Graphic*, Tess is more likely to feel she can begin her life again: 'mastered her, no longer counteracted by external pressures'.

9. *eaten of the tree of knowledge*: This allusion is to the tree of the knowledge of good and evil in the garden of Eden, with Tess as Eve. See Genesis 3, and Milton's *Paradise Lost*.

10. *O ye Sun . . . Him for ever*: Tess's litany comes from the canticle 'Benedicite, Omnia Opera' (known also as 'The Song of the Three Children'), in the 'Order for Morning Prayer', *The Book of Common Prayer*. Hardy is presumably using 'psalter' to mean a 'prayer-book' or 'missal', since he mentions the '*Benedicite*' by name two paragraphs below.

11. *polished brass knobs on their horns*: Furbank points out that these knobs 'would have been attachments to protect other animals from the sharp points of their horns' (p. 425).

CHAPTER XVII

1. *I knowed . . . her marriage*: In later editions Crick does not know Joan Durbeyfield at all. Thus, he greets Tess by telling her 'as a lad I knowed your part o' the country very well . . . Though I've never been there since' (1895).

2. *William Dewy by name*: William Dewy, his son Reuben and grandson Dick feature in *Under the Greenwood Tree*. See also 'The Oxen' (*Moments of Vision* (1917)).

3. *'Tivity Hymn*: Gibson suggests this may be Isaac Watts's 'Nativity Hymn' (1707), 'which has the first line, "Come let us join our cheerful songs" ' (p. 382).

4. *one cow*: In *Graphic* Hardy inserted a paragraph explaining why Tess does not dwell on Angel: because everything else is novel too, and 'She was regarding, speculatively, the current of her own life which, beginning in the mists around her birth-year, stretched forward through her past to her present, and onward to her future'.

5. *Low Church . . . High*: The High Church represents 'the "Catholic" side of the [Church of England], emphasizing the role of tradition, sacraments, and authority'; the Low Church or Evangelical Church 'represents an emphasis on the spiritual transformation of the individual by conversion and the "serious" Christian life resulting therefrom'; while the Broad Church 'deemphasized the doctrinal and ecclesiastical issues that separated' High and Low, by stressing 'the national and inclusive character of the church' and opening it 'to advances in modern thought, particularly biblical criticism' (Mitchell, 361, 272-3, 93). See also Chapter XXVII.

CHAPTER XVIII

1. *the child of his old age*: Angel is twenty-six now (pp. 117, 162) and the Reverend Clare is 'about sixty-five' (p. 157), which makes him about thirty-nine when Angel is born.

2. *Look into this book . . . a minister of the Gospel*: Hardy based this episode on an incident involving his friend Horace Moule, who is thought to be a model for aspects of Clare's character (see *Biography*, 294 – 5). Moule's strained relations with his father came to a head when in 1858 he ordered a copy of Gideon Algernon Mantell's *The Wonders of Geology* (1848), which Moule then gave to Hardy.

3. *redemptive theolatry*: The doctrine that Christ died on the cross to redeem mankind.

4. *thimble-riggers*: Swindlers who challenge bystanders to guess which of three thimbles has a pea under it.

5. *Indeed opine . . . very truth*: Browning, 'Easter-Day' (1850), Section VIII. This poem, published with a companion, 'Christmas-Eve', is in the form of a dialogue on the difficulties of faith.

6. *Article Four . . . by the Declaration*: Article Four of the Thirty-Nine Articles holds that Christ was physically raised from the dead. The Articles and the *Book of Common Prayer* set out the doctrine of the Church of England, to which all ministers must declare their adherence at ordination. The doctrinal indefiniteness of the Articles was the subject of much controversy among Low Church and Broad Church Anglicans in the nineteenth century.

7. *the removing . . . may remain*: Hebrews 12: 27. Hardy came to believe that the Church had in fact moved forward: in the prefatory 'Apology' in *Late Lyrics and Earlier* (1922), he wrote of advances in 'men in certain worthy but small bodies of various denominations, and perhaps in the homely quarter where advance might have been the very least expected a few years back – the

English Church – if one reads it rightly as showing evidence of "removing those things that are shaken"'. Angel is, however, also being ironized in his zeal for 'reconstruction', since Hardy believed for a long time that the endemic crisis of faith in England had provoked 'a childish back-current towards a belief in magic rites' (*Life*, 359), such as Tess's Pagan appropriation of Church litanies, a regression decidedly attractive to Angel. This allusion to Hebrews is not present in MS nor in *Graphic*.

8. *that it may be used . . . man, father*: Angel is more earnest and less intent on shocking his father in MS. and *Graphic*, in which he 'pleaded': 'that I may put it to other uses, father'.

9. *the pitiable dummy known as Hodge*: This phrase and much of the descriptive and explanatory material here were drawn by Hardy almost word for word from 'The Dorsetshire Labourer'. Hodge is the generic name for English agricultural labourers. In the holograph marginal emendations in Hardy's study-copy of 1912, he adds that the farm-folk were 'personified *in the newspaper press* as the pitiable dummy . . .'

10. *The thought of Pascal's . . . hommes*: From the 'Préface Général' to Blaise Pascal's *Pensées* (1670), which may be translated as: 'The more intelligent a man is, the more likely he is to appreciate distinctiveness in others. Ordinary people discern no difference between men.'

11. *some mutely Miltonic . . . Cromwellian*: Adapted from Thomas Gray's 'Elegy Written in a Country Church-Yard' (1751), stanza 15: 'Some mute inglorious *Milton* here may rest,/Some *Cromwell* guiltless of his Country's Blood'.

12. *road to dusty death*: *Macbeth*, V.v.22–3: 'And all our yesterdays have lighted fools/The way to dusty death'.

13. *ignes-fatui*: Will-o'-the-wisps: the phosphorescent lights seen hovering or flitting over marshland, caused by the spontaneous combustion of gas from decaying vegetation. Omitted in 1892.

14. *the constraint . . . to be watched*: Tess traces patterns with '*gaucherie*' (social awkwardness) in MS. and *Graphic*. However, it is insisted in MS. that her discomfort was 'the outcome of a vague under-thought only in Tess of Clare's presence. Her primary thoughts were miles away from him.'

CHAPTER XIX

1. *What of . . . Yes, sir*: In MS. and *Graphic*, Angel at first asks whether death is one of Tess's 'indoor fears' (she answers no); an earlier layer of MS. has her confess: 'I am rather afraid of – of – myself'.

2. *the ache of modernism*: Angel's musing on Tess's unwittingly sophisticated melancholy modulates into the general observation of the narrator's – the celebrated Hardyan 'ache of modernism' ('approximating to the spirit of modernism' in MS. and *Graphic*). See David J. de Laura, ' "The Ache of Modernism" in Hardy's Later Novels', *ELH* 34 (1967), 380–99.

3. *advanced ideas . . . grasped for centuries*: In the *Academy* in February 1892, William Watson criticized Hardy's own 'over-academic phraseology' in *Tess*: 'Possibly Mr Hardy intends some self-reference of a defensive sort when he observes that ["advanced ideas are really . . . the latest fashion in definition"] – touching which, one is impelled to ask – Are the words in *logy* and *ism* necessarily more accurate instruments of thought than simpler phrases?' (Cox, 198).

4. *Valley of Humiliation*: See John Bunyan, *The Pilgrim's Progress*, Part I (1678). MS. augments the allusion: there Tess encounters 'Giant Despair'.

5. *the man of Uz . . . not live alway*: Job (see Job 1 and 7. The quotation is Job 7: 15–16).

6. *like Peter the Great . . . yard*: In order to learn naval architecture Peter the Great (1672–1725) worked for a brief period as a carpenter in Dutch and English shipyards.

7. *an American or Australian Abraham . . . his spotted and his ring-straked*: Abraham was the great Hebrew leader who left Mesopotamia to found a new nation in Canaan, the Promised Land (see also Chapter LII). See Genesis 30, which tells of Jacob's bargain with Laban to remove all the speckled, spotted and ring-straked (brindled) animals from his flock.

8. *the poor Queen of Sheba . . . in me*: 1 Kings 10: 1, 4–5, in which the Queen of Sheba came to challenge Solomon with 'hard questions': but when she had 'seen all Solomon's wisdom, and the house that he had built . . . and his ascent by which he went up unto the house of the Lord; there was no more spirit in her'.

9. *why the sun shines . . . the unjust alike*: Matthew 5: 45: 'your Father which is in heaven . . . maketh his sun to rise on the evil and on the good, and sendeth rain on the just and on the unjust'.

10. *There's the Billetts . . . song a'most*: This sentence about the lowered families was added to 1891.

11. *Paridelles*: Furbank notes: 'Paridels are mentioned as landowners in the parish of Melbury Osmond . . . in J. Hutchins, *History and Antiquities of the County of Dorset*, vol. iv, p. 437' (p. 427).

12. *in Palestine*: In the Crusades.

CHAPTER XX

1. *Another year's instalment . . . inorganic particles*: Compare 'Proud Songsters' (*Winter Words* (1928)):

> These are brand-new birds of twelve-months' growing,
> Which a year ago, or less than twain,
> No finches were, nor nightingales,
>> Nor thrushes,
>> But only particles of grain,
>>> And earth, and air, and rain.

2. *the merest stray phenomenon*: Angel's developing consciousness of Tess – and his own idealization – is more marked in MS. and *Graphic*, where she is the 'merest ideal phenomenon'.

3. *the Resurrection hour . . . Magdalen*: In John 20: 1, Mary Magdalene arrives at the sepulchre at dawn, 'when it was yet dark', to find the stone 'taken away'. For Victorian readers 'Magdalen' was just as likely to denote the archetypal fallen woman, as the historical figure of the Gospels (Luke 7: 36–50).

4. *phosphorescence*: Tess had professed her belief that 'our souls can be made to go outside our bodies', and this is one of several examples of the visible or separate soul that surrounds her in these scenes.

5. *a whole sex condensed . . . Artemis, Demeter*: Hardy is rebelling against this condensation in *Tess*. Artemis is the Greek goddess of chastity, Demeter the goddess of fruitfulness.

CHAPTER XXI

1. *Marian*: The original is identified in *Life* (p. 30):

it was about this date that he formed one of a trio of youths who taught in the Sunday School of the parish, the vicar's sons being the other two, where as a pupil in his class he had a dairy-maid four years older than himself, who afterwards appeared in *Tess of the d'Urbervilles* as Marian – one of the few portraits from life in his works. This pink and plump damsel had a marvellous power of memorizing whole chapters in the Bible, and would repeat to him by heart in class, to his boredom, the long gospels before Easter without missing a word . . .

2. *Conjuror Trendle's son in Egdon*: Conjuror Trendle appears in 'The Withered Arm' (*Wessex Tales* (1888)).

3. *Conjuror Fall . . . when I was a boy*: Conjuror Fall appears in *The Mayor of Casterbridge*.

4. *Holy Thursday*: Ascension Day.

5. *for ravaging her trustful innocence*: *Graphic* bowdlerizes this to: 'for trifling with her feelings'. In 1912 Hardy emended it further to 'for ravaging her virgin innocence'.

6. *– and more*: Izz's insinuation of how far she would go with Angel was added to 1891, to lay the ground for Chapter XL.

7. *more woman than either*: Not in the Ur-*Tess*.

CHAPTER XXII

1. *the self-controlling sense . . . by him*: In MS. and *Graphic* Tess respects Angel's 'purity of mind and chivalrous sense of duty'. The younger Angel is more passionate and more solicitous in MS.

CHAPTER XXIII

1. *She had now . . . first excursion*: In MS. and *Graphic* Hardy retains something of the hesitancy and reserve that characterized Tess at Trantridge: 'It was seldom that Tess went about in company, but they had urged her, and to please them she had consented to accompany them to-day.'

2. *Sun's-day*: Hardy emphasizes the pagan origins of the day of religious observation: on the sun in the novel, see Bullen, 'The Gods in Wessex Exile: Thomas Hardy and Mythology'.

3. *That-it-may-please-Thees*: *The Book of Common Prayer* dictates that the Litany – in which supplications to bless the queen and royal family, magistrates, etc. are led by 'That it may please thee' and responded to with the refrain 'We beseech thee hear us, good Lord' – be sung or said after Morning Prayer on Sundays, Wednesdays and Fridays.

4. *un-Sabbatarian*: Angel is no strict observer of the sabbath.

5. *sermons in stones*: From *As You Like It*, II.i.16–17:

> Finds tongues in trees, books in the running brooks,
> Sermons in stones, and good in everything.

6. *I'll carry you . . . of you*: In *Graphic*, Angel offers to wheel the girls in a wheelbarrow. The ridiculousness of this contrivance has often been commented upon, but Hardy still manages to retain the sexual overtones. Angel instructs them to 'sit upon the top, and put your arms round my shoulders', and as the 'rickety conveyance . . . rocked and groaned', Retty 'kept exclaiming hysterically that he would upset her, and clasped his shoulders tightly, full of

more emotions than one'. Angel still exclaims 'O Tessy!', moreover, while 'pressing close against her'.

7. *A time to embrace . . . from embracing*: Ecclesiastes 3: 5.

8. *Three Leahs . . . one Rachel*: See Genesis 29, in which Jacob, who is in love with Laban's daughter Rachel, works seven years for the father but is cheated on his wedding night into sleeping with her sister Leah. Jacob decries the fraud and claims Rachel as his wife, in return for another seven years' work. She is childless, while Leah bears him four sons. Thus, Angel works for his one Rachel.

9. *dress herself up*: Changed to 'deny her love' in 1892.

CHAPTER XXIV

1. *Thermidorean weather*: 'Thermidor' was the name given to the period of hot weather between 19 July and 17 August in the French Revolutionary calendar.

2. *And as Clare was . . . silent Tess*: In the early stages of MS. 'the young people' – that is, Tess, Izz, Marian and Retty – are 'oppressed by the outward sultriness no less than inwardly by their consuming devotion to Angel Clare'. Hardy altered this, however, to focus on Clare: 'And as Clare was oppressed by the outward heats so was he burdened inwardly by a growing madness of passion for the seductive Tess.'

3. *the old Elizabethan simile of roses filled with snow*: As in stanza 2 of 'There is a Garden in her Face' (in *The Third and Fourth Book of Airs* (1618)) by Thomas Campion (1567–1620):

> Those cherries fairly do enclose
> Of orient pearl a double row,
> Which when her lovely laughter shows,
> They look like rose-buds filled with snow.

4. *aura*: A gentle breeze, or the current of air produced from a discharge of electricity.

5. *He had been . . . tender conscience' sake*: In the Ur-*Tess*, Angel is a more ardent lover, who had been on the point of 'violently' kissing that mouth, and proclaims himself 'passionately' devoted. His sensuality is inevitably attenuated when Hardy begins to emphasize his Shelleyan idealism and fastidiousness (see Chapter XXXI, note 6).

PHASE THE FOURTH

The Consequence

CHAPTER XXV

1. *noctambulist's face*: See Chapter VI, note 2. Angel's noctambulism ('night-walking') features again in Chapter XXXVII.

2. *Crowds of men . . . are to me*: *Crossing Brooklyn Ferry* (1881–2), ll. 3–4, added in 1891.

3. *novelty . . . started up elsewhere*: *Graphic* here adds Angel's wonderment at the 'mighty personality' that has influenced everything (later in the chapter in this edition): 'What mighty force had shifted the centre of his interests thus? A simple country-girl. He stared with wonder into himself at the mastering heat engendered in him by this something which had arisen as an exhalation out of such infinitesimally small and hitherto disregarded surroundings.'

4. *unsympathetic First Cause*: There are echoes of the 'Immanent Will' of Hardy's thought here: the unconscious 'Supreme Mover', 'limited in power, unknowing, or cruel' (*Life*, 302).

5. *pleasure girdled . . . pain*: From the chorus 'Who hath given man speech?' in Swinburne's *Atalanta in Calydon* (1865), ll. 1069–70:

> And circled pain about with pleasure,
>
> And girdled pleasure about with pain.

It is the gods who, in this chorus, 'very subtly fashion/Madness with sadness upon earth' (ll.1055–6).

6. *Antinomianism*: That is, Mercy is well-versed in Antinomian beliefs: the pre-eminence of grace over moral law, or more generally the superiority of human living to any law, compulsion or human regulation. See Chapter XLIV, notes 5 and 7.

7. *the impassioned . . . living, intensest*: At different stages, the heathens are 'summer-tipsy', 'summer-basking', 'summer-scented' and 'sun-flushed, summer saturated' (all in MS.); and 'summer-steeped' (1892). In 1895, Hardy added 'their rosy faces court-patched with cow-droppings'. Tess is variously the 'most tender' of them all, the 'most impassioned, most venust, most tender one' and the 'most living, tenderest, intensest' (all in MS.: Hardy's coinage 'venust' – meaning beautiful and sensual – was singled out by Mowbray Morris in his letter to Hardy rejecting the novel: see 'A History of the Text').

8. *Wycliff, Huss . . . life and thought*: John Wyclif (*c.* 1330–84), English theologian, philosopher, church reformer and promoter of the first complete translation of the Bible into English, was a forerunner of the Reformation; he charged the Church to renounce its worldly possessions, and in 1378 began a systematic attack on its beliefs and practices. The Bohemian religious reformer Jan Huss (*c.* 1370–1415) was a transitional Reformation figure whose thinking anticipated the Lutheran Reformation by a century; he was convicted of heresy at the Council of Constance and burned at the stake. Martin Luther (1483–1546) was the founder of the sixteenth-century Reformation and of Protestantism, and John Calvin (1509–64) was the follower and systematizer of Lutheranism. The Reverend Clare is a member of the Evangelical faction of the Church of England, which stresses the preaching of the gospel, the primacy of the personal conversion experience and active evangelism. His 'Apostolic simplicity' indicates that he follows as closely as possible the simple life-style of the Apostles ('primitive simplicity' in MS.).

9. *Paul of Tarsus . . . less a Christiad than a Pauliad*: The centrality of St Paul in the Reverend Clare's beliefs shows the powerful conflict in Christian thought between salvation through faith, and salvation through good works. Predictably, he 'hates' St James, who preached that faith without good works was a dead faith (in MS. Hardy had him 'secretly' hating St James). To take the New Testament as a book more of Paul than of Christ shows that Clare believes Paul's teachings are as fundamental as Christ's.

10. *a renunciative philosophy . . . Leopardi*: Clare's fierce Calvinistic determinism is likened by Hardy, first, to the unremitting pessimism of Arthur Schopenhauer (1788–1860). In March 1888, Hardy noted down a synopsis of Schopenhauer's position from *Encyclopaedia Britannica*:

True life begins only when we have learnt that happiness is impossible by means of gratifying the cravings of desire.

The central principle of pessimism (Schopenhauer's) asserts that in the order of nature, i.e. – so long as the will to live remains unbroken, happiness in the true sense is impossible. (*Literary Notebooks*, I, 203, no. 1529)

Giacomo Leopardi (1798–1837) was a revolutionary lyric poet and scholar whose poetry was deeply despairing. The reference to them was added in 1891.

11. *the Canons and Rubric*: Respectively, the laws of and the regulations for the conduct of worship in the Church of England.

12. *if Greece . . . not Palestine*: Angel's ideas derive from Matthew Arnold, whose 'Pagan and Mediaeval Religious Sentiment' (1877) Hardy read in early 1880, and quoted from in his *Literary Notebooks*: '*Greece* – a country hardly less important than Judaea' (I, 130, no. 1178). Compare Sue Bridehead's hostile reaction to the model of Jerusalem in *Jude the Obscure* (II.v).

13. *Its transcendental . . . another planet*: In *Graphic*, this reads:

The two extremes of its aspirations – on the terrestrial hand a suppression of the natural; on the celestial, soul-insurance – were as remote from his own as if . . . [from] another planet. The world's *raison d'être* was quite other in their eyes than it was in his. Having almost forgotten that classes of society existed, as such, that denominational antagonisms in religion existed, he had forgotten still more.
The 'geocentric view' places the earth at the centre of the universe, with heaven (literally) above and hell below.

14. *nymphs and swains*: The semi-divine maidens who inhabited nature, and the bucolic lovers, in classical mythology.

15. *non-evangelical*: Clare's brothers are studiously Broad Church.

16. *Correggio's Holy Families . . . any personal objection*: Hardy uses the comprehensive genealogy of Angel's father's beliefs and the detailed description of his brothers to draw attention to Angel's roots in evangelical morality and his liberal upbringing, which will turn out to be decisive in his later actions when he is 'surprised back into his early teachings' (Chapter xxxix). The 'Holy Families' of Correggio (1494–1534) include his *The Madonna of the Basket* (1520–26), in the National Gallery; Hardy described the paintings of Velázquez (1599–1660) in the National Gallery as 'natural & expressive rather gloomy' (*Personal Notebooks*, 111).

17. *Diocesan Synod and Visitations*: The Church of England is governed through synods – ecclesiastical councils of bishops and clergy which represent their diocese – and overseen by the General Synod, the highest governing body. In the nineteenth century the synod members administered the diocese by 'visitations' to parishes.

18. *high thinking may go with plain living*: From Wordsworth's sonnet 'Written In London, September 1802' (1807), ll. 11–14:

> Plain living and high thinking are no more:
> The homely beauty of the good old cause
> Is gone; our peace, our fearful innocence,
> And pure religion breathing household laws.

19. *dapes inemptæ*: Unbought meal. Hardy adapts 'dapes inemptas adparet', l. 48 of Horace's *Epodes*, II ('Beates ille'), a paean to rural self-sufficiency and to the role of the 'modest helpmeet' in preparing and serving the home produce.

CHAPTER XXVI

1. *your goings-out and your comings-in*: Compare Psalm 121: 8: 'The Lord shall preserve thy going out and thy coming in'.
2. *altar . . . call it one day*: Mercy has obviously picked up fashionable High Church notions.

3. *a Pauline view of humanity*: Interpreted variously as 'Pauline charity' – implying that the Reverend Clare unconsciously elevates Tess with her pure humanitarian heart – and as purity-as-abstinence: that he unconsciously damns her.

4. *full of poetry . . . paper-poets only write*: A recurring idea in Victorian fiction: Will Ladislaw, in George Eliot's *Middlemarch* (1871–2), exclaims to Dorothea Casaubon: 'You *are* a poem' (II.xxii).

5. *Christologist*: A person who enquires into the nature and personality of Christ, including his function as Redeemer, the mystery of the Incarnation and the validity of his prophecies and miracles.

6. *ghostly legend of the coach-and-four*: Related in Chapters xxxiii and li.

7. *exclaim against their own succession*: In *Hamlet*, II.ii. Rosencrantz informs Hamlet that the tragedians of the city are no longer popular because of the fashion for child players who inveigh against adult companies. Hamlet remarks that 'if they should grow themselves to common players . . . their writers do them wrong, to make them exclaim against their own succession' (341–4).

8. *Thou fool . . . required of thee*: Luke 12: 20. A parable against covetousness. What is the value of storing up wealth and possessions, and taking 'ease' to 'eat, drink, and be merry', Jesus tells his followers, when God can claim your soul at any moment?

9. *Being reviled . . . unto this day*: In 1 Corinthians 4: 12–13, Paul beseeches the Corinthians to follow him, laying out as his credentials the revilements, persecutions and defamations he has suffered in Christ's name. Both this passage and that of Luke (note 8) claim that 'whatsoever ye have spoken in darkness shall be heard in the light' (Luke 12: 3).

10. *may spring . . . seed some day*: The parable of the sower is told in Luke 8.

CHAPTER XXVII

1. *Talbothays having no resident landlord*: The absent landlord is a constant in the social landscapes of Hardy's fiction. Compare Flintcomb-Ash in Chapter xliii.

2. *as Eve at her second waking . . . regarded Adam*: This complex simile seems to be an allusion to *Paradise Lost*, Book V, in which Adam finds 'unawakened Eve/ With tresses discomposed, and glowing cheek,/As through unquiet rest' (9–11). His whispering wakes her, and she turns a 'startled eye' (26) on him and tells him of her dream, in which she is tempted to taste the fruit of the tree of 'interdicted knowledge' (52). This is Eve's second waking (she recounts how she 'first awaked' in Book IV).

3. *echoed*: *Graphic* adds: 'the entanglement with D'Urberville seeming startlingly real and irrevocable all of a sudden'.

4. *Tractarian . . . Pantheistic as to essence*: The Tractarian or Oxford Movement was an ultra-High Church movement led by John Henry Newman (1801–90). It set forth its doctrines and practices in ninety *Tracts for the Times* (1833–41), which Newman edited. Hardy is thinking, perhaps, of the Roman Catholic phraseology that characterizes the devotional poetry of the Tractarian John Keble's widely circulated *The Christian Year* (1827), which in Tess's mouth is transformed into the 'Fetichistic' utterances (xvi) of a Pantheist (one who believes God is everything and everything is God).

5. *Leave thou . . . melodious days*: Tennyson, *In Memoriam* (1850), XXXIII, 5–8. The poet is addressing the dead Hallam whom he imagines to be looking down upon his sister's devout and hopeful prayer from 'a purer air,/Whose faith has centre everywhere'. He implores Hallam not to cast doubts into her mind. An allusion that shows how in Angel's mind it is Tess's body and its relation with 'outdoor nature' that is one with God: 'sacred be the flesh and blood/To which she links a truth divine' (ll. 2–3, 11–12).

6. *in season or out of season*: 2 Timothy 4: 2: 'Preach the word; be instant in season, out of season; reprove, rebuke, exhort with all longsuffering and doctrine'.

CHAPTER XXVIII

1. *sigh gratis*: *Hamlet*, II.ii.316–17: 'the lover shall not sigh gratis': that is, shall not sigh for no payment. Love-making, in other words, is its own reward.

2. *her sense of incompetence . . . himself*: Hardy later moderates Angel's view: 'her modest sense of incompetence in matters social and polite' (1912).

3. *mourn silently . . . phlegmatic negative*: In *Graphic*, Tess is anxious about her 'marriage' to Alec: 'She had decided that the marriage with D'Urberville could not be a real one, and had come away in that belief. Yet there would surge up now the startling thought more continually, suppose it should be half-real? Anything could be done with a special licence. Moreover, if not legally valid, was it not morally so? With such disturbing fancies she worried herself.'

4. *her soft arm*: MS. and *Graphic* continue: 'He had done this more than once, though from motives of delicacy, or otherwise, he had seldom pressed her lips.' In 1891 and all later editions Clare vows not to kiss Tess on the face 'until he had obtained her promise' (Chapter XXIX).

5. *a coquette of the first urban water*: As accomplished and artificial as a coquette

from the city: a telling reminder of Angel's apparent experience with urban coquettes, and a further complication of the Nature–Art antithesis in women (see also Arabella in *Jude the Obscure*, who uses sexual artifice almost instinctually).

6. *to snatch . . . shut upon her*: An echo of Andrew Marvell's 'To His Coy Mistress' (1681), ll. 43–4: 'And tear our pleasures with rough strife/Through the iron gates of life'. Hardy thus indicates that Tess's resistance breaks down under the mounting force of her passion, but also in part because she recognizes that Angel perceives her 'scrupulousness' as 'coyness'.

7. *love's counsel would prevail*: In MS. Tess is even prepared to become Angel's mistress: 'As a path out of her trying strait poor Tess might even have accepted another kind of union with him, purely for his own sake, had he urged it upon her; that he might have retreated if discontented with her on learning her story. To be a cloud in his life was so cruel to him that her own standing seemed unimportant beside it; and she could not master herself sufficiently to give him up altogether.'

To the beginning of the following paragraph *Graphic* adds: 'Yet would it not be a wicked sin against him – sincere, honourable gentleman that he was – to give way thus with sealed lips? But how be frank with him without endangering her very purpose in giving way?'

CHAPTER XXIX

1. *This question . . . amusement to others*: Hardy explores this question most fully in *The Hand of Ethelberta* (1876), in which the eponymous heroine tells stories professionally for the amusement of others; her career culminates with her telling the painful story of herself. *Graphic* adds Tess's thoughts that 'her own case was so much graver than that woman's. It concerned the virtue and moral validity of a rite.'

2. *much longer*: In MS. the narrator adds: 'It was the nineteenth century and the tone of the time, even in farms and dairies, was grown to be that women should capitulate gracefully, resistance being always tempered by the thought that the sex is rather plentiful, not as in the days of the Sabines' (the Sabine women were abducted by Romulus and his men, according to legend, because of the shortage of women). This hint of Tess's anxiety that Angel might give up and choose elsewhere if she keeps resisting him belongs to an earlier conception of her.

3. *decide it*: In MS. and *Graphic*, Tess tries to bring herself to tell Angel: 'The thought so weighed on her that she kept asking herself if it would not be well before the sun set to fling herself upon his neck, and tell him her story. She had sought an opportunity for doing it, and yet she had held her tongue.'

CHAPTER XXX

1. *of Caroline date*: From the reign of Charles I (1625–49) or Charles II (1660–85).

2. *a poor enough terrestrial star*: This image connects Talbothays ominously with the wider sphere of 'modern life' and Tess's view of the earth itself as a 'blighted' star (Chapter IV). It also indicates how Tess is connected with earthliness: see Chapter XXXI and note 3.

3. *of more importance to Talbothays Dairy*: Snell links the development of the railway system in Dorset (after 1857) with 'the growing urban demand for dairy produce, consequent upon rising urban living standards' (*Annals of the Labouring Poor*, p. 377).

4. *I sometimes wonder ... of the circumstance*: Angel is probably referring to the political philosophy of collectivism, which was becoming increasingly popular in England. Emma Hardy copied a long excerpt from an article on collectivism and Anarchism by Emile de Laveleye (1822–92) in the *Fortnightly Review* (April 1883). Laveleye, who is also mentioned in 'The Dorsetshire Labourer', wrote that one important meaning of collectivism was state ownership of the soil, '& this is the system which is being now so much discussed in England, under the name of *nationalisation of the land*' (*Literary Notebooks*, I, 151, no. 1296).

5. *I sometimes ... born*: Compare Chapter XII, in which Tess says this to Alec, and 'Tess's Lament' (Appendix IV).

6. *appetite for joy*: From Browning's *Paracelsus* (1835), Part I 'Paracelsus Aspires', ll. 86–91:

> When Festus learns
> That every common pleasure of the world
> Affects me as himself; that I have just
> As varied appetite for joy derived
> From common things; a stake in life, in short,
> Like his ...'

This appetite 'stimulates all creation' in MS. and *Graphic*.

7. *was not to be controlled ... rubric*: Hardy's language nicely imitates the stifling effect of pedantry and abstract thought. *Graphic* puts it differently: 'a vague sense of self-abnegation on the score of a moral precontract. It could obstruct emotion, but could not quench it.'

CHAPTER XXXI

1. *last-century hand*: 'I' and 'J' were not distinguished in English until the seventeenth century, and the habit of writing the personal pronoun as 'J' persisted much longer in some areas.

2. *haunting episode of bygone days*: *Graphic* alters to: 'haunting transaction of the past, the binding force of which still remained upon her conscience, concealed as it might be by overgrowths'. The bogus marriage allowed Hardy to exploit Alec's (contractual) hold over Tess, and in subsequent editions he continues to underscore her shamed feelings of Alec as rightful husband.

3. *a touch of earth*: An ironical echo of Tennyson's *Lancelot and Elaine* (1870). Elaine, scorning Arthur, tells Lancelot that the one '. . . who loves me must have a touch of earth;/The low sun makes the colour' (133–4). A further allusion to the red light with which Tess is associated in these chapters and the earthliness which the celestial Angel does not yet understand; and to the mock knightly romance underlying Alec's relationship with Tess which resurfaces mockingly here in Angel's chivalry (see note 6 below).

4. *knew all . . . should know*: An ironical allusion to Alexander Pope's *An Essay on Man* (1733–4), IV.390: 'Thou wert my Guide, Philosopher, and Friend'. Significantly, the poem ends (IV.398) proclaiming '. . . all our *Knowledge* is, *Ourselves to Know*' – foreshadowing Clare's failure.

5. *singularly free from grossness*: The vexed conflict between a man's grossness and his spiritual aspirations is central in *Jude the Obscure*. The likeness between Angel and the spiritual Sue Bridehead is therefore important.

6. *less Byronic than Shelleyan*: In keeping with the romance motif of the dark and light heroes, Alec is the dark, carnal, Byronic hero (Arthur in the Arthurian typology); and Angel is the fair, intellectual, Platonic Idealist, Shelleyan hero (Lancelot). 'Hardy is both repelled by, and attracted to, the ethereal, fastidious nature of Shelley's love poetry. It seems significant that Hardy associates the least attractive traits in his two main characters [Angel and Sue Bridehead] with Shelleyan notions' (*Literary Notebooks*, I, 366); significantly, it is only in 1892 that Hardy introduces the word 'fastidious' ('it was a fastidious emotion'). On Hardy and Shelley, see Michael Millgate, *Thomas Hardy: His Career as a Novelist* (1971; Houndmills: Macmillan, 1994), esp. pp. 299ff.; and Pinion, *Thomas Hardy: Art and Thought*, esp. pp. 93–6 and 148–57.

7. *periphery*: Le Gallienne's critical review (see Chapter VI, note 2) cited this word as an example of 'a defect in Mr. Hardy's style which is continually making one grind one's teeth'. Hardy changed it to 'surface' in 1892.

8. *true, and honest . . . of good report*: Philippians 4: 8: 'Finally, brethren, whatsoever things are true, whatsoever things are honest, whatsoever things are just, whatsoever things are pure, whatsoever things are lovely, whatsoever things are of good report; if there be any virtue, and if there be any praise, think on these things.'

9. *When shall the day be*: Angel appears to be quoting from a folk-song: compare 'Pretty Miss, Will You Wed?', which concludes: 'When shall be our wedding day?/Why I think tomorrow'.

CHAPTER XXXII

1. *I have decided on a licence*: Rather than have notice of the forthcoming wedding read out in the church for three successive Sundays, where all the parish would hear it, Angel chooses to apply for a marriage licence.

2. *That never . . . amiss*: From 'The Boy and the Mantle', which tells of a magic mantle only the pure can wear. *Graphic* has two stanzas after 'Guénever':

> One while was it gule;
>   Another while it was green;
> Another while it was plaided;
>   Ill it did her beseem.

> Another while it was black,
>   And bore the worst hue.
> 'By my troth,' quoth King Arthur,
>   'I think thou be not true!'

(In F. J. Child (ed.), *The English and Scottish Popular Ballads*, 5 vols. (1882–98), vol. 1, no. 29.)

CHAPTER XXXIII

1. *his arm*: In MS. Tess is more self-conscious and her beauty more openly sexualized. Initially Hardy added: 'By looking down she avoided catching the observers' eyes, but her mouth she could not hide'; this he emended to 'her elasticity she could not hide'.

2. *mistake*: Hardy originally included (and then deleted) the remainder of the remark in MS.: 'unless I make a great mistake, no maid'.

3. *This*: In *Graphic*, Hardy uses a different device:
But she did not go to bed. She bethought herself of a story which she had seen in an old periodical in the parlour downstairs, and had been so arrested by its title that she

had brought it up to her room to read . . . The tale was entitled 'Marriage in Jest and in Earnest' – this being what had originally attracted her – and, in her present high-strung mood, she wondered how she could have postponed the reading for so long.

The story was, in brief, a very old-fashioned one of two persons who had been tempted to go jestingly through the marriage ceremony together in the presence of a parson, with some other mock formalities, to find to their horror, some time after, that they were legally man and wife. Tess did not quite see the probability of the thing; nevertheless, this . . .

4. *still doubtful . . . received it*: In MS. and *Graphic*, Angel's lack of reaction causes Tess to be: 'for the first time gay, notwithstanding her due sense of the solemnity of the step that she was about to take'. Hardy compounds her doubts in 1892, however, in which she feels 'guiltily doubtful'.

5. *overwhelmed her . . . at this late moment*: In 1912, Tess knows that there is still time to confess: 'she had jumped at [the incident of the letter] as if it prevented a confession; but she knew in her conscience that it need not; there was still time.'

6. *the Angel whom St John saw in the sun*: Revelation 19: 17: 'And I saw an angel standing in the sun; and he cried with a loud voice, saying to all the fowls that fly in the midst of heaven, Come and gather yourselves together unto the supper of the great God.' This leads into an ambiguous image for the prospective wedding-feast in Revelation, which resonates with the aristocratic corruption suggested in the D'Urberville coach and the decaying postilion: 'That ye may eat the flesh of kings, and the flesh of captains, . . . and the flesh of all men, both free and bond, both small and great.' In 1892, Tess's 'condition of exaltation' is amended to 'condition of mind'.

7. *calmed down*: Hardy explained Tess's feelings in MS. and *Graphic*: 'And it was then that a suddenly-renewed sense that she had deluded by her muteness him whom she only lived to please – that she had deprived him of opportunity to retreat, began to horrify her.'

8. *These violent delights have violent ends*: *Romeo and Juliet*, II.vi.9. Friar Laurence's warning against loving immoderately (violent delights 'in their triumph die, like fire and powder,/Which, as they kiss, consume', he continues) is a response to Romeo's 'come what sorrow can,/It cannot countervail the exchange of joy/That one short minute gives me in her sight' (3–5).

9. *That's bad*: 'Cockcrow at an unusual time is almost universally held ominous' (Firor, 12). See also Luke 22: 60–62 for the best-known example of the thrice-crowing cock.

CHAPTER XXXIV

1. *As all visitors . . . in his dreams*: Here the narrator's change to present tense suggests the language of a tour-guide. Replicas of these portraits (of Turbervilles) hang in the Dorset County Museum. Reference to them occurs first in *Graphic*.

2. *Clare touched hers under the water*: For the motif of hands under water, see *Under the Greenwood Tree* (II.vii), 'Under the Waterfall' (*Satires of Circumstance*) and Emma Hardy, *Some Recollections* (London: Macmillan, 1961), p. 57. See also J. O. Bailey, *The Poetry of Thomas Hardy: A Handbook and Commentary* (Chapel Hill, N.C.: 1970), pp. 292–3.

3. *to whom the use of them . . . rightly belong*: In MS. and *Graphic*, Mrs Pitney's jewels were willed as the 'absolute property' of Angel's wife. The change from an outright gift to an heirloom will become critical when Tess needs money.

4. *folks mops and brooms*: Half-drunk. *OED* notes: 'an allusion to the drinking that took place at the hiring fairs . . . at which maids carried mops or brooms in token of the capacity in which they wished to be hired'.

5. *an Aldebaran or a Sirius*: Stars which emit flashes of coloured light. Aldebaran is a reddish giant star in the constellation Taurus; the blue-white Sirius, the Dogstar, is the brightest star in the night sky, and a bad omen.

6. *To begin*: In MS. Angel's confession began originally:

> 'Tess, have you noticed that though I am a parson's son, I don't go to church?'
> 'I have – occasionally.'
> 'Did you ever think why?'
> 'I thought you did not like the parson of the parish.'
> 'It was not that, for I don't know him. Didn't it strike you as strange that being so mixed up with the church by family ties and traditions I have not entered it but have done the odd thing of learning to be a farmer?'
> 'It did once or twice, dear Angel.'

A sheet containing 'To begin . . . strange company for St Paul' was pasted over this, and it is probably one of the places where Hardy went on to say 'much more on religion as apart from theology', which he decided to omit, as he remarked in a letter to Frederic Harrison (1 January 1892; *Collected Letters*, I, 251). This change establishes Angel as a hypocrite, and brings the sexual double standard into greater prominence.

7. *a stickler for good . . . do now*: Angel's priggishness is tempered in 1892, which has him 'a believer in good morals', and no longer exempting himself from impurity: 'I admired spotlessness, even though I could lay no claim to it, and hated impurity, as I hope I do now.'

8. *plenary inspiration*: The belief that the authors of the Bible were infallible because they were divinely inspired; and thus that the Bible is literally accurate.

9. *Be thou . . . in faith, in purity*: 1 Timothy 4: 12: 'be thou an example of the believers, in word, in conversation, in charity, in spirit, in faith, in purity'. An interesting choice of text, since Angel is much more deeply the son of his Pauline father than he realizes.

10. *Integer vitæ*: Horace, *Odes* I.xxii: The two lines below are as translated by Hardy himself (see *Collected Letters*, I, 282). In MS. and *Graphic*, Hardy has: 'O Fuscus, has no need of spear and bow.'

11. *Well, having felt this so strongly . . . fell*: In 1892, Angel concludes: 'Well, a certain place [i.e. hell] is paved with good intentions, and having felt all that so strongly'. This addition looks forward to the road paved with Angel's moral intentions.

12. *a Last Day luridness*: Bathed in the red light of adultery, Tess imagines the reckoning fires of the end of the world in the coals.

13. *her acquaintance . . . drooping down*: In *Graphic*, Tess enters upon the story of 'the visit with D'Urberville to the supposed Registrar's, her abiding sense of the moral validity of the contract, and her wicked flying in the face of that conviction by wedding again. She murmured the words without flinching, and with her eyes fixed on the fire.'

PHASE THE FIFTH

The Woman Pays

CHAPTER XXXV

1. *auricular impressions*: Hardy puns on the two meanings of 'auricular': pertaining to the ear (confessions made privately into the confessor's ear), and to the heart (after the auricle: the two upper cavities of the heart).

2. *were nothing . . . not weep*: MS. and *Graphic* have: 'might have seemed to show an insufficiently deep nature, but it showed nothing except his own sense of the inadequacy of his accents to convey the complexity of his ideas and the perfunctoriness which comes of heart-sickness.'

3. *How can forgiveness . . . as that*: 'Considering all the circumstances of the scene we take this to be one of the most unconsciously comical sentences ever read in print,' wrote Mowbray Morris, 'Culture and Anarchy', *Quarterly Review* (April 1892; Cox, 215). Hardy responded in 1892 by adding a dash between 'grotesque' and 'prestidigitation', as if Angel fumbles for the word – which means 'sleight of hand' – in his overwrought state, and by making the following sentence begin: Angel 'paused, contemplating this definition'.

4. *He paused . . . jumped up*: In MS. and *Graphic*, this moment is reserved for Tess's awakening to the full consequences: 'Tess could be seen rising slowly and sadly as if lifted by an invisible hand. In rising she turned away from him; but in a moment she turned quickly back again, fuller perception having quite changed her.'

5. *To*: In 1892, this is prefaced by: 'These were the first words of antagonism.'

6. *Behold, when thy face . . . the crown shall be pain*: From the chorus, 'Not as with sundering of the earth', from Swinburne's *Atalanta in Calydon*, ll. 1852–5.

7. *more sinned against than sinning*: *King Lear*, III.ii.60: It is Lear himself who feels more sinned against, just as it is Angel who blindly feels himself the victim.

8. *I cannot help . . . want of firmness*: Clearly we are meant to be critical of Angel here, but the narrator too has implied as much in setting out Tess's passivity in terms of her father's want of energy.

9. *It was said . . . a long while after*: The narrator momentarily distances himself by assuming the voice of the tale-teller, projecting the narration into the future and casting the story as legend. Gibson (pp. 387–8) notes echoes of stanza 3 of Hardy's poem 'Beyond the Last Lamp' (*Satires of Circumstance*) in the cottager's return 'just as slowly':

> When I retrod that watery way
> Some hours beyond the droop of day,
> Still I found pacing there the twain
> >   Just as slowly, just as sadly,
> >   Heedless of the night and rain.
> One could but wonder who they were
> And what wild woe detained them there.

10. *Cistercian abbey*: Based on Bindon Abbey near Wool, founded 1172. The Cistercian order was a severely ascetic offshoot of Benedictine monasticism founded in 1098 by St Robert of Molesme. These well-organized farming and marketing communities flourished in the twelfth century.

11. *A bough of mistletoe*: Millgate notes the source in a visit of Hardy's in autumn 1888 to Woolcombe, 'an estate (so he had learned from Hutchins) once in the possession of one of [the] branches of "the Dorset Hardys"'. At Evershot station, where he disembarked, he found 'some mistletoe' that had been there 'ever since last Christmas (given by a lass?), of a yellow saffron parchment colour' (*Biography*, 293).

12. *passion's slave*: *Hamlet*, III.ii.68–70: 'Give me that man/That is not passion's slave, and I will wear him/In my heart's core'.

13. *The little less, and what worlds away*: Browning, 'By the Fireside' (1855), l. 192. In MS., Hardy quoted:

> The little more, and how much it is!
> And the little less, and what worlds away!
> How a sound shall quicken content to bliss,
> Or a breath suspend the blood's best play,
> And life be a proof of this! (ll. 191–5)

This poem, with its declaration that 'If two lives join, there is oft a scar', is much quoted in Hardy's fiction (see especially *Jude the Obscure*, II.1 and IV.v). Like Angel, however (see Chapter XXXVII, note 9), Hardy characteristically overturns Browning's optimistic view.

CHAPTER XXXVI

1. *a lotus-headed column*: In ancient Egyptian architecture, the bell-shaped capitals of columns were sometimes decorated in paint or light bas-relief with lotus flowers and buds.

2. *ashes of their former fires*: An adaptation of lines (116–17) from Byron's *The Giaour* (1813):

> Snatch from the ashes of your Sires
> The embers of their former fires.

Hardy copiously marked his 1864 edition of Byron's *Poems*, and included a line from *The Giaour* in his 'Studies, Specimens &c.' notebook from the 1860s (see Pamela Dalziel and Michael Millgate (eds.), *Thomas Hardy's 'Studies, Specimens &c.' Notebook* (Oxford: Clarendon Press, 1994), pp. 37, 125).

3. *Indeed I cannot*: Under the 1857 Matrimonial Causes Act it was possible for a man to divorce his wife if he could prove her adultery, and for a woman to divorce her husband if she could prove adultery and one other serious offence (such as violence, desertion or extreme cruelty). It cannot apply since Tess's involvement with Alec took place before she was married: this is clarified in *Harper's Bazar*, in which Clare says 'For what happened before our marriage? Indeed I cannot.'

4. *If you . . . promise me to*: Angel's slightly paternal tone is altered in 1892: 'You must not dare to think of such a horrible thing! How could you! You will promise me as your husband to . . .'

5. *She did not raise her eyes*: In later editions many of the phrases and gestures which suggest Tess's feelings of shamed servitude are removed: here, for example, she does raise her eyes (1892).

6. *made her unseemly . . . Apostolic Charity*: Drawn from the Apostle Paul's description in 1 Corinthians 13: 4–5: 'Charity suffereth long, and is kind; . . . Doth not behave itself unseemly, seeketh not her own, is not easily provoked, thinketh no evil . . .'

7. *that man lives*: In *Graphic*, Angel then points out that: 'he [Alec] is your husband in the sight of heaven, if not really?' Hardy reincorporated Angel's realization in 1895: 'he being your husband in Nature, and not I.'

8. *better endure . . . than fly to others*: *Hamlet*, III.i.78–82:

> But that the dread of something after death,
> The undiscovered country, from whose bourn
> No traveller returns, puzzles the will,
> And makes us rather bear those ills we have
> Than fly to others that we know not of . . .

The extent of Angel's despair is borne out in this allusion to the religious dread underlying his moral dread.

9. *You shall be born*: 'Le voeu' (1865), by René François Armand Sully Prud-homme (1839–1907). In 1888 Hardy quoted and annotated an article by F. W. H. Myers in *Nineteenth Century* 23 (May 1888) on 'The Disenchantment of France', and recorded: 'The *Condamnés à naître* (M. Sully-Prudhomme in the poem Le voeu)' (*Literary Notebooks*, I, 218, no. 1629).

10. *vitalizations*: An example of Hardy deliberately choosing a word for several meanings. To vitalize is to endow with life; also, to animate; or, in another sense, to put life into a literary or artistic conception. Here its meaning – children – is rendered into an ugly abstraction to suggest how painful the realization is to Tess at this moment when she suddenly confronts what Sue Bridehead was to call, echoing Shelley, the 'Shapes like our own selves hideously multiplied' (*Jude the Obscure*, V.iv).

11. *The heart of woman . . . bitterness*: From 'The heart knoweth his own bitterness; and a stranger doth not intermeddle with his joy' (Proverbs 14: 10).

CHAPTER XXXVII

1. *which, as usual was loosely nailed*: To alert occupants to intruders; or because stairs were not in general tightened from above with nails but from beneath using wedges (which could be tightened with a tap to prevent creaking); or because it is the step which turns the corner.

2. *washed the handrail . . . steady heads*: Initially Hardy wrote that after the autumn rains, 'only the handrail was above the water' (MS.). The rail itself, therefore, 'of sawn wood, flat on the top' (*Graphic*) formed the perilous walk-way, which overly sensationalized an already pseudo-gothic melodrama.

3. *the empty stone coffin . . . without a lid*: In Bindon Abbey, such a coffin is reputedly that of Richard de Maners (*c.* 1310).

4. *Clare then . . . alongside*: In MS. and *Graphic* Clare lays Tess on a monk's grave in the cloister-garden and lies 'down himself beside her'.

5. *like a Samson shaking himself*: Samson shakes himself after waking from the sleep in which Delilah cuts off his hair and takes his strength from him (see Judges 16: 19–20). (Compare Chapter XLV, p. 306).

6. *withstood her*: MS. and *Graphic* continue: 'But she was too honest to succeed with men, who suffer artifice gladly, not as fools but as wise. Clare had, in truth, feared some such final outburst from her, with good reason.'

7. *In her submission . . . that acquiescence*: In 1912: 'Pride, too, entered into her submission – which was perhaps a symptom of that reckless acquiescence'.

8. *agreed*: The jewels are Tess's outright property in MS. and *Graphic*, and Angel deposits them in her name and gives her the banker's receipt 'so that she could get them on application'; he also advises her that she 'can turn them into money' if necessary. Later in MS. and *Graphic* Angel estimates their worth at several hundred pounds.

9. *God's not . . . the world*: The well-known lines from Browning's *Pippa Passes* (1841) – from I 'Morning', 221–4, 227–8 – read:

> The year's at the spring
> And day's at the morn;
> Morning's at seven;
> The hill-side's dew-pearled; . . .
> God's in his heaven –
> All's right with the world!

In MS. and *Graphic*, Angel actually quotes the lines correctly, but 'in a peculiar tone of his own'.

CHAPTER XXXVIII

1. *when such changes were made*: On the calendar set for the hiring of rural workers, see Chapters XLVI (and note 4) and XLIX.

2. *not a lesson*: The mishap 'had been lying in wait for Tess in her future by its own contrivance and whim' in MS.

CHAPTER XXXIX

1. *staring and ghastly . . . by Van Beers*: On a journey to Europe in 1876, Hardy almost certainly visited the Wiertz Museum, Brussels: 'The pictures of Antoine Wiertz (1806–65) were profoundly macabre, intensely violent, and highly melodramatic, but they were calculated to appeal to Hardy's temperament, with its penchant for the grotesque' (J. B. Bullen, *The Expressive Eye: Fiction and Perception in the Works of Thomas Hardy* (Oxford: Clarendon Press, 1986), p. 24).

Bullen points out that Wiertz's painting was often compared with that of his fellow-countryman Jan Van Beers (1852–1927), and that Van Beers's work was on show in London in 1887.

2. *This is the chief . . . Pagan moralist*: Marcus Aurelius (121–180), from *The Thoughts of Marcus Aurelius Antoninus* (Hardy treasured his 1862 copy, a New Year's gift from Horace Moule, inscribed with this quote: see *Biography*, 87). See also *Life*, 182–3, and *A Laodicean* (IV.1).

3. *Let not . . . the Nazarene*: These words of Jesus, 'the Nazarene', appear in John 14: 27. The juxaposition of these maxims makes explicit the parallels between the pagan and Christian worlds.

4. *the Empire of Brazil*: Hardy drew upon his memory of the disastrous scheme to entice British emigrants to Brazil in 1872, reported in *The Times*. See Norman Page, 'Hardy and Brazil', *Notes and Queries* 228 (August 1983), 319–20.

5. *a good thing could come out of Nazareth*: From John 1: 46, in which Nathanael asks this of Philip, who leads him to Jesus; a bitterly ironical allusion.

6. *Who can find . . . excellest them all*: Angel's father in fact reads only selections from Proverbs 31: verses 10, part of 15, 17–18 and 27–9. Most significantly, he omits verse 11: 'The heart of her husband doth safely trust in her, so that he shall have no need of spoil.'

7. *who knew neither the world . . . in their own hearts*: 'From fornication and all other deadly sin, and from all the deceits of the world, the flesh and the devil [*Good Lord, deliver us*]' ('The Litany' in *The Book of Common Prayer*). Cf. Chapter XIV and note 11.

8. *failure*: MS. and *Graphic* continue: 'When he pulled up his blind to look out at the night, the familiar objects were there in shape truly, but they had put on new aspects. The shrubs rubbing on the adjoining wall scraped forth the statement, "This is what you have brought us to. We were planted to give pleasure to serene and thankful eyes, not to be blighted by ill-omened rays from yours." '

9. *slave to custom and conventionality*: Hardy was an avid reader of John Stuart Mill as a young man. In the late 1860s, he read and annotated the chapter on individuality in Mill's *On Liberty* (1859) which argued that 'it is the privilege and proper condition of a human being, arrived at the maturity of his faculties, to use and interpret experience in his own way. It is for him to find out what part of recorded experience is properly applicable to his own circumstances and character' (*On Liberty* (London: 1867), p. 33).

CHAPTER XL

1. *Thou art in a parlous state, Angel Clare*: In *As You Like It* Touchstone says: 'Why, if thou never wast at court, thou never saw'st good manners; if thou never saw'st good manners, then thy manners must be wicked; and wickedness is sin, and sin is damnation. Thou art in a parlous state, shepherd' (III.ii.40–44).

2. *The dairyman . . . rid of her*: Marian has in fact already 'left to look for employment elsewhere' (p. 252). Hardy corrected this in 1895: thereafter the dairyman 'has got rid of her'.

3. *"'Twas down in Cupid's Gardens" and "The Tailor's Breeches"*: Barrineau notes: ' "Cupid's Gardens" is a popular song about Cuper's Gardens, a pleasure garden forced to close in 1753 by the popularity of Vauxhall. The speaker is a sailor who goes to the gardens to look at the flowers and find a lover. "The Tailor's Breeches" is a bawdy ballad about a tailor who loves wine and women "exceedingly well". He gets drunk, and in order to win a woman, trades his breeches for her petticoat. His reward is that she steals his breeches, watch, and money' (p. 401).

4. *kissing the . . . rod*: To 'kiss the rod' is to accept chastisement submissively. Angel recklessly decides he will not act as convention dictates. The text has 'kiss the pedagogic rod' but the gloss is referring to the conventional saying, not this version of Hardy's.

5. *affection*: *Graphic* omits most of the discussion after Angel admits he is separated from Tess for 'personal' reasons and turns his proposal into a bitter joke: '. . . affection, and the conversation was continued on the subject of Brazil, Clare asking her jestingly if she would like to go with him. Concerned to find from her affirmative that she took the question seriously, he said no more on that matter, and then lapsed into silence.'

6. *have laid down her life for 'ee*: 'Greater love hath no man than this, that a man lay down his life for his friends' (John 15: 13).

7. *the prophet on the top of Peor*: In Numbers 23–4 the prophet Balaam is enticed by Balak, king of Moab, to curse the Israelites from the top of Mount Peor, but 'the spirit of God [comes] upon him' (24: 2) and he finds he can only bless them; likewise, Izz cannot curse Tess.

8. *to act wisely and well*: The irony is that the three have 'loved not wisely, but too well' (*Othello*, V.ii.344).

9. *a dying man to the dying*: Gibson (p. 389) notes that this is 'probably an echo of the words of the noted English nonconformist divine, Richard Baxter (1615–91): "And as a dying man to dying men!" '

NOTES

CHAPTER XLI

1. *passing mean . . . hers at all*: This is more or less what Tess feels in MS. and *Graphic* in which she *can* sell the jewels: 'there was something repugnant to her sentiments to make away with a wedding-gift of such a marked character, as it would probably be painful to Angel if they were ever united again'.

2. *on Brazilian plains*: Hardy mistakenly situates Curitiba on the low plains: it is more than 3,000 feet above sea level.

3. *Black Care*: Horace, *Odes*, III.i.40: 'Black Care sits behind the horseman.'

4. *she refrained . . . had come*: Tess justifies her decision not to engage in indoor work in *Graphic*:

To indoor work, indeed, Tess had never taken kindly. Mantua-making she hated, so far as she knew anything of it: she could not stitch gloves with rapidity sufficient to earn a maintenance, as some girls in the district were wont to do; and upon the whole the work she was compelled to seek was the work she preferred – that which involved living in the open air. Of the winter wind she knew the worst, and of the bitter sky; but not of man's ingratitude. The possibilities of harm from artificial livers had, so far, surprised her.

This omission, which Hardy decided upon presumably to play down any hint that Tess could have avoided her fate, removes information about the labour-market for women in the region: Snell shows an overwhelming majority were engaged to indoor work – either in service, or in the sweated labour of hand-stitching (*Annals of the Labouring Poor*, p. 404).

5. *Tess*: MS. and *Graphic* continue: 'But a crushing sense that persecution followed her wherever she went, and that the answer would have to be given as a penance, blinded her to the perception that she would have been justified in denying his right to question her.'

6. *All is vanity*: Ecclesiastes 1: 2. 'Vanity of vanities, saith the Preacher, vanity of vanities; all is vanity.'

7. *worse than vanity*: 1892 names them: ' – injustice, punishment, exaction, death'.

8. *fallen one by one as she had heard them*: Hardy abhorred cruelty to animals for whatever reason; see, for example, the harrowing description of the starving horses in *The Hand of Ethelberta*; Jude and Sue listening to the 'agonies of rabbits' caught in traps in IV.11 of *Jude the Obscure*; and 'The Puzzled Game-Birds' (*Poems of the Past and the Present* (1901)).

9. *Nature*: Undecided about what should rightly be opposed to the 'arbitrary law of society', Hardy made several adjustments: 'the moral nature of man' in MS., and 'the moral nature' in *Graphic*.

CHAPTER XLII

1. *The maiden's mouth . . . her head*: From Swinburne's 'Fragoletta' (1866), ll. 41, 44–5.

2. *bosomed with semi-globular tumuli*: Hardy extended this landscape metaphor in 1892, adding 'as if Cybele the Many-breasted were supinely extended there'. Cybele is a goddess represented with many breasts.

3. *molested*: In 1892, Hardy changed to 'clipsed or colled' (hugged or kissed), which is at once more direct and (as dialect) more evasive in its implication of sexual violence.

4. *Old Lady-Day*: Lady Day is the feast of the Annunciation of the Blessed Virgin; in the Gregorian calendar, it falls on 25 March. But Old Lady-Day, fixed by the older Julian calendar on 6 April, continued to be celebrated in some counties. (For the calendars, see Chapter 11, note 5.) Lady-Day is a 'quarter-day' (see Glossary).

CHAPTER XLIII

1. *The swede-field . . . set hacking*: See the poem 'We Field-Women' (*Winter Words in Various Moods and Metres* (1928)) on turnip-hacking at Flintcomb-Ash.

2. *some early Italian conception of the two Marys*: Mary the mother of God and Mary Magdalen. Bullen argues that Hardy uses Italian art to strike a 'contrast between the stark realities, the cruelty and the violence of the present, and the gentleness, the dignity and the humanity of a mythical past' (*The Expressive Eye*, p. 25). In addition, 'many of the scenes' in *Tess* recall the 'amplitude and warmth of the south', which Hardy had visited for the first time in 1887 (p. 191).

3. *and what would . . . such a consummation*: Hardy deleted this hopeful clause in 1895, and inserted at the beginning of the following paragraph: 'Marian, primed to a humorous mood, would discover the queer-shaped flints aforesaid, and shriek with laughter, Tess remaining severely obtuse.'

CHAPTER XLIV

1. *powers of renunciation*: Which are 'fixed rather by her affection than by her sycophancy' in MS. and *Graphic*. This limit and its consequences shocked and offended many readers who expected unlimited powers of renunciation in fallen women: Lionel Johnson, for example, recommended Tess to read

Thomas à Kempis, following the lead of that exemplary renunciatory Victorian heroine, George Eliot's Maggie Tulliver (in *The Mill on the Floss* (1860)): *The Art of Thomas Hardy* (London: Mathews and Lane, 1895), pp. 248–9.

2. *Cross-in-Hand . . . miracle, or murder, or both*: The legend of the Cross-in-Hand (also known as Cross-and-Hand and Crossy-Hand, perhaps alluding to the figure of a woman with crossed hands once engraved on it), is given in Chapter XLV (which relates that 'a human hand' is carved on it), and in Hardy's poem 'The Lost Pyx' (*Poems of the Past and the Present* (1901)).

3. *Publicans and Sinners . . . Scribes and Pharisees*: In Mark 2: 16, the scribes and Pharisees see Jesus eating with publicans and sinners and righteously question his disciples. The Christian compassion of the Clares, in other words, would override their righteous judgement of Tess.

4. *there was nothing left . . . farm*: In 1912, Tess intends to return to Emminster when 'she could again summon courage to face the vicarage'.

5. *ranter*: Includes two sorts of nonconformist preacher, both suggested here: one who preached in the open air (or, as here, in barns and other shelters) in the style of the early Methodists; and one who belonged to an antinomian sect and preached the dominance of grace over law (see note 7 below, and Chapter XXV, note 6).

6. *declamatory . . . dialectician*: That is, he wins over his congregation by force of impassioned rhetoric and not by argument.

7. *O foolish Galatians . . . crucified among you*: St Paul's epistle to the Galatians 3: 1, which continues by urging his correspondents that 'no man is justified by the law in the sight of God . . .: for, The just shall live by faith' (3: 11).

PHASE THE SIXTH

The Convert

CHAPTER XLV

1. *transfiguration . . . almost ferocious*: Alec's complete change allows Hardy to show explicitly what has been implicit in the description of the Clares: the sexual mastery underlying religious fanaticism; the paganism underlying the Pauline fundamentalism of the Reverend Clare; and the close relationship between theolatry and Tess's worship of Angel.

2. *Tess's energies . . . atrophy of his*: Another reference to the story of Samson and Delilah, this time relating to Alec; and a return to the language of energy and atrophy associated with Tess.

3. *her Cyprian image . . . extinguished*: The legend is untraced. However, the 'Cyprian image' is presumably Aphrodite, the entry on whom in Hardy's well-marked copy of Sir William Smith's *A Smaller Classical Mythology* (London: John Murray, 1889) relates how she was born on the sea and 'floated gently in a sea-shell first to Cythera and then to Cyprus'. Moreover in the description of Alec's evangelical 'fire', his displaced sexual ardour is explicitly linked with other images of fire, suggesting that Hardy may be casting him as Aphrodite's ugly and lame husband, Hephaestus, the god of fire. If so, the allusion implies that Alec is Tess's 'rightful' husband, and Angel the lover.

4. *question of Church and State . . . saith the Lord*: Alec refers to the fundamental difference between the established Church of England and the radical nonconformist 'wing' to which he belongs. In 2 Corinthians 6, from which Alec quotes (verse 17), St Paul exhorts his readers to flee the society and pollutions of idolaters; and prefaces this by showing that he has proved himself a faithful minister of God by enduring suffering and ridicule. Compare the Reverend Clare in Chapter XXVI (and note 9).

5. *the first-fruits of the Spirit*: Romans 8: 23. St Paul goes on to say that even such believers 'groan within' themselves, waiting for 'the redemption of our body'.

6. *those who came to scoff. . . pray*: A paraphrase of ll. 179–80 in Oliver Goldsmith's *The Deserted Village* (1770): 'Truth from his lips prevailed with double sway,/ And fools, who came to scoff, remained to pray'.

7. *fleshly tabernacle*: A common biblical epithet, but in a novel which repeatedly invokes Milton, Hardy may be thinking specifically of *Paradise Regained* (1671), which describes the 'True image of the Father . . . /. . . enshrined/In fleshly tabernacle, and human form,/Wandering the wilderness' (IV, 596–600).

8. *far removed from the charm . . . tragic blackness*: A much repeated idea in Hardy, who believed that 'To find beauty in ugliness is the province of the poet'; and 'After looking at the landscape by Bonington in our drawing room . . . I feel that Nature is played out as a Beauty, but not as a Mystery. I don't want to see landscapes, i.e., scenic paintings of them, because I don't want to see the original realities – as optical effects, that is. I want to see the deeper reality underlying the scenic, the expression of what are sometimes called abstract imaginings'; for 'if Nature's defects must be looked in the face and transcribed, whence arises the *art* in poetry and novel-writing? which must certainly show art, or it becomes merely mechanical reporting. I think the art lies in making these defects the basis of a hitherto unperceived beauty, by irradiating them with "the light that never was" on their surface, but is seen to be latent in them by the spiritual eye' (*Life*, 222, 192, 118).

9. *would have helped him . . . to that end*: Alec uncannily usurps the family place of the strayed Angel.

CHAPTER XLVI

1. *to save time*: For 1900, Hardy added: 'It was my old mother's dying wish.' Alec's stratagem of producing the licence is not introduced until 1891.

2. *I cannot stand your looks*: Compare Sue's imploring speech in *Jude the Obscure* (VI.11): 'Don't turn away from me! I can't *bear* the loneliness of being out of your looks!'

3. *The unbelieving husband . . . by the husband*: 1 Corinthians 7: 14. The allusion also hints at Angel's absence, as the next verse states: 'if the unbelieving depart, let him depart'.

4. *Candlemas Fair*: The Feast of the Purification of the Virgin, on 2 February. There were two major hiring fairs each year: this and one at Martinmas (11 November). See also *Far From the Madding Crowd*, Chapter VI, and *The Mayor of Casterbridge*, Chapters XXII and XXIII.

5. *I believe in . . . and so did my dear husband*: The sermon on the mount (Matthew 5–7) is the longest and fullest record of Christ's teaching. Tess's adherence to its 'spirit' is further evidence that her faith, like Clare's, is held in deep suspicion of the dogma of organized religions: for her the New Testament is a Christiad not a Pauliad.

6. *Here she gave her negations*: What Tess does not believe remains unspoken; more crucially, the narrative never gives any evidence of Tess as a reasoning being, but simply 'a vessel of emotions' (Chapter XLVII). Thus, the reader cannot judge how far her 'negations' are simply mechanical repetitions of Angel's or, as we may suspect, a genuine convergence of them with her own. Similarly, Angel's syllogisms (see a few paragraphs later) are not specified. In MS. and *Graphic*, Tess does not give her negations.

7. *Dictionnaire Philosophique to Huxley's essays*: The *Dictionnaire Philosophique* (1764) was written by Voltaire (1694–1778), who bitterly opposed organized religions, but believed in a righteous God. Thomas Henry Huxley (1825–95), the celebrated Victorian agnostic, had published essays since 1863; his *Collected Essays* (1894) ran to nine volumes. In 1892 he wrote, 'I have a great respect for the Nazarenism of Jesus – very little for later "Christianity"' (Leonard Huxley, *Life and Letters of Thomas Henry Huxley* (New York: Appleton, 1901), II, p. 361).

8. *like the devils I believe and tremble*: 'Thou believest that there is one God; thou doest well: the devils also believe, and tremble' (James 2: 19). This recalls the Reverend Clare's hatred of St James's theology of good works, and also points out how hollow Alec's 'faith without works' is and how dangerous Clare's theology is.

9. *you withdrew yourself . . . one victim*: Though Alec admits that Tess is his victim, in claiming that she 'withdrew' herself he also implies that she had given herself. Hardy altered this in 1900 to: 'you took yourself off from me', but reverted to the earlier reading in 1912.

10. *worshipped on the mountains . . . serve in the groves*: When 'the children of Israel . . . forgat the Lord their God', they 'served Baalim [in] the groves', not Jehovah on the mountain-tops (Judges 3: 7); see also 2 Kings 17.

11. *servants of corruption . . . their beginning*: 2 Peter 2: 19–20. Ominously for Tess, verse 18 reads: 'For when they speak great swelling words of vanity, they allure through the lusts of the flesh, through much wantonness, those that were clean escaped from them who live in error.'

12. *witch of Babylon*: In Revelation 17: 5 the Whore of Babylon is described as the Mother of Harlots.

13. *his conversion*: The extensive changes to Alec in 1902 culminate with the confirmation that it was 'his whimsical conversion, which was perhaps the mere freak of a careless man in search of a new sensation, and temporarily impressed by his mother's death'.

CHAPTER XLVII

1. *primum mobile*: The prime mover: in Aristotle's philosophy, it is the first cause of all change, and is therefore not itself subject to change.

2. *a creature from Tophet*: Like a visitant from the valley of fire near Gehenna outside Jerusalem, a kind of hell where idolatrous Jews burnt their sons and their daughters (see Jeremiah 7: 31). In *Paradise Lost* (I, 403–5), Milton writes that Satan 'made his grove/The pleasant valley of Hinnom, Tophet thence/And black Gehenna called, the type of hell'.

3. *a strange northern accent*: Suggests that the Tophet from which the engine-man brings his fire and smoke is a northern industrial city.

4. *his Plutonic master*: Pluto was the god of the underworld in classical mythology.

5. *not stop either*: In 1892, Hardy, considering the unlikelihood of Tess being able to work without respite, has Marian change places with her: 'sometimes . . . for half an hour in spite of Groby's objection that she was too slow-handed for a feeder'.

6. *For some probably economical reason*: The narrative is evasive about the women doing the work of men, though Hardy claims in 'The Dorsetshire Labourer' that women were chosen because they were paid lower wages. In *Annals of the*

Labouring Poor, Snell argues that women working on threshing machines would have been 'almost unheard-of by the 1880s in this region' (p. 392). Compare the reappearance of Car Darch and her sister in Chapter XLIII.

7. *the seven thunders*: During the Last Days in Revelation 10: 1–3, an angel comes down from heaven with a little book and cries with the roar of a lion, after which seven thunders are heard.

8. *Weltlust*: Pleasure in things of the world (German). Compare Hardy's rather different use in *The Mayor of Casterbridge* to describe Lucetta's pleasure in shaking the hand of the 'royal personage': 'The proceedings had been brief – too brief – to Lucetta, whom an intoxicating *Weltlust* had fairly mastered; but they had brought her a great triumph nevertheless' (Chapter XXXVIII).

9. *Hymenæus and Alexander . . . learn not to blaspheme*: From 1 Timothy 1: 20; St Paul exhorts Timothy to hold faith and a good conscience, for others have made 'shipwreck' of their faith (1: 18–19). Like Alec, Hymenæus and Alexander had both made a profession of the Christian religion but lost their faith.

10. *the bachelor-apostle*: St Paul. Alec's repeated references to the example and epistles of Paul show how he has modelled himself on the 'chief of sinners' who is, with St Augustine, the most celebrated of converts; and he uses Paul's fabled bachelorhood to frame his own conversion in terms of sexual restraint.

11. *let go the plough*: See Luke 9: 62: 'And Jesus said unto him, No man, having put his hand to the plough, and looking back, is fit for the kingdom of God.'

12. *you can have the religion of loving-kindness . . . dogma*: Tess is summarizing a long line of free-thinkers from Voltaire to Huxley, and Hardy himself. At the heart is an idea of sincerity, which Hardy felt at this time was being deeply compromised by dogma: a note of 7 October 1888 reads: 'The besetting sin of modern literature is its insincerity. Half its utterances are qualified, even contradicted, by an aside, and this particularly in morals and religion. When dogma has to be balanced on its feet by such hair-splitting as the late Mr. M. Arnold's it must be in a very bad way' (*Life*, 224).

13. *And she shall . . . better with me than now*: Hosea 2: 7 has 'lovers', but otherwise Alec quotes accurately. The prophet is referring to idolatry. Ethelberta uses this same quotation in *The Hand of Ethelberta* (Chapter XXXVII) to express her scruples about leaving her first love for a richer man.

CHAPTER XLVIII

1. *like a Jacob's ladder*: See Genesis 28: 10–12. Jacob dreams of a ladder 'set up on the earth, and the top of it reached to heaven: and behold the angels of God ascending and descending on it'.

2. *the Giant's Hill by Abbot's Cernel*: The naked giant carved in the chalk hillside overlooking Cerne Abbas possibly dates from Roman times.

3. *Pandemonium*: A place of lawless violence, uproar and confusion; and 'the high Capital/Of Satan and his peers' in *Paradise Lost* (I,756–7).

4. *bled calf*: Alec's grotesque sacrificial simile refers to the process of sticking or bleeding calves so as not to colour the veal at slaughter (sticking is described in the well-known pig-killing scene in *Jude the Obscure*, I.x).

5. *my last state . . . my first*: Luke 11: 26, in which Jesus preaches on the perils of an imperfect repentance and conversion. The sinner who believes the devil has gone finds: 'seven other spirits more wicked than himself; and they enter in, and dwell there: and the last state of that man is worse than the first'. Tess fears she will fall into temptation again; the allusion also echoes Alec's situation, of course.

CHAPTER XLIX

1. *this may hasten . . . to Angel*: In MS. and *Graphic*, the Reverend Clare decides that no more letters should be sent on, 'or he and they will cross in mid-ocean'.

2. *as Abraham might have mourned . . . together*: The story of Abraham's willingness to sacrifice his son Isaac is told in Genesis 22: 1–14.

3. *Who was the moral man . . . among things willed*: In MS. 'among things conceived'. Writing in the *Illustrated London News* in 1892, Clementina Black felt that the sentiment that 'a woman's moral worth is measurable not by any one deed, but by the whole aim and tendency of her life and nature' was the 'essence' of the book (Cox, 187). Compare Tess's thoughts on 'sins . . . of inadvertence' in Chapter LI.

4. *her residence . . . her feelings*: In MS. and *Graphic*, Tess sends Angel her address at Flintcomb-Ash, and Angel does write to her: see note 6 below.

5. *Was not the gleaning . . . the vintage of Abi-ezer*: From Judges 8: 2; the metaphor in Judges refers to the victory of the Israelites over the Midianites which the Ephraimites jealously wanted to be part of; Gideon, the general of the Israelites, pacifies them by assuring them that cleaning up after the battle is more honourable than actually winning it.

6. *response to the entreaty*: Tess is less confident in 1892: her expectation 'was alternately great and small. What lessened it was that the facts of her life which had led to the parting had not changed – could never change; and that, if her presence had not attenuated them, her absence could not.'

In MS. and *Graphic*, the vision arouses Angel to write to Tess at Flintcomb-Ash:

It resulted in his writing her a passionate letter, declaring that he forgave her all, and would return in a few weeks. But that letter she never received. Using the direction of Flintcomb-Ash that she had given him, he addressed her in her married name, which her reticence had never allowed her to assume; and when, in the course of a month, the missive reached the post-office of that village, it was promptly returned to the head-office as being that of a person unknown. The result was less to be deplored in that he was unable to return as soon as he had stated, but the assurance might have for the moment cheered, though it would afterwards have disappointed her.

Meanwhile, Tess's warm outpouring lay awaiting him in a drawer at Emminster Vicarage; its ardour pitifully wasting itself on the cold darkness and impercipience of that receptacle, like a star whose rays reach no inhabited planet.

7. *I have parks . . . I did grow*: Furbank notes that 'I have parks, I have hounds' is a 'version of . . . "The Farmer's Toast" ' (p. 435); Barrineau adds: 'It is a rollicking drinking song sung by a farmer who feels wealthy as long as his friends are around him drinking . . . "Such a beauty I did grow" has not yet been located' (p. 406).

8. *To perfect . . . deep desire*: It is her 'whimsical desire' from 1892. MS. and *Graphic* added that 'These preferences of Clare's, if ever he had expressed them, must have been pronounced in the most careless fashion; probably had depended so entirely upon the mood of the moment that he would have disowned them the next day. But Tess never thought of that; to her his estimates were as permanent as those of a divinity . . .'

CHAPTER L

1. *the witches . . . ducked*: According to Firor, ' "pricking the witch" is a device that has long been held the most efficacious among the simpler countercharms against witchcraft' (p. 91). In *The Return of the Native* (III.11), Susan Nunsuch pricks Eustacia Vye with a long stocking-needle to end the spell on Susan's son Johnny. Ducking is the better-known test for a witch: if she sinks, she is innocent; if not, she is a witch.

2. *the 'pillar of a cloud' . . . light by night*: An allusion to the Israelites' flight from Egypt: 'And the Lord went before them by day in a pillar of a cloud, to lead them the way; and by night in a pillar of fire, to give them light; to go by day and night' (Exodus 13: 21).

3. *the old Other One*: The devil. Compare Alec's epithet for himself as the 'old Adam' in Chapter XLV.

4. *Empress, the way . . . said Eve*: *Paradise Lost* IX, 626–31. Satan, 'the wily adder', lures Eve towards the Tree of Knowledge, and he is like 'a wandering fire' which 'misleads the amazed night-wanderer from his way' (625, 634, 640).

5. *'liviers' were disapproved of . . . it was never renewed*: The 'liviers' were lifeholders: tenants who occupied their houses for a succession of lives (three in Durbeyfield's case). These 'half-independent villagers', as Hardy calls them in 'The Dorsetshire Labourer', were more and more often dismissed upon the cessation of the lifehold. Snell notes that these non-migratory small-holders were the focus of considerable class tension in Dorset (*Annals of the Labouring Poor*, p. 381). See also the following chapter.

CHAPTER LI

1. *The labourers . . . introduced from without*: For Hardy, the term 'labourer' suggests industrial work: the workfolk, Hardy writes in 'The Dorsetshire Labourer', are 'under the constant attrition of lives mildly approximating to those of workers in a manufacturing town'.

2. *These annual . . . on the increase here*: Snell argues that 'in Hardy's time the yearly hiring system . . . had become a very minor aspect of the labour market' (*Annals of the Labouring Poor*, p. 394).

3. *The Egypt of one family . . . changed and changed*: Hardy explicitly associates the collapse of rural social structures under industrialization with Tess's (and others') increasing wanderings: both are linked to the Fall, as well as to the exodus from Egypt.

4. *The village had formerly contained . . . by machinery*: This passage is reproduced almost word for word from 'The Dorsetshire Labourer'.

5. *A sudden rebellious . . . the window-panes*: In 1892, Hardy shifted this letter-writing scene until after the reappearance of Alec; thus, Tess's 'sense of injustice' arises not in response to the villagers who evict the Durbeyfields but to him.

6. *Here we suffer . . . no more*: From the Sunday School hymn, 'Heaven Anticipated' (1832), by Thomas Bilby.

7. *Not in utter nakedness . . . do we come*: From stanza V, 63–4, of Wordsworth's ode 'Intimations of Immortality from Recollections of Early Childhood' (1807):

> Our birth is but a sleep and a forgetting:
> The soul that rises with us, our Life's star,
> > Hath had elsewhere its setting,
> > And cometh from afar:
> > Not in entire forgetfulness,
> > And not in utter nakedness,
> But trailing clouds of glory do we come
> > From God who is our home:
> > Heaven lies about us in our infancy! (V, 58–66)

MS. quotes a different passage from the poem: 'Thou little child, yet glorious

in the might/Of heaven-born freedom on thy being's height' (VIII, 122–3).
8. *asked her mother*: In 1892, Joan adds 'Your husband?', to which Tess replies 'in stony hopelessness': 'No. He'll never, never come'. In 1900, this scene ends: 'It was not her husband, she had said. Yet a consciousness that in a physical sense this man alone was her husband seemed to weigh on her more and more.'

CHAPTER LII

1. *the hexagon to the bee*: Hardy's description of the Lady-Day migration is adapted from 'The Dorsetshire Labourer', where this simile is used.
2. *Ark of the Convenant*: The sacred chest containing the Ten Commandments is described in Exodus 25.
3. *The distance was great . . . lodgings somewhere*: In MS. and *Graphic* (in part):
Later in the day they reached the top of a hill which formed part of the upland dividing the Vale from Shottsford-Forum. They had all walked up because of the steepness, and while the horses stood to breathe themselves Tess looked around. The country was more open now; high downs had taken the place of the small fertile fields, and a great deal of the country was uninclosed [*sic*]. A man on a pony could be seen advancing along the road in front, and when he beheld the nature of their waggon load he hastened towards them . . .
'Well, I am sent on to tell 'ee that the rooms at Shottsford be let . . .'
Tess gazed desperately at the waggon of goods. The cold watery sun-light of the gusty evening peered invidiously between the spokes of the waggon-wheels upon the crocks and kettles which swung from the axles; upon the bunches of dried herbs shivering in the wind, . . . exposed to the vicissitudes of a wild roofless hillside for which they were never made. Round about, Hod-Hill, Hambledon, Bulbarrow, and other commanding eminences, looked on imperturbably.
The man went his way, and the defenceless family turned to each other . . .
4. *inscribed*: The gothic lettering reads: The Door of the Sepulchre of the Venerable D'Urberville Family (Latin).
5. *The old order changeth*: Tennyson, *Morte d'Arthur* (1842): 'The old order changeth, yielding place to new' (l. 240).

PHASE THE SEVENTH

Fulfilment

CHAPTER LIII

1. *Crivelli's dead Christus*: The *Pietà* of Carlo Crivelli (*c.* 1435–*c.* 1493) in the National Gallery, which Hardy knew (see Bullen, *The Expressive Eye*, p. 142 and plate 2).

2. *Has any letter . . . he asked*: In 1891, Angel does not receive Tess's long first letter in Brazil: it is on its way back to Emminster, and he will read it in a few days (in earlier versions he must wait a fortnight). In 1892, however, he intercepts it before he returns, adding here: 'I received the last you sent on by the merest chance, and after considerable delay through being inland; or I might have come sooner.' In later versions, therefore, Angel's homecoming, prompted by his own sudden insight, is hastened by her letter.

3. *O why . . . your hands!* – *T.*: As Hardy originally conceived it, in Ur-*Tess*, Tess's letter read:

> Sir: May your son's wife take the liberty of asking you to do her a kind service? If my husband should ever return and inquire for me, or is inclined to seek me, please to inform him that it is my particular request that he do not seek me. Things have happened which make it quite impossible for us to live together, or even be friendly again, and it is far better we should not try to do otherwise than continue the strangers we have been for so long.
>
> T. D'Urberville.

4. *her letter*: 1892 adds: 'showing that her estimate of him had changed under his delay – too justly changed, he sadly owned'.

5. *which alters when it alteration finds*: From Shakespeare's Sonnet 116, 'Let Me Not to the Marriage of True Minds': 'love is not love/Which alters when it alteration finds' (2–3).

6. *virtual Faustina . . . a queen*: Annia Galeria Faustina, the cousin and wife of the Roman emperor Marcus Aurelius, was reputedly unfaithful; the virtuous Cornelia was the wife of Tiberius Sempronius Gracchus and bore him twelve children; Lucretia, the beautiful and virtuous wife of the nobleman Lucius Tarquinius Collatinus, was raped by Sextus Tarquinius; Phryne (Greek for 'The Toad' because of her sallow complexion) was a famous Greek courtesan; the 'one deserving to be stoned' is the adulteress whom Christ pities in John 8; Bathsheba was married to Uriah the Hittite and committed adultery with King David, whom she married after he had arranged Uriah's death.

7. *unmanned him quite*: In 1892, Angel hunts out the letter he had received in Brazil, and the 'sentences touched him now as much as when he had first perused them'. It is after rereading, therefore, that he 'determined that he would no longer believe in her more recent and severer regard of him'.

CHAPTER LIV

1. *a tale that is told*: In 1912, Hardy emended to 'a tale told by an idiot', clarifying the allusion to the soliloquy in which Macbeth exclaims that life:

> . . . is a tale
> Told by an idiot, full of sound and fury,
> Signifying nothing. (V.v.26–8)

CHAPTER LV

1. *the prophet's gourd*: Jonah, displeased that God had spared Nineveh from the destruction he had prophesied, sat outside the city: 'And the Lord God prepared a gourd, and made it to come up over Jonah, that it might be a shadow over his head' (Jonah 4: 6). God kills the gourd the next day with disease.

2. *passed as a married woman*: Tess passes as 'Miss D'Urberville' in *Graphic*, and lives alone. Alec sometimes stays in another set of rooms as her cousin.

3. *Too late, too late*: Cf. Christina Rossetti, 'The Prince's Progress', ll. 481–4:

> 'Too late for love, too late for joy,
> Too late, too late!
> You loitered on the road too long,
> You trifled at the gate . . .'

4. *you have come*: In response to the first reviews, many of which condemned Tess for returning to Alec, Hardy tried to explain her motivation. In his own study copy of 1912, he added: 'These clothes are what he's put upon me: I didn't care what he did wi' me! The step back to him was not so great as it seems. He had been as husband to me: you never had!' See also the following note.

5. *silence*: In 1892, Hardy added: 'But he had a vague consciousness of one thing, though it was not clear to him till later; that his original Tess had spiritually ceased to recognize the body before him as hers – allowing it to drift, like a corpse upon the current, in a direction dissociated from its living will.'

CHAPTER LVI

1. *bound to some Ixionian wheel*: Ixion was bound to a revolving wheel of fire in punishment for boasting of his seduction of Hera.

CHAPTER LVII

1. *enlightenment*: In 1892: 'shining light'.

2. *her Antinous, her Apollo even*: The beautiful Antinous (*c.* 110–30) was a favourite of the Roman emperor Hadrian, and was deified by the Emperor after his death (he drowned in the Nile). (Hardy has 'Adonis' in MS. and *Graphic*.) Apollo, the sun god, is the model for masculine beauty.

3. *steer in a general northerly . . Channel*: In 1892, Angel suggests they 'steer in a general way towards the interior of the country, where we can hide for a time, and are less likely to be looked for than anywhere near the coast . . . Later on, when they have forgotten us, we can make for some port.'

4. *Bramshurst Manor-house*: 'Moyles Court, three miles north-north-east of Ringwood' in F. B. Pinion, *A Hardy Companion*, p. 246 (see Appendix II).

5. *Atalanta's race*: Atalanta was a swift huntress in Greek mythology – a lesser form of Artemis – who offered to marry anyone who could outrun her, but those whom she overtook she speared. Hippomenes (or Milanion) challenged her and was given three golden apples of the Hesperides by Aphrodite; when he dropped them, Atalanta stopped to pick them up, losing the race. Thus they married. See Chapter XIV, note 10.

CHAPTER LVIII

1. *fetch tea, bread . . . beyond*: In 1892, Hardy, realizing that the couple could not make tea without lighting a fire and alerting neighbours, added 'a small tin kettle and spirit-lamp' to Angel's purchases, 'that they might get fire without smoke'.

2. *she is my sister-in-law*: Under English law, Angel cannot marry 'Liza-Lu. The Deceased Wife's Sister Marriage Act (which would have made it possible) was not passed until 1907. See Diane M. Chambers, 'Triangular Desire and the Sororal Bond: The "Deceased Wife's Sister Bill" ', *Mosaic* 29 (1996), 19–36, and Judith Weissman, 'The Deceased Wife's Sister Marriage Act and the Ending of *Tess of the d'Urbervilles*', *American Notes & Queries* 14 (1976), 132–4.

3. *death had not divided us*: In 2 Samuel 1: 23, Saul and his son Jonathan are lamented by David: 'in their death they were not divided'.

4. *Did they sacrifice . . . behind it*: As Angel suggests, Stonehenge, the most important shrine in pagan Britain (begun in 1900 BC), was dedicated to sun-worship, and was also believed to have been used for human sacrifice.

5. *Like a greater . . . not answer*: In Matthew 27: 14 when Jesus is accused by the chief priests, the elders and Pilate, he 'answered . . . never a word'.

CHAPTER LIX

1. *Giotto's 'Two Apostles'*: This picture 'is now thought to be the Two Haloed Mourners from the *Burial of St John the Baptist* by Spinello Aretino' (Bullen, *The Expressive Eye*, p. 21n).

2. *the President of the Immortals . . . sport with Tess*: The 'Æschylean phrase' was claimed by Hardy to be a literal translation of l. 169 of *Prometheus*. In response to the controversy surrounding it, he wrote in *Life*:

Among other curious results from the publication of the book was that it started a rumour of Hardy's theological belief which lived, and spread, and grew, so that it was never completely extinguished. Near the end of the story he had used the sentence, 'The President of the Immortals had finished his sport with Tess', and the [first five] words were, as Hardy often explained to his reviewers, but a literal translation of Aesch. *Prom.* 169: . . . The classical sense in which he had used them is best shown by quoting a reply he wrote thirty years later to some unknown critic who had said in an article:

'Hardy postulates an all-powerful being endowed with the baser human passions, who turns everything to evil and rejoices in the mischief he has wrought,' another critic taking up the tale by adding: 'To him evil is not so much a mystery, a problem, as the wilful malice of his god.'

Hardy's reply was written down but (it is believed), as in so many cases with him, never posted; though I am able to give it from the rough draft:

'As I need hardly inform any thinking reader, I do not hold, and never have held, the ludicrous opinions here assumed to be mine – which are really, or approximately, those of the primitive believer in his man-shaped tribal god. And in seeking to ascertain how any exponent of English literature could have supposed that I held them I find that the writer of the estimate has harked back to a passage in a novel of mine [*Tess*], printed many years ago, in which the forces opposed to the heroine were allegorized as a personality (a method not unusual in imaginative prose or poetry) by the use of a well-known trope, explained in that venerable work Campbell's *Philosophy of Rhetoric* as "one in which life, perception, activity, design, passion, or any property of sentient beings, is attributed to things inanimate." ' (p. 256)

In *Graphic*, Hardy wrote that 'Time, the Arch-Satirist, had had his joke out with Tess.'

3. *As soon as . . . and went on*: Compare the closing lines of *Paradise Lost*: 'They hand in hand with wandering steps and slow/Through Eden took their solitary way' (XII, 648–9).

APPENDIX I

Prefaces to the Fifth and Later Editions

PREFACE TO THE FIFTH EDITION (1892)

This novel being one wherein the great campaign of the heroine begins after an event in her experience which has usually been treated as extinguishing her, in the aspect of protagonist at least, and as the virtual ending of her career[1] and hopes, it was quite contrary to avowed conventions that the public should welcome the book, and agree with me in holding that there was something more to be said in fiction than had been said about the shaded side of a well-known catastrophe. But the responsive spirit in which *Tess of the d'Urbervilles* has been received by the readers of England and America, would seem to prove that the plan of laying down a story on the lines of tacit opinion, instead of making it to square with the merely vocal formulæ of society, is not altogether a wrong one, even when exemplified in so unequal and partial an achievement as the present. For this responsiveness I cannot refrain from expressing my thanks; and my regret is that, in a world where one so often hungers in vain for friendship, where even not to be wilfully misunderstood is felt as a kindness, I shall never meet in person these appreciative readers, male and female, and shake them by the hand.

I include amongst them the reviewers – the great majority[2] – who have so generously welcomed the tale. Their words show that they, like the others, have only too largely repaired my defects of narration by their own imaginative intuition.

Nevertheless, though the novel was intended to be neither didactic nor aggressive, but in the scenic parts to be representative simply, and in the contemplative to be oftener charged with impressions than with opinions,[3] there have been objectors both to the matter and to the rendering.

Some[4] of these maintain a conscientious difference of sentiment[5] concerning, among other things, subjects fit for art, and reveal an inability to associate the idea of the title-adjective[6] with any but the licensed[7] and derivative meaning which has resulted to it from the ordinances of civilization. They thus ignore, not only all Nature's claims, all æsthetic claims on the word, but even the[8] spiritual interpretation afforded by the finest side of Christianity:[9] and drag in, as a vital point, the acts of a woman in her last days of desperation, when all her doings lie outside her normal character.[10] Others dissent on grounds which are intrinsically no more than an assertion that the novel embodies the views of life prevalent at the end of the nineteenth century, and not those of an earlier and simpler generation – an assertion which I can only hope may be well founded. Let me repeat that a novel is an impression, not an argument; and there the matter must rest; as one is reminded by a passage which occurs in the letters of Schiller to Goethe on judges of this class: 'They are those who seek only their own ideas in a representation, and prize that which should be as higher than what is. The cause of the dispute, therefore, lies in the very first principles, and it would be utterly impossible to come to an understanding with them.'[11] And again: 'As soon as I observe that any one, when judging of poetical representations, considers anything more important than the inner Necessity and Truth, I have done with him.'

In the introductory words to the first edition I suggested the possible advent of the genteel person who would not be able to endure the tone of these[12] pages. That person duly appeared, mostly mixed up with the[13] aforesaid objectors. In another of his forms he[14] felt upset that it was not possible for him to read the book through three times, owing to my not having made that critical effort which 'alone can prove the salvation of such an one.' In another, he objected to such vulgar articles as the Devil's pitchfork, a lodging-house carving-knife, and a shame-bought parasol, appearing in a respectable story. In another place he was a gentleman who turned Christian for half-an-hour the better to express his grief that a disrespectful phrase about the Immortals should have been used;[15] though the same innate gentility compelled him to excuse the author in words of pity that one cannot be too thankful for: 'He does but give us of his best.' I can assure this great critic that to exclaim illogically against the gods, singular or plural, is not such an original sin of mine as he seems to imagine. True, it may have some local originality; though if Shakespeare were an authority on history, which perhaps he is not, I could show that the sin was introduced into Wessex as early as the Heptarchy[16] itself. Says Glo'ster to Lear,[17] otherwise Ina, king of that country:

> 'As flies to wanton boys are we to the gods;
> They kill us for their sport.'

The remaining two or three manipulators of *Tess* were of the sort[18] whom most writers and readers would gladly forget; professed literary boxers, who put on their convictions for the occasion; modern 'Hammers of Heretics';[19] sworn Discouragers, ever on the watch to prevent the tentative half-success from becoming the whole success;[20] who pervert plain meanings, and grow personal under the name of practising the great historical method. However, they may have causes to advance, privileges to guard, traditions to keep going; some of which a mere tale-teller, who writes down how the things of the world strike him, without any ulterior intentions whatever, has overlooked, and may by pure inadvertence have run foul of when in the least aggressive mood. Perhaps some passing perception, the outcome of a dream-hour, would, if generally acted on, cause such an assailant considerable inconvenience with respect to position, interests, family, servant, ox, ass, neighbour, or neighbour's wife. He therefore valiantly hides his personality behind a publisher's shutters, and cries 'Shame!' So densely is the world thronged that any shifting of positions, even the best warranted advance, hurts somebody's heels.[21] Such shiftings often begin in sentiment, and such sentiment sometimes begins in a novel.

T. H.
July 1892

PREFACE TO THE OSGOOD, MCILVAINE
'WESSEX NOVELS' EDITION (1895)

The foregoing remarks were written during the early career of this story, when a spirited public and private criticism of its points was still fresh to the feelings. The pages are allowed to stand for what they are worth, almost word for word;[22] but probably they would not have been written now. Even in the short time which has elapsed since the book was first published, some of the critics who provoked the reply have 'gone down into silence',[23] as if to remind one of the infinite unimportance of both their say and mine.

In the present edition it may be well to state, in response to inquires from readers interested in landscape, pre-historic antiquities, and especially old English architecture, that the description of these backgrounds in this and its companion novels has been done from the real. Many features of the first two kinds have been given under their existing names; for instance, the Vale of Blackmoor or Blakemore, Hambledon Hill, Bulbarrow, Nettlecombe Tout, Dogbury Hill, High-Stoy, Bubb-Down Hill, The Devil's Kitchen, Cross-in-Hand, Long-Ash Lane, Benvill Lane, Giant's Hill, Crimmercrock Lane, and Stonehenge. The rivers Froom or Frome, and Stour, are, of course, well known as such. And in planning the stories the idea was that large towns and points tending to mark the outline of Wessex – such as Bath, Plymouth, The Start, Portland Bill, Southampton, &c. – should be named outright. The scheme was not greatly elaborated, but, whatever its value, the names remain still.

In respect of places described under fictitious or ancient names – for reasons that seemed good at the time of writing – discerning persons have affirmed in print that they clearly recognize the originals: such as Shaftesbury in 'Shaston', Sturminster Newton in 'Stourcastle', Dorchester in 'Casterbridge', Salisbury in 'Melchester', Salisbury Plain in 'The Great Plain', Cranbourne in 'Chaseborough', Cranbourne Chase in 'The Chase', Beaminster in 'Emminster', Bere Regis in 'Kingsbere', Woodbury Hill in 'Greenhill', Wool Bridge in

'Wellbridge', Hartfoot or Harput Lane in 'Stagfoot Lane', Hazelbury in 'Nuttlebury',[24] Bridport in 'Port-Bredy', Maiden Newton in 'Chalk Newton', a farm near Nettlecombe Tout in 'Flintcomb-Ash', Sherborne in 'Sherton Abbas', Milton Abbey in 'Middleton Abbey', Cerne Abbas in 'Abbot's Cernel', Evershot in 'Evershead', Taunton in 'Toneborough', Bournemouth in 'Sandbourne', Winchester in 'Wintoncester', and so on. I shall not be the one to contradict them: I accept their statements as at least an indication of their real and kindly interest in the scenes.

January 1895

PREFACE TO THE MACMILLAN WESSEX EDITION (1912)

The present edition of this novel contains a few pages that have never appeared in any previous edition. When the detached episodes were collected as stated in the preface of 1891, these pages were overlooked, though they were in the original manuscript. They occur in Chapter x.

Respecting the sub-title, to which allusion was made above, I may add that it was appended at the last moment, after reading the final proofs, as being the estimate left in a candid mind of the heroine's character – an estimate that nobody would be likely to dispute. It was disputed more than anything else in the book. *Melius fuerat non scribere.*[25] But there it stands.

The novel was first published complete, in three volumes, in November 1891.

T. H.
March 1912

Notes

1. In 1895 Hardy altered to: 'treated as fatal to her part of protagonist, or at least as the virtual ending of her enterprises'.

2. 'by far the majority' (1895).

3. 'convictions' (1895).

4. 'The more austere' (1895).

5. 'opinion' (1895).

6. 'sub-title adjective' (1912).

7. 'artificial' (1895).

8. 'They ignore the meaning of the word in Nature, together with all æsthetic claims upon it, not to mention the' (1895).

9. 'of their own Christianity' (1895).

10. 'and drag . . . normal character' omitted from 1895.

11. *Correspondence between Schiller and Goethe from 1794 to 1805* (trans. L. D. Schmitz) (1871), I, 58.

12. 'endure something or other in these' (1895).

13. 'appeared among the' (1895).

14. 'In one case he' (1895).

15. Andrew Lang, whose critical notice in the *New Review* in February 1892 (Cox, 195–7) particularly galled Hardy:

Not surprisingly, Lang felt himself licensed by such comments to repeat and elaborate his earlier strictures. Whether or not it was he who (as Hardy suspected) originated the term "Tessimism" as a synonym for pessimism, he certainly took Hardy to task in the November [1892] number of *Longman's* [Cox, 238–43] not only for that pessimism but also for his dubious morality and his defects of style and taste. Although Hardy kept public silence thereafter, his hostility towards Lang . . . never abated. (*Biography*, 321)

16. The Heptarchy was the Anglo-Saxon division of England into the seven kingdoms of Wessex, Sussex, Essex, Kent, East Anglia, Mercia (an early kingdom in central England), and Northumbria.

17. 'in *Lear*' (1895); *King Lear*, IV.i.36–7.

18. 'the predetermined sort' (1895).

19. Gibson notes: 'Johann Faber (1478–1541) was a German opponent of the Reformation who earned the name, Malleus Haereticorum' (p. 377).

20. 'whole success later on' (1895).

21. 'galls somebody's kibe' (1895); see *Hamlet*, V.i.139–41.

22. 'worth, as something once said' (1902).

23. See Psalm 115: 17.

24. Called 'Nuzzlebury' in 1891.

25. 'It would have been better not to write it' (Latin).

The Landscapes of Tess of the D'Urbervilles

There are four distinctive Wessex landscapes in *Tess*, corresponding to four of the six main geographical regions of Dorset: the heavy clayland of the Vale of Blackmoor, the rich heathland valleys of the Frome, the forbidding chalk upland of Flintcomb-Ash and the fringes of the great barren heathland which impinge upon the paths of the heroine's journeys.[1] (These are indicated on the accompanying map, as are Tess's journeys.) Unlike Hardy's other novels, which (with the notable exception of *Jude the Obscure*) settle upon particular districts and are unified to some degree by the dominant complexion of the landscape, *Tess* exploits the diversity and distinctiveness of the Wessex landforms and agricultural practices, and each of its four 'intrinsically different' (XVI) settings 'becomes an arena, its peculiar character contrasted with the others, in which Tess acts out a part of her life'.[2]

Most of the action in the first five phases centres upon the 'rival vales' (XVI) of Blackmoor and the Froom (the Frome): 'the valley of her birth and the valley of her love' (XLII). The Vale of Blackmoor, where the novel opens, is characterized by the heaviness of its soil and its 'languorous' atmosphere. It is bounded to the south by the chalk ridge that forms the edge of the cretaceous upland which will feature so prominently later in the novel – the same flat and featureless landscape which Tess approaches from the south-west (after working as a milkmaid in the small dairies to the west, near Port Bredy) when she comes to Flintcomb-Ash. Viewed from the Vale of Blackmoor, however, this chalk ridge is a striking and dramatic series of hills rising over 800 feet. These are Hardy's 'Wessex Heights': Hambledon Hill, Bulbarrow, Nettlecombe-Tout, Dogbury, High-Stoy and Bubb Down.

The 'fertile and sheltered' vale of Blackmoor is separated from the Valley of the Great Dairies by the belt of heathland ('the intervening uplands and lowlands of Egdon' – XVI) which encroaches from the south-east and meets the dip-slope of the chalk upland. This intervening flat and brown terrain serves to keep apart the two emotionally charged landscapes of Blackmoor and the Valley of the Great Dairies. With its 'vast flat' meadows – 'a level landscape compounded of old land-scapes long forgotten, and, no doubt, differing in character very greatly from the landscape they composed now' (XVII) – the Froom valley is a 'green trough of sappiness and humidity' (XXVII), which lacks 'the intensely blue atmosphere' of Blackmoor Vale 'and its heavy soils and scents' (XVI). Where the latter is characterized by heaviness, the former is all lightness: the waters of the Froom are clear and rapid, 'with pebbly shallows that prattled to the sky all day long', unlike the waters of Blackmoor, which are 'slow, silent, often turbid; flowing over beds of mud into which the incautious wader might sink and vanish unawares' (XVI).

To the south and east of Blackmoor Vale, and on the north-eastern edge of the chalk upland, lies The Chase (Cranborne Chase), the 'truly venerable tract of forest land, one of the few remaining woodlands in England of undoubted primæval date'. When Tess returns to Marlott after her stay on the Stoke-D'Urberville property at Trantridge (the real-life Pentridge), near Chaseborough, she finds that 'the soil and scenery differed much from those within Blakemore Vale'.

Flintcomb-Ash Farm lies on the exposed chalk upland – the 'cal-careous downs and corn-lands' – south of Blackmoor Vale. It is 'fifteen miles' walk' from Marlott. This landscape of 'stony lanchets or lynchets' (XLIII) is whitey-brown, virtually tree-less and crossed with white dusty lanes. It is difficult to locate an 'original' of the farm with any precision: emblematically, it lies in the stretch of land between the two valleys (XLII), and in that sense represents Tess's absence from those valleys. F. B. Pinion argues that 'Hardy's topography suggests that [Flintcomb-Ash] was south of Church Hill, a chalky plateau north-east of Alton Pancras, with the "summits" of Nettlecombe Tout to the east and Bulbarrow further away to the north-east. It was, in fact, first called "Alton Ash Farm". Hardy's map of Tess's "wander-ings" places it further east, however, almost south of Nettlecombe Tout' (*A Hardy Companion: A Guide to the Works of Thomas Hardy and their Background* (London: Macmillan, 1968), p. 332 – referred to below as 'Pinion'). On the evening of the threshing, the light falls towards the

Route 1: Tess's Journey from Flintcomb-Ash to Emminster,
Chapter XLIV

Route 2: Tess's Journey from Flintcomb-Ash to Marlott,
Chapter L

Route 3: The flight of Tess and Angel from Sandbourne,
Chapters LVII and LVIII

0   5   10 Miles

0   5   10 Km

SHERTON-ABBAS

BLACKMOC

VALE

Nuzzle

Dogbury
Hill

Route 1

King's Hintock

Bubb
Down

Nettle

Crimmercrock
Lane

Eversheads

High-Stoy

Flintcomb
Ash

Benvill Lane

Abbot's
Cernel

Long-Ash Lane

Emminster

Chalk Newton

Weath

PORT BREDY

Casterbridge

Ev

DEADMAN'S BAY

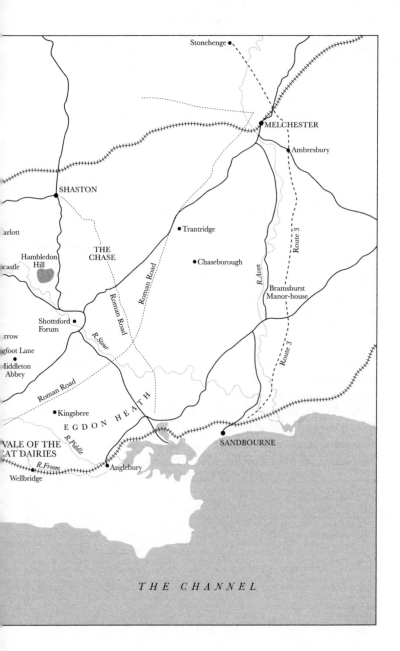

Stonehenge ●

● MELCHESTER

● Ambresbury

SHASTON

arlott

● Trantridge

THE
CHASE

Hambledon
Hill

castle

● Chaseborough

R. Avon

Route 3

Bramshurst
Manor-house

Roman Road

Roman Road

Shottsford
Forum

R. Stour

rrow

gfoot Lane

Route 3

*Aiddleton
Abbey*

Roman Road

● Kingsbere

E G D O N   H E A T H

R. Piddle

SANDBOURNE

VALE OF THE
EAT DAIRIES

R. Froom

● Anglebury

Wellbridge

T H E   C H A N N E L

Giant of Abbot's Cernel as the moon rises over Middleton Abbey and Shottsford, which places Flintcomb-Ash somewhere between Alton Pancras and Melcombe Bingham.

Emminster (Beaminster) is a 'hill-surrounded little town' with its 'Tudor church-tower of red stone' (xxv); between it and Blackmoor lies 'the elevated dorsal line of South Wessex' (XL). Tess makes her way there from Flintcomb-Ash: 'Keeping the Vale on her right she steered steadily westward; passing above the Hintocks, crossing at right-angles the high-road from Sherton-Abbas to Casterbridge, and skirting High-Stoy or Rubdon Hill. Still following the elevated way she reached Cross-in-Hand . . . Three miles farther she cut across the straight deserted Roman road called Long-Ash Lane; leaving which as soon as she reached it she dipped down the hill by a transverse lane into the small town or village of Evershead, being now about half-way over the distance.' (From 1892 Tess skirts 'Dogbury Hill and High-Stoy, with the dell between them called "The Devil's Kitchen"'.) The second half of her journey is 'through a more gentle country, by way of Benvill Lane' and 'about noon she paused by a gate on the edge of the basin in which Emminster and its Vicarage lay' (XLIV).

The novel ends with the meandering route traced between two locations on the fringes of the novel's central landscapes: Sandbourne (Bournemouth) and Stonehenge.

Readers wishing to look further into the topography should consult H. C. Darby, 'The Regional Geography of Thomas Hardy's Wessex', *Geographical Review* 38 (1948), 426–43; Andrew Enstice, *Thomas Hardy: Landscapes of the Mind* (London: Macmillan, 1979), esp. Chapter 6; and John Barrell, 'Geographies of Hardy's Wessex', *Journal of Historical Geography* 8 (1982), 347–61.

KEY TO PLACE NAMES IN TESS OF THE D'URBERVILLES

Abbot's Cernel	Cerne Abbas, north of Dorchester
Ambresbury	Presumably Alderbury. Not mentioned from 1892, when Angel and Tess have to walk through Melchester to cross the river
Anglebury	Wareham
Benvill Lane	'The upper part of the road leading from Evershot to Toller Down; the road beyond leads down to Beaminster' (Pinion, 241)
Bubb Down	Near Melbury Bubb (see *Bulbarrow*)
Bulbarrow	Also known as Bealbarrow, south of Sturminster Newton; one of the hills rising from a chalk band stretching from Cerne Abbas in the direction of Shaftesbury which overlooks Blackmoor Vale
Casterbridge	Dorchester
Chalk-Newton	Maiden Newton
Chaseborough	'Cranborne, a small market town south of the Blandford–Salisbury road' (Pinion, 274)
Crimmercrock Lane	'Originally "Cromlech Crock lane", part of the road from Maiden Newton, leading up to Toller Down on its way to Crewkerne' (Pinion, 289)
Dogbury	Lies near High-Stoy (a landmark in *The Woodlanders*); one of the hills rising from a chalk band (see *Bulbarrow*)
Egdon Waste	Egdon Heath extends from Higher and Lower Bockhampton in the west to an area north of Poole Harbour in the east
Emminster	Beaminster, north of Bridport
Evershead	Evershot, north-west of Dorchester
Greenhill	Woodbury Hill
Hambledon Hill	One of the hills rising from a chalk band (see *Bulbarrow*)
High-Stoy	A 'wooded hill on the chalk downs south of Blackmoor Vale' (Pinion, 366); see *Bulbarrow*

Hintocks	Woodland village settings of *The Woodlanders*, based on Melbury Osmond, Melbury Bubb and Melbury Sampford, north of Maiden Newton
Kingsbere-sub-Greenhill	Bere Regis in Dorset. The family vault of the Turbervilles lies beneath the south aisle of Bere Regis church
Lew-Everard	'The name is derived from Lewell Mill in the valley by the Frome river, and Frome Everard, the old name for Stafford House ... and indicates West Stafford' (Pinion, 389)
Long-Ash Lane	'Part of the old Roman road from Dorchester to Yeovil and Ilchester' (Pinion, 393)
Lullstead	Lulworth (?)
Marlott	Village of Marnhull, near Shaftesbury in the Vale of Blackmoor (which Hardy spells 'Blackmoor' and 'Blakemore' throughout *Tess*).
Melchester	Salisbury
Middleton Abbey	Milton Abbas, due east of Cerne Abbas
Millpond St Jude	Milborne St Andrew (although Pinion notes that 'Hardy's directions are wrong, and perhaps deliberately so' – p. 416)
Nettlecombe-Tout	South-west of Bulbarrow; one of the hills rising from a chalk band (see *Bulbarrow*)
Nuzzlebury	Hazelbury Bryan, in the Blackmoor Vale, beneath Bulbarrow. Changed to Nuttleberry in 1895; and becomes 'the Lane inn' in 1912.
Port Bredy	Bridport
Rubdon Hill	Near High-Stoy on the chalk escarpment
Sandbourne	Bournemouth
Shaston	Hill-town of Shaftesbury, overlooking Blackmoor Vale. In MS. and earlier editions, Durbeyfield is walking home from Stourcastle (Sturminster Newton, which lies on the river Stour) not Shaston in 1; because of this change,

	Hardy mistakenly reintroduces 'the hill-town called Shaston' in v
Sherton Abbas	Sherborne
Shottsford-Forum	Blandford Forum, to the north and east of Cerne Abbas
St Catherine's Hill	St Giles Hill, which overlooks Winchester
Stagfoot Lane	'Hartfoot Lane, a small village among the chalk hills between Nettlecombe Tout and Bulbarrow which overlook the Vale of Blackmoor' (Pinion, 479)
Valley of the Great Dairies	Valley that stretches from Dorchester to Wool
Trantridge	'Generally thought to be Pentridge, from its proximity to Cranborne, the "Chaseborough" of *Tess*' (Pinion, 492)
Var or *Froom*	River Frome
Weatherbury	Puddletown, north-east of Dorchester. (In M S. and *Graphic* Tess's lift takes her not here but to Millpond, near Weatherbury)
Wellbridge	Wool, between Dorchester and Wareham (once known as Woolbridge). 'On the northern side, across the five-arched Elizabethan stone bridge, stands the "Caroline" manor-house which belonged to the Turberville family' (Pinion, 505)
Wintoncester	Winchester

Notes

1. Only the limestone Isle of Purbeck, which features so heavily in Hardy's last novel, *The Well-Beloved*, and the hilly clayland of Western Dorset, do not get mentioned in *Tess*.

2. Andrew Enstice, *Thomas Hardy: Landscapes of the Mind* (London: Macmillan, 1979), p. 116.

The Graphic *Illustrations*

Even before Hardy delivered the first part of the manuscript provisionally entitled *Too Late Beloved* to the conservative newspaper syndicate of Tillotson & Son, he sent in August 1889 'a list of some scenes from the story, that your artist may choose which he prefers'. Typically Hardy took a lively interest in the illustration of his works; he made suggestions to those artists with whom he had direct contact, providing sketches or a photograph to indicate local colour or the proper curve of a chin. In his correspondence with Tillotson, therefore, Hardy recommended scenes that would 'make an effective picture' in the family newspapers to which the work would be marketed.[1] But when Tillotson's cancelled the contract, they returned everything. Hardy's list of scenes and three illustrations, now lost, were apparently not passed along to the *Graphic*. In all likelihood the magazine, known for the high quality of its artwork, preferred to commission one of its own most eminent artists: Hubert Herkomer, who had no contact with Hardy until after publication.

The *Graphic*, a large-format family weekly that addressed a prosperous audience, advertised itself in the *Newspaper Press Directory* as independent, 'admirably illustrated' and 'combining literary excellence with artistic beauty'.[2] An issue would normally carry a full-page cover image, a dozen pictures accompanying current news articles such as the visit of the French fleet or a report on Lord Randolph Churchill's trip to South Africa, a selection of gallery art, a page-long comic strip and lavish pictorial advertisements. Several numbers in 1891 extensively covered the wedding of Princess Louise to Prince Aribert of Anhalt, in honour of which the German emperor visited England. As Hardy's novel was appearing, the *Graphic* ran political articles about

PLATE I   *Tess flung herself down upon the undergrowth of rustling spear-grass as upon a bed.*

a civil war in Chile, sketches about an African chieftain and reports on farming in Australia or Argentina. Artists whose work appeared in 1891 were Robert Barnes and Arthur Hopkins (both had illustrated novels by Hardy), Frank Brangwyn, Joseph Nash and Lawrence Alma-Tadema; their style ranged from brusquely realistic to lushly romantic, indicating the eclectic visual taste of the readers.

That readership was what the assistant editor William Locker called a 'peculiar *clientele*'. In a letter of 25 June 1890 warning Hardy of improprieties in *A Group of Noble Dames*, Locker noted that stories in the magazine were read aloud by fathers to their families. He rejected as 'hopeless' certain stories, and demanded cuts or bowdlerization of 'questions of childbirth, and those relations between the sexes over which conventionality is accustomed (wisely or unwisely) to draw a veil' in order to protect 'the delicate imaginations of young girls'.[3] One issue raised by the illustration of *Tess of the D'Urbervilles*, then, is the impact of the *Graphic*'s policies on the selection of the scenes (twenty-five) to be illustrated.

Many suggestive descriptions of violence or of physical desire remain in the serial text, and a surprising number of these attracted illustrations, such as the death of the horse Prince (IV),[4] Tess awakening amid a field of fatally wounded pheasants (XLI) and the murder of Alec (LVI). Some of the sensual scenes highlighted by an illustration, which one might have thought would concern editorial sensitivities, are Tess's first visit to Trantridge, when Alec insists on thrusting a strawberry into her mouth (V); the meeting between Tess and Angel in the uncultivated dairy garden, where 'the floating pollen seemed to be his notes made visible' (XIX); Angel's ecstatic embrace of Tess while she is milking (XXIV); and Angel sleepwalking with Tess in his arms to the cloister garden (XXXVII).

Even in modern unillustrated editions, these moments have continued to arrest readers' attention. Yet the thematic weight of such images strongly indicates that the board and editors of the *Graphic* were not involved in selecting the passages to be illustrated. To be

PLATE II *They reached the cloister-garth, where were the graves of the monks. Upon one of these graves he carefully laid her down.*

sure, there may have been a tacit line between what the 'hatchet men' rejected in a text[5] and what was acceptable in serious visual depiction, a possibility raised by the 'fine' academic art printed in the journal during 1891, e.g. the 22 August number reproduced *La Cigale* by Henrietta Rae, depicting a nude musician curled up in a forest (from the Royal Academy), while the preceding week showed P. H. Calderon's *St Elizabeth of Hungary's Great Act of Renunciation*, in which the saint bends over naked on her knees before an altar with nuns and a monk looking on severely. Whatever the contradictions of the *Graphic*'s illustration policy, it seems clear that the editor Arthur Locker left the decisions about what to engrave to the illustrator.

The publisher's choice of an illustrator for *Tess* was Hubert Herkomer (1849–1914). A regular contributor to the journal, Herkomer had emigrated from Bavaria as a child to the United States before moving to England in 1857; he had studied at Southampton, Munich and South Kensington. In 1869, the sale of a picture of two gypsies to the *Graphic* for £8 released Herkomer from part-time work as a mason and musician. In the 1870s he contributed to *Good Words for the Young*, the *Illustrated London News*, *London Society* and the *Cornhill Magazine*.[6]

Herkomer specialized in rural or proletarian subjects charged with human suffering such as the blind weaving baskets, the unemployed or those on strike – topics that made Vincent Van Gogh particularly admire him.[7] *Hard Times* (1885) depicted rural hardships similar to those described in *Tess*, when 'Hundreds of honest labourers wandered through the country in search of work.'[8] *The Last Muster*, which sold for £1200, won a Medal of Honour at the International Exhibition in Paris (1878). Herkomer became an Associate of the Royal Academy in 1879 and at Ruskin's suggestion was named Slade Professor of Art at Oxford University (1885–94); he was ennobled by the German

PLATE III   *On going up to the fire to throw a pitch of dead weeds upon it, she found that he did the same on the other side. The fire flared up, and she beheld the face of D'Urberville. The unexpectedness of his presence, the grotesqueness of his appearance in a gathered smock frock, such as was now worn only by the most old-fashioned of the labourers, had a ghastly comicality that chilled her as to its bearing. D'Urberville emitted a low, long laugh.*

emperor in 1899 (adding 'von' to his name), became a Chevalier in the Légion d'Honneur in 1900 and was knighted in 1907.

In 1883 Herkomer had founded a school of art at Bushey, outside London, which he directed until 1904. By then five hundred students had attended, the majority of them women. Herkomer charged only fees for costs, not tuition; he derived his income from sales of his landscapes, genre paintings and portraits of leading figures such as John Ruskin, Alfred Tennyson, Richard Wagner, Lord Kitchener, Queen Victoria and the Prince of Bavaria. At Bushey, to achieve 'plein air' effects, Herkomer devised a portable studio and glassed in an area where his students could paint animals under natural light.

In his autobiography Herkomer emphasized his early formation as an illustrator: 'it left me with an ineradicable love of black-and-white art', which 'trains the mind to *see subjects*; it exercises the sense of design; and it increases powers of drawing'. Engraving for the *Graphic* was also well paid and respected. Herkomer reported that the founder of the journal had 'trained' the public taste rather than cater to it; he 'dictated to the public, and never allowed his shareholders to dictate to him; his one aim was high art'.[9] Herkomer experimented technically: he invented a new white ground that made etched lines appear dark to the engraver and perfected 'electro-deposition' in a process he called Herkomergravure. In terms reminiscent of Hardy, he wrote that engraving had absorbed him for a quarter of a century, as a 'well-beloved' that he pursued in ever-new forms, including lithography.

Herkomer resisted the 'mere copying of the objects'. In a chapter on portraiture, he wrote: 'Paradoxical as it may sound, a portrait may be *like*, and yet not life-like, and contrariwise'. Art deals with impressions: 'Truth in art is what it seems to the individual, and not what it is'. Realistic attention to detail, then, becomes a way to resist a conventional treatment that seeks the 'pattern': 'Whatever the cause of its origin or continuation, convention is a hard thing to kill'.[10]

By virtue of his favoured subject matter and of his aesthetic philosophy, therefore, Herkomer was an appropriate choice to illustrate a novel that exposed rural poverty and raised questions about the nature of representation. Herkomer, however, drew only six of the engravings for *Tess*; he shared the task with three of his students: Ernest Borough

Johnson (1867–1949), Daniel A. Wehrschmidt (1861–1932), and Joseph Syddall (*fl.* 1898–1904). This was not unusual considering the deadlines under which twenty-five wood engravings were to be produced. Herkomer's decision to collaborate was of a piece with his efforts to advance his students' careers both in commercial engraving and through exhibitions. Johnson (who provided six illustrations, five of which were printed in the US editions) found the greatest professional success. While still a student he showed *Her Daily Bread* at the Royal Academy. Headmaster for fifteen years in the Art Department of Chelsea Polytechnic, he also taught painting and drawing at the London School of Art and published books in the field. Johnson acquired a reputation for shocking realism and dark tonalities; his dramatic composition and careful shading skilfully depict inner struggle and repressed desires. For example, Johnson's engraving of Tess in despair, having 'flung herself down upon the undergrowth of rustling spear-grass as upon a bed', picks up the sexual implications of the text. The conflicts between 'palpitating misery' and momentary 'shoots of joy' spring to view in this agitated, arched figure (XXVIII). It is certainly a moment when, as Hardy puts it, 'sex takes the outside place in the presentation' (XXVII), yet Johnson's voyeurism mingles with an achieved interiority. Wehrschmidt, who anglicized his name as Veresmith, eventually became an Art Master at Bushey for twelve years; a successful portrait painter and graphic artist, he exhibited at the Royal Academy. Wehrschmidt completed eight of the illustrations, while Syddall did the other five. Syddall's career is less well documented, although he exhibited portraits at the Royal Academy.

The styles of the four artists, as displayed in the *Tess* engravings, are distinctly different. So different are they that Carroll A. Wilson commented on the 'strangely unlike' depictions of Tess and Angel, who shift in shape and manner from week to week.[11] These interpretations unintentionally reinforce the effect that Tess passes through successive 'phases' lacking organic unity: the cut of Tess's chin, the slant or arch of her brows, the texture of her hair and her mysterious 'peony' mouth all vary disconcertingly. Both Alec and Angel in the early numbers seem boyish, their faces lacking modelling, and their shifting images therefore remind us of changes in character. Development, however, is undercut because of the weaker delineations by Syddall and Wehrschmidt. Syddall's sketches of rural life use a scratchy, light touch to establish an airy background for figures without much definition or depth. His realism was challenged by a US reviewer in *Harper's New Monthly Magazine* for putting 'the milkmaid on the wrong side of the cow'.[12] Under Wehrschmidt's pen the characters seem stiffly conventional.

The strongest images and the most consonant with each other are those drawn by Herkomer and Johnson. Herkomer's illustrations demonstrate his powerful sense of form and control of line in the service of character and dramatic effect.[13] What Hardy shows in the novel, for example, in the tragic separation of Tess and Angel pulled apart by feelings working at a tangent, finds expression not only in the meeting of sexual drives with the death drive in Angel's embrace of Tess on the tomb, but in Herkomer's delineation of the failure of Angel's sleepwalking gaze to meet Tess's yearning eyes (XXXVII).[14]

The images produced by the four artists coincide in their common assumption of a perspective with Tess as the object of attention. As N. N. Feltes has observed, the text often locates the reader within Tess's consciousness, looking outward, but the illustrations consistently position the reader facing Tess, whether viewing her from behind her mother, Alec or Angel. In considering a drawing by Wehrschmidt where Angel confronts Tess on a landing above him, Feltes concludes that this angle of vision presents Tess 'not as the conscious agent in a complexly determined moment but as a woman who has been accosted while alone, who yet is protected by rules of decorum . . . so necessary to the commodity-text'.[15] Tess, of course, is the primary commodity offered for consumption by these images. Yet one of the rules of decorum followed in the majority of the images is the separation of the lovers: whether Angel is jumping up and knocking over his stool to embrace Tess, standing at the bottom of the stairs instead of right next to her on the landing or watching over her outstretched on an altar stone at Stonehenge, space as a rule protects Tess from too physical a visualization of their relationship.

Although the artists must not have collaborated very closely, the mosaic of scenes does develop into a highly patterned sequence.

Undoubtedly this structure in part reflects Hardy's own overdetermined layering of patterns – natural, historical, legendary, social and others.[16] Thus the homecoming scene that Herkomer selected for his first, double-page spread introducing the novel, when Tess returns to her dreary cottage from club-walking, prepares the reader for the many other homecomings, arrivals and departures that map the peregrinations of Tess and Angel.

The predominant tone is dark, with sharp chiaroscuro contrasts that set off the figure of Tess and reinforce the pattern of death, beginning with Prince collapsed in the roadway, followed later by the groaning pheasants, a darkly immobile Alec and Tess herself, whose final rest at Stonehenge foreshadows her execution. But there is also a visual chain of gardens, linked to more extensive motifs of fertility: the gift of strawberries to Tess by Alec, who is linked by other details to Satan in the garden of Eden; Angel's hesitant approach to Tess in the untended, blighted garden at Talbothays; the ruined cloister garth or churchyard at Wellbridge; and the infernal burning vegetable plot at Marlott, drawn with brilliant melodrama by Herkomer to evoke both Alec's aggression and his underlying connection to Tess, victim and victimizer. Life and death meet in this garden plot, whose pollarded thorn trees with arching whips of branches bracket the doomed pair on one side, met by flickering flames and smoke on the other. At their best, these illustrations capture the movement of the narrative, including its contrasts and ironic qualifications.

The dramatic impact of this last scene serves to remind us that Herkomer's involvement with *Tess of the D'Urbervilles* did not stop with its serial publication. Inspired by his love of theatre design and acting, Herkomer began making films in 1912 and established a film studio with his son; they contracted to produce *Tess* but went out of business before the film could be made.

The three-volume first edition of *Tess of the D'Urbervilles* was not illustrated, while the US one-volume edition published in January 1892, like the version in *Harper's Bazar*, used eleven of the *Graphic* illustrations. The collected edition of 1895–6 provided a map of Wessex and an etching of the Wellbridge Manor House 'drawn on the spot' by H. Macbeth-Raeburn. Not until 1926, when Hardy agreed to an edition of 325 copies printed on large paper with the plates of the 1912–13 Wessex Edition, was the novel again fully illustrated, with forty-one wood engravings by Vivien Gribble.

Margaret R. Higonnet

Notes

1. *Collected Letters*, I, 197.

2. Cited by N. N. Feltes, *Modes of Production of Victorian Novels* (Chicago: University of Chicago Press, 1986), pp. 83–4.

3. Dorset County Museum, quoted in Gatrell, 81–2.

4. Readers who consult the serial should note that its numbering of chapters differs from 1891.

5. Gatrell, 92.

6. Philip V. Allingham, 'Six Original Illustrations for Hardy's *Tess of the D'Urbervilles* Drawn by Sir Hubert von Herkomer, R. A., for *The Graphic* (1891)', *Thomas Hardy Journal* 10 (1994), 54.

7. Lee M. Edwards, 'The Heroic Worker and Hubert von Herkomer's "On Strike"', *Art Magazine* 62 (1987), 31.

8. E. Grant Longman and Horace C. White, *Bushey Then and Now*, Booklet 1 (Bushey, 1974), p. 20.

9. Sir Hubert von Herkomer, *The Herkomers* (London: Macmillan and Co., 1910), II, pp. 158, 162–3.

10. Ibid., II, pp. 123, 126, 121.

11. Carroll A. Wilson, *Descriptive Catalogue of the Grolier Club Centenary Exhibition of the Works of Thomas Hardy* (Waterville, Maine: Colby College Monograph no. 9, 1940), cited in Arlene M. Jackson, *Illustration and the Novels of Thomas Hardy* (Totowa, N. J.: Rowman and Littlefield, 1981), p. 57.

12. 'Editor's Study', *Harper's New Monthly Magazine* (June 1892), 152.

13. See Allingham, 'Six Original Illustrations', 52–69.

14. This scene, which violates the rule of decorous separation, immediately precedes the moment when Angel will kiss her lips a second time and fall asleep beside her, the symbolic 'spurt of mental excitement which had produced the effort . . . now over'.

15. Feltes, *Modes of Production of Victorian Novels*, p. 73.

16. See Gillian Beer, *Darwin's Plots* (London: Routledge and Kegan Paul, 1983).

A Poem Relating to Tess

TESS'S LAMENT

(from *Poems of the Past and the Present* (1901))

I

I would that folk forgot me quite,
          Forgot me quite!
I would that I could shrink from sight,
          And no more see the sun.
Would it were time to say farewell,
To claim my nook, to need my knell,
Time for them all to stand and tell
          Of my day's work as done.

II

Ah! dairy where I lived so long,
          I lived so long;
Where I would rise up staunch and strong,
          And lie down hopefully.
'Twas there within the chimney-seat
He watched me to the clock's slow beat –
Loved me, and learnt to call me Sweet,
          And whispered words to me.

III

And now he's gone; and now he's gone; . . .
          And now he's gone!
The flowers we potted perhaps are thrown
          To rot upon the farm.

And where we had our supper-fire
May now grow nettle, dock, and briar,
And all the place be mould and mire
      So cozy once and warm.

IV

And it was I who did it all,
      Who did it all;
'Twas I who made the blow to fall
      On him who thought no guile.
Well, it is finished – past, and he
Has left me to my misery,
And I must take my Cross on me
      For wronging him awhile.

V

How gay we looked that day we wed,
      That day we wed!
'May joy be with ye!' they all said
      A-standing by the durn.
I wonder what they say o'us now,
And if they know my lot; and how
She feels who milks my favourite cow,
      And takes my place at churn!

VI

It wears me out to think of it,
      To think of it;
I cannot bear my fate as writ,
      I'd have my life unbe;
Would turn my memory to a blot,
Make every relic of me rot,
My doings be as they were not,
      And leave no trace of me!

'Saturday Night in Arcady', 'The Chaseborough Dance' and 'The Midnight Baptism'

When Hardy 'dismembered' *Tess* for publication in the *Graphic*, he decided to publish the excised sections as separate stories. The first, the Chaseborough dance scene and the rape–seduction in The Chase (Chapters x and xi), was published in the *National Observer* as 'Saturday Night in Arcady'. The other, Chapter xiv, appeared in the *Fortnightly Review* as 'The Midnight Baptism'. Most of this material was duly reinstated when Hardy pieced 'the trunk and limbs of the novel together' for the first volume edition, but readers familiar with *Tess* will immediately notice the absence of the Chaseborough dance scene in the Penguin edition, which is based on 1891. That scene, as it was reinstated in 1912 in the Wessex Edition, is reproduced below.

A. SATURDAY NIGHT IN ARCADY

(*National Observer*, Special Literary Supplement, 4 November 1891)

The *National Observer* (formerly *Scots Observer*), an imperialistic and anti-democratic periodical, was driven by W. E. Henley's autocratic style and reflected his militant Conservatism. It had a modest circulation (seldom more than one thousand copies), but a considerable reputation for shocking or offending its readers, which may have prompted Hardy to choose it. According to Jerome Buckley, 'Henley refused to cater to the respectability of "decent Englishwomen". He bemoaned the fact "that the theory and practice of British art [were] subject to the influence of the British schoolgirl, and that he [was] unworthy the name of artist whose achievement [was] of a kind to call a blush to the cheek of youth". Sex, he declared, was "the great subject, the leaven of imaginative art"' (*William Ernest Henley: A Study in the Counter-Decadence of the 'Nineties* (New York: Columbia University Press, 1945), pp. 156–7).

He was masterful, supercilious, coarse; and Big Beauty (as she was called) could not bring herself to encourage him. But he won her. This was how and when.

The farm had an abiding defect. It was a drinking farm. It had always been a trouble to the parson in this respect; and since the son of its owner had arrived at man's estate the failing had become more marked. The staple subject of conversation in the fields was on the uselessness of saving money; and sundry smock-frocked arithmeticians, leaning on their ploughs or hoes, would enter into calculations of great nicety to prove that parish relief was a better provision for a man in his old age than could possibly result from the savings practicable upon their wages during a whole life-time. It was quite true; and they made merry while their blood ran warm.

The chief pleasure of these philosophers lay in going every Saturday night when work was done to a decayed market-town two or three miles off; and, returning in the small hours of next morning, to spend Sunday in sleeping off the dyspeptic effects of the curious compounds sold to them as beer by the monopolizers of the once independent inns. Under pressure Beauty at length consented to go with the rest. It was dark by the time they arrived. They parted for marketing; and her own purchases having been quickly executed she began to look about for the other cottagers for the sake of their company home.

She could not find them, and she was informed that the majority had gone to what they called a private little jig at the house of a hay-trusser and peat-dealer who had transactions with their farm.

Approaching the hay-trusser's she could hear the fiddled notes of a reel proceeding from some building in the rear; but no sound of dancing was audible: an exceptional state of things for these parts, where, as a rule, the dancing drowns the music. She traversed the dwelling, and went up the path to the outhouse whence the notes came.

It was a windowless erection used for the storage of peat, and from the open door there floated into the night a mist of yellow radiance, which at first she thought must be illuminated smoke. But on drawing near she perceived that it was a cloud of buoyant particles lit by the candles within, whose glimmer made staves of sheen upon the exhalation.

Through this she beheld indistinct forms racing up and down to the figure of the dance, the silence of their footfalls being at last accounted for. The revellers were footing the tune on a floor lying overshoe in 'scroff' – the powdery residuum of the peat lately stacked there – the stirring of which by their turbulent toes and heels had also produced the dense nebulosity that involved the scene.

Through this floating, fusty *débris* of a late geologic period, mixed with breathings, odours, and perspirations from the dancers, and forming altogether a sort of vegeto-human pollen, the muted fiddles feebly pushed their notes, in marked contrast to the spirit with which the measure was trodden out.

They coughed as they danced, and laughed as they coughed. There could barely be discerned of the rushing couples more than the high-lights. The indistinctness shaped them to satyrs clasping nymphs – a multiplicity of Pans whirling a multiplicity of Syrinxes; Lotis attempting to elude Priapus[1] – and always failing.

At intervals a couple would approach the doorway, and, the haze no longer veiling their features, the demi-gods resolved themselves into the homely personalities of Beauty's next-door neighbours. In two or three short hours had the village migrated from its roof-trees and metamorphosed itself thus madly.

'When be any of you going home?' anxiously asked the girl of some Sileni[2] of the throng who sat on hay-trusses by the wall.

'A'most directly,' they replied, as they skimmed the dust from their beer with the forefinger.

But the dance in hand merged in another, and another still. She became restless and uneasy: yet having waited so long it was necessary to wait longer; the roads were lonely.

'Don't 'ee be nervous, my dear good soul!' expostulated between his coughs a young man with a wet face, and a straw hat so far back upon his head that the brim encircled it like the nimbus of a saint.

'What's yer hurry? To-morrow's Sunday, thank God, and we can sleep it off. Now do ye, my dear, have a turn with me?'

She did not abhor dancing, but she shunned it here. The movement grew more passionate. The fiddlers behind the luminous pillar of cloud now and then varied the air by playing on the wrong side of the bridge, and on the tail-piece, and with the back of the bow. But it did not matter: the panting shapes spun onwards.

They did not vary their partners if their inclination were to stick to the same ones. Changing partners simply meant that a satisfactory choice had not been made; and by this time every couple was suitably matched. It was then that the ecstasy and the dream began; in which emotion was the matter of the universe, and matter but an adventitious intrusion calculated to hinder you from spinning where you wanted to spin.

Suddenly there was a dull thud on the ground: a couple had fallen, and lay in a mixed heap. The next couple, unable to check its progress, came toppling over the obstacle; and an inner cloud arose amid the general mist, in which a twitching entanglement of arms and legs was discernible.

'The Lard-a Lard! An you shall catch it for this, my gentleman, when you get home!' burst in feminine accents from the heap: the voice of the unhappy partner of the man whose clumsiness had caused the mishap – a partner who happened to be also his recently married wife.

A loud laugh from behind Big Beauty's back united with the squabbling within the outhouse. She looked round and saw the red coal of a cigar. The man she avoided – the son of her employer – was standing there alone. He beckoned to her, and she reluctantly retreated with him.

'Well, mine! what are you doing here?'

She was so tired that she confided her trouble to him – that she was waiting for their company home because the road at night was strange to her.

'I rode in to-day,' he said, 'and intended to ride back. But come to The Stag, and the horse shall be put into a gig, and I'll drive you.'

Her mistrust of him was such that, with all their tardiness, she preferred to walk home with the villagers. 'No,' she said, 'I will not go.'

'Very well, Madam Independence: please yourself.'

He said this and departed. The mishap to the dancers had checked the merriment, and in no very good humour they soon prepared to leave. Their bundles and baskets were all gathered up, and in a few minutes, when the clock-chime sounded half-past ten, they were straggling along the lane which led out of the town towards the village.

It was a three-mile walk, along a dry, white road, made whiter now by the light of the lately risen moon.

She soon perceived as she walked in the flock, sometimes with this one, sometimes with that, that the fresh night air was producing staggerings and serpentine courses among the men who had partaken too freely; some of the more liquor-loving women also were wandering in their gait – to wit, the dark girl Car Darch, dubbed Queen of Spades; Nancy Serjeant, the Queen of Diamonds; and the young married woman who had tumbled down. Yet, however terrestrial and lumpish their appearance just now to the mean, unglamoured eye, with themselves the case was different. While they marked the road with a pattern like the map of St Paul's course in the Euroclydon,[3] they nevertheless knew that they were skimming along like swallows, were full of original and profound thoughts; themselves and surrounding Nature forming an organism of which all the parts harmoniously and joyously interpenetrated each other. They were as sublime as the moon and stars above them; and the moon and stars were as ardent as they.

Big Beauty, however, had undergone such painful experiences in this kind at other times that the discovery of their condition spoilt the pleasure she was beginning to feel in the moonlight journey. Yet she still stuck to the party for reasons above given.

In the open highway they had progressed in scattered order; but now their route was through a field-gate, and, the foremost finding a difficulty in opening it, they closed up together.

This leading pedestrian was Car, the Queen of Spades, who carried a wicker-basket containing her mother's groceries, her own draperies, and other purchases for the week. The basket being large and heavy, Car had placed it for convenience of porterage on the top of her head, where it rode onwards in jeopardized balance as she walked with arms akimbo.

'Well! . . . Whatever is that a-creeping down thy back, Car Darch?' said one of the group suddenly.

All looked at Car. Her gown was a light cotton print, and from the back of her head a kind of rope could be seen descending to some distance below her waist, like a Chinaman's queue.

' 'Tis her hair falling down,' said another.

No: it was not her hair; it was a black stream of something oozing from the basket; and it glistened like a slimy snake in the cold, still rays of the moon.

' 'Tis treacle,' said an observant matron.

Treacle it was. Car's poor old grandmother had a weakness for the sweet stuff: honey she possessed in plenty out of her own hives; but treacle was what her soul desired, and Car had been about to give her a treat of surprise. Hastily lowering the basket the dark girl found that the vessel containing it had overturned within.

By this time there had arisen a shout of laughter at the extraordinary appearance of Car's back, which irritated the dark queen into getting rid of the disfigurement by the first sudden means available, and independently of the help of the scoffers. She rushed excitedly into the field they were about to cross, and, flinging herself down upon the grass, began gyrating horizontally upon her back, and dragging herself hither and thither upon her elbows, to wipe the hind part of her bodice and gown as well as she could without taking them off.

The laughter became louder: they clung to the gate, to the posts, rested on their staves as a support against the weakness engendered by their convulsions at the spectacle of Car. She who had hitherto held her peace forgot her dignity at this wild moment: Big Beauty could not help joining with the rest, in that intense low laugh of hers which shook her shoulders.

It was a misfortune to her in more ways than one. No sooner did the dark queen hear the soberer, richer note among those of the other workfolk than a long-smouldering sense of rivalry inflamed her to madness. She sprang to her feet, and closely faced the object of her dislike.

'How darest th' laugh at me, hussy!' she cried.

'I couldn't really help it – when t'others did,' apologized the girl.

'Ah! th'st think th' beest everybody, dost n't? because th' beest first favourite with master just now! But stop a bit, my big beauty, as he calls ye – stop a bit! I'm as good as two of such! Look here – here's at 'ee!'

To her dismay the dark queen began stripping off her gown – which for the added reason of its ridiculed condition she was only too glad to be free of – till she had bared her plump neck, shoulders, and arms to the moonshine, under which they looked as luminous and beautiful as some Praxitelean creation, in their possession of the faultless rotundities of a lusty country woman.

She closed her fists and squared up to the young offender.

'Indeed, then, I shall not fight!' said the other with dignity. 'And if I had known you was of that sort I wouldn't have so let myself down as to come with such a whorage as this!'

The rather too inclusive definition brought down upon the fair speaker's unlucky head a torrent of vituperation from the other women, particularly from the Queen of Diamonds, who, having stood in relations to their ruling young man that Car had also been suspected of, united with the latter against the common supplanter. Several other women also chimed in with an animus which none of them would have been so fatuous as to show but for the rollicking evening they had passed. Thereupon, finding that a pretty girl was getting unfairly browbeaten, the husbands and lovers tried to make peace by defending her; but the result of that attempt was directly to increase the war.

The young woman was indignant and ashamed. She no longer minded the loneliness of the way and the lateness of the hour; her one object was to get away from her dear friends as soon as possible. Surely there was not another such a set of farmfolk in the county. Her suspicions of the farm before coming there, gathered from casual reports, were only too true. She knew well enough that the better among them would repent of their passion next day. They were all now inside the field, and she was surreptitiously edging away from them to rush off alone, when a horseman emerged almost silently from the corner of the hedge that screened the road, and the son of their employer looked round upon the scene.

'What the devil is all this row about, workfolk?' he asked.

The explanation was not readily forthcoming, and in truth he did not require any. Having heard their voices while yet some way off, he had ridden creepingly forward, and learnt enough to satisfy himself. Big Beauty, preparing to make a run for it, was standing apart from the rest, close to the gate. He bent over towards her. 'Jump up behind me,' he whispered, 'and we'll get shot of the screaming cats in a jiffy!'

She felt almost ready to weep, so vivid was her sense of the crisis. At almost any other moment of her life she would have refused his proffered aid and company, as she had refused them several times before. And even now the loneliness would not of itself have forced her to do otherwise; neither would the attack of the women. But coming as the invitation did at the particular juncture when defeat and indignation at these adversaries could be transformed by a spring of the foot into a triumph over them, she abandoned herself to her impulse, put her toe upon his instep, and leapt into the saddle behind him. The pair were speeding away into the distant grey by the time that the contentious revellers became aware of what had happened.

The Queen of Spades forgot the stain on her bodice, and stood beside the Queen of Diamonds and the new-married staggering young woman, with a gaze of fixity in the direction in which the horse's tramp that bore their supplanter along was diminishing into silence on the road.

'What be ye looking at?' asked a man who had not observed the incident.

'Ho-ho-ho!' laughed dark Car.

'Hee-hee-hee!' laughed the tippling bride, as she steadied herself on the arm of her fond husband.

'Heu-heu-heu!' laughed dark Car's mother, stroking her moustache as she exclaimed laconically, 'Out of the frying-pan into the fire!'

And then these children of the open air, whom even alcohol could scarce injure permanently, betook themselves to the field path; and as they went there moved onward with them, around the shadow of each one's head, an opalized circle of glory, formed by the moon's rays upon the glistening sheet of dew. Each pedestrian could see no halo but his or her own, which never deserted the head-shadow whatever its vulgar unsteadiness might be; but adhered to it and persistently beautified it: till the erratic motion seemed an inherent part of the irradiation, and the hot fumes of their breathing a component of the night-mist: and the spirit of the hour, and of the moonlight, and of Nature, seemed harmoniously to mingle with the spirit of wine.

Meanwhile the vanished twain cantered along for some while without speech, the girl as she clung to her knight still panting in her triumph yet in other respects dubious; though she had not heard the old woman's laconic cry, 'Out of the frying-pan into the fire.'

'Neatly done, was it not, dear?' he said by-and-by.

'Yes,' said she. 'I suppose I ought to be much obliged to you.'

'And are you?'

She did not reply.

'Why do you always dislike my kissing you?' continued he.

'Because I don't love you.'

'You are quite sure?'

'Quite. I am angry with you often.'

'Ah! I half-feared as much.' Nevertheless, he seemed not to object to that confession: anything was better than frigidity. 'It has not been on account of my love-making?'

'Sometimes – too many times.'

'Every time I have tried?'

She was silent; and the horse ambled along for a considerable distance. Having undergone the excitement of the quarrel, and it being the end of a long day, she was inexpressibly weary. He seemed to notice it, and, withdrawing his feet from the stirrups, turned sideways on the saddle, and enclosed her waist with his arm to support her, saying, 'Mayn't I for once treat you as a lover?'

She drew a quick, pettish breath of objection, writhing uneasily on her seat; looked far away, and murmured, 'I don't know – I wish – how can I say yes or no when —'

He kept his arm where he had placed it, and she expressed no further negative. Thus they sidled onwards, descended a hollow, and ascended on the other slope to the margin of a wood through which their journey lay. At the rise they met a pedestrian going in the opposite direction; but as he passed behind their backs neither of the two observed him.

When they had withdrawn he turned and looked after them, which he had plenty of time to do, the heavily weighted horse moving but slowly. They ascended the white road higher and higher, until they suddenly disappeared from the moonlight and were absorbed into the shade of the trees.

He resumed his journey towards the town, and from that moment no living soul saw either of the pair till noon on the day following, when Big Beauty was perceived for a minute or two in the garden by some of her fellow-villagers who had walked with her the night previous. On Monday, when they were in the fields as usual, they spoke of her.

'How pale and thoughtful she do look,' said one.

'All her hontishness gone!' said another.

'Quite a tractable girl!' said a third.

It was true; she seemed even glad of their friendship. She looked troubled, regretful. She resented nothing that they said to her: even when they asked her at what time four-legs brought her home, and whether it was quite soon enough to make the breakfast-kettle boil.

They observed that to him she was deferential thenceforward, that she started when he came into the field and when he joked jokes of the most excruciating quality she laughed with a childlike belief in them.

Two or three months afterwards she was called away from the farm to her native place, many miles off, by the sickness of a relative, which necessitated her giving up her engagement here. He made no objection to her going, and on parting she gave him her mouth to kiss, not her cheek as at one time. She implored him not to desert her. He said he would not; that the parting would not be for long; that he should soon come to see her.

But he never went.

B. THE CHASEBOROUGH DANCE
(In 1912 Wessex Edition)

. . . This had gone on for a month or two when there came a Saturday in September, on which a fair and a market coincided; and the pilgrims from Trantridge sought double delights at the inns on that account. Tess's occupations made her late in setting out, so that her comrades reached the town long before her. It was a fine September evening, just before sunset, when yellow lights struggle with blue shades in hair-like lines, and the atmosphere itself forms a prospect, without aid from more solid objects, except the innumerable winged insects that dance in it. Through this low-lit mistiness Tess walked leisurely along.

She did not discover the coincidence of the market with the fair till she had reached the place, by which time it was close upon dusk. Her limited marketing was soon completed; and then as usual she began to look about for some of the Trantridge cottagers.

At first she could not find them, and she was informed that most of them had gone to what they called a private little jig at the house of a hay-trusser and peat-dealer who had transactions with their farm. He lived in an out-of-the-way nook of the townlet, and in trying to find her course thither her eyes fell upon Mr d'Urberville standing at a street-corner.

'What – my beauty? – You here so late?' he said.

She told him that she was simply waiting for company homeward.

'I'll see you again,' said he over her shoulder as she went on down the back lane.

Approaching the hay-trusser's she could hear the fiddled notes of a reel proceeding from some building in the rear; but no sound of dancing was audible—an exceptional state of things for these parts, where as a rule the stamping drowned the music. The front door being open she could see straight through the house into the garden at the back as far as the shades of night would allow; and nobody appearing to her knock she traversed the dwelling and went up the path to the outhouse whence the sound had attracted her.

It was a windowless erection used for storage, and from the open door there floated into the obscurity a mist of yellow radiance, which at first Tess thought to be illuminated smoke. But on drawing nearer she perceived that it was a cloud of dust, lit by candles within the outhouse, whose beams upon the haze carried forward the outline of the doorway into the wide night of the garden.

When she came close and looked in she beheld indistinct forms racing up and down to the figure of the dance, the silence of their footfalls arising from their being overshoe in 'scroff' – that is to say the powdery residuum from the storage of peat and other products, the stirring of which by their turbulent feet created the nebulosity that involved the scene. Through this floating fusty *débris* of peat and hay, mixed with the perspirations and warmth of the dancers, and forming together a sort of vegeto-human pollen, the muted fiddles feebly pushed their notes, in marked contrast to the spirit with which the measure was trodden out. They coughed as they danced, and laughed as they coughed. Of the rushing couples there could barely be discerned more than the high lights – the indistinctness shaping them to satyrs clasping nymphs – a multiplicity of Pans whirling a multiplicity of Syrinxes; Lotis attempting to elude Priapus, and always failing.

At intervals a couple would approach the doorway for air, and the haze no longer veiling their features, the demigods resolved themselves into the homely personalities of her own next-door neighbours. Could Trantridge in two or three short hours have metamorphosed itself thus madly!

Some Sileni of the throng sat on benches and hay-trusses by the wall; and one of them recognized her.

'The maids don't think it respectable to dance at "The Flower-de-Luce,"' he explained; 'they don't like to let everybody see which be their fancy-men. Besides, the house sometimes shuts up just when their jints begin to get greased. So we come here and send out for liquor.'

'But when be any of you going home?' asked Tess with some anxiety.

'Now – a'most directly. This is all but the last jig.'

She waited. The reel drew to a close, and some of the party were in the mind for starting. But others would not, and another dance was formed. This surely would end it, thought Tess. But it merged in yet another. She became restless and uneasy; yet, having waited so long, it was necessary to wait longer; on account of the fair the roads were dotted with roving characters of possibly ill intent: and though not fearful of measurable dangers, she feared the unknown. Had she been near Marlott she would have had less dread.

'Don't ye be nervous, my dear good soul,' expostulated, between his coughs, a young man with a wet face, and his straw hat so far back upon his head that the brim encircled it like the nimbus of a saint. 'What's yer hurry? To-morrow is Sunday, thank God, and we can sleep it off in church-time. Now, have a turn with me?'

She did not abhor dancing, but she was not going to dance here. The movement grew more passionate. The fiddlers behind the luminous pillar of cloud now and then varied the air by playing on the wrong side of the bridge or with the back of the bow. But it did not matter; the panting shapes spun onwards.

They did not vary their partners if their inclination were to stick to previous ones. Changing partners simply meant that a satisfactory choice had not as yet been arrived at by one or other of the pair, and by this time every couple had been suitably matched. It was then that the ecstasy and the dream began, in which emotion was the matter of the universe, and matter but an adventitious intrusion likely to hinder you from spinning where you wanted to spin.

Suddenly there was a dull thump on the ground: a couple had fallen, and lay in a mixed heap. The next couple, unable to check its progress, came toppling over the obstacle. An inner cloud of dust rose around the prostrate figures amid the general one of the room, in which a twitching entanglement of arms and legs was discernible.

'You shall catch it for this, my gentleman, when you get home!' burst in female accents from the human heap – those of the unhappy partner of the man whose clumsiness had caused the mishap; she happened also to be his recently married wife – in which assortment there was nothing unusual at Trantridge, as long as any affection remained between wedded couples; and, indeed, it was not uncustomary in their later lives, to avoid making odd lots of the single people between whom there might be a warm understanding.

A loud laugh from behind Tess's back, in the shade of the garden, united with the titter within the room. She looked round, and saw the red coal of a cigar: Alec d'Urberville was standing there alone. He beckoned to her, and she reluctantly retreated towards him . . .

C. THE MIDNIGHT BAPTISM: A STUDY IN CHRISTIANITY
(*Fortnightly Review*, May 1891)

This issue of the liberal *Fortnightly Review* (edited by Frank Harris) also included an instalment of George Meredith's novel *One of Our Conquerors*. Margaret Oliphant, reviewing *Tess* in *Blackwood's Magazine* (March 1892; Cox, 203–4), affected 'tremendous objection' to the fact that 'what we must call the naughty chapters have had to be printed surreptitiously, in what we presume ought to be described as elderly Reviews, while the rest has come out in the cheerful young newspaper open to all men'.

They were harvesting in Sixty-Acres, and the revolving arms of the painted reaping-machine glared red in the sun against the pale brown corn, while the knives of the instrument clicked like the love-call of the grasshopper. At each circuit of the field the brass star on the forehead of the leading horse glistened suddenly into the eyes.

As the morning wore on the standing wheat was reduced to a smaller and smaller area in the middle of the field. Rabbits, hares, snakes, rats, mice, all retreated inward as into a fastness, unaware of the ephemeral nature of their refuge and of the doom awaiting them later in the day when, their covert shrinking to a more and more horrible narrowness, they were all huddled together, friends and foes; till the last few yards of upright stalks fell also under the teeth of the machine, and every creature of them was put to a fearful death by the sticks and stones of the harvesters.

Upon the fallen corn in the rear of the machine the binders had set to work, some of them men, but the majority women, or rather girls. A singular charm was added to these latter by their out-door employment. The men were personalities afield; the women were almost a portion of the field; they had somehow lost their individuality, and assimilated themselves to their surroundings.

They wore drawn cotton-bonnets with great flapping curtains to keep off the sunburn, and gloves to prevent the stubble from wounding their hands. The eye was attracted by one who appeared in a pink cotton skirt; but it was not on account of the garment, nor even because she could boast of the most flexuous outline, the finest figure of the group; rather from a certain listlessness which characterized her: she never turned her head like the other women, who often gazed around them. She seduced attention precisely because she did not demand it. Her bonnet was pulled so far over her brow that not an inch of her face was disclosed while she worked; but her complexion might have been guessed from a stray twine or two of shady hair which extended below the curtain of her bonnet.

Her binding proceeded, indeed, with clock-like indifference and monotony. From each sheaf last finished she would draw a handful of straw by the ears, to form a bond, patting their tips with her left palm to bring them even. Then stooping low, she moved forward, gathering a proper quantity of the cut corn against her knees. Next pushing her left hand under the bundle, with the end of the bond in her fingers, she met it with her right on the other side; holding in a lover-like embrace the sheaf thus formed, on which she knelt while bringing the ends of the bond together and tying them, beating back her skirts now and then when lifted by the breeze. A narrow stripe of her naked arm was exposed between the buff leather of the gauntlet and the sleeve of her gown; and as the day wore on the feminine smoothness of the skin became scarified by the stubble, and bled visibly.

At intervals she stood up to rest, and to re-tie her disarranged apron, or to pull her bonnet straight. Then could be seen the oval face of a handsome young woman about eighteen years of age, with dark eyes, and heavy tresses which seemed to seize in a lazy cling anything they fell against. The cheeks of the damsel were paler, the red lips thinner, than is usual with country-bred girls.

The movements of the other women were more or less similar to hers, the whole bevy of them drawing together like dancers in a quadrille at the completion of a sheaf by each; every one placing her sheaf on end against those of the rest, till a shock of ten or a dozen was formed. As the hour of eleven drew near a close observer might have noticed that every now and then the glances of the girl in the pink frock flitted wistfully, even anxiously, to the brow of the hill, though she did not for a moment pause in her sheafing. On the stroke of the hour a group of children, their ages ranging from about thirteen to five years, rose above the stubbly convexity of the field. The young woman with the clinging hair flushed a little, but still she did not pause. The eldest of the children, a girl in a mud-coloured triangular shawl whose corner draggled over the stubble, brought what at first sight seemed to be a doll, but proved to be a very small infant in long clothes. Another brought some lunch. The harvesters ceased working, took their provisions, and sat down against one of the shocks. Here they fell to, the men plying pretty freely a stone jar which had been hidden under a sheaf, and passing a cup round to each. The aforesaid young woman had been one of the last to suspend her labours. She sat down at the end of the shock, her face turned quite away from her companions. When she had deposited herself a man in a rabbit-skin cap and with a red handkerchief tucked into his belt, held the cup of ale over the top of the shock toward the girl in pink. But she did not accept his offer. As soon as her lunch was spread she called up the biggest of the children, evidently her sister, and took the baby from her, who, glad to be relieved of her burden, went away to the next shock and joined the rest of the children playing there. The other, with a curious, stealthy, yet courageous movement, and with a still rising colour, unfastened her frock and began suckling the child.

The men who sat nearest considerately turned their faces toward the other end of the field, some of them beginning to smoke; one, with absent-minded fondness, regretfully stroking the jar that would no longer yield a stream. All the women but the youthful one with the baby fell into animated talk, and adjusted their disarranged knots and bows. When the infant had taken its fill the young mother sat it upright in her lap, and, looking into the far distance, dandled it with a gloomy indifference that was almost dislike. Then all of a sudden she fell to violently kissing it some dozens of times, as if she could never leave off, the child crying at the vehemence of an onset which strangely combined passionateness with contempt.

'She's fond of that there child, though she do say she wishes the baby and herself, too, were underground,' observes one of the other women in an undertone.

'She'll soon leave off saying that,' replies her neighbour. 'Lord, 'tis wonderful what a body can get used to in time!'

The harvest-men rose from the shock of corn, stretched their arms, and extinguished their pipes. The horses, which had been unharnessed and fed, were again attached to the scarlet machine. The spouseless mother, having quickly eaten her own meal, beckoned to her eldest sister to come up and take away the baby; then, fastening her dress, she put on the buff gloves anew, stooped to draw a bond from the last completed sheaf for the tying of the next, and worked on automatically as before.

At dusk that evening they all rode home in one of the largest wagons on the farm, in the company of a broad, tarnished moon which had risen from the ground to the eastward, its face resembling the outworn gold-leaf halo of some worm-eaten Tuscan saint. The pink girl's female companions sang songs, and, looking toward her, could not refrain from mischievously throwing in a few verses of the ballad about the maid who went to the merry greenwood, and came back a changed person. But they were sympathetic, and glad to have her among them again, the event which had made of her a social warning having also for the moment made her the most interesting inhabitant of the village. Their friendliness won her still further away from herself, their lively spirits were contagious, and she became almost gay.

But a quick period was put to this unauthorized indulgence in good spirits. When she reached home it was to learn to her grief that the baby had been taken ill quite suddenly since the afternoon. Some such collapse had been probable, so tender and puny was its frame; but the event came as a shock nevertheless.

The baby's offence against society in coming into the world was forgotten by the girl-mother; her soul's desire was to continue that offence by preserving the life of the child. However, it soon grew clear that the hour of emancipation for that little prisoner of the flesh was to arrive even earlier than her worst fears had conjectured. And when she had discovered this she was plunged into a misery which transcended that of the child's simple loss. Her baby had not been baptized.

She had drifted into a frame of mind which accepted passively the consideration that if she should have to burn for what she had done, burn she must, and there was an end of it. Like all village girls, she was well grounded in Scripture, and knew the histories of Aholah and Aholibah, and the inferences to be drawn therefrom. But when the same question arose with regard to the baby, it had a very different colour. Her darling was about to die, and no salvation.

It was now bedtime, but she rushed down stairs and asked if she might send for the parson. The moment happened to be one when her father's sense of respectability was at its highest, and his sensitiveness most pronounced, for he had just returned from his evening booze at the public-house. No parson should come inside his door, he declared, prying into his affairs just then, when, by her shame, it had become more necessary than ever to hide them. He locked the door and put the key in his pocket.

The household went to bed, and, distressed beyond measure, the girl retired also. She was continually waking as she lay, and in the middle of the night found that the baby was still worse. It was obviously dying quietly and painlessly, but none the less surely.

In her misery she rocked herself upon the bed. The clock struck the solemn hour of one, that hour when thought stalks outside reason, and malignant possibilities stand rock-firm as facts. She thought of the child consigned to the nethermost corner of hell, as its double doom for lack of baptism and lack of legitimacy; saw the arch-fiend tossing it with his three-pronged fork, like the one they used for heating the oven on baking days; to which picture she added many other curious details of torment. The lurid presentment so powerfully affected her imagination in the silence of the sleeping house that her night-gown became damp with perspiration, and the bedstead shook with each throb of her heart.

The infant's breathing grew more difficult, and the mother's mental tension increased. It was useless to devour the little thing with kisses;

she could stay in bed no longer, and walked feverishly about the room.

'Oh, merciful God, have pity; have pity upon my poor baby!' she cried. 'Heap as much anger as you want to upon me and welcome, but pity the child!'

She leaned against the chest of drawers, and murmured incoherent supplications for a long while, till she suddenly started up. 'Ah! perhaps baby can be saved! Perhaps it will be just the same!' She spoke so brightly that it seemed as though her face might have shone in the gloom surrounding her.

She lit a candle, and went to a second and third bed under the wall, where she awoke her little sisters and brothers, all of whom occupied the same room. Pulling out the washing stand so that she could get behind it, she poured some water from a jug, and made them kneel around, putting their hands together with the fingers exactly vertical. While the children, scarcely awake, awe-stricken at her manner, their eyes growing larger and larger, remained in this position, she took the baby from her bed – a child's child – so immature as scarce to seem a sufficient personality to endow its producer with the maternal title. The mother stood erect with the infant on her arm beside the basin, the next sister held the Prayer Book open before her, as the clerk at church held it before the parson, and there and then this emotional girl set about baptizing her child.

Her fine figure looked singularly tall and imposing as she stood in her long white night-gown, a thick cable of dark, braided hair hanging straight down her back to her waist. The kindly dimness of the weak candle abstracted from her form and features the little blemishes which sunlight might have revealed – the stubble scratches upon her wrists, and the weariness of her eyes – while her high enthusiasm had a transfiguring effect upon the handsome face which had been her undoing, showing it as a thing of immaculate beauty, with an impress of dignity that was almost regal. The little ones kneeling round awaited her preparations, their sleepy eyes, blinking and red, full of a suspended wonder which their physical heaviness at that hour would not allow to become active. The eldest of them said listlessly, 'Be you really going to christen him, Sis?' and the girl-mother replied in a grave affirmative.

'What's his name going to be?'

She had not thought of that, but a name came into her head as she proceeded with the baptismal service, and now she pronounced it. '*Sorrow*, I baptize thee in the name of the Father, and of the Son, and of the Holy Ghost.' She sprinkled the water, and there was silence.

'Say "Amen", children.'

The tiny voices piped in obedient response, 'A-men!'

Sis went on: 'We receive this child' – and so forth – 'and do sign him with the sign of the Cross.' Here she dipped her hand into the basin, and fervently drew an immense cross upon the baby with her forefinger, continuing with the customary sentences as to his manfully fighting against sin, the world, and the devil, and being a faithful soldier and servant unto his life's end. She duly went on with the Lord's Prayer, the children lisping it after her in a thin gnat-like wail, till, at the conclusion, raising their voices to clerk's pitch, they again piped into the silence, 'A-men!'

Then their sister, with much augmented confidence in the efficacy of this sacrament, poured forth from the bottom of her heart the thanksgiving that follows, uttering it boldly and triumphantly, in the stopt-diapason note which her voice acquired when her heart was in her speech, and which will never be forgotten by those who knew her. The ecstasy of faith almost apotheosized her; it set upon her face a glowing irradiation, and brought a red spot into the middle of each cheek, while the miniature candle-flame, inverted in her eye, shone like a diamond. The children gazed up at her with reverence, and no longer had a will for questioning. She did not look like Sissy to them now, but a being large, towering, and awful, a Divine personage with whom they had nothing in common.

Poor Sorrow's campaign against sin, the world, and the devil was doomed to be of limited brilliancy – luckily perhaps for himself, considering his beginnings. In the blue of the morning that fragile soldier and servant breathed his last; and when the other children awoke they cried bitterly, and begged Sissy to try to find another.

The calmness which had possessed the girl since the christening remained with her in her baby's loss. In the daylight, indeed, she felt her terrors about his soul to have been somewhat exaggerated; whether well founded or not she had no uneasiness now, reasoning that if Providence would not ratify such an act of urgency, she, for one, did not value the kind of heaven lost by the irregularity – either for herself or for her child.

So passed away Sorrow the Undesired – that intrusive creature, that bastard gift of shameless Nature who respects not the law; a waif to whom eternal time had been a matter of days merely, who knew not that such things as years and centuries ever were; to whom the cottage interior was the universe, the week's weather climate, new-born babyhood human existence, and the instinct to suck human knowledge.

Sis, who mused on the christening a good deal, wondered if it were doctrinally sufficient to secure a Christian burial for the child. Nobody could tell this but the parson of the parish, and he was a new-comer, and a very reserved man. She went to his house after dusk, and stood by the gate, but could not summon courage to go in. The enterprise would have been abandoned if she had not by accident met him coming homeward as she turned away. In the gloom she did not mind speaking freely.

'I should like to ask you something, sir.'

He expressed his willingness to listen, and she told the story of the extemporized ordinance, and its reason, owing to her father's pride and the baby's illness. 'And now, sir,' she added earnestly, 'can you tell me this – will it be just the same for him as if you had baptized him?'

The dignity of the girl, the strange tenderness in her voice, combined to affect the Vicar's natural feelings – or rather those that he had left in him after ten years of endeavour to graft technical belief on actual scepticism. The man and the ecclesiastic fought within him, and the victory fell to the man. 'My dear girl,' he said, 'it will be just the same.'

'Then will you give him a Christian burial?' she asked quickly.

The Vicar felt himself cornered, 'Ah – that's another matter,' he said.

'Another matter – why?' said she rather warmly.

'Well – I would willingly do so if only we two were concerned. But I must not – for parochial reasons.'

'Just for once, sir!'

'Really I must not.'

'Oh, sir, for pity's sake!' She seized his hand as she spoke.

He shook his head.

'Then I don't like you!' she burst out. 'And I'll never come to your church no more!'

'Don't talk so rashly, Sis.'

'Perhaps it will be just the same to him if you don't? . . . Will it be just the same? Don't speak, sir, as parson to sinner, but as you yourself to me myself – poor me!'

How he reconciled his answer with the strict notions he supposed himself to hold on these subjects it is beyond a layman's power to tell, though not to excuse. Somewhat moved, he said in this case also, 'It will be just the same.'

So the baby was carried in a small deal box, under an ancient woman's shawl, to the churchyard that night, and buried by lantern-light, at the cost of a shilling and a pint of beer to the sexton, in that shabby corner of the enclosure where the nettles grow, and where all unbaptized infants, notorious drunkards, suicides, and others of the conjecturally damned are laid. In spite of the untoward surroundings, however, Sis bravely made a little cross of two laths and a piece of string, and having bound it with flowers, she stuck it up at the head of the grave one evening when she could enter the churchyard without being seen, putting at the foot also a bunch of the same flowers, in a little jar of water to keep them alive. What matter was it that on the outside of the jar the eye of mere observation noted the words, 'Keelwell's Marmalade'? The eye of maternal affection did not see them in its vision of higher things.

Notes

1. *The indistinctness . . . Priapus*: In Greek mythology satyrs were wild, licentious woodland gods who worshipped Dionysus; nymphs were beautiful semi-divine maidens found throughout the natural world. The nymph Syrinx threw herself into a river to escape from Pan (the Greek god of herds and shepherds). Hearing her call for help, the gods changed her into reeds, which produced

a plaintive melody when Pan sighed through them. This became Pan's pipe. Likewise, Lotis was changed into a shrub (the lotus) to escape the pursuing Priapus, god of fertility.

2. *Sileni*: Silenus was the old schoolmaster and foster-father of Dionysus. Sileni here refers to the drunken older men.

3. *Euroclydon*: A strong cold Mediterranean wind; it wrecked St Paul on his way to Rome (see Acts 27: 14).

GLOSSARY

Abbreviations
adj. adjective
adv. adverb
excl. exclamation
interj. interjection
phr. phrase
pron. pronoun
prs.p. present participle
pst.p. past participle
sb. substantive
sb.pl. substantive plural
vb. verb

achromatic, adj.	colourless
Agape, sb.	'love-feast' held by the early Christians in celebration of the Lord's Supper
amuck, adv.	(run) viciously, frenzied for blood (from Malay word for homicidal frenzy)
andirons, sb.pl.	metal stands for supporting burning wood on a hearth
Anno Domini, phr. (Latin)	in the year of our Lord, in the Christian era
apostacy, sb.	abandonment of religious faith, vows or principles
apple-blooth, sb.	apple blossom
architrave, sb.	main beam resting immediately on the upper member of the capital of a column
Aurora, sb.	Aurora Borealis, the northern lights
autochthonous, adj.	native
baint, vb.	are not

ballyragging, prs.p.	abusing
Bantam, sb.	small domestic fowl
barton, sb.	farmyard, enclosure
bill-hook, sb.	implement for lopping and pruning
bizarrerie, sb. (French)	strangeness, weirdness
black-pot, sb.	black pudding, sausage made principally of blood and suet
blower, sb.	contrivance fixed over a fire for producing a draught
bolt, vb.	sift
boreal, adj.	from the north; the boreal wind is the cold north wind
Brahma, sb.	Mediterranean breed of chicken
brake, sb.	thicket, brushwood
broad-cloth, sb.	quality double width black cloth
carking, adj.	burdensome
centurions, sb.pl.	Roman soldiers
Chapel-of-Ease, sb.	chapel for the use of remote parishioners
cheese-wring, sb.	press for separating curds and whey in cheese-making
chimney-corner, sb.	warm seat within a fireplace
chimney crooks, sb.pl.	hooks hanging over the chimney
chitterlings, sb.pl.	smaller intestines of pigs, cooked as food
clipsed, pst.p.	embraced
cob, sb.	sturdy short-legged horse
Cochin, sb.	large chicken of Asian breed
coll, vb.	kiss and embrace
convenances, sb.pl. (French)	conventional proprieties
cowcumber, sb.	cucumber
crape quilling, sb.	transparent gauze-like silk fabric formed into pleats or folds
crowfoot, sb.	plant of genus *Ranunculus*
crush, sb.	crowded social gathering
Cubit's lags, phr.	Cupid's legs
cuckoo-spittle, sb.	a frothy secretion left by insects on plants

cwoffer, sb.	coffer, chest
dand, sb.	dandy
Daze, interj.	Damn
deparked, adj.	(park) cut up into paddocks
determined, adj.	terminated
diment, sb.	diamond
dimity, sb.	cotton fabric with raised stripes or checks
dog-days, sb.pl.	the hottest days of summer, when the Dog star is set; the most unwholesome weather
dogs, sb.pl.	irons which support burning wood in a fireplace
drachm, sb.	one-eighth of an ounce
drave, vb.	toil
durn, sb.	door-post
eastings, sb.pl.	turnings to the east end of the church (to recite the creed, etc.)
éclat, sb. (French)	brilliant success
en, pron.	him, it
fairlings, sb.pl.	gifts bought at a fair
fatness, sb.	fertility of the soil
felloes, sb.pl.	outer circles of the wheel, attached by spokes
fess, adj.	proud
fibrils, sb.pl.	small fibres
flexuous, adj.	sinuous; by extension: full of natural grace
foot-higgler, sb.	dealer who buys and sells by picking up and delivering goods on foot
gallantry, sb.	conduct of a gallant; sexual intrigue or immorality
gallied, adj.	worried, scared
gallopade, sb.	lively dance of Hungarian origin
gin, sb.	trap
glane, sb.	sneer
gnomic texts, sb.pl.	books of maxims or aphorisms
good hussif', sb.	bag containing needlework items
gr't-grandfer, sb.	great-grandfather

guindée, adj. (French)	stiff and prim
haggler (higgler), sb.	small goods dealer, middle man
hag-rode, adj.	plagued with nightmares
het, vb.	gulp down
higgling, adj.	dealing in goods by cart; variant of 'haggling'
hobble, sb.	troublesome business
hogs'-backs, sb.pl.	sharply crested ridges
holmberry, adj.	holly-berry colour (i.e. bright red)
hontishness, sb.	haughtiness
'hor's-bird, sb.	('hore's bird) bastard
kex, sb.	dry, usually hollow, stem of certain plants
lanchets (lynchets), sb.pl.	beds of flint
larry, sb.	noisy celebration
lath, sb.	piece of split timber about an inch wide
leads, sb.pl.	milk-pans (made from lead)
leery, adj.	empty, hungry, exhausted, faint
limed, adj.	spread with a sticky substance called birdlime, made from holly bark; used to catch small birds
long-dog, sb.	greyhound
lords and ladies, sb.pl.	wild arum
Maltese Cross, sb.	cross with arms which broaden outwards, often indented at the ends
mampus, sb.	crowd
market-nitch, sb.	customary market-day tipple
mid, vb.	may, might
milchers, sb.pl.	milkers (i.e. dairy cows)
mommet, sb.	scarecrow
mullioned window, sb.	window divided into lights (separate perpendicular panes) with bars
nammet-time, sb.	mid morning or early afternoon meal in the fields
nap, sb.	like the surface of a cloth in which the fibres have been raised, cut, and smoothed
nater, sb.	nature

'nation, excl.	damnation
niaiseries, sb.pl. (French)	sillinesses
night-rail, sb.	wrapper or dressing-gown
nott, adj.	hornless
'Od rot, phr.	God rot
off-license, sb.	an establishment licensed to sell liquor for consumption off the premises
Olympian, adj.	relating to the gods of Greek mythology, who resided on Mount Olympus
one-handed clock, sb.	clock with hour-hand only
out of her books, phr.	out of her favour
pachydermatous, adj.	thick-skinned
Papistical, adj.	Roman Catholic
partie carrée, sb. (French)	party of four
pattens, sb.pl.	wooden overshoes
petite mort, sb. (French)	faintness
pinner, sb.	pinafore (i.e. apron)
plashed, plashed down, adj.	pleached; made into low hedges
plim, vb.	swell
poppet, sb.	dear; doll (a term of endearment to a child)
post-chaise, sb.	four-wheeled carriage for rapid transportation of passengers and mail
professed, adj.	professional
pummy, sb.	apples crushed to pulp for cider
quadrille, sb.	square dance for four couples containing five complete figures
quarter-day, sb.	Lady-Day, Midsummer Day, Michaelmas and Christmas Day: days when quarterly payments are due, and tenancies and work contracts begin and end
quarter-hogshead, sb.	small cask
queue, sb.	hanging pigtail
quickset, sb.	plant, especially hawthorn, set to grow as a hedge

randy, sb.	party
reared, pst.p.	roused
reed-drawing, sb.	process for preparing straw for roofing thatch
reed-sparrow, sb.	common British bird, *Emberiza schoeniclus*, which frequents reedy places
roof-tree, sb.	roof
rozums, sb.pl.	strange people (from 'a quaint saying')
scram, adj.	puny, contemptible
sedge, sb.	rushlike plant of the genus *Carex* growing in wet places
shadder, sb.	shadow
shade, sb.	shadow
sheaf-pitcher, sb.	one who pitches the sheaves to the loader or feeder on the thresher
siliceous, adj.	rich in silica
slack-twisted, adj.	spineless, shiftless
sommat, summat, pron.	something
spear-grass, sb.	presumably spear-wort, *Ranunculus flammula*
springe, sb.	snare for catching small game
stale, vb.	urinate
starve-acre, adj.	barren
steading, sb.	farm outbuildings
stooded, pst.p.	bogged down
stubbard-tree, sb.	variety of apple tree
stuff, sb.	woollen fabric
subtilized, adj.	refined
sumple, adj.	soft, supple
teave, vb.	struggle
term, sb.	statue or bust representing the upper part of the body and terminating below in a pillar or pedestal
thirtover, adj.	obstinate, perverse
thistle-spud, sb.	tool for weeding out thistles
tilt-bonnet, sb.	sun-bonnet
tole, vb.	entice, draw

517

touchwood, sb.	wood converted into an easily ignitable substance by the action of certain fungi
tranter, sb.	carrier; one who transports goods
traps, sb.pl.	personal possessions
trencher-woman, sb.	woman with a hearty appetite
trilithon, sb.	two vertical stones supporting a third laid across them
trowing, prs.p.	believing
twang, sb.	taint
unceiled, adj.	unplastered; without a ceiling
vamp, vb.	tramp
wafer, sb.	small round disk of wax used to seal letters
wales, sb.pl.	welts; vertical ribs in knitted clothing
whickered, pst.p.	sniggered or giggled
withy basket, sb.	plaited willow basket
withy-bed, sb.	willow plantation
wold, wuld, adj.	old
zeed, zid, vb.	saw

THE STORY OF PENGUIN CLASSICS

Before 1946 ... "Classics" are mainly the domain of academics and students; readable editions for everyone else are almost unheard of. This all changes when a little-known classicist, E. V. Rieu, presents Penguin founder Allen Lane with the translation of Homer's *Odyssey* that he has been working on in his spare time.

1946 Penguin Classics debuts with *The Odyssey*, which promptly sells three million copies. Suddenly, classics are no longer for the privileged few.

1950s Rieu, now series editor, turns to professional writers for the best modern, readable translations, including Dorothy L. Sayers's *Inferno* and Robert Graves's unexpurgated *Twelve Caesars*.

1960s The Classics are given the distinctive black covers that have remained a constant throughout the life of the series. Rieu retires in 1964, hailing the Penguin Classics list as "the greatest educative force of the twentieth century."

1970s A new generation of translators swells the Penguin Classics ranks, introducing readers of English to classics of world literature from more than twenty languages. The list grows to encompass more history, philosophy, science, religion and politics.

1980s The Penguin American Library launches with titles such as *Uncle Tom's Cabin*, and joins forces with Penguin Classics to provide the most comprehensive library of world literature available from any paperback publisher.

1990s The launch of Penguin Audiobooks brings the classics to a listening audience for the first time, and in 1999 the worldwide launch of the Penguin Classics website extends their reach to the global online community.

The 21st Century Penguin Classics are completely redesigned for the first time in nearly twenty years. This world-famous series now consists of more than 1300 titles, making the widest range of the best books ever written available to millions—and constantly redefining what makes a "classic".

The Odyssey continues ...

The best books ever written

PENGUIN CLASSICS

SINCE 1946

Find out more at www.penguinclassics.com